Praise for Laura Childs's C

Featured Selection of
"Highly recommended

"Childs is a master of Southern local color, and, of course, every chapter offers delectable descriptions of aromatic teas and scrumptious quiches and cakes, with recipes."
—*Publishers Weekly*

"You'll be starved by the end and ready to try out the recipes in the back of the book . . . enjoy!"
—*The Charlotte Observer*

"Murder suits Laura Childs to a Tea."
—*St. Paul Pioneer Press*

"The perfect series for tea and mystery lovers."
—*The Tea Caddy*

"Tea lovers, mystery lovers, [this] is for you. Just the right blend of cozy fun and clever plotting."
—Susan Wittig Albert, bestselling author of *Bleeding Hearts*

"Delightful!"
—*Tea: A Magazine*

"Engages the audience from the start . . . Laura Childs provides the right combination between tidbits on tea and an amateur-sleuth cozy."
—*Midwest Book Review*

"A delightful cozy that will warm readers the way a good cup of tea does. Laura Childs describes the genteel South in ways that invite readers in and make them feel welcomed . . . Theodosia and her friends are a warm bunch of characters . . . A delightful series that will leave readers feeling as if they have shared a warm cup of tea on Church Street in Charleston."
—*The Mystery Reader*

"Along the way, the author provides enough scrumptious descriptions of teas and baked goods to throw anyone off the killer's scent."
—*Library Journal*

"This mystery series could single-handedly propel the tea shop business in this country to the status of wine bars and bustling coffeehouses."
—*Buon Gusto (Minneapolis, MN)*

"If you devoured Nancy Drew and Trixie Belden, this new series is right up your alley."
—*The Goose Creek (SC) Gazette*

"Gives the reader a sense of traveling through the streets and environs of the beautiful, historic city of Charleston."
—*Lakeshore Weekly News (Minnetonka, MN)*

Tea Shop Mysteries by Laura Childs

DEATH BY DARJEELING

GUNPOWDER GREEN

SHADES OF EARL GREY

THE ENGLISH BREAKFAST MURDER

THE JASMINE MOON MURDER

CHAMOMILE MOURNING

BLOOD ORANGE BREWING

DRAGONWELL DEAD

THE SILVER NEEDLE MURDER

Scrapbooking Mysteries by Laura Childs

KEEPSAKE CRIMES

PHOTO FINISHED

BOUND FOR MURDER

MOTIF FOR MURDER

FRILL KILL

Anthology by Laura Childs

DEATH BY DESIGN

Death
by Design

LAURA CHILDS

BERKLEY PRIME CRIME, NEW YORK

THE BERKLEY PUBLISHING GROUP
Published by the Penguin Group
Penguin Group (USA) Inc.
375 Hudson Street, New York, New York 10014, USA
Penguin Group (Canada), 90 Eglinton Avenue East, Suite 700, Toronto, Ontario M4P 2Y3, Canada
(a division of Pearson Penguin Canada Inc.)
Penguin Books Ltd., 80 Strand, London WC2R 0RL, England
Penguin Group Ireland, 25 St. Stephen's Green, Dublin 2, Ireland (a division of Penguin Books Ltd.)
Penguin Group (Australia), 250 Camberwell Road, Camberwell, Victoria 3124, Australia
(a division of Pearson Australia Group Pty. Ltd.)
Penguin Books India Pvt. Ltd., 11 Community Centre, Panchsheel Park, New Delhi—110 017, India
Penguin Group (NZ), Cnr. Airborne and Rosedale Roads, Albany, Auckland 1310, New Zealand
(a division of Pearson New Zealand Ltd.)
Penguin Books (South Africa) (Pty.) Ltd., 24 Sturdee Avenue, Rosebank, Johannesburg 2196,
South Africa

Penguin Books Ltd., Registered Offices: 80 Strand, London WC2R 0RL, England

Copyright © 2006 by Gerry Schmitt.
Keepsake Crimes copyright © 2003 by Gerry Schmitt.
Photo Finished copyright © 2003 by Gerry Schmitt.
Bound for Murder copyright © 2004 by Gerry Schmitt.
Cover art by Dan Craig.
Text design by Stacy Irwin.

First edition: July 2006

Library of Congress Cataloging-in-Publication Data

Childs, Laura.
    Death by design / Laura Childs.—1st ed.
      p. cm.
    Contents: Keepsake crimes—Photo finished—Bound for murder.
    ISBN 978-0-425-21000-0
    1. Women detectives—Louisiana—New Orleans—Fiction. 2. New Orleans (La.)—Fiction.
  3. Scrapbooks—Fiction. 4. Detective and mystery stories, American. I. Title: Keepsake crimes.
  II. Title: Photo finished.   III. Title: Bound for murder. IV. Title.

PS3603.H56D43 2006
813'.6—dc22

                                      2006040744

PRINTED IN THE UNITED STATES OF AMERICA

10 9 8 7 6 5 4

Contents

Author's Foreword

The following three Scrapbooking Mysteries take place in the city of New Orleans. They were written prior to Hurricane Katrina when the Big Easy, as that soulful city is known, was going about its business, unprepared for the catastrophic events that were about to take place.

Since those terrible days of Hurricane Katrina, so many readers of the Scrapbooking Mystery series have written me to ask if family and friends are safe. They are fine, thank you. And blessings on your head for your concern.

As a shy afterthought, many readers also wanted to know if Carmela, the main character of the series who runs a scrapbook shop in the French Quarter, also survived. In other words, would the Scrapbooking Mystery series continue?

The answer is a resounding yes. Carmela and her supporting cast of characters will reappear in the fourth Scrapbooking Mystery, *Motif for Murder*. In her own inimitable way, Carmela will help customers salvage water-damaged photos, aid in fund-raising, and, yes, get pulled into a perplexing murder mystery.

In fact, she will carry on just as New Orleans itself has been carrying on of late, with bustling grace and insouciant dignity.

So please enjoy the Scrapbooking Mysteries—and know there will be many more to come set in the fine city of New Orleans.

Laura Childs

Death
by Design

Keepsake Crimes

This book is dedicated to my dad,
who died a few short months before I became
a published author.

Acknowledgments

A million thanks to my husband, Bob, who urged me to pursue this scrapbooking theme; to mystery great Mary Higgins Clark who has been so encouraging with every book I write; to my agent, Sam Pinkus; to Henri Schindler, Mardi Gras float designer, historian, and author, and Stone and Joan in New Orleans who revealed the fascinating world of Mardi Gras parades, float dens, and balls; to my sister, Jennie, who was this book's first reader and critic; to my mother who always believes in me, no matter what; to Jim Smith, dear friend and tireless cheerleader; to my Chinese shar-pei dogs, Madison and Maximillian, who were the inspiration for little Boo; to everyone at Berkley who was so enthusiastic about a scrapbooking series; to all the thousands of scrapbookers out there who are so marvelously creative; and to readers of my Tea Shop Mystery series who expressed genuine excitement over my new series.

Chapter 1

CARMELA BERTRAND SPUN out a good fifteen inches of gold ribbon and snipped it off tidily. "This," she told the little group of scrapbookers clustered around her table, "gets added to the center panel." Heads bobbed, and eager eyes followed Carmela's hands as she punched two quick holes in the scrapbook page, then deftly threaded the ribbon through.

The ladies had been asking about wedding scrapbooks, and Carmela had come up with a layout that was easy for beginners yet elegant in appearance. Color photos of a bride and bridesmaids were alternated with squares of embossed floral paper, three down and three across, like a giant tic-tac-toe board. A diamond-shaped card, perfect for personal jottings, was positioned in the center.

As Carmela's hands worked to fashion a bow, her mind was working overtime. She had about a gazillion things to do on this late February afternoon. Call her momma, pick up batteries for her camera, check with her friend, Ava, about the Mardi Gras parade tonight, figure out just what the heck she was going to wear.

But there was time, right? Sure there was, there *had* to be time.

Willing herself to calm down, Carmela pushed an errant strand of hair from her face and took a deep breath.

People always asked Carmela if she'd gotten her name because of her hair. Dark blond, shot through with strands of taffy and caramel, it offered a startling contrast to the clear, pale skin of her oval face and blue gray eyes that mirrored the flat glint of the Gulf of Mexico.

Of course, Carmela didn't have the heart to tell folks she'd been born hairless, just like a baby opossum.

Over the years Carmela had chunked and skunked her hair, as Ava laughingly called it, in an effort to shed her cloak of conservatism and adopt an image that was a trifle more outgoing and a little more . . . well, hip.

Too often, people thought her reserved. Not so, she told herself. She only *looked* reserved. Inside was a zydeco-lovin', foot-stompin' Cajun. Well, *half* Cajun anyway. On her mother's side. Her father had been Norwegian, which, when she thought about it, probably *had* given her a slight genetic tendency toward wearing beige and voting Republican.

When she was little, before her dad died in a barge accident on the Mississippi, he'd jokingly told her she was Cawegian. Half Cajun, half Norwegian.

Carmela had been enchanted by that. And as she got older, chalked up her orderly sense of design to her Norwegian side, her passion for life to her Cajun side. It made her uniquely suited for New Orleans, a city that was eccentric, fanciful, and profoundly religious, yet casually tossed ladies' panties from Mardi Gras floats.

Carmela had taken to New Orleans like a duck to water. The Crescent City, the City That Care Forgot, the Big Easy. Only lately, things hadn't been so easy.

Carmela finished with a flourish. "There," she told her group. "The amazing Technicolor wedding layout."

"How very elegant," marveled Tandy Bliss. She slid a pair of bright red cheaters halfway down her bony nose and studied Carmela's handiwork. Tandy was a scrapbook fanatic of the first magnitude and one of Carmela's regulars at Memory Mine, the little scrapbooking store she owned on the fringe of the French Quarter in New Orleans. "But didn't you mention something about using vellum?"

Carmela dug into her pile of paper scraps and came up with a quick solution. "Three-inch squares of vellum go here and here," she said as she slid the thin, transparent paper atop the floral paper. "Gabby, you want to hand me those stickers?"

Gabby Mercer-Morris, Carmela's young assistant, passed over a sheet of embossed gold foil stickers. Carmela peeled one off gingerly and pressed it at the top of the vellum to anchor it.

"What a lovely, soft look," marveled Byrle Coopersmith. This was her first scrapbooking class, and she was wide-eyed with excitement. "I had no idea scrapbooks could be so elegant."

"People are always amazed at the sophisticated looks you can achieve," explained Carmela. She picked up a sample vacation scrapbook she'd created and flipped through the pages for all to see. "See . . . you can highlight a single photo by creating a gangbuster layout around it, use several photos for a fun montage effect, or turn your page into a kind of travel journal by incorporating your own personal notes and clippings. No matter what you do, scrapbooking is all about preserving memory in a very personal way." She passed the album to Byrle, who accepted it eagerly. "Think about it," continued Carmela. "Most people have snapshot collections that document all sorts of precious events: new babies, weddings, graduations, vacations. But what do they do with them?"

"Stick 'em in little plastic albums," said Tandy in her soft drawl. "Which is so *borrring.*"

"You got that right," said Carmela.

"Or toss 'em in shoe boxes like I used to," piped up a fifty-something woman with the incongruous name of Baby. Baby Fontaine was on the far side of fifty, but her tiny figure, pixie blond hair, peaches and cream complexion, and genteel accent lent a youthful aura. And Baby's friends, in no hurry to abandon the familiar, endearing moniker that had been bestowed on her back during her sorority days, continued to call her Baby.

There were five of them seated around the table. Carmela and her assistant, Gabby. And Tandy, Byrle, and Baby.

Tandy had found her way to Carmela's shop when it first opened, almost a year ago, and she was practically a fixture now. Tandy had completed elaborate scrapbooks that celebrated her wedding anniversary, vacations in Maui, and all of her children's varied and sundry accomplishments. Now she was working on a combination journal/scrapbook that documented her family heritage. Blessed with six grandchildren, Tandy had also done scrapbooks on each of the little darlings. And with two more grandchildren on the way, Tandy was now mulling over creative ways to showcase sonograms.

From out on the street came a loud hoot followed by raucous laughter.

"Parade goers," pronounced Tandy. She wrinkled her nose, swiveled her small, tight head of curls toward Gabby. Her smile yielded lots of teeth. "You going tonight?" she asked.

Gabby glanced down at her watch. "Are you kidding? I wouldn't miss it. Stuart's picking me up in . . ." She frowned as she studied the time. ". . . half an hour." Then, glancing quickly at Carmela, she asked, "I can still borrow your digital camera, right?"

"Not a problem," replied Carmela. "Knock yourself out."

"And we *are* closing at five today, aren't we?" said Gabby.

Carmela nodded again. "If we don't, we'll all be trapped here," she joked. Carmela loved her location next to one of the romantic, tucked-away courtyards on the edge of the French Quarter. With the gently pattering three-tiered fountain, overflowing pots of bougainvillea, and tiny, twinkling lights adorning the spreading acacia tree, it was a truly magical setting. But when Mardi Gras was in full swing, as it certainly would be tonight with the traditionally raucous Pluvius parade wending its way through downtown, the ordinarily manageable throngs of tourists would swell to an enormous, rowdy crowd. And that was way over here on Governor Nicholls Street. By the time you got to Bourbon Street, with its jazz clubs, daiquiri bars, and second-floor balustrades lined with shrieking, bawdy revelers, the scene would be utter chaos.

"Stuart got us an invitation to the Pluvius den," boasted Gabby.

The den she was referring to was the big barnlike structure down in the Warehouse District. Here, amid great secrecy, the Pluvius krewe had constructed twenty or so glittering Mardi Gras floats that would be revealed to appreciative crowds when their gala parade rolled through the streets of New Orleans in just a matter of hours.

The Stuart that Gabby gushed over so breathlessly was her husband of two months, Stuart Mercer-Morris. Mercer-Morris wasn't just a politically correct hybrid of their two last names, it was Stuart's family name. The same Mercer-Morris family that had owned the Mercer-Morris Sugar Cane Plantation out on River Road since the mid-1800s. The same Mercer-Morris family that owned eight car dealerships.

Baby nodded her approval. "It's a kick to visit the dens. Del's in the Societé Avignon, so you can believe we've done our fair share of preparade partying." Baby rolled her eyes in a knowing, exaggerated gesture, and Tandy and Beryl giggled. "Lots of mud bugs and hurricanes," Baby added, referring to those two perennial New Orleans favorites, crawfish and rum drinks.

Carmela was only half listening to Baby's chitchat as she studied a New Baby Boy scrapbook page she was planning to display in her front window. Then she let her eyes roam about Memory Mine, the little scrapbooking store she had created.

Memory Mine had been her dream come true. She'd always "shown a creative bent" as her momma put it, excelling in drawing and painting all through high school, then graduating with a studio arts degree from Clarkston College over in nearby Algiers. That degree had helped land Carmela a job as a graphic designer for the *Times-Picayune*, New Orleans's daily newspaper. Once she'd mastered the art of retail advertising, she'd parlayed her design experience into that of package goods designer for Bayou Bob's Foods.

Bayou Bob, whose real name was Bob Beaufrain, fancied himself a marketing maven and spun off new products at a dizzying rate. Carmela designed outrageous labels for Big Easy Etouffee, Turtle Chili, and Catahoula Catsup. In Carmela's second year on the job, just after she married Shamus Allan Meechum, Bayou Bob hit it big with his Gulfaroo Gumbo and got approached by Capital Foods International. Not one to pass up a buyout opportunity, Bayou Bob sealed the deal in three days flat. Carmela may have sharpened her skills as a package goods designer, but she was suddenly out of a job.

She trudged around to design studios and ad agencies, showing her portfolio, schmoozing with art directors. She got positive feedback and more than a few chuckles over her Turtle Chili layouts, along with a couple of tentative job offers.

But her heart just wasn't in it.

Deep inside, Carmela nursed a burning desire to build a business of her own. She was already consumed with scrapbooking, as were many of her friends, and New Orleans still didn't have the kind of specialized store that offered albums, colorful papers, stencils, rubber stamps, and punches, the scrapbooking necessities that true scrapbook addicts crave.

Why not do what she loved and fill the niche at the same time?

With a hope and a dream, Carmela put together a bare-bones business plan and shared her idea with husband Shamus. Turned out, he was as fired up as she was, proud that his wife had "*gumption*," as he put it. Shamus, who was pulling down a reasonably good salary from his job as vice president at his family's Crescent City Bank, even offered to foot the rent for the first four months.

Locating an empty storefront on Governor Nicholls Street, Carmela set about masterminding a shoestring renovation. Once the site of an antique shop, the former owners had packed up their choicest items and fled to Santa

Fe, where competition in the antique business wasn't quite so fierce. Abandoned in their wake were a few of their clunkier, less tasty pieces. An old cupboard, a tippy library table, a dusty lamp.

The jumble of furniture hadn't deterred Carmela in the least. She took the old cupboard, gave it a wash of bright yellow paint, and lined it with mauve fabric. By adding a few painted shelves, the newly refurbished cupboard became the perfect display case for papers, foils, and stencils.

Likewise, the old library table, which had probably been too ponderous to transport, was also put to good use. Carmela shoved it into the back of the store, jacked up the errant leg, bought a dozen wooden chairs at a flea market, and declared the table "craft central." For five dollars an hour, scrapbookers were welcome to sit at the table and use all the stencils, punches, paper cutters, and calligraphy pens they wanted, as well as dip into a huge bin of scrap paper.

Flat files were added, as well as displays of albums, photo mats, how-to books, acid-free pens and adhesives, markers, brass stencils, scissors, and card stock. The walls were lined with wire racks that held hundreds of sheets of different papers that featured all manner of designs and colors.

Shamus had encouraged Carmela every step of the way. After all, she'd been a designer and had a real knack for teaching others how to piece together a great layout. And Shamus had been bragging-rights proud that his wife was able to demonstrate such business smarts. In New Orleans, a woman-owned business, albeit a small one, was still as scarce as hen's teeth.

But all that had been a year ago, when life had seemed as eternally bright as sunlight on Lake Pontchartrain. Because four months ago, Shamus up and left her. Had tossed his jockey underwear into his suitcase, grabbed his football trophies and camera gear, and taken his leave from their home in the rather elegant Garden District. Reluctantly (or so he said) and pleading the Gauguin precedent, Shamus left in his wake a closet full of three-piece suits, a rack of wing tips, and his rose gold wedding band.

Carmela bit her lip as she passed a piece of teddy bear art over to Tandy. Shamus's parting words still stung like nettles.

The rat had told her he craved space, that he desperately needed breathing room. He'd pleaded and cajoled, telling her he *despised* banking, that he needed a respite, a time-out from *everything* in his life. Tearfully, Shamus told her he wanted to focus on photography and that he needed to find a renewed sense of *balance* in his life.

Carmela had been stunned. She thought Shamus *loved* banking. She thought Shamus had *found* balance. She thought Shamus loved *her*.

But there was something else, something that didn't sit right. All this raw emotion from a good old boy who tended to display his feelings only in such instances as a superlative bourbon mash or a well-thrown Tulane touchdown, had seemed, well . . . forced.

Why, suddenly, seemingly overnight, had Shamus, *her* Shamus, become a touchy-feely, need-my-space, got-to-break-free-and-grow kind of guy?

Très strange.

Carmela wasn't sure, she hadn't yet found *concrete* proof, but Shamus's departing words had sounded suspiciously as though he'd been reading from a TelePrompTer. As though the words had been . . . borrowed? Had a few key phrases in Shamus's exit speech been culled from the current crop of self-help books? Yeah . . . maybe.

Carmela had even racked her brain, trying to remember if she'd heard some of those same phrases uttered by Dr. Phil on *Oprah*. Could be.

Whatever fishy circumstances had surrounded Shamus's departure, Carmela's humiliation hadn't ended there.

Two weeks after Shamus traded their large brick home in the Garden District for the bare-bones privacy of his family's old camp house in the Barataria Bayou, her in-laws had come a-knocking. Led by Glory Meechum, Shamus's overbearing older sister, the in-laws had politely yet resolutely asked her to vacate the premises of what, they explained, was technically *the family's* house.

Never mind that Shamus had also slapped *the family* in their collective faces when he renounced his vice presidency from their beloved Crescent City Bank. Blood was thicker than water and, right or wrong, the family was abiding with Shamus's decision.

What could she do? In New Orleans, the only thing thicker than blood was gumbo.

Carmela abided by her in-laws' wishes, making it clear to them that, when it came to cordiality and common decency, she regarded the Meechum family as being on a par with the Manson family.

Loading her few personal possessions into the vintage Cadillac she'd dubbed Samantha, Carmela and her dog, Boo, set off for her momma's house in Chalmette. They spent five days there. Carmela wandered the woods and piney forests where she'd grown up, sat by the edge of Sebastopol Pond, and grieved. Boo, her little fawn-colored shar-pei, kept her company, gazing at her with a perpetually furrowed brow and sorrowful eyes. And when Carmela cried long, mournful sobs, the dog with the chubby face sighed deeply as well, the picture of soulful love and canine understanding.

Like pages in a scrapbook, Carmela looked back over her time with Shamus. She worried about what was good and true and okay to keep, what should be chucked out. Or at least stored in a file in the bottom drawer.

It wasn't easy; her defeat was so recent.

On the fifth day spent at her momma's, Carmela finally came around to worrying about *her* life, *her* future. She decided that was the most important thing now.

With a heavy heart but a clear head, she assured her momma that she was okay. Not exactly great yet, but she thought she'd be able to find her way there in her own good time.

Carmela and Boo drove back to the French Quarter, sacked out on a futon in her scrapbooking shop for a few days, then finally located a tiny garden apartment just two blocks from her store. The rent was right, the atmosphere slightly decadent, and the decor showed promise. Tucked behind Ava Grieux's little tourist-trap voodoo shop, Carmela's new apartment boasted coral red walls and all the incense she cared to inhale.

"ARE YOU going to the Pluvius parade?" Gabby asked Carmela. Gabby was pretty and twenty-two, with dark hair and even darker eyes, primly turned out today in a pistachio-colored cashmere twinset and elegantly draped gray slacks. Carmela, on the other hand, with her newfound single status and French Quarter lifestyle, was now veering toward clothes with a slightly more flamboyant style. Today she wore slim black jeans and a hand-painted black denim jacket shot through with wisps of gold and mauve.

"I wouldn't miss tonight's parade for the world," Carmela assured her. "I ran into Jekyl Hardy at the French Market the other day, and he was telling me that all this year's floats have these fantastic *oceania* themes. Sea serpents and jellyfish and flying pirate ships."

Jekyl Hardy was chief designer for the Pluvius floats and a dear friend of Carmela's. They'd gone to art school together and both volunteered with the Children's Art Association.

Gabby followed Carmela the few steps over to a flat file, where Carmela rummaged for paper. "I don't suppose you're going with Shamus?" Gabby asked quietly. Gabby was a newlywed of four months and regarded marriage as a holy sacrament and the Mount Olympus of feminine accomplishment. Gabby had confided to Carmela that she prayed to Saint Jude, the patron saint of lost causes, every night to help mend her and Shamus's differences. She also assured Carmela that she would light a candle each week until the two were once again reunited.

Carmela had thanked Gabby warmly, then suggested she might want to purchase those candles in bulk.

"I only ask," continued Gabby, "since I know Shamus used to be a member of the Pluvius krewe." They were back at the table again, and Carmela slid a sheet of calico-printed paper to Baby, a sheet of rose-printed paper to Tandy.

"That's no longer an option for my dearly departed husband," Carmela told her. Dearly departed was the term she most often used in polite society.

"Oh, I'm sorry, dear," said Byrle. She looked up with a distracted air. "Your husband is dead?"

Carmela smiled pleasantly. "No, just living in the bayou." She saw that Byrle was trying to fit way too many photographs onto a single page. Reaching a hand across the table, Carmela slid three of the photos off the page that Byrle seemed to be struggling with. "Try it with just these five," suggested Carmela. "And maybe . . ." She reached behind her and grabbed a sheet of lettering. ". . . this nice blocky typeface."

"Dead, living in the bayou . . . same thing," Tandy said with an offhand shrug.

"Pardon?" said Gabby. She peered at Tandy as a frown creased her forehead. She was never quite sure when Tandy was serious or just teasing her.

"A few years back," said Tandy, "my husband's uncle, Freddy Tucker, moved to the bayou out near Des Allemands. He had some romantic notion about living in harmony with nature, if you can call alligators and snakes nature. Anyway, after a while the poor fellow went sort of feral." Tandy glanced up to find a half circle of startled faces. "You know," she explained, "Uncle Freddy started picking fights whenever the relations got together for weddings or funerals."

"Sounds normal to me," said Baby. She had cousins who hailed from down in Terrebonne Parish, also hard-core bayou country, so nothing surprised her.

"Eventually, Uncle Freddy just stopped coming to town," said Tandy. "We never saw him again."

Gabby stared at Tandy, fascinated. She was the only one in the group "from not here," as they say in New Orleans. Which meant Gabby hadn't been born and bred in New Orleans and was sometimes overwhelmed by their offbeat brand of humor.

"You never saw him again?" asked Gabby, looking unsettled.

"Nope," cooed Tandy happily. "We don't really know what happened to Uncle Freddy. I suppose the old coot could still be out there, unless he got bit by a cottonmouth or something."

"Do you think that'll be the case with Shamus?" Gabby asked Carmela. "That he'll continue to live out at his camp house, I mean. Not get bit by a cottonmouth."

Carmela frowned as she snipped a piece of powder-blue gingham-patterned paper with her wavy-edged scissors. "No," she said. "No such luck."

AVA GRIEUX swept through the front door of Memory Mine with her red opera cape trailing grandly behind her and a king cake clutched in her hands.

"Afternoon, ladies," she greeted them. Ava Grieux was tall and sinewy, with a tousled mane of auburn hair and porcelain skin. Ava Grieux, formerly Marianne Sommersby and first runner-up in the Mobile, Alabama, Miss Teen Sparkle Pageant, had been brought up to believe that a lady should never set foot in the sun without benefit of hat or parasol. That Southern notion, instilled by her mother and grandmother, had stuck with her, and now, at age thirty, Ava still had a flawless if not somewhat luminous complexion. Never mind that she'd changed her name and now ran a slightly tacky voodoo shop that catered shamelessly to tourists with its overpriced candles and herbal love spells stuffed into little silk bags and tied with ribbon.

"Have a piece of king cake, Gabby," urged Ava as she set the goody in the middle of the table. "You can afford the calories."

King cake, to the uninitiated, is basically braided coffee cake topped with frosting and liberally sprinkled with purple and green granulated sugar. It's a de rigueur Mardi Gras treat and always features a plastic Mardi Gras baby baked inside. Whatever lucky person chomps a molar down on the tiny plastic toy is then beholden to provide the *next* king cake.

"Just who are the Pluvius queen candidates this year?" asked Tandy, breaking off a piece of king cake and suddenly getting swept up in the Mardi Gras spirit.

"Swan Dumaine and Shelby Clayton are the front-runners," said Baby with a knowing smile. "The other four girls are all very pretty and sweet, but they don't count. They're not *seriously* in the running." Baby was well versed in the social intricacies and political strata of Mardi Gras. Back in their debutante days, both her daughters had been queen candidates as well as reigning Mardi Gras queens for the Societé Avignon.

Ava Grieux flashed a broad smile at Carmela. "Just for you, my dear . . . batteries." She tossed a small brown paper sack onto the table.

"Batteries," exclaimed Carmela. "Thank you, Ava, you're my saving angel!" Carmela tore the batteries out of their blister pack, then quickly inserted them in the digital camera she'd promised to lend Gabby.

"Honey, you're not eating any king cake," said Tandy to Ava.

Ava made a face, held out one of her arms. "I think I'm gettin' crepey."

"You're what?" said Baby.

"You know those little dingle bags that hang down from the inside of your upper arms?" asked Ava. "I think I'm gettin' those."

Carmela glanced at Ava's arms. They were as sleek and toned as ever.

"Do you-all have any barbells I can borrow?" Ava asked Carmela.

"Soup cans," pronounced Baby.

"Pardon?" said Ava.

"You can use cans of soup instead of barbells. To do arm curls," said Baby. She pantomimed the exercise.

"Then, once you've worked up a real appetite, you can heat up the soup and really chow down," laughed Tandy.

"Listen," Ava said to Carmela, rapidly losing interest in her dingle bags, "I have to head back to my shop. I've got two customers stopping by to pick up masks."

In the past year, Ava had taken up the ancient art of mask making. She was hoping to eventually go legit and convert her store from a voodoo trinket shop to an upscale *atelier* that offered custom leather mask making. And she was off to a rousing good start. Ava already had more than two dozen customers who'd ordered custom masks for this year's Mardi Gras festivities.

"You come bang on the door when you're ready, honey, okay?" said Ava. "Then we'll head on down to the parade."

"Gotcha," nodded Carmela as Ava slipped out in a flurry of red fabric.

The two women were going to the Pluvius parade later tonight and had plans to hopefully meet up with friends and watch the parade over near the French Market.

Carmela turned back to her group. "Remember, after today, we won't have any formal classes. Until Mardi Gras is over, that is."

They nodded sagely. They knew that from now until next Tuesday, Fat Tuesday, which was still a week away, there'd be a parade almost every night and the entire French Quarter would be clogged with revelers.

"And we'll be closed all day Fat Tuesday," Carmela added.

JOSTLING DOWN Rampart Street two hours later, Carmela was amazed by the hordes of revelers, most of whom were clutching little plastic *geaux* cups, or to-go cups, purchased from the various bars. They were still five blocks from the parade route, and already it was impossible to walk on the sidewalk.

"Come on!" Ava grabbed Carmela's hand and tried to speed her along. "If we cut down Cabildo, then hook a right into Pirate's Alley, we can pop out near Jackson Square," she suggested.

Carmela was still wearing her black denim outfit, but Ava had changed into red hip-hugger snakeskin slacks, a skintight black nylon T-shirt emblazoned with a glitter skull, and what appeared to be a spring-loaded bra. Her ensemble would have drawn stares in any other part of the country, but it was arguably a tad conservative for Mardi Gras. Because, as the two women jostled their way through the French Quarter, the costumes worn by the myriad revelers and sightseers were amazing to behold.

Venetian lords and ladies clad in elegant velvets and brocades sported gilded bird masks with hooked beaks. A man in a swirling black *Phantom of the Opera* cape had somehow engineered an enormous crystal chandelier to hang above his head. Drag queens in full costume and makeup were trying to outshine the leather bondage aficionados, and a man wearing a suede spotted-dog costume walked a real spotted dog on a leash.

These costumed and coiffed revelers were accompanied by legions of Peking Opera performers, swashbuckling pirates, hooded monks, knights in armor, and even a cardinal in a mitered hat. They all jostled together, funneling down the narrow avenues of the French Quarter toward the parade route, their glittery costumes sparkling under neon lights.

Carmela stopped nearly a dozen times to snap pictures, using her little auto-focus Leica, since she had lent her digital camera to Gabby. She was determined to create three or four scrapbook pages that would showcase tonight's parade and serve as a knockout window display. Hopefully, her pages would inspire others to seek out her scrapbooking know-how and help fuel a demand for all the special green and purple paper, gold lettering, and Mardi Gras stamps and stickers she'd stocked up on.

"Over here, Carmela. Quick!" Ava beckoned to her from a spot she'd commandeered directly in front of two young men who were perched atop a twelve-foot-high stepladder, with a homemade viewing platform.

Carmela slipped into place just as the first marching band blared its way down Decatur Street, the brass section prancing and strutting in true Mardi Gras style.

Behind them, two dozen flambeaus twirled their flaming naphtha-fueled torches, dancing for coins, as has been the tradition for almost a hundred years.

Then, as the first floats rolled by, strands of purple and gold beads began to sail overhead. These were traditional Mardi Gras throws being tossed to the eager crowd by Pluvius krewe members who rode atop the floats. It wasn't long before ordinarily decorous women were shouting at each other and elbowing one another out of the way, getting embroiled in heated disputes over exactly *who* a strand of colored beads had been intended for.

Cries of "Throw me somethin', mistuh!" rang out as a starfish-themed float and a giant dolphin float glided by. The soft Cajun dialects mingled with the flat, nasal sound of tourists from up North, and lilting tones of African Americans blended with the soft, easy strains that were distinctly Baton Rouge.

It's a gumbo of dialects, thought Carmela, as the parade seemed to kick into high gear and the night became a whirlwind of bright colors, loud music, and frenzied activity. Giant heads with gaping grins loomed from prows of floats that sparkled with thousands of tiny lights.

Carmela executed a deft leap and a one-handed catch and settled another strand of Mardi Gras beads around her neck. "Look," she nudged Ava, "there's the sea serpent float Jekyl Hardy mentioned."

Plumes of smoke from the carefully concealed dry ice machine billowed into the night air, and a motorized head and tail wagged from side to side as the enormous green and yellow sea monster suddenly dominated the street. The scene was kitchy, totally over the top, and truly awesome to behold. All Carmela could do was grin from ear to ear as more strands of plastic beads rained down around her.

Then, just when the massive sea serpent float was directly in front of them, it shuddered to a stop.

Taken aback, the crowd stared curiously up the steep sides of the float. Twenty feet above them, some kind of disturbance seemed to be taking place. Men in white silk robes and white plastic masks milled about, talking in urgent voices and bending down over something.

Carmela's first thought was that there might be a mechanical problem with the sea serpent. Or that the crew had run short of beads or coins.

But, suddenly, the *whoop whoop* of a police siren sliced through the din of the parade noise. A murmur rose from the crowd, and people pressed closer to the float, craning their necks upward. It was obvious something more serious in nature was taking place up top. But what?

A police cruiser, its blue and red lights pulsing, wove its way between a marching band and group of flag twirlers. With a squeal of brakes, the cruiser pulled in front of the float, and two police officers jumped out. They rushed immediately to the side of the float and extended their arms upward.

Suddenly, from high above, a body was dangled over the side.

"Someone's ill," Carmela said to Ava. "I think they're trying to get him down off the float."

The crowd, sensing a defining moment, suddenly hushed.

Ava nodded. "Must have drunk too much or took sick."

The men atop the float seemed hesitant in their attempt to pass the body down to the two police officers. The sick krewe member, still clad in his fluttering white tunic and mask, hung uncertainly over the side of the float. From street level, the police continued to stretch their arms upward, ready to catch him.

A dozen hands seemed to release the body all at once, and it appeared to hang in midair for a split second. Then the police below grappled to catch the falling man. They fumbled for a brief moment, then got purchase on the body. Gently lifting the man down, they laid him on the pavement.

Carmela edged forward to see what was going on.

One of the police officers knelt down and carefully peeled the plastic mask from the face of the injured krewe member.

A gasp went up from everyone nearby. The poor man's eyes had rolled back in his head, and only the whites of his eyes were showing. His face was literally blue.

"His breathing must have stopped," said Ava. "Or he choked on something."

"My God," said Carmela, squinting at the downed man. "I think I know that poor soul. I think it's Jimmy Earl Clayton!"

"He might be gone," Ava pronounced in a matter-of-fact tone.

"Don't say that," admonished Carmela as two more sirens pierced the night with boisterous whoops. "Here come the paramedics now. Maybe he just had too much to drink." It was no secret that krewe members riding on floats often drank to the point of complete inebriation.

"He's sure feelin' poorly," said Ava in a classic understatement.

A second police car, as well as a red and white ambulance, pulled up alongside the float.

Two paramedics, looking very polished and professional in their crisp white uniforms, hopped from the ambulance and sprinted for the man who lay sprawled in the street. The two newly arrived police officers pulled open the back door of the ambulance and unloaded a metal gurney. It jittered across the uneven road surface as they wheeled it over, stopping just short of the body.

Both paramedics were on their knees, crouched over the inert man.

Carmela strained to hear what was being said but could only catch fragments of conversation.

". . . needs an airway," said the first paramedic.

". . . so swollen, I can't see his . . ." came the panicky reply from the second paramedic. He probed at the mouth of the collapsed man with latex-gloved hands, obviously frustrated in his attempt to establish an airway.

The two paramedics remained bent over the man, working on him furiously. Then Carmela saw one of the paramedics pull a small instrument from his medical bag. A sharp glint of metal told Carmela it must be a scalpel.

"Traching him," murmured a man next to her.

Carmela peered intently at the scene in front of her and saw that one of the paramedics was, in fact, performing an emergency tracheotomy. Crouched on the pavement, a single wavering flashlight held by one of the police officers, the circumstances were primitive at best. She prayed the paramedic was blessed with a steady pair of hands.

Finally, their emergency procedure seemingly accomplished and an airway established for Jimmy Earl, the police and paramedics rolled the inert man onto a stretcher. Then they scrambled to their collective feet and rushed him to the back door of the ambulance. As they slid the poor man in, one of the paramedics jumped in beside him. Then the door was slammed shut, and the other paramedic clambered into the driver's seat. Lights flashed, the engine roared to life, and the siren gave a single plaintive *whoop* as the ambulance screeched off down the street.

Chapter 2

THE WALLS IN Carmela's apartment were painted coral, a rich, satisfying red that matched the tumble of bougainvillea that sprang from the brown ceramic pots crouched outside her front door. Her furnishings were mostly thrift-shop finds. Chairs and couches with classic lines that she'd slipcovered in crisp, natural beige cotton.

Ava Grieux had donated a couple of sisal rugs, claiming they were "too upscale" for her shop, whatever *that* meant.

The rest of the furnishings were little touches Carmela had found in the bargain back rooms of French Quarter antique shops. An ornate framed mirror with some of the gilt scuffed off. A piece of wrought iron that had once been part of a balustrade on some grand old home and now functioned as a dandy shelf for Carmela's collection of antique children's books. Brass candleholders that were so oversized they looked like they must have once resided in a church.

It wasn't the sprawling grandeur of the Garden District, that was for sure.

But her apartment *did* reflect the quirky charm and old-world ambiance of the French Quarter. Punchy yet relaxed, a little bit decadent, definitely Belle Epoque. A distinct flavor that could only be found in this birthplace of New Orleans.

Carmela knew that most visitors, once captivated by the French Quarter's spell, would give their eyeteeth to live here. And all she had to do was get tossed out of her own home. Correction, get tossed out of *Shamus's* home.

Carmela was in a downer mood tonight and knew it. Then again, who wouldn't be after seeing poor Jimmy Earl Clayton get handed down from his sea serpent float and laid out pathetically in the middle of the street for all to see?

It was an ignominious moment for one of the Pluvius krewe's big muckety-mucks. And not exactly the best way to cap off their gala torchlight parade.

Had Jimmy Earl been resuscitated at the hospital? Carmela wondered. She certainly hoped so. They'd probably taken Jimmy Earl to Saint Ignatius Hospital, where they had a crack ER team.

The more Carmela thought about it, the more she figured the poor man must have suffered some sort of cardiac incident. That would account for his terrible palor, his inability to breathe, right?

Jimmy Earl was young, mid-thirties, still in fairly good shape. But in a city that dined nightly on crawfish bisque, deep-fried shrimp, andouille sausage, fried oyster po'boys, and bread pudding with whiskey sauce, early onset heart attacks weren't exactly unheard of.

Carmela grabbed a carton of orange juice from her small refrigerator and poured herself a glass. Stepping out of her shoes, she padded back across the floor to an antique wicker lounge chair that had been bolstered with down-filled cushions. She flopped down and nestled in. Stretching her legs out, she caught the matching footstool with her toe, pulled it toward her.

Ah, that was better. Now she could kick back and relax. Carmela took a sip of juice, savoring the sweet, fruity taste, and closed her eyes.

For one split second tonight, when she'd seen that poor limp body in the white mask and tunic being hauled off the sea serpent float, Carmela had experienced a terrible moment when she'd imagined that it might be Shamus. Somehow, her mind had flashed on the idea that Shamus had been up there, riding in the Pluvius parade with his old krewe, and that something bizarre had befallen him.

But, of course, she'd known it *couldn't* have been Shamus. Shamus wasn't a member of the Pluvius krewe anymore. When he renounced his old life, he'd renounced *everything*. Gone cold turkey. Bid adios to her, his job, his social obligations.

There was no way Shamus would have been riding on that float.

Experiencing an unexpected flood of relief, Carmela was suddenly angry with herself.

Why had she thought it might be Shamus? How had *that* thought insinuated itself in her head?

Better yet, why would she even care? Wasn't she still furious at Shamus? Yes, she was. Of course she was.

Footsteps scraped across cobblestones in the courtyard outside her door and Boo, suddenly roused, let loose with a mournful howl. In almost perfect synchronization, the doorbell rang.

Carmela pulled herself out of the chair, ambled to her front door, opened it as much as the safety chain would allow.

Two uniformed police officers peered in at her.

"Ma'am?" said one.

"Yes?" said Carmela pleasantly.

The two officers continued to stare in at her.

Suddenly, reluctantly, Carmela had a pretty good idea of why the two policemen were here.

"Has something happened at the store?" Carmela asked then sighed deeply. Most business owners, the *smart* business owners, reinforced their store windows with wooden barriers and chicken wire during Mardi Gras. It was a good preventive measure that kept the party hearty hordes from trampling or pushing their way through your plate-glass windows. If the police were here, it was a pretty good indication something like that had happened. That the front window had been busted in or at the very least cracked. Darn. And she'd just put in a brand-new display.

"Ma'am . . ." one of the officers was saying.

"It's the front window, isn't it?" said Carmela as she unhooked the chain and reluctantly pulled the door open. "I could just kick myself. I *knew* I should have—" she began, even as she wondered if her insurance would cover it.

"It's not your window, ma'am," said the officer whose name tag read Robineau. He hesitated. "We're here about your husband."

Carmela was so surprised she took a step backward. Boo, who'd been milling about at her knees for the past minute, suddenly pressed forward for a good, investigatory sniff of the two men who stood in the doorway.

"My husband?" said Carmela. *What could this be about?*

"Yes ma'am," said Officer Robineau as he continued in that maddeningly polite procedural manner that many policemen adopt. "You are the wife of Shamus Allan Meechum?"

"*Estranged* wife," Carmela replied. "Shamus and I are separated."

"Well, ma'am," continued Robineau, "Mr. Meechum's been taken in for questioning."

Carmela frowned. *Why would the police want to question Shamus? What on earth has he done to warrant being taken into custody by the police? Gotten drunk and propositioned one of New Orleans's social doyennes?* Carmela cleared that thought from her mind. *No, that would be no big deal. During Mardi Gras that kind of social impropriety was par for the course.*

"He's been arrested?" Carmela asked with some trepidation.

"No, ma'am," the second policeman, Officer Reagan, chimed in. "Not formally charged, nothin' like that. It's just like my partner said. Mr. Meechum is being *questioned*." Officer Reagan paused. "We'd like to ask you a few questions as well."

"You want to tell me exactly what this is about?" Carmela asked, a note of suspicion creeping into her voice.

Officer Reagan, who bore the sad look of a betrayed bloodhound said, "Your husband is being questioned concerning the apparent murder of Jimmy Earl Clayton."

Stunned, Carmela put a hand to her heart. "Jimmy Earl is dead?"

Officer Reagan nodded slowly.

This was shocking news to Carmela. Somehow, she'd been fairly sure the brilliant doctors at Saint Ignatius would work their medical magic on Jimmy Earl. That they'd EKG, EEG, or ECG him so he'd live to play the fool in yet another Mardi Gras celebration.

And what is this about Shamus? Why on earth would the police think he is involved?

"Oh, no," said Carmela, "poor Jimmy Earl. Such sad news. I thought for sure he'd . . ." her voice faltered. "I hoped it was something the doctors could easily fix. But this . . ." Shaking her head, Carmela motioned the two officers in. "Perhaps you'd better come in . . . tell me all about it."

Chapter 3

THE SUN WASN'T up yet, but something was making a dreadful racket.

Carmela lay in bed in a half-dream state, trying in vain to figure out what was going on. Flag twirlers in spangled uniforms and shiny white boots pranced in front of a green and yellow float. Then the float ground to a halt, and a giant phone was handed down to her.

What? Oh, oh. Phone, she finally decided.

Carmela fumbled for the pale blue princess phone she'd ripped from the wall in the butler's pantry the day she'd vacated Shamus's home.

"Hello," she croaked.

"Carmela." The voice was a deep, languid drawl.

Carmela uttered a sharp intake of breath. It was the rat himself: Shamus.

"What?" she mumbled. Lifting her head, she peered at the oversized dial on her vintage clock radio. It read a big five-fifteen. She hadn't slept more than six hours. No wonder she felt tired and crabby.

"Are you insane?" Carmela groaned into the phone at Shamus, already knowing the answer. "Because it's so early the *birds* aren't awake. It's so early the morning shift of bartenders down on *Bourbon Street* hasn't come on yet."

"Carmela, I need to talk to you." Shamus's voice was soft yet insistent.

Carmela grimaced. She hated that soft, wheedling tone. It drove her crazy and got to her practically every time.

She closed her eyes, tried not to conjure up a mental picture of him. It didn't work. In her mind's eye she could still see Shamus. Tall, six feet two, and the proud possessor of a lazy smile that tended to be devastating when he decided to turn it up a notch or two. Shamus had a sinewy body, strong hands, flashing brown eyes. And a soft accent. His mother hailed from Baton Rouge, and he carried her soft-spoken ways.

"What about?" Carmela asked. She pretty much knew what Shamus was going to say, but she didn't feel like making it easy for him. She swung her legs out of bed, hit the sisal rug, scrubbed the bottoms of her feet back and forth across the bristles, as though the rug were a loofah, and she could magically rub some energy into herself. Positive energy that would fortify her against Shamus.

"You heard what happened to Jimmy Earl Clayton?" Shamus asked her.

"You know something, Shamus?" she told him. "I was *there*. I was standing in front of the French Market when the entire Pluvius parade ground to a halt and the police had to lift the poor man down from his sea serpent float." Carmela didn't know why she was suddenly so defensive, but she couldn't seem to help herself. When they were living together, she'd always thought they brought out the best in each other. Now that they were apart, Shamus most definitely brought out the worst in her.

"You're not going to believe this, Carmela," Shamus roared back, "but the police questioned *me* last night. Me!" She could hear both anger and anxiety in his voice. "In fact, they held me at the police station until almost two in the morning!"

"I've got news for you, Shamus, they came and talked to me, too," Carmela fired back.

"What?" said Shamus, genuinely stunned. "When?"

"Last night," she told him. "Around ten, ten-thirty. They came to my apartment. The exceedingly small apartment I was forced to move into after you unceremoniously dumped me. The one I retreated to after your lovely sister ousted me from our former home."

"Carmela, we've been over this," Shamus said plaintively. "I didn't dump you; I love you. You're my wife."

"Let's see now," she said. "Would that be your have-and-to-hold-till-death-do-us-part wife? Or your I'll-get-back-to-you-when-I'm-good-and-ready wife?"

"*Carmela.*"

Oh man, she thought, *there's that insidious, wheedling tone again.*

"Carmela," repeated Shamus. "What did they want with you?"

"They wanted to know if I'd seen you last night. I told them I hadn't seen your sorry ass since you stuffed your argyle socks into your banjo case and boogied on out the door."

"Guitar. You know darn well I play guitar."

"Sweetheart, I don't care if you switched to a cello and joined the Boston Symphony. The police wanted to know if you were acquainted with Jimmy Earl Clayton."

"What did you tell them?" asked Shamus.

"I told them everybody and his brother from here to Shreveport was well acquainted with Jimmy Earl Clayton. The man was your basic Southern boy mover and shaker. Rated several column inches per week in the business section as well as a few mentions in our somewhat questionable society pages. And I use that term loosely, society being what it is today."

"That's it?"

"Of course that's it, Shamus. I even gave you the benefit of the doubt. I assumed you had absolutely nothing to do with this."

"You assumed right, darlin'."

Darlin'.

"So what was it that prompted the police to come knocking on my door then?" asked Carmela, more than a little peeved.

"Nothing. I was taking pictures of the Pluvius floats, for Christ's sake. I suppose I was in the wrong place at the wrong time, that sort of thing."

"And you just happened to snap a few photos of the sea serpent float," said Carmela.

"Yes."

"That's it?"

"Of course, that's it," said Shamus. He paused. "Well, I might of had words with Jimmy Earl."

"Words," Carmela repeated.

"Yes, words," Shamus said crossly.

"What exactly did you say to Jimmy Earl?" asked Carmela.

"What does it matter what I said?" Shamus answered in a huff. "It was nothing. Just because something happened to Jimmy Earl Clayton later on, doesn't mean it had anything to do with me. I'm truly sorry the man is dead, but I can assure you, I had nothing to do with it."

A tiny pinprick of heat slowly ignited behind Carmela's eyes. It spread into her forehead and set her nerves to jangling. Carmela knew what was happening. She was getting one of her Shamus headaches. They swept over her whenever he acted this way. Belligerent, aggressive, manipulative. In other words, your typical Southern male.

"I have to go, Shamus," she told him. "Nice talkin' to you. Bye-bye." Carmela slapped the phone back in its cradle, flopped back into bed. She lay on her back, staring up at the lazily spinning ceiling fan.

Just when you think you're safe, she thought to herself. *Just when you think your heart won't hurt again. What was it the Tin Man said when Dorothy was about to leave Oz and fly back home to Kansas? "Now I know I've really got a heart because I can feel it breaking."*

Carmela pulled the covers over her head. Did she want to be married to this clod, or should she go ahead and get that divorce? Which was it going to be? Door number one or door number two?

Carmela lay there trying to release the tension from her body. If she could just relax and clear her head. Maybe catch a couple more hours of sleep . . .

Nope. No way, nohow. Try as she might, counting sheep, counting her chickens before they were hatched, counting on her own resourcefulness, she couldn't fall back to sleep. That vision of Jimmy Earl Clayton being dropped from the float and laid out on the pavement seemed burned in her memory. It played over and over in her head like a bad news bulletin on CNN.

Do the police really think Shamus had something to do with it?

She shook her head in disgust. *Preposterous. Shamus may be a louse, he might even turn out to be a sneaky two-timing bum, but no way is he a killer.*

Carmela pulled herself out of bed, crept to the little kitchen, brewed a pot of nice, strong, chicory coffee. Scrounging one of yesterday's beignets, she went out to sit in the courtyard. Wisely, Boo remained tucked in her cozy little dog bed, the L.L. Bean version that had cost way more than Carmela's down comforter.

The sun, just beginning to peep over the crumbling brick wall that separated her little slice of the world from the rest of the French Quarter, felt warm on her shoulders. The steady drip-drip of the fountain was somehow reassuring.

Sipping her coffee, Carmela tried to banish thoughts of Shamus from her mind.

Begone, she commanded, as she let her eyes take in the beauty of the courtyard garden. The wrought-iron benches, the lush thickets of bougainvillea, the old magnolia tree dripping with lacy fronds of Spanish moss. Against the brick wall, tender green shoots of cannus peeped up through the dirt, and tendrils of tuberose curled on gnarled pine trellises that had been cut and woven by hand more than a hundred years ago.

There was a powerful amount of history here in the French Quarter, Carmela told herself as she took a fortifying sip of hot coffee. Which would make it a logical place to begin one's life anew.

Chapter 4

"KETAMINE," EXCLAIMED GABBY. "What on earth is ketamine?" She stared at Tandy Bliss in wide-eyed amazement.

Tandy had shown up promptly at ten o'clock. A packet of photos that showcased two of her grandchildren, wide-eyed, grubby-faced, and cooing over last night's Pluvius parade, were clutched in her hot little hands. Carmela figured Tandy must have hit the one-hour photo mill at first light.

"Sweetie," said Tandy, obviously enjoying her inside track, "don't you ever watch *Sixty Minutes*? Haven't you ever heard of *club drugs*?"

Gabby shrugged. The only clubs she was familiar with were the boisterous, rollicking clubs in the French Quarter. Jasmine's, Dr. Boogie's, Moon Glow. She assumed some drug trafficking went on there. But didn't it go on most everywhere now?

"Ketamine as in Special K," explained Tandy. "It's the stuff kids are always OD'ing on at raves."

"Oh," said Gabby as understanding began to dawn. "Come to think of it, I *have* heard of Special K. And raves. Aren't those like . . ." She searched for the right words. ". . . . *unauthorized* parties for high school kids?"

"More like *illegal*," snapped Tandy.

Standing behind the counter, listening intently, Carmela gave an involuntary shudder. How on earth did something like that connect with Jimmy Earl? *Or Shamus*, she mentally added. *Or Shamus*.

"Here's the thing," said Tandy as she waggled her index finger and moved closer to the counter. Carmela and Gabby, fascinated by her words, leaned in to listen, even though no one else was in the shop yet. "Poor Jimmy Earl had a whopping dose of this Special K stuff in his bloodstream."

The news of Jimmy Earl's death had made front-page headlines in the *New Orleans Times-Picayune*, though the story that followed was short, with very few details. Carmela knew it was only a matter of time, however, before a mix of rumors and truth concerning Jimmy Earl's demise would spread like wildfire throughout the city.

Gabby frowned. "Isn't too much of that stuff like *poison*? Where did you hear this?" she demanded. "And are you sure it was ketamine?"

"Darlings," Tandy's hyperthyroidal eyes got even bigger, "I heard it first-person from CeCe Goodwin, Darwin's sister-in-law." Darwin was Tandy's husband. "I'm not sure you-all know this," continued Tandy, "but CeCe is a nurse over at Saint Ignatius. And," she added triumphantly, "she just happened to be on duty last night when Jimmy Earl Clayton was brought in to the emergency room, all pale and white on a stretcher!"

That level of confirmation was good enough for Gabby. "Wow," she breathed. "Do they know how he overdosed? I mean, it *was* an overdose that killed him, right? Or did someone . . . what? Put it in his drink?"

"Nobody's saying anything about that yet," said Tandy. "Of course, it's possible Jimmy Earl could have taken the drugs himself. He *did* have a slight tendency to overdo."

Slight tendency, thought Carmela, *now there's an understatement.* She recalled seeing Jimmy Earl Clayton at a Garden District party one night doing the Macarena on top of someone's Louis XVI table, stoned out of his mind. Then there were his so-called after work "martini races" at Beltoine's. Those were legendary. And he'd once tossed his cookies on the eighteenth green at the Belvedere Country Club in full view of the clubhouse after he'd imbibed in a few too many bourbons. *No,* she thought, *Jimmy Earl Clayton hadn't been just a social drinker; he had darn near achieved professional status.*

"I'm sure the police will explore all possibilities," continued Tandy. "They're *extremely* clever when it comes to things like toxicology screening and forensic tests." Tandy talked as though she'd just earned a master's degree in criminal justice. "They can run tests that narrow everything down to the nth degree," she added.

Carmela listened intently to Tandy. That was exactly what the police had told her last night when they revealed that Jimmy Earl had been poisoned. *No wonder Shamus had been heartsick and worried this morning,* thought Carmela. *Being accused of such a heinous crime. And poor Jimmy Earl. Dead from an overdose of a drug that was popular, easy to obtain, and so very lethal.*

Still, there was no way Shamus would ever have been involved.

Jimmy Earl had so loved to party, Carmela mused. So there was that possibility. It wouldn't be the first time a white-collar business type had been caught using drugs. Just look at the popularity of cocaine. It was not only rampant these days, cocaine was most often the drug du jour among executives. Jimmy Earl could have just as easily developed a taste for club drugs. It happened. God knows, it happened.

On the other hand, Jimmy Earl was also a high-test financier. He was one of the senior partners in Clayton Crown Securities. Clayton Crown was one of the few independently owned brokerage firms left in New Orleans, and they handled millions, maybe billions, in stocks, bonds, mutual funds, and corporate financing. They also engineered mergers and acquisitions. Shamus had mentioned Clayton Crown on more than one occasion and had obviously had a lot of respect for them. In fact, Clayton Crown was considered a major player in New Orleans.

But as head of a prominent company like that, it was also possible Jimmy Earl had courted a few enemies over the years. Sooner or later, investors lost money, mergers went sour, financing fell through.

The question was, would someone have gone so far as to *kill* Jimmy Earl? Carmela thought about this for a moment, didn't come up with anything definitive. That would be a good question for Miss Cleo's Psychic Hotline, she decided.

"What happened to the float?" Carmela asked Tandy as an afterthought.

"Impounded," said Tandy. "Apparently, poor Jimmy Earl really choked down a megadose so they're checking *everybody* out."

The tightness in Carmela's chest loosened a notch.

"So . . ." said Gabby, unwilling to let the issue of Jimmy Earl Clayton's death go, "they *are* surmising that someone put ketamine in his drink?"

"Honey, nobody knows for sure yet," said Tandy. "But I'm not surprised that Jimmy Earl ingested so much," she sniffed. "Given the way most of those men tipple all that whiskey." Tandy gave a tight nod of her curly head, then headed for the back table to work on what would be her fourteenth scrapbook.

"GABBY, THIS couldn't be our last sheet of purple foil." Carmela stood at the paper cabinet, pulling open drawers, riffling though stacks of colored paper. She was feeling slightly discombobulated by Tandy's news as well as her obvious excitement over all the gory details.

Gabby looked up from the counter. "I think it is. Didn't you order more?"

Purple, green, and gold were the official colors of Mardi Gras, and Carmela knew that, over the next few weeks, everybody and his brother would be looking for those specific colors when they put together scrapbooks to showcase their Mardi Gras photos.

"I ordered a ream of foil paper. What's happened to it?"

Gabby frowned as though trying to recall. "I think Baby bought a hundred sheets for wrapping party favors. Then, the other day, while you were at lunch, some of the people from the Isis krewe came in and bought a whole bunch more. What with your regulars . . ." Gabby's voice trailed off uncertainly.

"I get the picture," said Carmela. "But we're going to need more. Pronto."

"Can you put an order in?" Gabby asked as she stood at the counter, arranging packets of foil stickers.

"I'll place an order online," Carmela assured her. "That way we'll get free shipping, and the order should be processed today."

"Good." Gabby looked up as the bell over the door sounded. "Oh, hi there," she said as Baby walked in, accompanied by one of her spectacularly beautiful daughters.

"You remember Dawn, don't you, everybody?" asked Baby as she proudly thrust her daughter in front of her. Dawn possessed the same classic features as her mother, but at twenty-five was a far younger and perkier version.

"Of course," said Carmela, greeting her warmly. "And this is Gabby, my assistant."

"Hello," said Dawn pleasantly as she pushed back a tendril of golden blond hair. "Hi, Tandy," she waved a hand toward the back of the store.

"Hi, sweetie," replied Tandy, barely looking up from her stack of photos.

"You heard about Jimmy Earl?" asked Baby.

Everybody nodded.

"Tragic," breathed Baby, "simply tragic."

"Tandy's husband's sister-in-law was there," said Gabby. It was a tangled reference, but Baby and Dawn seemed to pick up on it right away and nod expectantly. "She was right there in the emergency room when Jimmy Earl was brought in," finished Gabby with great enthusiasm.

Baby cranked her patrician brows up a notch and turned to study Tandy. "You don't say," she murmured. "Was the poor fellow still alive, do you know?"

"Dead as a doornail," said Tandy as she flipped through her stack of photos like playing cards.

"I heard they found drugs in his bloodstream," volunteered Dawn.

"Ketamine," called Tandy from the back, not wanting her inside information to be overshadowed by anyone else.

"Such a sad business," said Baby. "I think I'll make a crab étouffée to take over to Rhonda Lee." Rhonda Lee was Jimmy Earl's wife. Technically his widow now. "What do you think, honey?" She turned to Dawn.

"Crab's good," said Dawn.

"You know, the Claytons only live a few blocks away," Baby added. "It just goes to show you never know when or where tragedy's going to strike." There were murmurs of agreement from the women, then Baby shook her head as if to clear it. "On a happier note, I was telling Dawn about the wedding scrapbook pages you showed us yesterday."

"Ya'll know I just got married this past fall," said Dawn, brightening immediately. "To Buddy Bodine of the Brewton Creek Bodines. And I *still* haven't got my reception pictures in any semblance of order. Mama did my wedding album, of course, but these . . ." She sighed dramatically and held up a large fabric-covered box that presumably contained a jumble of reception photos. "I thought maybe ya'll could help," she finished with a pleading note.

"You thought right," said Carmela, draping an arm around Dawn's shoulders and leading her to the table in back. "In fact I just got a *load* of new albums and papers in. Here . . ." Carmela got Dawn and Baby seated at the table, then moved to a flat file cabinet and slid open a drawer. Drawing out an album with a thick cover of cream-colored, nubby paper embossed with tiny hearts, she passed it over to them.

Dawn fingered the thick paper. "I *adore* this cover, it's so tactile."

"That's because the paper's handmade," Baby quickly pointed out.

"And I absolutely *love* the almond color," said Dawn, "it's so much more elegant than just plain old pasty white. And those little hearts are *perfect*. So romantic."

"I've got some great papers, too," said Carmela, smiling at Dawn's over-the-top enthusiasm. "Some are mulberry, handmade in Japan. One even has cashmere fibers woven in."

CARMELA HAD almost forgotten about Jimmy Earl's demise by the time Donna Mae Dupres walked into her shop. A rail-thin little woman in her sixties with a tangle of gray hair, it was rumored that, in her youth, Donna Mae Dupres had been wilder than seven devils. But whatever mischief she had wrought and hearts she had broken had now been replaced by matronly decorum, for Donna Mae Dupres was a tireless fund-raiser and chairman of Saint Cyril's Cemetery Preservation Society.

Saint Cyril's, like all the ancient cemeteries in New Orleans, had been built aboveground back in the late 1700s. With constant outbreaks of yellow fever killing off large numbers of the population, early settlers had still found it nearly impossible to bury the bodies of their dead in the ground. The city of New Orleans, it seemed, was situated a good six feet *below* sea level. So the water table had a nasty habit of eventually returning their loved ones to them. An alternative method was hastily and cleverly devised. The aboveground tomb.

Carmela had been commissioned by Saint Cyril's Preservation Society to design a history scrapbook commemorating this historic old cemetery with its whitewashed tombs, historic monuments, and black wrought-iron gates. Quite a creative coup and the first *commercial* scrapbook project she'd ever received.

"Look what someone just donated, dear," said Donna Mae, handing a yellowed and tattered brochure to Carmela. "It's the program for the dedication of Saint Cyril's back in 1802."

Carmela accepted the fragile program. From the condition of the faded, half-shredded paper, it had obviously been forgotten for decades in someone's old trunk. And, over the past hundred years, it had been subjected to all manner of heat, mildew, mold, and insects.

"I'll get this treated with archival preserving spray right away," Carmela promised. "Like some of us, it doesn't need any more age on it."

"We located a few more black-and-white photos, too," said Donna Mae, handing over a large manila envelope. "And I asked some of the older folks to write down their recollections, just as you suggested."

"Wonderful," said Carmela. "That way this scrapbook can be an interesting amalgam of photos, news clippings, and written history."

Donna Mae beamed. "And you'll have a sample page or two to show the committee by the end of next week?"

"Count on it," Carmela assured her.

"Isn't that a coincidence," remarked Tandy as the door closed on Donna Mae Dupres. Tandy's eyes sparkled, and a curious smile occupied her thin face.

"What is?" asked Carmela.

"You're creating a scrapbook for Saint Cyril's," said Tandy, nodding at the packet of photos in Carmela's hands.

"Yes," said Carmela slowly, still wondering what coincidence Tandy was referring to.

"And the Clayton family plot is in Saint Cyril's," continued Tandy. "That's where poor Jimmy Earl will be laid to rest."

CARMELA WAS hunched over her iMac in her little office at the back of the store when Gabby poked her head in.

"Jekyl Hardy's on the phone," Gabby announced. She looked at the computer screen. "You got the order in okay?"

Yes, mouthed Carmela as she picked up the phone. "Jekyl, hey there," said Carmela.

Jekyl Hardy was a whirling dervish of a man who, for the better part of the year, made his living as an art and antiques consultant. When Mardi Gras rolled around, however, you could usually find Jekyl Hardy at the Pluvius or Nepthys dens, where he served as head designer and float builder for both krewes. Lean and wiry, dark hair pulled snugly into a ponytail, Jekyl Hardy was usually attired in all black. And since he was constantly overbooked, Jekyl was generally in a state of high anxiety throughout Mardi Gras—at least until the last beads were tossed and the queens were crowned on the final Tuesday night.

"Carmela, my most darling and favorite of all people," came his intense voice at the other end of the phone. "Do you know your name was mentioned in passing regarding our fair city's latest brouhaha?"

"What are you talking about, Jekyl?" She had a pretty good guess as to what Jekyl meant but still held out a faint glimmer of hope it might be something else.

"I'm referring to the untimely demise of Jimmy Earl Clayton," said Jekyl. "My phone's been ringing off the hook. As you know, I'm doing the decorations for the Pluvius Ball next Tuesday night." He paused dramatically. "And now there's a slight rumble the ball may be canceled altogether."

"Out of respect for poor Jimmy Earl?" asked Carmela.

"I suppose that would be the general idea," said Jekyl. "Although, from what I've heard about Jimmy Earl, the man didn't garner all that much respect when he was alive." Jekyl Hardy cackled wickedly, pleased with his offbeat brand of gallows humor. "But, Carmela, this nasty innuendo about your ex," Jekyl continued. "Very, very bad. Word on the street is that Shamus is suspect numero uno, the odds-on favorite for the moment."

"Not *my* favorite," replied Carmela.

"I admit it's all circumstantial," said Jekyl. "On the other hand, Shamus does posses a fairly famous temper and has been known to dip his beak in the demon rum. It's a fairly damning combination. I mean, *I* was running around like a chicken with its head cut off last night, trying to get the damn floats out the door, and I *still* noticed Shamus staggering around, sucking down hurricanes like they were Pepsi Colas."

"Shamus always does that at Mardi Gras," said Carmela. "Hell, Jekyl, the whole of New Orleans does."

"Point well taken," agreed Jekyl. "The question is, what's to be done now? What kind of damage control can you engineer?"

"There's nothing to do," said Carmela. "Except let the police do their job. I'm sure they'll blow off all the nasty rumors and innuendos soon enough and get on with their job."

"Which is?" said Jekyl.

"Figuring out who *really* did away with poor Jimmy Earl Clayton," responded Carmela. "Or, rather, I should say determine how he died. Since nothing's really been proven yet."

"Carmela," gushed Jekyl Hardy, "you're such a linear thinker. I absolutely *adore* that aspect of your brain. Me, I'm far too right brain. Just not enough balance between the cerebrum and the cerebellum, I guess. Or does it all take place in the cerebral cortex? I can't remember. Anyway, next question. What lucky gent is squiring you to the Marseilles Ball this evening?"

"No one," said Carmela. "I'm not going."

"But, darlin', you have your beauteous costume all figured out!" protested Jekyl.

Carmela grinned. To pass up a Mardi Gras ball was heresy for a Mardi Gras fanatic like Jekyl Hardy.

"Well," blustered Jekyl, "you most definitely *are* going, and don't bother trying to weasel your way out of it. You'll go with me."

"I don't think so—" protested Carmela.

"Mm-mn, case closed," declared Jekyl over her protests. "I'll meet you in the lobby of the Hotel Babbit at eight o'clock sharp. Okay?"

"Okay," sighed Carmela.

"And you *are* wearing that delightful black-and-gold creation, correct?"

Carmela sighed again. "If you say so." She wasn't sure she wanted to go flouncing into one of the biggest Mardi Gras parties of the year with her décolletage in plain sight while her soon-to-be-ex-husband was being speculated on so freely. On the other hand . . . what could she do? Shamus was surely innocent, right?

Chapter 5

GRANGER RATHBONE PAUSED on the sidewalk outside Memory Mine and narrowed his eyes as he stared in the store's front window. Gazing past his own reflection of a lanky, long-jawed man with an unruly shock of gray-brown hair, he could see a young woman standing at the counter. She seemed to be arranging various sheets of paper into some kind of display. Handling them with great care, as though the darn things were terribly fragile or expensive or something.

Granger Rathbone spat on the pavement, ran his rough knuckles across the lower half of his pockmarked face. *Women's stuff.* He snorted to himself. *Frilly, silly, women's stuff.* He glanced at the old-fashioned sign that read *Memory Mine, Scrapbooking Shop.* And underneath in smaller type, *Where Memories Are Made.*

Yeah, right, he thought, *memories.* He had a head full of memories, didn't he? Memories of a childhood spent up on the Saint Louis River. Gettin' the tar whupped out of him by his pa. His ma running off and leaving him and his squalling little sister behind.

Ain't got no time for memories like that, Granger Rathbone told himself. *Or for women who think such things are important.*

Gabby smiled sweetly at the man entering the scrapbooking shop and wondered briefly if he might be lost.

In fact, she was about to direct him to the CC Jazz and Social Club two doors down, when the rather rough-looking man reached into the breast pocket of his rumpled brown sport coat, pulled out a leather wallet, and snapped it open in her face.

"Detective Rathbone here to see Carmela Bertrand," he said with a curl of his lip. "You her?"

"No . . . no, I'm not," stammered Gabby. She was dismayed to see that Detective Rathbone seemed to take great enjoyment in the fact that he'd deliberately flustered her. "Carmela," Gabby called out.

Bent over the craft table in back, Carmela looked up expectantly. In an instant she caught the look of intimidation on Gabby's face, the smug look on the face of the man who had just entered her store. And she knew in a heartbeat that something was up. *Who is this person?* she wondered. *Cop? Private investigator?*

Carmela sauntered to the front counter slowly, taking careful stock of the man who gazed at her with such guarded interest as well as bold-faced arrogance. A cool smile settled across her face as she made up her mind to deal with this better than she'd dealt with Officers Robineau and Reagan last night. "I'm Carmela Bertrand, the owner," she said. "May I help you?"

"Damn right you can," replied the man. "Name's Granger Rathbone. I'm with Homicide. Need to ask you some questions."

"Concerning what?" Carmela said pleasantly. Now that she'd had some time to get used to the idea of Shamus being branded a murder suspect, she wasn't quite as spooked as she had been last evening. Besides, she knew that the charge or rumor or whatever it was, was entirely without basis.

"You know darn well why I'm here," spoke Granger Rathbone. "Your husband—"

"Ex-husband," said Carmela.

"I've got it on good authority you're still married to Mr. Shamus Allan

Meechum," said Granger Rathbone. "In the eyes of the law that makes him your old man."

"That makes him nobody's old man," Carmela replied breezily. "Case in point, Shamus is a relatively *young* man. Chronologically he's thirty-four. Although, as far as maturity level goes, one might peg him at around sixteen."

There was a titter from the back room. Tandy.

Granger Rathbone narrowed his eyes at Carmela. He'd dealt with smartass women like this before. Women you couldn't intimidate, couldn't seem to ruffle. *That's just fine,* he thought, *she'll whistle a different tune when her old man's hauled in and put behind bars and she has to scramble to make bail. She'll be sobbin' her heart out then.*

Granger Rathbone struck a casual pose and pulled out a black leather notebook.

"Shamus much of a drinker?" he asked.

"He likes his bourbon now and then." Carmela paused, managed an innocent smile. "I'll bet you do, too."

"You're just full of answers, aren't you, lady?" snarled Rathbone. "How about drugs. Does your husband do drugs?"

"Hardly," replied Carmela, determined not to let herself be outwardly intimidated by this thug. Gabby, on the other hand, was fairly trembling as she hovered nearby.

"Know if Mr. Meechum ever *deals* drugs?" asked Rathbone.

Carmela let a long beat go by before she said anything. Then she looked carefully down at her watch and gave Granger Rathbone a reproachful look. "Gosh," she said, "I'd really love to help with this thing, but I've got a scrapbooking class starting in about two minutes."

"We can do this another time," Granger Rathbone said as he fixed her with a hard-eyed gaze.

"Better phone ahead," suggested Carmela with as much sincerity as she could muster. "Things tend to get a little crazy around here." She turned to leave him, then hesitated. "Oh," she said, as though the thought had just popped into her head. "Next time, instead of stalking in here, trying to intimidate everyone in sight, why don't you call Seth Barstow's office first. Perhaps you've heard of his law firm, Leonard, Barstow and Streeter? Well, the thing of it is, Seth is my attorney. And if you have any more questions, I'm sure Seth can arrange a time and proper place when we can all sit down together and talk."

His black notebook snapped closed like an angry alligator as Granger Rathbone leaned forward, his pebbly cheeks flaring with color. "Think you're pretty hot stuff, don't ya, lady? Think you can outsmart me." He shook his head from side to side, curling his lip in disdain. "We'll just see about that." With that, Rathbone stalked out of her store.

"Whew," breathed Gabby after the door had slammed behind him. "I can't believe you handled him the way you did. You didn't even seem like you were a bit . . . *Carmela?*"

Gabby watched with surprise as Carmela staggered around to the back of the counter and eased herself down onto a wooden stool. Her face was white, and she looked about ready to faint.

"Don't tell me that was all an act," sputtered Gabby, a slow smile beginning to spread across her face.

Carmela bobbed her head, seemed to be having trouble catching her breath.

"Honey . . ." she grasped for Gabby's hand, "I haven't done that much playacting since sixth grade when I was sadly miscast for the part of Lisle in the *Sound of Music*."

"You mean Seth Barstow *isn't* your attorney?" asked Gabby.

Carmela's face assumed a thoughtful look. "Well, I've certainly *met* the man before. So he could probably *be* my attorney if I paid him a handsome retainer."

Peals of laughter erupted from the back of the room. Baby and Dawn had left an hour ago to attend a luncheon, but Tandy had stuck around.

"Hooray for Carmela," chuckled Tandy as she waved a clenched fist in the air. "That Granger Rathbone is a real rotten egg. He was suspended from the police force last year for roughing up a prisoner he was transporting. I can't imagine how the man ever got his job back. He must have had a stroke of luck and nabbed some poor city official on a drunk driving charge. Applied some not-so-subtle pressure."

"Good lord," said Gabby, "it's beginning to sound like Shamus might really be in trouble."

Carmela nodded her head thoughtfully, and a look of concern stole across her face. "Although I'd probably be the first to proclaim his innocence, it feels like there aren't a lot of people rushing to be in his corner."

Tandy and Gabby exchanged meaningful glances. They were slowly coming to the same conclusion.

"He'll be okay, Carmela, I know he will," Gabby assured her. "You both will."

"I sincerely hope so," said Carmela as the front door to her shop flew open and three of her scrapbooking students eagerly pushed their way in.

Chapter 6

TUCKED BETWEEN RICHAUD'S Jazz Club and Toulouse's Live Seafood Bar, the Hotel Babbit wasn't a five star, but it certainly gave an impression of genteel elegance and respectability. To the busloads of tourists who wandered the French Quarter, shooting endless rolls of Kodachrome, the Hotel Babbit was roundly regarded as elegant. Its bright red carpet was appropriately plush, the velvet couches in its lobby, rendered in a sturdy, commercial bastardization of Louis XVI, appeared fairly sumptuous. And palmettos, graceful though slightly dusty, framed the lobby's battered wood reception desk, completing the illusion of a grand hotel. Though it had slipped a bit from grace, the Hotel Babbit was still highly regarded as having one of the best ballrooms.

Jekyl Hardy was five minutes early. In any other hotel in any other city, a man dressed in a red sequined Mephistopheles suit, complete with a tail and carrying a matching pitchfork, would be regarded as highly suspect. In New Orleans it was de rigueur.

Carmela bounded up the stairs of the Hotel Babbit, her black-and-gold dress trailing in bountiful swirls behind her. Costumed as a French courtesan this evening, Carmela's low-cut dress of panne velvet was cinched with a wide-laced corset, and her face was concealed by a gold lamé bird mask with a four-inch beak that Ava Grieux had custom designed for her.

Jekyl Hardy grasped Carmela's hands and kissed her chastely on the cheek. "Careful with that beak, my dear," he warned. "It could be classified as a lethal weapon."

In the Cotillion Ballroom, the Marseilles Ball was in full swing. The ballroom was packed with costumed revelers as a thirty-piece band blared out jazz standards. People danced, cavorted, drank, and screamed in amusement at each other's costumes. Purple, green, and gold bunting was strung across the ceiling in a wonderfully tangled web. Gigantic gold coins, some ten feet across, decorated the walls and served as a historic testament to the various krewes that made Mardi Gras such a delightful spectacle. The Bachus, Proteus, Endemion, Zulu, and Rex krewes were internationally known. These were the big krewes, the high-profile krewes, that had no trouble attracting Hollywood celebrities as their grand marshals. These were the krewes that drew over five million free-spending tourists to the city of New Orleans year after year to partake in the excitement of Mardi Gras.

Ava Grieux came flying across the dance floor toward Carmela and Jekyl. Dressed in an angel costume, complete with wings and a sparkling halo that bobbed provocatively above her head, Ava had a date in tow who was dressed head to toe in a furry costume.

Is he a Wookiee from Star Wars? Carmela wondered. *Or maybe he's just supposed to be an oversized dormouse from* Alice in Wonderland. *It really is a coin toss.*

"I heard you had some trouble at the shop today," Ava said as she grabbed Carmela's arm.

Jekyl Hardy was immediately concerned. His black, greasepaint-enhanced eyebrows shot skyward. "Trouble? Tell us what happened, Carmela? Fess up!"

Carmela rolled her eyes. "It was nothing, really. A detective by the name of Granger Rathbone stopped by to ask a couple questions about Shamus."

"Hey, girl," said Ava, "this is starting to get *serious*." Her halo bobbed wildly. The look on her face said she was clearly concerned.

"No, it's not," protested Carmela. "Because Shamus didn't *do* anything. This is all going to blow over; I guarantee it."

Ava suddenly turned to her escort, the Wookiee-dormouse. "Honey, could you run get us a couple drinks?" Then, remembering her manners, Ava made hasty introductions. "Ricky DeMott, these are my dear friends, Carmela Bertrand and Jekyl Hardy."

There were quick nods of acknowledgment among the group.

"Nice costume," said Jekyl Hardly, running his hand appraisingly down the arm of the Wookiee-dormouse's costume. "What is that? Washable acrylic?"

"I think so," said Ricky. "My sister made it. Oh, hey, you're the float guy," he suddenly exclaimed. "The designer who masterminds all those great floats. I recognized you from an article in the paper. Cool. Wait till I tell my friends I met you."

"The drinks, sweetie," Ava reminded him gently.

"Sure thing," said Ricky as he scampered off.

"That Granger Rathbone is a paid thug," said Jekyl, shaking his head. "You watch your step around him," he admonished Carmela. "Tell Shamus to be careful, too. This Jimmy Earl Clayton thing is far from over."

"I haven't really spoken with Shamus in weeks," said Carmela, then suddenly remembered that wasn't true at all. Shamus had called her just this very morning. How strange, she thought, that already their conversation seemed so distant. Just like their marriage.

"The best thing you can do is stay away from him," advised Jekyl. "Until this thing settles down."

"Right," agreed Carmela, wondering if that really was the best thing to do. Then, for her own peace of mind, Carmela decided to put all thoughts of Shamus and Jimmy Earl Clayton out of her head.

Got to concentrate on having a good time, she told herself. *Isn't that why I came tonight? For a little dancing and flirting? Got to get back into circulation. Life goes on . . . or at least I hope it does.*

The band, feeding off the frenzy of the crowd, was dishing up a wild rendition of Professor Longhair's "Go to the Mardi Gras." Carmela danced with a man in a purple Barney costume, was cut in on by a pirate who had a live parrot perched on his shoulder. Then, as she joined a snaking conga dance line, Carmela found herself behind a very brawny man decked out in full Scotsman's tartans, clutching at his exceedingly short kilt.

As interesting as the prospect appeared, she decided it might be more prudent to sit this one out. Time to head for the bar.

Of course the bar was five deep in people. Everyone was waving money in the air, vying for the attention of the two overworked bartenders. All had the same goal, to wrap their hands around a hurricane, mint julep, daiquiri, or even a cosmopolitan.

When Carmela finally jockeyed to the front of the pack, she ordered a soft drink. Weary and warm from the night's revelry, she was, most of all, just plain thirsty.

As Carmela sipped her cola and stuffed a couple dollars in the tip jar, a familiar face caught her eye.

"Dace?" she said, sidling over to the man on her left. "Dace Wilcox?"

A tall, lean man with ginger-colored hair and soft brown eyes turned his attention toward her. He was dressed in a skeleton costume but had his mask, a black plumed affair, dangling from one arm.

"Yes ma'am?" he said cordially.

Carmela slid her gold mask up. "It's Carmela Bertrand. We were on a Concert in the Parks committee together a couple years ago." She remembered Dace Wilcox as being a conscientious and concerned committee member, one who was zealous in marshaling funds and mindful of dollars being spent.

As recognition dawned, Dace Wilcox flashed her a friendly grin and touched a finger to his forehead in a salute. "Of course. Nice to see you again, Miss Bertrand."

Carmela suddenly realized that Dace probably didn't know she'd been married. Or realize that she was now separated. But, surely, Dace must know Shamus, Carmela decided. Because she was almost certain that Dace Wilcox was also a member of the Pluvius krewe.

"You used to be in the Pluvius krewe, right?" said Carmela.

"Still am," said Dace as he downed the last of his drink.

"Then you must know Shamus Meechum," she said. "He's my—"

Dace fixed his gaze on a point slightly higher than Carmela's head. "No," he said, cutting her off. "Can't say as I do."

"Shamus Meechum of the Crescent City Bank Meechums?" Carmela continued. "Surely you—"

"Nope, sorry," said Dace. His voice was friendly enough, but his eyes slid away, seeking out someone in the crowd.

Carmela had the distinct feeling that Dace Wilcox was definitely not telling the truth. *The man has to know Shamus, right? So what's going on here?* Then she shrugged to herself as Dace melted into the crowd.

Maybe she was wrong. Maybe Dace Wilcox really *didn't* know Shamus. No point in browbeating the man. If he said he didn't know Shamus, she ought to take him at face value.

SOME FORTY minutes later, Carmela and Jekyl Hardy were seated at a table in the Praline Queen, a colorful neighborhood restaurant and bar located in Jekyl's beloved Bywater District. Because the Praline Queen was notorious for its jumbo stuffed artichokes, spicy gumbos, and sinfully rich praline pie, it drew customers from all over the city. From the French Quarter, Warehouse District, Garden District, even folks who lived across the river in Metairie.

Tonight was no exception. The open kitchen revealed a frenzied knot of white-coated chefs working at breakneck speed to keep pace with orders. Flames danced above the grill as great slabs of barbecue ribs were slathered with mind-bending sauces and fillets of catfish and skewers of gulf shrimp were plopped on the grill to sizzle and hiss.

Carmela and Jekyl shared a stuffed artichoke, dipping each tender morsel in the zesty lemon and garlic remoulade that accompanied it. Now Carmela was enjoying a bowl of oyster stew while Jekyl dug into a heaping mound of boiled crawfish.

"I'm about ready to go insane," declared Jekyl. "The floats for the Nepthys krewe *still* aren't finished for Saturday night, and I'm supposed to conduct a connoisseurship class that morning. How everything got mishmashed on top of one another *I'll* never know."

Carmela smiled. Jekyl was notorious for taking on ten projects at once, then flipping out from the stress of it all. Then again, there seemed to be a lot of stressed-out folks these days. Didn't everybody have a scrip for Prozac? Wasn't Valium making a big comeback?

"What are you going to cover in your connoisseurship class?" Carmela asked him.

"Oh . . . restorations, fakes and frauds, periods and styles," answered Jekyl. "Same old same old, except for the fact that the ladies still lap it up."

Carmela nodded. Jekyl Hardy had been blessed with an unerring eye for quality and a gift for imparting his knowledge in a nonthreatening, easy-to-digest sound-bite manner. He was expert in discussing oil paintings, old silver, porcelain, and even furniture.

"I take it this is your usual audience?" asked Carmela. Jekyl was wildly popular among the ladies who resided in the immense homes in New Orleans's famed Garden District. Where *she* had lived not that many months ago.

"The usual," agreed Jekyl. "Although most of them have major parties cooking over the next few days, so I don't know how *they're* going to find time, either. But I talked with Ruby Dumaine this afternoon," he said, "and she assured me there's still going to be at least a half-dozen ladies in attendance."

Carmela suddenly perked up her ears. Ruby Dumaine was the wife of Jack Dumaine, the remaining senior partner in Clayton Crown Securities, now that Jimmy Earl Clayton was dead.

"Ruby mentioned that her husband, Jack, is going to deliver the eulogy tomorrow morning at Jimmy Earl's funeral," said Jekyl. He gave a practiced twist of his wrist and snapped the head off another crawfish. "Do *you*, by any chance, have plans to don a black shawl and be in attendance at Jimmy Earl's funeral?" he asked.

Carmela tossed a handful of oyster crackers into her stew. "You know," she mused, "I hadn't really thought about it." Truth be known, she *had* pondered the idea, she just didn't care to admit her rather morbid curiosity to Jekyl.

"For the time being, your life seems to be inexplicably woven into this

Jimmy Earl thing," said Jekyl. "So I figured you'd want to be present for the final disposition." His voice betrayed a somewhat sly tone.

This is the man who advised me to stay under the radar until everything blows over. Oh well, Jekyl likes his fun.

Carmela gazed at Jekyl's purposely bland expression across the table from her. *Attend Jimmy Earl's funeral. Interesting idea.*

Carmela tested the notion in her mind.

The service will be held at the Clayton family crypt in Saint Cyril's Cemetery, of course. Which is the very same cemetery I've been asked to create the scrapbook for. So . . . I could probably finesse my appearance at Jimmy Earl Clayton's memorial service. People wouldn't consider my attendance all that strange.

There was another reason Carmela was suddenly liking this idea quite a bit. Someone had brazenly offed poor Jimmy Earl Clayton the night of his big Mardi Gras parade. And though it was fairly doubtful the culprit had been Shamus, her ex-husband extraordinaire, it surely *had* to be someone fairly close to Jimmy Earl. Didn't it?

Would the culprit, the murderer, dare to show his face at Jimmy Earl's funeral? And if so, will I be able to figure out who it is?

Perhaps the perpetrator of the deadly deed would conduct himself in a highly suspicious manner. Or throw himself on poor Jimmy Earl's coffin out of guilt or remorse. Carmela considered this for a scant moment.

Hardly. Times are tough. And guilty consciences are in exceedingly short supply these days.

Twenty minutes later, Carmela and Jekyl stood in line at the cash register to settle their tab. As she studied the collection of Mardi Gras paraphernalia that hung on the wall behind the cash register, Carmela heard her name called. A long, low, teasing call.

"*Car-mellll-a.*"

She whirled about, looking to see who had spoken. Searching the faces crowded around the various tables, she saw no one gazing in her direction. In fact, everyone seemed immersed in their own conversations or focused intently on chowing down. Frowning slightly, Carmela scanned the crowd again. Nope. Not a soul she recognized.

Turning back to Jekyl Hardy, accepting the couple dollars in change he stuffed in her hand, Carmela once again heard someone call to her.

Only this time it was a teasing, slightly more menacing threat.

"*Your old man's gonna be in the paper tomorrow, Carmela.*"

Jekyl Hardy heard it, too, furrowed his brow. "Let it go," he advised as he took Carmela's elbow and steered her out the door. There was a sudden burst of laughter behind them and a loud hiss just as the door slammed shut.

"Neanderthals," grumped Jekyl.

That's it, Carmela decided. *Pencil me in for that funeral tomorrow. In fact, I'm gonna try to get a front-row seat for Jimmy Earl's big send-off!*

Chapter 7

A JUMBLE OF white, sun-bleached aboveground tombs stretched as far as the eye could see. Some were simple rounded tombs that contained a single casket; others were elaborate mausoleums adorned with crosses, statues of saints, and wrought-iron embellishments, built to hold the remains of entire families. One of the strangest features of many of these older, ornate tombs was the one-way trap door built into the floor of the tomb. After a body had laid in state for a decent interval of time, that trap door could be flipped open, and the bones of the deceased could be discreetly disposed down a chute, where they would mingle with all the former relations who'd been buried there.

A block away, at the far end of Saint Cyril's Cemetery, a jazz combo played a mournful tune, while a tight clutch of mourners swayed rhythmically. Such was the business of funerals and burials in New Orleans's old cemeteries.

"Get up here," whispered Tandy. Dressed in a black suit with a vintage black pillbox hat perched atop her tight curls, Tandy had been discreetly worming her way to the front of the group, with Carmela in tow, for the past twenty minutes.

A minister had opened the services for Jimmy Earl with somber prayers and a rousing oratory. Now he had succeeded in coaxing most of the mourners into joining him in a fairly dismal and off-key rendition of "Nearer My God to Thee," the song most noted for having been played by the *Titanic*'s shipboard orchestra as the ill-fated luxury liner headed for the briny depths of the Atlantic.

Carmela tuned out the awful singing and turned her thoughts to the vicious innuendos that had appeared in this morning's *Times-Picayune*.

True to the anonymous heckler's promise of last evening, Shamus had indeed been mentioned.

Not by name, of course. Bufford Maple, the opinionated boor of a columnist who had penned the piece, was much too smart for that. Bufford Maple had been a columnist at the *Picayune* for as long as anyone could remember, although calling him a columnist was putting a pretty glossy spin on things. Rather, Bufford Maple was a nasty viper who liked nothing better than to pontificate, spout off, and launch personal attacks against selected targets.

It had also been suggested more than once that an under-the-table agreement could often be struck with Bufford Maple whereby, for the right amount of money, he would launch an all-out public attack on one's enemy.

When Bufford Maple penned this morning's vitriolic piece, he must have been as elated as a pig in mud.

While not naming names per se, Bufford Maple had managed to insinuate and imply that a certain *"banker turned swamp rat"* had a very nasty bone to pick with a certain *"well-heeled businessman."* Bufford Maple went on to write that this *"cowardly swamp rat"* had plotted and schemed and finally brought about this *"poor businessman's death."*

The rest of the column had been a diatribe about *"swift apprehension"* and *"just punishment."*

Even though Carmela was still hopping mad at Shamus, she had been stung mightily by the nasty innuendos that Bufford Maple had flung. As she glanced about the group of at least a hundred mourners, she wondered if they had all read the article, too. And judging by the pairs of eyes that had flicked across at her, then looked quickly away, she guessed most of them had.

THE OFF-KEY hymn drew to a conclusion, and Jack Dumaine, Jimmy Earl Clayton's business partner, proceeded to take his place front and center of the group. Gazing tearfully down at Jimmy Earl's deluxe mahogany coffin, Jack Dumaine let fly with his eulogy.

Tuning out Jack Dumaine's quavering voice as it seemed to rise and fall like a politician's speech, Carmela focused her gaze squarely on Jimmy Earl's coffin. With the morning sun glinting off its shined-up facade, it looked a bit like an old Lincoln Continental that had been tricked out with all the options money could buy. Ivory handles, engraved brass name plate, carved geegaws and knobs. She guessed that no expense had been spared for Jimmy Earl's final send-off.

Fixing her gaze on Jack Dumaine, Carmela decided he looked exactly like the exceedingly prosperous businessman that he was. Jack Dumaine's stomach protruded like a dirigible from between the lapels of his sedate black suit coat. His pants seemed to be held up by industrial-strength suspenders. Jack Dumaine was obviously a man who loved New Orleans and indulged freely in its rich bounty. He was a hale-and-hearty good old boy and a world-class gourmand.

Jack's trio of chins wobbled, and his head seesawed like a bobble-head doll as he addressed the group of mourners.

"Jimmy Earl was my best friend," Jack declared with heartfelt zeal, his voice climbing with trembling fervor. Reverently, he placed his chubby right hand over the broad expanse of his chest to emphasize this point. "In the sixteen years we-all were together in business at Clayton Crown, Jack and I might have had ourselves a few rough moments, but we never disagreed on the fine points."

"Like making a shitload of money," Tandy whispered in Carmela's ear. Carmela had to agree with her. Ensconced in huge Garden District mansions, the Claytons and the Dumaines had never seemed to want for anything.

Jack Dumaine continued with his eulogy. "Jimmy Earl was an entrepreneur and a community benefactor," he intoned as he grabbed his lapels and scanned the faces in the crowd. "He was a good father, beloved husband, and a damn fine bass fisherman."

Standing at her husband's side, Ruby Dumaine nodded her punctuation at the tail end of every line Jack Dumaine delivered. Ruby was fifty-something, with a mass of reddish blond curls pulled into a flouncy pompadour atop her head. Poured into a black jersey wrap dress, Ruby didn't look all that bad from a distance. It was only up close and personal that you noticed the slightly wonky eye job.

Easing her digital camera out of her purse, Carmela snapped a couple shots of Jack Dumaine in all his oratorical splendor. Then Carmela aimed her little camera at the crowd that spread out on either side of Jack and clicked off a few more shots. Glancing at the digital counter, she saw that her memory card would easily hold another forty or so shots. Gabby had obviously not taken all that many shots the other night when she borrowed the camera.

As Carmela continued to shoot, ostensibly for a *Funerals Then and Now* section in the Saint Cyril's scrapbook, nobody seemed to notice, since the camera was far smaller in size than her usual Leica. Or better yet, nobody seemed to care.

Of course, funerals in New Orleans were unlike funerals anywhere else. Carmela knew that you could probably haul a Hollywood movie crew in and film the whole shebang for posterity, and nobody would seriously bat an eyelash. Plus, New Orleans funerals were notoriously quirky. Dogs, cats, horses, mistresses, illegitimate children, obscure heirs—you name it—he/she/it had all been in attendance at various New Orleans funerals.

As Carmela continued taking pictures with her digital camera, she scanned the crowd. Mostly Garden District folk, businessmen and their wives. The Taylors, the Coulters, the Reads. Baby was there, too, looking very cool and blond, a little Grace Kellyish, on the arm of her swarthy husband, Del. Two rumpled-looking men who looked like they might be reporters, perhaps sent by Bufford Maple, hung out on the sidelines.

Sitting at the head of the casket, perched on black metal folding chairs, were Rhonda Lee, Jimmy Earl's widow, and her daughter, Shelby.

Carmela's heart especially went out to the girl. Shelby was a beautiful young woman: tall, coltish, with beautiful olive skin and long, tawny blond hair. She was perhaps eighteen at best, a freshman at Tulane. Carmela knew it wasn't easy to lose your father at such a young age. God knows, she'd lost her dad when she was just ten.

A couple days ago, Baby had informed them all that Shelby was one of the finalists for queen of the Pluvius Ball. In light of all that had happened, Carmela wondered if Jimmy Earl's only daughter would still grace the lineup of queen candidates next Tuesday. She thought probably not.

As Carmela continued to gaze at Shelby, Rhonda Lee suddenly shifted her gaze toward Carmela. Rhonda Lee Clayton was short, puffy-faced, with a sleek helmet of brown hair. Hate filled her eyes.

Stung for a moment by the overt hostility she saw there, Carmela quickly lowered her camera and looked away.

Was it possible Rhonda Lee actually *believed* the terrible rumors that seemed to be circulating? That Rhonda Lee actually thought Shamus had been responsible for her husband's death? Carmela sighed. Of course, it was possible. Anything was possible.

SURPRISINGLY, AT the conclusion of the graveside service, Jack Dumaine and his wife Ruby came crunching across the gravel to speak with Carmela and Tandy. Carmela had met the Dumaines over the last couple years at various social and business functions that Shamus had dragged her to. And, of course, they were members of the Pluvius krewe. A somewhat enigmatic couple, they had a peculiar tendency to jump in and finish each other's sentences.

"A lovely tribute," said Tandy, grasping Jack's hand in a goodwill gesture.

"This is the saddest day of my life," declared Jack tearfully. "Jimmy Earl was like . . ." He hesitated.

"Like a brother to him," filled in Ruby Dumaine. "And, don't you know, our dear girls practically grew up together."

Ruby Dumaine was referring to their daughter, Swan, who was standing some twenty feet away, looking morose and talking with Shelby Clayton and several other young women.

"When Jimmy Earl collapsed on that float . . . it was like a member of my family died," said Jack tearfully.

"You were riding on the sea serpent float together?" said Carmela.

Jack nodded sadly, then unfurled a large, white handkerchief, held it to his nose, and blew loudly. "It's a bad business about Shamus," he rumbled solemnly, directing his gaze at Carmela. His eyes, buried in the massive flesh of his face, looked like glinting little pig eyes. Blowing his nose again, hitting yet a higher octave, Jack shook his giant head regretfully. "A real bad business."

"Bad business," echoed Ruby as the two of them slid off into the crowd.

Carmela watched Jack Dumaine lumber off toward the minister and wondered, *What exactly did Jack Dumaine mean by that remark? And whose corner is he in, anyway? Does Jack think Shamus is guilty? Or innocent?*

"I thought I'd find you here," murmured a clipped, slightly menacing voice at Carmela's elbow. "Catch the paper this morning?" Granger Rathbone's eyes glinted like an alley cat who'd just spied a cowering mouse.

"Granger Rathbone," Carmela muttered as she turned to face him. "Tandy, have you met the illustrious Mr. Rathbone?"

Tandy fixed Granger with a hostile gaze. "You were in such a rush yesterday, I'm afraid we didn't have the pleasure of a formal introduction. Such a pity."

Carmela smiled at Tandy. For someone who weighed barely a hundred pounds soaking wet, this gal was certainly blessed with *beaucoup* guts.

"Tell Shamus to call me," snarled Granger as he moved off. "I've got more questions."

"Tell him yourself," snapped Carmela.

Tandy gave Carmela a playful punch on the arm. "You go, girl! Don't let that little dog turd push you around."

Then, when Granger Rathbone was out of earshot, Tandy asked in a somewhat more worried tone of voice, "Have you talked with Shamus, honey? 'Cause things really *are* getting weird."

"I guess you saw this morning's newspaper?"

"Honey, I guarantee that, right after checking out Jeane Dixon and Dear Abby, *everybody* read Bufford Maple's column. Heck, the darn thing's probably on the Internet by now, whirling around out there in cyberspace."

"It's drivel," said Carmela.

"Of course, it's drivel," said Tandy. "But it's drivel people are starting to pay attention to." She squeezed Carmela's hand, then added, "Girl, you have to *do* something."

Somewhat unnerved by Tandy's words, Carmela turned to gaze toward the crowd that lingered, seemingly reluctant to disperse.

Last night she'd almost convinced herself that the real culprit might show up here today. *Had he? Well, if he had, there'd been no dramatic graveside confession, no bolt of lightning that had shot from the sky and singled him out. There had only been more heavy-handed insinuations against Shamus.*

Are witnesses being interviewed? Carmela wondered. *And if so, who? And, if things continue to go against Shamus, will formal charges be filed?*

Oh lord, thought Carmela. Why couldn't Shamus have kept his size-eleven Thom McAns parked safely under his desk at the Crescent City Bank? Why couldn't he have gone on doing his mortgage banking thing during the day and plunking his banjo while relaxing on the side portico at night? Better yet, why hadn't their life just gone on and on and on instead of him acting like such a dunce? And why was Shamus suddenly in this terrible fix?

As Carmela and Tandy wound their way through the tangle of tombstones and graves, they could see the very proud Ruby Dumaine dragging her daughter, Swan, over to a cluster of women. Even from forty feet away, they could hear Ruby's high-pitched bray.

"Swan's going to be Pluvius queen this year!" bragged Ruby. "Just look at her, isn't my girl absolutely *gorgeous*?"

Swan, who was indeed very pretty, squirmed uncomfortably under the heavy-handedness of her mother's words.

"This will be a year to remember for all of us," continued Ruby Dumaine. "Swan's official coming out as a New Orleans debutante *and* the beginning of her reign as Pluvius queen. Don't you know, her poppa and I are *soooo* proud."

"Does she know something we don't?" asked Tandy out of the corner of her mouth. "Swan has to get *elected* first, doesn't she?"

Carmela, again wondering whether poor Shelby Clayton had, in fact, formally withdrawn from the queen contest, shook her head in disgust at Ruby Dumaine's braggadocio manner. "Poor girl," she said, "to have such an overbearing momma."

Chapter 8

"HAVE YOU SEEN this?" asked Gabby, not long after Carmela returned to the store. She hesitantly held up a copy of the *New Orleans Times-Picayune*.

"Yes," Carmela sighed, "I read it first thing this morning."

"And you *still* went to Jimmy Earl's funeral?" asked Gabby, surprised.

"I'm afraid so. I thought maybe I'd be able to—" Carmela stopped in midsentence. *She'd be able to what? Figure out what really happened? Yeah, right. Lotsa luck, kiddo.*

"I thought I'd shoot some current photos of Saint Cyril's for the scrapbook," Carmela told Gabby instead.

Gabby seemed to accept that as a plausible answer. "Oh, right. I can see where you might want to do that," she said.

Fifty minutes later, Baby pushed her way through the front door of Memory Mine.

"Carmela, honey, I'm *really* sorry I didn't get a chance to talk to you at Jimmy Earl's funeral. Del wanted to leave immediately so he could get back to his office." Del was a hotshot attorney.

Carmela waved a hand. "Not a problem. As it was, my time was fairly well occupied."

Baby blinked her blue eyes in a quizzical gesture.

"Oh my, yes," continued Carmela. "Fending off Granger Rathbone, getting hate looks from Rhonda Lee . . ."

"Say, Rhonda Lee *was* in a fairly foul mood, wasn't she?" gushed Baby as she shifted her scrapbooking bag off her shoulder to the front counter. "Of course, the poor woman was burying her husband. I suppose you wouldn't classify that as a major social event where you were obligated to appear totally hidebound and *proper*."

"Ruby Dumaine would have," said Tandy as the front door closed behind her and she hastened to join in the conversation. "She was all gussied up, with her hair in those weird little wiener rolls."

Gabby put a hand to her face and laughed, despite herself. "Oh no!"

"My gosh," said Baby, "did you get a load of that wrap dress Ruby was wearing! Did that look go out in the seventies, or did I miss something?"

"Maybe she just dresses vintage," suggested Gabby. "There are lots of stores where you can get stuff like that today."

"Vintage shmintage," hooted Tandy. "Ruby just pulled it from the back of her closet. That old gal is so tight with her money she doesn't throw a thing away!" This produced absolute howls from the women, including Gabby, who normally refrained from gossiping and cracking jokes at the expense of others.

"Say now," said Baby, delicately wiping tears from her eyes. "Carmela mentioned something last week about making keepsake boxes. What say we press her into action and have her deliver a quick lesson?"

"Carmela?" said Tandy eagerly. "Would you?"

Carmela nodded. *Why not? The store isn't particularly busy today. My two best customers are here. And keepsake boxes really are a terrific project.*

"Say," said Tandy suddenly. "You're open tomorrow, right?"

"Right," said Carmela, reaching under the counter for her stash of brown kraft-paper boxes.

"Well, CeCe Goodwin is planning to stop by," said Tandy.

"For heaven's sake," exclaimed Baby as they all walked back to the craft table. "You don't mean Darwin's sister-in-law, do you?"

"The one who's a nurse?" asked Gabby, suddenly interested.

Tandy nodded. "Yup. CeCe's off for the rest of the week now, and she wants to work on some scrapbook pages. Remember, Carmela, CeCe was in a few months ago?"

"She worked on her vacation pictures," said Carmela as she set an array of small cardboard boxes, some square, some round, and some octagonal, in the middle of the table. "From when she went to Saint Barth. That's great, it'll be nice to have her back again."

And nice to perhaps get a firsthand account of Jimmy Earl's demise, Carmela thought to herself. For CeCe, who was a nurse at Saint Ignatius Hospital, had been on duty the night Jimmy Earl had been lifted down from his float and rushed to the emergency room.

"Okay," said Carmela, holding up one of the cardboard boxes, "they're rather lowly looking boxes right now, but once you get going, I guarantee they'll be reincarnated in some very marvelous ways. Gabby, if you could get my plastic box . . . the one filled with rubber stamps and stamp pads . . ."

"Sure thing," said Gabby, hopping up.

"And a few sheets of pale yellow parchment paper," added Carmela. "I'll grab a couple bottles of paint . . . let's see, probably the gold, the bronze, and the almond . . . and some brushes."

"I love this already," declared Baby as Gabby and Carmela pulled craft supplies out of the various cabinets and scattered them in the middle of the table.

"Start with your sheet of parchment paper," instructed Carmela. "Then use one of these stiff brushes to stipple on a couple layers of paint. You can work light to dark or dark to light, it doesn't matter, but strive for a nice *aged* look. Think of how the gilt frame on an antique mirror looks. Or maybe an old hand-painted music box. Then, once you've built up your layers of color and your ink has dried, you'll start rubber stamping some of these flower motifs." Carmela held up a tray that held a selection of rubber stamps. "Be sure to trade off on different floral designs, though, and vary the sizes. Use black ink or sepia for stamping the flower outlines." Carmela placed the rubber stamps in the center of the table. "Once your flowers are stamped on in a pattern you like, we'll color them in using varying hues of yellow, gold, and bronze. That will give your sheet an amazing variety of gold tones and mottled hues."

"This is great!" declared Tandy as she grabbed a brush, gingerly dabbed it into one of the dishes of paint Gabby had poured out, then began carefully stippling her parchment.

"Once you get your sheet of parchment painted and stamped exactly the way you want it," continued Carmela, "you'll decoupage that sheet onto your cardboard box. From there, it's simply a matter of adding extra touches."

"Like what kind of touches?" asked Gabby, fascinated by this new dimension to crafting.

"Charms threaded on gauzy ribbons, Roman numerals, even tiny photos," said Carmela. "You could even add a string of antique beads, little gold keys, old coins, you name it."

For the next twenty minutes, heads were bent diligently over their sheets of parchment, as Baby, Tandy, and Gabby transformed their paper into gilded sheets that carried an old world, hand-rubbed look.

As they worked, Carmela gazed around her shop happily. *This is what it's all about,* she decided. *Everyone absorbed by the activity of their craft, excited over creating something that's both beautiful and one of a kind.*

And, since the women were all working diligently on their keepsake boxes, Carmela decided this was the perfect time to finish up the place cards she'd begun for the Claiborne Club.

The Claiborne Club was a private club over on Esplanade Avenue that had been in existence since the mid-1800s. Housed in an Italianate mansion with Greek columns, stained-glass windows, and dark woodwork, and surrounded by an ornate wrought-iron fence, the Claiborne Club had once been the cloistered sanctuary of New Orleans's power elite. It was where men had finalized business deals over lunch, smoked cigars till the air turned blue and, in general, gotten away from it all. As a final testament to an earlier, male-dominated era, brass spittoons had ringed the Claiborne Club's mahogany bar.

But that had all changed. In the mid-seventies, the businessmen's wives decided to claim it as their own. Out went the old mahogany bar and the brass spittoons that had ringed it; in came a silver tea service, Spode dinnerware, and Chippendale furniture. Bathrooms were enlarged, urinals yanked out of the walls, and counter space and pink lightbulbs installed.

A few weeks ago, Alyse Eskew, the Claiborne Club's event coordinator, had asked Carmela to create a couple dozen place cards for a special brunch that was being held at the Claiborne Club on Lundi Gras, this coming Monday.

For these place cards, Carmela had, in turn, asked Ava Grieux to design a plaster mold of a miniature carnival mask. Once that mold had hardened, Carmela had soaked two dozen sheets of thick, handmade paper in water, then pressed each sheet over the mold to create an individual paper mask. When each sheet of paper had dried and formed in the exact shape of the mask mold, Carmela had trimmed and gently rounded the bottom part of each paper mask. Top edges were cut and crimped to create the look of cascading hair.

Now, as Carmela sat at the craft table surrounded by Baby, Tandy, and Gabby, she took a soft piece of cloth, dipped it into a puddle of purple pearlescent paint, and dabbed it gently across the cheeks of each paper mask. She repeated that process using green paint for the hair and luminous bronze paint over the eyes and nose. After a good hour of painting, Carmela had two dozen colorful, gilded mask faces. Once the paint was dry, she would attach a purple tassel to the right side of the mask and a gold name tag strung on tiny pearls to the other side.

"My gosh, Carmela," said Tandy as she squinted over her glasses. "Those little masks are wonderful! I can't believe all the crafts that seem to spin off from scrapbooking and your collection of wonderful papers!"

Tandy was right. Scrapbooking was only the tip of the iceberg. The same techniques used for scrapbooking could be employed to create beautiful journals as well as family history books. And the fabulous arsenal of paper she had amassed was perfect for creating invitations, tags, cards, and even picture frames. Likewise, the rubber stamps the ladies were using to emboss their keepsake boxes could just as easily be creatively employed to decorate scrapbook pages.

Laying in a more substantial supply of rubber stamps and inks would probably be her next big investment, Carmela had decided. Why, you could do incredible things using rubber stamps! You could even use them to apply the most marvelous designs to flowerpots, jars, velvet pillows, and even evening bags!

IT WAS quarter to one, and nobody was showing signs of quitting or even a slowdown in enthusiasm. So Gabby was tasked with running down the block to the Orleans Market to bring back a sack full of po'boys and a couple pints of coleslaw.

Po'boys were the quintessential New Orleans sandwich. They usually consisted of a long French roll stuffed with fried shrimp, fried oysters, or meatballs. Of course, po'boys could also veer toward being highly creative, with fillings of crab, roast beef, deli cheeses, or ham, usually slathered with Creole mustard or *mynaz*, which is what everyone in New Orleans called mayonnaise.

"Byrle!" called Tandy, who was in the middle of biting into her very squishy po'boy sandwich. "You made it!"

Byrle Coopersmith, whose first experience at Memory Mine had been this past Tuesday, came hurtling toward the craft table.

"Do you think I could get out of my house today?" Byrle exclaimed loudly. Then, without waiting for an answer, declared, "Of course not. The Wicked Witch of the West called to request a recipe for pickled okra that I *know* I've already given her a zillion times."

"Who's the Wicked Witch of the West?" asked Gabby.

"Zelda Coopersmith," answered Tandy. "Byrle's mother-in-law and queen bee of the New Orleans Garden Club." Tandy paused, an impish grin dancing on her face. "I prefer to address *my* mother-in-law as Mum-zilla."

"And my kids . . ." continued Byrle as she shook her head in mock despair. "Sometimes I want to string the little darlings up by their thumbs." Byrle swiveled her head and flashed a quick smile at Carmela, who was quietly listening as she worked. "Hello again," said Byrle pleasantly. "Could you please tell me what those delightful little masks are all about?"

"Carmela's doing place cards for a luncheon at the Claiborne Club," volunteered Tandy. "Aren't they adorable?"

"Too cute," said Byrle as she hoisted a floral duffel bag onto a clear spot on the craft table. "And look at those little boxes. What do you call those?"

"Keepsake boxes," said Baby. "Don't you just love them?"

"I do," declared Byrle. "Gonna have to make me one of those, once I finish up my scrapbook."

Carmela smiled over at Byrle. "Before you get started, can I interest you in half a sandwich? We've got lots."

Byrle waved a hand. "Thanks, but I just choked down a candy bar on my way over."

"A woman after my own heart," murmured Baby, who was notorious for her passion for chocolate and her firm belief that chocolate should definitely be acknowledged as one of the four major food groups.

CARMELA TOUCHED the tip of her index finger to the face on one of the masks. It came away clean, which meant the paint had dried.

Good, decided Carmela. *While Byrle works on her scrapbook and Tandy, Baby, and Gabby finish their keepsake boxes, I'll letter names onto these tags to finish them off.*

She pulled out the luncheon list Alyse had faxed her a couple weeks ago, counted the names again just to make sure, then laid out two dozen gold tags. With a ruler and a pen filled with special disappearing ink, Carmela drew a quick guideline across the lower length of each tag. Then, using a calligraphy pen, she meticulously hand-lettered each name onto the tag. By the time Carmela finished hand-lettering the final name, the guidelines she'd drawn on the first few tags had begun to disappear. Gradually, all the lines would disappear. Using this disappearing ink was a technique Carmela often employed in scrapbooking. It was perfect when you wanted to add a bit of text under a picture or write a poem or fun phrase on a page.

Next, Carmela dabbed a cloth in gold paint, then buffed the gold around the edges of each tag to give it a soft, rich look. Then she attached each of the finished name tags to the finished masks. Leaning back, she admired her handiwork.

"Those are spectacular," commented Byrle.

"I wish I would've asked you to do the invitations for my party," lamented Baby. "Then they really would've been special."

Baby and her husband, Del, were having their traditional Mardi Gras party this Saturday night at their large Garden District home. This year Baby had mailed out invitations in little silver picture frames, which were just as spectacular in their own right.

Tandy stood up to stretch. Her keepsake box was looking good, she decided. That brass dragonfly charm she'd added to the top of it looked really fun. Now she was debating about adding a ribbon edging around the bottom of the box. It had definitely progressed from a little box made of kraft paper to something that looked like a gilded treasure from the turn of the century. "My gosh," Tandy exclaimed, suddenly glancing at her watch. "It's almost three o'clock. We've been at this for *hours*."

Chapter 9

THE INFAMOUS STREETCAR named *Desire* had been retired way back in 1948. And, while the Regional Transit Authority has memorialized the name by emblazoning it on a city bus that dutifully chugged along New Orleans city streets, something seemed forever lost in the translation.

But the St. Charles Avenue streetcar was still very much alive and operating.

Hopping on at Canal Street and Carondolet in the French Quarter, a rider could travel on the old-fashioned trolley through some of New Orleans's most historic and picturesque neighborhoods for the bargain price of one dollar each way.

Rather than pull her vintage Caddy, Samantha, out of her carefully guarded parking space, Carmela had opted to pack up her finished place cards and ride the trolley to the Claiborne Club to deliver her handiwork.

Bells clanged, metal wheels clicked steadily, and passengers shouted with glee as the old green trolley zoomed down St. Charles Avenue past LaFayette Square, around Lee Circle, and through the bustling CBD, or central business district.

As the trolley approached the fashionable Garden District, noses were suddenly pressed to windows, the better to catch a glimpse of the elegant old mansions, stately live oaks draped in Spanish moss, and Gothic-looking wrought-iron fences. For here was antebellum Louisiana at its finest. Novelist Truman Capote and French Impressionist Edgar Degas had both called the Garden District home for a short while. Jefferson Davis, president of the Confederate States of America, had died here. And though many of the old homes now exuded a patina of age, they were still quite spectacular.

Carefully gathering up her package, Carmela hopped off the trolley at Fourth Street and walked a block over to Prytania. As she strode down Prytania, just blocks from where she had lived not so long ago with Shamus, she could see a spill of women on the steps of the Claiborne Club. Probably, they'd just emerged from one of their afternoon teas and were hanging around to chitchat and speculate whose daughter or granddaughter would be chosen as reigning queen this year by the various Mardi Gras krewes.

As she approached the front door, the gossip and chatter suddenly died out, and Carmela found herself edging her way past a half-dozen women who stood on the front steps eyeing her cautiously.

"Afternoon," she said, smiling and nodding, determined to maintain her poise.

"Afternoon," came cool replies back as heads nodded imperceptibly.

Good lord, thought Carmela as she pushed her way through the ornately carved doors of the old mansion into what was now the lobby and reception area. *What's going on here? The sins, or in this case, alleged sins, of the husband are suddenly (and rather rudely!) being heaped on the head of the soon-to-be ex-wife? Talk about jumping to conclusions and being utterly unfair.*

"Hey there, Carmela," called Alyse Eskew as she spotted Carmela from her office. "I was just about ready to take off."

Carmela walked into Alyse's office, set her box down on top of Alyse's rather disorganized-looking desk. "Special delivery," she said.

"You finished the place cards!" exclaimed Alyse. "Ooh, I can't wait to take a peek." She popped up from her chair and wrestled the top off the box. Then, upon seeing the finished place cards, Alyse's face lit up with joy. "Oh, my gosh," she marveled. Then, carefully lifting one of the masks out, she cradled it in her hand. "These are beautiful," she crooned. "You've absolutely outdone yourself, Carmela. I know everyone is going to be extremely pleased with these. In fact, I'd say they're probably going to be viewed as Mardi Gras collectibles."

"Great," said Carmela, pleased at the thought. "It was a fun project to do."

Alyse grabbed the box and moved it over to an equally crowded credenza that sat against a wall in her office. "I'm going to put these over here for safe-keeping, since we don't need them until next Tuesday."

"I take it they're going to be used for a luncheon?"

"That's right," said Alyse. Her thin shoulders rose in a shrug; her face assumed a harried look. "And I don't mind saying we've been absolutely *inundated* lately. We're catering luncheons, morning cream teas, afternoon high teas, receptions, you name it. It seems that the wives and daughters of almost every Mardi Gras krewe want to hold some special event. Of course, most of the events have to do with queen candidates and such." Alyse focused weary eyes on Carmela. "And since we're smack-dab in the middle of Mardi Gras, there doesn't even seem time to breathe. But I imagine you know what that's like," said Alyse. "Your shop must be busy, too."

"Fairly busy," said Carmela. "Although the brunt of our business will come right *after* Mardi Gras, when people are most eager to incorporate their recent photos and mementos into scrapbooks."

"Good for you," said Alyse as she walked Carmela out.

Gazing about at the lovely interior of the Claiborne Club, Carmela remarked casually, "You know, I've been asked to join the Claiborne Club a number of times. Next time around, I think I just might seriously consider it."

The smile froze on Alyse's face.

Oh, no, thought Carmela. *Not you, too.* "Is there a problem?" Carmela asked innocently.

Alyse fumbled to cover her faux pas. "It's just that . . . well, the club is not actually *accepting* new members at the moment. And you understand, of course, that if one is fortunate enough to be nominated, that nomination has to be *seconded* by at least three long-standing members . . ."

"Of course," said Carmela. Looking down, she saw that her hand was gripping the doorknob so hard her knuckles had turned white. "I understand completely."

Chapter 10

MILD TEMPERATURES AND a mass of warm air billowing up from the Gulf of Mexico had rushed smack-dab into a degenerating yet static cool front. And now fog, a vaporous haze that cast a scrim over the entire French Quarter and put everything into soft focus, had seeped in. In this strange atmosphere flickering gas lamps looked even more romantic. Old weathered wooden buildings, painted shades of bottle green and indigo blue like so many Caribbean cottages, took on a misty feel. Curlicued wrought-iron balustrades that topped the second stories of so many French Quarter buildings virtually disappeared. Even the clip-clop of the horse's hooves that pulled the jitneys filled with tourists down Bourbon Street sounded muffled tonight. Redolent with atmosphere, the area suddenly felt very much like the Vieux Carré, or French Quarter, of a century ago.

As Carmela turned down the arched walkway that led to her courtyard apartment, she could hear Boo's insistent, high-pitched bark.

"What's going on?" she asked the little dog as she stuck her key in the rusty old gate that cordoned her courtyard off from the walkway.

Boo's inquisitive little shar-pei face pushed up at her. Carmela could see a torrent of shredded paper in the dog's wake.

At the same moment Carmela entered her courtyard, Ava Grieux peeked out the French double doors at the back of her voodoo shop and gestured at Carmela through the glass. Holding up one finger, she mouthed, *Be right there*. Then, moments later, Ava shut off her shop lights and let herself out the back door.

"How long has she been outside?" Carmela asked, surveying the damage.

"I let her out maybe ten minutes ago," said Ava. "Fifteen at the most." She grinned and shook her head at Boo. "Amazing, isn't it? You'd swear a team from the FBI had swooped in here and gone through your garbage."

"Maybe they did," said Carmela. "Or at least a few spies from the New Orleans Police Department."

"Uh-oh," said Ava. "Have you been having problems with Granger Rathbone again?"

"You might call it that," replied Carmela. "The little slug accosted me at Jimmy Earl Clayton's funeral this morning."

Ava fixed Carmela with a level stare. "You showed your sweet little innocent face at Jimmy Earl's final send-off? Girl, you are seriously endowed with chutzpah."

Carmela tried to gather up the worst of the shredded paper while Boo followed behind her at a safe distance. The little dog was looking decidedly guilty. A shred of green plastic clung to her lower lip, snippets of newspaper were caught between her toes.

"That little dog works so fast I bet she could get a job shredding documents at a Swiss bank," volunteered Ava, determined to cheer Carmela up.

Carmela didn't answer.

"Look," said Ava, snatching up some of the shredded paper, "I think Boo might have even torn up Bufford Maple's column." Ava put her hand atop Boo's furry brow and petted her gently. "Good girl, you still love your daddy lots, don't you?"

"Don't," Carmela warned.

"Carmela," said Ava, finally, "you need to seriously chill out. Stay home, put your feet up, have a glass of wine. *Good* wine. Maybe even get a little snockered if you feel like it. And try to forget about all this stuff, because it's not worth worrying your head over. You know as well as I do that excessive worry only leads to crow's-feet. And you are far too young to begin a costly and somewhat tedious regimen of Botox or laser resurfacing."

"Ava," said Carmela, turning to face her. "I'm at the point where I'm not so sure Shamus is innocent anymore." There was a note of desperation in her voice. "I want to *believe* he is, but there is some very negative energy swirling around."

"Mm-hm," agreed Ava. "That there is. And you are certainly in need of a walloping dose of *gris gris*." *Gris gris* was the term for good luck. "But I don't think white candles and herbs in velvet bags are gonna do it, *chérie*."

"Neither do I," said Carmela. She paused dejectedly and thought for a moment. "Ava, you know as well as I do that Shamus is hotheaded as all get out. And he was seen arguing with Jimmy Earl Clayton. Seen, apparently, by a lot of people. What would that suggest to you?"

"That Shamus is hotheaded and ill-tempered?" said Ava. She sauntered over to the trash can, lifted the lid, and stuffed a glut of papers inside. "No surprises there. You *knew* all that when you married the man, right? Now what you *really* got to figure out is *why* somebody wanted Jimmy Earl Clayton out of the way. You've got to look for motive." Ava paused. "Did Shamus have motive?"

Carmela gave serious consideration to Ava's question. "I really don't think so."

Ava threw her hands in the air. "There you go. Then he's probably innocent."

"Right," said Carmela, grabbing Boo's collar and giving her a tug. "But who's the nasty fruitcake who did away with Jimmy Earl?"

"That, my dear," said Ava, "is the sixty-four-thousand-dollar question."

ONE OF the most popular theories holds that Jambalaya is directly descended from the rice dish, *paella*, which was brought to New Orleans by the Spanish. Over the years, Cajuns, Creoles, African Americans, Haitians, French, and just about everyone else in and around New Orleans fell in love with and adopted that steamy, spicy rice dish. They improved it, fiddled with it, and created endless varieties of rice until it finally evolved into the unique delta staple that's known today as jambalaya.

As a rule, jambalaya contains a savory mixture of andouille sausage, crawfish, shrimp, and chicken. But jambalaya can actually be made from any combination of the aforementioned ingredients. What's *really* indispensable, of course, are spices. Tabasco sauce, pepper, garlic, fresh parsley, thyme, and chili powder are *de rigueur*, with liberal amounts of onions and bell peppers tossed in as well.

For the last forty minutes Carmela had been dancing around her kitchen, chopping, blanching, peeling, coring, seeding, and dicing. She was bound and determined to give her mind a rest from the debacle of Jimmy Earl Clayton's murder and the nasty accusations that seemed to be piling up against Shamus. Cooking seemed as good a refuge as any.

Now she was ready to simmer most of her ingredients atop the stove in a large pan for an hour or so. Then, once everything was tender and aromatic, she'd toss in the seafood and sausage and finish the whole dish off for another thirty minutes. And, per her momma's stern advice, she would scrupulously avoid *stirring* the rice dish toward the end of the cooking process so it for sure wouldn't lump up.

As the big blue enamel kettle hissed and burped atop the stove, Carmela *did* help herself to a glass of wine. She yanked the cork from a nice crisp bottle of Chardonnay she'd lifted from Shamus's private stash before she left.

Grasping her glass of wine, Carmela poured out a cup of dry dog food for Boo, topped it with a dollop of cottage cheese, then finally settled into her wicker easy chair. Even though she'd vowed not to let herself get overwrought about this whole mess, she found her thoughts once again turning toward the man who had once made her life seem joyful and rich, then had haphazardly turned everything ass over teakettle: Shamus Allan Meechum.

Good lord but the man was maddening! And to skip out on her as he had. What had been his plan, anyway? Keep your fingers crossed behind your back when you mumble the old marriage vows, then hit the fast-forward button? Hold everything, whatever happened to the pause button?

Maybe she should be glad Shamus was up to his armpits in trouble. Glad he was getting some form of comeuppance for his reckless ways.

Am I glad?

No, not really.

And did she honestly believe that Shamus was involved in Jimmy Earl Clayton's demise? Well, she'd be the first to admit it didn't look good. Shamus *did* have a famously hot temper, that was for sure. And certain events in his life *had* proved that Shamus wasn't always a colossally clear-headed thinker or was immune from acting the fool.

There had been that silly business about stashing a goat in the dean's office when he was a senior at Tulane. In addition to consuming a perfectly good leather couch, the goat had committed a nasty indiscretion on the dean's Aubusson carpet. Besides rating a couple inches in the newspaper, that goat incident had almost kept Shamus from being admitted to graduate school. But then his family had stepped in. God forbid the pride of the Meechum clan didn't continue on and earn his MBA.

There had also been some problem with a belly dancer from Meterie that Shamus had hired for Joe Bud Kerney's bachelor party. Besides her penchant for Casbah-style dancing, Miss Meterie also had a nasty little habit of picking pockets. So, while she'd been charming her audience with the dance of the seven veils, she'd also been pocketing Rolexes and pinching Diners Club cards.

Shamus had also been involved in something a few months ago, just before he'd walked out on her. Carmela recalled hearing Shamus on the telephone, angry and insistent, telling Seth Barstow, one of Crescent City Bank's corporate lawyers, to *handle it. It* being something that had to do with construction loans and land zoning. She'd asked Shamus what the heck was going on, but he'd never made her privy to any of the details. Again, his family had swooped in and supposedly taken care of things. The big fix, as he always called it.

Will they be able to fix things this time? Carmela wondered.

That would remain to be seen.

THUMBING THROUGH a catalog of rubber stamp art, enjoying her steaming bowl of jambalaya, Carmela had finally been able to calm down. In fact, she was determined to look ahead and plan for the future, especially when it came to her little store, Memory Mine. She was particularly excited by the variety of decorative rubber stamps that were available: fanciful stamps depicting trailing vines, elegant picture frames, fans, filmy summer dresses blowing on hangers, tiny ballet slippers, filigree designs, and teacups.

All would lend delightful extra touches to wedding and anniversary scrapbooks and would also be perfect should her customers decide to create invitations for engagement parties, baby showers, and such.

Just as Carmela was imagining how a pair of doves would work on a sheet of soft blue-flecked paper with a deckled edge, the phone rang.

She kicked the footstool out of the way, hoping for a telemarketer to take her excess energy out on.

"Carmela," came a rough purr.

Oh shit. It's Shamus.

"Where are you?" asked Carmela.

"Can't say, darlin'."

"You mean you *can't* say because you've somehow lost your memory and are wandering around the parishes of Louisiana in a delirium, or you *won't* say?"

There was quiet laughter. "Your phone could be tapped."

Darn Shamus, Carmela thought to herself, *why does he have to go and act all spooky and mysterious? Like he's playing Mission Impossible or something.*

"This isn't a game, Shamus. And my phone isn't tapped. Where are you?"

"Why do you want to know?"

"Why?" said Carmela, feeling her blood pressure begin to inch up. "Because I just won the lottery, Shamus. A hundred million dollars. And I want to give you half. *Helloooo.* Why do you *think* I want to know?" Carmela hissed.

"Because last time I looked, I was still your *wife,* that's why. Even though half of my queen-sized bed is decidedly unoccupied." She paused. "And because, Shamus, whether you want to admit it or not, you're in deep doo-doo."

"I know, darlin', that's why I called. I don't want you to worry."

"Worry?" said Carmela. She suddenly shifted the tone of her voice. "Why would I worry?"

"Because you worry about everything," laughed Shamus.

"I do not," said Carmela, indignant now.

"Of course you do. You used to worry about the baby birds that fell out of their nests in the oak tree out back. I came home once and you were using this teeny tiny little eyedropper to—"

"That's different," said Carmela. "Those were creatures."

"Listen, honey," said Shamus. "If you need to get in touch with me, you just get a message to a guy named Ned Toler. He owns a boat place out in the Barataria Bayou, in a little village called Baptiste Creek. If you bring him a six-pack of Dixie Beer, he'll know it's really you."

"Where are you going to be?" asked Carmela.

"Around," said Shamus. "But don't worry." There was a sharp *click*, and the line went dead.

Damn. He hung up on me again.

Sprinting across the room, Carmela grabbed for her purse, then threw herself back in her easy chair. She dug for her address book, fumbled for the phone number of his family's camp house, then punched the number into the phone, determined to call him back, *finish* this conversation once and for all.

But the phone out there just rang and rang. She could picture it, an old black enamel wall phone, hanging on the wooden wall of the two-room camp house that sat on stilts above sluggish brown-green water.

Probably Shamus wasn't staying there anymore, Carmela decided.

Then where is he? And why has he gone into hiding?

Because he's guilty?

Oh please. Say it ain't so.

Chapter 11

GLORY MEECHUM WAS a woman who still put a great deal of faith in girdles. Nice, durable, reinforced panty girdles designed to smooth out unsightly blips and bulges and carefully encase both thighs.

Glory Meechum also had a penchant for floral-print dresses. Not demure daisies or elegant roses but big, splotchy prints of indeterminate floral and fauna origin. Certainly not as nature had intended.

When Carmela looked out the window Friday morning and saw Glory Meechum steamrolling down Governor Nicholls Street, headed straight for Memory Mine, her first thought was that Shamus's older sister looked like an overstuffed parlor chair.

Then the door flew open, and Glory Meechum exploded inward. Plunking her sturdy black leather Queen-of-England-style purse on the front counter, Glory planted chubby hands on Lycra-encased hips.

"You've got to help me!" she wailed loudly at Carmela.

Keenly aware that both Baby and Tandy were sitting at the back table and that Gabby was close by in the storeroom, Carmela willed herself to stifle any unseemly urge to giggle. The idea of Glory Meechum coming to *her* for help was over-the-top ridiculous. Glory had barely even been present at their wedding ceremony and her thinly veiled dislike for Carmela had always hung between them.

Carmela also made up her mind to handle Glory with a fair amount of decorum and try her very best to forestall any shouting match that might threaten to erupt. On Glory's part, not hers.

"Glory, what's wrong?" Carmela asked with as much civility as she could muster.

Glory fixed beady, bright eyes on Carmela. "That nasty little Granger Rathbone came looking for Shamus yesterday. Poking his nose into things over at the house."

The *house* Glory was referring to was one of three elegant manses in the Garden District that were owned by the Meechum family. According to the Meechum family's whims, these houses were allowed to be occupied by whomever was most recently married in the family or needed a place to live. Not necessarily in that order and certainly not a family dictum that had ever applied to Carmela.

"Well, have you seen him?" Glory demanded.

Carmela shook her head regretfully. "No. Sorry."

"Have you *talked* to him?"

Carmela hesitated. "No," she said finally. *If Shamus wants to talk to his sister, he'll call her, right?*

Glory Meechum threw her hands up in the air, exhaled a gush of air through her nostrils. Her sigh emerged as a distinct snort. "Then, where in heaven's name *is* he?" Glory demanded.

"Glory, I don't know," said Carmela. "Shamus left me, remember?"

Glory Meechum flashed Carmela an exasperated look, a look that said *Oh, give me a break.* "Yes, yes, of course," said Glory hastily, "but I thought for sure you two would keep *in touch*. That your little spat would eventually blow over."

If you thought we just had a little spat, then why was I asked to vacate the house?

But Carmela held her tongue. She simply replied, "Sorry I can't help you, Glory." *Gosh,* she thought, *I wish my momma hadn't instilled so much civility in me. This really could have been fun. Sport, actually.*

There was a scrape of chair legs against the wooden floor as Tandy slid her chair back a few inches, jockeying for a better position from which to observe Glory Meechum's rantings.

"Don't get me wrong," thundered Glory as she snatched up her purse and hung it possesively in the crook of her hefty arm. "It's not Granger Rathbone who concerns me. He's not nearly smart enough. What worries me is who Granger might be working for." With that, Glory Meechum spun on her sensible low heels and darted out the door.

"Who was *that*?" asked Gabby. She emerged from the storeroom with an armful of paper and a startled look on her normally placid face.

"That, my dear girl, was Glory Meechum, Shamus's big sister," answered Tandy, obviously relishing the heated exchange she'd just witnessed. "Isn't she a doozy? The old gal really fancies herself the matriarch of the family."

Gabby put a hand to her heart. "I don't mind telling you, that lady frightened me to death. I found the stencils and paisley paper I was looking for five minutes ago, but I was afraid to come out. I thought she might take off on *me*!"

Baby waved a manicured hand dismissively. "Glory barks like a rabid Rottweiler, but I doubt there's much real bite in her." Baby, who owned four Catahoula hounds, adored making dog analogies. There had even been Mardi Gras queen candidates who, over the years, had been referenced as poodles, poms, and pugs.

"Here's that picture frame stencil you wanted," said Gabby, passing the stencil, along with a stack of mauve cardstock, to Baby.

"Thank you, dear," said Baby, who was bound and determined to finish off her daughter's album of wedding reception pictures with a real flourish.

"If you slide the stencil right to the edge," suggested Gabby, "I think you can cut two frames from one—" The ringing of the telephone interrupted her.

"Memory Mine," answered Gabby as she snatched up the phone. Listening for a second, she nodded. "Yes, she's here. Hang on, please." Gabby punched the hold button, then turned toward Carmela. "It's for you. Something about your lease?"

"My gosh, don't tell me you've been here a full year already!" exclaimed Tandy. "*Tempus fugit,* how time *does* fly."

Carmela picked up the phone. "This is Carmela."

The crackly voice of Hop Pennington from Trident Property Management greeted her on the other end of the line.

"Carmela," he said cheerfully. "I might have a spot of bad news for you. That nice fellow who has the space next door to you . . ."

"The art dealer?" said Carmela. "Bartholomew Hayward?" Barty Hayward was a self-styled antique impresario with delusions of grandeur. Carmela saw the delivery trucks pulling up at the back door of Barty Hayward's store. She knew most of his antiques were really replicas and reproductions, and that Barty carefully and surreptitiously aged and distressed them in the workroom behind his store.

"That's the fellow," chirped Hop. "He might need your space."

Hold everything, thought Carmela, *just what the heck is going on here?*

"What if I need *his* space?" replied Carmela, thinking quickly.

"What?" sputtered Hop. From the surprise in his voice, Carmela knew he obviously hadn't considered *that* scenario. "What are you talking about?" asked Hop.

"Does Bartholomew Hayward have an option on my space?" asked Carmela. She knew that in order for someone to *really* force her out of her retail space, they had to have some kind of option clause written into their lease. And probably hers, too. And she didn't recall seeing anything like that.

"Well, he doesn't have an option per se," Hop replied slowly. "It's more like a gentleman's agreement. Should Mr. Hayward wish to—"

"Tell Mr. Hayward that you're terribly sorry, but my space simply isn't available. In fact, I'm probably going to want to sign a five-year lease this time around. Business is booming. And I like it here."

"Carmela . . ." wheedled Hop Pennington, "it doesn't work that way."

"Sure it does," said Carmela. "In fact, I bet this whole thing will work out just fine if we're all decent and honest and civilized about it."

"You know, sugar," said Hop Pennington, "I don't *own* the building. I just work for the management company. I'm really just the hired help."

Like that makes everything all right? thought Carmela.

"I understand," said Carmela. "I meant nothing personal. By the way, Hop, who *does* own the building?"

"Investors," replied Hop vaguely.

"Which ones?"

"Ah . . . private ones."

Carmela hung up the phone, more than a little miffed, verging on cold fury. *Is this another subtle pressure being exerted from somewhere? And if so, who was doing the exerting?*

"CeCe!" called Tandy, who was right in the middle of cutting a group of so-so color photos into small slivers with the idea of piecing them together to form a collage. "I'm so glad you could make it." CeCe Goodwin, a petite woman with green eyes and a modified shag haircut, strode through the shop and back to the craft table.

"Hello there," she said to Carmela, sticking her hand out in a friendly, forthright gesture. "It's great to see you again." CeCe hoisted a plastic shopping bag into a clear spot on the craft table. "As you-all can probably see, I'm in photo hell right now. I *love* taking pictures, but my hours at Saint Ignatius are crazy, and I am definitely *not* making time for myself." CeCe paused, looking around the table at all the friendly, welcoming faces. "You know . . . not enough bubble baths, candlelit dinners with my hubby, flower arranging, or scrapbooking. Boo-hoo," she finished with a goofy smile.

"Let's see what you've got there," said Carmela as CeCe dug into her shopping bag and began scooping out piles of loose color photos.

"CeCe," exclaimed Tandy as she watched Carmela and CeCe lay stacks of pictures out on the table, "you've got as many pictures of your dogs as you do of your kids."

"Smart woman," noted Baby. "See, she *does* have her priorities straight after all. What are their names?"

"Andrew and Livia," said CeCe.

"She meant the dogs," said Tandy.

"Oh," said CeCe. "Coco and Sam Henry."

"They sound like people names," observed Gabby.

"Well, dogs are people, too," said CeCe as she dug into her pile of photos. She turned toward Carmela with an imploring look. "Can you help me, or am I totally beyond redemption?"

Carmela had to laugh. CeCe was turning out to be a real card. In fact, after the earlier antics of Glory Meechum and the sleazy tactics of Hop Pennington, CeCe Goodwin was a welcome breath of fresh air.

"Why don't we start by organizing your photos," suggested Carmela. She reached behind her, pulled a handful of oversized, clear plastic envelopes off the shelf. "Let's put dogs in one, kids in another," said Carmela. "Vacation photos, relatives, whatever, in the rest."

"Got tons of husband stuff, too," said CeCe.

"Fine," laughed Carmela. "We're an equal-opportunity scrapbooking store. We'll allot your husband an envelope as well." She smiled down at CeCe. "Want a cup of tea or bottle of juice?"

CeCe shook her head. "No thanks. Don't want to get my hands sticky."

"How are the arrangements going for your party tomorrow night?" Gabby asked Baby as she continued to cut out a series of ornate frames.

Baby looked over at Gabby and grinned, her pixie face suddenly all aglow.

"Fantastic! You-all know I'm using that new caterer, Signature & Saffron, over on Magazine Street?"

"Mmm," said Tandy squinting, "I've heard wonderful things about them. They're very avant-garde and *chichi*. Or at least that's what I read in that fancy magazine, *New Orleans Today*. So what delightful little tidbits are in store for us, if I may be so bold as to inquire?"

Delighted that she'd finally been asked, Baby's face lit up with anticipation. "For appetizers they're doing miniature crawfish cakes, andouille sausage bites, and scallop ceviche. Doesn't that all sound dreamy?"

"Are you serving the little crawfish cakes with remoulade sauce like Liddy Bosco did a couple weeks ago?" asked Tandy.

"No, honey, if I remember correctly, that was a *Creole* remoulade that Liddy served," Baby pointed out. "Signature & Saffron is doing a *French* remoulade."

"What's the difference?" asked Gabby.

"Oh, the French remoulade has capers and anchovies but is *sans* tomato sauce," said Baby conspiratorially. "And it's got a much lighter touch. Effortless, one might say."

"Especially effortless if one is having the entire gala affair catered," said Tandy with a wry grin. She reached over and patted Baby's wrist just to let her know she was kidding, not criticizing. "Then what about your main entrées, honey?" Tandy asked. "What'cha gonna serve for that?"

Baby leaned back, clearly in heaven. "Tiny roasted squab, sweet potato galette, pumpkin risotto, creamy coleslaw of cabbage and jicama . . ."

The women all groaned in anticipation as Baby ticked off her rather fantastic menu.

"I can't *wait*," declared Gabby. "Everything sounds simply divine."

"Divine," echoed Tandy, nodding her approval.

"ISN'T THIS a cozy little group," pronounced the rather shrill voice of Ruby Dumaine.

"Hello there, Ruby," called Baby, looking up from the scrapbook album she was putting together for her daughter. "Long time no see." Since she had just seen Ruby Dumaine at Jimmy Earl Clayton's funeral yesterday morning, her comment was obviously intended to be humorous.

But Ruby Dumaine wasn't laughing. Dressed in a suit that could only be called crustacean coral, her face was set in a grim mask that would have given even the statues on Easter Island pause.

"Carmela," Ruby called out in her loud bray, "I have a serious emergency, and I need your help *tout de suite*."

Carmela scrambled to the front of her store to see what she could do for Ruby.

"I am in dire need of a guest book," said Ruby, rolling her eyes as though it was the most important thing in the world. "Specifically for use by my dear daughter, Swan. Don't you know, so many folks will be dropping by our home over the next couple days to congratulate her. In fact, we're having a group of people in tonight, then again on Sunday night after the big Bachus parade."

Carmela nodded, even as she grabbed four albums off the shelf to show Ruby.

"And, of course," continued Ruby, "we'll be doing a fancy barbecue Monday night, after everyone returns from watching the Proteus parade. And then there's the Pluvius queen candidate luncheon on Tuesday." She threw up her hands as though it was all too much for her, though the smile of self-satisfaction on her face said she was relishing every single moment.

"Of course," said Carmela. She especially knew about the Pluvius queen candidate luncheon. She'd designed the place cards, after all.

"Any one of these albums should work beautifully for you," said Carmela as she laid them out carefully on the counter.

Ruby Dumaine fingered the smaller of the four albums, one with a brilliant purple satin cover and creamy pages rimmed with a fine gold line. "This is nice . . ." she began.

The satin cover was a bright royal purple, the purple of kings and queens and royal heraldic banners. Carmela had chosen it specifically for Mardi Gras, since purple, green, and gold were the official Mardi Gras colors. Purple for justice, green for faith, and gold for power.

"This must be a very exciting time for Swan," offered Carmela as she watched Ruby deliberate.

Ruby turned wide eyes on her. "Exciting?" she trumpeted as though Carmela had dared to trivialize the events she'd just spoken of. "This is the most *important* thing that's ever *happened* to us!"

"I'll bet it is," said Gabby pleasantly as she brought two more albums to the front of the store for Ruby's perusal.

But Ruby Dumaine had already made up her mind. She abruptly thrust the purple album into Carmela's hands. "I'll take this one," she said. "It should do very nicely."

"What's got into her?" asked Gabby as the door closed behind Ruby Dumaine.

Carmela gave a quizzical smile. "Mother-of-the-queen-candidate jitters?" She was amused to observe that Ruby had also been wearing squatty little low-heeled shoes that must have been dyed to perfectly match her suit. And that the leather on one heel had split.

Gabby nodded knowingly. "You're right. Must be jitters. Wonder if I'll be that nuts when I have a daughter?"

"You'll probably keep the poor girl under lock and key," came Tandy's voice from the back.

"No," said Gabby, "but I know Stuart will."

"I guess Shelby Clayton has dropped out as Pluvius queen candidate," said Tandy as she pushed her cropped photos around, trying out different arrangements.

Baby slid one of the frames she'd punched out on top of a photo and positioned it on a sheet of creamy paper that had a background of tiny silver wedding bells. "It should be a shoo-in for Ruby's daughter then," she murmured. "Oh well . . ."

"Carmela," said Tandy suddenly, "are you *ever* going to show us what you're working on for Saint Cyril's?"

BABY TOOK off at noon to have a final powwow with her florist, but CeCe and Tandy stayed at the store. Gabby fired up the toaster oven in the back room and toasted bagels for everyone, while Carmela broke out a batch of sour cherry cream cheese spread she'd whipped up a couple days ago.

After the women had munched their bagels, they went back to their scrap-booking projects. CeCe continued to doggedly organize her photos while Tandy worked on her own album even as she paid rapt attention to Carmela's efforts on the Saint Cyril's scrapbook.

"I'm going to create an art montage for the introduction page of the scrapbook," Carmela explained to them. "A kind of establishing visual that will set the tone all the way through." She fingered a nubby piece of paper. "I'll start with this five-by-seven-inch piece of beige paper, then stamp it in brown sepia using this oversized rubber stamp that depicts an architectural rendering."

"Looks like the doorway to an Italian villa," said Tandy, peering over her glasses.

"Or a home in the Garden District," suggested Gabby enthusiastically. She had a serious case of I-want-to-live-there.

"Actually, the design is taken from the front of a Roman tomb," said Carmela. "I'm hoping it will pass for one of the family crypts in Saint Cyril's."

"Perfect," breathed CeCe. "You could have fooled me."

"Okay," said Carmela, "so first I stamp the architectural rendering using brown ink so it looks like sepia. Then I'm going to write over it using a copper ink."

"What are you writing, honey?" asked Tandy, as Carmela began writing in a flowing longhand.

"It's a French inscription I found on one of the old tombs at Saint Cyril's," said Carmela.

"Neat," allowed Tandy. "What does it say?"

"Something about peace and eternal rest," said Carmela.

"Then what?" asked Gabby, fascinated.

"Now I take these dried acanthus leaves and tie them at the top of the page with some metallic copper ribbon," said Carmela, as she punched two holes, then threaded the ribbon through.

"Wow," enthused Gabby, "the folks at Saint Cyril's are going to love this."

"You think?" said Carmela. "But wait, I'm not done yet."

"What else?" asked Tandy.

"This finished piece gets mounted on this dark reddish brown paper, which is just slightly larger. You see," said Carmela, "it gives it a sort of float-ing mat look. Then I paste *that* onto a slightly larger ivory sheet of paper with a deckled edge."

"Wow," said Tandy, impressed.

"It's elegant and somber," said Gabby, eyeing it carefully, "but very scrap-booky." She sounded slightly envious that Carmela was able to put together such a pretty art montage with seemingly little effort.

"Hey, everybody," CeCe exclaimed suddenly, "I think I've finally got my photos organized!"

Tandy stood up and arched her back in a leisurely stretch. Her collage had actually worked out far better than she'd hoped. Once she'd trimmed away the uninteresting backgrounds and pieced together the shards of what was left, she got a pattern going that was not unlike a stained-glass window. In fact, there was real charm to the jumbled image.

"Isn't this interesting," commented Tandy as she picked up one of the envelopes that CeCe had sorted photos into and riffled through it.

"Those pictures are all from Bobby's Tulane days," pointed out CeCe. "His birthday is in a couple weeks, so I thought I'd pull together a bunch of mementos and stuff and make him a little memory book. Bobby pretends to be so tough, but he's really sentimental as hell. You should see him . . . blubbering away at weddings, funerals, football games . . . that sort of thing."

CeCe had, indeed, pulled together a great many photos of her husband, Bobby. Plus she'd thrown in clippings that related to his fraternity days, an old homecoming button, and a frayed blue ribbon he'd won at a state track meet.

"Darwin's a big softy, too," said Tandy, referring to her own husband. "When he participates in those catch-and-release fishing tournaments, he gets *so* upset if he can't get the hook out clean," said Tandy as she continued to peer into the envelope. "If some poor fish gets a torn lip or starts gasping and goes belly up, Darwin really feels bad."

"The strong but sensitive type." CeCe grinned. "I know what you mean."

"You're right about a memory book being a good birthday present for him," continued Tandy, "and what great stuff you have to work with. Carmela, do you still have those brown leather-looking photo corners?"

Carmela nodded as she worked. "I'm pretty sure we do."

"They'd look nice and masculine with all this stuff," said Tandy.

"I agree," said Carmela. "Especially if CeCe chose one of the old-fashioned photo albums with the black pages."

"Oh, my gosh, would you look at this!" said Tandy as she held up a photo and stared pointedly at it.

"Oh, that's just one of Bobby's old fraternity pictures," remarked CeCe. "Wasn't he adorable? Wasn't he young?"

"Wasn't Shamus in Phi Kappa Sigma?" asked Tandy suddenly.

Carmela's head spun around like a gopher popping up out of a hole. "Yes, he was," she replied as she paused in her careful application of gold paint to the deckled edges of her montage.

"Lord honey," exclaimed Tandy excitedly. "I think this fellow in the picture *is* Shamus. Come over here and look for yourself."

Frowning slightly, Carmela stood up and made her way around the table.

"Right here," said Tandy, pointing with a carefully manicured index finger. "See the fellow with the silly grin, standing behind the beer keg?"

Carmela peered at an old color Polaroid that was starting to go orange with age. It *was* Shamus. But seeing Shamus in the old photo didn't surprise her half as much as recognizing the young man who was posed next to him. Because it was none other than Dace Wilcox!

The same Dace Wilcox who'd claimed he didn't know Shamus. Or even remember Shamus from the Pluvius krewe!

Why had Dace lied? Carmela wondered. *Was he trying to hide something, or had he simply forgotten?*

"Gabby," said Carmela suddenly. "You were at the Pluvius den the other night. Do you remember seeing this man, Dace Wilcox?"

Gabby came around the table and studied the picture, cocking her head to one side. She nodded. "Yes, I know Dace Wilcox. Or at least I've *met* him. And he was there."

"Talking to Shamus?"

Gabby thought for a moment. "Don't think so."

There followed a long moment so pregnant with silence you could've heard a pin drop.

"Was he talking with Jimmy Earl?" asked Carmela.

Gabby continued to study the old Polaroid of Shamus and Dace, taken at the Phi Kappa Sigma fraternity at Tulane.

"I *think* I might have seen the two of them talking," said Gabby finally.

"Just so we're absolutely clear on this, Gabby, you saw Dace Wilcox talking with Jimmy Earl Clayton," said Carmela.

Gabby nodded her head again. "I'm pretty sure I saw 'em together." Her brows knit together as she suddenly realized what she'd just said. Then she added, "Just before the floats rolled out of the den."

Chapter 12

AT TWENTY TO five, the store was deserted, all the papers, stencils, and fancy-edged scissors put away in drawers and cupboards for the weekend. Still, Carmela was reluctant to leave. She wandered about the store, snapping out display lights and fretting about the strange events of the day.

Seeing Dace Wilcox's picture next to Shamus's had been a stunner. And learning that Dace might have been talking to Jimmy Earl Clayton right before he died was downright eerie.

Was it possible Dace Wilcox was not what he appeared to be? That he'd had some sort of bone to pick with Jimmy Earl Clayton? If Dace had somehow engineered a nasty "accident" using a lethal dose of ketamine, how convenient to help steer the rumors and innuendoes to point toward Shamus.

The call she'd received earlier from Hop Pennington didn't help things either. In fact, it had left her feeling terribly unsettled. Carmela loved her retail space and dearly wanted to remain there. *Had* to remain there, really, if she had any notion of supporting herself as she continued to grow her fledgling business.

Is the landlord trying to ease me out? Or is Hop Pennington just trying to cut a better deal so he can garner a fatter commission check? And who the heck is the property owner anyway?

Now that Carmela thought about it, she realized she didn't have a clue. Of course, there was a legitimate reason for that. When she was setting up the store a year ago, Shamus had volunteered to handle that aspect of the business. She had located the empty space on Governor Nicholls Street, but Shamus had volunteered to negotiate the lease for her.

Curious now and hungry for information, Carmela wandered back to her office, plunked herself down behind the tiny desk that was wedged between a counter that held a paper cutter and one of the flat files where their expensive handmade papers were stored.

Reaching down and pulling open a file drawer, Carmela's fingers flipped across the hanging files with their hand-lettered labels. Way in the back was a file marked *Lease*. After she'd signed the lease, she'd stuck the document in there without really reading it or giving it a second thought. She'd just assumed Shamus would deal with the lease again when it was time to renew.

And wasn't that a nice assumption. Welcome to never-never land, dear girl.

Carmela pulled the lease out and studied the first page. It was printed on company letterhead and listed Trident Property Management at the top of the page. Their address, phone number, and fax number were printed below.

Carmela dialed the phone number listed on the lease. It was doubtful anyone would still be in the Trident offices. Still . . . she could try.

"Hello," said a voice on the other end of the phone. It was a woman's voice. Probably a secretary or the front-desk person. At least it wasn't Hop Pennington who answered.

"I'm glad I caught you," said Carmela, with a friendly greeting. "I didn't know if anyone would still be there."

"Well, I'm the last one here," said the woman, a touch of impatience in her voice. "I was just about to lock up and make my escape."

"Listen," said Carmela, thinking quickly. "My boss wanted me to call and get some numbers."

The woman on the other end of the line sighed heavily. "Now? Late Friday afternoon?" Clearly this was an imposition.

"Yeah," said Carmela, trying to match her tone. "I was trying to get out of here myself. Don't you just love bosses and their last-minute requests?"

"Tell me about it," said the woman, warming up to Carmela now. "What property was your boss interested in?"

Carmela racked her brain, wondering exactly how to play this out. She'd seen the blue and green Trident Property Management signs all over town.

They were a fairly big outfit. They handled leasing and the management of lots of different commercial properties.

Carmela took a stab at it. "Trident has some property for lease down on Bienville, right?"

"You mean the new Rampart Building?"

"That's it," said Carmela. She held her breath as she heard papers rustling. "My boss talked to someone about square footage and lease rates for the second and third floors."

"Gosh," said the woman. "I don't have that kind of information. That building's so new it's not even handled by property management yet. It's still in the initial leasing stage, so everything is being handled out of the executive office."

Bingo, thought Carmela. *Now we're getting somewhere.*

"Who should I ask for at the executive office?" asked Carmela.

"I suppose you'd want to chat with one of the partners," said the woman. "Although I seriously doubt they're still there. Anyway, tell your boss to get in touch with Mr. Michael Theriot. He's the managing partner. He handles day-to-day operations and works up lease proposals, that sort of thing."

"And the other partner?" asked Carmela.

"That would be Mr. Maple," said the woman. "You want the number?"

Carmela was suddenly stunned beyond belief. "Mr. Maple?" she asked in a hoarse voice. "Would that be Mr. Bufford Maple, the newspaper columnist?"

"Yes," said the woman pleasantly. "Would you like his number?"

Chapter 13

THE GOLD STATUE of Hermes, winged courier and messenger of the Greek gods, cut through the night like the illuminated prow of a ship. Horsemen in flowing gold robes clattered down the street, flanking the gleaming Hermes float on either side. Costumed jesters in billowing purple and gold silks accompanied the contingent as they strutted along, balanced on six-foot-high stilts.

Brass bands blared, the flambeaus twirled their torches and handfuls of shimmering blue, purple, and pink doubloons were flung into the crowds.

And even though the entire Vieux Carré seemed caught up in the grip of Mardi Gras madness, Carmela wasn't. Heresy as it might be for a native New Orleanian, her heart simply wasn't in it.

She had allowed herself to be dragged along tonight by Ava Grieux on the pretext (Ava's) that it would be *good* for her.

It wasn't.

Try as she might, Carmela just couldn't seem to make walk-around drinks and catching beads and shiny candy-colored souvenir doubloons her A-number-one priority. And when Ava confided to her that she had a serious *in* with one of the bar owners who could get them *upstairs* to one of the coveted second-floor wrought-iron balconies, that was the final straw. Because cavorting on a wrought-iron balcony, being urged on by hundreds of leering, drunken men on the street below to *pleeease* waggle her bare ta-tas just wasn't the kind of evening she had in mind.

No, while everyone around her carried on with wild abandon, Carmela's mind was running through the *other* things she could be doing if she'd stayed home tonight. Like defrosting her refrigerator. Hemming that silk skirt she'd bought on sale last fall. Wrestling Boo into a half nelson and trying to clip her pointy little toenails (what Baby would no doubt call a *peticure*). Maybe even phoning that dirtbag Granger Rathbone and telling him to back off, to take a hard look at a couple of *other* suspects.

Like the illustrious newspaper columnist Bufford Maple, who just *happened* to be the owner of her building. And who might be, for whatever reason, trying to ease her out even as he used his newspaper column to cast nasty suspicions upon her soon-to-be ex.

Or how about the standoffish Mr. Dace Wilcox? Dace had just happened to conveniently forget that he and Shamus had been in the Pluvius krewe together. And Dace had been seen talking with Jimmy Earl Clayton just before Jimmy Earl gasped out his final breath. She had it on good authority from Gabby.

Carmela grabbed Ava's arm as they pushed their way through the crowd inside the Blind Tiger. "Ava, I'm going to duck out," she told her friend.

Ava stopped in her tracks to stare blandly at her. A waiter with a tray of drinks held over his head had to quickly divert with a minimum of rum and bourbon sloshing. "Please tell me you're leaving me because you've got a hot date," pleaded Ava.

"I am," said Carmela. "I have."

"Liar," snorted Ava. "You're just pooping out on me." But when she saw the look of real worry on Carmela's face, she immediately relented. "All right, you're excused for tonight. Go directly home, do not pass go, do not collect two hundred dollars."

"I am going home," said Carmela.

"It's probably a good thing," said Ava. "I don't mind telling you, you're not exactly a barrel of belly laughs tonight." She put her arms around Carmela, pulling her into a gentle hug. "Poor girl, feelin' so sad."

"I've got to figure a couple things out," said Carmela. She had to shout at the top of her voice to make herself heard in the noisy bar.

"I know you do," said Ava, shouting back. "Be careful, though. Play it safe, okay?"

Carmela nodded, then headed out the door. Once she found herself on Bourbon Street, it was a palpable relief, even though the crowds that milled about were still overwhelming. Strangely enough, Bourbon Street had been named for the French family of Bourbons and not the drink itself, like most people assumed.

When Carmela was finally a good five blocks away from all the pandemonium, she ducked into a little neighborhood grocery store.

"Going to the parade?" the man behind the counter asked her. He was dressed in a Robin Hood costume, complete with tunic, loden green tights, and a jaunty cap with a pheasant feather stuck in it.

"Eventually," she told him, dumping her groceries on the counter.

"Party hearty," was Robin's parting shot as she pushed her way out the door.

When Carmela got to Governor Nicholls Street, she saw that Ava Grieux had wisely covered her store windows with a grid of chicken wire. She'd done the same thing at Memory Mine a couple days ago. Neither of their shops were on the parade route per se, but that didn't mean that Mardi Gras revelers were immune from flinging the occasional liquor bottle or getting into skirmishes and shoving each other around. It happened, and it happened with regularity in the French Quarter.

Arriving home, Carmela snapped the leash on Boo, the leash she'd bought at the Coach store back when she'd had money. Then she took the little dog for a brisk walk around the block. Boo, with her canine sensitivity, must have picked up on the Mardi Gras mood because, much to Carmela's consternation, Boo seemed to make a huge production out of staring pointedly at every costumed person who walked by.

Finally arriving back home, Carmela got around to putting her groceries away, then slumped into her wicker chaise.

Walking Boo hadn't really cleared her head at all. In fact, it had just served to make her feel more nervous and apprehensive. On the other hand, one thing *had* crystallized in her mind. And that was that maybe the police should be hassling Dace Wilcox instead of Shamus.

Should she call Granger Rathbone? He probably wasn't in his office this time of night, but she could leave a message on his voice mail or something. *Hey Granger, why don't you take a good hard look at Dace Wilcox while you're at it.*

Would that be way too forward? Naaah.

Because the thing of it was, old Dace Wilcox *had* been hanging around Jimmy Earl Clayton the other night. And even though this fact was predicated on Gabby's recollection being correct, Carmela knew that Gabby rarely misspoke. If Gabby said Dace was there, Dace had surely been there.

So now we've put Dace Wilcox in the immediate vicinity of Jimmy Earl Clayton right before the sea serpent float rolled out the door. Right before Jimmy Earl cacked on his lethal drink of rum and ketamine.

That could mean that, hopefully, Shamus *was* innocent. And that maybe, just maybe, if Dace *hadn't* had a hand in offing Jimmy Earl, he still might know considerably more than he let on.

Carmela looked up the central number for the New Orleans Police Department. She punched in the digits, then asked to be connected with Homicide. When a very bored, gum-snapping secretary came on the line, Carmela asked for Granger Rathbone and got his voice mail instead.

That's okay. It's what you expected.

When the beep sounded, Carmela mustered up all her courage and outrage and left a message that, to the best of her recollection, went something like, "Hey Granger, you sack of shit. Why don't you take a look at Dace Wilcox while you're at it."

While it probably wasn't the most friendly or eloquent of messages, Carmela figured it would do the trick in at least garnering Granger Rathbone's attention. *And that was the whole point, wasn't it?*

Now, what was she going to do about Bufford Maple? *Is he a member of the Pluvius krewe?* That she'd have to find out. *And is Bufford Maple trying to ease me out of the building he owns?*

Good question. For now she didn't have an answer. But she'd find one. Sooner or later, she'd find one.

Shucking out of her blue jeans and poppy red cashmere sweater, Carmela pulled on a comfy oversized sweatshirt that came down to her knees. The front of the voluminous shirt proclaimed *Voulez Bon Ton Roulez*. Let the Good Times Roll.

That's right, she thought. And that was exactly what she was going to do tomorrow. Roll. She'd fire up her '88 Cadillac Eldorado and blow out the carbon as she barreled down Highway 23 to the Barataria Bayou.

She'd tote along that six-pack of Dixie Beer she'd bought at the little grocery store tonight, then stashed in her refrigerator to chill. She'd see what she could find out from Shamus. And try to hold his feet to the fire so she could get some real answers to her questions.

Chapter 14

IN THE MURKY depths of the Barataria Bayou, saltwater intrusion from the Gulf of Mexico has created a primordial tangle that yields a frightening but amazing habitat for animal and plant life. Among lurking, waterlogged trees, alligator, opossum, and nutria flourish. So do the dreaded cottonmouth and water moccasin.

But the Barataria Bayou is also a fisherman's paradise. Redfish, black drum, sheepshead, speckled trout, and black bass are easily caught here. No wonder herons with six-foot wingspans, Mississippi kites, and magnificent bald eagles wheel casually overhead, scanning the brackish waters intently.

Shamus was ostensibly holed up in or near his family's old camp house at the far end of the Barataria Bayou just east of Baptiste Creek. So, early this morning, Carmela had loaded Boo and her cooler into her trusty Cadillac, Samantha, stoked up with Premium at Langley's Superette, then pointed the broad nose of her gas guzzler southwest down Highway 23. Passing through the towns of Port Nickel, Jesuit Bend, and Naomi, Carmela continued on down some sixty miles or so to Myrtle Grove. From there she maneuvered her way over fifteen twisting miles of seashell roads through dank swampland and the occasional dark piney forest until she arrived at the tiny village of Baptiste Creek.

Truth be known, *village* might have been putting it kindly, for the term conjured up romantic images of quaint shops and picturesque vistas.

Baptiste Creek was more on the order of a rough-and-tumble fish camp. Rough because most of the inhabitants were fishermen and trappers by trade. Tumble because that's what a lot of the buildings seemed to be in the process of doing.

Carmela didn't have any trouble locating Toler Boat and Bait. Their international headquarters consisted of a ramshackle, once-canary-yellow building that was now weathered mostly silver gray and featured a motley collection of old fishnets, alligator hides, and antique tin signs nailed to its roof and outside walls. It was what an avant-garde installation artist might call an architectural *objet trouvé*, a treasure trove of found objects.

From the rear of Toler Boat and Bait, a rickety dock extended out into a dank slough. Roped to this dock were a half-dozen boats that creaked and rocked as they tugged gently at their moorings.

On one side of the shack, a skinny man wearing overalls, a blue T-shirt, and a straw hat was painting foul-looking brown stuff onto the bottom of a boat that had been hoisted up onto two sawhorses. Carmela saw immediately that the boat was a pirogue, a shallow, flat-bottomed boat used for travel in the bayou. In fact, before the advent of fiberglass and aluminum, Cajuns had traditionally hollowed out pirogues from cypress logs.

"Ned Toler?" Carmela called.

The man stuck his brush in the can of brown goo and gave her an appraising glance. Brown as a nut, his face careworn and lined from a life spent outdoors, Ned Toler appeared to be in his early sixties. Interestingly enough, Ned Toler also had one brown eye and one blue eye. A half-dozen spotted hounds lay snoozing on the ground around him.

Carmela hoisted her six-pack of Dixie Beer and dangled it provocatively in front of him.

A wide smile suddenly creased the man's face, revealing a glint of white teeth. "Carmela?"

She nodded.

Ned Toler's big paw swiped at the six-pack. It was, Carmela thought to herself, much like a brown bear effortlessly grabbing a jar filled with honey.

"Thought you might show up," Ned Toler told her as he cranked the cap off one of the long necks. The *whoosh* of the twist top coming off was followed by an appreciative *"Aaah"* from Ned as he tilted the amber bottle back and let malty brew roll down his throat.

When he had drained half the bottle, Ned wiped at his mouth and flashed Carmela a contented smile. "He ain't here."

"Do you know where he is?" asked Carmela, her hopes of finding Shamus and really talking to him suddenly dashed.

"Nope." Ned Toler glanced over at her car. She'd pulled it off the gravel road and parked it halfway in the weeds. "Nice car." He squinted at it again. "Eighty-seven?"

"Eighty-eight."

"That your dog inside?" Boo was jumping about excitedly, lathering up the rear windows and making a general mess.

Carmela nodded. "Yes."

"What the hell kind of dog is it?"

"She's a Chinese shar-pei," said Carmela.

"You don't say," said Ned, starting toward the car. "Exotic breed, huh? Looks a little like a crissy-cross between a boxer and a basset hound. You know, 'cause of all that wrinkly skin."

Carmela walked over to the car and opened the rear door so Boo could jump out. She immediately gave Ned Toler a tentative slobber, then turned her attention to the pack of leggy brown-spotted hounds that were edging toward her.

"Play nice," Ned admonished his motley band of dogs. "She's a little lady from the city."

Boo, who was suddenly in seventh heaven to be cavorting with a passel of other dogs, bounded off energetically with her newfound friends.

Ned Toler wandered back to the boat and the six-pack. Picking up his brush, he resumed his painting or waterproofing or whatever it was he was doing.

"I'd still like to go out to the camp house anyway," Carmela told him.

Ned Toler bit his lower lip as he worked. "It's your choice. Boat rental's five dollars an hour."

Carmela considered the twisting maze of swamp, the purple water hyacinth that was so rampant it often choked off entire channels, and the towering stands of bald cypress that enveloped Baptiste Creek and stretched beyond it for many dark miles. The journey to the camp house could be a daunting one. And then, of course, one could always run into *el lagarto*. Literally translated as "the lizard," it was what early Spanish sailors had called the alligator.

"What if I get lost?" Carmela ventured.

"Cost you more then," responded Ned. "All that wasted time spent wandering around in the swamp, tryin' to find your way back."

"And if I hired a guide . . . ?" Carmela slipped out of the cardigan she'd thrown on earlier. The sun was shining down, and the air was redolent with humidity and the sweet smell of water lilies and wild camellias. She'd forgotten just how truly lovely it could be out here.

Ned Toler sucked air through his front teeth. "I'm pretty busy right now."

"I can see that," said Carmela. She paused. "I'd certainly make it worth your while."

Ned pulled the battered straw hat from his head and scratched his lined forehead thoughtfully. "Twenty dollars says I can run you out there right now." He checked his watch, an old Timex stretched around his wrist on what looked to be a snakeskin band. "But we gotta be back by two."

"What happens at two?" asked Carmela.

"Gotta get ready for my date," Ned Toler said with relish. "Takin' the widow Marigny to a *fais-dodo* at the church over in Taminy Parish."

A *fais-dodo* was a Cajun shindig. A big party with lots of food and dancing.

"They gonna have a crawfish boil and cook up some gumbo and frog's legs, too," continued Ned Toler. "Plus they got a pretty good zydeco band that cranks up early."

"Okay," said Carmela, who didn't have a lot of trouble conjuring up a vision of Ned Toler doing the Cajun two-step with the widow Marigny. "Deal." She looked around for Boo but didn't see her.

"Don't you worry none about your little dog," Ned Toler assured her. "She won't go nowhere. My hounds stick closer to home than a wood tick on a possum. They'll take good care of her." Ned Toler snatched up the remaining beers and headed for the dock. "Come on then."

Carmela pulled a pair of sunglasses from her bag and slid them on. Following Ned Toler onto the rickety dock, she was surprised at how lighthearted and at home she suddenly felt out here.

Cajun country. That had to be it.

Her momma had grown up not far from here, in a little shrimping village over on Delacroix Island. She herself had never lived out here, of course, had only really lived in Chalmette and, more recently, in New Orleans proper. But she'd visited out here plenty of times. Had enjoyed some week-long stays with her cousins during the summer when she was young. The mists that crept in at twilight, the cry of screech owls, and the sharp, hoarse bark of the alligator raised goose bumps on a lot of people who ventured out this way. Sent them scurrying right back to the apparent safety of the city. But not Carmela. She liked the wildness of the bayou, the abiding sense of being surrounded by raw nature. It was somehow very comforting. And peaceful, too.

Isn't it funny, Carmela thought to herself, *that Shamus grew up in relative luxury in the Garden District but chose this as a place to hide out. To try to find himself.*

Had something of her rubbed off on him? Hmm. Now there was a weird thought.

Chapter 15

THE MEECHUM FAMILY'S camp house, located at a promontory point at the far end of the Barataria Bayou, had been constructed some eighty years ago. Each one of the cypress and cedar boards had been split, sawed, planed, and nailed in place by hand.

Viewing the camp house from a distance as Carmela was now, coming up the river in Ned Toler's sputtering motorboat, the structure appeared fairly substantial. Built on stilts and hunkered into a grove of saw palmetto and tupelo gum trees, it looked impervious to the occasional hurricane that lashed its way in from the Gulf of Mexico. Windows that were hinged on top and opened outward to allow breezes to sift through could be battened down in a heartbeat. The steeply pitched roof shed water easily. The cypress and cedar boards were thick and sturdy. An open-air porch wrapped around the front and sides.

As Ned's boat puttered up to the small dock, he reached over and handily tossed a rope around one of the wood pilings. Then Ned snugged his watercraft up close, allowing Carmela to jump out.

She'd been here twice before, always with Shamus. The first time had been when they'd returned from their honeymoon in Paris, and Shamus still had a couple days before he had to get back to his job at the bank. That had been a wonderful couple of days. Evenings they snuggled together in the double bed upstairs in the loft and talked about their future. Mornings Carmela had struggled good-naturedly to cook bacon and grits on the old-fashioned wood-fired stove.

Carmela's second visit to the camp house had been last spring. Shamus had wanted to come out here and take photographs of the azaleas and water hyacinths that were in bloom. Back then he'd been mumbling and grumbling about how much happier he'd be if he were a photographer instead of a banker. About how much happier he'd be if he could work outdoors. Of course, back then she hadn't really *heard* what he was saying.

Skipping lightly up a path of crushed oyster shells, Carmela climbed the steep, sturdy stairs and found herself on the wide porch that spanned the camp house on three sides. With its roof of pressed tin, she could imagine sitting out here in a storm. You could put your feet up on the railing, watch the bursts of heat lightning. Or listen to the beat of the rain, cozied up under a homemade quilt in one of the old cane chairs.

Carmela could hear the jangle of keys as Ned Toler came up the stairs behind her, pulling a heroic ring of keys from his pocket.

But the door to the camp house stood wide open.

Frowning, Carmela stepped over the threshold into the camp house.

The place looked like a hurricane had whipped through.

"Oh no!" exclaimed Carmela. Someone had obviously ransacked the entire place. What had been a fairly utilitarian and orderly little home was now an utter mess.

Carmela stared in dismay at the jumble of papers, dishes, knickknacks, and utensils that littered the planked wooden floors. The simple wooden chairs, so spare in their design, were overturned and strewn everywhere. One of the chairs had been completely smashed.

Ned Toler pushed in behind her. He held up a hand, indicating she should remain quiet. He stood, head cocked, listening for anything or anybody that might still be around, but the intruders seemed to be long gone.

"Damn," he said. "I was just out here day before yesterday, and everything was fine."

"Was Shamus here then?" asked Carmela.

"Yeah," said Ned Toler. Striding around, with his brow furrowed, his face displayed a fair amount of displeasure. "What a mess," he snorted as he grabbed a cane chair and set it upright.

"Who would do this?" said Carmela.

"Who's ever got it in for Shamus, I s'pose," barked Ned.

The main floor of the house was a combination living room–kitchen area with a small partitioned-off storage room. Upstairs was the bedroom loft.

Ned clumped up the narrow flight of steps that led to the loft. "It's all catawampus up here, too," he called down to Carmela. "Damn."

"How else would somebody get out here if they didn't come through Baptiste Creek village?" Carmela called to him.

Ned Toler came clumping back down the stairs, looking grim. "Lots of ways, really. There's fishermen and sightseers that come through here all the time. That's why I make it a point to check out here every few days. No tellin' when somebody decides to play squatter." Ned shook his head angrily again. "We've had people camp out here and help themselves to firewood and such, but nobody ever broke in and *trashed* the place before."

"What now?" said Carmela, looking around at the devastation and noting that a venerable old cypress table now had a broken leg.

"Now I better get back quick and grab a couple new locks." Ned Toler frowned at his wristwatch. "Then I'll run back out and install 'em. Tomorrow, I'll come back and sort things out as best I can."

Carmela nodded. There was nothing to be done here.

What had the intruder been looking for? she wondered. *Clues as to Shamus's whereabouts? Or something else?*

She shrugged, puzzled, and followed Ned back to the boat. *Have to think about it later. Like Ned Toler said, he wants to get back quickly.*

Back at the village of Baptiste Creek, Carmela thanked Ned Toler for his trouble, then headed off to round up Boo. She found the little dog snoozing in the sun with Ned Toler's hounds. Clipping a leash to Boo's collar, Carmela pulled her away from her hound dog friends and started for her car. Then, at the last minute, she decided to investigate a little food stand that had seemingly sprung up like a mushroom in her absence. Somewhat lifted out of her low mood by the dazzling array of fresh produce and home-canned goods, Carmela bought a dozen fresh brown eggs from the old woman who was manning the stand, then added a loaf of prune bread and a couple jars of homemade pepper jelly to her order. The boudin sausage, a Cajun sausage of pork and rice, looked wonderful, but Carmela passed. Just way too many calories.

"Lagniappe," said the old woman with a shy smile as she pressed a little package of bourbon balls wrapped in cellophane into Carmela's hand as she handed over her change. Lagniappe was a word that meant "a little extra." It was a charming custom that still flourished in many parts of Louisiana. Grocers giving a little extra to a customer's order, restaurants adding a little something on the plate of a favored patron, ordinary folks sharing the bounty of their garden with their neighbors.

IT WASN'T until Carmela was driving back to New Orleans, with a dozen or so miles racked up on the odometer, that she slowly became aware of the blue car behind her.

She studied the innocuous-looking dark blue sedan in her rearview mirror. *Am I being followed?* she wondered. *And, if so, what the heck is this all about?*

Carmela speeded up. The blue car behind her immediately sped up. She eased off the gas a bit. So did the blue car.

Okay, genius, she told herself. *You're being followed. You figured that out all right. Now what would old Kojak do?*

In the next half mile, Carmela got her big chance. Just past an old gray clapboard church with a flickering blue neon sign out front that proclaimed *Jesus Saves*, she swerved off the main highway onto a narrow little trail marked Two Holes Swamp Road. It was a dirt road she'd traveled a few times before. It was also one that wound circuitously through a generous portion of the Barataria Bayou, then eventually snaked back and hit Highway 23—*if* you knew exactly where to turn. The operative word being *if*, since Two Holes Swamp Road had more darn spur roads and offshoots than a tangle of wild grapevine.

Right now, Carmela's Cadillac, Samantha, was bumping along, kicking up a voluminous trail of dust. She figured it had to be completely obscuring the vision of the driver behind her. *Piece of cake,* she thought. *I ought to lose this joker in a matter of minutes.*

Carmela narrowed her eyes and pushed her foot down hard on the accelerator as she spun down the narrow dirt road. Dear Samantha, always hungry for a hit of high octane, guzzled deeply and responded with another appreciative burst of speed. But the driver in the blue car, seemingly unfazed by the dust she'd been kicking up, stuck tenaciously behind her like a burr.

Now what? she wondered.

With a flash of inspiration, Carmela cranked open her sun roof, then dug her right hand into the sack of eggs that rested precariously on the seat beside her. She waited until the car pursuing her was lined up directly behind her, then eased the little brown egg onto the roof and let it roll backward.

The egg skittered and danced along her car's roof like a billiard ball, then slid down the back window and bounced off the trunk like a missile spat from a grenade launcher. Hitting the windshield of the car behind her, the little brown egg landed with a deadly splat, obliterating the vision of the driver.

Rocketing down the dirt road, Carmela wove the Caddy from side to side, kicking up a barrage of dust and debris. Now the windshield of the car behind her, coated with sticky egg yolk, had become a virtual magnet for dirt.

"He goes to get that car cleaned up," Carmela advised Boo, "the seven ninety-nine econo-wash isn't gonna cut it. That boy's gonna have to pop for the fourteen-dollar suds-o-mania with plenty of hot carnauba wax!"

Approaching a Y in the road, Carmela barely hesitated as she navigated toward the right fork. This road was slightly narrower and bumpier, and as the bayou closed in around her, fronds of palmetto swatted at her windshield.

Peering in her rearview mirror, she saw that the driver of the blue car either didn't see her make the cut or chose not to follow.

When Carmela finally passed an old wooden sign that pointed toward a dilapidated boat launch, she knew the next left turn would loop her back to the highway.

Hah! It would almost be worth it to double back and see where that blue car ended up!

But Carmela didn't. She was anxious to get on back to New Orleans. To get home. After all, like Cinderella who'd bumped about in the dust all day, she had to get all cleaned up and pretty for a very fancy party tonight at Baby Fontaine's.

Chapter 16

THE HOT, NEEDLELIKE spray from the shower pinged against Carmela's back and shoulders. After rattling around Jefferson Parish for the better part of the day hunting for Shamus and eluding whatever obnoxious oaf had been tailing her, Carmela was anxious to shrug off any dust and residual bad karma she might have picked up and start the evening in splendiferous freshness.

Which meant emerging from her shower all pink and wet like a freshly netted gulf shrimp, then slathering on her favorite shea butter lotion. Once said lotion had been absorbed into her skin and her hair had been tousled and finger-combed into a semblance of the choppy do that Mr. Montrose Chineal had perfected at the Looking Glass Salon a scant two weeks ago, Carmela plunked herself down in front of the old vanity her momma had given her to do her makeup.

The vanity was an old-fashioned fifties-style piece of furniture. Big round mirror, sunken table in the center, drawers to either side. Carmela had a clear memory of being maybe six or seven years old and watching her momma get ready to go out with her daddy on Saturday nights. Her mother's *toilette* had always seemed like such an elegant ritual. Makeup dabbed on just so, dark eyeliner applied, fingers dipped into shimmering pots of colorful lip gloss, finishing spritz of floral perfume.

She remembered the look her momma and every other woman had tried to affect some twenty years ago. Big hair, big shoulders, big eyes. A vision that was slightly disco, a little bit *Dallas* TV show, and a little bit New Orleans. Nothing that would qualify as the natural look.

The phone rang, rousing Boo from one of her snory little dog dreams and causing her to utter a high-pitched yip.

"Shush," warned Carmela as she picked up the phone.

"You ready?" came a sharp voice. It was Ava, checking up on her.

"Almost," said Carmela.

"Honey, I've poured myself into my gold silk dress and, I don't mind telling you, it's pure evil. I only hope you can boast the same."

"I didn't know I was vying for runner-up in the Miss Slinky Tits contest."

"Life's a contest," shot back Ava.

Still holding the phone, Carmela studied her image in the mirror. *Hmm, not bad.* "I'll try not to disappoint you, Ava," she told her friend.

"Try not to disappoint faster. This girl is ready to party."

"Five minutes," said Carmela. "I'm heading down the home stretch even as we speak."

"Hey, did you see him?" asked Ava.

"Nope," replied Carmela. "Nobody home out there."

Carmela dropped the phone in its cradle and finished dabbing on her makeup, using a light touch with the eyeliner and mascara, preferring to adapt a softer, more natural look.

Thank goodness Baby's party hadn't been designated a costume ball, she thought to herself. There were *so* many costume parties during Mardi Gras. And by last count, she'd already attended four. Instead, Baby had carefully specified on her invitation that the evening would be *"black tie or suitably elegant attire."* Which was just hunky-dory with Carmela, since it offered the pluperfect opportunity to wear the black slit skirt and matching camisole bodice she'd bought in a wild fit of madcap spending right after the holidays.

Zipping the pencil-thin skirt, pulling the laces of the bodice tight, Carmela marveled to herself how she wouldn't have dreamed of wearing an outfit like this a year ago. Back then, life with Shamus had always seemed like it should be fairly proper and filled with decorum. He'd been a banker, she a banker's wife.

On the other hand, dressing like this was decidedly fun. She was young and attractive and, when she wasn't mooning about Shamus, could almost manage vivacious. So why on earth shouldn't she dress the part? Besides, Ava Grieux had threatened to put a curse on her head if she didn't start getting her head in the game.

Ava Grieux would have also whispered in her ear, *"If you've got it, flaunt it, kiddo."* But then again, Ava had long legs, a mass of curly auburn hair, and a body with seriously dangerous curves. In other words, an awful lot to flaunt.

Pulling open the closet door, Carmela searched for her shoes. Ah, there they were. Black suede, very strappy and sexy. Perfect. She studied her toenails for a moment, glanced at the clock. She had one minute before she was supposed to meet Ava. Carmela grabbed for her nail buffer and gave them a quick shine. There. She straightened up, stared at herself in the mirror, decided she was pleased with the pretty lady who smiled back. She hadn't quite achieved drop-dead vamp. No, that role still belonged to Ava for now. But still . . . she was looking mighty fine.

Chapter 17

MARK TWAIN ONCE wrote, "There is no architecture in New Orleans, except in the cemeteries." But anyone who has actually wandered the tree-bowered lanes of the elegant Garden District might hasten to take exception to Mr. Twain's somewhat flippant remark. For here are huge, elegant homes that resonate with history, with architectural symbolism, and with such pure Southern style that you feel like you've slipped back a hundred genteel years in time.

Just as the French Quarter is revered for its bawdy clubs, posh shops, cutting-edge restaurants, and picturesque architecture, the Garden District is the *pièce de résistance* of residential bliss. Once the sight of the great Livaudais plantation, the Garden District is now a grand dowager neighborhood filled with Victorian, Italianate, and Greek Revival homes that stand shoulder to elegant shoulder alongside each other. And just as its name implies, the Garden District delivers gardens galore. Gardens awash with camellias, azaleas, and crape myrtle. Gardens that echo with pattering fountains, chirping birds, and the quiet crunch of footsteps on pebbled walkways. Even private, hidden gardens enhanced with crumbling Roman-style columns, cascading vines, and greenery-shrouded loggias.

Tonight, as Carmela and Ava hopped from Carmela's car, the Garden District seemed to resonate with excitement. Up and down Third Street, homes were ablaze with lights, and stretch limousines rolled up, one after the other, to drop off elegantly attired couples. Strains of music from the hired jazz trios, bands, and combos echoed throughout the neighborhood.

"Don't you just love the smell of money?" exclaimed Ava as she adjusted a shimmery little shawl about her bare shoulders.

"What does money smell like?" Carmela asked with amusement.

Ava scrunched up her shoulders in a gesture that was pure Marilyn Monroe. "Like this!"

As Carmela and Ava hastened down the sidewalk, drawn like moths to the light, it seemed that *everybody* in the Garden District was throwing a party tonight. But on this sparkling evening, with lights blazing from every window and tiny garden lights dotting the path to her door, none of the houses seemed so grand as Baby Fontaine's.

Baby stood in the entry of her Italianate home, looking cool and pixieish in a shimmery emerald green strapless gown. Her husband, Del, who was her physical opposite, swarthy and dark, wide-shouldered and tall, held court next to her.

"Carmela! Ava!" cried Baby as two maids, specially employed for this grand evening, ushered the two women through the wrought-iron and glass double doors. Rushing to embrace them, Baby bestowed enormous air kisses which, of course, were eagerly returned.

"Gosh, this is absolutely stupendous," said Ava, dropping her shawl a little lower to show off her spectacular décolletage and gazing about at the interior of Baby's house. The walls of the front entry were covered with pale pink silk fabric. Ornate plasterwork and carved cypress moldings crowned the room, an enormous crystal chandelier dangled overhead, a huge circular staircase curled upward.

Peering down the center hallway, Ava could see a grand living room furnished with Louis XVI furniture and hung with original oil paintings to her right, a spectacular library with floor-to-ceiling bookshelves on her left.

"Baby, I really love your house," gushed Ava.

Baby waved a hand in a dismissive gesture. "Oh, it's just home," she said. "Casa Fontaine."

But Ava was still very impressed. "I do believe this is even nicer than Anne Rice's behemoth over on First Street." Ava had once peeked inside when she delivered some of her voodoo trinkets for use as favors at a Halloween party.

"Well, *we* certainly think so," allowed Baby. "And thank heavens we're located over here on Third Street. We don't get quite the hordes of sightseers that First Street or Washington Avenue or some of the other streets in the Garden District do."

"Lafayette Cemetery and Commander's Palace *are* awfully big draws," allowed Ava, referring to City of Lafayette Cemetery No. 1, a historic cemetery crowded with family tombs and wall vaults that abutted the Garden District, and Commander's Palace, the famed restaurant from whence Emeril Lagasse got his start.

Del put an arm around Baby. "If we start drawing crowds, honey, we'll just go on ahead and charge admission," he said in a leisurely drawl.

Baby batted her blue eyes at her husband. "Trust Del to find a way to turn a profit! Now, you two girls run along and kindly enjoy yourselves," she urged Carmela and Ava. "Gabby and Stuart are already in there somewhere, cooing like lovebirds and acting like the newlyweds they are. Say, that Stuart *is* a handsome devil, isn't he? And Tandy and Darwin are here, too. Although I think Darwin is huddled in the library with a bunch of menfolk, puffing on one of those awful cigars that Edgar Langley imports illegally from Cuba. I don't understand *what* the fascination is, those things stink to high heaven. We're probably going to have to air the place out for at least a week!"

"Is Jekyl Hardy here?" asked Carmela.

"He's here somewhere," said Baby. "And he was so worried about finishing up some of his floats. But then he got one of his assistants to oversee the final preparations, and he made it here just the same." She smiled, pleased. "*Everyone's* here tonight."

Del put a hand on his wife's bare shoulder. "Course they are, darlin'. Nobody in their right mind would miss one of *your* parties."

"My gosh," exclaimed Ava as Carmela propelled her toward the bar. "Baby's husband seems like he might be from one of those old Southern aristocrat families whose ancestors fought with Andrew Jackson."

"Actually," said Carmela, "I think Del's great-great-grandfather *did* fight with Andrew Jackson."

"Cool," exclaimed Ava. "Very cool."

THE PARTY was, as Ava put it, a blast. Beautifully dressed women and elegantly attired gentlemen rubbed shoulders and exchanged outrageous compliments and pleasantries. Crystal tumblers and champagne flutes were filled and refilled, and melodious strains from a string quartet drifted gently from room to opulent room.

Carmela drifted from room to room, too. Ava had disappeared almost immediately in a flurry of golden silk, having laid eyes on two thirty-something men she deemed "extremely interesting." In Ava-speak it meant the two men were bachelors whom she was itching to subject to her rigorous yet surreptitious questioning. For when it came to determining a man's merit as a "likely prospect," Ava was definitely an analytical left-brain type. And her scrutiny rivaled the process used for admitting prospects to the FBI Academy. Carmela had even kidded her about being a "profiler."

"Carmela," squealed Gabby as she waved from across Baby's glittering living room. "Come say hello to Stuart. He's absolutely *dying* to see you again."

Carmela threaded her way through a sea of silk-covered sofas and ottomans, noting that Stuart Mercer-Morris looked nowhere near dying to see anyone. Rather, his youthful face bore a somewhat bored, been-there-done-that look. It was, Carmela figured, the jaded countenance of a young man who was raised with money, lived with money, would always have a plenitude of money.

"Carmela darlin'." Stuart greeted her with a chaste peck on the cheek and a hearty handshake. Carmela noted it was not the limp-rag grasp that many New Orleans males reserved for the fairer sex. Then again, Stuart had gone to an East Coast school. Princeton. Or maybe it had been Harvard. Carmela couldn't recall exactly which one, except that it was one of those stalwart, preppy institutions where women were refreshingly considered the intellectual equal of men. Quite unlike little Clarkston College over in Algiers, where she'd attended school. There, they still elected a Crawfish Queen, Cotton Blossom Queen, and Sternwheeler Queen. Of course, there was never a crawfish, cotton blossom, or sternwheeler *king*. Gosh, life just wasn't fair.

"Gabby is always regaling me with the most marvelous stories about the things that go on in your shop," said Stuart pleasantly. "It would seem the problems of the world get sorted out there. Or at least the social peccadilloes of greater New Orleans."

"I've always thought we'd make a good premise for one of those reality TV shows," said Carmela. "Just prop a camera in the corner and see what goes on when you get a pack of Southern women together."

"What would you call it?" asked Gabby, clapping her hands together, caught up in the fun of the moment.

Carmela thought for a moment. " 'Cotton Mouths'?"

"Ah, very good," said Stuart with a somewhat forced smile on his face. He snaked one arm about Gabby's waist possessively. "And how is your husband, Shamus?"

Carmela kept her smile plastered on her face, maintained her voice at an even pitch. "Gone," she said. She hoped it sounded like a casual, offhand remark.

"But not forgotten," added Gabby, who suddenly looked a trifle nervous at the turn the conversation had taken.

"Shamus had such a promising career," continued Stuart. "I was so sorry to hear he'd left his position at the bank."

"And so was his family," said Ava, joining the conversation as she slipped in next to Carmela. "They probably haven't had a Meechum go rogue on them in the entire history of the family. Honey," Ava said, focusing her big, brown eyes directly on Carmela. "You have *got* to pay a visit to the buffet table. The food those caterers laid out is simply out of this world."

"Thanks for the save," Carmela whispered to Ava as they pushed their way through the crowd and headed for the buffet table in Baby's enormous dining room. "Stuart and Gabby are *so* hung up on my separation, it's beginning to get out of hand. I was afraid Stuart was going to start reciting pithy little quotes about Mars versus Venus."

"Oh, honey," said Ava as she fluffed back her hair and reached for a bone china buffet plate, "don't you know that touchy-feely caring-sharing thing is just a clever ruse with Stuart? The man owns car dealerships, for goodness sakes. He was just trying to soften you up so he could move in for the kill and sell you a nice big Toyota."

"You think Stuart knows what I drive?" grinned Carmela as she grabbed a gleaming white plate bordered by pink roses.

"*Everybody* knows what you drive," quipped Ava.

Baby's description of the menu a few days earlier had been vastly underplayed. For here was a buffet that was truly sumptuous. Enormous silver chafing dishes offered up their bounty of Oysters Bienville, crawfish cakes with red bean relish, and cunning little eggplant pirouges, tiny little eggplants that had been hollowed out and stuffed with crabmeat and melted cheese.

The overhead lights in the dining room had been purposely dimmed and

giant candelabras with sputtering pink candles placed strategically on the table
to lend a warm, mellow glow.

Truly, Baby's new caterers, Signature & Saffron, had come through like
troopers. And they were even handling food for three other major parties taking place in the Garden District this evening.

Carmela dug an enormous silver serving spoon into an ocean of okra
gumbo and transferred a helping to her plate. At the next chafing dish she
reached for the fried plantains and succeeded in covering up part of the pink
rose border on her plate. She cast an appraising eye down the table at the
dishes she *hadn't* tried yet, and decided she could probably cantilever a tiny
sliver of duck au jus on top of her pork roulade.

"You're going for the double-decker," said Ava, impressed. She never
knew Carmela could eat so much.

"Tonight I am," said Carmela as they moved down the line.

"If I eat too much, I'm for sure going to bust the seams of this dress," declared Ava. But Carmela noticed that didn't stop her from helping herself to a
little of everything.

Carmela was munching a crawfish cake and balancing a ramos fizz when
Jekyl Hardy came rushing up to her some ten minutes later.

"Car-*mel*-a!" he exclaimed, planting a giant kiss on her cheek.

"Jekyl, hi," she said. "Have you tried the food yet?"

Jekyl rolled his eyes. "Let's not go into that right now. Suffice it to say I
stormed the table with Tandy." He grabbed her arm. "But right now, my dear,
you are going to have your fortune told!"

"What are you talking about?" asked Carmela as Jekyl pulled her along
with him and she practically had to toss her empty plate, Frisbee-style, to one of
the tuxedo-clad waiters who was clearing away dishes and wineglasses.

"I'm referring to Madame Roux or Lou or whatever her name is," said
Jekyl. "Baby hired a fortune-teller for the evening. Isn't that an absolute
kick?"

Ensconced in Baby's solarium on a Chinese-style settee, Madame Roux
wasn't so much a fortune-teller as she was a reader of tarot cards.

"See," said Jekyl proudly as he prodded Carmela into the solarium ahead
of himself, "you've just got to have a go at it."

"Come in," Madame Roux beckoned to Carmela. "Open your heart and
mind, and let Madame Roux see what the tarot has divined for you." Clad in
a flowing hot pink robe, armloads of bangle bracelets, and a Dolly Parton wig
with a slightly pinkish cast, Madame Roux looked not so much like a fortune-
teller as a flamboyant senior citizen dressed for a hot date at the bingo parlor.

"I'm not a big believer in fortune-telling," Carmela confided to Madame
Roux as she sat down on the low stool that faced her. "I think people create
their own destinies."

Madame Roux shuffled the cards like a practiced blackjack dealer, then
fanned them out on the table between them. "I do, too, *chèrie*," she said with

a slight French accent. "The cards only point out choices; *you* make the final determination."

"So what do I do?" asked Carmela, feeling kind of silly.

"Choose three cards," Madame Roux instructed. "The first card will reveal your past situation, the second card your present situation, and the third card your future. But . . ." She held up her hand with theatrical flair. "Choose carefully."

Carmela grinned. *Past, present, and future, huh? Okay, this should be interesting.*

She indicated her first card. Past. Madame Roux plucked it from the line of fanned-out cards and turned it over. It was the queen of wands.

Madame Roux crinkled her eyes in a smile. Or as much as one could crinkle when wearing double sets of false eyelashes. "You have always been very sympathetic and friendly," said Madame Roux. "You were brought up to have a kind nature and also to be a good hostess."

Carmela returned Madame Roux's smile politely. "Not as good as Baby Fontaine is," she quipped.

"Now you must select the card that indicates your *present* situation," continued Madame Roux, unfazed.

Carmela chose a card from the middle.

Madame Roux turned it over, revealing the six of swords. A tiny frown crossed her face. "Difficulties. Anxieties."

Carmela shrugged. "A few, yes." *Well, that was a strange choice of cards. Probably won't come up again in a zillion years, right?*

"And now your future card," urged Madame Roux.

Carmela pointed to the last card on the far right. "That one."

Madame Roux flipped it over. It was the hierophant card. The ancient Greek priest who was the interpreter of mysteries and arcane knowledge.

"What does it mean?" asked Carmela as she studied the card. Her final choice of cards *looked* fairly benign. An ancient priest sitting between two Greek columns with a gold key at his feet. Still, it could probably be interpreted any number of ways.

"The meanings are varied," said Madame Roux. "Mercy, kindness, forgiveness."

"All good things," said Carmela. "And what does the key mean?"

Madame Roux studied the card. "Not completely clear," she said, "but it *should* be revealed soon enough."

Carmela continued to take this experience with a grain of salt. "So this is a short-term reading?" she asked, her bemusement apparent. This was like one of those psychic hotlines on TV, she decided. Got to flash a disclaimer that said, "For entertainment purposes only."

Madame Roux's eyes sparkled darkly as they met hers. But even as her eyes were filled with kindness, they also projected a certain seriousness. "You will know about the key in a matter of days, *madame*," said Madame Roux.

"Well, thank you," said Carmela, standing up. She dug in her evening bag for a tip, but Madame Roux held up her hand.

"Not necessary," Madame Roux told her. "Everything has been taken care of."

There were loud giggles and a shuffle of feet behind Carmela. Obviously other guests were waiting their turn to commune with Madame Roux.

Carmela turned around to leave and almost ran smack-dab into Ruby Dumaine.

"Carmela!" exclaimed Ruby loudly. Her round face was pink and flushed, her manner bordering on boisterous. A glass of champagne was clutched tightly in one hand. It was obviously not her first.

"Hello, Ruby," said Carmela. She noted that Ruby was dressed not unlike Madame Roux. Lots of flashy jewelry, a hot pink dress that swirled around her.

Ruby leaned unsteadily in toward Carmela. "A little bird told me someone was *very* mad at you!"

Carmela favored Ruby with a wry smile. Ruby Dumaine was notorious for hinting at little bits of gossip and then dropping nasty clues.

"Let me guess," said Carmela, playing along with Ruby the best she could. "The garden club booted me off their roster for failing to produce a single Provence rose." Carmela moved a few steps away from Ruby, noting that the woman was a notorious space invader.

Ruby Dumaine rolled her eyes in an exaggerated gesture. "*Noooo,*" she said.

"On the other hand, I'm not even *in* the garden club anymore," laughed Carmela. *Have I exchanged enough polite banter with Ruby to pass as being sociable?* she wondered. *Can I please exit stage left now?*

But Ruby was in an ebullient mood. "If I recall, Carmela, when you resided in this rather hoity-toity neighborhood not so very long ago, you managed to coax a fair amount of flowers into bloom."

Carmela heard familiar voices and glanced sideways. Tandy Bliss and Jekyl Hardy were bearing down on her. Bless them. Rescue was in sight.

"Ah, you'll have to take that up with Glory Meechum, matriarch of the Meechum clan," said Carmela to Ruby. "For, alas, I am no longer a resident of this glorified zip code."

"Matriarch," shrieked Jekyl, moving in next to Carmela. "Doesn't that word conjure up images of incredibly stolid-looking women wearing togas and metal helmets?"

"I think you're confusing matriarchal images with opera icons," said Tandy. She smiled perfunctorily at Ruby. "Hello there," she said.

"Oh, but I *adore* opera," protested Jekyl. "It's just those enormous opera singers that put me off. Stampeding across the stage as they do. Opera is so refined, so genteel. The art should reflect that, should it not?"

"But then the singers wouldn't be able to *project*," argued Tandy. She flashed Carmela a look that said, *We'll get you out of here in a minute.*

Jekyl favored Tandy with a sly smile. "But *you* do. You can talk louder than a foghorn in a hurricane when you want to. And you're only . . . what . . . a hundred pounds?"

"Please," said Tandy. "I tip the scales at ninety-eight pounds." In her short black dress with its teeny, tiny spaghetti straps, Tandy looked even skinnier.

Jekyl Hardy gave an elaborate shrug, as though he'd proven his point. "See."

Carmela was pleased to see that her friends were now on either side of her, ready to spirit her away from Ruby.

But Ruby Dumaine wasn't so easily put off. "Carmela," she began again, "you *are* being whispered about. People are saying *terrible* things."

Jekyl Hardy peered at Ruby peevishly. "Who's got their undies in a twist over some insignificant slight on Carmela's part?"

"Wrong," interrupted Tandy. "When Carmela slights someone, *if* she slights someone, it's significant. They *stay* slighted."

"Good girl," laughed Jekyl. "No sense pussyfooting around."

"It's Rhonda Lee," Ruby blurted out loudly. "Rhonda Lee Clayton thinks Shamus is responsible for her husband's death." Ruby's eyes blazed wildly as she stared directly at Carmela. "And she's positive that *you're* covering up for him!"

Carmela was suddenly dumbfounded. "She thinks *I'm* covering up for him?" she said to Ruby. "Does Rhonda Lee know that Shamus and I are separated? That we have been for almost six months now?" Carmela almost reeled from the impact of this nastiness. "Aside from the fact that Shamus had nothing to do with Jimmy Earl's death," she added. *I hope,* said a little voice inside her.

Ruby Dumaine nodded slowly, obviously pleased at the impact her words had on Carmela. "Rhonda Lee has been telling *everyone* that it's all part of your master plan." Ruby smiled, looking decidedly like the cat that just swallowed the canary.

"*My* master plan?" Now Carmela's voice carried real outrage. "The woman is insane."

Tandy rolled her eyes. "Why do I feel like I'm standing in Pee-wee's Playhouse where things are getting crazier by the minute?"

"You're right," said Jekyl. "Time to take our leave."

"Bye-bye, Ruby," said Tandy as they propelled Carmela down the hallway and away from Ruby Dumaine.

"Whew," said Jekyl when they were out of earshot. "What was *that* all about?"

"I think the old bat's been drinking absinthe," said Tandy.

"Actually," said Jekyl, "Ruby was drinking a French fizz. Pernod and champagne."

"A hooker's drink," sniffed Tandy.

"This is such craziness!" said Carmela, still smarting from the nasty gossip Ruby had been so happy to spread. Her angst and frustration were obvious. What started out as a lovely evening had suddenly taken a nasty twist.

"Do you know what?" said Tandy in a low voice. "The insidious thing is that people *do* listen to Rhonda Lee."

Jekyl's face was suddenly lined with concern as he stared at Carmela. "They do," he said. "Carmela, do you know if Shamus has a lawyer? A good one?"

"I don't know. Probably," said Carmela, recalling Shamus's many phone conversations with the attorneys who were kept on retainer by his family's Crescent City Bank.

Tandy gave a quick look around to make sure no one was listening in on their conversation. "Do you even *know* where Shamus is, Carmela?"

Carmela shook her head. Tears had begun to gather in her eyes and threatened to spill down her cheeks. *Why,* she wondered, *am I getting so damned emotional about this all of a sudden?*

"My God," exclaimed Jekyl, peering at her. "You still love Shamus!"

Carmela shook her head fervently. "I don't. Absolutely not."

"Yes, you do!" Jekyl insisted.

"Leave her alone," hissed Tandy. "Can't you see she's upset?" Tandy slipped a thin arm around Carmela's waist and pulled her close. "Don't you dare make her any more worried than she already is," she sternly admonished Jekyl.

"Sorry," said Jekyl. "Really. I had no intention of . . . ah . . . upsetting Carmela."

"I think the two of us better go outside for a little fresh air," Tandy announced imperiously. She grabbed Carmela's elbow and began to lead her through the crush of people that buzzed about the makeshift bar in Baby's game room. "S'cuse us, s'cuse us," Tandy intoned as they pushed their way through the crowd, heading for the French double doors that led to the patio outside.

JUST AS they had for last year's big party, Baby and Del had hired two different musical groups: a string quartet that played in one corner of the living room from seven-thirty until about nine o'clock, and a zydeco band that had as its venue an enormous white tent in the Fontaines' backyard.

Carmela's and Tandy's heels clacked across the bricks of the patio as they crossed toward the tent. They could see that the zydeco musicians were just starting to warm up, and a few couples were already lolling about the dance floor in anticipation of the music. Carmela knew it wouldn't be long before the entire crowd, lured by the rousing music and wildly engaging beat, would thunder outside, lubricated with drink and ready to cut loose. And Carmela also knew that once the really wild music started, the party would go on until God knows when.

"Tandy," said Carmela, "you go on back in. Let me take a breather by myself."

Tandy's pencil-thin eyebrows shot up, and her face suddenly assumed a worried look. "Are you sure, Carmela? Because you seemed awfully upset in there."

Carmela sighed deeply. "Ruby Dumaine just got the best of me for a moment. Plus I went out to Shamus's camp house today and found it totally trashed."

"Oh, no!" exclaimed Tandy. "Who on earth would want to—" She stopped suddenly, bit her lip. Obviously, someone *did* want to discredit Shamus or cause him serious problems.

"I'm pretty sure Shamus *is* in some sort of trouble," confided Carmela. "I just don't know what kind." She was also recalling the blue sedan that had followed her for a while this afternoon. Suddenly her rollicking adventure didn't seem quite so rollicking anymore.

"Jeez," breathed Tandy. "So your ex is seriously on the lam. I didn't know old Shamus had it in him. The Meechums always seemed like such a prim and proper family. The kind of people who are born with the proverbial stick up their butts, if you know what I mean."

Tandy's somewhat unkind characterization of Shamus and his family brought a wry smile to Carmela's face. "Lots of people think that," she admitted. "But the fact remains, Shamus is an *honest* person, a *good* person." Carmela wanted to add, *Except with me,* but she didn't. Instead she simply added, "I can't believe Shamus was in any way involved in Jimmy Earl's murder."

"Course he wasn't, honey," said Tandy. "Ruby Dumaine is just a big old loudmouth pea hen. She's got nothin' to do all day but fret, bug her daughter Swan to death, and spend Big Jack's money as fast as he makes it. It's a lethal combination. Breeds contempt of others."

"I think you're right," said Carmela.

"I *know* I'm right," responded Tandy. "Now you go on and take a few minutes to pull yourself together, then I want you to march that cute little tush of yours back here. I am hereby issuing strict orders that you're to be on that dance floor shaking your booty in approximately five minutes. Okay?"

She didn't know how much booty shaking she'd be doing, but Carmela decided the easiest thing to do was agree with Tandy. "Okay," she told her.

Tandy leaned forward and gave Carmela a motherly peck on the cheek. "Good girl."

Standing on the side portico, some twenty feet away, Dace Wilcox had just witnessed this exchange between Carmela and Tandy. And, from the depths of the shadows, he was staring at them intently.

Chapter 18

SLIPPING DOWN A stone walkway into the shrouded depths of Baby Fontaine's backyard garden, Carmela was decidedly glad to have a few moments away from the crush of the party. It had been wonderful to see all her friends, and the food was truly delightful. But why did catty old Ruby Dumaine have to bring everything to such a screeching halt?

Did Rhonda Lee Clayton *really* believe there was some *master plan*? And was Rhonda truly spreading stories about her and Shamus?

And why did I get so teary-eyed just a few moments ago?

As a gust of cool air swept through the sweet olive and boxwood trees, stirring the shrubbery around her, Carmela gave a little shiver. Clutching her arms to her chest, she was still reluctant to go back inside. Like an F5 tornado, the party was swirling at a feverish pitch. Men were drinking, women were flirting outrageously, the zydeco band was about to cut loose big time. But then again, that's what a Mardi Gras party was all about. The word *carnival* was derived from a Latin word meaning "farewell to flesh." And the whole concept of the Mardi Gras *carnival* was to eat, party, drink, live fast and hard, and commit more than a few sins. Because once Ash Wednesday arrived, you had to slam on the brakes and observe forty long days of denial.

A glint of moonlight illuminated a stone bench just ahead of her. Carmela walked over and sat down, still reluctant to return to the party. Out here, she could still *feel* the residual rush of the party and hear the muffled voices and musical strains. But it was removed, filtered, safer.

As Carmela stared into the darkness of the garden around her, she could hear the strains of "If Ever I Cease To Love." As the official Rex anthem, it was played constantly during the Rex parades and the Rex krewe's imperial receptions. Today, most of New Orleans viewed the song as the official Mardi Gras ballad.

> If ever I cease to love
> May sheeps' heads grow on apple trees
> If ever I cease to love
> May the moon be turn'd to green cheese

Humming along to the haunting tune, Carmela *still* couldn't get Ruby Dumaine out of her head.

What is her problem? thought Carmela. *Why is Ruby so all-fired set on spreading rumors, on promoting Rhonda Lee's paranoia? Is this just sport on her part? Does she just want to see Shamus's ears get nailed to the wall?* Carmela shook her head regretfully. There were a lot of things she was having trouble figuring out. Like why did Bufford Maple, the columnist, seem to have it in for both her and Shamus? And what was Dace Wilcox's connection to all this, if anything?

Carmela stood up, strolled to the back gate, and pushed it open. Now she found herself in the middle of a narrow cobblestone alley that ran between the backyards of a half-dozen enormous houses. A hundred years ago, this had been the carriage lane, the tradesman's and servant's entrance. Now BMWs, Porsches, and Audis were the only vehicles that rumbled down this lane. And tonight, hired car parkers had jammed extra vehicles up and down the length of it, narrowing the roadway even more.

Gingerly, Carmela eased her way past the parked cars. She was beyond the boundaries of Baby's estate now and staring at the back of the house next to them. These neighbors were throwing a party, too, albeit a smaller, more sedate one. If there was such a thing as a sedate Mardi Gras party.

Carmela paused, ready to turn back toward Baby's house, when she was suddenly stopped in her tracks. Parked across the alley from her was a dusty blue car.

Is this the car that followed me today? Parked right here? Whoa, better take a closer look.

Even in the dim light Carmela could see the windshield had streaky smears on it.

Egg yolk? Gotta be.

She blinked, looked around, wondered again whose car this was and did they live around here or had they just popped in for a visit?

Well, the car's parked directly behind this palatial home with the peaky, almost Chinese-like roof. This would be the place to start. So . . . take a look? Not take a look?

Carmela's eyes sought out a glowing window on the second floor. And there, sitting just a few feet from the window, talking on the phone or maybe to somebody else who was in the room, was Swan Dumaine, Ruby and Jack Dumaine's daughter!

How bizarre, thought Carmela. *This is Ruby and Jack Dumaine's home!* And on the heels of that came the thought, *It also feels like a scene out of the movie,* Rear Window.

All her sensibilities told Carmela to just walk away. Yet she was drawn by the thought of the blue car. *Was the driver of the blue car a guest in Jack Dumaine's house? And who exactly was this person who found her trip down to the Baritaria Bayou so all-fired interesting?*

Carmela tiptoed down a gravel path toward the back of the house, acutely aware of rocks crunching underfoot.

Can anyone hear me? Will someone come dashing out of the house? Is anyone even in there besides Swan?

As if in answer to her question, a muffled roar of applause emanated from the tent in Baby's backyard. Then the zydeco band started up with what sounded like a cataclysmic crash.

Carmela put a hand into a clump of bushes and parted it slightly, the better to catch a glimpse of the lower floors.

Is Jack Dumaine home? Or is he down the street, prowling around at Baby's party, too? Spreading the Dumaine good cheer, same as his wife.

Carmela suddenly caught a flicker of movement on the first floor of the house.

Somebody's in there. Somebody's home.

Her curiosity made her bold. Creeping closer to the house, Carmela peered in through draperies that were not fully drawn.

Jack Dumaine was sitting behind a massive wooden desk in what had to be the library. Behind him, bookcases lined the walls, and books with leather bindings gleamed in the low light. A Tiffany lamp with a dragonfly motif sat on Jack's desk. It was one of the old ones, a mosaic of brown and gold glass with a burnished brass lamp base. Surrounded by all that apparent luxury, Jack was smoking a cigar and haranguing an unseen person who seemed to be perched at a right angle to his desk.

Who was Big Jack chewing out, anyway? It couldn't be Ruby; she was still at the party across the way.

Jack Dumaine was angry, though. Extremely hot under the collar. Red-faced, with thunderclouds for eyebrows, he bounced up and down in his leather chair, speaking with great force and stabbing the air with his cigar, as if to underscore each point he was making. Since Carmela couldn't hear Jack Dumaine's words and could only see his angry expressions, it was like watching the antics of an overwrought mime.

Who are you talking to, Big Jack? What poor soul is sitting in the hot seat across from you getting royally drilled?

Feeling with her toes, which were by now half frozen, Carmela gingerly shuffled her way around the bush. Then she took a deep breath and leaned toward the window, peering between Ruby Dumaine's not-quite-closed curtains of green velvet.

Carmela was rocked by who was sitting across from Big Jack.

Ohmygosh, it's Granger Rathbone!

Granger Rathbone sat in a high-backed chair that was set at an angle to Jack Dumaine. His pockmarked face was set in grim repose, and he looked like a bobble-head doll, as he bobbed his head and nodded while Jack lectured to him.

So what is Granger Rathbone doing in Jack Dumaine's library? wondered Carmela. *Has Jack Dumaine got Granger on his payroll? Did Jack Dumaine* kill his business partner, Jimmy Earl Clayton, and now he's enlisted Granger Rathbone to help him cover it all up?

Maybe, could be were the answers that came back to her.

And on the heels of that happy thought came the grim realization: *They're trying to set Shamus up!*

Suddenly panic-stricken, Carmela tried to halt her runaway thoughts. *Are they? Really?*

She backed slowly away from the window. *Let's just think about this for a minute,* she told herself. *Someone murdered Jimmy Earl Clayton by feeding him a megadose of ketamine. And a lot of people close to Jimmy Earl seemed to be growing increasingly suspicious of Shamus. But nobody had uncovered any hard evidence that linked him to the deed. So far, this whole thing against Shamus was being fueled only by rumors and innuendos.*

The thing she had to decipher was, *who exactly was doing the fueling?* Jack Dumaine and Granger Rathbone? Or were they working on something else?

Could Bufford Maple or Dace Wilcox have a motive as well?

Carmela quietly exited Jack Dumaine's yard, pondering the whole mess. One thing was for sure, Jack Dumaine seemed to have Granger Rathbone in his hip pocket. And that wasn't good. That wasn't good at all. Granger Rathbone was a nasty, vindictive cop of the worst kind. And in New Orleans, cops had power. A lot of power.

As Carmela stood in the alley, she heard the back door open and a low mumble of voices, then footsteps crunch on gravel.

Somebody's coming!

Diving behind a silver BMW, Carmela ducked down and held her breath. As the footsteps passed close by, she allowed herself a quick peek.

It was Granger Rathbone, all right. *What a creep.* Remaining in her hiding spot, Carmela waited until she heard his car door open, then slam shut, hesitated as the engine revved and turned over. Then headlights flared, and Granger's blue car swept noisily down the alley away from her.

So that's who'd been following her today. Quite probably, the old boy had gotten her phone call from the previous night and categorically blown off her suggestion to take a look at Dace Wilcox. But he *had* decided to follow her out to the bayou this afternoon in hopes of finding Shamus.

Finding Shamus for who, though? For the New Orleans PD or for Jack Dumaine?

There was also another possibility that loomed large.

Had Granger Rathbone trashed Shamus's camp house?

Carmela considered the idea for a moment. Somehow, it didn't feel right. Granger Rathbone would have had to sneak out there earlier, then wait around for her.

No, the most plausible explanation was that Granger had followed her, plain and simple. Hoping, of course, that the trail would lead to Shamus.

As Carmela stood behind the silver BMW pondering this new twist, one of the garage doors across the alley suddenly emitted a loud *cha-clunk*, then began to rise. Easing back into the shadows, she watched carefully. And, in the dim light from the overhead bulb that hung in the center of the garage, she recognized the somewhat ample profile of Jack Dumaine.

Jack Dumaine is going somewhere! And he was agitated. In fact, he looked as though he was in a powerful hurry as he tried to insert his bulk into the front seat of his jumbo-sized Chrysler Voyager.

Where's he off to? Carmela wondered. Then just as quickly decided, *There's only one way to find out.*

In a flash, she scampered through the side yard between Baby's house and the neighbor's big money pit of a home. When she hit Third Street, Carmela darted left, sprinted the length of a city block in what had to be record time, then dove into her car.

Raised by a careful Norwegian father who had always worn a belt *and* suspenders, Carmela, too, was a careful, cautious person. She always kept a spare key under the dashboard. She grabbed for it now, jammed it into the ignition, and cranked the engine hard. It was quicker than pawing through her evening bag in the dark.

As the Caddy came to life with a roar, Carmela pulled out into the street, then experienced a moment of high anxiety. *Which way is Jack Dumaine headed? Should I flip a U-turn or continue on straight ahead?*

It was a fifty-fifty proposition, with no time to get overly analytical or toss a coin. *Straight,* Carmela decided.

At the corner of Chestnut she hooked right and was rewarded with a glimpse of Jack Dumaine's fat-ass Chrysler, just a block ahead of her.

Awright, good call, she told herself.

Carmela settled in behind Jack Dumaine, staying a safe distance behind him. As they puttered along, Carmela decided that Jack Dumaine drove his car the same way he walked. Ponderous bordering on lugubrious. Jack's car seemed to lurch forward slowly as though he kept tapping the brake every few seconds instead of just proceeding smoothly.

They bumped down Washington until it turned into Palmetto, then hit the Airline Highway. This was the side of New Orleans that wasn't so quaint and pretty. Lots of fast-food franchises, neon lights, tacky rib joints, and drive-through daiquiri bars.

Jack Dumaine eased his car onto Airline Highway and headed west. But rather than working up a full head of steam, he stayed in the right lane, carefully observing the fifty-five-mile-an-hour speed limit. A mile later, his right-turn signal pulsed, and Jack turned off. Carmela followed, again keeping her distance behind him. Driving down a side street now, Jack wove his way past an all-night rib joint, a seedy office building, and the Calhoun Motel.

Jack made a slow, wide turn into the motel's parking lot.

Cutting her headlights, Carmela rolled in behind him. She stopped her car in a shadowy part of the parking lot and waited. Watched as Jack Dumaine pulled into a parking space, then eased himself out of his vehicle and stretched languidly. A sharp *bleep* sounded as Jack Dumaine locked his car with his electronic key. Then Jack strode confidently toward the door of one of the motel rooms.

Carmela tried to time her drive-by so she'd be rolling past the motel room at the exact same moment the door opened and Jack slipped inside.

It worked like a charm.

Because just as the door opened and light shone out into the dark parking lot, Carmela was rewarded with the surprise of her life. Rhonda Lee Clayton, Jimmy Earl's grieving widow, stood in the doorway to greet Jack, wearing a black-and-gold floor-length caftan and a pussycat smile on her face.

Chapter 19

JACK DUMAINE AND *Rhonda Lee Clayton. Rhonda Lee Clayton and Jack Dumaine.* The words played over and over in Carmela's brain like a feverish mantra. What *were* the two of them doing together?

Canoodling, that much was obvious. But what were they *really* doing together?

Had Jack and Jimmy Earl's partnership not been as cozy as Jack had made it out to be? He'd certainly sung Jimmy Earl's praises to high heaven and made their partnership sound like a mutual admiration society when he'd eulogized him at the memorial service a scant two days ago.

Could it be that Rhonda Lee was the *real* partner in the company, the silent partner, and Jimmy Earl had just been a figurehead?

No, that didn't make any sense either, Carmela decided. Jimmy Earl had been quoted frequently in the business pages. And he'd gotten lots of little blurbs written about him in some of the smaller business magazines attesting to the fabulous deals he'd engineered. So Jimmy Earl *had* to have been a real partner in his own right, despite all his pathetic frat boy antics.

So maybe Big Jack had just plain offed Jimmy Earl in a straight-ahead murder?

Yeah, that's gotta be the answer, figured Carmela. *Jack offed his partner to gain control of the company and bed Rhonda Lee.*

On the other hand, that answer seemed far too pat.

For one thing, Rhonda Lee was no great prize.

No, Carmela decided, there was something else going on. Something she hadn't figured out yet.

Turning the key in her lock, Carmela let herself into her apartment. Even before she flipped on the lights, she knew she wasn't alone. Someone was in there with her. Someone who had obviously become a new best friend with Boo. Could it be Granger Rathbone? Maybe. Pity Boo had such poor taste.

"Awright," Carmela called into the darkness with as much bravado as she could muster. "Let's cut the games. I know you're in here."

The cushions in the wicker chair gave a muffled squeak as someone shifted their body weight and reached for the ginger jar lamp that occupied the adjacent table.

There was a bright flash, and then Carmela was staring wide-eyed at her soon-to-be ex-husband. "Shamus!" she exclaimed. This *was* a surprise.

"Howdy, Carmela," he said, returning her greeting.

She stared at him, hating the insolent look he wore on his face. Or maybe it was just his confidence. Shamus had always been a supremely confident being. Even when he played varsity football at Tulane, he was the kind of guy who could drop a pass and still walk off the field looking like a winner.

What the hell, Carmela decided, it didn't matter. What *did* matter was that she was getting more and more angry with every second that passed.

"Brushing up on your breaking and entering?" she asked him.

He responded by shifting his long legs off the ottoman and giving it a gentle pat, trying to entice her to come sit down next to him.

She sauntered over carefully, plunked herself down.

"Nice dress," he remarked, reaching for the laces of her camisole.

Carmela held up a cautionary index finger. "That's off limits," she told him sternly.

He pulled his hand back, favored her with a lazy smile. "Still, you're looking quite delicious," he said.

Carmela didn't answer him. What she wanted to say was, *No, you're looking good.* Because damned if he wasn't. Shamus's olive skin, brown eyes, and shaggy, slightly sun-streaked hair were pure eye candy. Very appealing. In fact, he looked happier and healthier than when he'd been living with her. Being on the run seemed to agree with him.

Damn, she thought, *how can it be? It just doesn't make sense. Then again, nothing seems to make sense.*

She also noticed that Shamus hadn't abandoned his Rolex Datejust and his Todd loafers. He may have ditched her, but he'd kept his toys. She guessed the Meechum family trust was still operating in full force.

"I came looking for you today," she told him. "I was out at the camp house."

"Yeah, I heard," said Shamus. Boo came pattering over to him and rested her head on his knee. Shamus reached down and gently kneaded the dog's tiny, flat ears. "Good girl," he cooed to her.

"It's been totally trashed," Carmela told Shamus. She was trying not to let his apparent affection for Boo get under her skin. How could Shamus be so sweet and attentive to a little dog and act like an inconsiderate louse with her?

"I'm not surprised," said Shamus.

"Everybody thinks you're on the lam," Carmela told him.

Shamus gave a disinterested shrug. "If that's what everybody thinks, then I suppose I am," he said.

Carmela was beginning to get very frustrated by his apparent lack of concern for himself. "People are accusing you of murder, Shamus! They're trashing your camp house and saying incredibly nasty things about you. Doesn't that bother you just one teeny tiny bit?"

Shamus turned liquid brown eyes on her. "Should it? Should I really care what vitriolic lies are being spewed out about me?" he asked her.

Carmela was flustered. This was not the hardheaded banker of the notoriously conservative Crescent City Bank that she'd known and loved. "No, but—" she started.

"But what?" he asked. His flashing eyes challenged her.

"But you should at least *defend* yourself," she sputtered. Carmela stopped abruptly, tried to pull herself together. Why did she feel like she was suddenly playing one of the lead roles in a romantic comedy from the '40s? One of those frothy, fast-moving films where the leading man and woman constantly snapped and snarled at each other, yet everyone knew they were madly in love and would end up happily-ever-aftering at the end of the picture.

Will Shamus and I end up back together at the end of the picture? Somehow it doesn't seem like a Hollywood ending is on the horizon.

"I saw Jack Dumaine with Rhonda Lee!" Carmela suddenly blurted out.

"Where?" asked Shamus.

"Tonight. At the Calhoun Motel. A hot sheet joint just off Airline Highway." Burned in Carmela's mind was the vision of Rhonda Lee Clayton in her sixties-style earth mother caftan. It was an image that projected far more than she cared to know about the woman.

"You don't say," said Shamus. "With the grieving widow, no less. I'm amazed Big Jack is still out wolfing around. My hat's off to the old boy."

"Shamus," said Carmela, "I think Big Jack is trying to set you up. In fact, I'm pretty sure he is."

Shamus leaned back and steepled his fingers together, looking as though he was lost in deep, impenetrable thought. Carmela had seen him do this before. It meant Shamus was stalling. Or, worse yet, merely toying with her.

"Let me get this straight," said Shamus. "You think that just because Jack Dumaine decided to have a toss in the hay with Rhonda Lee . . . that he's plotting to set me up? Destroy my career and my good family name?"

"Well, yes. He certainly could be," said Carmela. "Beside the fact that he's sleeping with his dead partner's wife, Jack Dumaine also seems to have Granger Rathbone in his hip pocket."

"Really," said Shamus. "And what do you make of that?"

"Duh," said Carmela. "A setup?" *Jeez*, she thought, *is this boy dense or what? Or just in very serious denial?*

"You're right," Shamus said finally. "It doesn't look good."

Aware that her skirt was beginning to ride up, Carmela shifted about on the ottoman, trying to smooth it down and assume a slightly more decorous pose. Shamus's eyes followed every aspect of her struggle.

"Shamus, tell me something," she said finally. "What words did you have with Jimmy Earl, right before he climbed up on that big green float and took a drink that snuffed out his gray matter?"

"Nothing that would interest you, my dear."

"Try me." Carmela stood up suddenly, placing her hands on her slim hips and gathering her face into a semblance of a thundercloud.

Shamus flashed a smile at her. "God, you're a pretty thing."

"Shamus . . ." Carmela's voice carried a warning tone.

He threw up his hands in mock defeat. "Okay, okay, you win. If you must know, Jimmy Earl called me an asshole."

"The man *did* have a way of making sense of things," Carmela said with the beginning of a wry smile. She paused, staring into Shamus's intense brown eyes. He didn't seem all that amused by her banter. "Okay, Shamus, I'll bite. Why did Jimmy Earl call you an asshole?"

"For leaving you."

Carmela gave an audible snort. "I don't believe you."

"Honey, you can believe whatever you want, but I swear on a stack of Bibles . . . on my momma's grave, in fact . . . that it's true."

"Where were you today?" Carmela asked him.

Shamus gathered his long legs beneath him and suddenly stood up. He stepped close to Carmela, towering over her. He looked like he was about to wrap his arms around her, then he suddenly seemed to do an about-face. "You came to see me today," said Shamus. "I told you not to."

"You said that if I needed to get hold of you to contact Ned Toler," replied Carmela. "That's exactly what I did. Followed your wishes to the letter of the law, in fact."

Shamus thought for a second. "You're right."

"I'm sorry the camp house got trashed," she told him. He was still standing way too close to her. It angered her and made her feel shivery at the same time. *Oh God*, she asked herself, *why do I suddenly turn into a gelatinous mess when I'm around this man?*

Shamus shook his head sadly. "One of my macro lenses got smashed."

"Where were you?" Carmela asked him. "Where are you hiding out?"

Shamus gazed down at her with a look of complete innocence. "Hiding? I wasn't hiding. In fact, today I was driving up and down the River Road."

Carmela frowned. *He was driving around? Doing what?* "Doing what, I might ask?"

"If you must know," said Shamus, "I was photographing some of the old plantations. The Destrehan, the Laura, the Houmas House," said Shamus, naming some of the more famous plantations that graced the scenic River Road just north of New Orleans. Shamus shrugged his shoulders and rotated his head as though he was trying to work out a few muscle kinks. "You might not believe this, Carmela, but I truly believe I'm finally doing my best work ever."

Carmela regarded him as you would a seriously demented person. "Your best work?" she exclaimed. "Shamus, I hate to be the one to break the news to you, but *you don't work*! You quit your job at the bank to run off and cohabit with alligators and possums. And, in case you're not entirely plugged into reality, might I remind you that your name keeps coming up in connection with a *murder* investigation!"

But Shamus was already moving swiftly across the room, heading for the door.

"Yeah," he muttered with his back to Carmela, "ain't it a bitch." He yanked open the door and slipped out without bothering to say good-bye.

Carmela ran to the door, pulled it open, fully prepared to hurl a nasty invective at him.

But Shamus had already melted into the dark.

From the *click click* of toenails, Carmela knew that Boo had followed her across the room. She slammed the front door shut, fixed the security chain in place, and looked down at Boo. "If that cad comes back here, I want you to bark your head off," she told the dog. "Better yet, you have my permission to bite him in the ass."

Boo gazed placidly at Carmela, then her nose crinkled up in a tired doggy yawn.

"Some help you are," said Carmela with disgust.

It was only after she'd crawled into bed and pummeled her pillow for a while that Carmela realized she'd completely forgotten to ask Shamus about any possible connection he might have to Dace Wilcox or Bufford Maple.

Damn, she thought, *there are still so many loose ends.*

Chapter 20

"WHERE DID *YOU* disappear to last night?" came a shrill voice.

Carmela sat up in bed and rubbed her eyes. *How did I get the phone to my ear, and who is this person shrieking at me and drilling me for answers?*

"Ava?" she said, a giant question mark in her voice.

"Of course, it's Ava," came the reply. "Who were you expecting? Madame L?" Madame L, or Marie Laveau, was an early nineteenth-century folk heroine who was a hairdresser, volunteer nurse, and voodoo queen.

"I had to take off in a hurry. Sorry," said Carmela.

"You should be. I hope it was with a man."

"Actually, it was," said Carmela. Jack Dumaine was nobody's idea of a dream date, but she had, technically, taken off with him. Or at least taken off *after* him. On the other hand, Carmela decided, Jack just might be Rhonda Lee Clayton's idea of a dream date. Truth was indeed stranger than fiction.

"I'm glad to see you're back in the social swing," said Ava, her voice dripping with praise. "I told you it was like riding a horse. You fall off, you get right back on again."

"I'm not sure that's the best analogy," offered Carmela.

There was silence as Ava took a few moments to contemplate this. "You might be right," she admitted. "Okay, how about this. Men are like shoes. They start to crimp your toes, you toss 'em out and get a new pair."

"I'll go along with that," yawned Carmela.

"Listen," said Ava, "I've got an idea you're really going to adore. How's about you and me meet at Brennan's for brunch. Say about tenish? We can indulge ourselves with praline pancakes dripping with syrup, an order of thick-sliced bacon, and a dollop of bread pudding with brandy sauce. Of course, we might want to indulge in one of their deliciously refreshing hurricanes to wash it all down." For a woman who was worried about busting dress seams last night, Ava certainly seemed to have changed her tune.

Carmela sighed. Brennan's hurricanes were notorious. Triple shots of rum mingled with fresh-squeezed fruit juices, crushed ice, and a floral garnish. You didn't need more than a couple of those to start seeing the world through rose-colored glasses. But instead of saying yes, Carmela flopped back on her pillow and snuggled in. "Ava, I have to take a rain check, okay?" she told her friend.

"You're not alone!" came Ava's delighted shriek. "The fair maiden's bed is finally *ocupado*!"

"No, I'm alone," Carmela hastened to tell her. "But I have some figuring out to do."

"Life-decision figuring out or more mundane stuff like deciding whether to pay the rent or pop for a new cashmere sweater?"

"Both," said Carmela.

"Okay," agreed Ava, "I can see you've got a lot on your plate—other than praline pancakes, that is. But I'm gonna call you later."

"Do that," said Carmela.

Hanging up the phone, Carmela stared at the whitewashed ceiling and the ceiling fan that swished slowly overhead. That was the way her mind felt. Like it was going in endless circles. Trying hard to figure things out but always ending up back where she started. It was frustrating. And downright debilitating in a strange kind of way.

* * *

A VACUUM cleaner howled from somewhere deep within the old house when Carmela banged on Glory Meechum's screen door some fifty minutes later. It felt strange to be back in the Garden District, just a few blocks from where she'd been last night. She wondered vaguely if the big white tent was still flapping in Baby and Del Fontaine's backyard. Or had it been struck down at first light?

"Glory?" Carmela shouted. "It's me. Carmela. Are you home?" Carmela banged on the door again. Nothing. Maybe they couldn't hear her in there.

Wait a minute, what am I thinking? Of course they can't hear me in there. With that vacuum cleaner blasting away, it sounds like the motor pit at the Indy 500.

Frustrated, Carmela reached down to grab the door handle. She was just about to pull it open and step inside when the ample form of Glory Meechum suddenly loomed behind the screen. Off in the distance, but farther away now, as if the vacuum cleaner had moved into another room, the mournful howl continued.

Does Glory make her poor maid clean on Sunday, too? Carmela wondered. Then she decided to shelve that thought. Of course she did. Glory Meechum's behavior often bordered on obsessive-compulsive.

Is the iron unplugged? Better check it again. Lights off? Got to make sure. Definitely a touch of the old OCD.

Shamus had told her it was a harmless little foible. That Glory was really a sweet and gentle person. Carmela wasn't so sure. She thought, if probed deeply enough, Glory Meechum might reveal a fairly dark side, kind of like that wacko, Annie Wilkes, from the Stephen King novel, *Misery*.

"What do you want?" demanded Glory Meechum. She'd opened the screen door, but with her arms folded across her sizable chest, she still blocked the entrance to her house.

"Good morning to you, too," said Carmela pleasantly. "It *is* a gorgeous day, isn't it?" She tried to smile her most convincing smile. This was, thought Carmela, the same technique you'd use to handle a large, hostile dog. Stand your ground, smile, betray not one iota of fear.

Glory Meechum, with her sensible housedress, helmet of gray hair, and no-makeup complexion, stared at Carmela and her sudden cheeriness as though she were a strange science project that had been unceremoniously dumped on her doorstep.

But Carmela's upbeat approach was obviously working, because Glory seemed to soften just a tad. Her countenance lost its hard, accusing look, and she gazed at the pecan trees and flowering oleander in her yard as if finally seeing them for the first time. "Yes," Glory replied briskly, "it is a very nice day."

"Glory," said Carmela, still on her best behavior, "may I come in for a moment?"

Glory nodded abruptly and stepped back, admitting Carmela to her inner sanctum.

Carmela, walking a few steps ahead of Glory, turned toward the living room.

"No," said Glory hurriedly, grabbing at her arm. "That's just been freshly cleaned. Let's go sit in the dining room instead."

Glory's dining room was really the old breakfast nook. But it was still big enough to accommodate a rather nice Sheraton table that easily seated twelve. Carmela supposed there might be extra leaves, too, to enlarge the table even more. Although Glory Meechum certainly didn't impress her as an entertaining hostess with the mostest.

Light spilled into the dining room from a trio of windows that overlooked the bucolic and somewhat overgrown backyard. Carmela realized she'd only been in this room once before. That was well over a year ago, when she and Shamus were planning their wedding and Glory had thrown what they'd laughingly referred to as the "grand inquisition dinner." Most of Shamus's family had been in attendance that evening, and it was amazing how prophetic their little nomenclature had turned out to be.

Glory plunked herself down on a dining room chair, causing it to utter a sharp *creak*. "What do you want?" she asked. Clearly, Glory was not a woman who felt she had to ease gracefully into a conversation.

Carmela decided the smartest thing to do was play this by the book.

"Glory," she began, "when you paid a visit to my scrapbooking shop the other day, you were awfully upset."

Glory's full lower lip seemed to protrude a tad more than was normal. "Still am," she told Carmela with all the aplomb of a petulant five-year-old.

"And you asked me to help you," said Carmela.

Glory Meechum sat there like a lump, surrounded by an uncomfortable silence.

Wow, thought Carmela, *Glory must have colossally lost it the other day. Is that regret showing through right now or just stubborn reluctance?*

"I think we could help each other," prompted Carmela. This whole conversation was proceeding with a lot more difficulty than she'd thought it would. In fact, trying to get a response from Glory was like trying to yank out teeth.

Glory folded her flabby arms across her chest in one of her favorite poses. "How so?" she demanded.

Carmela took a deep breath and began. "I think we both know that Shamus is in some kind of trouble," she said. "What the exact nature of it is, I have no idea. But, what I *am* proposing is that we pool our resources in an effort to unearth a clue or two."

"And how would we go about that?" asked Glory Meechum in her flat tone.

"Shamus still has his office at the Crescent City Bank, does he not?" asked Carmela. Carmela knew for a fact that he did. In fact, Glory probably kept Shamus's office looking like a shrine, the way some parents do with their children's rooms, even though the little darlings have long since departed the old homestead.

What did they call that? Carmela wondered. *Probably Whatever Happened to Baby Jane syndrome.*

"Yes," said Glory somewhat reluctantly. "Shamus *does* still have his office at the bank." She paused. "We're *holding* it for him." Disappointment and disapproval were evident in her voice.

"Then I'd propose we start there," said Carmela.

"At the bank," said Glory. "Going through confidential records." Glory Meechum had stonewall in her voice.

Uh-oh, thought Carmela. She shifted in her chair, bent forward, and tried to project what she hoped was a kinder, gentler sort of conspiracy. "Not snooping," she told Glory. "Sifting through *information*. Information that might give us a clue as to what's going on."

Glory continued to stare at her with reluctant, hooded eyes.

"You saw the column Bufford Maple wrote," prompted Carmela. "That had to sting. And you've no doubt heard the innuendos."

Glory's head nodded ever so slightly.

Did the other guy just blink? wondered Carmela. *Am I starting to actually get somewhere?*

"And, of course, Granger Rathbone stopped by here the other day," continued Carmela. "I'm sure his little invasion of privacy angered you. In fact, I *know* it did." *That's right,* Carmela told herself, *play on the woman's paranoia.*

"Granger Rathbone is a very hostile person," spat Glory.

Touché, thought Carmela. *The pot calling the kettle black.*

But Carmela's words were working on Glory. Because Glory was beginning to get wound up, actually seemed to be seriously considering the need for taking action. Glory's eyes shone brighter, and her hands began to clench ever so slightly. A good case of outrage was starting to smolder deep within.

"Okay, then," said Carmela. "For sure we can't just stand idly by. We've got to take a proactive stance."

The spark inside Glory Meechum suddenly ignited into a white-hot flame. "If Shamus won't lift a hand to clear his good name, then we'll do it for him," proclaimed Glory. "If not for your own family, then who else? Am I right?"

"You are *so* right," declared Carmela fervently as the whine of the vacuum cleaner suddenly sounded nearby. She wanted to leap up on the table and declare *Liberté, Égalité, Fraternité,* even as she wondered to herself, *Does that family thing still include me? Am I still technically part of the Meechum clan?*

Chapter 21

THEY'D BEEN AT it for well over an hour. Bent over stacks of files that had been pulled from Shamus's desk drawers in his office at the Crescent City Bank.

Glory Meechum had produced a giant ring of keys that had admitted them into the bank lobby, taken them beyond the teller cages, and finally into the inner sanctum of executive offices. As a senior vice president herself, Glory had punched in the code numbers on the various keypads at the different checkpoints to alert the security company that she was in the bank but that everything was just fine.

Strangely enough, Glory had left Carmela alone for most of the time. She had hung around for the first twenty minutes, while Carmela went through Shamus's appointment book and desk drawers, then poked through a few piles of paper that sat on his credenza. But then Glory had drifted down to her own office, and now Carmela could hear the faint strains of a radio playing. Well, that was just fine with her. It was easier to work alone than under Glory Meechum's stolid gaze.

Carmela sighed and gazed around Shamus's office. It was just as she'd suspected it would be. Like a scene out of *The Day the Earth Stood Still.*

Shamus's calendar was still turned to the day he'd walked out, some six months ago. His pen lay where he'd set it down. A letter was waiting to be signed. Carmela glanced at it, hoping it wasn't an important letter, that some poor soul hadn't put his entire life on hold while waiting to hear if his mortgage application had been approved.

But, no, it was just something about interest rates. Besides, Shamus hadn't handled residential loans, he'd only worked on commercial loans. *What did they call that again?* Carmela wondered. *Oh, yeah, mortgage banking.* She guessed that telling people you were a mortgage banker sounded a whole lot fancier than just saying you were a loan officer. People who worked in banks were funny that way. They always had to have a fancy title.

She'd also learned long ago that, in a bank, everybody and his brother-in-law was a vice president. Those titles were handed out like candy to kindergarten kids. Apparently, customers felt much happier and more secure when they knew they were dealing with a vice president. Of course, they probably still got the same crappy service, but since it was coming from a vice president, there was justification for it, right? After all, vice presidents were busy people! Vice presidents had a lot on their plate! Vice presidents were . . . *vice presidents!*

Carmela snorted. *Hah! Right. Just like Shamus and Glory and the rest of the Meechum family*. Their big break had really come from having a great-great-granddaddy who'd had the cold cash and the good foresight to start a bank. Then, all the following generations of Meechums really had to do was tread carefully in the proverbial family footsteps. If the bank's interest rates on savings accounts and CDs weren't too high, and if the bank was prudent when extending loans, then the business would essentially be self-perpetuating.

Carmela had even learned early on from Shamus how exceedingly simple it was to start a bank. All you needed was about a hundred thousand dollars in your hot little hand, and you could go ahead and apply for that all-important charter from the federal government. A hundred thousand dollars—that was all it took! Far less than most people paid for a house these days!

Then again, Carmela had decided that a lot of things in business didn't make sense. How could a giant accounting firm with everything to lose cover up for an unscrupulous utility? How could major corporations suddenly go bankrupt? Who was the genius who thought they could sell fifty-pound bags of dog food via the Internet? Wasn't anybody thinking? Wasn't anybody looking ahead? Wasn't anyone minding the store?

Kneeling down in front of a squat, silver filing cabinet, Carmela pulled out the top drawer. Running her fingers across the plastic file tabs, she skimmed the labels. Delphi Corp., deYoung & Company, Crowell Ltd., Theriot & Partners. Everything very neat and businesslike.

Wait a minute. Theriot? Why did that name sound so darned familiar?
Carmela racked her brain.

Oh no! Theriot. Isn't that the name of Bufford Maple's partner? Sure it is. Theriot is one of the men who owns Trident Realty!

Carmela ripped the file folder from the cabinet, eager to see what was inside.

The top sheet was an application for a bridge construction loan, whatever that was. An application that had been turned down. By Shamus.

That's it? Shamus turned Theriot and maybe Bufford Maple down for a loan? A bridge loan? That's why they're trying to set him up?

Carmela frowned, slumped down into a sitting position, cross-legged on the carpet.

It doesn't seem earth-shattering enough, it doesn't make sense, and it for sure doesn't seem related to Jimmy Earl Clayton's death.

Also, what about Big Jack Dumaine? I thought he was the guy trying to set Shamus up to take the fall?

Carmela skimmed through every paper contained in the folder. There were about ten pages. Nowhere did she find a mention of Jack Dumaine. Or even Jimmy Earl Clayton.

How strange, thought Carmela. *Here I thought I was on to something big, and everything I've found so far has just made things even more confusing and tangled.*

"Carmela!" Glory Meechum's shrill voice roused Carmela from her jumble of thoughts.

"I'm almost done, Glory," Carmela called back. She grabbed the Theriot file, hesitated a split second, then folded it in half and jammed it in her handbag.

Have to give this a little more thought, she decided with a slight twinge of guilt. At the very least she could possibly bring it up to Shamus. That is, if the old boy came skulking by her apartment for another nocturnal visit.

Carmela sprang up from her cross-legged position on the floor and yanked open the office door. "Hey there," she said to Glory, who stared in at her with suspicious eyes.

"You find anything?" demanded Glory.

Carmela assumed a wistful expression and shook her head sadly. "No, not really." She hoped she projected total innocence and guile.

"Hmph," said Glory. "Chased all the way down here on Sunday for naught."

Carmela smiled ruefully. *I'm back to being the family dingbat again,* she decided. *I was Glory's big ally for a few short moments, but now I'm relegated to dingbat status once again. Well, at least it's a role I've had some experience with.*

IT WAS still early, just two in the afternoon. So Carmela popped back to her apartment, changed into jeans and a yellow Spider-Man T-shirt that Ava had talked her into buying, then hustled Boo into the backseat of her car. For the past couple years, she'd been serving as a volunteer for the Children's Art Association. Started by a community-minded group of artists and craftspeople, the Children's Art Association taught drawing, painting, and crafts to kids between the ages of eight and fifteen at various neighborhood centers around the city.

Today, Carmela was headed for the Chamberlain Center out near Audubon Park. If memory served her correctly, Jekyl Hardy should be there, teaching the kids the fundamentals of still life drawing.

He was there, all right, along with a couple other volunteers. They were warning a group of squirming kids to *"Please do not eat the apples, oranges, grapes, and pears. Please do not eat any of the props!"*

Carmela saw that, like kids everywhere, they were steadfastly ignoring the volunteer artists' pleadings. Orange peels littered the floor as the rowdy children feasted mightily on the forbidden fruit and drew on each other's faces with paint.

"Carmela!" exclaimed Jekyl Hardy when he saw her. "Come over here and help me! These little darlings are completely out of control."

He good-naturedly snatched a pear from the sticky hands of a beautiful little African American girl. "Ariella," he warned. "You've already eaten two apples. These are to paint!" She giggled and proceeded to mix her yellow with her blue to produce a luminous pool of green.

"Good," Jekyl told her as she made an artful brushstroke across her canvas, "that's a very auspicious start. Oh, you brought your dog," he exclaimed to Carmela. "She's very cute." Jekyl knelt down and faced Boo. "Can you shake?" he asked her. "Can you shake hands?"

Boo, an old pro at shaking hands, promptly sat on her butt and stuck her right paw in the air. "Good girl," said Jekyl. He took her paw, pumped it gently, then released it. Boo, loving the attention, promptly stuck her left paw out at him.

"Oh, I see she's ambidextrous," laughed Jekyl, patting her. "That talent can come in handy."

"She's a show-off," said Carmela. "And don't let that sweet little face fool you. She'll steal one of those oranges if you don't watch out. Toss it around like a tennis ball and then eviscerate it."

Jekyl Hardy threw up his hands. "So what else is new? Oh, honey," he said, clasping Carmela's arm tightly. "I am *sooo* sorry about last night. I didn't mean to get you all upset. And I really didn't foresee the bizarre antics of Ruby Dumaine. I think Tandy was right, she must have been sipping absinthe."

"I believe it," said Carmela. "That woman packs a lot of punch when she sets her mind to it."

"But hey," said Jekyl. "What's with you? Where did you sneak off to last night? Did you go out chasing leads in the great Shamus mystery? Or were you just chasing around?"

"Jekyl, you have no idea," sighed Carmela. "This whole thing just gets stranger and stranger."

"Do tell," said Jekyl. He turned to the little boy at the table next to him. "Carlyle, I love that arrangement. So unconventional. Now don't be afraid to add in some highlights. Red on top of purple is *good*."

As she was watching Jekyl interact with the kids, Carmela felt a tug on the back of her T-shirt. "Can we take your dog outside and play with him?" asked a little boy.

"Her name is Boo, and she's a she," said Carmela. "And yes, you certainly may. But please lead her out this side door here so you'll be in the fenced-in play area, okay?"

Two more kids put their hands gently on Boo's shoulders and marched out to the playground with her. *Gosh,* thought Carmela, *this is nice. This is so sane after hanging out with the likes of Glory Meechum this morning.*

Jekyl Hardy turned back to Carmela with a smile. "Now, what were you saying?"

"Jekyl, you did the floats for the Pluvius krewe . . ." said Carmela.

"Indeed I did," declared Jekyl. "Twenty magnificent oceania-themed beauties. Some of my finest work, I might add."

"Do you know a Pluvius krewe member by the name of Theriot?

Jekyl Hardy rolled his eyes upward, thinking. "Theriot . . . Theriot . . . *Michael* Theriot? Yes, I think I might have bumped shoulders with him. Is he a somewhat portly fellow?"

"I have no idea," said Carmela. "I've never met him."

"You know who's probably more plugged in?" said Jekyl. "My assistant, Thomas Waite." Jekyl pulled a tomato-red StarTac from his pocket and

promptly hit the speed dial. "Thomas knows *everyone*," Jekyl assured
Carmela. "And he keeps lists of all the Pluvius committees."

"Thomas?" said Jekyl when his call was finally answered. "Yes, it's Jekyl
here. Say, a dear friend of mine is trying to glean some information on one of
the Pluvius krewe members. A Mr. Michael Theriot. Do you know him?"

Jekyl winked at Carmela and gave an exaggerated nod as he listened to
Thomas on the other end of the line. Finally, Jekyl thanked his assistant and
hung up.

"Here's the scoop," said Jekyl in a conspiratorial tone. "Michael Theriot
is one of the newer Pluvius members. And by that I mean maybe two or three
years with the krewe, since some of the other fellows have been with it for just
eons. It seems this Theriot is some kind of real estate mover and shaker, or
claims he is, anyway. Of course, you never know for sure with these business
types. I say give me an artsy type any day. They may be poor as church mice,
but they're generally a lot more honest. Anyway," continued Jekyl, "this Theriot has a reputation as a real gung-ho volunteer. He was on the parade route
committee, the marching band committee, and the refreshment committee."

Carmela stared at Jekyl. "The refreshment committee," she repeated.

"Yes," said Jekyl. "And Thomas says that—oh, my God!" Jekyl suddenly
clapped a hand over his mouth. "You don't suppose . . ." His eyes widened; his
mouth fell open. "I mean, are you thinking what *I'm* thinking?" he sputtered.
"That horrible thing with Jimmy Earl? Wow . . . I wonder if the police took a
hard look at who was serving drinks that night. Or who *mixed* the drinks."

"I always assumed they did," said Carmela. "Now I'm not so sure."

THE CHOKING sounds coming from the backseat of Carmela's car weren't
good. Gazing in her rearview mirror to make sure she wouldn't sideswipe anyone, Carmela swerved over to the curb. She was just in time to see a spurt of
yellow foam issue from Boo's gaping mouth.

"No you don't!" Carmela was out of her car in a split second. "Not on
Samantha's backseat!" She yanked open the rear door and grabbed the terry
cloth towel she kept stashed back there for just such occasions. She positioned
it under Boo's chin in anticipation of a second outpouring. Annoyed, Boo
promptly jerked her head away and gave a violent shake. Tendrils of yellow
gunk flew everywhere, decorating the interior of Carmela's car.

"Boo, we talked about this," said Carmela firmly. "No oranges and no
spinning on the merry-go-round. Evidently you once again flung caution to
the wind and did both." Carmela mopped gingerly at the backseat of the car.
Boo, who seemed to have made a speedy recovery, now licked her paws happily with that amazing nonchalance dogs often have. *Sick? Who me? Nah.
Never happened.*

As Carmela pulled into her parking space in the alley behind her apartment, Ava was just returning from a trip to the market. "Hey," she called to
Ava, "you ever make it to Brennan's?"

Ava shifted her grocery bag from one arm to the other. "No. I ended up at Cardamom's with some other friends. Obviously not you."

Carmela jumped from her car, hauled Boo out of the back.

"What's that awful smell?" asked Ava, wrinkling her nose.

"Air freshener," said Carmela. "That car wash down on Marais Street is letting me try out some new chemicals they developed. Smells real bad at first, but then the interior of your car reverts to that pleasant new car smell."

Ava narrowed her eyes. "Well, it smells like dog puke, if you ask me. In fact, it's amazing what companies will try to foist on an unsuspecting public."

"Hey," said Carmela. "Why don't you come over for dinner tonight. I made jambalaya the other night, and I've still got gallons."

"Why don't you come to the Bachus parade with me?" asked Ava. "I'm supposed to meet Smoochy Peabody and some of his friends over at Tipitina's."

"To tell you the truth, Ava, I'm kind of paraded out," admitted Carmela. In the final twelve days of Mardi Gras there were something like fifty different parades. The whole thing could really set your head to spinning.

Ava brushed back a mass of auburn hair and rocked back on the heels of her espadrilles. "You want to talk, huh?"

"Kind of," admitted Carmela.

"You found something out today?" inquired Ava.

"I did," said Carmela, "but I'm not exactly sure what it means."

Ava put a hand to the side of her face to shade it from the late-afternoon sun. "To tell you the truth," she said, "I'm a little bit paraded out myself. What say I drop by in an hour or so? Would that work?"

"I'll heat up that jambalaya," said Carmela. "And chill a bottle of wine."

"You might want to chill two bottles," suggested Ava. "And while you're at it, better wipe that yellow glop off your dog's chin."

Chapter 22

CARMELA AND AVA chatted their way through dinner, helping themselves to extra large servings of Carmela's very excellent jambalaya, slices of prune bread, and sipping the crisp white Vouvray they'd uncorked. They talked about Baby's party, the strange tissue paper–looking dress that a woman by the name of Magdalen Dilworth had worn, and about the Swedish crystal chandelier Jekyl Hardy had apparently found for a song at an antique sale over in Destrehan. They even skirted around the issue of the amazing disappearing Shamus but never did attack it head-on.

Now, with the dishes piled in the sink and the second bottle of wine uncorked, they were ready to get down to it.

"You found something out about Shamus today," began Ava. She was lounging at the little dining table while Carmela made a pretense of rattling dishes in the sink. "How did this all come about?"

Carmela abandoned the dishes and came over and sat down across from Ava. "I paid a little visit to Glory Meechum, Shamus's sister," said Carmela.

Ava made a face. "Always a challenge dealing with the queen of the harpies."

"Actually, Glory wasn't in *that* bad a mood," said Carmela. "I've seen worse."

Ava shivered. "Tell the story."

"Well, long story short," said Carmela, "I talked Glory Meechum into escorting me to the Crescent City Bank office and letting me snoop around inside Shamus's office," said Carmela.

Ava took another sip of wine. "And what incredible findings were unearthed from his inner sanctum?" asked Ava. "Gold from Carthage? Tutankhamen's Treasure?" Ava paused dramatically. "Wait just a minute, that stuff is already in the British Museum, isn't it? Silly me."

Carmela pulled the stolen file from her handbag, unfolded it as best she could, and handed it to Ava. "I found that," she said.

Ava set her glass of wine down, uncrumpled the folder. "You didn't find it, you pilfered it."

"Well, yes," admitted Carmela.

"Good girl," said Ava as she opened the manila folder. "And who exactly is this Theriot fellow?"

"Part owner in a real estate company," said Carmela. "Trident Realty."

Ava nodded, then spent a good three or four minutes poring through the documents. Finally, she frowned, then looked up at Carmela. "What?" said Ava. "I don't see any connection."

"Neither do I," replied Carmela.

Ava stared blandly at her. "Then why did you steal it? Or is this just a practice exercise for some far grander cat burglar caper?"

"The thing of it is," said Carmela, "I *know* there's some important tidbit of information in that file. But I'm just not seeing it."

"Okay," said Ava. "Let's try to be analytical and completely emotionless about this, which is no small task when you're of the female persuasion and have just downed a few glasses of wine."

"Agreed," said Carmela, taking another sip of wine.

"However," continued Ava, "let's try to recall every single detail concerning this entire Shamus mess. Going back to the absolute very beginning."

"The very beginning," agreed Carmela.

"We were at the parade . . ." Ava prompted.

"And saw Jimmy Earl Clayton collapse on his float," said Carmela.

"And then right after that, all sorts of strange rumors started flying," said Ava. "About Shamus."

"It was like someone was feeding them," said Carmela. "Busily fanning the flames." She hunched forward and stared at Ava. "And then Bufford Maple wrote a nasty column implicating Shamus."

"Right," nodded Ava. "It ran the day of Jimmy Earl's funeral, which I'm sorry I missed since, aside from Baby's party, it seems to have been one of the pivotal social events of the season."

"Then Hop Pennington, one of the property managers from Trident Realty, called and tried to muscle me around," recalled Carmela. "He said Bartholomew Hayward from next door wanted my space."

"Oh no," said Ava, dismayed. "They can't do that. That's the absolute *perfect* space for you!"

"Don't I know it!" responded Carmela. She was still ticked off by Hop Pennington's macho power play attempt. "And get this, afterward I called and schmoozed the receptionist at Trident Realty. And I found out that the company is owned by Bufford Maple and Michael Theriot."

"Bufford Maple penned the nasty column, and now we have Michael Theriot's bank folder in front of us," finished Ava. "With a turndown from Shamus."

"Right," said Carmela.

"But people get turned down for these kinds of loans all the time," said Ava. "That's not a reason to try to pin a murder on somebody. Unless, of course, *they're* the murderers and they need a handy pigeon to foist the blame on."

"I hate to think of Shamus as a pigeon," said Carmela.

Ava stared at her. "What do you think of him as?"

Carmela shrugged. "I don't know. My soon-to-be ex, I suppose."

"A couple weeks ago a very smart and together lady I know referred to him as a cad, a rat, and a louse."

Carmela squirmed uncomfortably.

"It's happening, isn't it?" said Ava, emitting a huge sigh.

"What's happening?"

"You're starting to feel *sorry* for him."

"I—" began Carmela.

"Don't!" admonished Ava. "This changes *nothing*. Shamus is still the man who boogied on out of your life with no just cause. He's still the man who left you in the lurch. You know," said Ava, peering carefully at her, "Shamus *could* be a murderer. He's secretive enough. And he's colossally hotheaded."

Ava's harsh words cut Carmela to the quick. *Shamus a murderer? My Shamus? Well, the man who used to be my Shamus? No, I still don't believe it. Or maybe I just don't want to believe it.*

"Up until this afternoon, I harbored a funny feeling about Dace Wilcox. I thought that he might be a suspect in Jimmy Earl's demise," said Carmela. "When I ran into him at the Marseille Ball, he pretended he really didn't know

Shamus. Then later on at the shop, CeCe and Tandy discovered an old photograph that proved Dace *did* know Shamus. In fact, the two of them were in the same fraternity together. And then when we started talking about Dace, Gabby said that Dace Wilcox had been talking to Jimmy Earl right before he climbed up on his float."

"Hmm," said Ava. "Dace Wilcox. Yes, you mentioned him before. He's kind of a wild card in all this, isn't he?"

"And let's not forget about Granger Rathbone," said Carmela. "He's been harassing me *and* trying to locate Shamus. Plus I found out that Granger Rathbone is very tight with Jack Dumaine. Might even be working for him on the side."

"This *is* getting complicated," acknowledged Ava.

"I also have a slight confession to make," said Carmela. "I *followed* Jack Dumaine last night. That's where I disappeared to," admitted Carmela.

Ava's eyebrows shot up. "Followed him as in *tailed* him?" asked Ava. "PI style?"

Carmela nodded.

"Jeez, you really are a squirrel," said Ava.

"Thanks a lot," said Carmela.

"So where did our boy Jack run off to?" asked Ava.

"To the Calhoun Motel over near the airport," said Carmela. "Where he met up with one Rhonda Lee Clayton. She'd already reserved a trashy little motel room and was obviously expecting him."

"What?" Ava squawked. "Big Jack Dumaine had a clandestine rendezvous with Rhonda Lee? Jimmy Earl's *widow*?"

Carmela nodded, pleased that she'd been able to arouse so much outrage from Ava. "What do you think it means?" she asked excitedly. Maybe Ava could offer some insight as to this strange alliance.

Ava's face was a mixture of curiosity and shock. "It means the two of them are either thick as thieves or else that love is completely blind."

Chapter 23

IT WAS A show of solidarity that warmed Carmela's heart. Baby and Tandy were standing on the sidewalk outside Memory Mine, waiting for her when she arrived for work Monday morning.

"Hey, talk about a surprise!" exclaimed Carmela. "I didn't think anyone would show up today!"

"We didn't want you to be alone," said Tandy.

Carmela's smile immediately slid off her face. "What's wrong?" she asked.

"She hasn't heard the news," said Baby to Tandy. "I *told* you this would come as a complete surprise."

"What's going on?" asked Carmela. Watching the two women fidget, Carmela was growing more and more nervous.

"Del heard a rumor via the old boy's grapevine," said Baby.

"About what?" asked Carmela, instantly on the alert. She knew that, as a high-profile attorney, Baby's husband was privy to all sorts of inside information.

"Now don't come all unglued, sweetie, but Shamus has been hauled in for questioning again," finished Tandy.

Carmela put a hand to her mouth. "Oh no." Her voice was a hoarse whisper; the ring of keys she had clutched in her hand suddenly clattered to the pavement. *They found Shamus*, she thought to herself. *Or at least caught up to him.*

Tandy knelt down to scoop up the dropped keys. "Let me get those," she said.

Carmela turned to face Baby. "What else did Del say? Did he know if the police had any hard evidence against him?"

"Shush, dear." Baby put a hand on Carmela's shoulder. "That's all we know for now. Just that Shamus is being questioned again. Del has court all day today, so he'll be able to keep an ear open. Plus he knows where I'll be. He promised to call if there's any news."

Tandy put the key in the lock, fought with it for a couple seconds, then finally wrestled the door open. "C'mon, Carmela," she said in her characteristic upbeat, no-nonsense style. "There's really nothing you can do. So the best thing is to just stay busy."

Promptly at 9:00 A.M. Gabby came marching into Memory Mine and handed Carmela a steaming cup of café au lait that she'd fetched from the Merci Beaucoup Bakery down the street. Carmela, sitting at the back craft table with Tandy and Baby, murmured a quiet *"Bless you"* as she accepted the cup.

Unsnapping the white lid, Carmela took a sip of the hot, steaming coffee. "This really hits the spot," she declared as Gabby continued to stare at her silently. She took another sip. All the while, Gabby's eyes never left her.

"What?" asked Carmela finally. *"What?"*

Their antennae suddenly up and sensing an impending problem, Tandy and Baby squirmed at the sudden tension developing between Gabby and Carmela.

"Stuart says I have to quit," said Gabby quietly.

Gabby's words hit Carmela like a bolt from the blue. "Gabby, what are you *talking* about? Why on earth would you quit?"

Gabby hung her head. "Stuart thinks it's for the best. Until this whole mess is resolved."

"This whole mess meaning . . ."

"Well . . . Shamus and everything," stammered Gabby.

"And this is *Stuart's* idea, not yours?" said Carmela, peering up at her.

Gabby's pleading face spoke volumes. "Oh, Carmela, you *know* I don't want to leave you in the lurch like this." Gabby looked like she was about ready to cry.

"Don't you think you should make up your *own* mind?" Carmela asked her gently.

"Honey," said Tandy, suddenly interjecting herself into the conversation, "are you suddenly experiencing a tremendous hormonal imbalance at your tender young age? I mean, what *is* this all about? Why on earth would you be doing this?"

"Because I promised Stuart that I would love, honor, and obey him?" ventured Gabby, her voice quavering wildly.

"Obey!" snorted Tandy. She glanced around the table, realized she had overreacted a bit, decided to try to diffuse the situation. "Is *that* all! Thank goodness, I thought we really had ourselves a big hairy *problema* here."

Baby, ever the diplomat, gave a gentle laugh. "Isn't that the cutest," she said as she continued to thread pink ribbon through the top of a scrapbook page that she'd just punched with little *V*s. "Spoken like a new bride. All sweet and innocent and still agog over the joys of marriage."

"But so misguided," added Tandy. This time she leveled a somewhat more accusing gaze at Gabby.

"Sakes, yes," agreed Baby. She gently took one of Gabby's hands in her own, focused her baby blue eyes on the girl. "Honey," said Baby, with all the sincerity she could muster, "you're a married woman now. You have to learn how to *handle* your man."

"But Stuart thinks—" began Gabby again.

"It doesn't matter what *Stuart* thinks," snapped Tandy. "What do *you* think?"

Tears were streaming down Gabby's face now. "Carmela," she implored, "*help* me! You know I don't want to quit for good. Just for a while. Until things blow over."

Carmela leapt from her chair and swept Gabby into her arms. "I know that, dear," she told her. "Don't worry about it, okay?"

Gabby continued to sniffle. "It's just that . . . well, somebody broke into our house last night while we were over visiting Stuart's cousin. And now Stuart is mighty jittery."

"Oh no!" said Tandy. "Why didn't you say something sooner? Now *that's* a different story."

"Dear lord," said Baby, clapping a petite hand to her chest. "Did you-all lose your valuables? Your silverware and jewelry and such?"

Gabby continued to sob. "Some jewelry, yes. My ruby ring and the cameo I inherited from my grandmother. But the worst of it is that our house looks like we were positively *invaded*! The robbers emptied out all the drawers and messed things up pretty bad." Gabby wiped at her streaming eyes. "It looks like a hurricane blew through. I have no idea where to even start."

AS IF Carmela didn't have enough going on in her life, business was positively booming at Memory Mine this morning. A gaggle of tourists had come pouring in, delighted to have found a dedicated scrapbooking store.

"We're from a little town in Ohio," said one of the women excitedly, "and we don't have a real scrapbooking store."

"Right," echoed her chubby friend who had just picked out a pair of scallop-edge scissors along with a pair that would create a lacy Victorian edge. "We have to pick stuff up at the mall whenever we can. Or drive up to Dayton when they have their scrapbooking conventions."

There's gotta be something strange in the ozone, Carmela marveled to herself. *My assistant quit, everything's in turmoil, and suddenly customers are pouring in here like crazy.*

"Tandy," called Carmela, as she tried to ring up three customers at once even as she was trying to explain molding mats to another. "Do you by any chance know how to operate a cash register?"

Tandy's eyes grew big. "Me? Uh . . . no." Obviously, it had been more than a few years since Tandy had held down a job.

As the door flew open once again, Carmela's first thought was, *We stuff one more body in here, and the fire marshal's gonna shut us down.*

But it wasn't another customer, it was Ava. She took one look around, saw the panic on Carmela's face, and plunged right in.

"You want to put that on your charge card?" she drawled as she plucked the Visa card from the hand of a woman hovering near the cash register. "No problem, sugar."

Sure enough, within five minutes, Ava had cashed out half of the customers and was now showing a die cutter and some alphabet templates to two other women.

"You're a lifesaver!" Carmela whispered to Ava when she had a spare moment.

"Where on earth is Gabby?" asked Ava. "She call in sick today?"

"Not quite," said Carmela.

Ava rolled her eyes. "Oh, oh, *that* doesn't sound good."

"It's not," Carmela told her.

BY NOON things had settled down, and Carmela, buoyed by her windfall of business, had phoned a nearby deli and had salads delivered for everyone. She, Ava, Tandy, and Baby sat munching them now at the back table. They rehashed events at Baby's party, still awestruck by the food and giggling over some of the more colorful characters who had been in attendance.

"So tell me about the incredible disappearing Gabby," Ava finally prompted as she carefully spooned vinaigrette over her spinach and citrus salad.

"She just up and quit," pronounced Tandy.

"Well, it wasn't quite *that* abrupt," said Baby. "Her husband sort of strong-armed her into it."

"Plus her house was broken into," said Tandy, gesturing with a forkful of greens.

Ava shook her head. "This crazy city. They feed us all sorts of statistics that are supposed to convince us crime is on the *decrease*, then you hear something like this." She shook her head again. "Poor Gabby. She's having a tough time right now, but I think she'll be back."

"I *know* she will," said Carmela confidently. "Gabby loves this store almost as much as I do."

"We all love it," declared Baby.

"Ava," said Tandy, "what about *your* store? I would think you'd be jumping right about now. I mean, tomorrow's the big one . . . Fat Tuesday!"

"Tyrell's at the store today. He's even better at working the crowd than I am." Tyrell Burton was Ava's sometime assistant, a twenty-two-year-old African American who was also a grad student in history at Tulane. Tyrell's great-grandmother was purported to have emigrated from Haiti and been known to dabble in voodoo lore. Needless to say, Tyrell took great delight in his rather strange pedigree and never tired of spinning a few good yarns for the tourists.

"But the *real* reason I stopped by," said Ava, "was to give you a heads-up on something." She paused, unsure of just how to relate her story. "The thing of it is, Carmela, I just stopped over at Bultman's Drug Store to pick up some photos I left to be developed."

Carmela nodded. She'd used Bultman's many times herself before she'd switched to digital photography a month or so ago. Bultman's was just down the block from Memory Mine and awfully handy. She still sent a lot of her customers there, since Bultman's offered photofinishing in both matte and high gloss.

"So I picked up my photos from that fellow Dirk who's always at the counter," continued Ava. "You know, the one with the pierced tongue and bowl haircut?"

Carmela nodded. She knew Dirk. Everybody knew Dirk.

"Anyway, he asked about you," said Ava.

"What about me?" said Carmela, stabbing at an oversized crouton.

"Well," said Ava, "here's where the story starts to get a little strange. It seems that someone had just been there ten minutes earlier asking if there were any photos for you."

Carmela gave Ava a quizzical gaze. "Somebody tried to pick up my photos?" *What is this all about? Jekyl Hardy trying to do a good deed, maybe?*

"According to Dirk, this *person* said they were running errands for you and wanted to know if your photos were ready."

"But I didn't drop anything off to be developed," said Carmela. "Now that I've gone digital, all I have to do is *print* photos off my computer." She thought for a minute. "And I *still* haven't used up all the shots on my Leica."

The last time I used that camera was the night Jimmy Earl died, thought Carmela.

"I know that, honey," said Ava patiently, "but the point is, somebody was trying to pick up your photos." Ava paused. "You don't think that's a trifle strange?"

"I don't think it's strange at all," said Tandy. "I leave my film all over town. I'd be *delighted* if one of my friends volunteered to pick up my finished photos."

Carmela shrugged. "I don't know, Ava. In the scheme of things, it doesn't seem worth worrying about." She stood up and stretched. And, as if on cue, the front door burst open and four women with delighted grins lighting up their faces poured into her shop.

"Good afternoon," Carmela called to them. "Welcome to Memory Mine."

Chapter 24

CARMELA'S SCRAPBOOK FOR Saint Cyril's Cemetery was coming together nicely. Over the past week, in stolen moments here and there, she'd put together the introduction page as well as two double-page spreads. The material the Preservation Society had provided her with had been rich, indeed, and Carmela was quite pleased at how good everything was looking. In a couple days she would present her initial work to Donna Mae Dupres and her cemetery preservation group and, hopefully, get their final blessing to complete the project.

"Carmela, what *are* you doing with those photographs?" asked Tandy. She had watched Carmela take two perfectly good photographs, a black-and-white photo and a color photo, then cut them both into strips. Now, Tandy's curiosity had gotten the better of her.

"Oh," said Carmela, "it's a fun technique I picked up at a scrapbooking convention last year. You take a color photo that you like and also have it printed in black and white. Then you cut *both* photos into strips and weave them together."

"What?" said Baby, her interest piqued. "This I have to see."

"Here," said Carmela, laying the photo strips out. "What you do is alternate strips, see? A color strip, then a black-and-white strip, then a color strip again. When you weave the photo back together, you achieve a kind of checkerboard result. Or mosaic. It doesn't really matter what you call it, the results are just wonderfully effective."

"Wow," said Baby, watching as Carmela's deft fingers wove strips from the two photos into a single, finished piece.

"Isn't that a great effect?" asked Carmela. "The color strips make it look contemporary, but the black-and-white strips give it an aged feel."

"I love it," said Tandy, "but how do you keep all the various strips in place?"

"Turn it over gently and use some photo-safe adhesive tape," said Carmela.

"Saint Cyril's is going to absolutely *love* this," said Tandy. "Can I look at the rest of what you've done?"

"Sure," said Carmela. She slid the pages she'd already completed and carefully encased in plastic sleeves across the table to Tandy.

Together, Tandy and Baby studied Carmela's handiwork. They were obviously impressed.

"You know what you're missing?" asked Tandy, rubbing at the tip of her nose.

"What's that?" replied Carmela.

"You don't have any photos of the oven crypts."

Oven crypts were walls of crypts with front openings that looked something like bread ovens. When they were first built, they housed the final remains of indigents. Today, however, the oven crypts were much in demand by ordinary families. Coffins were slid into these so-called ovens and, after a couple years of New Orleans's heat and humidity, a sort of natural cremation took place. The contents and the coffins were reduced to almost nothing. The human remains were then swept back into a kind of pit in the rear of the oven crypt and the pieces of the coffin removed. The real estate, such as it was, was now available for yet another occupant.

"I *thought* I had some," said Carmela, as she shuffled through the various envelopes of photos that the Saint Cyril's group had given her. After a fairly thorough search, however, it appeared she *didn't* have any photos of the oven crypts.

"And you're right, Tandy," said Carmela. "The oven crypts *are* historically significant. Some of them are even older than the family and fraternal organization crypts."

"Plus they form the outside walls that surround Saint Cyril's," Baby pointed out. "That's important, isn't it?"

"I'd say it's critical," said Carmela. "Which means I'd better stop by Saint Cyril's tomorrow morning and shoot a few photos. I just hope it doesn't rain." Carmela noted that the day had started out partly cloudy and was rapidly becoming overcast. Fact was, the weather forecasters *were* predicting rain for Mardi Gras day tomorrow.

"I hope it doesn't rain on our parades!" declared Baby.

"But if it does rain, your photos might turn out nice and eerie," suggested Tandy. "Very funereal."

"The problem is," said Carmela, studying her pages, "I'm not exactly shooting for eerie. Saint Cyril's Cemetery Preservation Society specifically requested historic."

"I suppose a preservation group would look at it that way," allowed Tandy. "Most of the time, folks are so rabidly obsessed with our cemeteries and the notion that New Orleans keeps its dead so close by, you sometimes *forget* there's a historic aspect."

"It's those darn vampire stories," said Baby, shaking her head. "Just way too much vampire lore and mythology. Outsiders probably think we walk around with garlic wreaths strung around our necks."

TANDY PASTED a final Raggedy Ann sticker on her scrapbook page. She'd titled her page, "When I Grow Up . . ." and below her headline of colorful, bouncing type had created a photo montage of Julia, her two-year-old granddaughter, interspersed with Raggedy Ann stickers depicting the beloved doll in various astronaut, karate, and nurse costumes. "Uh-oh," she said, glancing up toward the front window. "Incoming."

Carmela looked up just in time to see Rhonda Lee Clayton, Jimmy Earl's widow, pulling open the door to her store. She winced and jumped out of her chair. The set of Rhonda Lee's jaw and the fiery look on her face told her this wasn't going to be pretty.

"I don't think Rhonda Lee's here to make a scrapbook," said Baby in a low whisper.

Rhonda Lee Clayton launched into her tirade before the door swung shut and whacked her on the backside.

"I'm going to shut you down if it's the last thing I do!" Rhonda Lee screamed at Carmela. Rhonda Lee, dressed in a long, black skirt and oversized sweater, suddenly seemed to bear a striking resemblance to the Wicked Witch of the West.

"Rhonda Lee, take it easy," cautioned Carmela. "What's got you so upset?"

"Upset? Upset?" shrilled Rhonda Lee. "I'm more than a little *upset*!" Her normally pale face had two rings of color high on her cheeks, making her look even more hysterical.

Tandy, never one to be left out of a good catfight, decided to interject herself into the fray. "Hey Rhonda Lee, how do?" She gave a friendly wave from where she sat at the back table.

"Stay out of this, Tandy," Rhonda Lee snapped. "This is between me and Carmela!"

"Rhonda Lee," said Tandy sharply, "don't go postal on us." She stood up and advanced on the screaming woman. "You're a lady, remember? Ladies don't go postal."

"I'll do whatever I want!" spat back Rhonda Lee. "My husband is *dead*!" She turned wild eyes on Carmela. "And it was *your* husband who killed him!"

What is this, wondered Carmela, *some kind of delayed stress reaction?*

Now it was Baby's turn to wade into the fracas. "For heaven's sake, Rhonda Lee," said Baby, adjusting the silk Hermes scarf draped about her neck, "you are *so* over the top. Ya'll know Shamus wouldn't hurt a fly. Besides," she said, adding a modicum of logic, "he's a Meechum. And you know the Meechums are a good, upstanding New Orleans family."

I wouldn't be so sure of that, Carmela thought to herself.

"Of course Shamus didn't have anything to do with poor Jimmy Earl's death," said Carmela, putting a real note of authority in her voice this time. No way was she going to back down to *this* woman.

Rhonda Lee dug in her purse for a hankie, then dabbed at her eyes. "My life is *ruined*," she moaned. "My *daughter's* dreams are completely shattered. And all because of Shamus Meechum." Rhonda Lee gazed about Memory Mine with a wild look in her eyes. "I'll shut you down!" she declared again. "As God is my witness, I'll shut you down! Then you'll see what it's like to have *your* life in shreds!"

Carmela gazed at Rhonda Lee with what could only be called bemused pity. In fact, she might have allowed herself to be halfway intimidated by this woman's threats if she hadn't just seen Rhonda Lee grinning ear to ear in the doorway of a room at the Calhoun Motel two nights ago. Opening the door of her somewhat *déclassé* motel room to the likes of Jack Dumaine, the partner of her dearly departed husband. On the other hand, Rhonda Lee *had* just lost her husband, which meant she should still be accorded a small amount of leeway. Very small.

But Rhonda Lee was fixated on how she was going to ruin Carmela. "I'll put you out of business," she cried again. "Have the landlord padlock your door!"

As Carmela stared at Rhonda Lee Clayton and listened to her rantings, she suddenly found herself wondering if this was just an idle threat, or did Rhonda Lee really know something? "Rhonda Lee," said Carmela suddenly, "do you know who owns this building?"

That question halted Rhonda Lee in her tracks. Rhonda Lee blinked, her nostrils flared, and her mouth opened and closed like a fish gasping for air. "Whaaat?" she croaked.

"Do you know who owns this building?" Carmela asked again. This time her voice rang out with even more authority.

Rhonda Lee was temporarily derailed by Carmela's bravado. And she also seemed to interpret Carmela's question as some sort of *trick*. She clenched her jaw tightly and pulled herself up to her full height, which was difficult, Carmela noted, when you were only five foot two. "I can find out!" Rhonda Lee spat at her. "I have *friends*."

I'll just bet you do, thought Carmela. She almost said, *Like Jack Dumaine?* She would have loved to see the look of utter surprise on Rhonda Lee's face, but she held her tongue instead. No sense revealing her cards at this stage of the game. Especially when she wasn't sure what game was even being played out here.

"Rhonda Lee," said Carmela slowly, wondering if she could somehow get a piece of the puzzle to click into place, "do you know anything about Jimmy Earl being involved with Bufford Maple and a fellow named Michael Theriot?"

"What is she *talking* about!" shrilled Rhonda Lee to Tandy. "Will somebody *please* tell me what she's babbling about?"

Rhonda Lee was so worked up that every time she spoke, spit flew out of her mouth. It wasn't pretty, although at this point, it was starting to seem pretty darn funny.

Baby put a hand on Rhonda Lee's shoulder. "Maybe it's time you get going, dear," she suggested in a gentle yet firm tone. Clearly, Baby had grown tired of Rhonda Lee's hysterics.

Tandy closed in on Rhonda Lee's other side. "Gosh, look at the time, Rhonda Lee. Don't you have to be somewhere? Sure you do."

They escorted Rhonda Lee to the front door of the shop, trying to usher her out as gently as possible. Carmela remained standing where she was. Her friends were doing a masterful job with what had been a totally whacked-out situation. For that she'd be eternally grateful.

There were a few more muffled exchanges, then the front door banged shut. Tandy turned and threw her hands in the air. "What a fruitcake," she declared.

"Bonkers," said Baby. "Absolutely bonkers."

Is she really? wondered Carmela. *Or does Rhonda Lee know something but is just too upset to piece together what she knows?*

AS CARMELA was about to flip the light switch and lock up for the day, the phone rang.

Sighing, she contemplated not even answering it, but her conscience got the better of her. *Hey lazybones, it's a business, remember?*

She groaned and reached for the phone. "Good afternoon," she said. "Memory Mine Scrapbooking."

"Carmela?" came the voice on the other end of the line. "Hi, there. It's Alyse Eskew at the Claiborne Club."

The Claiborne Club, thought Carmela. *Lucky me. The club that isn't sure they want to admit any new members right now. I guess Alyse's remark about that has really stuck in my craw, as my momma would say.*

"Hello Alyse," said Carmela with not much enthusiasm.

"I'm glad I caught you," Alyse purred. "I know how busy you are."

"Mm-hm," replied Carmela.

"Say Carmela," asked Alyse, "do you still have that list we faxed you?"

Carmela's mind was blank for a moment. "The list?" *What list is Alyse babbling about?*

Alyse gave a nervous titter. Obviously, this conversation wasn't all that pleasant for her, either. "You know, the one you used when you created all those adorable place cards, then hand-lettered the names onto them?"

Carmela was suddenly confused. "You wanted the list *back*? I'm not sure

I even have it anymore." *Probably tossed the darn thing out,* she thought to herself.

Then Carmela added, more out of curiosity than anything, "Isn't that luncheon being held tomorrow?"

"Yes, but we're just tidying up loose ends," Alyse assured her. "Trying to keep our records in order."

"Sure," muttered Carmela. "Whatever. If I run across it, I'll pop it in the mail to you."

Carmela dropped the receiver back in its cradle, feeling distracted. *Who cares about a dopey list when Shamus is probably still downtown being beaten with a rubber hose? Give me a break!*

Chapter 25

RAIN LASHED AT the windows, pounded on the roof, gushed in torrents down the drain spouts. Cozied inside her apartment, Carmela figured that to-night's big Orpheus parade would *have* to be declared a washout. How could the floats and bands even survive in weather like this?

In fact, with this much rain pouring down, New Orleans would be lucky if Canal Street didn't flood completely and revert to being a real canal again! Carmela was so focused on the storm that when someone pounded on her door, she wasn't even sure if she was hearing right.

But when she finally threw the door open, there was Ava, looking soaked and disheveled.

"Didn't you hear me out there?" Ava grumped. She shed her raincoat like a snake shedding its skin, then did another little shake and dance that left a large puddle on the floor.

Carmela rushed to get her a towel. "I'm sorry," she apologized. "The storm was making so much noise I couldn't tell *what* was going on."

"Pour me a glass of wine, and all is forgiven," said Ava, deciding that she'd pouted long enough. Plopping into one of the chairs that surrounded Carmela's small wooden dining table, Ava ran long fingers through her tousled hair and gazed at the colorful papers and tags that were spread out on the table. "What's all this?" she asked.

Carmela set two glasses of wine down. "Tags," she told her friend. "I'm trying to put together a sample scrapbook page that's really an assembly of tags with photos mounted on them."

Ava studied the montage Carmela had assembled so far. It was really quite striking, all sorts of travel photos mounted on tags and then pasted on a terrific map background. She squinted. The map had to be either the Caribbean or Hawaii. She wasn't exactly sure which, since she'd popped her contacts out a few minutes ago.

"I swear," said Ava taking a sip of her wine, "I believe you could incorporate toilet paper rolls into a scrapbook page and make it look good."

"Now that *would* be a challenge," admitted Carmela. "But you didn't brave thunder and lightning to pay me a social call tonight, did you?"

"Aren't you the little psychic," said Ava. "Let's just wrap a turban around your head and call you *Madame* Carmela. Set you up in business in the back of my store. But, no, you're right. Tandy called earlier. She was worried about you and asked me to stop by and check on you."

"Did she tell you what happened after you left?"

Ava nodded. "That Rhonda Lee Clayton is truly certifiable. I can't believe you didn't just haul off and smack her one."

"I thought about it," admitted Carmela. "But mostly I just felt sorry for her."

"I'm surprised you didn't inform her in no uncertain terms that her little secret is out of the bag. I think it's shameful the way she's carrying on with her dead husband's partner."

Boo crept over to lie next to Carmela, and she dropped her hand to rub the little dog's furrowed head. "I think Rhonda Lee knows something," said Carmela.

"Knows what?" asked Ava, yawning.

"I think if Rhonda Lee could pull herself out of her hissy fit, she just might be able to put two and two together and figure out who killed her husband," said Carmela.

Ava stared at Carmela. "Yeah? Then why doesn't she just boogie on down to police headquarters and yak her little head off? Start *cooperating* with them?"

"Because Rhonda Lee doesn't know what she knows," said Carmela.

Ava blinked. "You think Rhonda Lee's little pea brain actually knows something but she doesn't know *what* she knows?" Ava repeated. "Is that what you're saying?"

Carmela nodded thoughtfully. "Pretty much."

"Are we talking repressed memory syndrome?" asked Ava. "Like that episode we saw on *Oprah*?"

"I wouldn't say it's that clinical," said Carmela. "But I do think that Rhonda Lee Clayton, in her own stumbling, bumbling way, just might know why Jimmy Earl was killed. She just hasn't put the pieces together."

"Assembly required," said Ava. "She ain't no Nancy Drew."

"You got that right," said Carmela.

"But you, on the other hand," said Ava, "are foaming at the mouth to take a crack at a perfectly good mystery that really could stand to remain unsolved. You want to figure out every precise little detail." Ava raised one eyebrow at Carmela. "You'd just love that, wouldn't you?"

Carmela rubbed at her temples as though she suddenly had a headache. "Ava, don't."

"You really don't need to keep picking away at this," Ava told her, "out of misplaced loyalty to that hairball Shamus."

"We've been over this before," said Carmela tiredly. "Maybe I *am* an idiot, but I still feel compelled to help him."

"So you can negotiate a better settlement," said Ava. "Really stick it to the Meechums when you start divorce proceedings."

"Yes . . . no," said Carmela.

Ava stared at Carmela, then shook her head. "I can tell by the look on your face, you've still got it bad for him, don't you?"

Carmela didn't say anything. She just felt defeated. Defeated and tired. All this intrigue was swirling around her, and she didn't seem to be able to make heads or tails out of anything. Hell, she didn't even have a *date* these days. Rhonda Lee thought *her* life was in shreds, and she at least had a *paramour.* Two nights after she tucked old Jimmy Earl into the family crypt at Saint Cyril's, she was out catting around. No Heartbreak Hotel for her, just a hot night at the Calhoun Motel!

"Don't you ever watch those TV shows where a bunch of clever, witty women sit around talking about how great it is to be independent?" asked Ava. "Didn't you ever think how nice and self-respecting it would feel to actually *be* one of them?"

"Listen to *you,*" said Carmela. "First thing you do when you meet a man is interrogate him, try to determine if he's got the makings for a perfect matrimonial candidate."

"I daresay I'm not *that* obvious," said Ava.

Carmela folded her arms and stared back at Ava. One corner of her mouth twitched.

"I *am?*" screeched Ava. "Oh, no. You think so, *really?*"

AFTER AVA left, Carmela moped about her apartment. Somehow the tags didn't seem all that intriguing anymore for the travel layout. Maybe she should start over, she decided. Try to do a sample page using torn pieces from old maps and then integrate some luggage templates.

At ten minutes to eight, Carmela snapped on the TV and turned to one of the local cable channels. Regular programming had been preempted tonight so they could cover the Orpheus parade. The newscaster, sent out to do a remote broadcast, was huddled pitifully beneath an enormous striped umbrella that rocked precariously in the gale and threatened to blow away. Yet the newscaster, Fred Something, continued to reassure his TV audience that the Orpheus parade was *still* going to roll. In fact, Fred was fairly certain that this single stalled cell that was delivering such a walloping rain to New Orleans would soon rumble on over into neighboring Mississippi.

Carmela was just about to fix herself a grilled cheese sandwich when the phone rang.

"Hello?" she said.

"Carmela, dear, I suppose you're planning to stay in." It was Jekyl Hardy.

"Absolutely," replied Carmela. "How about you? You're not going to the Orpheus parade are you? I figured it would be canceled, but now they're saying it's still going to roll."

"Word is the start time's been delayed an hour. Apparently the National Weather Service is making all sorts of optimistic predictions."

"So I heard."

"They're holding all the floats in the den, plus they packed in a bunch of bands and marchers, too. It's absolute bedlam. But they're still going to roll, come hell or high water."

That's Mardi Gras for you, thought Carmela. *Act of God, act of war, and the parades still roll.* At least it was something that could be counted on, like death and taxes.

"So the thing of it is," said Jekyl, "I'm sitting here in a restaurant over on Esplanade, sipping Bloody Marys and doing oyster shooters with some of my die-hard float-builder friends."

"Having a better night than I am," quipped Carmela.

"Don't be so sure," said Jekyl. "I think the vodka they're pouring is about two hours old. Anyway, I don't want to schlep my costume home in the rain tonight, so do you mind if I stash it at your store?"

"Be my guest," said Carmela. "You still have the key, right?" She'd given Jekyl a spare key a couple months ago, in case he needed to raid her stash of paper and ribbon for float-making supplies. Whenever he stopped by, he left a detailed list. Then she'd tally it up later and send him an invoice.

"Still got it," said Jekyl. "Will I see you tomorrow when I stop by to pick my costume up?"

"Not sure," said Carmela. "I'm officially closed, but that doesn't mean I might not be in the back room catching up on busywork."

"Okay, love, see you when I see you."

"Bye, Jekyl," said Carmela. As she hung up the phone, she suddenly decided she really was hungry. What did she have in her larder that would be even easier than a grilled cheese sandwich? Bowl of cereal? Cup of yogurt? Or had she fed the last of the yogurt to Boo?

Carmela ambled into her small kitchen and pulled open the door of the refrigerator. When the phone shrilled a few minutes later, she realized that she'd been standing there staring at the somewhat meager contents, balanced on one leg like a sand crane, completely tranced out.

Jekyl again, Carmela thought to herself as she reached for the phone. *He's gonna spin some farfetched story and try to coax me out into the night. He's probably worried that I'm home alone again,* she decided as she picked up the phone.

But it wasn't Jekyl Hardy's voice that greeted her. It was the slow, slurry voice of Rhonda Lee Clayton.

"Carmela," she said, her tongue sounding thick. "It's Rhonda Lee."

What's with this? thought Carmela. And then immediately wondered, *Has Rhonda Lee been drinking? Or is she just tooted up on medication? A little Xanax or a hit of Valium?*

"Hello, Rhonda Lee," said Carmela. She was about to say, *Well this is a surprise,* but decided not to. It would be too much of an understatement.

"Carmela," said Rhonda Lee. Her voice suddenly carried that ebullient tone that users often get.

"Rhonda Lee," Carmela repeated cheerily, suddenly unsure of what to say and starting to feel like a complete idiot.

"I might have been a little . . . uh . . . *harsh* today," said Rhonda Lee.

Rhonda Lee apologizing for her little tantrum this afternoon? Well, this is history in the making.

"I'm sorry . . . ah, Car*me*la," said Rhonda Lee, carefully pronouncing each and every syllable. Rhonda Lee's voice suddenly sounded sleepy.

"Rhonda Lee?" asked Carmela. "Are you all right? Are you at home?" God forbid that this woman was out driving around playing Chatty Cathy on her cell phone.

"Fine, fine, fine," Rhonda Lee said in a drowsy, singsong voice. "Just hanging around the old homestead."

"Are you alone?" asked Carmela. It suddenly occurred to her that Rhonda Lee might have taken an overdose of something. *Like Jimmy Earl had?*

"My beautiful daughter is here with me," said Rhonda Lee, suddenly sounding slightly more lucid. She sighed deeply. "I'm okay. *We're* okay."

Is there a point to this conversation? Carmela wondered. *Or is this just a rambling apology?*

"Carmela," began Rhonda Lee, "I think you might have been right . . ."

Okay, I'll bite, thought Carmela.

"Might have been right about what, Rhonda Lee?" asked Carmela.

"I went through some papers in Jimmy Earl's desk," said Rhonda Lee.

Carmela stood stock-still. *Ohmygosh.*

There was a sharp *clink* and then a *thunk*. Carmela figured Rhonda Lee must be helping herself to another drink.

"Are you still there, Rhonda Lee?"

A few seconds went by before Rhonda Lee answered her. "I'm here. I've got some . . . uh . . . papers."

"Could I see them, Rhonda Lee?" asked Carmela. "Will you let me look at them?"

"Sure."

It's that easy? thought Carmela. *She said "Sure" just like that?*

Yeah, but she's been drinking. Is drinking. So what do I do now? Strike while the iron is hot?

Carmela squinted toward the window. Rain was still pelting down outside. Not exactly a great night to be dashing over to Rhonda Lee's house.

"Can I come over now, Rhonda Lee?" asked Carmela. *Damn, how would she even get through the traffic on—*

"Now?" said Rhonda Lee, sounding startled. "No. Oh no. Tomorrow."

"I can stop by tomorrow?" said Carmela. *Get this confirmed; set up a specific time.*

"I'll come to *you*," said Rhonda Lee. "At your store. Tomorrow . . ." There was a long pause as Rhonda Lee struggled to get the word out. ". . . afternoon," she finished.

"Rhonda Lee," protested Carmela, "it's gonna be a madhouse down here in the French Quarter. It'd be a whole lot better if I . . ."

But Carmela was talking to dead air. Rhonda Lee had hung up.

Carmela stood with the receiver clutched in her hand. Tomorrow afternoon. She'd have to wait until Rhonda Lee Clayton stopped by Memory Mine tomorrow afternoon. But then maybe, just maybe, she'd start to get some answers.

Chapter 26

THE MORNING DRIZZLE didn't seem to dim the enthusiasm of the Fat Tuesday revelers as tourists and locals alike thronged the streets of the French Quarter. Many wore rain garb with costumes peeking out; most had the ubiquitous *geaux* cups clutched in their hot little hands. And those in the know, which was just about everybody these days, were headed for Bourbon and St. Ann Streets, where the ladies on the second-floor balconies, lubricated by liquor and urged on by a crowd that often numbered in the thousands, would be jitterbugging and proudly displaying their ta-tas.

Carmela hadn't really planned to go in to her shop today at all, would have rather headed right for Saint Cyril's Cemetery to photograph the oven crypts. But Alyse Eskew's call late yesterday had set her teeth on edge and caused her to completely forget about bringing her digital camera home with her, so a quick trip to Memory Mine was in the cards.

Pushing open the door to Memory Mine, Carmela flipped on the lights and kicked the door shut. What she'd do, she decided, was grab the camera and hoof it the eight or ten blocks over to Saint Cyril's Cemetery. If she was really lucky, she'd be able to click off a few shots between raindrops. Then she'd zip back here to the shop and download the photos to her computer. Viewing them on her monitor, a fairly new Hitachi with great color resolution, she'd know immediately if she had her shot. If everything looked okay, she'd go ahead and print them out on special photo paper. Then, she'd sit tight and wait for Rhonda Lee Clayton to show up. That is, assuming the somewhat mercurial Rhonda Lee was still coming and wasn't curled up in bed nursing a hangover.

That was the plan for sure, Carmela decided, as she dug in her desk drawer, searching for her little camera.

Pawing through a tangle of papers, disks, and scrapbook supply catalogs, Carmela swore that she was going to get organized one of these days, even if it killed her. She couldn't live her life in perpetual disarray, could she? Maybe she should take up the art of feng shui; then at least there'd be a Zen-like semblance of order to her disorder.

Where is that darn camera anyway? she wondered as Jekyl Hardy's costume, hanging in the corner of her office, suddenly caught her eye. Seeing the red sequined suit hanging there made her stop and smile. Jekyl's prized devil costume. A sequined red suit complete with top hat and glittery pitchfork. *People in New Orleans truly are mad,* she decided. To spend all year planning for Mardi Gras and then spend a month's salary or more on a costume was . . . what? Insane? No, it only looked insane if you didn't live here. But, if you were born and bred in New Orleans, that madness was forever in your blood, part of your visceral heritage. And, sure as shit, the minute Mardi Gras was finished and Ash Wednesday rolled around, you'd find yourself dreaming about *next* year's exotic costume or big party idea.

Her fingers skittered across the plastic edge of the camera. *Okay, here it is,* she told herself.

Now, is there enough space left on the card?

Carmela flipped the switch on and checked the counter. It looked like . . . what? Maybe twenty shots left?

That's it? What have I been shooting lately?

Carmela racked her brain.

Oh, wait a minute. Gabby used it the night she and Stuart went to the Pluvius den. And then I snapped quite a few shots a few days later at Jimmy Earl's funeral. And, of course, nobody's bothered to download any of the images to the computer yet. Well, it really shouldn't be a problem. After all, I only need a couple good shots, right?

As Carmela headed down Prieur Street toward Saint Cyril's Cemetery, she felt completely out of step with the rest of the world. Or, at least the world of the French Quarter. Because while she was heading out of the *Vieux Carré*, it seemed that everyone else was spilling into it.

The French Quarter was definitely ground zero today; streets were cordoned off for twenty blocks. And the few blocks surrounding Jackson Square and the French Market were pandemonium, pure and simple.

Yes, thought Carmela, *today the French Quarter is bursting with parades, marching bands, jazz groups, street performers, strippers, and a couple million costumed revelers. To say nothing of the oyster bars, jazz clubs, street vendors, horse-drawn jitneys, and paddle wheelers sitting over on the Mississippi.*

ST. CYRIL'S cemetery looked almost abandoned, Carmela decided as she squeezed through the half-open front gates. No visitors in sight, no funerals in full swing. Just row upon uneven row of whitewashed tombs that stood out in sharp contrast to the muddy earth. Rain was still sifting down in a fine mist, and when lightning pulsed from purple, billowing clouds overhead, the old tombs seemed to glow with their own eerie brand of electrical energy.

Carmela shivered. She'd never been here alone before. And as familiar as she was with the many cemeteries tucked in and around the city of New Orleans, she'd never seen one this empty. So utterly devoid of any human life-forms. Then again, she'd never visited a cemetery on Fat Tuesday before.

Well, she decided, as she made her way down one of the lanes, she'd snap her photos and get out. Luckily, the rain *seemed* to be letting up a touch. So she just might get a good shot of the wall ovens. Which were . . .

Carmela stopped in her tracks and gazed around. She'd entered Saint Cyril's from the Prieur Street entrance, so the wall ovens had to be . . . where?

Her eyes skimmed the tops of tombs, trying to determine just exactly where the wall ovens were located.

If that was the Venable monument up ahead, then the wall ovens should be to her left. Correct?

Carmela hooked a left and threaded her way through Saint Cyril's. This was one of New Orleans's oldest cemeteries, and many of the tombs clearly betrayed their age. Stone faces of angels and saints that had been lovingly carved more than a century ago had been melted by the ravages of time. Many tombstones were badly cracked and chipped and tilted at awkward angles. As Carmela skipped by one row of tombstones, they appeared to gape at her like broken teeth.

Her nerves may have been slightly frayed, but her sense of direction was intact. Carmela spotted the wall ovens from forty feet away.

Good, she breathed. *I'll take a couple quick shots and get out of here. It's way too creepy without anyone around.*

Stopping at a large, flat tomb, Carmela set her purse down and pulled the camera out. She turned it on and checked the battery. The green glow told her everything was a go.

Putting the camera up to her eye, Carmela framed the shot.

No, I can get closer yet.

Keeping the camera to her eye, she moved a few steps toward the wall ovens, thinking how nice it was to finally be working with an auto-focus camera. So much easier.

She paused, rather liking the composition of her shot. The viewfinder told her she'd be able to capture three of the wall ovens head-on. It was a good shot. Told a complete story.

And that's what a good scrapbook layout is all about, right?

Holding her breath, Carmela was about to click the shutter when she heard a faint crunch of gravel.

She clicked the shot anyway, then whirled about quickly.

Nothing. Nothing but white, bleached-out tombs.

Am I hearing things? Probably. Gotta stop being so jumpy.

She put the camera to her face, deliberately hesitated, then fired off three more shots.

Still hearing things? No . . . it's just that . . . what?

Something *felt* different.

Like *what?*

Like the *air* had been disturbed.

Carmela was suddenly conscious of her heart beating a little quicker, the hair on the back of her neck suddenly beginning to rise.

You're crazy; there's nothing here, she told herself.

Still . . .

Carmela fired off five more shots, then got the hell out of there. Walked briskly to the Roman Street entrance instead of going back to the Prieur Street entrance. *Better to walk around the outside wall of the cemetery,* she decided, *even if it is the long way. There are people out here. Living people.*

Chapter 27

THE FEELING THAT she was being followed stayed with her all the way back to her shop.

You're being paranoid, Carmela told herself. *Nobody's dogging your footsteps; nobody's brandishing an umbrella with a poison tip. Stop running old James Bond movies in your head!*

But even lecturing herself sternly didn't stop Carmela from glancing in shop windows to see what shimmering reflection might be hovering behind her. And once she even stopped dead in her tracks and turned around to scour the crowd. But all she saw was a marauding band of pirates, a couple people in goofy-looking bird costumes, and a person in a red and yellow clown suit.

Hardly, she told herself.

The phone was ringing as she pushed her way into Memory Mine. Leaning across the counter, Carmela swiped the phone off the hook. "Hello," she answered breathlessly.

"I thought you weren't gonna be there." It was Ava.

"If you didn't think I was going to be here, why did you call?" A fair question, Carmela decided.

"Don't know," said Ava. "Force of habit?" They *did* tend to call each other a lot.

"You finish all your masks?" asked Carmela. She knew there were at least a dozen different masked balls tonight and that Ava had been hustling her buns to get a couple last-minute orders finished.

Ava sighed. "Just barely. I'm still putting the finishing touches on one. Gold paint with lots of red and purple feathers. Very exotic and hot looking. Think Rio and conga lines. Then I'm gonna zip down to Canal Street and catch the Rex parade."

"Isn't Rex already rolling?" Carmela asked. She knew Rex usually hit downtown right around noon. That's when all hell broke loose.

"I was just listening to the radio, and the announcer said they're way backed up," said Ava. "Not all the Zulu floats have gone through yet." Zulu was the parade *before* Rex.

"So what else is new," said Carmela. *Will Rhonda Lee be able to make it to my shop at all? Maybe I should call Rhonda Lee at home, just to double-check . . .*

"Oops, gotta go," chirped Ava. "Customers."

"Talk to you," said Carmela. She hung up the phone and stood there, gazing about her empty store. *Okay, what's next on the agenda? Oh yeah. Download the photos.*

It took her but a minute to pop the card out of her camera and insert it into her computer. Then she was clicking her way through the roster of photos that, up until now, had been stored on the camera.

The first shots, of course, were the photos Gabby took the night she and Stuart went to the Pluvius den.

The night of the Pluvius *parade*, Carmela reminded herself. The night Jimmy Earl Clayton ingested his fateful dose of ketamine.

Gabby had taken the usual jumble of shots. Close-ups of Stuart talking with various people. A couple of Stuart hanging off a mermaid float. One with him cuddling up to the oversized mermaid. Gabby certainly was enamored of old Stuart, thought Carmela. Then decided her sour-grapes attitude wasn't particularly cordial. Just because *her* marriage didn't work out all that well . . .

There were other shots, too. Shots that showed frantic volunteers putting finishing touches on a Poseidon float and a seahorse float. A couple that showed Jekyl Hardy looking like he was ready to tear his hair out. One close-up of a large silver papier-mâché octopus that had obviously just lost a tentacle. *Probably that's why Jekyl was tearing his hair out,* Carmela decided.

There was even a shot of Jimmy Earl Clayton. Standing with two other men, raising their glasses in a boisterous toast.

Interesting, thought Carmela.

The next few shots weren't so interesting. Wide shots. Mostly just photos that recorded the frantic last-minute activity in the den.

Carmela scanned them quickly, was about to delete the ones that weren't particularly good, when something caught her eye.

Who is that? Is that Dace Wilcox in the photo? Sure it is.

Carmela studied it.

Gabby had caught Dace Wilcox in profile. He looked like he was talking to a couple of the float builders.

Hmm. No. Nothing here.

Carmela flipped through a few more shots.

Here's a shot of Ruby Dumaine. With her philandering husband, Jack.

Carmela clicked to the next shot.

Ruby again. This time alone.

Doing what? Carmela hit a couple buttons to enlarge the photo. *Nope, that doesn't work. I need to enlarge just the lower right portion of the photo.*

She made a few adjustments on her computer. There, now she had it.

She stared at the photo, frowning.

Ruby was holding a drink out to Jimmy Earl's daughter, Shelby.

Okay.

Carmela forwarded to the next shot. In this photo Jimmy Earl had grabbed the glass and was waggling a finger at his daughter!

Carmela stared at the screen. *What was going on here?* She wasn't sure, but she had a feeling it might be bad *juju*, as Ava would say. Really bad.

Feeling discombobulated, Carmela stood up, stretched her arms overhead, blew out a couple deep breaths.

A jittery feeling had suddenly insinuated itself in her body. Nerves, a little hit of adrenaline, whatever you wanted to call it, had definitely gotten her going.

Carmela sat down in front of her computer again. She thought for a couple seconds, then pulled open the bottom drawer of her desk, started pawing through papers.

It was here before, she told herself. At least she *thought* she'd put it there.

She shuffled through the stamp catalogs again, a few old invoices that had been marked paid, flyers for scrapbooking classes that had come and gone.

Ah, there it was. The list of names for the Pluvius queen luncheon that Alyse Eskew had been so hot to trot over.

Carmela scanned the list, blinked a couple times, set it aside. She rubbed the top of her head in an unconscious gesture, as if trying to stimulate her brain cells.

What's so strange about this list? Something.

Carmela shook her head. *No, it's just a list. Nothing more.*

But the odd feeling persisted, and a germ of an idea was definitely rattling around in her brain.

Carmela picked up the list, studied it again. *Think,* she prodded herself. *What's off about it?*

A name is missing.

She bit her lip, thinking. *Whose?*

Shelby Clayton. Jimmy Earl's daughter. She had always been one of the front-runner candidates for Pluvius queen.

And in that same leap of consciousness, Carmela thought, *So what? Shelby Clayton dropped out of the running for Pluvius queen after Jimmy Earl died.*

Carmela slumped back in her chair, then immediately straightened back up again.

Hold everything! How can that be? I received this list long before Jimmy Earl died from his overdose of ketamine! Unless . . .

"Oh my God," breathed Carmela. There was a sudden pounding in her ears as it dawned on her what might have taken place.

Someone drew up a nasty plan to insure that Shelby Clayton wouldn't be a queen candidate!

Jimmy Earl hadn't been killed over a business deal at all! Jimmy Earl had been sacrificed so his daughter would drop out . . .

Holy smokes! Could that be right?

Carmela paced nervously about her store, thinking.

Okay, try this on for size, she told herself. *What if poor Shelby Clayton had been the intended target all along? And Jimmy Earl, her father, had simply gotten in the way?*

Carmela reeled at the idea. Strode back into her office, dropped into her chair.

Would someone commit murder just for the sake of their daughter being named Pluvius queen? Was that possible?

Deep in her heart, Carmela knew it was possible. That it could happen. In Texas, not that long ago, a woman had taken out a contract on a sixteen-year-old girl just so her own daughter would be insured a slot on the cheerleading squad!

Crazy? Yeah. But there are lots of crazy people in the world.

The bell over the door sounded.

Rhonda Lee? Already? Oh, no, the poor woman. Can't let her know about this yet . . .

Carmela looked up from her computer, her expression one of consummate grief and commiseration.

How am I ever going to—

Carmela was stunned to see a red and yellow clown costume materialize before her eyes.

What the—?

"Hello, Carmela." The flint-edged voice of Ruby Dumaine rang out in the stillness of the deserted shop.

Carmela's eyes turned to saucers; she tasted bile in the back of her throat. *Ruby. Oh no!*

Ruby Dumaine reached up and pulled a curly purple wig off her head. She flashed Carmela a supremely confident smile above the pistol she had pointed directly at her. Curiously, Ruby balanced the pistol in her hand with a confident, relaxed manner. It made Carmela think Ruby had done this before. That Ruby might be an old pro with a pistol.

Careful, a warning bell sounded in Carmela's head. *Don't want to mess with an old pro.*

"Ruby!" said Carmela, fighting to keep the panic from her voice. "What a surprise."

"Oh, I don't think you're all that surprised to see me here," said Ruby Dumaine. Her voice was smooth and dangerous. She edged into Carmela's office carefully, and her eyes darted toward Carmela's computer monitor.

"Well, isn't that sweet," Ruby Dumaine purred as she stared at the screen. "A lovely little photo show. Planning to immortalize me in one of your silly little scrapbooks?"

"Just reviewing a few shots," said Carmela, trying to stay cool. *Now what?* she wondered. *Got any great ideas? Noooo, not really.*

"Yes, let's run through those shots," said Ruby. "Let's see what that dim-witted assistant of yours really captured."

"You broke into Gabby's house," said Carmela, staring at her. Ruby Dumaine had slathered white greasepaint on her face and outlined her lips with coral lipstick. Not only did she look like a clown, she looked like a parody of an older woman who was hooked on using way too much makeup. The Tammy Fay syndrome.

Shit. And I'll bet Ruby was there in the cemetery with me, too. No wonder I came down with a bad case of the creeps.

"Of course I paid a visit to Gabby," said Ruby. "I figured she still had the camera."

"And then you tried to pick up my photos," added Carmela. Suddenly, the pieces of the puzzle were coming together with dizzying speed. And she didn't much like the picture that was emerging.

"I didn't realize you'd gone digital," said Ruby. "Silly me; guess I'm going to have to take the plunge into cyberspace myself."

Carmela also knew, with complete and utter clarity, that it had been Ruby Dumaine who strong-armed Alyse Eskew into calling her and trying to get the list back.

Nobody noticed that Shelby Clayton's name wasn't on the list? No, of course not. Ruby drew up the list with zealous glee and probably hadn't given a second thought to the fact that Shelby's absence from the list might be a dead giveaway. It hadn't occurred to Ruby until now. Now that things are getting a little too hot.

Dead giveaway, thought Carmela. *Ha-ha.*

"Know what else I did?" bragged Ruby Dumaine. "I talked that idiot Rhonda Lee into calling you last night."

"You did? How?" Carmela regretted her question the minute the words flew from her mouth.

But Ruby just smiled. "I have my ways. Suffice it to say she's just a drunken pawn, doesn't understand a thing. In fact, I'm sure she'll be thrilled to death when my own daughter, Swan, is crowned Pluvius queen tonight."

Thrilled to death. Once again, an interesting choice of words, thought Carmela.

Carmela mustered up her nastiest sneer. "You'll never get away with this!" she told Ruby with far more conviction than she felt.

"I already have," smirked Ruby Dumaine. "Now, there's just one final little item I'm going to enlist from you. In fact, it'll help me tie up an awful lot of loose ends." Ruby paused, flashed a horrible barracuda smile. "Your confession."

"What?" said Carmela, stunned.

"You're going to pick up your pen and write out your confession. About how Shamus killed Jimmy Earl Clayton and you gave him your very capable assistance."

"Dream on," said Carmela.

Ruby shifted the gun slightly to focus on the space between Carmela's eyes. *I've always been partial to that space,* Carmela decided. *Okay, fine, I'll pick up the damn pen and humor this crazy lady.*

Carmela searched around on the top of her desk. *Too messy,* she thought wildly. *Gotta get organized.* Her fingers hit a green plastic pen that lurked under a pile of papers. It was the pen with the disappearing ink. *Ahh . . . there you go! I finally caught a break.*

Ruby dictated a somewhat rambling statement, which Carmela diligently wrote out word for word on a piece of plain white paper. Ruby scowled at Carmela's efforts, watching her over the pistol, moving her lips as she read the statement back. Then she gave a quick nod. "Sign it," she ordered.

Carmela signed it.

Ruby snatched the paper from Carmela's hands, folded it in half, and tucked it inside her red leather purse.

A clown with a designer purse, thought Carmela. *If this wasn't Mardi Gras, people would for sure know she was fruit loops.*

"Stand up," commanded Ruby. She gestured wildly with the pistol, and Carmela reluctantly scrambled to her feet.

"Is that your costume?" asked Ruby, gesturing toward Jekyl Hardy's devil suit.

"No," Carmela told her.

"Put it on anyway."

Carmela slid the jacket off the hanger and put it on. The shoulders were too big and the sleeves way too long.

"Excellent," said Ruby. "Trousers, too." She leaned forward with a stupid grin on her face. "Remember, dearie, it's Mardi Gras! We wouldn't want to rouse suspicion."

Carmela grabbed the trousers and stepped into them, pulling them up over her own black slacks. All the while she was hoping someone or something would intercede.

What was it that always saved the day in a Greek tragedy? Deus ex machina. God by machine. That was when a person or deity came crashing into the final scene to resolve a conflict. The Greek dramaturge's version of the cavalry arriving.

That single idea fueled Carmela's hope. Maybe Jekyl Hardy would show up to retrieve his devil costume. Or Ava would get worried and peek in the window. Or maybe Rhonda Lee would get it together and drop by for their chat. Unfortunately, Carmela noted, none of those possibilities seemed to loom large on the horizon.

"Is your car parked nearby?" asked Ruby. She was tugging the purple clown wig back on over her red curls. If she didn't look so terrifying, it would have been ridiculous.

"Not really," said Carmela.

"Where is it?"

"Um . . . in an alley off Esplanade Avenue," said Carmela. She decided it was better to tell the truth than lie about it. If Ruby decided to march her to her car, maybe she'd be able to figure out *the great escape* on the way. Flash a signal to someone. Or wrest herself away. Or get a bullet in the back of her head. No, she decided, the latter was not such a good option.

"Perfect," cooed Ruby. She hefted the gun again. "Let's march."

There was a famous quote that went something like, "Never argue with people who buy ink by the gallon." Carmela thought there should be another version that said, "Never argue with crazy people who carry guns." Because as Ruby marched her down the street, Carmela realized just how helpless she was.

Here they were, in the middle of Mardi Gras, for goodness sakes, and she couldn't do a thing.

"You live around here?" asked Ruby after they'd gone the requisite two blocks or so.

"No," said Carmela. *My apartment is barely fifty feet away, and Boo is in there all by herself. I'll die before I let Ruby near my dog.*

"You sure?" Ruby Dumaine cocked her head like an inquisitive crow, staring at Carmela with glazed eyes.

Carmela shrugged. "I just park my car here," she answered.

Ruby seemed to accept the answer at face value. *Good,* thought Carmela, *she's not as shrewd as she thinks she is. And she obviously didn't do her homework.*

Carmela showed her the old Cadillac.

"Perfect," said Ruby. "Unlock it, and let's get in. And don't try anything funny. I have very good reflexes."

I'll bet you do, thought Carmela.

Carmela inserted the key in the ignition, turned on the engine. It did its rough *tocka-tocka-tocka* for a couple minutes, warming up. "Where to?" Carmela asked as she buckled her seat belt.

"Back to Saint Cyril's," Ruby told her. She ignored her seat belt and half turned in her seat, focusing her hostile gaze on Carmela.

Carmela could barely contain her surprise.

Ruby waggled the gun in her face again. "Just drive," she said in a tired voice. "Don't piss me off any more than you have to, okay?"

Carmela negotiated the car out of her parking space, headed down to Barracks Street. Luckily, the streets this far over weren't blocked off yet, and she was able to head over to North Rampart, then hang a right to Prieur.

"That's it," said Ruby, catching a glimpse of the cemetery a few blocks away. "Go in the front entrance. The Prieur Street gate."

"Ruby . . ." began Carmela. "I don't know what you've got planned, but you'll never—"

"Honey, you don't know *what* I've got planned," Ruby spat out. She snaked a hand into her purse and fumbled around. She pulled out Carmela's confession as well as a large, rusty key.

Skeleton key? thought Carmela. *What's that for?*

Ruby saw the consternation on Carmela's face and favored her with a thin smile. "In case you don't know, the Dumaines also have a family crypt at Saint Cyril's. Six generations are interred there. And probably a few other various and sundry bodies as well." Ruby let loose a crazed chortle and gazed hungrily at Carmela. "I don't think one more body would put a strain on the accommodations. There's not all that much of you."

Carmela felt her hands go numb and her knees begin to tremble. *Ruby is going to try to force me inside the family crypt. If all goes well with Ruby's bizarre plan, I'll die of starvation, and there'll be nothing left of me. Barely a few bones.*

Ruby waved the signed confession at Carmela and jangled the key in her face. "Keep driving," she snarled. "Don't slow down now."

Is this the key the tarot cards revealed for my future? Is this how my life is supposed to end?

Carmela's brows furrowed together. No, she told herself. *We all have a part in creating our own destinies. We just have to act on our impulses, take advantage of situations. That's what spells the difference!*

Carmela's right foot crunched down hard on the accelerator, and the old Cadillac shot ahead with a burst of speed.

"That's the spirit," roared Ruby. "Zoom zoom, hurry it along!"

Up ahead Carmela could see the wrought-iron gates of Saint Cyril's Cemetery coming into view. She'd walked through those gates barely an hour ago. Actually, she'd more or less *squeezed* through them, since the gates weren't completely open, more like standing ajar. When she'd arrived here earlier, she'd just figured the caretaker had hastily unlocked them, then been distracted by something.

That's it, thought Carmela. *I'll aim for the gates. I'll drive this big honkin' car right into the wrought-iron gates and send this crazy lady clear through the windshield!* Carmela clutched the steering wheel and tried to brace herself.

Good-bye, Samantha. Please forgive me. You've been a great car.

At the last minute, Ruby saw Carmela's plan written on her face. "Stop it!" she screamed. "Don't you dare crash this—!"

Finally hearing fear in Ruby's voice, Carmela took a deep breath, even as she tried to relax every muscle in her body as her car slammed into the giant pair of black wrought-iron gates that loomed at the entrance to Saint Cyril's Cemetery.

The air was filled with screams, the sickening screech of grinding metal, and the high-pitched shatter of glass as the car gunned its way up one of the wrought-iron gates. Then, back tires still churning and burning rubber, the car began to roll to its side. As if in slow motion, passengers, papers, and bits of Mardi Gras costumes all tumbled wildly in the car. And the last thing that flitted into Ruby Dumaine's consciousness was the realization that the ink on Carmela's signed confession had somehow faded into oblivion.

Chapter 28

SUNLIGHT. A WHITE blur of a costume. And definitely a splitting headache.

Carmela was also cognizant of buzzing voices and soft footsteps padding around her. She knew she should try to open her eyes. But it all seemed too much. Too painful to even contemplate.

What's going on? Am I lying on the pavement in the middle of Mardi Gras with a bullet through my head? Is someone in a white chicken costume flapping about in a panic?

Carmela fought to open one eye. It fluttered mightily before she managed to get it to remain open and focus. The white chicken costume wasn't a costume at all; it was a nurse's uniform.

She decided to go for the other eye, too. *Live a little,* she prodded herself. *That is, if I'm still alive.*

Both eyes fluttered open, and she stared into the anxious faces of Tandy Bliss, Ava Grieux, Baby Fontaine and . . . Shamus? Oh my.

Carmela made a feeble effort to sit up, decided her head hurt too much. "I'm not dead?" she croaked. "This isn't heaven?"

"Close to it," said Ava kindly. "You're still in New Orleans."

"Mardi Gras?" rasped Carmela.

"The poor girl's delusional," sobbed Tandy.

"Quick, get her a sip of water," Baby directed the nurse. "Her throat is bone dry. Listen to that poor rattly little voice."

Ava clutched at Carmela's hand. "You're in the hospital, honey. You're going to be okay. No broken bones, but you're a little shook up."

"Samantha?" Carmela croaked again.

"Who's Samantha?" asked the nurse. "Was she the victim in the clown costume? The one they had to subdue?"

"Samantha's her car," murmured Ava. She smiled at Carmela, shook her head. "She didn't make it. Samantha was totaled. I'm sorry, kiddo."

Carmela sipped greedily at the water the nurse offered her. Then she licked her lips.

"Ruby?" she asked.

"Broken collarbone, broken arm, broken jaw," said Tandy, happy to deliver such dreadful news. "They've got her all trussed up."

"And in traction, too," added Baby helpfully. Her blue eyes were bright with tears.

"Here?" asked Carmela. She had to know. She'd been dreaming about Ruby Dumaine for the last couple hours. Sick, drug-induced dreams that had made Ruby seem larger than life. Like some rampaging *thing* that couldn't be stopped. Lying here, feeling completely helpless, Carmela didn't even like the idea she might be in the same *building* as Ruby Dumaine.

"No. They moved Mrs. Dumaine to the state hospital early this morning," said the nurse.

"Ladies," said Shamus, finally speaking up. "Could you give the two of us a few minutes alone?"

There were knowing glances all around, then Ava, Baby, Tandy, and the nurse shuffled out into the hallway and pulled the door closed behind them.

Shamus moved around to the side of Carmela's bed so he could be close to her. Carmela could smell his spicy aftershave. It smelled nice. Like their bathroom used to smell after he showered and shaved.

"I was so worried about you, darlin'." Shamus bent down and kissed her cheek gently. In his navy cashmere sweater and khaki slacks he looked like a college kid.

"I was worried about me," said Carmela. "Oh, no . . ." Once again she tried to struggle to a sitting position. "Poor Boo! She's been stuck in my apartment for—" Carmela began.

"Shhh, Boo's fine," said Shamus, patting her shoulder. "She stayed with me last night. At Glory's."

Carmela winced. "Glory'll make Boo sleep outside," she whispered. "She hates dogs."

"Honey . . . no." Now Shamus's fingers caressed the top of Carmela's bandage-wrapped head. "Boo slept on the bed with me all last night. She's fine, really. In fact, she's having the time of her life chasing the vacuum cleaner around."

"Is Ruby hurt real bad?" Carmela asked in a small voice.

"You banged her up pretty good," said Shamus. Carmela could tell he was trying to put a lighthearted spin on things, but his face was tight with concern.

"I thought Jimmy Earl was killed because of a real estate deal," said Carmela. "I thought Bufford Maple and Michael Theriot were involved."

"They *are* involved in a real estate deal," said Shamus, looking grim now. "Just not the one you were hell-bent on pursuing. Maple and Theriot are under investigation by the SEC for real estate fraud. Phony bonds and some mortgage flipping."

"What's mortgage flipping?" asked Carmela.

"It's kind of like a real estate ponzi scheme," explained Shamus. "You trade properties back and forth to avoid taxes and declare paper profits. Dace Wilcox has been investigating them for several months now."

"Dace?" said Carmela weakly. "I thought he might be involved with Jimmy Earl, too."

"He was, but as an investigator. Dace is a special agent for the IRS, although it's not widely known. Just as well to keep it under wraps."

Carmela settled back against her pillows. *Boy, did I have a wrong number with Dace! Who knew he was working on the side of justice?*

"What about Jack Dumaine? And Granger Rathbone?" asked Carmela.

"Apparently Jack hired Granger to try to figure out how much I knew. You see, I was the whistle-blower on the deal. Maple and Theriot also tried to tap Crescent City Bank for financing and, in reviewing some paperwork that came over from Clayton Crown Securities, a few things started to look hinky. Anyway, you kind of got pulled along for the ride." Shamus ducked his head. "Sorry about that."

"So Jack Dumaine was involved in this real estate fraud, too?" said Carmela.

"Yes, he was," said Shamus. "But apparently not Jimmy Earl. Strangely enough, Jimmy Earl seems to have been the innocent one."

"But Jack knew what Ruby did to Jimmy Earl? With the ketamine?" asked Carmela.

Shamus shook his head. "No. Jack was as shocked as we are. At least that's what he claims."

Carmela snuggled against her pillow, trying to digest all these layers of information. "Jack Dumaine and Rhonda Lee Clayton are having an affair," she told Shamus. Her voice was still hoarse, almost husky sounding.

"You mentioned that the other night, remember?"

Carmela blinked. "I did?"

Shamus leaned over and kissed her on the forehead. The small part that wasn't bandaged. "You look so helpless lying there," he said, the words catching in his throat.

"I'll be just as helpless when I get out of here," said Carmela. "Poor Samantha . . . completely totaled." She sighed. "I really loved that old car."

"I know you did," said Shamus slowly. "Think you can get used to driving something else?"

"I suppose I'll have to," said Carmela. "Eventually."

"Why not right now," said Shamus. His right hand dug into the pocket of his khaki slacks and Carmela heard a faint, metallic *clink*.

Suddenly, a set of car keys dangled before her eyes.

"What's that?" Carmela asked warily.

"Keys to your new car," said Shamus.

She peered at him. A shit-eating grin was spread across his handsome face. *Oh no.*

"You bought me a car," she said. She was shocked. *What does this mean? He loves me, he loves me not? Oh, I wish my poor head didn't ache so much. If ever there was a time I needed to think straight, it's right now.*

"Don't think about it so hard," said Shamus, watching her closely.

Carmela sighed and closed her eyes. "Don't try to read my mind," she murmured, feeling slightly perturbed. She lay there for a moment until one eye peeked open, then the other. Now the slightest hint of curiosity danced in her blue eyes. "What exactly did you buy?"

"Mercedes." The pride was evident in his voice. "Five hundred SL."

Carmela was shocked. "No way!"

"I can see you in a Mercedes," said Shamus. "Classy woman, classy car."

"There's no way I can accept this." Carmela turned her head so she wouldn't have to look at the keys that dangled from his fingers.

This is nuts. Plus everything's happening way too fast. In warp speed, as a matter of fact.

"Look, you've got a concussion," Shamus told her. "You're not thinking straight yet. So just . . . think about the car. Okay?" His face shone with kindness and concern.

Carmela stared at him. Damn, he looked good. Cute, eager to please. Just like the fella she married that fine day at Christ Church. "Okay," she finally answered. "I'll think about it."

"Good." His hand brushed her shoulder. "Better get some sleep now. I'll stop by again later, okay?"

"Okay," she said and closed her eyes again, half aware of a whispered exchange at the door.

More than anything, Carmela wanted to drift off to sleep, but someone was standing at her bedside, plucking at the sleeve of her stylish polka-dot hospital johnny. She lifted a lid tiredly. It was Ava. "What?" she asked her friend.

"You're going to accept it, right?" said Ava expectantly.

Carmela shook her head. "I can't."

"Honey," said Ava, dangling the keys in front of Carmela's face. "The keys I have clutched in my hot little hand are for a Mercedes Five hundred SL. We're talking three oh two horsepower with a V-eight engine. Sticker priced at over eighty-five grand. Like it or not, you just grabbed the brass ring!"

"It doesn't seem right," said Carmela stubbornly. "Especially since Shamus and I seem headed for divorce."

"Now you're headed for divorce," said Ava. "Two days ago, you were sticking by him out of loyalty."

"Shamus is a good man, and I love him dearly. But he's having trouble with the commitment part," sniffled Carmela.

"All men have trouble with the commitment part," answered Ava. She pulled a half dozen tissues from the box near the bed, stuck them in Carmela's hand.

Carmela held one up to her leaky eyes, sighed heavily.

"You know," said Ava in an upbeat, conspiratorial tone, "there are lots of mechanical devices on the market today that can bring pleasure to a woman. But the best by far is a Mercedes-Benz!" She gently placed the car keys in Carmela's hand.

Carmela closed her fingers around the shiny new keys. There was no denying it, a Mercedes-Benz *was* an awfully nice car. Beyond nice, actually. Bordering on splendiferous. She narrowed her eyes, gazed down at the keys. With the sun pouring in her hospital window, the keys looked like they were plated in twenty-four-karat gold. Like keys to a magical kingdom. The promise of something new and bright, like sunlight bouncing off Lake Pontchartrain.

She thought back to the tarot card reader at Baby's party. Maybe *these* were the keys in her future. *Could they be?*

"You think I should accept?" said Carmela, trying to stifle a yawn. *Damn, I'm feeling tired.*

"I think it would be *rude* not to," said Ava, doing a masterful job of maintaining a straight face.

Carmela's fingers closed tightly around the keys as she smiled up at Ava. "You know what?" she said. "I think you may be right."

Scrapbooking Tips from Laura Childs

Words Add Impact

Be sure to add snippets of poetry, favorite sayings, or your very own jottings to your scrapbook pages. One easy way is to compose your words on a computer using a nice, funky type, then output those words on a sheet of see-through vellum. You can tear around your words to achieve a deckled-edged cloud effect or even cut the vellum into a square and lay it across your photo for a ghost effect.

Tag, You're It!

Have you seen the wonderful tags that are available in various shapes, sizes, and colors? They really add interest to a scrapbook page. You can paste smaller photos on tags, rubber stamp the tags, or add stickers if you want. And be sure to thread a piece of ribbon, lace, or raffia through the punched holes in your tags to complete the look!

Charm-ing Ideas

Tiny charms and other three-dimensional objects really make scrapbook pages come to life. Depending on the story your page is telling, think about adding tiny brass keys, old coins, paper butterflies, scrabble tiles, tiny beads and buttons, even little squares of foil that you've embossed.

Brush It Up

When using embossed papers as backgrounds, drybrush a little bit of gold acrylic paint over a few select areas to add elegant highlights.

Try Your Hand at Painting

Why not create your own scrapbook background page? Try painting a beach scene with white clouds, scalloped waves, and gentle, undulating yellow sand. Once you lay your summer photos over it and rubber stamp a fish and starfish, you might be surprised at how impressive your artwork looks!

Personalize Your Scrapbook Covers

Buy a simple album and make your own elaborate cover. Silk flowers and ribbons are easily glued on. You can use charms, beads, quilted squares, or a piece of needlepoint. Lace and dried flower petals also lend an elegant touch. Or get a yard of fabric and cover the entire book!

Adding Dimension to Your Scrapbook

A tiny mirror surrounded with lace, an old embroidered hankie, paper dolls, even a tiny locket or string of inexpensive pearls adds a personal touch and is very symbolic of a keepsake motif.

Scrapbooks Can Be More Than Just Scrapbooks

You can create a special book that you use for journaling, sketching, jotting down poems or special phrases, or even recording vacations, special events, favorite memories of your children, or your best recipes.

Favorite
New Orleans Recipes

Carmela's Jambalaya

¾ cup chopped onion
½ cup chopped celery
¼ cup chopped green pepper
¼ cup minced fresh parsley
1 clove garlic, minced
2 tbsp. butter
2 large tomatoes, skinned and chopped
2 cups of chicken stock
1¼ cups water
1 tsp. sugar
½ tsp. dried whole thyme
½ tsp. chili powder
¼ tsp. black pepper
¼ tsp. Tabasco sauce
2 cups browned sausage or cooked ham
1 cup uncooked long-grain rice
1½ pounds fresh medium shrimp

Using a Dutch oven, sauté onion, celery, green pepper, parsley, and garlic in butter until vegetables are tender. Stir in tomatoes, chicken stock, water, sugar, thyme, chili powder, black pepper, Tabasco sauce, and sausage or ham. Bring to a boil, then stir in rice. Cover, reduce heat, and simmer for 25 minutes. While mixture cooks, peel and devein shrimp. Add to rice mixture and simmer uncovered for an additional 10 minutes. Yields 6 servings.

Prune Bread

5 cups all-purpose flour
8 tsp. baking powder
1 tsp. salt
1 tsp. nutmeg
¼ tsp. ginger
½ tsp. cinnamon
1 cup sugar
2½ cups chopped prunes
4 eggs, lightly beaten
2½ cups milk
½ cup shortening, melted

In a large mixing bowl, combine flour, baking powder, salt, nutmeg, ginger, cinnamon, sugar, and prunes. In a separate bowl, beat eggs, milk, and shortening, then add to flour mixture, stirring until moistened. Pour into two 9" × 5" greased loaf pans. Bake at 350 degrees for 1 hour. Cool in pans for 10 minutes, then remove bread from pans and cool on wire rack.

Baked Oysters with Blue Cheese
(For the adventuresome eater!)

½ lb. peeled young potatoes
4 tbsp. milk
4 tbsp. olive oil
2 tbsp. chopped parsley
2 dozen fresh oysters with shell
Salt and pepper
2 egg yolks
4 tbsp. dry white wine
⅔ cup cream
3 oz. crumbled blue cheese

Cook potatoes in salted, boiling water until tender. Drain well and mash with fork, adding in milk, olive oil, and parsley. Open oysters and separate the bodies from the shell. Reserve the juice and set aside. Discard top shell, wash bottom shell carefully. Beat egg yolks together with wine in double boiler and cook until mixture doubles in volume. Continue to beat while cooking. In another pan, mix together cream and blue cheese. Bring to a boil for 2–3 minutes, then remove from heat. Add oyster juice and fold this mixture gently into the egg yolks. To serve: Fill oyster shells with mashed potatoes. Put oysters on top, and cover with sauce. Place under grill for 5 minutes until mixture becomes golden brown. Add salt and pepper to taste. Serve hot.

Fried Okra

1 lb. okra
3 tbsp. all-purpose flour
2 egg whites
1½ cups soft bread crumbs
Vegetable oil
Salt

Wash okra and drain well. Remove tip and stem end, then cut okra into ½" slices. Coat okra with flour. Beat egg whites until stiff peaks form, then fold in okra. Stir in bread crumbs, coating okra well. Deep-fry okra slices in hot oil until golden brown. Drain on paper towels and sprinkle with salt. Yields 4 servings.

Ava's Favorite Rum Hurricane

2 oz. dark rum
2 oz. light rum
1 tbsp. passion fruit syrup
2 oz. apricot nectar
2 oz. strawberry nectar
2 tsp. grenadine
2 tsp. lime juice

Shake well with ice and strain into a hurricane-shaped glass filled with ice. Beware!

Carmela's Sour Cherry
Cream Cheese Spread

4 oz. cream cheese
2 tbsp. chopped dried sour cherries
2 tbsp. slivered almonds
1 tsp. honey
1 tsp. fresh lemon juice
1 drop of almond extract

Mash softened cream cheese in a bowl; add in the rest of the ingredients plus a dash of salt. Spread on toasted English muffins or bagels. (Note: In a pinch you could use sour cherry jam.)

Photo
Finished

This book is dedicated to my husband,
Dr. Robert Poor.

Acknowledgments

Heartfelt thank-yous to mystery great Mary Higgins Clark; my wonderful agent, Sam Pinkus; my sister, Jennie, who is always first reader and critic; my mother, who devours books and asks for more (I can't write that fast—no one can!); good friend and cheerleader Jim Smith; all the tea drinkers and scrapbookers who have been so wildly enthusiastic over this series; all the marvelous writers and editors who have been so kind in their reviews; all the hard-working booksellers who put my books on their shelves and into the hands of readers; and to all the enthusiastic readers who enjoy both the Scrapbooking Mysteries and the Tea Shop Mysteries. I continue writing because of you!

Chapter 1

THE LAST THING Carmela Bertrand wanted was a cocoa-almond body scrub that would leave her smelling like a Zagnut bar. But that was what Jade Ella Hayward was trying to push on her. Tonight of all nights. When Carmela had twenty scrapbook fanatics crammed into her tiny little shop in the French Quarter, primed and pumped and ready for an all-night crop.

"No, thanks, Jade Ella, really," protested Carmela. As it did for so many women who lived in New Orleans, the high humidity seemed to keep Carmela's skin hydrated and free of tiny lines. Or maybe it was just her youth or the sparkling blend of DNA her parents had gifted her with.

"Look," said Jade Ella, batting dramatic, kohl-rimmed eyes, "you helped me out by taking those great photos. See . . ." She shoved a newly printed flyer at Carmela. "I even used one on the cover of my new brochure."

"That was nothing," protested Carmela. "A happy accident."

Jade Ella held up a finger adorned by a sparkling citrine that was roughly the size of a Buick. "And Spa Diva's just opened, so now's the time to come and enjoy a little complimentary pampering. Before the crowds hit. Before we become a *huge* success."

Spa Diva was the newest, ritziest day spa in New Orleans and Jade Ella Hayward its major investor. A pantheon to women's desire for the latest in beauty, hair treatments, and pampering, Spa Diva was located in a rehabbed shotgun house on the upper stretch of Magazine Street, where dozens of decorators' studios and art galleries were clustered.

Carmela's blue eyes crinkled politely as she quickly ran a hand through her mane of tawny blond hair. She had nothing against spas; she'd just never had much use for them. Hadn't had *time* for them since she'd opened Memory Mine, her little scrapbooking shop, over a year earlier.

But the very insistent Jade Ella was the estranged wife of Bartholomew Hayward, the proprietor of Menagerie Antiques, which sat right next door to Carmela's shop. Bartholomew Hayward did a land-office business selling eighteenth-century oil paintings and antique furniture. And he had always struck Carmela as the sort of fellow it might be best to tread lightly around.

So Carmela accepted the complimentary spa certificates and thanked Jade Ella profusely. It was the best way she could think of to get Jade Ella on her way and herself back to the gaggle of customers who were clamoring for attention.

"Why don't you and your friend, Ava, come in next Saturday," shrilled Jade Ella as she zipped her marabou-trimmed ivory satin jacket and slung her jewel-encrusted Fendi bag over her shoulder. Waggling her fingers at Carmela, Jade Ella disappeared out the door and into the Saturday night throng. "Tootles," she sang over her shoulder.

Gazing out her front window at her own slice of the French Quarter, Carmela experienced the slight contact high that always seemed to reverberate in the two-hundred-year-old neighborhood also known as the Vieux Carré.

She knew that right now, over on Bourbon Street, raucous music clubs and strip bars were huckstering in visitors like mad, even as house bands banged out funky, eardrum-busting tunes.

A few blocks over, on Royal Street, the atmosphere would be slightly more rarefied. Antique shop windows gleaming with captivating treasures: oil paintings, antique silver, and elegant estate jewelry from a more genteel era. Flickering candlelight would beckon seductively from behind the paint-peeling shutters of old-world restaurants, and the clink of crystal and pop of the wine cork, along with the tantalizing aroma of Creole and Cajun cuisine, would lure hungry visitors like moths to the flame.

And here, on Governor Nicholls Street, the hand-lettered sign hanging in her front window boldly proclaimed CROP TILL YOU DROP! TONIGHT!

Carmela grinned widely as she suddenly caught sight of a small woman with a cap of tight red curls barreling down the street. Then, a moment later, Tandy Bliss, laden with bulging scrapbook bags, shouldered open the painted blue door and tumbled in.

"Tandy!" exclaimed Carmela, rushing to embrace her dear friend and newest guest. "We weren't expecting you for another four days and now here you are!"

"Honey, my sanity was severely in question," declared Tandy wearily, adjusting scrapbooking bags on her small frame like a wrangler adjusting a pack horse. "Darwin wasn't one bit happy with me, but I had to bail." Darwin, Tandy's husband of twenty-five years, had "volunteered" Tandy to stay with his sister, Elvira Bliss Wilkerson, up in Ponchatoula. Tandy was supposed to help with the kids while Elvira was in the hospital.

"How did Elvira's surgery go?" asked Carmela as they pushed their way past the two large folding tables she'd wedged into her shop to handle customer overflow, and headed for the big craft table at the back of the store.

Tandy stopped dead in her tracks and planted bony hands on slim hips. "Are you *kidding*?" she said, her voice rising to a decibel level that could only be called shrill. "Elvira wasn't even *in* the hospital! She gave us this big song and dance about needing my help because she had to undergo major surgery. And then all they did was scrape her feet!"

The dozen or so women who were packed in at the two temporary craft tables collectively stopped what they were doing and stared at Tandy. Looking askance as well, Carmela ran a hand through the tawny mass of shoulder-length hair that framed her face.

"She had her feet scraped?" said Carmela. She paused. "What exactly *is* that, anyway?"

Waving a hand disdainfully, Tandy continued her journey toward the back of the crowded shop. "Search me," she said. "Something to do with bunions and calluses. Or maybe it's blisters and hammer toes. Anyway," Tandy proclaimed, "I'm here to tell you that Elvira and that insurance agent husband of hers spawned four totally hideous children. Bona fide hellions, every one of them."

Tandy slung her scrapbook bags down on the big wooden table at the back of the store and grinned widely at the women sitting there. "Hey there, chickens, I'm ba-ack," she announced in a singsong voice.

Baby Fontaine and Byrle Coopersmith, two of Carmela's regulars, murmured warm hellos. They were used to Tandy's antics and crazy greetings. Since they were all scrapbook fanatics of the first magnitude, they saw each other almost every day. But Gabby Mercer-Morris, Carmela's young assistant, immediately jumped up to give Tandy a big hug.

Tandy reciprocated the hug and delivered a quick peck on the cheek to Gabby. Then she turned her attention back to Carmela. "But enough about my trials and tribulations," said Tandy. "Look at the gang *you* pulled in tonight, Miss Smart Business Lady. What have you got here? Almost twenty people?"

Carmela nodded and gave an appreciative gaze about her scrapbooking shop. Truth was, she was utterly thrilled at the turnout for her first all-night scrapbook crop. Besides her regulars like Tandy, Baby, and Byrle, another *sixteen* women had shown up. Hunkering down at the tables and ponying up twenty dollars each for unlimited use of Carmela's ample stock of stencils, punches, sheets of peel-off lettering, colored pens, and fancy-edged scissors.

As a lucky strike extra, Carmela and Gabby were also planning to serve steaming mugs of homemade shrimp chowder, as well as all the pecan popovers and honey butter a hungry scrapbooker cared to snarf.

After getting Tandy settled in, Carmela threaded her way back through the tables, giving a suggestion here, passing out pens and scissors there. She couldn't help but feel a burst of pride at how well her little scrapbooking shop was doing. She'd logged long hours and suffered sleepless nights to pull off her business venture. And now that she had eighteen months of real-time business ownership under her belt, she was feeling a lot more confident, a lot more hopeful that she'd be able to continue eking out a small but respectable profit.

But being an independent woman had recently taken on a new meaning for Carmela. Because besides being financially independent, she'd been forced to reclaim her independence as a single woman, too, when Shamus Allan Meechum, her husband of barely one year, had walked out on her. Had literally slipped out the back door of their Garden District home one afternoon and boogied his way into seclusion at the Meechum family's camp house in the Barataria Bayou.

Had Carmela been shocked by this turn of events? Truth be told, she'd been rocked to the core.

Had she subsequently been filled with doubt, self-recrimination, and guilt over her part in the breakup? Hell no.

Carmela's estranged husband had always been a strange duck. The youngest one in the Meechum clan, the same Meechums who'd owned and operated the high-profile Crescent City Bank for the past hundred and twenty years, Shamus had been born with a silver shoehorn in his Gucci loafers. He'd been a trust fund kid who'd coasted blissfully through most of the major chapters of his life. Shamus had attended the right school (Tulane), played the right sport (varsity football), lived in the right part of town (the Garden District), and celebrated life's holidays, holy days, and personal triumphs at the right restaurants (Antoine's or Galatoire's—jackets and reservations always required).

Carmela had been the one wild card aspect in Shamus's life. Unlike Shamus, she was not descended from old French and English families, but instead laid claim to being half Cajun and half Norwegian. Or Cawegian, as her dad had always joked. Plus Carmela had been born and bred in the more blue-collar city of Chalmette.

But their courtship, seemingly unhampered by social conventions, had been passionate, romantic, and swift. They were both people who spoke their minds freely, were fiercely independent yet ruled by deep-seated emotion, and were, in general, prone to acting impetuously.

Only, to Carmela's way of thinking, Shamus had been a little *too* impetuous.

Because, unlike most members of the Meechum clan, Shamus hadn't fallen in love with the variances and vicissitudes of the banking business. Shamus was moody, some would say a dreamer. Shamus had an artistic bent, as did Carmela. In fact, Carmela had always figured the "art factor" was what had attracted them to each other.

Still, Shamus had gone into the banking business per his family's wishes, diligently learning the ins and outs of mortgage banking, calmly dealing with slightly nefarious real-estate developers, carefully parsoning out loans, and, along the way, building a solid reputation and nice little fiefdom for himself.

Then all hell had broken loose. First, Shamus left banking. Two days later, he left Carmela.

Carmela suddenly blinked back tears at the searing memory of Shamus's unexpected departure.

Good heavens, don't let the waterworks turn on now, Carmela told herself as she quickly bent down at the nearest table, where Dove Duval and Mignon Wright were busy with a craft project that involved Chinese paper fans. *After all, the man's been gone for over a year.*

"These look fantastic," Carmela told the two women. Dove and Mignon had rubber-stamped various Chinese characters onto heavy white card stock, tinted those images with bronze and gold paint, then cut them out and adhered them to bright red Chinese fans. As a finishing touch, they were adding more stamped images and attaching old Chinese coins and red tassels to the fans' black lacquer handles.

"The fans are announcements for a party I'm throwing in a few weeks," Mignon told Carmela. "Aren't they fun?" She smiled up at Carmela, eager for approval.

"Your invitations are absolutely delightful," Carmela told Mignon and Dove. "But the two of you are almost finished. What are you planning to work on the rest of the night? I hope you brought along lots of photos so you can work on a few scrapbook pages."

"Oh, we have to leave early," explained Dove, who was already making motions to pack up her craft bag.

"But we'll be back next week," Mignon assured Carmela. "I'm thinking of decorating some little tins to match. You know, to hold party favors?"

Carmela was always amazed at how the whole scrapbooking thing spilled over so wonderfully into dozens of other projects. Scrapbooking itself was fantastic, of course, what with all the album choices and gorgeous papers that were available. But enhancing your page layouts with stickers, rubber stamps, tags, tiny charms, and ribbons inevitably led to so many more craft projects. Carmela noted that tonight about half the ladies were working on scrapbooks per se, while the other half were creating cards, invitations, tags, and stamp collages. One woman had a tea party planned for the upcoming holidays, so she was crafting darling little invitations that also featured a small side pocket. When her invitations were finished, she'd be able to tuck a small tea bag inside as well.

Darling, really darling, thought Carmela. *I should do some of those pocket-style invitations for my Christmas window display. Didn't I just see some boxes of spiced holiday tea down the street at the Ashley Place Gift Shop? Sure I did. Those would work perfectly.*

Carmela squeezed past the two folding tables back to where her regulars were holding court and sat down.

"Look at this, Carmela," said Gabby. "Tandy brought jars of strawberry jam for us." Gabby was her usual prim-looking self tonight, attired in a silk blouse and wool slacks, her fine brown hair held back in its inevitable pageboy by a black velvet ribbon.

Tandy continued to unearth jars of strawberry jam from her seemingly bottomless bag and slam them down on the big wooden table that normally served as the epicenter for Carmela's "craft central."

Gabby picked up one of the jars and studied the viscous red contents. "This looks absolutely delicious."

Tandy nodded her head of tight curls and squinted at Gabby. "It should be, honey. Ponchatoula lays claim to being the strawberry capital."

"Of the state?" asked Gabby, who was the only one sitting at the table who was, as they say, "from not here." In other words, not a native of Louisiana.

"Of the universe," cackled Tandy. "Every place I went people plied me with strawberry goodies. I came home with strawberry jam, strawberry sauce, strawberry preserves . . . why, one of Elvira's cousins even presented me with a bottle of homemade strawberry vodka. The darn stuff is candy apple pink!"

"I bet that strawberry vodka would make one heck of a Cosmopolitan," offered Baby. Baby Fontaine was fifty-something, very pixieish. And, with her immaculately coifed blond hair and bright blue eyes, she was still a stunner. Carmela thought Baby still possessed the vivaciousness of the sorority girl she'd been when she'd gotten her nickname. And, of course, her nickname still suited her perfectly.

"Oh, I don't know about that," murmured Gabby. "Martini drinkers are awfully *particular*."

"You talking about your husband, honey?" asked Baby. Gabby was married to Stuart Mercer-Morris. The Mercer-Morris family that owned *beaucoup* plantations and car dealerships.

Gabby nodded. "Stuart's a martini purist. His idea of the perfect dry martini is a big splash of gin and then a contemplative moment where he only *imagines* a shot of vermouth."

"No olive?" asked Tandy.

Gabby shook her head.

"You say the vodka's pink?" asked Carmela with a crooked grin. "Maybe you could create a vodka drink that's an homage to the end of the Cold War." She waited a beat, then dropped her punch line. "Call it Pinko."

"Love it!" giggled Baby.

"Gosh, Carmela," exclaimed Gabby, "you really should be in marketing."

"I *was* in marketing," Carmela reminded her. "Two years of designing labels for Turtle Chili, Catahoula Catsup, and Big Easy Étouffée." Carmela had been, in fact, low man on the totem pole when she'd worked for the in-house design group at Bayou Bob's Foods.

"We're delighted you chose to open your scrapbook shop instead," said Baby, reaching across the table to squeeze Carmela's hand. "We *love* coming here."

A door scraped open at the very back of the shop.

"Judging from all that raucous laughter, I guess everyone has thoroughly embraced the idea of an all-night crop," called a familiar voice.

Carmela's head whirled around. "Ava?"

"Who else?" said Ava. The back door closed behind her with a *whoosh* and she sauntered in, leading a small fawn-colored dog on a leash. A very wrinkled dog.

"Hey there, Boo," exclaimed Gabby, easing off her chair and kneeling down to pet Carmela's little dog. Boo, every inch a lady, held out her delicate shar-pei paw in greeting.

Ava shrugged out of her fringed leather jacket and tossed back her wild mane of auburn hair. "We just had a nice walk-walk, then we did our doo-doo in the alley," said Ava. "Now we're here to say hewwo to Momma."

Gabby took Boo's paw in her hand and waved it at Carmela. "Hewwo, Momma," she said in a high-pitched voice.

"Good lord," declared Tandy. "Why is it people always feel compelled to talk baby talk to dogs?" Although Tandy was crazy over kids, especially her grandchildren, no one would ever call her a pet fancier.

"Because dogs are just like children," offered Baby, who had reared and loved dozens of blue-eyed Catahoula hounds of her own. "Dogs are gentle, innocent, trusting creatures."

"*Hell-o,*" said Tandy. "You honestly think *children* are innocent, trusting creatures? You'd change your tune fast enough if you were stuck with my sister-in-law's tribe. Those kids make the bushmen of Borneo look like a bunch of Methodist ministers." She paused, gazing around the table at the bemused group. "Don't take that the wrong way," she told them. "*I'm* Methodist."

"Anyway," said Ava, "I assume it's okay for Boo to stay?"

There were affirmative murmurs from everyone as Gabby unfurled a blanket for Boo to cozy up on.

"Just don't let her nibble any glue sticks," advised Carmela. "She has a very touchy tummy."

"Tell me about it," said Ava, unsnapping Boo's leather leash. "One time Boo gnawed apart a sisal rug in my store and then oopsied all over the floor. Afterward, we had to pull strands of sisal out of her mouth like we were reeling in fishing line. Lucky it didn't get kinked around her—"

Carmela stood up so fast her chair almost tipped over. "Ava, do you think you could help Gabby serve the popovers? She's been keeping everything warm in the back office."

"Oh, sure thing," said Ava, checking her watch. "Gosh, it's after nine. I guess you guys are pretty hungry by now."

Ava Grieux, formerly Mary Ann Sommersby of Mobile, Alabama, was the proprietor of the Juju Voodoo and Souvenir Shop over on Esplanade Avenue. Carmela had met Ava after she was tossed out of Shamus's Garden District home by Glory Meechum, Shamus's older sister. Ava lived in an apartment above her voodoo shop and managed the two little apartments on the bougainvillea-filled courtyard behind her shop where Carmela had finally ended up renting a place.

"Whatcha serving, honey?" asked Tandy as she pulled a scissors from her bag and proceeded to cut a deckled edge on a sheet of mulberry paper. She was going to use it as a backdrop for a grouping of photos.

"Shrimp chowder and pecan popovers," said Carmela. "The chowder recipe is one of my momma's favorites and the popover recipe is Baby's."

Baby nodded and adjusted the Hermès silk scarf that sat coiled like a perfect smoke ring around her neck and shoulders. "Actually, my Aunt Cecily's," she amended. "She grew up on a pecan plantation in Bossier Parish, don't you know?"

Carmela turned toward one of the flat files to pull out a sheet of vellum paper to also try with Tandy's scrapbook layout when a second sharp rap sounded at the back door.

Baby arched her perfectly waxed eyebrows. "Another late arrival?"

Carmela frowned. "We weren't expecting anyone else." The cobblestone alley out back was awfully dark and dreary. And, besides the utterly fearless Ava, nobody in their right mind ever came in that way.

Indeed, the alley behind Memory Mine and the neighboring Menagerie Antiques was so dark and narrow it was used only for deliveries to the various neighboring businesses.

Carmela hurried to the back door, flipped the latch, and pulled the door open.

"Carmela," said a deadpan voice.

Bartholomew Hayward, proprietor of Menagerie Antiques, stood gazing at her with a look of sublime dissatisfaction on his normally unhappy face.

"Barty," Carmela said. "Come in. You just missed Jade Ella. She stopped by a few minutes ago."

Bartholomew followed Carmela a few steps inside, pointedly ignoring her reference to his soon-to-be ex-wife. "*You're* certainly open late," he said in a tone that was almost accusing.

"We're having an all-night crop," Carmela explained. She waved a hand to indicate the three tables of women who were engrossed in their various scrapbooking and craft projects. She noted that Dove Duval and Mignon Wright, who'd been seated at the first table, had finished packing their craft bags and were now headed out the front door.

Bartholomew Hayward continued to stand in Carmela's back hallway like an imperious ballet master surveying his ballet corps. "You're going to have to move your car," he announced in a petulant tone.

Gabby poked her head out of the temporary kitchen that was really Carmela's office. "Billy said it was okay to leave Carmela's car there."

Carmela flashed an inquisitive glance at Gabby.

"I took him a popover and some honey butter maybe an hour ago," Gabby explained.

"Well, it *isn't* all right," said Bartholomew. "In fact, Billy had no right to grant you permission. I'm expecting a delivery later on and I'm sure you're well aware that parking is absolutely *horrendous* around here. Besides which, those two parking spots out back are specifically leased to *me.*"

"I'll move my car," Carmela assured him. She sure didn't need Bartholomew Hayward creating a stinky scene when the evening seemed so alive with creativity and wonderful karma.

"Excellent," said Bartholomew. He still wore a dubious expression on his face, which indicated it wasn't *really* excellent at all. In fact, he looked as though he didn't quite believe Carmela. Or had expected her to put up more of a fuss.

Ava strolled out of the back office carrying a silver tray piled high with giant pecan popovers. "Hey, Barty, grab yourself a popover," she said, tipping the tray toward him.

"No, thank you," he said in his clipped tone. Then he spun on his heels and was out the back door in a flash.

"Bring those right over here, Ava, *I'd* love one," said Tandy after the door had swung shut behind Bartholomew. "That man is *such* a sourpuss," she declared. "I wish Billy wasn't working for him, but the boy is just nuts over antiques." Billy Cobb was Tandy's nephew. He'd been working as an assistant to Bartholomew for the past six months or so.

"Billy plans to open his own antique shop someday," added Tandy, obviously proud of her nephew.

"I bet he will," said Baby, ever the cheerleader.

"Do you know Billy goes cruising up the River Road in that old truck of his, going to tag sales and yard sales?" said Tandy. "When he finds something nice, like an old wooden ice chest or a picture frame, he brings it home and refinishes it. Does a remarkable job, too. Then he takes his restored treasures over to the Sunday flea market at the fairgrounds in Livingston Parish. Lenore says he's already cleared something like two thousand dollars."

"Billy has a very enterprising spirit," said Gabby. "Plus I think some of Bartholomew Hayward's customers find him far nicer to deal with than Barty himself."

"Lord sakes, don't ever say that in front of Barty," warned Tandy. "He'd fire Billy for sure if he thought his customers were tight with him." She shook her head in a gesture of exasperation. "If you only knew what that poor boy puts up with . . ."

Carmela nodded. She had a pretty good idea of how tough it might be to work for Barty Hayward. The man was a legend in his own mind. Arrogant, overbearing, and not particularly friendly. Plus his prices were awfully high and the authenticity of his furniture often seemed questionable.

"Billy's a good kid," said Carmela as she slid a sheet of pink vellum in front of Tandy. "I'm sure he'll do fine."

"I hope so," said Tandy as she moved one of her family photographs around, looking for the best placement on the page.

"How about using this vellum to ghost over that group shot of your grandkids?" asked Carmela.

Tandy beamed. "Perfect," she declared. "Give it a nice soft-focus quality."

Gabby emerged from Carmela's office, balancing another heavy tray laden with mugs filled with steaming shrimp chowder. "Now be careful everyone," she warned. "Push your scrapbooks and such aside. We don't want any accidental spills ruining all your hard work." There was a two-minute flurry while everyone slipped photos, papers, and projects into plastic protective envelopes. Then, as Gabby began to pass around mugs of chowder, the aroma of shrimp, onions, and cayenne pepper permeated the air.

"Is this strictly formal or are we allowed to dunk?" asked Baby as she tore off a hunk of popover and tentatively dipped it into her chowder.

"Please do," insisted Carmela. "And you'll have to adhere to our strict rationing policy tonight. Due to our overzealous kitchen crew, you're expected to snarf down a minimum of three popovers per person!"

"Yum," said Tandy, who weighed barely a hundred pounds soaking wet.

"Carmela," said Gabby, returning from her rounds with an empty tray. "Your car?"

"Holy smokes," said Carmela, scrambling to her feet. "I almost forgot." She dug in her jeans for the keys. "Barty's probably going to have a hissy fit if I don't get moving."

Gabby set down the tray and put out a hand. "Here, give me the keys. I'll go move your car."

"You sure?" asked Carmela. She'd parked out back a few hours earlier to make it easier to ferry in boxes of rubber stamps, colored ink pads, and a lacquer tray filled with fun earrings and pendants. She'd created the pendants by pressing rubber stamps into clay. Because they were somewhat sizable, the pendants hadn't been completely dry, and it had been just her luck to bobble the tray in the dark. Almost as though she'd had a premonition that Barty Hayward was skulking around somewhere, trying to prohibit any possible infringement on his parking spaces.

"You should stay here at the store," said Gabby. "After all, it's your show."

"I don't think you're going to have much luck finding another parking space close by," Carmela told Gabby. Indeed, parking in the French Quarter was nearly impossible. Police cars continually prowled the narrow streets and any cars parked in unauthorized zones were immediately towed. "You'll probably have to drive way over to Esplanade." Esplanade was where Carmela lived. Where *her* overpriced monthly parking spot was located.

"No problem." Gabby grinned. "Besides, I always wanted to get behind the wheel of your Mercedes and take it for a spin."

"Then knock yourself out," she said, passing the keys to Gabby and suddenly recalling the circumstances that had precipitated her getting the sharp little 500 SL. An issue involving Shamus had come to a head the previous March. On Mardi Gras day, in fact. And her beloved vintage Cadillac, the one she'd nicknamed Samantha, had been completely totaled in a nasty accident.

Overcome with a sense of love, shame, drama, indebtedness, whatever, Shamus had decided to present her with a brand-new Mercedes sports car. It was a hot and truly gorgeous car, and Carmela had been consumed with countless hours of guilt once she'd finally accepted it.

But I also love that car, Carmela reminded herself. *And back then,*

Shamus was making positive signs toward reconciliation. Funny how all that seems to have totally evaporated. So what should I do now about what appears to be a somewhat murky future? File for divorce and move on? Yeah, maybe. Keep the car? Oh sure.

"That's a cute sweater," remarked Baby, as Gabby shrugged into a heavy cardigan. I like that nubby look."

"Gettin' cold out," said Gabby, grabbing her purse. "Be back in ten minutes. Fifteen at the most."

PULLING OPEN the back door, Gabby stepped outside and was immediately enveloped in darkness. *Spooky*, she thought to herself and wished she'd asked someone to keep a watchful eye out, just until she climbed into Carmela's car and popped the locks on the doors.

As Gabby headed for the car, strains of music drifted out from the C.C. Club next door and from Dr. Boogie's down the block. At the end of the block, where the alley emerged onto Royal Street, there was a muffled *clunk*, then the crash of glass.

Startled, Gabby's head jerked, and she scanned the alley warily. She didn't see anyone lurking in the shadows. Still, this wasn't the best place to be walking alone on a Saturday night.

She tossed the car keys up in a casual, whistling-in-the-dark sort of gesture. But grabbing for them, Gabby fumbled the recovery and was dismayed when she heard a faint *clink* as they hit the ground.

Gabby peered downward.

A sudden scraping noise, dull but distinct, sounded somewhere off to her right.

Gabby froze, her attention suddenly riveted on the hulking metal Dumpster some twenty feet away. She wondered if someone might be over there. Crouched down. Hiding.

As if on cue, the moon slid out from behind flimsy cloud cover and spilled eerie light into the dark alley.

And at that very moment, someone . . . Gabby's fleeting impression was that it might have been a woman . . . bolted from behind the Dumpster and headed down the alley toward Royal Street. But whoever it was kept close to the rear of the buildings as they ran, staying in darkness.

Heart pounding wildly, Gabby put a hand to her chest, trying to steady her nerves, willing herself to breathe a sigh of relief.

That's when she saw the body.

A man. Sprawled directly in front of her on the cobblestones, limbs awkwardly askew. Surrounded by a puddle of shiny black . . . ohmygod . . . was that blood?

Gabby let loose a blood-curdling scream. A scream that began in the pit of her stomach, resonated in her throat, and cut through the raucous night sounds of the French Quarter like a knife.

* * *

CARMELA, WHO was seated closest to the back door, heard Gabby's shriek of terror. And pounded out the door in a flash. Ava, no slouch herself in the reaction department, was right behind her.

"Gabby!" cried Carmela, bursting through the door, fully expecting to find her assistant half beaten to death or in the process of being kidnapped.

Instead, like Lot's wife turned to a pillar of salt, Gabby was standing stock still in the middle of the alley.

Carmela pulled up short beside her. "Gabby?" she asked quietly, staring at Gabby's stunned face. Clearly, something was very wrong. Gabby appeared to be in shock.

Gabby's eyes were round as saucers as she pointed toward the ground. "Look," said Gabby, her voice sounding tremulous and disconnected.

Carmela's eyes, which were adjusting rapidly to the darkness now, followed Gabby's finger downward. To the body that lay sprawled on the ground.

"Holy shit!" exclaimed Ava, who had skidded to a stop directly behind Carmela and also spotted the body. Ava spun on her fashionably stacked mock croc heels and bounded back into the scrapbook store. "Somebody call nine-one-one," she yelped. "We need an ambulance out back! Now!"

Still paused in the alley, Carmela gazed down at the body with a mixture of curiosity and horror. Close as she could tell, the person sprawled on the cobblestones was Bartholomew Hayward.

Oh my god . . . but I just talked to Barty Hayward a few moments ago. What could have happened? Who could have . . . ?

Suddenly, almost in a gesture of reverence, Gabby knelt down beside Bartholomew, as though she were preparing to minister to the body. Gabby's hand reached out tentatively, then stopped just inches short of Bartholomew's neck. There, imbedded to its hilt, was a large orange-handled scissors.

Carmela sensed more than saw that Gabby was about to reach for the protruding scissors. Was going to grasp it and pull it from the poor man's neck.

Carmela, figuring it had to be the murder weapon, suddenly barked at Gabby: "Don't touch that!"

Reacting to the harshness in Carmela's voice, Gabby snatched her hand away as though she'd just been burned.

Heavy footsteps sounded behind them. Now all of Carmela's customers were pouring out the back door into the alley. The mournful wail and advancing *whoop whoop* of sirens mingled with the strains of jazz and Zydeco music, creating a strange, disjointed cacophony.

A light burst on above the back door of Menagerie Antiques, and a metal door clanked open. Billy Cobb, Bartholomew Hayward's young assistant, emerged, looking startled.

"What's wrong? What's going on?" called Billy. "I heard someone scream." Billy stopped in his tracks the instant he spotted the body, then turned to stare at Carmela, who stood closest to it. "Is that Mr. Hayward?" Billy asked in a small voice. "Is he all right?"

Carmela reached down and gently touched the pulse point on the other side of Bartholomew Hayward's neck. There was nothing to indicate the man was still alive. No movement, no breath sounds, no pulse.

Tentatively, Billy Cobb crossed the twenty feet of alley that separated them.

"Is Mr. Hayward all right?" Billy asked again. His face looked pinched and pale in the dim light, his demeanor hushed.

Carmela straightened up, placed her hands firmly on Gabby's shoulders, walked the girl back a few paces. She was keenly aware that, in a city that boasted forty-one cemeteries, swarms of vampire groupies, and an ever-increasing murder rate, death rubbed familiar shoulders with everyone each and every day. Still . . . in the trickle of moonlight, Barty Hayward's blood glistening like India ink against the pavement was a shocking affront to the senses.

"No, Billy," said Carmela slowly. "Mr. Hayward is definitely *not* all right." Swiveling her head, Carmela saw concern turn to horror on the faces of her customers who were fanned out behind her. *This evening's over,* she thought.

As they all huddled wordlessly, waiting for the paramedics and police to arrive, Carmela's mind flashed on the image of the little sign that still hung in the front window of her store: CROP TILL YOU DROP.

Prophetic words, indeed.

Chapter 2

SILVERWARE CLINKED GENTLY against china, crystal champagne glasses sparkled under antique chandeliers, soft jazz mingled with gentle Southern drawls. At a side table, a chef in a white smock and towering white hat sizzled fresh creamery butter along with sugar, brandy, and egg yolks in a brass chafing dish, creating the perfect sauce to complement the restaurant's heavy-duty bread pudding.

Ava stared over her camellia blossom–garnished mimosa at Carmela. "So Tandy was pretty upset," said Ava. It was an understatement and she knew it.

"Hysterical," said Carmela. "In fact, Melinda Harper finally had to slip her a Valium." Carmela paused, took a quick sip of her own drink, smiled at Ava. "Never underestimate the power of a tried-and-true drug. Especially one from the eighties."

"Didn't the police explain to Tandy that the only reason they wanted Billy down at the station was to give a statement?" asked Ava. "I mean, it's not like they wanted to *arrest* the boy or anything."

"Tandy's always been a little"—Carmela paused, searching for the right phrase—"high strung."

"Unlike the two of us," said Ava, unfurling her white linen napkin and settling it across her lap. "Modern women who are utterly unflappable and totally grounded."

"Completely," agreed Carmela, who had been known to go ballistic over a millipede in the bathroom or a speck of dust on her contact lens.

The two women were sitting in Bon Tiempe, a new restaurant located in the Bywater area that had recently received rave reviews for its Sunday brunch. Bon Tiempe, which translated literally as "good times," was housed in what had once been a rambling old Victorian mansion. Now it was a rambling old Victorian restaurant. Its interior was painted a restful sage green; its wood-planked floors were strewn with faded Aubusson carpets. Overhead, mood lighting was delivered compliments of tinkling glass chandeliers, many salvaged from old plantations.

Bon Tiempe's furnishings were a charming mishmash of styles and eras. Comfortable parlor chairs sat next to Queen Anne chairs, with a couple upholstered Sheraton chairs scattered in for good measure. Sturdy wooden tables of pecan, oak, and pine were set with tall white tapers in silver candleholders and fresh flowers in cut-glass vases. Against the wall was an ornate marble-topped buffet, a curious piece of furniture with carved wooden shelves below and a curlicue wrought-iron backsplash. Today, the buffet was laden with straw baskets overflowing with breads, croissants, and other assorted pastries, as well as large platters of smoked fish and cheese.

With its creaking doors, sagging floors, and atmosphere of genteel decay, Bon Tiempe was definitely in keeping with the general aura that pervaded the whole of New Orleans.

"I'm sorry your all-night crop came to such a screeching halt," said Ava. After the discovery of Bartholomew Hayward's body in the alley, nobody had felt much like scrapbooking.

Carmela shrugged. "Try, try, again."

"You *will* do it again?"

"Oh sure," said Carmela. "But probably not until spring. After Mardi Gras, when things have settled down."

Ava took another sip of her mimosa and gave Carmela a searching look. "Who do you think did it?" she asked in a loud whisper.

Carmela shrugged, shook her head. She'd been asking herself that same question for the past fifteen hours. It was highly probable that the previous night's tragic events had been a random robbery, a casualty of life in the charming but rather dangerous French Quarter, where great architecture rubbed uneasy shoulders with bad behavior. On the other hand, Bartholomew

Hayward could have been purposely singled out. Someone *could* have wanted the man out of the way for good.

"No idea," Carmela told Ava. "But the whole event does inspire chills."

"What do you . . . *did* you know . . . about Bartholomew Hayward?" asked Ava.

Carmela had to think about Ava's question. Bartholomew Hayward had always been rather standoffish and sour, barely exchanging more than a few sentences with her in the eighteen months since her scrapbook shop had moved in next to him. The displays in Barty Hayward's front window had always been tasty . . . mostly spectacular oil paintings, Tiffany lamps, and Chinese vases. But some of the larger pieces in his store, particularly the furniture, seemed . . . questionable. On the few occasions Carmela had stayed late to work on the books, redo her front window, or complete a scrapbook project, she'd noticed covered trucks rumbling up to Bartholomew Hayward's back door. Trucks that seemed to be filled with fairly new pieces of furniture. Carmela knew that in the antique business, it wasn't unusual for middlemen or dealers to take an old serving board or dressing table, break it up, and then use a smattering of the authentic parts to construct three or four *new* pieces.

But rather than relating all this to Ava, Carmela simply said, "Bartholomew Hayward always seemed like pretty much of a loner."

"Uh-huh," said Ava. "Which explains why he's in the throes of a nasty divorce." Ava extended a hand and wiggled her fingers, beckoning Carmela to give her more. "But you must have *some* suspicions."

Carmela shook her head. "Nothing specific. Although I don't think it was random like one of the police detectives theorized last night."

"Cold-blooded murder then," whispered Ava, obviously enjoying this immensely.

"Or some sort of confrontation gone bad," surmised Carmela. "The assault itself on Barty might not have been premeditated." She paused. "But it might have . . . *evolved* into murder?" She tried the idea out, decided it might hold water.

"With who as a suspect?" prompted Ava.

"Could be anyone," replied Carmela. "A disgruntled customer, a vendor who got stiffed, an unhappy employee."

"Employee? Good heavens, you're not thinking of Billy Cobb, are you?" exclaimed Ava.

"No, not Billy." Carmela smiled. "He's a good kid. And apparently a very hard worker. Really, the murderer could be anyone." Carmela picked up one of the menus the waiter had left for them and scanned the list of entrees. Everything sounded incredible. "We should think about ordering," she told Ava.

Ava squinted at the freshly printed parchment paper where the entree choices were listed. "Escolar," she read slowly. "Wasn't Escolar the name of a drug kingpin?"

"That's Escobar," said Carmela, thinking. *Oh, oh. I forgot how picky Ava can be when it comes to food.* "Escolar is particularly tasty, with nice firm white meat."

Ava wrinkled her nose. "I think I might need somethin' a tad more traditional," she drawled. Ava was okay with familiar fare such as crawfish étouffée and blackened catfish, but she was having trouble with the notion of grilled escolar served over sweet red peppers and lavishly garnished with tarragon butter.

"What do they call this style of food again?" Ava asked.

"Local food critics, such as they are, credentialed or not, have dubbed it Cajun Fusion," replied Carmela.

"Mmm," murmured Ava, clearly not impressed. "Look at this," she went on, scanning the menu. "Crab fritters on avocado with citrus dressing. Everybody knows you serve crab fritters with red beans and rice. Honey, this is more like Cajun *Con*fusion."

"Bon Tiempe's supposed to be one of the hottest places in town," said Carmela. "Of course, that doesn't mean it's the best," she hastily explained. There was a greasy little hole-in-the-wall joint down the block from her that served the best oyster po'boys, bar none.

Ava laid her menu down and gazed around. Every table was filled, the bar was bustling, and a line had formed just inside the front door. "The joint *does* seem to be jumping," she admitted. Languidly, she lifted her hair from off the back of her neck and let it fall in lush waves. "And the owner, the good-looking fellow who's standing over there talking to the woman with the peculiar red hair. What's his name? Craig? . . . Grigg?"

"Quigg," said Carmela. "Quigg Brevard."

"He's not only adorable," said Ava in a stage whisper, "I hear he's the last of a dying breed . . . an eligible bachelor."

"I hadn't really thought about it," replied Carmela, who actually *had* thought about it, but didn't want to stare at the man and make an idiot of herself.

"Well, *he's* noticed us. In fact, oh . . . hang on to your pantyhose, sweet-ums . . . I think *Monsieur le restaurateur* is charting a direct course to our table!"

Carmela had met Quigg Brevard, Bon Tiempe's owner, at a dinner party some two months earlier. In fact, she'd found herself seated next to him. Quigg Brevard had proved to be charming, witty, and handsome.

So why don't I want anything to do with him? wondered Carmela. *Shamus is history and life has to go on, right? Kind of like the Big Muddy, which, come hell or high water, just keeps rolling toward the Gulf. Maybe I'm scared to do something. I'm afraid to take a chance and put myself out there like a yutz. Yeah, that's probably it. That and the fact that I'm still carrying this darned torch.*

Quigg Brevard had indeed made a beeline for their table.

"I heard you had some trouble at your store last night," he said, flashing a wide, dimpled grin at Carmela. Obviously, he remembered her rather well.

"Not exactly at my store," said Carmela. She suddenly felt slightly flushed and wondered if it was the mimosa cocktail she'd just tossed down or because Quigg Brevard's piercing brown eyes were focused so intently on her.

"Hi, I'm Ava Grieux," said Ava, delicately offering a hand to Quigg. "And technically, the murder occurred *behind* Carmela's store. In the alley."

"Charmed to meet you, Miss Grieux." Quigg executed a gentlemanly half-bow. "And you're looking particularly lovely this morning also, Ms. Bertrand."

Carmela smiled back at him, giving praise to the heavens that she'd taken time to apply eyeliner and had worn her almost-Chanel jacket.

"How did you hear about Barty Hayward?" Ava asked. "Was it on the news?"

Quigg tugged at the perfect cuffs of the perfect white shirt that peeked from his impeccably tailored navy jacket. "Are you kidding?" he asked, his expressive eyebrows shooting up. "Rumors have been spreading like wildfire. Half the people eating here are speculating about Barty Hayward's demise. And those are people who live all over the city . . . in the French Quarter, Faubourg Marigny, Garden District, and here in the Bywater. I tell you, *everybody's* heard about it by now. And everybody's got a theory."

There was a sudden cataclysmic crash as the chef at the marble-topped sideboard drove a meat cleaver down, lopping off the head of a giant smoked sturgeon.

So shattering was the noise that Carmela and Ava both flinched.

"Hah!" exclaimed Quigg. "That fellow's probably in a *good* mood over the news."

"The chef?" asked Carmela, with a slight frown, wondering why on earth the chef would be happy over news of Barty's death.

"That's Chef Ricardo Gaspar," explained Quigg, lowering his voice. "Poor fellow's restaurant went belly-up last year when Bartholomew Hayward pulled the plug on financing."

Carmela turned in her chair to study the chef, a swarthy, determined-looking man with dark eyes and sharp features.

"I heard about that," said Ava. "A group of businessmen put money into a couple restaurants that didn't work out."

"That's not exactly true," said Quigg. "The backers, the consortium, really didn't give the restaurants much of a chance to find their niche or turn a profit. From all reports, Chef Ricardo was doing a fabulous job running Scaloppina. The place was steadily picking up steam and they'd garnered some very favorable reviews. But"—he gestured with his hands—"what can you do in six months? In my estimation, it takes a good two years to get a place up and running and really find your market."

"Who else was backing Chef Ricardo's restaurant?" asked Carmela. "Besides Bartholomew Hayward?"

Quigg shrugged. "I don't remember the names of the individual investors. All I know is it was a consortium of fellows. Called themselves Parasol Partners."

Chef Ricardo's cleaver came down again with a murderous thud and diners at several tables turned to stare.

"I'll bet *he* remembers," said Ava, nodding wide-eyed at Chef Ricardo, who returned her gaze then gave a flirtatious wink.

"You do get that feeling, don't you?" said Carmela.

Quigg Brevard grinned widely, showing off perfect Chiclet teeth. "In the end, their loss was our gain. We're delighted to have Chef Ricardo on staff, though he is temperamental."

"You've had problems?" asked Carmela politely.

Quigg shrugged. "We've had our share of jealousies and pissing matches, the usual stuff that goes on in restaurant kitchens. You know, petty political maneuverings that end in a scuffle, a few copper pots being hurled. A minor stabbing . . ."

"A stabbing?" asked Carmela. That sounded a lot more serious than simple political maneuvering.

"Well, not a stabbing per se," laughed Quigg. "Let's just say someone got in the way of a fillet knife."

"Ouch," said Ava.

"In the way of one of Chef Ricardo's knives?" Carmela persisted.

Realizing he'd probably said too much already, Quigg held up his hands in a gesture of appeal. "Understand, dear ladies, my *sous*-chef hails from Ecuador, my *saucier* is a native of Haiti, and my pastry chef came here from the Dominican Republic. When Latin tempers flare, unhappy words are often exchanged and unfortunate things occur in the heat of the moment." He paused. "But enough of kitchen politics. Have you made your selection yet?"

Ava screwed up her face in a look of abject concern. "I'm just not sure about this Cajun Fusion thing."

"Perhaps you'd be happier with something else?" Quigg observed.

Ava batted her false eyelashes. "I would." She hadn't been first runner-up in the Mobile, Alabama, Miss Teen Sparkle Pageant for nothing.

"I could have the kitchen prepare something slightly more traditional," offered Quigg. "*Pain perdu* perhaps, or trout meunière?" *Pain perdu* was the Creole version of French toast, made with French bread. Trout meunière was pan-fried trout with a rich butter sauce.

"*Pain perdu* would be wonderful," said Ava, "along with some of that thick sliced bacon."

"I'll tell your waiter, Jerome," said Quigg. "Now remember"—he held up a finger—"don't judge us entirely by today's menu. I can assure you we haven't abandoned the roots from whence we've come. Tomorrow is Mud Bug Monday: boiled crawfish and hush puppies. And every fourth Thursday is Chicken Pickin' Thursday. Fried chicken with snap peas, dirty rice, and buttered biscuits." He flashed another of his megawatt smiles. "Ya'll come back now, ya hear?" And he was off to greet a new gaggle of guests who'd just flocked through the front door.

"He likes you," whispered Ava.

"He's very nice," replied Carmela, thinking that Quigg Brevard seemed more taken with Ava.

"No, I mean he *really* likes you. As in, don't be surprised if he asks you out," said Ava.

Carmela's cheeks suddenly glowed a bright pink. "I'm still married," she told Ava. It wasn't a very good excuse, but it was all she had at the moment.

"I've been meaning to talk to you about that," said Ava, assuming a stern expression. "I thought you finally decided to file those papers. Get the ball rolling on the big D. Make it official."

"I've been awfully busy," lied Carmela.

"You've been a coward," accused Ava. "Face it, cookie, Shamus is history. He's not coming back. He's gone wild mustang on you. He got himself a snort of freedom and he likes it too much to give it up." Ava paused, realizing she'd maybe come across a little too rough. "I'll tell you one thing," she said, her voice softening. "Cut yourself loose from Shamus Allan Meechum and you'll find a whole new world opening up for you. Nice respectable men like Quigg Brevard. You could do worse."

"Agreed," said Carmela, fumbling in her purse for a Rolaid.

Do I have heartburn? No, just a broken heart. Will the Rolaid fix it? Hey, at least a girl can pretend.

Twenty minutes later, Carmela was scraping up her last morsel of escolar when what seemed to be a full-scale shouting match suddenly erupted in the kitchen. There was a quick shuffle of footsteps as Quigg Brevard hustled the length of the dining room, then pushed his way through the swinging door into the kitchen. A sudden sharp increase in the decibel level ensued, then the door swung closed with a *thwack* and silence prevailed.

"Fun place to work, huh?" remarked Ava.

"Reminds me of the Gator Grove Cafe over in Algiers," said Carmela. "When I was waiting tables senior year in college, a fry cook tried to eviscerate a surly busboy with a potato peeler."

"That'd do the trick," Ava said with a nod.

"Can I interest you in dessert, ladies?" Their waiter, Jerome, was suddenly hovering tableside, probably nervous about the shouting match that had gone on in the kitchen. "Bread pudding or our homemade granita?"

"Nothing for me," said Carmela.

"Bread pudding," said Ava. "But don't just drizzle a teeny bit of sauce on it. Really drench it."

The waiter bowed, a faint smile playing at his lips. "As you wish, *madame*."

"How can you eat like that and stay a size six?" asked Carmela. She herself was an eight and had to constantly struggle to keep a tight rein on things.

Ava sighed. "Actually, I've let myself go. I've been trying to convince myself that cellulite is really fancy French fat, but it's not working."

Carmela stared across the table at Ava. She had the lean, sinewy body of a New York fashion model.

"Now Sweetmomma Pam is entirely different," said Ava. "She's blessed with a fiery metabolism. That old lady can chow down like a stevedore and never gain an ounce."

"How *is* Sweetmomma Pam?" Carmela asked. Sweetmomma Pam was Ava's maternal grandmother. She'd blown into town a few days ago on the pretext of sightseeing and was just about driving poor Ava bonkers. That was one of the reasons Ava had wanted to go out to brunch today. To get a much-needed reprieve from Sweetmomma Pam.

"She's a TV junkie," said Ava.

"Watching soaps?" asked Carmela.

"No, ordering stuff off infomercials. Yesterday Sweetmomma Pam decided she simply couldn't live without a Flowbee and some kind of greaseless chicken cooker." Ava paused. "Yech, who'd want to eat greaseless chicken?"

"I've seen the ads for the chicken cooker thing," said Carmela. "But what on earth is a Flowbee?"

Ava made a face. "Some kind of weird attachment you stick on the end of your vacuum cleaner. It sucks up your hair and cuts it at the same time."

"Let's hope," said Carmela, "that Sweetmomma Pam never discovers the Internet. Or eBay!"

"Amen," said Ava, as her bread pudding was delivered to their table.

Carmela continued to listen with great amusement to Ava as she babbled on about the trials and tribulations of having a seventy-nine-year-old woman as her houseguest. More than once, she had to put down her fork and indulge in a good belly laugh.

Sweetmomma Pam is something else. Or maybe this rum sauce is finally getting to me, loosening me up. Anyway, it feels good to laugh.

Still, all through dessert, Carmela kept a watchful eye out for the hot-tempered Chef Ricardo.

Chapter 3

AT THREE THIRTY that afternoon Carmela found herself back at Memory Mine. By the time Bartholomew Hayward's body had been packed into the ambulance the night before, by the time they'd all finished giving statements to the police, it had been too late to do more than a cursory cleanup.

The place was still a mess.

Papers, stencils, colored markers, and orange-handled scissors were scattered everywhere. Her back office was catty-wampus and redolent with the remains of shrimp chowder and now-petrified popovers. And the two big folding tables she'd rented from Party Central had to be taken down and stashed somewhere until they could be returned. After all, tomorrow was Monday. Business as usual.

Business as usual. Right. I wonder what business will happen next door tomorrow. Will Billy open up the shop and soldier on, trying to run things? Or will Jade Ella, Barty's soon-to-be ex who hasn't spoken to him in months, suddenly step in to manage things?

She shrugged. There was also the possibility that Menagerie Antiques might just remain dark and shuttered, an ominous reminder of that night's terrible events.

Carmela worked quickly, staying focused on her tasks and making short order of the cleanup. Luckily, the shop was compact in size and fairly well organized. It was easy to replace pens, colored pencils, all the various pairs of scissors with their decorative edges . . .

Scissors. Oh, please don't tell me I stock the same brand of scissors that ended up in Barty Hayward's throat last night!

Carmela rushed to the front of the shop where she had a display of Sure Cut and KeenCo scissors. She scanned the ripple, scalloped, and wave-edged scissors, too, which were packaged in clear blister packs and hung on metal holders.

No. Whew. I didn't think so.

For some reason, Carmela felt relieved. As though she, personally, were somehow off the hook.

But at the same time, she also knew she probably shouldn't have let Gabby go tripping out into the back alley so late at night. That had probably been poor judgment on her part. After all, stumbling upon Barty Hayward's dead body would probably leave the poor girl spooked for quite some time.

Carmela nursed her guilt until all the rubber stamps were put away, all the various 8½" × 11" and 12" × 12" papers were gathered up, checked to make sure there weren't any crinkles or folded corners, then carefully returned to their rightful places in the flat files.

Now, the last thing I have to do is break down these darned folding tables.

Carmela grunted and groaned, until she had the metal legs folded flat and the heavy six-foot tables leaning up against the back wall.

No, this is not going to work. Sure as shootin' we're going to want to dig into those files first thing tomorrow. Okay then, where can I stash these tables until I get someone to help me return them?

There was only one place. Outside. In the back alley.

Eeeyuh. Really? Out there?

Tentatively, Carmela pushed open the back door. She knew in her heart that the tables would be fine if left out here overnight. In fact, if Billy Cobb came in to work tomorrow, and she had a feeling he probably would because he was just that kind of fellow, she could get Billy to help her move them into his back workroom for safekeeping. There was always plenty of space in the workroom.

Tugging, shoving, and grunting, Carmela maneuvered the two tables outside and down the two back steps. With one final effort, she muscled them into place and propped them up against the dingy back wall of her store.

When Carmela was satisfied that the tables blended in fairly well with the dark bricks of the building and probably wouldn't be noticed by anyone passing by, she breathed a sigh of relief. That job was finally done.

Carmela turned around slowly and stared down the alley that, just eighteen hours earlier, had been the scene of a violent and terrible crime.

The words *returning to the scene of the crime* suddenly rumbled through her brain, causing her to shudder. She noted that, already, the October sun hung precariously low and the back alley was etched with shadows.

Last night, black and yellow crime scene tape had been taped and strung everywhere, like a crazed spider's web. Now, just a few desultory strands remained to flap in the wind. A few cars had undoubtedly roared through here, the drivers oblivious.

Carmela stared at the spot where Bartholomew Hayward had been murdered. There was no white chalk outline of the body like you always saw in movies, just a splotch of red spray paint at the point where Bartholomew Hayward's head had connected with the rough cobblestones.

And where the orange scissors had connected with him.

The police had been super diligent last night about taking crime scene photos and had gone to great lengths to attempt to obtain fingerprints. Now, fine white powder covered everything. It clung to the back door of Carmela's shop and the back door of Menagerie Antiques. Powder residue also covered the Dumpster and nearby telephone poles. The darned stuff had even been on

Carmela's car this morning, until she'd run it through the Suds-o-Matic up on Marais Street.

Carmela stared around, her natural curiosity aroused. It was a trait that sometimes got the best of her, often led her into trouble. Today that curiosity was prodding her to wonder exactly how the night's murderous events had played out.

Let's see, how had Gabby told it? Oh, yeah . . .

Carmela took four measured steps forward.

Gabby said she was right about here when she heard the sound of a bottle breaking at the far end of the block. She tossed the car keys up in the air and missed the catch. Then, just as she heard the keys drop, she heard something . . . a noise . . . over by the Dumpster.

Carmela's eyes were naturally drawn to the big brown hulking Dumpster.

So someone had been hiding beside or behind the Dumpster. Then when Gabby paused, or looked over, or whatever she did, they sprinted off down the alley.

Carmela now focused on the back door of Menagerie Antiques. She wondered if somebody had shown up at Barty's back door and lured him outside. Or some kind of furniture shipment had arrived.

Hadn't he said a shipment was coming? Sure he did. Then why didn't I hear the truck?

The answer to that was simple. Because everyone had been talking, laughing, and having a grand old time. Because the noise level inside Memory Mine had been pretty high that night.

Crossing her arms, tapping a foot against the cobblestones, Carmela continued to puzzle out what might have taken place.

Okay, let's just say somebody came knocking at Barty's back door. Barty stepped out, closed the door behind him. Then Barty and his unknown assailant began to talk, argue, struggle, whatever. Then this unknown assailant stabbed him.

Carmela stared down at the red squirt of paint that delineated where Bartholomew Hayward's body had lain.

Then maybe this assailant was startled when he heard Gabby click open the back door. So he squirreled himself behind the Dumpster. That would be the most logical hiding place.

Carmela paced off a few steps to the Dumpster.

She hesitated a split second, then squeezed in between its rusting hulk and the grubby brick wall. Glancing about, she didn't see anything that struck her as particularly interesting. Or threatening. More fingerprint-dust residue. A couple cigarette butts lying on the ground, stuck between the cracks of cobblestones. Gingerly, Carmela lifted the heavy lid of the Dumpster and peered in. A malodorous scent wafted up from its dark interior. Stale beer, rotted food, Lord knew what else.

Okay, stick with this, she told herself as she let the lid slam down. *What happened next?*

When Gabby heard a weird noise and looked around, the murderer . . . because this wasn't just an assailant anymore, but a bona fide murderer . . . tore off down the alley.

Carmela eased herself out from behind the Dumpster and started walking slowly down the alley in the same direction Barty's murderer had fled. In her mind's eye, she was trying to picture the exact escape route the perpetrator might have taken. Head down this alley, pop out on Royal Street, get lost in the crowd. Pouf, it was that easy.

A few shreds of newspaper swirled about Carmela's ankles as she continued down the alley. A couple *geaux* cups, plastic take-away glasses from a nearby bar, had rolled up against a brick wall.

The police searched around for clues, but came up empty.

The closer Carmela got to Royal Street, the more she knew her search was futile. Not much here. An empty cigarette pack, a smashed whisky bottle. Obviously not a highly trafficked alley.

Nothing, she thought. *No wonder the police are positively clueless.*

Five feet from the end of the alley, a faint glint caught Carmela's eye. She stopped and leaned down. Studied the shiny little object. Couldn't believe her eyes!

That's one of my pendants! I must have dropped the darn thing last night when I bobbled the tray climbing out of my car.

Carmela frowned and stared at the embossed gold disk with the fleur-de-lis design. It was definitely one she'd painstakingly stamped out of clay then rubbed with gold paint some two days ago.

But how the heck did the darned thing get way down here?

Carmela reached down to pick up the pendant, hesitated, suddenly inhaled sharply.

One edge of the pendant was seriously flattened. And bore a rather strange impression. One she certainly hadn't stamped there.

Oh my god!

Could it be . . . a partial imprint from the heel of a shoe?

Carmela's eyes bugged out as she was struck with the full implication.

Did Barty Hayward's murderer step on this? The darned thing had obviously been lying somewhere near my car. And neither the clay nor the paint was completely dry. Could the clay pendant have clung to the bottom of the murderer's heel, then suddenly flown off right here? Sure, it could have.

Carmela's theory sounded plausible to her, but would the police see it the same way? No, probably not.

They'd already called in their detectives, uniformed officers, and crime scene technicians to the scene. The whole lot of them had shuffled around, scowling, smoking, cracking jokes, and making official grumblings. Then they'd packed up and left. Hadn't really bothered to quiz her or her customers all that much.

So what do I do now?

Her instincts told her exactly what to do.

Reaching into her pocket, Carmela pulled out a Kleenex tissue. Carefully, without touching the top of the little hand-crafted medallion, she scooped it up.

Okay, now what?

Carmela stared at the squashed medallion.

What I should do is take a digital photo. Then show it to Gabby or Tandy or Baby and see what they think. It's got these weird initials on it. Maybe they'll know if that's a designer logo or something.

The notion encouraged her. At least she'd be doing *something* positive.

Can I get a good enough photo of it?

That thought made her smile.

Of course I can, especially if I sprinkle the medallion with some of that embossing powder I use to enhance rubberstamped images on cards and invitations. After all, embossing powder probably isn't all that different from the powder real forensic labs use.

As she hurried back to her store, Carmela found herself on edge and curiously excited.

Look at me. All worked up over finding what could turn out to be a very weird clue to a real-life killer. Am I completely nuts or what?

Please, she told herself, *don't even answer that.*

Chapter 4

THEY SAY THE devil sometimes pops up when you least expect him. Unpredictably, unforeseeably, certainly unwelcome. Such was the case when Carmela heard a sharp knock on her door that evening.

She glanced at her watch. Nine o'clock. *Who's plotzing around out there this time of night? Ava? Can't be, I just had a gab with her an hour ago. Told her all about the medallion with the heel impression.*

Carmela rose from the creaky wicker chaise lounge where she'd been curled up, surfing her seventy-five cable channels, searching for a scintillating forensic TV show, and padded to the front door in her stocking feet. Rolling over in her cozy L. L. Bean dog bed, Boo uttered a half-hearted yip, then dropped her head back onto the pillow. A wet snore gurgled from her well-padded muzzle.

Some watchdog you are, thought Carmela.

Carmela peered through the peephole in the door. Shamus Allan Meechum was standing there in the small courtyard outside her apartment. Her tall, curly-haired, good-looking, soon-to-be ex-husband.

Shamus! What the heck does he want?

Reluctantly, Carmela took the chain off the door and let him in.

"Hey, babe." Shamus gave a lazy smile as he brushed by her, his larger-than-life personality immediately insinuating itself in the confines of her small apartment.

Carmela closed the door and gave a quizzical glance.

What just happened here? I was cozied up, skimming a magazine and surfing channels, when suddenly this big galoot breezes in and changes the entire character of my place.

She peered at her apartment with its coral red walls, earth-tone sisal rug, and flea market furniture that had been reupholstered in cream-colored cotton duck fabric. Along with some antique-shop buys, most from scratch-and-dent rooms, she'd managed to concoct a semblance of casual chic. But Shamus's presence seemed to throw off the whole *atmosphere*. Suddenly, everything felt tilted and out of focus.

The notion that Shamus had waltzed in and impacted the character of her home greatly perturbed Carmela. Which meant she didn't waste time with pleasantries.

"What do you want?" she asked Shamus bluntly.

Shamus, ever the Southern gentleman, favored Carmela with a look that fairly dripped with concern. "I've been worried about you," he said in the soft accent he'd picked up from his mother, who hailed from Baton Rouge.

"Why?" Carmela asked in a neutral tone.

"Carmela," Shamus replied with what seemed like genuine surprise. "I heard about Bartholomew Hayward's murder last night." He shook his head. "Poor Barty. Terrible thing. He went to Tulane, you know."

"Do tell," said Carmela. Shamus had gone to Tulane and considered all Tulane alumni kindred spirits.

"And for his murder to have taken place in the alley behind your shop," continued Shamus, "well, that's just way too close for comfort!"

"Oh, that." Carmela resumed her position on the chaise lounge, crossed her legs, stared pointedly at the television set. The minute Shamus had brought up Barty Hayward's murder, she'd decided she wasn't going to tell him about the little medallion she'd found in the alley. The one that carried the mysterious heelprint with the initials GC.

Carmela had never encountered a designer with the initials GC, but that didn't mean she couldn't start looking. Who knew, maybe an Internet search would turn something up.

Without waiting to be invited, Shamus plopped himself down next to Carmela, put a hand on her bare ankle. "You're always in the wrong place at the wrong time, aren't you?" he remarked. A Cheshire cat grin lit his handsome face; his brown eyes sparkled.

Carmela fought the urge to reach down for one of her loafers and whack Shamus upside of the head.

"I'd say I was certainly in the wrong place at the wrong time two years ago," she replied. "On June twelfth." June twelfth was their wedding date. She was always very careful to refer to June twelfth as their wedding date and not their anniversary. After all, anniversaries were what *married* people celebrated. Married people who lived together and honored those little ol' vows of love, honor, and respect.

"Say now, darlin'," purred Shamus, "that's not very sweet. I myself harbor extremely fond memories of that particular date."

Fond memories. Carmela stared at her loafers again, felt her fingers twitch. *The man is a cad, an absolute cad.*

"So," said Shamus. "Do the police have any suspects? Or, at the very least, a best guess?"

Carmela picked up the TV remote control, turned the volume down a notch.

"No," she said. "Do you?"

Her question was meant to be smart-ass and facetious, but Shamus immediately assumed a thoughtful expression.

"Since you ask, I'd probably have to put my money on Jade Ella."

Carmela hesitated for a split second, then clicked the television completely off. Shamus suddenly had her clear and undivided attention.

"Talk to me," she said.

Shamus smiled a lazy smile. He knew Carmela was intrigued by what had occurred the night before even though she was scared to death by it, too.

"Jade Ella Hayward was in the process of divorcing Barty," said Shamus.

Carmela nodded. "I know that. I know Jade Ella. She even stopped by the shop last night. Said she *adored* the idea of an all-night crop but was far too busy generating some buzz for the grand opening of Spa Diva."

Shamus nodded. "I heard she was involved in that. So how'd you two get so buddy-buddy?"

Carmela shrugged. The two of them *weren't* particularly friendly. "She stopped by the shop a couple times," replied Carmela. Jade Ella usually came into Memory Mine right after she paid a quick visit to Bartholomew Hayward's shop. On more than one occasion, Carmela had heard their voices raised in bitter argument through the not-so-substantial wall that separated the two businesses.

But, hey, everybody fights, Carmela told herself. *Shamus and I fight. Fought. That's certainly not grounds for murder, is it?*

She peered at Shamus.

From love to hate in the blink of an eye. One day you're head over heels in love, the next day your man is boogying out the door. Or cheating on you. Can emotions flip-flop that fast? Oh yeah. Sure they can. I guess they can.

"You know that Jade Ella absolutely *despised* Barty," said Shamus. "Thought he was a real horse's patoot."

"She was right on that count," said Carmela.

"I also heard Jade Ella poured a fortune into Spa Diva and was frantic over the possibility of being screwed royally in the divorce."

There it is. The D-word, thought Carmela. *Funny how neither one of us has ever verbalized that word before in the other's presence.*

"Were Barty and Jade Ella's divorce papers final?" Carmela asked, painfully aware she'd probably be filing her own divorce papers pretty soon. If she intended to get on with her life, that is.

"Nope," said Shamus, looking pleased. "Nothing was final. *Nada.*"

"So now that Barty's dead, Jade Ella inherits everything?"

Shamus leisurely crossed one long leg over the other. "Looks that way." He reached for a strand of Carmela's hair, fingered it gently. "I love your hair that way. That tawny color really makes your skin glow."

"Thank you." Ava had talked Carmela into letting her hair grow out a little. Now, instead of the chunked and skunked, short and choppy do Carmela had been sporting, her face was framed with softer, slightly more blond locks. Carmela thought her new look made her look more vulnerable. Ava said it made her look predatory.

"So you're saying Jade Ella had a motive for wanting to be rid of Barty Hayward," said Carmela.

Shamus shrugged. "I guess so. I don't know." He smiled lazily at her. "What did you do today?" he asked as Boo finally roused herself from her bed and came over to greet Shamus.

"Went out to brunch with Ava," said Carmela. "Ate too much."

"Ava Grieux, the infamous serial dater," said Shamus, rubbing Boo's tiny triangle-shaped ears. "Hey there, Boo Boo, you like that?" In response, Boo snuggled closer.

"Ava's not a serial dater," said Carmela. "She's just picky. And why shouldn't she be? Given the choice of men in this neck of the woods."

Shamus glanced sideways at her. "Am I supposed to be insulted by that remark?"

"Depends," said Carmela, treading cautiously. "Depends on whether you're back on the market or not."

"I did get a rather gracious invitation to participate in next month's Most Eligible Bachelor Auction," said Shamus. "The one to benefit the Tulane Music Society."

The Most Eligible Bachelor Auction was your basic beefcake venue: a dozen hunky, single men auctioned off for dinner dates to women who had too much time on their hands and too much money. Carmela thought the whole thing was pretty pathetic.

"Did you take them up on it?" Carmela asked him.

"'Course not, darlin'," purred Shamus. "I'm married to you."

Carmela's thumb sought out the On button and clicked the TV picture back on.

"What else did you do today?" Shamus asked.

Carmela stared past him. "Went grocery shopping. Took Boo for a walk."

Shamus waited, obviously expecting Carmela to ask about his day. She chose not to give him the satisfaction.

Shamus's brows suddenly met in a pucker. "You know, Carmela, this is no way to engineer any sort of reconciliation."

Her mouth flew open in surprise. *Who said anything about a reconciliation? That sure came zooming out of left field. And what's this "engineer" business? That's certainly not the correct usage of a verb. Especially when you team it with reconciliation.*

"You're full of shit, Shamus," said Carmela, turning up the full volume of the TV.

"And you're totally hostile," said Shamus.

They pointedly ignored each other for a few minutes. Boo, sensing discord in the ranks, skulked back to her bed. Finally, the anger between the two of them began to dissipate.

"Okay," Carmela said finally. "Sorry."

"Apology accepted," said Shamus.

"But," said Carmela, unwilling to let the subject simply drop, "we have major issues to deal with . . . and I think we need to face reality."

Darn, she thought, *why do I suddenly sound like Dr. Phil?*

"You're not going to threaten to give back the car, are you?" asked Shamus, sidestepping the larger issue. "Because I'm *not* going to take it back," he insisted.

Carmela made a face. Obviously Shamus was in no mood to talk about reconciliation or divorce. Then again, he never seemed to be.

"It's *your* car," continued Shamus.

Carmela stared at him, let a few beats go by. "Ok*aaay*," she relented, experiencing a slight sense of triumph at the look of genuine consternation on Shamus's face. No way was she *really* going to give the car back. She might be colossally ticked at Shamus and ready to divorce him, but she wasn't an idiot. No sir, that little 500 SL was a thing of sheer beauty. V8 engine, 302 horsepower.

Plus, as Ava had helpfully pointed out, the Mercedes had proven to be an incredible man magnet. You could park that puppy anywhere and suddenly, like magic, men came crawling out of the woodwork to drool over it.

"I have a marvelous idea," said Shamus enthusiastically. "Why don't you and I go away together? Spend some time alone?"

Carmela lifted an eyebrow and stared at him. What was this happy crap? They could spend a few nights together, but not their lives?

"We'll drive up to Lafitte's Landing Plantation Inn, get a little hideaway," rhapsodized Shamus. Lafitte's Landing Plantation Inn was an elegant Greek Revival plantation up the Great River Road, just north of New Orleans. Tucked in among other old Victorian and "steamboat" Gothic plantations, it had been turned into an inn some twenty years ago and was famous among honeymooners as well as couples seeking to rekindle romance. The plantation was situated right next to Houmas House, where the Bette Davis movie *Hush, Hush, Sweet Charlotte* had been filmed.

Carmela continued to gaze at Shamus, amazed any man could possess so much unmitigated gall. Shamus had up and left her, bid adios to his job at the bank, and headed off to concentrate on his photography, for goodness' sake! Plus, he'd been spotted squiring various women around town. Carmela sighed heavily. Bad behavior wasn't even the term for it. It was more like bad judgment. Then again, this *was* Louisiana. A state where married governors, senators, and various and sundry politicos routinely courted younger women. Without causing any collateral damage to their careers.

Shamus was still on a roll. "How about this coming Friday?" He sidled closer to her.

"No. Absolutely not," Carmela told him.

"Why not?" Shamus asked.

Carmela folded her arms protectively across her chest. "Because, among other things, I have previous commitments." She was, once again, close to losing her temper.

"Like what?" Shamus challenged.

"Besides being busy at the shop," said Carmela, "this Saturday is Halloween."

"So?" said Shamus.

"The Art Institute's Monsters & Old Masters Ball is this Saturday evening," said Carmela. Monsters & Old Masters was one of the New Orleans Art Institute's big fund-raisers. As Baby had proclaimed, Monsters & Old Masters was rife with the three F's: food, fun, and fund-raising. In this case, the Art Institute was hoping to finance new art acquisitions.

"Not a problem," said Shamus. "I was going to attend myself. Better yet, we can go together."

"Sorry," said Carmela. "But I'm sitting with Baby and Del. They already reserved a table for eight. Besides," she added, "I'm likely to be busy. I've been tapped to create menu cards and twenty description tags for the art and floral displays that are going to be on view."

Shamus ducked his head and threw her an inquisitive look. With his tousled brown hair and slightly olive skin, he looked youthful and boyish. And, truth be told, quite adorable.

Quit it, Carmela told herself. *This marriage is over.* Fini. Finito. *Down the toilet.*

"Okay then," said Shamus. "Grant me another simple favor. Come to dinner with me Tuesday night at Glory's."

"At Glory's?" Carmela's voice rose in a sharp squawk. Glory Meechum was Shamus's older sister and the self-proclaimed matriarch of the Meechum clan. Glory had also led the charge to force Carmela out of Shamus's palatial home in the Garden District after he'd skipped out on her and fled to his family's camp house. Suffice it to say, Glory was not high on Carmela's top ten list of amusing dinner companions.

"Come on, Carmela," said Shamus. "It'd mean a whole lot to her. Hell, it'd mean a lot to *me.*"

Carmela narrowed her eyes, wondering if the invitation to Lafitte's Landing Plantation Inn had simply been a red herring.

Maybe Shamus was confident I'd turn him down on that, and dinner at Glory's was what he'd been angling for all along. Am I nuts to think this way? Yeah, probably. But Shamus makes me nuts.

Shamus scrambled to his feet and flashed her a winning smile. Carmela recognized it immediately. It was his touchdown smile. The same confident, slightly arrogant smile he'd always worn when he played varsity football at Tulane. The smile that, even when his team got royally trounced, said *I did my best, I sure as hell played to win.*

"Tell you what," said Carmela. "I'll be your date Tuesday night, but I'm going to need a small favor in return. Quid pro quo."

"Such as?" said Shamus.

"I'll go with you to Glory's dinner party, but you have to pick up the two tables stashed behind my store and return them to Party Central."

Shamus considered this for a few seconds.

"Deal?" pushed Carmela.

"Deal," said Shamus. "Glory's going to be thrilled."

Carmela gave a disdainful snort. "Glory *hates* me."

"Carmela," said Shamus in a hurt tone of voice, "Glory's your sister-in-law. Of course she doesn't hate you."

"Then how come she banished me from your house after you walked out on me?"

Shamus threw his hands in the air. "That doesn't mean Glory *hates* you, honey. It's just . . ."

"It's just what?" demanded Carmela. She clambered to her feet and placed her hands on her hips, pretty sure now that she'd been blindsided on the dinner invitation.

"It's . . . it's just the way some families are," stammered Shamus.

He leaned down, brushed his lips across the top of her head in a quick semi-kiss, and headed for the door. As the door flew open and chill air wafted in, Carmela was surprised to see a mixture of confusion and unhappiness on Shamus's departing face.

And deep within her heart, in the part where she tried to suppress her true feelings for him, Carmela felt a painful stab.

Chapter 5

"GABBY, I'M SO sorry about Saturday night," Carmela apologized for about the twentieth time. "I should *never* have let you go out back by yourself."

"Carmela, it's okay, really," said Gabby. "I'll get over it. I *am* over it."

It was Monday morning. Gabby had shown up on time at nine o'clock, looking slightly subdued, but certainly no less enthusiastic about her job as Carmela's assistant.

"I was afraid Stuart wouldn't let you come back to work," said Carmela. Gabby's husband of barely two years was a combination worrywart and hard-ass. Stuart was also, as Tandy whispered when Gabby was absent from the shop, a male chauvinist pig. Only Tandy never actually *said* the word, she just spelled it out: p-i-g.

"My coming back to work here *was* an issue," Gabby admitted. "But I promised Stuart I'd never venture into the back alley again, even during day-time hours." Gabby grimaced. "Stuart's not particularly happy making that concession, but I wasn't about to give up a job I love." Gabby adjusted her black velvet headband and nervously picked at a mythical speck of lint on her camel-colored sweater. "Besides, it's not as though murder was a rare occur-rence around here."

Gabby was right. New Orleans was infamous for its nasty murder rate, and the French Quarter had always been a hotbed of trouble. Hot music, hot women, hot tempers.

Gabby smiled broadly. For her the issue was closed. "Okay to put the OPEN sign on the front door?" she asked Carmela as the phone on the front counter shrilled.

"Please," said Carmela.

Gabby flipped over the sign, then swiped at the telephone. "Hello." She listened for a few seconds, then held it out to Carmela. "It's Tandy and she's super upset!"

"Tandy," said Carmela, taking the phone.

"The police kept him until *five* in the morning and now they've called him in again," said the tearful voice on the other end of the phone.

"You mean Billy?" Carmela gasped. *Of course Billy. Who else?*

"It's downright crazy," shrilled Tandy. "Insane. Billy had absolutely *noth-ing* to do with Bartholomew Hayward's death! You know that and so do I!"

"Of course he didn't," said Carmela. "The police are probably just trying to put together a possible timeline or something. Or they're quizzing Billy about acquaintances of Barty's, fishing around for possible suspects."

"No, they're not," blubbered Tandy. "They keep asking Billy about the latex gloves."

"What about latex gloves?" asked Carmela.

"The police found a box of them in Barty's workroom." Tandy paused and there was a loud honk as she blew her nose. "Carmela, this is awful!" she cried. "The police think that, just because they couldn't find any fingerprints, Billy might be involved!"

Billy Cobb involved? No way. Billy was a good kid. Bright, polite, upstanding. Right?

"Has Billy got an attorney?" asked Carmela. She knew that even if you were totally innocent, it was always smart to be represented by a crackerjack attorney. A lot of people learn that one the hard way.

"I already called Baby," sniffled Tandy. "And Del's agreed to represent Billy." Baby's husband, Del Fontaine, was a high-powered attorney and senior partner with the law firm Jackson, Fontaine & DeWitt.

"Okay, honey," said Carmela. "Let us know if you hear anything."

"I might be coming in later," said Tandy.

"Really?" said Carmela, surprised by Tandy's remark.

"There's nothing *else* to do right now," said Tandy, her voice quavering wildly.

Twenty minutes later, Baby Fontaine and her daughter Dawn Bodine, who'd married into the Brewton Creek Bodines, pushed their way through the door. Shortly after that, Byrle Coopersmith, another of Carmela's staunch regulars, also arrived. They were all shocked to hear that the police were now eyeing Billy Cobb as a possible suspect.

"But those latex gloves were used for stripping and shellacking," argued Gabby. "Everybody knows that."

"Sure," said Carmela. "Even *I* keep a box of latex gloves in the store. For when I work with glass paints and things. It doesn't make *me* a murderer."

"Didn't you try to take over part of Barty's space a few months ago?" asked Baby.

"I did," said Carmela.

Baby put a finger to her mouth. *"Ssshhh."*

"All this talk about murder is making me very jumpy," said Byrle. "Can't we just work on our projects for a while?"

"I'm making a vacation scrapbook," piped up Dawn. She was the youngest of Baby's daughters, youthful and vivacious, recently married and just back from a trip to Paris. Dawn was also the spitting image of her mother, only twenty-six years younger.

"What kind of album are you using?" Carmela asked Dawn.

Dawn held up a large square album with a plain cream-colored cover.

"This one. Momma got it for me." She smiled at Baby, who was sitting next to her.

"How would you ladies like a few ideas on how to create your own album covers?" asked Carmela.

"What fun!" exclaimed Baby, pulling out an album of her own. "We design all these wonderful scrapbook pages and sometimes forget that our album covers can be personalized, too."

"Let me show you one quick idea," said Carmela. "And then you can improvise and do your own versions."

"Freestyle," joked Byrle.

"Exactly," replied Carmela as she pulled open cupboard doors, gathering the materials she needed.

"Okay, then," said Carmela, spreading everything out around her. "I'm going to start with this Eiffel Tower rubber stamp. Using gold ink, I'm going to stamp an Eiffel Tower image onto a three-by-three-inch square of light blue card stock."

"You need the colored oil crayons, too?" asked Gabby, hovering nearby.

"Please," said Carmela. She took the box of crayons from Gabby and pulled out a dark blue and a purple crayon. As an afterthought she grabbed a pink oil crayon, too. "Now I'm just going to color in a little bit of the Eiffel Tower," said Carmela, rubbing the oil crayons on the inside and around the outer edges of the Eiffel Tower image.

"Pretty," said Byrle. "Now what? You smudge it?"

"Carefully smudge it," said Carmela. "A *controlled* smudge, like doing your eye shadow. To achieve a soft, almost pastel look. Then we trim the square with a deckle-edged scissors to get a nice torn-edge effect." Carmela trimmed the image, then carefully set it down on the table. It shone like an oversized French postage stamp.

"Now," said Carmela, "we'll take our album cover and adhere this dark blue and purple paisley paper to the right side. On the left side we'll use this light-colored cream and gold paisley paper." Carmela's hands worked swiftly with the papers and adhesive and, in a few minutes, the album cover had assumed a whole new look.

"That's gorgeous," said Dawn. "Very rich-looking. But what about the Eiffel Tower image?"

"I'm getting to that," said Carmela. "Now we take our deckle-edged Eiffel Tower square and paste it on. Not quite centered . . . maybe a little to the right." The Eiffel Tower image went on, then Carmela picked up a calligraphy pen.

"To add a finishing touch to our cover, I'm going to do some hand-lettering across the cream and gold paper." She uncapped a bronze-colored pen, paused for a moment, then bent over the album and began to write in a long, looping script.

Baby watched her closely. "'Paris, City of Light.' Beautiful. Now it's the

perfect album for preserving memories of Dawn and Buddy's Paris trip."
Baby's fingers touched the edge of Dawn's sleeve; she was clearly proud of her
daughter.

"Do you think I could do something similar using heart images?" asked
Dawn. "For an anniversary album?"

"I think hearts would be adorable," said Carmela. "We could even add
some heart-shaped charms for a dimensional effect."

"Could you attach charms to this?" asked Baby, indicating the album
cover Carmela had just completed.

"Oh, absolutely," said Carmela. "Tiny charms, stickers, gold tassels, a
wax seal . . . the more layers you put on, the more depth you achieve."

"Here are some rubber stamps with heart images," said Gabby, passing a
half-dozen rubber stamps to Dawn. "And this handmade mulberry paper has
tiny rosebud petals imbedded in it."

"Wow," said Dawn, clearly impressed.

"That paper comes in cream, white, and pink," said Carmela. "And I
think we also have some pretty gold paper with poetry verses etched in the
background. That would certainly go well with your romantic theme."
Carmela rose from her chair and headed for the front of the shop. "Let me
take a look."

As Carmela was searching through her stock of special papers, the phone
rang. She grabbed the handset.

"Hello," she said, fully expecting to hear Tandy once again.

But it wasn't Tandy. It was Lt. Edgar Babcock of the New Orleans Police
Department. Asking Carmela if she would kindly put together a list of customers who'd attended her scrapbook crop this past Saturday night.

"Sure I will, of course I will," Carmela replied into the phone. *God, am I
babbling? Sure sounds like it. Why am I suddenly nervous?*

"Today, if possible?" asked Lieutenant Babcock.

"Shouldn't be a problem," Carmela told him. She glanced toward the back
of the shop. Everybody seemed involved in their own projects and she was
pretty sure Gabby had kept that reservation list. Positive they had it, in fact.

Lieutenant Babcock's request had also made Carmela suddenly hopeful.

*If the police are looking at other people, surely that means they're not en-
tirely focused on Billy Cobb. On the other hand, they're starting to look at my
customers . . .*

"Shall I e-mail you the list or . . .?"

"I'd like to stop by and pick it up if I could," said Lieutenant Babcock.

"I'll have it ready," Carmela promised him.

"Problems?" asked Gabby as Carmela hung up the phone.

Carmela pulled the gold paper from the front display and hurried back to
her friends.

"Not a problem per se," Carmela answered slowly. "That was a police detective. He's asking for a list of Saturday night's customers."

"Do they suspect someone?" asked Gabby, suddenly looking worried again.

"No, I don't think that's it at all," said Carmela. "I think this is more routine than anything."

"Oh," said Gabby, not terribly convinced.

Uh-oh, thought Carmela. *I hope Gabby doesn't get Stuart all upset about this.*

"You know," said Baby, when there was a lull in the conversation, "there *is* someone who's royally pissed at Barty Hayward."

"Who's that?" asked Carmela. *And why am I not surprised?*

"Dove Duval," said Baby as she carefully traced out a heart-shaped photo frame for Dawn.

"Dove was here Saturday night!" gasped Gabby.

"And, as I recall, she left rather early," continued Baby, lifting an elegant hand and pushing a lock of blond hair behind her ear. "*Before* Gabby went out the back door and rather unceremoniously stumbled upon Bartholomew Hayward's bleeding body."

Gabby turned to Carmela. "That's right, she did. Remember? She and Mignon. They were the ones who bought a bunch of those new rubber stamps. I think they're planning to make holiday invitations or something."

"Will someone please tell me who Dove Duval is?" demanded Dawn. "And is this woman related to the Duvals who live over in St. Landry Parish?"

"She is," said Baby. "Sort of." Baby gazed around the table, her bright blue eyes lighting up as she told her story. "In case you hadn't noticed, Dove Duval is what you'd call a *faux* Southerner. Originally, she was the Mrs. of Dr. and Mrs. Marvin Fleckstein of Montclair, New Jersey. Marvin Fleckstein being a self-proclaimed orthodontia king. But, times being what they are, and marriages not always that permanent, Dove and the dentist decided to divorce a year or so ago. On a trip to New Orleans, where Dove came to heal her wounded psyche and dip her beak into what was supposedly a pleasingly plump settlement, Dove met up with a certain Taurean Duval. The husband market being as precarious as the stock market, Dove wasted no time. She pounced quickly and is now Mrs. Taurean Duval."

"What does Taurean Duval do?" asked Byrle.

"Owns the Dydee-doo Diaper Service," said Baby.

"This is all very interesting," said Gabby, a frown creasing her normally placid face, "but why on earth would Dove Duval have it in for Bartholomew Hayward?"

"I was getting to that," said Baby. "Apparently, in her headlong rush to become an instant Southern lady and receive friends and visitors in her newly acquired Garden District home, Dove Fleckstein Duval purchased an entire *truckload* of what was touted to be genuine Southern plantation antiques."

"Let me guess," said Carmela, "some of them turned out to be fakes."

"Yes!" exclaimed Baby. "How did you know?"

Carmela shrugged. She'd seen the trucks pulling up late at night to Barty's back door. She knew he'd been doing some heavy-duty distressing and refinishing in his back room. Many of the pieces Barty sold were genuine, but there couldn't be *that* much old pecan and cypress left on the face of the earth.

"So Dove Duval could have been more than just a little upset with Bartholomew Hayward," said Gabby. "She could have been furious."

"Why didn't she just sue him?" asked Byrle.

"She was probably too embarrassed," said Baby. "Wouldn't you be? After being flimflammed?"

"Then the question remains," said Byrle. "Was Dove furious enough to kill him? To stab him with scissors?"

The women all paused and looked at each other. In Louisiana, men had been known to kill each other in disputes over prized coon hounds. In many ways there was still a "shoot first, ask questions later" kind of mentality in the South. But did the transplanted Dove possess that same kind of hair trigger? That was the unanswered issue that seemed to perch like a giant question mark on the table.

"So tell me," said Dawn, breaking the tension of the moment, "did Dove Duval finally get rid of all the fakes Barty unloaded on her?"

"Yes, she did, honey," replied Baby. "Dove unloaded them at a flea market over in Baton Rouge. She has since hired a *professional* decorator in her quest to have her home featured in *Southern Living*." Baby paused. "I understand her new decor is quite eclectic."

"Define eclectic," said Byrle as she cropped a large photo into quarters, then prepared to edge each piece with gold foil tape.

Baby's face assumed an impish grin. "It means nothin' really goes together!"

"She should hire Jekyl Hardy," suggested Gabby. "He could get her home straightened out in no time." Jekyl Hardy was a design consultant and one of New Orleans's premier Mardi Gras float designers. He was also a dear friend of Carmela's and sole proprietor of Hardy Art & Antique Consultants. Besides having a real knack for design, Jekyl Hardy periodically gave seminars on art collecting and connoisseurship.

Carmela had remained silent yet highly attentive throughout Baby's story. Now she wondered if this might be the moment to tell everyone about the heelprint she'd found.

Tell them? Not tell them? What should I do?

It was a bit of a dilemma. Then again, there was the off chance someone might recognize the heelprint and shed some light on this whole thing.

Silently, Carmela slid a laser print onto the table. It was an enlarged printout of the enhanced heelprint that had been squashed into her medallion. Only she'd flopped the image so the initials, which had originally looked like interlocking G's, now clearly read GC. The same way you'd see them if you looked at the bottom of the shoe.

"What's this?" asked Byrle, turning the sheet toward her. "Another cover idea?"

"Better than that," said Carmela.

The women listened with rapt attention as Carmela told them how she'd found the little medallion halfway down the alley. And how she'd noticed the heelprint, thought it might be significant, and enhanced the slightly smudged image by sprinkling it with embossing powder.

"Wow," said Gabby, impressed. "You pulled a print. Just like on *CSI*!"

"Not exactly," said Carmela. "You make it sound like I followed crime scene protocol. Instead, it was more like stumbling upon the little clay medallion, then noticing the smudgy heelprint."

"You gonna show us the *real* forensic evidence, honey?" asked Baby, clearly fascinated by all of this.

"You really want to see it?" asked Carmela. She had initially thought the ladies might be a little put off by her amateur sleuthing. Quite the contrary. They seemed *mesmerized* by the idea of trying to track down Barty's killer.

Carmela placed the actual medallion in the center of the table while Gabby slipped into the back office and retrieved a magnifying glass.

"Let me take a peek," said Baby, reaching out a hand to Gabby.

Gabby handed her the glass.

Baby peered forward, studying the medallion with the heelprint. "This is the medallion you crafted from clay," she said. "And you think you dropped it when you got out of your car."

Carmela nodded. "I'm pretty sure I did."

"You're right," said Baby finally. "This definitely looks like it's been stepped on and kind of ground in by—what . . . maybe a lady's heel?"

"What are those, entwined G's?" asked Byrle. "Maybe a Gucci logo?"

Baby picked up a pencil, tapped at the page Carmela had printed out. "Not Gucci," said Baby. "The initials read GC. And see here, there's a little crosshatch pattern in the background."

Gabby took the magnifying glass back from Baby, stared at the now-squished medallion, then at Carmela's printout. Finally, she straightened up and looked around the table. "Anybody ever hear of a designer with the initials GC?"

"No designer I know of," said Baby, her hands unconsciously patting the gold and rust Versace scarf draped about her patrician neck.

"What about a local store?" asked Carmela. "It could be a private label thing."

But nobody could think of a store or clothing shop that had the initials GC.

"Y'all are completely forgetting about Jade Ella," said Byrle. "From what I hear, she and Barty were locked in the throes of a very nasty divorce."

"That's what Shamus said, too," said Carmela.

Gabby flashed Carmela an approving glance. "You're seeing Shamus again?" she asked hopefully.

"No," said Carmela. "Shamus just sort of . . . dropped in on me last night."

"Sounds romantic," said Gabby, ever hopeful that the couple's marriage would rebound.

"It wasn't, particularly," Carmela told her. She looked around into the hopeful faces of her friends. "Don't hold your breath concerning Shamus and me."

"Well, this information about Jade Ella and Dove is certainly intriguing," declared Baby, getting back to the main thread of their conversation. "It seems that both women had a serious ax to grind with Bartholomew Hayward."

Dawn nodded excitedly. "They really did, didn't they!"

"And both ladies generally wear high heels," said Baby, ever the fashion maven.

Gabby looked around the room, wide eyed. "I swear, it *did* kind of sound like someone in high heels taking off down the alley."

"So either Dove Duval or Jade Ella Hayward could be considered a suspect," said Baby.

"Or Chef Ricardo," said Carmela. "But only if he wears Cuban heels."

This new entry, tossed so casually into the pot, brought a stunned silence to the table.

Finally, Byrle spoke up. "Who on *earth* is Chef Ricardo?"

Carmela quickly related her brunch experience from the day before and explained about the withdrawal of financing from Chef Ricardo's ill-fated Scaloppina Restaurant.

Baby nodded. "That's right. I *heard* about that. In fact, I think Del's firm might have represented one of the parties in a lawsuit. Turned out to be a real mess."

"Buddy and I dined at Scaloppina once," volunteered Dawn. "They served the best crab risotto I ever tasted." She looked thoughtful. "Sad that the place had to close."

"And under unfortunate circumstances, it would appear," said Byrle.

"Sounds like Bartholomew Hayward might have had a few enemies," said Gabby.

There were nods all around.

"Since this appears to be a crime of passion," said Carmela, "what we need to do is try and figure out who hated Barty the most." She gazed about the table, studying the troubled faces of her friends. "Anybody got any bright ideas?"

No lightbulbs clicked on.

Chapter 6

TANDY CAME STEAMROLLING in just as Carmela, Gabby, and Baby were eating salads that had been delivered a few minutes earlier by the French Quarter Deli. Dawn and Byrle had packed up their craft bags and left an hour earlier.

"You poor thing," said Carmela, jumping up from the craft table to greet Tandy. "Come on back here and tell us what's going on. You want part of my salad?" she asked as she led Tandy toward the back. "Baby field greens with smoked turkey?"

Gabby and Baby focused looks of concern on Tandy. She seemed tired and distracted. Her usual tight mop of curls was frowsled. Already skinny to begin with, Tandy looked wan bordering on frail.

"Nothing to eat, no, thanks," said Tandy as she collapsed into the wooden chair Carmela pulled out for her.

Carmela stared pointedly at Tandy. "Things aren't going well," she said as she sat down next to her. It was a statement rather than a question.

"You wouldn't believe it," said Tandy. "This has turned into the worst possible nightmare." She leaned across the table and grasped Baby's hand. "Thank goodness Del agreed to represent Billy. He's the only bright spot in all of this."

"He's happy to help," Baby told her. "We all are."

"If there's anything I can do . . ." began Gabby.

Tandy flashed Gabby a sad smile. "You're a sweetheart, but . . . well, we're all just in a hold pattern for now. As you might expect, Donny and Lenore are absolutely hysterical." Donny and Lenore were Billy's parents, Donny being Tandy's younger brother.

"What news is there, if any?" Carmela asked, trying to steer Tandy away from the emotionalism of the issue and more toward actual facts.

Tandy leaned back and sighed. "Billy hasn't been formally charged with anything yet, but the police are completely hung up on those latex gloves."

"I can't see where the gloves are all that relevant," said Carmela. "Especially since Billy and Bartholomew Hayward and whoever else helped out in the back room wore them whenever they were doing furniture stripping or refinishing."

Tandy grimaced. "There's another little wrinkle."

"What's that?" asked Carmela, her ears perking up.

Tandy shifted uneasily in her chair. "The scissors that were found in Barty Hayward's neck?"

"Yes?" said Carmela. *Come on, Tandy, spit it out.*

"The police found a couple flecks of gold paint on them. Similar to the gilding used to touch up frames in Barty's workshop."

"Ouch," said Gabby.

"That's not so good," said Baby, commiserating.

"Still," said Tandy. "The gold paint can be *explained.* And the scissors could *still* have come from Bartholomew Hayward's workshop."

"Did Billy have any flecks of this gilt paint on his hands?" asked Carmela.

"No," said Tandy. "Which is why, I suppose, the police are looking at the latex gloves so hard."

"What possible motive do the police think Billy had?" asked Carmela.

"Oh, honey," said Tandy, "they'd sooner grill someone to death and figure all that out later. I tell you, it's a travesty of justice."

Baby nudged a sharp elbow into Carmela's side. "Tell Tandy about the heelprint," she said in a low voice.

"What heelprint?" asked Tandy.

Pulling out her medallion and her printout, Carmela quickly related her story of finding the wayward little medallion in the back alley, noticing the heelprint, then enhancing the heelprint via embossing powder and her computer.

Tandy was stunned. "This is fabulous, Carmela!" She leaned forward and planted a grateful smooch on Carmela's cheek. "This almost *proves* there was someone else in the alley that night."

"No, it doesn't," said Carmela.

"Hallelujah," sang Tandy, grinning ear to ear. "I'm going to tell Billy all about this wonderful *Exhibit A.*" She smiled over at Baby. "And Del, too. In fact, I see it as a major break in the case!"

"Please don't tell anyone," protested Carmela. *Holy smokes, we don't know a thing about this print and Tandy's already got her hopes up. Maybe I shouldn't have even told her about it.*

"Then I'm going to tell Billy that a star investigator is hot on the trail of the murderer," said Tandy with great excitement.

"You shouldn't get your hopes up based on this," said Carmela. "Even though a few of us have studied the heelprint, we're still utterly clueless."

"Hope is the one thing that will see us through this," said Tandy fervently as she dug in her voluminous leather purse and pulled out a set of keys. "Here," she said, shoving the keys toward Carmela. "Billy asked me to give you these."

Slowly Carmela accepted the keys. She knew exactly what they were for. They were the keys to Menagerie Antiques next door. *Gulp. What's all this about?*

"Billy said he *trusted* you," said Tandy. "You see, there are a couple customers who might stop by to pick up things. Billy thought if you had the keys to the store you could help out. As if you haven't done enough already!"

"How will I know who these customers are?" asked Carmela with a puzzled expression.

"Oh, you won't," said Tandy blithely. "In fact, it's pretty much a hit-or-miss proposition. But if a customer *happens* to stop by here, and they're clutching a receipt in their hot little hand, *then* you could let them in." Tandy paused, slightly out of breath. "Could you do that?"

Carmela nodded. "Sure." She figured it was the least she could do. Barty Hayward hadn't been a particularly hospitable neighbor, but Billy was always polite and friendly. Plus he *was* Tandy's nephew.

Baby reached out and grasped Tandy's hands. "Come back tomorrow, will you? No sense sitting around and just stewing. We'll have some fun designing labels." Baby tried to project an upbeat attitude. "You've got all those wonderful jars of strawberry jelly, I always make a gazillion batches of applesauce for the holidays . . ."

"Carmela makes her special caramel sauce," said Gabby jumping in, trying to keep the ball rolling.

"What do you say?" prompted Baby. "Are you game?"

"Okay," said Tandy as she gathered her coat around her. "Why not."

It wasn't until after Tandy had left that Carmela remembered several of *her* customers had been using gilt paint on Saturday night.

They were painting highlights on the edges of party invitations and scrapbook pages, weren't they? Uh-oh, please don't tell me it was one of my customers who stabbed Barty Hayward. Especially not . . . what's her name? . . . Dove Duval.

"ARE THOSE for this Saturday?" Baby asked Carmela, nodding at the array of colored squares and photo corners spread out on the table. "For the Monsters & Old Masters Ball?"

"They will be if I ever get them done," Carmela answered.

Monsters & Old Masters was actually a spin-off of the Art Institute's springtime Blooming Art Ball. During Blooming Art, two dozen pieces of artwork were selected for special display, and the same number of art patrons were tasked with creating floral arrangements that interpreted and complemented the artworks.

One year, Baby had been assigned a Claude Monet painting and she'd created a spectacular display of lilies and hyacinths floating in a Waterford crystal vase.

Because Blooming Art had proven to be a real money maker, and because party-hearty, costume-loving New Orleans folk were already head over heels in love with Halloween, Monsters & Old Masters, the slightly darker cousin to Blooming Art, was spawned.

Of course, the artworks that the museum selected had to remain in keeping with the Halloween theme. Which meant that many of the artworks had a spooky, slightly unsettling edge. Among the pieces selected by the current year's committee was a painting by American artist Josephus Allan of the Hudson River School, which depicted one of the Salem witch trials. Edward Hopper's American-nostalgia style of art was also represented. And, at the last minute, the committee had added a dark and moody seventeenth-century painting of Roman ruins to the twenty chosen pieces.

The autumnal floral arrangements were equally in keeping with the Halloween theme: flowers in subdued autumn colors, baskets of dried leaves and grains, twisted twigs, grapevines, and branches of bittersweet.

"I've been asked to create menu cards as well as descriptive tags for the art and floral pairings," Carmela explained to Baby. "It's kind of a fun little project."

"What's on the menu?" asked Gabby. She was eagerly looking forward to attending her very first Monsters & Old Masters Ball on Saturday night. Baby and Del, always so generous, had reserved a table for eight and invited Carmela and Ava, Gabby and Stuart, and Tandy and Darwin to join them.

"Let's see," said Carmela, consulting the list that had been faxed to her earlier. "Crawfish bisque, citrus salad, roast duck, sweet potato praline casserole, cranberry bread pudding, and lemon bars."

"To die for," moaned Gabby. "I can't wait!"

"The Art Institute always could put on a decent spread," commented Baby. She glanced at the red marbleized card stock on which Carmela had printed out the menu in twelve-point scrolling type. "That looks pretty. Now whatcha gonna do with it?"

Carmela picked up a rubber stamp and, above the headline that read MENU, stamped an image of a woman that had been taken from a seventeenth-century painting.

"First the artsy image," said Carmela. "Then we'll add a hint of mystery." She picked up a second rubber stamp and stamped over the first image, giving the woman an elaborate mask.

"Cute," said Baby.

"Now I'm going to faux finish these black photo corners using gold, red, and bronze-colored paint."

"Wow," said Gabby, suddenly getting interested. "Detail work."

"Then," continued Carmela, "I'll use the photo corners to mount the menu card onto a second and slightly larger card of marbleized *brown* card stock."

So intently was Carmela working that she barely heard the bell jingle over the door. Until the noise finally penetrated her consciousness and she looked up to find Jade Ella Hayward staring at her.

"Jade Ella!" Carmela must have jumped a foot. Here was the wife of the deceased Bartholomew Hayward studying her with the faintest of smiles on her face. Dressed in a spiffy poison green suede jacket and black leather slacks, rings sparkling from almost every finger, and her dark hair swooshing about her kohl-rimmed eyes and bright red mouth, Jade Ella had obviously not given a passing thought to looking the part of the grieving widow. She was her usual glam self.

"Carmela," said Jade Ella, in the clipped manner of speech she was famous for. "Have you seen Billy?"

A shocked silence followed her question. Baby and Gabby stared with open mouths.

Finally Carmela spoke up. "The police are talking to him."

"They are?" said Jade Ella, blinking, favoring them with a polite yet distant smile.

"Carmela means they're *talking* to him," said Baby, finally finding her voice. "About Barty's death."

Only then did Jade Ella seem to react. "You mean to say Billy's a *suspect*? Billy Cobb? Barty's assistant?" She paused, obviously digesting this. "Hmm."

Gabby, who was still surprised to find Jade Ella acting so chipper, finally stammered out, "I'm sorry for your loss, Jade Ella."

Jade Ella whirled toward her, eyes blazing. "Don't be. Barty and I weren't particularly close. In fact, we weren't particularly on speaking terms."

"Have you finalized funeral arrangements?" asked Baby, who was too well bred to be put off by Jade Ella's blasé attitude.

"At first I thought about having Barty cremated," said Jade Ella. "That way I could have the thrill of tossing his worthless ashes into a Dumpster behind the Wal-Mart store. But a small contingent of Barty's friends thought he deserved a slightly more dignified send-off. So, in consideration of those folks, as well as the many loyal customers he's managed to screw over the years, I've opted for a more traditional funeral." Jade Ella smiled broadly, enjoying her own theatrics. "The whole nine yards, in fact. Fancy-schmancy casket, ordained minister, final interment at Lafayette Cemetery No. 1." Jade Ella paused, her eyes flashing, silently daring anyone to make a comment. "Ain't that a kick?"

"It's very considerate of you," said Baby. Her patrician eyebrows were cranked up more than a few notches.

"Not really," said Jade Ella. "I myself, in keeping with my new Spa Diva image, will probably wear a red silk dress and dash off early for a fashionable luncheon at Galatoire's." She struck a dramatic pose. "I shall most likely order the trout amandine and a nice glass of Pouilly-Fuissé."

"You can't go wrong with Galatoire's trout amandine," Baby agreed.

Carmela feigned a cough to stifle her giggle. *Count on Baby for the perfect retort.*

"Listen, Carmela," said Jade Ella, "you used to do a lot of label designs, didn't you?"

Carmela nodded.

"Well, here's the thing," said Jade Ella. "I'm seriously thinking of launching my own line of cosmetics, too. I'd start by retailing them at Spa Diva. If that venture goes well, and I have no reason to believe it won't, I'll set up a website and maybe even get placement in a few upscale stores."

Carmela gaped at Jade Ella. Her idea *sounded* good, but rarely were new products launched with that much ease. And the money needed for private labeling and a marketing launch was enormous. Bordering on astronomical. Jade Ella didn't have that much money, did she? Or had Bartholomew Hayward carried a lot of insurance?

"Anyway," said Jade Ella, "I immediately thought of you as the package designer. You have such an artistic flair!"

"Thank you," said Carmela, doubting the project would ever come to pass.

"We'll put our heads together real soon," said Jade Ella, who was already making tracks for the door. "Ta ta." She waved a hand and a pair of large gold charm bracelets jangled noisily. "See you."

"I'd say that woman suffers from Mrs. Bling Bling syndrome," joked Baby after Jade Ella had gone. "Too much gold, too many gemstones. Worn all at once."

Carmela had to agree with Baby. Jade Ella was pushy beyond belief and always decked out like a show horse. Still, she was a female entrepreneur who had just launched her own business. And even though the add-on cosmetics line seemed awfully pie-in-the-sky, it was no small feat, especially in a city like New Orleans, for a woman to succeed. Carmela did wish Jade Ella well, even if she was put off by her attitude.

"Well, you could've knocked me over with a feather when Jade Ella told us about the funeral," announced Gabby. "How can a woman be so cool, so totally *arctic*, about her dead husband?"

"Give it a few years," laughed Baby. "The sanctity of marriage ain't always so sanctified." She paused, realizing what she'd said, then assumed a slightly embarrassed look. "Well, *some* marriages, anyway," she backpedaled. Baby paused, gathering her thoughts. "Did you know that Jade Ella has been dating Clark Berthume?"

"Seems to me I've heard that name mentioned in connection with money," said Gabby. "Is he one of those fellows with money?"

"Piles of it," replied Baby. "Old money."

"That's the best kind," agreed Gabby.

"Don't you remember, honey," continued Baby, "Clark Berthume runs that new photo gallery over on Toulouse Street? What's it called?"

"The Click! Gallery," said Carmela. "Click with an exclamation point at the end."

"The Click! Gallery," repeated Gabby. "Sure."

"I peeked in there a couple weeks ago," said Carmela. "They actually have some marvelous photos. Prints by Ansel Adams, Copanigro, and Minor White. Great stuff."

Truth be known, Shamus had confided to Carmela a few weeks earlier that he'd been angling to get a small show of his own in the back gallery at Click! He'd told Carmela that scoring his own show would finally validate his work. Carmela had told Shamus that his photos were terrific, always had been terrific, and if he wanted *real* validation, he should go out and earn a paycheck. Shamus had pouted, telling Carmela he felt hurt and grievously injured by her harsh response. Carmela had replied something to the effect of "tough cookies."

A sharp knock on the back door prompted an immediate look of anguish from Gabby. "I thought you said you were going to keep the back door locked," she exclaimed.

"I am," said Carmela. "And *please* don't fret over every bump and thump, because it's probably Ava. She still prefers to pop down the alley," said Carmela, scurrying to let her in. "Even after what happened."

"I've only got a moment," said Ava as she burst into the shop, "but I just had to stop and say hi, see what everyone's up to."

"Hi, Ava," called Baby.

Gabby eyed Ava suspiciously. "Have you lost weight?" Ava was dressed in skin-tight blue jeans and a low-cut cashmere sweater with froufrou feathery trim.

"It's just my long-line bra," Ava confided. "Holds all the fat and stuff in."

Gabby peered at Ava's thin frame. "You sure don't look like you have all that much to hold in," she said dubiously.

"Trust me, I do," said Ava. "Hey, remember that great quote . . . a woman can never be too rich or too thin?"

"I believe those words have been attributed to the Duchess of Windsor," offered Baby.

"Really?" said Ava. "Gosh, I thought it was Oprah. She's always so darned clever. Oh well." Ava whirled toward Carmela. "Hey girl, we still on for tonight?"

"Anytime after six," said Carmela as the phone started to ring. Ava was going to come over for dinner, then they were both going to work on projects.

"Carmela," called Gabby. "Phone."

"See y'all later," called Ava, dashing out the front door this time.

"Hello," said Carmela, taking the phone from Gabby.

"Carmela, you're going to kill me," said a tentative voice on the other end of the line.

"Natalie?" asked Carmela. Natalie Chastain was the registrar at the New Orleans Art Institute. "Let me guess," said Carmela. "You've got more changes."

"Yes, I do," came Natalie's anguished reply. "And for that I truly apologize. Problem is, the director *still* hasn't finalized his choices."

"I hope you don't have menu changes," said Carmela, alarmed. *Yikes. I just printed the darn things.*

"No," said Natalie. "That's the one thing that seems to be carved in stone, probably because the whole shebang is being catered. But it's the *only* thing, I'm afraid. I'm sorry to tell you, Carmela, that we've got more changes on the art and floral pairings." She paused. "Big surprise, huh?" Natalie had called Carmela twice already with changes. And Carmela had long since decided that the smartest thing to do was to leave most of Friday afternoon open. She'd wait and knock out the twenty description cards then, when it would be too *late* for changes.

"Don't worry, Natalie," said Carmela. "I'm set up to do typography at the last minute so you've got till maybe . . . Thursday." Carmela glanced toward the back of her shop where her new color printer sat hunkered on the counter. *Thank goodness,* she thought. *I can push a button and print out any script, typeface, or hand-lettered font and it still looks like I slaved for hours.*

"We're pulling our hair out over here," continued Natalie, still sounding desperate. "The publicity people . . . our curators . . ."

"What seems to be the problem?" asked Carmela, just to be polite.

"One minute a piece is in, the next minute it's out," said Natalie in a re-signed tone. "We're in complete chaos."

"How on earth are people going to get their floral arrangements done if they don't know which artwork they're supposed to be keying off?" asked Carmela.

"Good question," said Natalie. "But you'd be amazed at how forgiving some of our art patrons are. They think Monroe Payne walks on water. Which, when it comes to the rarefied realm of fund-raising and capital cam-paigns, he probably does." Monroe Payne was the New Orleans Art Institute's rather flamboyant director and a veritable pit bull when it came to wresting money from the town's movers and shakers.

Natalie hesitated. "Besides, not everyone actually creates their *own* floral arrangement."

"The shocking truth finally revealed," laughed Carmela.

"Well, don't tell anyone," continued Natalie. "But I think more than a few of our patrons have enlisted Teddy Pendergast at Nature's Bounty to de-sign floral arrangements for them." Nature's Bounty was the premier floral shop in New Orleans. They could always be counted on for hip, thematic, al-most Manhattanesque table arrangements. For one of Baby's summer dinner parties, Nature's Bounty had created a stunning centerpiece with calla lilies, cattails, and sea grasses sprouting from a giant clump of bright green moss. It had been a huge hit with her guests and subsequently copied by a few other Garden District hostesses.

"Just e-mail me the poop when you have it," Carmela told Natalie. "And don't worry, there's still time."

"Bless you," said Natalie.

Hanging up the phone, Carmela glanced toward the front of the store just as the front door opened and a man walked in. Hesitantly. He was in his midthirties and rather nattily attired in a houndstooth blazer and gray slacks.

Carmela decided he had to be from the police. Nobody else in the neighborhood dressed that well. In fact, most of the art and antique dealers shuffled around in worn jackets, hoping the local pickpockets would assume they were poor.

"Can I help you?" Carmela asked, going up to greet her visitor.

The man reached into his jacket pocket and pulled out a small black leather case. Flipping it open, he showed his ID. But not in an intimidating manner, just a low-key professional way.

Carmela glanced at the ID. "Lieutenant Edgar Babcock. Right. We talked on the phone."

"Actually we met the other night. Saturday night?" said Lieutenant Babcock. He flashed her a shy smile.

Carmela stared back at him. Tall, lanky, with ginger-colored hair, Lt. Edgar Babcock was not an unattractive man.

"You've come to pick up the list," said Carmela.

Now why am I suddenly acting so stiff and formal? Carmela wondered to herself. *Maybe because this guy is, as Ava would say, a bit of a hunk? Too bad Ava didn't stick around a little longer. She would've been intrigued by someone in law enforcement.*

Carmela glanced toward the back of the store where everyone was casting surreptitious glances toward the front.

"Uh . . . wait here a moment, okay?"

"Sure," said Lieutenant Babcock. He was suddenly busy, looking at the rack of pens and scissors that was just to the right of the front counter.

Carmela was back in a flash with the list. "Here it is," she said, holding out a sheet of paper.

Lieutenant Babcock accepted the list, folded it into quarters without looking at it, and slid it into the breast pocket of his blazer. "Thanks," he said.

"You're welcome," responded Carmela.

"Do you carry Gemini scissors?" Lieutenant Babcock suddenly asked her. His question obviously did not come out of the blue.

"No," Carmela said. "They're a good scissors when it comes to cutting paper, but the Sure Cuts are better." She continued staring at him. "Is that the kind you found sunk in Barty Hayward's neck? The Gemini?"

Lieutenant Babcock smiled at her. "Not necessarily."

Carmela continued to fix him with a questioning look. "I suppose you have to hold back some information," she said.

"Actually," said Lieutenant Babcock, "someone close to me is a scrapbooker."

"Your wife?" Carmela asked, glancing down at his ring finger.

He followed her gaze. "No, I'm not married. It's my sister. She's got a birthday coming up and that's one of the things on her list."

Carmela smiled at him. "Come back and I'll help you put together a little scrapbooker's gift bag," she told him. "Stencils, rubber stamps, some fun papers maybe."

"It's something to consider," he said.

"Whatever," she said, wondering if there really *was* a scrapbooking sister or if Lieutenant Babcock was just a very skillful interrogator.

"Listen," he said. "I know you gave a statement the other night, but if anything occurs to you, or anything strange happens, give me a call. Okay?"

She nodded.

Lieutenant Babcock pulled open the door, patted his jacket pocket. "Thanks for the list. We'll get back to you."

"Great," said Carmela as the door swung closed on him. Hesitating before she went back to rejoin the group, Carmela considered Edgar Babcock's words. *If anything strange happens . . .*

Anything strange? she thought to herself. *Who's he kidding? This is New Orleans. Everything is strange!*

Chapter 7

BIG EASY SHRIMP was one of Carmela's all-time favorite recipes. You sautéed plump Gulf shrimp in a pan with butter, onions, garlic, green peppers, tomatoes, and spices for barely twelve minutes, then dumped the whole thing on top of hot, steamy rice. And voilà! You had yourself a dinner to die for.

Tonight Carmela's Big Easy Shrimp was accompanied by a nice bottle of Chianti. Not the rough, slightly fermented version in the cheesy raffia basket that most people tippled during their el cheapo student days, but a lovely, lush Montepaldi Chianti. Bottled in a narrow, high-shouldered Bordeaux-type bottle, the Montepaldi was velvety rich, yet delicate in taste and scent. The perfect red wine to complement her seafood dish.

"This is *so* good," exclaimed Ava, digging into her second helping of Big Easy Shrimp. "I wish I knew how to cook. I mean *seriously*." Ava always claimed she followed the slash-and-burn method of cooking. Slash up some meat and vegetables, burn it in the pan.

"Cooking's fairly simple," Carmela told her between bites. "As long as you don't get too hung up on recipes and measurements."

"Is that a fact?" said Ava, reaching to pour herself another glass of Montepaldi. "I would think you'd *have* to measure carefully so things come out right."

"My momma always said cooking was truly about food chemistry," said

Carmela. "That it's more important to be tuned in to flavors and interactions between ingredients."

Ava grimaced. "Food chemistry. That sounds kinda grim and academic."

"It isn't really. For example, it's about knowing how to pair sulfur-based foods with sugar-based foods. Think how tasty onions are with rice."

Ava looked doubtful. "I don't know. I flunked home ec my senior year."

"Come on," laughed Carmela. "Nobody flunks home ec. Trigonometry and physics, maybe. Definitely calculus. But never home ec."

"Our teacher, Miss Fruth, *despised* me. Besides, I was more into class plays, cheerleading, and flag twirling," replied Ava.

"Then you didn't flunk home ec," said Carmela, "you flunked attendance."

One of Ava's crowning glories had come when she was named head flag twirler for the Jefferson High Martinettes. Then, right before graduation, high hopes for a beauty pageant career had led Ava to the Miss Teen Sparkle Pageant where she came in first runner-up. College hadn't interested her, so Ava went on to compete in the Miss Palmetto Contest, the Miss Yellowhammer Contest, and finally the Miss Alabama Contest. Ava was pretty, some might say beautiful, but she did have a certain edge. So when her pageant career didn't pan out as successfully as she hoped it would, Ava moved on to abbreviated careers. She worked as a cocktail waitress, skip tracer, paralegal, and photographer's assistant, which was her longest stint. But Ava finally touched on magic and found her calling: for two years, she'd been running the Juju Voodoo and Souvenir Shop in the French Quarter.

Visitors to New Orleans who came seeking a small touchstone of the Crescent City to carry home with them were captivated by the candles, charms, and trinkets that adorned Ava's shop. And Ava, who enjoyed spinning harmless stories about love charms and pink candles that inspired happiness and good fortune, went on to build a rather thriving business.

But, like Carmela, Ava was also blessed with a flair for the arts. And in the last year, her creative bent had led her to mask making. For the last Mardi Gras, Ava had received orders for more than three dozen custom leather masks. Fanciful bird masks with plumes and beaks, tiger masks, jeweled Venetian Carnivale masks, and even Renaissance masks. For Halloween, orders had once again poured in, and Ava was working frantically to put the finishing touches on the last of her elegant, handcrafted masks.

"Is Sweetmomma Pam still staying with you?" asked Carmela.

"Lord, yes," replied Ava.

"It must be fun having her around," said Carmela, whose own grandparents had long been deceased.

"Are you for real?" said Ava. "Today Sweetmomma Pam ordered a talking watch off some darned TV ad she saw on the cable sports channel. Popped for overnight delivery and put the whole thing on my Visa card."

"Can you send it back?" asked Carmela.

Ava shrugged. "Who knows. Anyway, we had a little talk and then she stomped out. Seems she's got some kind of *date*. Do you believe that? Sweet-momma Pam came here not knowing a soul and now she's cavorting around town like a prom queen."

Carmela stared at Ava. *A seventy-nine-year-old woman was out cavorting? Where? At the local bingo parlor?*

"Where'd she go?" Carmela asked.

"Some senior citizen dance," grumped Ava. "With a *date*. A man. Never mind that *I* haven't had a truly viable date in six months."

"Why, Ava, I do believe you're jealous," said Carmela.

"That's not the worst of it," continued Ava. "I think she might even have a better sex life than I do."

"No way," said Carmela, laughing.

"Listen, cupcake, I came home the other night and found Sweetmomma Pam on the couch, canoodling with Wendell Pickens," declared Ava.

"Wendell Pickens?" said Carmela, alarmed. "You mean the old guy who runs the fruit stand in the French Market? The one who juggles peaches and *cackles*?"

Ava rolled her eyes. "That's the one." She drained her wineglass and set it down with an air of resignation. "Can you believe it? I'm almost twenty-nine years old. I thought for sure I'd be *divorced* by now."

TWENTY MINUTES later, the dishes were cleared from the table and Carmela and Ava were busily working away, Carmela on her menu cards and Ava on a leather mask.

"I'm absolutely in love with that green mask," said Carmela. "But the whole thing seems like such a complicated process." Ava was assembling a mask of iridescent sea green leather. When all the parts were fitted together they would yield the elfin face of a sea nymph.

"Mask making actually *is* complicated," admitted Ava. "First you have to do sketches. You know, figure out what it's going to look like. Then you have to create a paper pattern. That can be anywhere from three to three hundred pieces for a single mask."

"Yikes," said Carmela. "What's the most complicated pattern you've ever done?"

Ava considered this for a minute. "Maybe a hundred and twenty pieces. When I did a really elaborate bird mask with a long beak and leather feathers."

Carmela nodded. "Then what?"

Ava picked up a leather-cutting tool to demonstrate the next step. "Then you cut out your pieces and trim the edges so each piece lies flat against the other," continued Ava. "Moistening and shaping the pieces comes next. Then, when they're dry, you start to assemble all of them."

"Using glue?" asked Carmela.

"A special leather glue," said Ava. "If I'm fastening several layers together or putting in an unusual crimp or bend, I also use a few grommets so the pieces stay where they're supposed to. Anyway, once the mask is assembled, I wet the whole thing again and begin sculpting."

"How do you do that?" Carmela was fascinated by the lengthy process. The only masks she'd ever made were some miniature pressed-paper ones. And Ava had helped her out by creating the initial mold.

"Honey, I use anything and everything I can find," said Ava. "Cuticle sticks, my fingers, a hair dryer. Leather is a very plastic material, so it moves and molds."

"You're really amazing," marveled Carmela. "The patterns, all those pieces . . ."

"Oh, give me a break," said Ava, pushing a frizzle of auburn hair out of her eyes. "And you're *not* creative? Look at all the stuff *you* do! Scrapbooking, rubber stamping, crime solving . . ."

"Crime solving?" said Carmela with feigned innocence.

"Don't play coy with me, cookie. I know you're dying to figure out who whacked Bartholomew Hayward."

Carmela snorted.

Ava peered at her sharply. "You are, aren't you?"

"Aside from the fact that it happened right behind my store and in front of my number-one employee, yes, I am," replied Carmela. "Especially if it will help bring some peace to Billy and Tandy and their family. Problem is, there seem to be a number of people who were pretty ticked off at Barty Hayward."

"The almost ex-wife," said Ava. "Jade Ella. The one who gave you those complimentary passes so we can get waxed, buffed, and sloughed at Spa Diva."

"She dropped by the shop today," said Carmela. "Claims she's going to launch her own makeup line and dance on her husband's grave."

"Charming lady," said Ava. "Enterprising and spiteful. Remind me never to get on her bad side."

"She also seemed surprised that the police were questioning Billy Cobb."

"Honey, *I'm* surprised the police are questioning him," exclaimed Ava. "He always seemed like a pretty innocuous kid."

Carmela took a deep breath. "Dove Duval was awfully upset at Barty Hayward, too."

Ava frowned. "Wasn't Dove Duval at your shop Saturday night?"

"I'm afraid so," said Carmela, who then proceeded to tell Ava about the load of faux antiques that Barty Hayward had stuck Dove with.

"Would you really kill someone over cheap replica furniture?" questioned Ava. "Personally, I think I would've just clobbered Barty with an andiron or something. Try to get him to see the error of his ways."

"Bartholomew Hayward didn't just stick Dove Duval with a load of bad furniture," said Carmela. "He made her look foolish. When a person is shamed or made to look ridiculous in front of others, that can often plant the seeds for bitterness and hatred. And serious retaliation."

"I see what you mean," said Ava thoughtfully. "And I gather from the way you quizzed Quigg Brevard yesterday that you have a few suspicions about his good-looking chef . . . what's the fellow's name? Have meat cleaver, will travel?"

"Chef Ricardo," said Carmela.

"Right," said Ava. "You think instead of snipping herbs for his remoulade sauce the good chef might have used his kitchen shears to snip Barty Hayward's jugular?"

"I think Bon Tiempe is close enough to Menagerie Antiques that, somewhere between the étouffée and the crème caramel, Chef Ricardo could have found time to hightail it over and do the deed," offered Carmela.

Ava beamed. "That's what I like about you, Carmela Bertrand. You're a very suspicious person. Always thinking the worst of people."

"I do not," said Carmela. "I'm just . . . careful. And realistic, too. I think it has something to do with my genetic code." Carmela's father, who had died in a barge accident on the Mississippi when she was just seven, had been one hundred percent Norwegian. Her mother, who lived across the river in Algiers, was full-blooded Cajun. It was a slightly hodgepodge pedigree, the Norwegian part tempered and cool, the Cajun part more than a little impulsive.

A tough balancing act. No wonder Shamus and I can't seem to find any middle ground.

"You were telling me earlier about the good-looking detective who dropped by your store?" prompted Ava.

"To pick up a copy of my customer list," said Carmela.

"Probably just a formality," said Ava.

"That's what they always say in the movies," said Carmela. *That's what they always say when they're really closing in on a suspect.*

"Well, life's pretty much a movie script, isn't it?" asked Ava. "Your life is, anyway. Mine's a colossal snooze right now." She stood up and stretched, arms overhead, her pink silk T-shirt lifting to reveal bare skin and an amazingly taut stomach. "Tell me," said Ava. "What's new on the home front with the wayward hubby?"

"Not much," said Carmela. She paused. "I told Shamus I'd go to dinner with him tomorrow night."

"A *date*," declared Ava, rolling her eyes. "Now doesn't that sound cozy as hell. And which five-star restaurant will be sending its minions out to bow and scrape in your glorified presence? Could it be Antoine's or Commander's Palace? K-Paul's or NOLA?" Ava rattled off the names of a smattering of crème de la crème restaurants in New Orleans.

Carmela made a wry face, knowing exactly what Ava's reaction would be. "It's not like that at all. Shamus and I aren't going on a *date* date. We're having dinner at Glory's house."

"Glory Meechum's? *Eeeyew*," grimaced Ava. "Big sister Glory has always impressed me as one hard-assed woman. In fact, truth be known and all cards face up on the table, Glory Meechum scares the bejeebers outa me. She reminds me of that crazy actress who played Jessica Lange's momma in that movie *Frances*. You know, the momma kept up a respectable appearance on the outside, but inside she had a very sinister soul."

"Shamus always speaks highly of Glory," offered Carmela.

"Isn't Glory the senior vice president at Crescent City Bank?" asked Ava. "Doesn't Glory control the distributions from Shamus's trust fund?"

"Well . . . yes. I suppose she does," said Carmela.

"There's your *real* family dynamics, honey. Shamus is a smart boy. No way is he going to bite the hand that feeds him." Ava picked up a camel-hair brush, dipped it in shimmering green paint, and deftly applied a few judicious highlights to one of her mask components. "On the other hand," she said, "every Southern family's got their fair share of crazies in the attic. Lord knows, I do."

Chapter 8

"YOU'RE LATE!" DECLARED Tandy as Carmela came chugging through the front door, more than a little behind schedule on Tuesday morning.

Carmela stopped dead in her tracks, then a huge smile spread across her face. "Tandy!" she cried. Sitting at the back craft table were Tandy Bliss, looking decidedly less frazzled, and Baby Fontaine, looking lovely as ever. Gabby hovered at the front counter, pulling out various scrapbook albums and extolling their merits for a couple of interested customers. "Need any help, Gabby?" Carmela asked.

Gabby shook her head. "We're fine."

"More than fine," said one of the customers with her, a small dark-haired woman with mischievous-looking eyes. "I'm just getting into this scrapbook thing and I adore it!"

"Watch out, it's contagious," Carmela told her as she hurried toward the back of her store.

"Look who's feeling considerably more chipper today," said Baby.

"Let me guess," said Carmela, "the police have shifted their focus off Billy Cobb."

"Nooo," said Tandy, "not entirely. But thanks to Baby's high-powered lawyering husband, they're being a tad more careful with their accusations."

"Hoo yah," said Carmela, sitting down at the table. "Glad to hear it. There's nothing better than having one of the city's movers and shakers on your side."

"Telling the New Orleans police when to move and what to shake," said Tandy.

Baby arched her neck, secure in the notion that one of her adopted baby chicks was happy and content for the time being. "Okay now," she said in her best schoolmarm voice, "Carmela promised to help us design labels today."

"I brought in a couple jars of that strawberry jam," said Tandy. She reached into her bag, plunked two squat jars on the table. They were the size of large squared-off mustard jars and had plain gold tops.

"And I brought along some of my applesauce," said Baby. Her jars were rounded and slightly taller, also with gold tops. "I adore giving these away during the holidays," she added.

"Which will be upon us sooner than we think," said Tandy.

"Amen," declared Baby. The two women stopped their amiable chatting to stare at Carmela.

"Well?" Tandy said, her eyes twinkling.

Carmela picked up a pen and paper. "How do you want your labels to read?"

"'Strawberry Jam,'" said Tandy without missing a beat.

"'Baby's Applesauce,'" said Baby, grinning. "I take great pride in ownership."

"Okay," said Carmela. "I'm going to spend five minutes on my computer doing the typography, then I'll print your titles out on beige parchment paper and we'll get to work."

"What should *we* do?" asked Tandy.

"Grab a bunch of rubber stamps and colored ink pads," said Carmela. "I know for sure we've got apple stamps as well as strawberry stamps, but you'll probably want to embellish your labels with other designs as well."

True to her word, Carmela was back in five minutes with multiple printouts. "Okay," she said, "now we'll fit the labels to your jars. Which means you have to decide if you want your words centered, or a little offset toward the top or bottom."

"Centered," said Tandy and Baby in unison.

Carmela held the printouts up to the jars, eyeballed the dimensions, then took them to the paper cutter in her office. After a bit of judicious trimming, the labels, though still undecorated, wrapped around their respective jars perfectly.

"I've given you both five sets of labels," said Carmela. "That way, using different stamps, colored inks, colored pens, and oil crayons, you can experiment and play to your heart's content." She shrugged. "You might love every one you come up with, or maybe just one design will trip your trigger. Then that'll be the one you'll want to replicate. Anyway, think of this as a kind of test kitchen," laughed Carmela. "And your number one goal is to have fun."

As Baby and Tandy labored away happily at the craft table in back, business was brisk that morning and Carmela and Gabby were kept hopping. One customer, a woman in the throes of scrapbook anxiety, was about to abandon hope at ever putting together a genealogy scrapbook until Carmela and Gabby shared a few tricks on mounting photos onto acid-free paper and showed her a variety of oversized envelopes, acid-free storage boxes, and craft bags for organizing and transporting her papers, photos, pens, and stencils.

A young art student came in, searching for Japanese handmade paper to incorporate into a collage project he was doing for class. Carmela showed him some sheets of paper made from bamboo leaves as well as sheets of kanji-printed tissue paper and the young man left happy as a clam, a brown bag tucked carefully under his arm with Carmela's gold MEMORY MINE sticker adorning it.

And two gray-haired ladies, regular scrapbook customers who'd driven down from Baton Rouge for the day, kept Carmela and Gabby digging through their files with requests for sports-themed paper and stickers. They both had grandsons who were excelling in soccer and football, they explained, and had declared themselves the self-appointed keepers of memories.

"Whew," said Gabby. "Busy day. But it sure is heart-warming to see regular customers come in."

Carmela nodded. She knew that regulars were the bread and butter of any retail business. The tourists, the one-time shoppers, just weren't enough to sustain a business. You had to have regulars. Which was why she worked so hard to offer promotions, scrapbook and stamping classes, frequent buyer specials, even the all-night crop. Every event she staged gave customers a good reason to come back.

Carmela was even noodling around the idea of offering a class in the next month, called Paper Moon. Introduce folks to some of the brand-new art papers, work in a little scrapbooking and holiday card making at the same time. Or, if she could twist Ava's arm, maybe even a paper mask making class in January to coincide with Mardi Gras, which kicked off the following month.

"Carmela," said Baby, "show Tandy one of the menu cards you designed for Saturday night."

Carmela pulled one down from the back counter, slid it across the table to Tandy.

"Ooh, this is special," Tandy exclaimed. "And I love that you painted the photo corners." She pulled off her glasses, red cheaters that she wore around her neck on a gold chain, and wiped at her eyes. "It's amazing what you miss when you don't stick around here."

Baby glanced quickly over at Carmela, then at Tandy. "After you left yesterday, Jade Ella stopped by," said Baby. She waited a moment, then let the other shoe drop. "She was looking for Billy."

Tandy gasped in surprise. "Are you serious? She didn't *know* the police were talking to him?"

"She acted like she didn't," said Baby. "What did you think, Carmela?"

"Hard to tell," said Carmela, "seeing as how Jade Ella's so wrapped up with this Spa Diva thing. On the other hand, she may just be playing it close to the vest. You know, see who shakes out as a suspect in her husband's murder."

"If you ask me," said Tandy, "I don't think she ever loved Barty Hayward in the first place. Jade Ella probably just married him for his money."

"Does he have money?" wondered Carmela. "Or just inventory?"

"I'll say one thing for Jade Ella," said Baby. "She's definitely one of those women who strive for a distinctive look. Like right now she's really into the whole glam thing, whereas a year ago she was wearing long, flouncy peasant skirts with lots of ethnic beads and baubles." Baby folded her arms across her chest. "I subscribe to the policy that Diana Vreeland, the former editor at *Vogue*, advocated. Miss Vreeland is dead now, God rest her oh-so-fashionable soul, but she firmly believed it was in the best interest of every woman to find a distinctive look and stick with it religiously. You know, wear a kind of uniform day after day."

"You mean like Hitler did?" asked Tandy.

"Exactly." Baby nodded. "Or Carol Channing."

Carmela shook her head. It wasn't often you heard the names Hitler and Carol Channing bandied about in the same conversation. Especially when it pertained to fashion. Oh well, they *were* a strange group.

CARMELA DIDN'T even recognize Dove Duval when she came striding through the door. Gabby, who was arranging a display of photo albums in the front window, obviously didn't either.

"Help!" Dove called out loudly, suddenly making her presence known to everyone within a three-block radius.

"Dove," said Gabby, realizing who it was and springing to her side. "What's wrong?"

In the back of the store, Tandy and Baby glanced up from their labels.

"I am in need of some ribbon," announced Dove. Her words came out *Ah-mmm en neeed.* "Hopefully," continued Dove, with a somewhat petulant expression, "with images of leaves on it."

"Carmela," called Gabby, "do we still have that velvet ribbon with the gold oak leaves?"

"Maybe a yard or two," said Carmela, hurrying toward the front of the store. She pulled open a drawer and pawed through it hastily. "As I recall, it might have been a moss green?" she said hopefully.

"Brown would be *so* much better," said Dove. She stood there with her arms across her chest, tapping one small foot. Her blond hair, cut in a choppy do, was slightly wind-tousled. Her face, though flawlessly made up, wore a hard expression.

"Brown it is then," said Carmela as she fished out a spool of brownish green ribbon. *Hey, hold this up to the light and the brown tints are fairly noticeable.*

Upon seeing the ribbon, Dove Duval finally allowed herself a small smile. "Perfect," she declared. "I was beginning to wonder if I'd *ever* finish my arrangement for Monsters & Old Masters." Wearing a self-satisfied grin on her face, this was Dove's not-so-subtle announcement to everyone in the shop that *she* was one of the chosen. That *she* was one of just twenty people who'd been selected to complete a floral arrangement for Saturday night's big bash. Carmela, on the other hand, knew this was a nice honor, but felt Dove was carrying on as if she'd just made the short list for the Nobel Prize.

"I hope you don't have to do an arrangement to complement the devil tapestry," said Carmela. Her good friend Jekyl Hardy was on the committee to select artworks for that year's Monsters & Old Masters and she recalled Jekyl laughing over one of the works, a Medieval tapestry with pitchfork-toting devils capering across the bottom.

On the other hand, Carmela thought to herself, *what a kick if Dove did draw short straw and ended up with that tapestry. From what Jekyl told me, it's pretty ghastly.*

"*Au contraire,*" said Dove, continuing to feign a Southern accent. "I lucked out and got that darling little owl painting by Rafael Rodrigue. You know, the one in the gold Renaissance-style frame?" Dove cocked a single eyebrow, again exuding a slight hint of superiority.

"*Owl in the Moonlight,*" said Baby, recalling the exact title. She had worked as a docent at the New Orleans Art Institute for years and was fairly knowledgeable when it came to its permanent collection. Carmela could have kissed Baby for her correct and rather snappy answer.

"Why, yes, that's it," said Dove Duval, a hint of uncertainty suddenly registering in her voice. It was slowly dawning on her that she wasn't the only one in the room who had an "in" with the museum crowd.

"What kind of arrangement are you doing?" asked Gabby, trying to diffuse the tension that suddenly hung in the air.

"Poppy heads, branches of curly willow, dried feverfew, and possibly some Dutchman's trousers if I can get them. All arranged in a moss-filled wire basket," Dove told her.

"Pretty," Tandy replied, although the brittle tone of her voice indicated otherwise.

But Dove Duval seemed not to notice. "How much ribbon is left?" she asked.

Carmela unwound the spool of ribbon and measured it against a yardstick that was taped across the back of the counter. "An inch short of two yards. Hope that's enough to do the trick."

"It's more than enough," Dove told her crisply. She turned to Gabby. "I need to pick up a few other things, too."

"Of course," said Gabby, reaching for a wicker shopping basket. "Not a problem."

*   *   *

"WHY DOES that woman put me on edge?" Carmela asked after Dove Duval had departed. "She's a good customer. I *try* to like her."

"Maybe because there's not all that much to like?" suggested Tandy.

"She's awfully pretentious," added Gabby. "Last Saturday night, right before the Bartholomew Hayward debacle, Dove was bragging to everyone about how she was probably going to get named to the museum's board of directors."

"Gosh," said Baby, crinkling her nose, "I just don't think that's going to happen in the near future. I really don't."

"Do you know something we don't?" asked Tandy.

"Could be," Baby replied as she applied streaks of both bright yellow and dark green oil crayon to her stamped apple leaf image, then smudged both colors gently to achieve a lovely shaded effect.

"Dove certainly seemed to be stocking up on things," remarked Tandy.

Gabby nodded. "I get the feeling Dove has been bitten by the entertaining bug and plans to design a lot of invitations. She bought card stock, raffia, some of those new brass templates, casting molds, some more gilt paint, and a new pair of scissors."

"Gilt paint?" said Carmela.

"Scissors!" yelped Tandy. "What kind?"

Gabby looked suddenly stricken. "Paper-cutting scissors. The stainless steel ones by Capers Cutlery."

The women glanced around the table at each other with wide-eyed looks. As if part of a Vulcan mind meld, everyone seemed to be focused on the same thought until Tandy finally asked: "What do you think Dove did with her old scissors?"

The tension was suddenly so thick inside Carmela's shop you could've cut it with a scissors.

Chapter 9

CARMELA COULDN'T EVER recall having been inside Glory Meechum's house when the vacuum cleaner wasn't rumbling full tilt. Cursed with a touch of OCD—obsessive-compulsive disorder—Glory always seemed to be embroiled in a cleanliness snit. *Take off your shoes, put a coaster under that drink, don't sit down till I put a doily on the arm of that chair, and for God's sake don't spill on the carpet.*

Visiting Glory was like some hellish trip back to the second grade. When teachers constantly hammered at you to wipe your feet, blow your nose, study hard, and flush.

To see Glory's Garden District house filled with guests was quite a shocker to Carmela. Normally taciturn and vaguely suspicious, Glory wasn't exactly a spitfire on the New Orleans social scene. In fact, the last social event Carmela remembered attending at Glory's house was the infamous Inquisition Dinner. When all the relatives had been present just before she'd married Shamus.

And hadn't that been a barrel of fun.

So this rather large person in the button-straining, splotchy floral print dress who was greeting guests and serving drinks couldn't be Glory Meechum, could it? wondered Carmela.

Maybe it's really Martha Stewart wearing a Glory costume. Spooky. And Halloween isn't until this Saturday.

Glory lumbered over to where Carmela stood uncertainly next to Shamus. Shamus fairly beamed at his older sister. Under Glory's close scrutiny, Carmela wanted to cower. Instead, she stood her ground and smiled.

Why do I suddenly feel like the too-small center on a football team, trying to muster up the courage to snap the ball while staring into a defensive line made up of three-hundred-pound gorillas?

After giving Shamus a perfunctory peck on the cheek, Glory wasted no time with snappy chitchat. "Drink, Shamus?" she asked. "Bourbon?"

Shamus nodded obediently. "Sounds good."

Carmela cocked an appraising eye at Shamus. Dressed in a navy blazer and khaki slacks, Shamus looked successful, purposeful, and focused. All the things he really wasn't.

Glory turned toward Carmela and focused hard, beady eyes upon her. "Carmela?" she said gruffly. "Glass of wine?"

"Merlot if you've got it," said Carmela, gazing around with a slightly dazed expression.

"No red wine," said Glory. "Only *white.*" A challenging look accompanied her retort.

"Fine," said Carmela. "White wine then." *Use your head,* she told herself. *Of course Glory isn't about to serve red wine. A drop or two might stain her precious carpet.*

"You still running that paper store?" asked Glory.

"Scrapbooking shop," replied Carmela.

"Whatever," said Glory as she wandered off toward the bar to alert her bartender.

"Well, this is fun," said Carmela, gazing up at Shamus. *Maybe, if I'm really, really lucky, the earth will open up and swallow me whole.*

"Carmela . . . don't," said Shamus. "Glory's trying, really she is."

"If that's trying, I'd hate to see how she handles oblivious," replied Carmela. "To say nothing of disdainful."

Shamus took Carmela's elbow and guided her toward the bar to collect their drinks. "The bourbon and a white wine?" Shamus said politely to the bartender, who was really Glory's gardener, Gus, tricked out in a white shirt and black cotton jacket. With the sleeves two inches too short for Gus's bony wrists, and the toggles fastened crookedly, Gus looked more like a disreputable waiter than a green-thumbed genius with magnolias and roses.

Shamus handed Carmela her glass of white wine. "Be nice," he said, smiling at her. "Try to meet Glory halfway."

"I'm always nice," she replied. "You're the one who's been acting like a pill."

Carmela noticed that Gus had plopped a colored umbrella into Shamus's bourbon. She figured it was Gus's notion of what a bartender was supposed to do. Shamus, on the other hand, simply glared at the offending umbrella, fished it out with his index finger, and flicked it into one of Glory's potted plants.

Glancing about, Carmela saw that Glory's ordinarily bare walls had been spiffed up. Now they were graced by a dozen or so of Shamus's photographs in contemporary-looking silver frames. Most were moody shots Shamus had taken of the bayous just south of New Orleans. Photos of old cypress trees shrouded in mist, a riot of blue iris that had just come into bloom, a few shots of palmetto forests, and even one of a lurking alligator. Carmela wondered if Shamus had shot that one using a telephoto lens.

"Your photos are very good," she told Shamus.

Shamus took a sip of bourbon and nodded, pleased that she'd noticed. "They are, aren't they. I'm getting so much better. Probably working up to my own show."

"You think so?" said Carmela.

"Oh yeah. For sure," said Shamus, gazing about the room.

The dinner party turned out to include more Meechum relatives than real invited guests, with Glory and Shamus's brother, Jeffrey, and a scattering of various and sundry cousins populating the premises. Plus, it wasn't a dinner party per se. Rather than seating everyone at her large Sheraton dining table, Glory had set up a small table with appetizers. Garden variety stuff, really. More in the genus *Munchies* than the phylum Appetizer. *Munchus ordinarus*, Carmela decided, since the offerings consisted of overcooked rumaki, tiny crab cakes, oversauced chicken drummies, and some cherry tomatoes that haphazardly squirted their red liquid contents when bitten into.

On her second trip to the appetizer table, in an attempt to snare a few pieces from a decent-looking wheel of Camembert that had just been brought out, Carmela ran into Monroe Payne. He was chatting with Glory, praising her to high heaven about something.

"Carmela," said Glory in her loud bray. "Have you met Monroe Payne? Monroe's our esteemed director at the New Orleans Art Institute." Glory pronounced his name *Mon*roe, putting the emphasis on the first syllable of his name.

Carmela smiled politely at Monroe, who was tall, lean, and slightly owlish looking with his round Harry Potter glasses and dark hair combed straight back.

"I think we said hello in the hallway a couple weeks ago," Carmela said as she balanced her glass of wine and plate of cheese bits while attempting to shake hands with Monroe Payne. "When I was over at the Institute meeting with Natalie Chastain," she explained.

"Of *course*," said Monroe, nodding. "You're doing some decorating for us."

"Actually," said Carmela, "I'm doing the menu cards and display tags for the Monsters & Old Masters Ball."

"*Wunderbar,*" said Monroe, flashing her a wide smile. "We're certainly all looking forward to *that*."

Standing at his side, Glory Meechum cleared her throat.

"I'm sure you're aware," said Monroe, still smiling at Carmela, "that Glory will be receiving a major award Saturday night."

"Mmm, yes," said Carmela noncommittally. *Glory is getting an award? Well, this is news to me. No wonder Shamus is being so solicitous. Glory obviously sent out the order to round up an audience and I'm one of the pigeons.*

"It's our Founder's Award," Monroe Payne went on to explain. "A most prestigious award that only gets handed out every couple years or so." Monroe turned his high-powered charm on Glory. "But Glory's been a most generous patron so the award is well deserved."

Glory fixed a hard stare on Carmela. "I hope you'll be joining us at my table, Carmela."

So that's what this little soiree tonight is all about, mused Carmela. *A prelude to Glory's award. A warm-up.*

If there was an uncomfortable moment or two, Monroe Payne didn't seem to be aware of it.

"I'm trying to convince Glory to underwrite one of our upcoming shows," Monroe confided to Carmela, while continuing to smile widely at Glory.

"Which show would that be?" asked Carmela, nibbling at her Camembert. *Ah, finally something tasty.*

"Feminist Art Perspectives of the Lower Mississippi," replied Monroe.

Carmela stole a quick glance at Glory's impassive face. *Glory underwrite a show on feminist art? Never happen. No way, no how. The word* feminist *doesn't exist in her lexicon.*

But Monroe continued to rattle on about Glory. "Don't you know," he told Carmela, "that Glory is one of our Gold-level patrons. Not only has she donated a significant number of artworks to our museum, but she has followed them up with generous *cash* gifts as well." Monroe paused dramatically and took a sip of his drink, trying to avoid the tiny purple umbrella that bobbed about, threatening to poke his eye out. "Everyone wants to donate works of art or have their money go toward *purchasing* works of art. But nobody ever wants their money to pay the heat bill or buy new display cases or pay the guards' salaries. But those are some of the necessary evils that are part and parcel of running a large museum." Monroe Payne gave a hangdog look, as though he sincerely regretted having to dirty his hands dealing with those particular necessary evils.

Carmela nodded politely. This was a side of Glory she didn't know much about. But having had up close and personal experiences with the strange and wily Glory Meechum, Carmela knew it was likely the woman had set up some sort of nonprofit foundation through the family's Crescent City Bank. That way Glory could appear civic-minded and magnanimous, while still getting a nice fat tax deduction.

"Did you know, Carmela," said Glory, "that Founder's Award recipients get to have their portrait painted?" She gazed down at the carpet, narrowing her eyes at some imaginary speck of lint. Carmela figured Glory was probably itching to pull the vacuum cleaner out of the closet for a fast touch-up. She also wondered if Glory was up to speed on the merits of a Flowbee attachment.

"That's great about the portrait," said Carmela, her mouth stuffed with cheese. "Terrific." This last word came out *terrifuff.*

"Monroe was also trained as a painter," added Glory. "In Italy." She was trying her darnedest to keep the conversation ball rolling.

Monroe laughed. "*Studied* painting. Years ago. And I was terrible. It's no wonder my professors urged me to switch to museology instead."

At that moment Glory's housekeeper, Gabriella, came and whispered something in Glory's ear.

"If you'll excuse me," said Glory, still being maddeningly polite as she scurried away.

Monroe gazed after Glory with watery eyes. "She's a wonderful woman," he told Carmela. "Generous to a fault."

"Mmm," murmured Carmela. *Is he talking about the same Glory Meechum who kicked me out of Shamus's house right after he rather unceremoniously took off? The same Glory Meechum who canceled all our joint credit cards? Who tried to get my name stricken from the rolls of the Garden Club?*

Monroe continued to mumble platitudes about Glory, but Carmela suddenly wasn't listening. Instead, she was intently watching Shamus as he talked and joked with a pretty young blond woman who was wearing a short black cocktail dress that had a keyhole cutout in back. Shamus's left hand kept wandering up to that keyhole cutout. *Flagrantly flirting right in front of the not-yet ex-wife,* she thought. *Where's my digital camera when I need it? Judge, take a gander at this photo of the unfaithful husband flirting outrageously with another woman. Mental cruelty of the worst kind, wouldn't you say?*

"Mrs. Meechum?" said Monroe, his voice firm, as though he were repeating himself. "Carmela?"

Carmela blinked, turned her head, stared into Monroe Payne's dark brown eyes. "I'm sorry," she said. "You were saying . . .?"

"That was some nasty business last weekend. With the fellow who owned the shop next to yours?"

"Bartholomew Hayward," said Carmela. "Yes, it was quite a shocker."

"Do you know . . . are the police close to catching someone?" Monroe asked. "Or has that already been in the papers? I've been so frantic at the Institute finalizing plans for Monsters & Old Masters, I'm afraid I haven't stayed all that well informed."

Carmela shook her head. "You haven't missed anything so far. But the police do seem to be focused on Billy Cobb, Barty Hayward's young assistant."

"From the hesitancy in your voice, I'm guessing you have other ideas," said Monroe. "Glory told me how you so cleverly helped Shamus out of a spot of bad luck this past year."

"Well, I wish I could shine that lucky star on Billy," said Carmela. "He's the nephew of one of my best friends and she's very upset that he's come under suspicion. Maybe you know my friend . . . Tandy Bliss?"

"Tandy and Darwin Bliss. Of course I know them," said Monroe. "It's good of you to be so involved. The world would be a far better place if more people were independent thinkers like you." He glanced around quickly, as if making sure no one would overhear. "You have a suspect in mind?" he asked.

Carmela pursed her lips and a tiny frown creased her forehead. "Not exactly. Let's just say I'm trying to follow up on a couple clues."

"Clues that the police uncovered?" said Monroe with an encouraging look.

Carmela hesitated, not wanting to say too much. "Actually, I think the police would pretty much *dis*count what I believe might be important."

"Then be careful," warned Monroe. "After having spent more years than I care to admit embroiled in the world of art and antiquities, I know that nefarious people abound. Which means that Bartholomew Hayward probably had any number of enemies."

Carmela considered Monroe Payne's words. They pretty much followed her line of thinking, too.

Monroe leaned toward her conspiratorially. "Lots of backbiting and strange goings-on in the art world," he murmured in a low voice. "Would you believe that a person who resides right here in our very own Garden District once tried to palm off a sixteenth-century painting that disappeared from the collection of a prominent Dutch family during World War II?" He reared back and shook his head. "Shameful."

"I hear a lot of stolen World War II artwork has resurfaced," said Carmela.

Monroe grimaced. "Has for some time now. It just isn't discussed in po-lite society."

"I'm getting that same feeling about Barty Hayward's murder," said Carmela. "Which is why all of us at the shop have been struggling to get a handle on it."

"Again," said Monroe, flashing her a concerned look, "please exercise caution."

"Don't worry," said Carmela. "I'm not about to stumble headlong into trouble. By the way, will you be attending Bartholomew Hayward's funeral tomorrow?"

One of Monroe's hands fluttered to his chest. "Unfortunately, I barely knew the man. How about you?"

"Yes, I believe I will be attending," said Carmela, making up her mind on the spur of the moment. She didn't really have a decent reason for going, only a huge dollop of curiosity.

Then, because Monroe Payne was still peering at her with a slightly in-quisitive smile, Carmela decided she'd better *come up* with a good reason to explain her attendance. "Since Barty Hayward was my neighbor," she said pi-ously, "it seems only proper."

"I agree," said Monroe, bobbing his head. "It's only proper."

Chapter 10

A SUBTROPICAL WAVE that had originated off the coast of Africa in mid-October had leisurely swooshed its way across the Atlantic and bumped into the broad area of low pressure that now hovered in the western Caribbe-an. Meteorologists, stunned to see signs of a hurricane percolating so late in the season, nevertheless recognized the telltale banding-type eye in their satel-lite imagery. Hoping the unseasonable storm would decelerate and peter out on its own, they were dismayed when a large mid- to upper-level trough moved into the central United States and slowly began edging the storm north-ward toward the Gulf coast.

Rain sputtered down on mourners that had gathered in Lafayette Ceme-tery No. 1 around the grave that would soon serve as Bartholomew Hayward's final resting place. Shivering against the raw wind, huddled under a cluster of black umbrellas, the morning's funeral contingent resembled a patch of slick, oversized toadstools.

Carmela had arrived a little late. Hurrying through the ornate black wrought-iron gate on Washington Avenue, she'd crunched her way down the white gravel lanes that wound past ancient above-ground tombs, then slipped into place next to Baby.

Someone, Carmela didn't know who, was right in the middle of a heartfelt eulogy to Bartholomew Hayward. The man, slightly built with an Ichabod Crane face and a terrible comb-over, was praising Barty's sense of humor and mourning the fact he'd no longer be part of the French Quarter.

Carmela gazed around curiously at the rest of the mourners. Most were sedate-looking males, probably antique shop owners. Bartholomew Hayward had been a member of a loosely organized group known as the Vieux Carré Antique Shop Owners. They sometimes organized antique shop "crawls" and advertised their various shops together.

True to her promise, Jade Ella was also present, wearing a flouncy, low-cut red dress and gobs of shining jewelry, clutching a Judith Leiber handbag that turned out to be a jeweled pig. Perched pertly on a black folding chair, Jade Ella did indeed look like Mrs. Bling Bling. Lots of rocks, lots of glam.

Could Jade Ella have knocked off her husband? wondered Carmela. *If she had, would she have shown up at his funeral flaunting a red dress and all that glitz? Only if she was certifiably crazy. Or maybe smart like a fox.*

Baby nudged Carmela with one shoulder. Dressed in a black suit with a nipped-in waist, Baby looked refined and elegant. Carmela herself had hurriedly tossed on a black cashmere crew neck sweater and black slacks that morning. In the dim light of her apartment, the outfit had seemed sedate, more than appropriate for a funeral. Now she suddenly felt like she was dressed like a second-story artist. All she needed was a black mask and bag to stash the goods in.

"Bad news," Baby whispered to Carmela.

Carmela frowned, not quite sure what Baby was referring to.

"It would appear our Billy skipped town last night," Baby said under her breath.

You could've knocked Carmela over with a feather.

"What?" she said, trying to exercise some restraint in her response. As it was, a few eyebrows shot up around her. "You gotta be kidding!" she hissed.

"Shush!" Baby put a finger to her mouth. People were definitely beginning to stare.

Carmela plucked at Baby's sleeve, but Baby merely shook her head and continued to focus on the proceedings. Any further elaboration of her tantalizing news would have to wait.

Two more eulogies droned by, then the minister passed out little paper songbooks. The mourners pulled themselves together and managed to belt out a slightly off-key rendition of "Amazing Grace." That concluded, a small contingent of the mourners, presumably the Tulane alums, broke into a rousing chorus of the Tulane Fight Song.

Green Wave, Green Wave
Hats off to thee.
We're out to
Fight Fight Fight
For our victory.

This college fight song was performed perfectly on key and with far more pep and energy than the sad hymn that preceded it.

Finally, the minister rendered his final blessing and Bartholomew Hayward's funeral was officially concluded.

"Baby!" cried Carmela, finally able to talk out loud. "What's up with Billy?"

Furrows appeared in Baby's patrician brow. "All I know is that Del was on the phone early this mornin' and that Billy was nowhere to be found."

"He'd been living at home?" asked Carmela.

Baby gave a brisk nod. "With his parents, Donny and Lenore."

"So what happened?" asked Carmela.

Baby dropped her voice a notch. "Apparently Billy went out last night and never came back."

"Is that a fact?" said Carmela, gazing across the open grave to where Jade Ella was smiling and shaking hands, bouncing about like a debutante at her coming-out party. Carmela had never, in her wildest dreams, imagined that Billy Cobb might be one bit guilty.

And now Billy's taken off into the night. Why? Is he actually running from the police?

She'd have to think about that one.

Why do people run from the police? Elementary, my dear Watson. Because they're guilty. But Billy isn't guilty, is he?

Carmela sighed. For all the thought she'd given this, she seemed to be going nowhere. And the meager clues she'd been able to garner seemed utterly useless. The little medallion with the GC insignia ground into it hadn't led anywhere. Maybe it never would.

"This sure throws a wrench into things," muttered Carmela.

"Doesn't it just," agreed Baby. She pulled a gold silk scarf from her perfect leather handbag and wound it around her neck.

"Tandy's gonna freak out," said Carmela.

"No, dear, Tandy's gonna go *ballistic*," said Baby. She hesitated, a slightly stricken look on her face.

"What?" asked Carmela, sensing more.

"There's more," said Baby, really looking worried now.

"Judging from the look on your face I'd say there's a real problem," said Carmela. "Tell me."

"It seems our Billy has a police record," whispered Baby.

"Oh, shit," said Carmela. "What? What'd Billy do?"

"Small potatoes stuff, mostly," said Baby. "A few years back, Billy stole a Jaguar XKE in order to impress a prom date."

"At least he exhibits good taste in cars," said Carmela. "What else?"

"He got pulled in for smoking pot," said Baby.

"*That's* not good," said Carmela.

"It's weird, isn't it?" said Baby. "I never in my wildest dreams saw this coming. I always figured Billy was clean as a whistle."

"Maybe he is," said Carmela. She was about to say more, when she saw Jade Ella heading toward them.

"Jade Ella," said Baby, extending a hand gracefully, "my sincere condolences."

"Ain't this a hoot?" exclaimed Jade Ella, taking Baby's hand. Her eyes shone brightly and her thick, dark hair swished at her shoulders. Carmela decided that Jade Ella looked a little like Cleopatra on Dexedrine. "Talk about dancing on someone's grave," Jade Ella babbled on. "But when your ticket is punched, what can you do?"

Carmela studied Jade Ella carefully. *Drugs. The woman has to be on drugs. Because Bartholomew Hayward had more than just his ticket punched. The poor man had his throat gouged open.*

"Will you keep the shop going?" Carmela asked.

"Why?" said Jade Ella playfully. "Do you need more space?"

"No," said Carmela slowly. "I was just thinking about the customers and the rather large inventory Barty has amassed. Business considerations, really."

Jade Ella waved a hand. "Not the sort of thing I want to worry about right now. The store will just have to take care of itself while I get Spa Diva up and running." She waggled a finger at them. "I expect the two of you to be among our first customers."

She doesn't know about Billy, Carmela suddenly realized. *She doesn't know that Billy's taken off. Should I tell her?*

Carmela gave a quick glance toward Baby, whose smile remained frozen in place.

Baby's not about to say anything. So neither will I. Jade Ella has such a snitty, irreverent attitude about her husband's death that I'll be darned if I'm going to bring her into the loop. Besides, she's just crazy enough to have masterminded some kind of weird plot against Barty.

Carmela watched as Jade Ella moved off into the crowd. Then, lost in thought, Carmela stared out across the white-washed graves. Lafayette Cemetery No. 1 was one of the city's oldest cemeteries and most of the graves testified to that fact. Many were cracked and crumbling. Lacy moss crawled up some of the tombs; sleeping angels, their faces eroded with time, kept watch on others.

This may be a place of dark beauty, Carmela thought to herself, *but it's also a place of unrelenting sadness.*

Baby touched at Carmela's elbow. "Sweetie," she said, "you seem so sad all of a sudden. Want to catch lunch at Commander's Palace?"

Carmela pulled herself from her dark thoughts and nodded. "Excellent idea." Commander's Palace was the rather tony restaurant directly across Washington Avenue from Lafayette Cemetery No. 1. A former speakeasy, the famed turreted turquoise and white Victorian building was the only restaurant to grace the Garden District and it was where TV chef Emeril Lagasse got his start. Though it had long since evolved into a New Orleans institution, Commander's Palace still enjoyed a reputation as one of New Orleans's premier restaurants.

Baby cast a worried glance at the sky as they hurried across the street. "This rain could put a terrible damper on Halloween."

"Weatherman says there's a tropical depression brewing out over the Gulf of Mexico," said Carmela.

Baby frowned. "Can't be. It's way too late in the season."

"Tell me about it," said Carmela. She'd lived in and about New Orleans all her life and the traditional hurricane season generally stretched from June to early October. Still . . . if an anomaly was going to occur, this seemed to be the place. New Orleans seemed to be ground zero for all manner of strange events, the least of which were hurricanes.

And don't forget, Carmela told herself, *New Orleans's most famous rum drink is named . . . what else? The Hurricane!*

COMMANDER'S PALACE was warm and cozy, the perfect rainy day lunch spot, and Carmela and Baby lucked out by scoring one of the coveted window tables. As Carmela dug in her black leather bag for a Kleenex, Baby spotted a packet of photos.

"May I?" she asked, plucking them from Carmela's bag.

"Go ahead," said Carmela. The photos were shots she'd taken a week earlier on a walk through Audubon Park, a 340-acre park that had once been an old sugar cane plantation. Carmela decided it might be fun to get someone's reaction to them.

"Oh, these are terrific," cooed Baby.

"Really?" Carmela hadn't counted on such a favorable review.

"Absolutely," said Baby as she eagerly scanned the photos. "Very professional looking. Did you print them yourself?"

Carmela nodded. Photography had changed so much in the last couple years, what with the advent of digital cameras and color printers. Color prints that used to take days and cost a pretty penny to process could now be done in minutes in your own home or office.

"You should have your own show," declared Baby. "You're certainly good enough."

"Hardly," said Carmela, but she was pleased all the same. When she and Shamus were first dating, she had taken a photography class with him, at his urging. It looked like all the lectures on lighting, composition, and visual text were paying off now.

Just as Carmela finished ordering her eggs de la Salle, a fabulous house specialty that was served with crab cakes and wild mushrooms, her cell phone shrilled.

"'Scuse me," she told Baby, who was still debating over whether to order the turtle soup. "It's probably Gabby at the store." Carmela snatched up her phone, punched on her Receive button, and said "Hello."

"I adore a woman with a morbid streak," came a rich, resonant male voice.

What? Who on earth is this? wondered Carmela.

"It's Quigg Brevard," the voice quickly explained. "I phoned your shop and your assistant assured me you were out wandering the byways of Lafayette Cemetery. I presume you were pondering the great hereafter and soaking up the mournful atmosphere."

"It wasn't exactly a pleasure jaunt," Carmela told him. "I was attending a funeral."

There was a short pause, then Quigg Brevard said, "Of course, for Bartholomew Hayward."

"Bingo," said Carmela, even as she wondered exactly why Quigg Brevard had called. *As if you don't know, you coy girl.*

"Listen," said Quigg, "I need to get some kind of scrapbook put together."

Oops, survey says . . . wrong answer! Better tuck that massive ego away for safekeeping.

"You being the proverbial scrapbook lady," continued Quigg, "I thought we could sit down and talk about a possible project."

"What kind of scrapbook are you thinking about?" asked Carmela. She put her hand across the phone and murmured a hasty "Sorry" to Baby. Baby, who was engrossed in perusing the wine list while reapplying her lip gloss, smiled and nodded, not in the least bit put off.

"Something that will showcase our party room and catering services," said Quigg. "And probably our wedding and banquet capabilities, too."

Carmela nodded. More and more, businesses were noting the merits of putting together scrapbooks to illustrate their products and services. Interior designers had been doing it for years, visually demonstrating to clients their befores and afters. Now floral designers, orthodontists, landscapers, and wedding planners were jumping on the bandwagon and flocking to her shop. Asking questions, taking lessons, buying supplies, and . . . praise be . . . even requesting that Carmela put together professional scrapbooks for them.

"When would you like to get together?" Carmela asked Quigg, mentally going over the free time she had available in the coming week.

Yeah, next week is pretty open, that should probably work.

"How about tonight?" Quigg proposed.

"Tonight?" squawked Carmela.

"Absolutely. No time like the present," Quigg said in his smooth yet en- thusiastic manner. "Why don't you drop by Bon Tiempe around sevenish? And please . . . come prepared for dinner. Plying you with fine food and wine is the least I can do for requesting your presence at such short notice."

Charmed and more than just a little bit intrigued, Carmela told Quigg that seven o'clock would work just fine with her. And as she slid her cell phone back into her purse, she decided she'd better make a detour back to her apart- ment after work. So she could slip into something a touch more appealing.

Chapter 11

THE FRENCH MARKET between Decatur and North Peters Streets had been standing for well over one hundred and fifty years. A large, almost open- air building, the French Market bustled with vendors, food stands, and sou- venir shops. Strands of braided garlic, known as prayer beads, hung from the rafters above the various farmers' market stalls that brimmed with brightly colored produce.

Here you could also buy grilled alligator on a stick, honest-to-goodness Creole pecan pralines, and jars of mind-blowing hot sauce.

At the uptown end of the market sat Café Du Monde. Open twenty-four hours a day, this landmark institution was famous for its beignets, square doughnuts sans holes and liberally sprinkled with powdered sugar, as well as its inventive blend of chicory coffee and steamed milk, known forever as café au lait.

As Carmela hurried down the jostling center aisle to meet Jekyl Hardy, she was reminded just how tacky, wacky, and infinitely appealing the French Mar- ket really was. Smells of cinnamon and cardamom perfumed the air, and a lovely mélange of accents—Creole, Cajun, Louisianan, and African Ameri- can—floated past her. Though Carmela didn't exactly have time for coffee with Jekyl today, she was here anyway. Because they were good friends, they tried to *make* time for each other at least once a week.

Lean and wiry, his dark hair pulled into a small, sleek ponytail, Jekyl Hardy sat at a creaky wooden table sipping a double espresso. Dressed impec- cably in his traditional black, Jekyl looked ethereal and slightly predatory, not unlike the infamous vampire Lestat who frequented New Orleans via Anne Rice's novels. As the head float designer for the Pluvius and Nepthys krewes, Jekyl Hardy was generally in a state of sublime excitation once Mardi Gras loomed on the horizon. But for right now, Jekyl was focused mainly on his business of art and antique consulting. As he'd once confided to Carmela, "the float building's for sport; the art and antiques consulting is for money."

Carmela slipped into the chair across from Jekyl. "Boo!" she said by way of announcing herself.

He gazed at her morosely. "Ugh. Don't remind me."

"Jekyl, you *love* Halloween. You're the only man I know who's got a walk-in closet devoted just to *costumes.*"

"I don't love it this year," he told her.

"What's wrong?" asked Carmela as she tucked her handbag under her chair, quickly ordered a coffee, and leaned in to listen to him.

"If I *ever* volunteer for Monsters & Old Masters again, kindly drag me into a swamp and shoot me with a silver bullet."

"That bad?" asked Carmela.

"How do I let myself get talked into these things?" moaned Jekyl. "It's taken a committee of five people *forever* to decide on twenty simple works of art."

Carmela grinned. Jekyl was notorious for letting himself get stretched too thin. He might be a whirling dervish of activity, but nobody could be a volunteer with the Children's Art Association, the Humane Society, and the Art Institute, head two float-building krewes for Mardi Gras, *and* run a consulting business. It wasn't humanly possible.

"Natalie told me the list of artworks would be finalized by end of day tomorrow," said Carmela. "Anyway, it *better* be. I'm the one doing the description tags for Saturday night's event."

Jekyl sighed, then took another sip of espresso. "Monroe Payne may be a wildly creative museum director, but he's also very well named. Just as his name implies, the man can be an incredible *pain.* He's constantly changing his mind."

"I met Monroe Payne the other night," said Carmela. "When I was at Glory's house."

Jekyl Hardy pulled his lips into a wicked smile. "Sleeping with the enemy, are we?"

"Nope," said Carmela, "just plain old socializing."

"Of that I approve," said Jekyl. "But I hope filing for divorce remains numero uno on your personal agenda, my dear Ms. Bertrand."

Carmela nodded her head in the affirmative.

"You sure about that?" prodded Jekyl. He'd been through more than a few go-rounds with Carmela on this divorce business. He pushing, she resisting.

Now Carmela looked downright sad. "Afraid so," she said.

Jekyl reached over and touched one of her hands. "Oh, honey, I didn't mean to make you upset. Honest."

Carmela managed a smile. "You didn't upset me, Jekyl. I upset me." *No,*

Shamus upset me. Still burned into her memory was the image of the blond in the black cocktail dress with Shamus's hand roving toward that keyhole cutout. *Cad.*

Jekyl waved a hand. "Sorry I'm so tediously distracted today, but I gave Natalie my solemn promise that I'd design a couple killer jack-o'-lanterns to light the museum's front entrance Saturday night . . . and now I have this last-minute *thing* I might have to do."

"What thing is that?" Carmela asked.

"There's a big antiques conference up in St. Louis this weekend, and one of the speakers, a real antiques honcho, had to cancel. So they called *me* this morning and asked me to pinch-hit. All expenses paid plus a fairly decent stipend." Jekyl rolled his eyes. "Plus there are undoubtedly *connections* to be made."

"You're going, aren't you?" said Carmela, always a big "seize the moment" proponent.

Jekyl Hardy fidgeted. "I don't know . . . "

They both paused, listening to the mellow saxophone strains that wafted over from nearby street musicians. Even in the rain, the street musicians were cranking out their moody, bluesy tunes. Carmela hoped the tourists were generous, pitching their quarters and dollar bills into the musicians' open, empty felt-lined cases. 'Cause these guys were *good.*

"Tell you what," said Carmela. "You go to St. Louis and I'll carve the jack-o'-lanterns for Natalie."

"How are you going to manage that, pray tell?" asked Jekyl. "Your schedule's got to be as jammed as mine."

"I'll corral Ava and we'll make time."

"Really?" asked Jekyl, a hopeful look lighting his face.

"No problem," said Carmela. "You go to St. Louis and be a star. Whip 'em into a frenzy with that great 'Fakes and Forgeries' talk you do."

Can I get all this done? Carmela wondered. *Sure I can. Of course I can. Gulp.*

"A thousand blessings on your head," proclaimed Jekyl.

BY THE time Carmela finished a few errands and got back to Memory Mine, it was after five. The sign hanging on the front door said CLOSED, and Gabby was nowhere to be found.

Of course Gabby's gone, Carmela told herself. *Closed means closed. Gabby went home to make dinner for Stuart, the car czar.*

Stuart was notorious for having low blood sugar. When Stuart didn't eat on time, all hell broke loose. He once gobbled half a dozen Three Musketeers bars during the last quarter of a New Orleans Saints game because he claimed he was suffering from a low blood sugar "attack" brought on by his beloved team's desultory performance.

Carmela shuffled back toward her office. She wanted to take a couple scrapbook pages with her to Bon Tiempe. Quigg Brevard might *think* he knew what he wanted, but Carmela still wanted to do a little show-and-tell. And she for sure wanted Quigg to look at the sample scrapbook pages she'd put together for Lotus Floral and the pages she'd done for Romanoff's Bakery.

Okay, where the heck are those pages? Where did I put them?

Carmela whipped open three drawers in the flat file in rapid succession, but came up empty. Frowning, she decided the pages had to be stashed somewhere in this cubbyhole of an office.

Cramped, crowded, and cluttered, her office wasn't exactly a model office deserving of a center spread in *Architectural Digest*. In fact, her office was definitely due for a makeover. Or a cleanup. Or maybe even a full-scale intervention.

Carmela wondered if there were twelve-step programs for junk junkies, then decided there had to be. There were twelve-step programs for everything else. Heck, there were probably twelve-step programs for people who ate glue.

Finally, in the bottom drawer of her battered wooden desk, Carmela found the scrapbook pages she'd been searching for.

Hah! Gotcha.

Now she had to beat feet home, hit the shower, and wiggle into a cute little dress.

Right?

As if in answer to her question, a sharp knock sounded at her back door.

Ava? No, can't be. Tonight Ava's supposed to be shepherding Sweet-momma Pam to an early dinner at Brennan's and then a jazz concert at Pete Fountain's club over in the Hilton.

So who's tapping on my back door? Quoth the Raven, Nevermore?

Carmela padded to the door and hesitated. Putting an ear to the heavy reinforced steel door, she listened for a couple seconds, but could hear nothing.

"Who's there?" she called, then added in an emphatic tone, "I'm sorry, but the shop is closed."

"Carmela?" came a low muffled voice. "It's me."

"Who's me?" she called warily.

"Billy. I—"

Flinging open the door, Carmela was stunned to find Billy Cobb standing at her back door. Looking utterly forlorn and bedraggled in a faded checked shirt and frayed blue jeans, he was the last person she expected to turn up here.

"Billy! What on earth . . . ?" Carmela began.

But Billy simply stared at her and continued to look mournful.

Carmela did a fast scan of the alley. Then she reached out, plucked at Billy's shirtsleeve, and reeled him in. "Get in here," she whispered hoarsely.

"Don't you know everyone is looking for you? The *police* are looking for you, for goodness' sake. And your poor family . . . well, they're worried sick!"

Under her prodding, Billy Cobb hustled himself inside and closed the heavy door behind him.

"Do you want to tell me what's going on?" Carmela asked.

Billy screwed up his face in a look of sublime unhappiness. "I . . . I don't know what's going on."

Always a results-oriented person, this was not the answer Carmela wanted to hear. She decided to take a different approach in her line of questioning.

"Billy, you didn't have anything to do with what happened last Saturday night, did you?" she asked.

"No, of course not!"

Carmela stared at him. He looked believable, sounded believable.

"The police are trying to railroad me," he protested.

"Any idea why?" she asked.

"I think because I'm convenient," he said, one hand raking through his mop of hair.

Carmela stared at Billy. He was a kid who'd been in trouble with the law, he wasn't a property owner or a business owner, and he happened to be in the wrong place at the wrong time. She was sure this wasn't the first time the police had taken the path of least resistance.

"Listen, Billy, did Bartholomew Hayward get a lot of late-night deliveries?"

Billy shook his head. "I dunno. If he did, he always took care of them himself."

"Do you have any idea who killed Bartholomew Hayward?" asked Carmela.

Something akin to fear crept into Billy's expression. "No, of course not," he answered. "But . . ." He cast his eyes downward.

"Billy," said Carmela, her voice softening, "has someone threatened you?"

Billy's mouth twitched, but no words issued forth. Finally he nodded. "Just tell my family I'm okay, will you? Can you do that for me?"

"I'd like to do more than that," said Carmela. "I'd like to help if I can."

"Then stay out of it," pleaded Billy. "Because right now, the best thing for me to do is disappear for a while." He spun back toward the door and grasped the doorknob.

"Billy," said Carmela. She grabbed a pad of paper, scrawled her cell phone number on it, and pressed it into his hand. "Call me, will you? Let me know you're okay."

Billy pulled open the door and a gush of cold, damp air swept in. He hesitated, his back to Carmela. "I'll try . . ."

And with that, Billy Cobb was out the door.

"Billy, please . . . ," said Carmela.

But he'd already melted into the darkness.

Chapter 12

THE DINNER HOUR at Bon Tiempe was even more appealing than lunch or brunch. Candles flickered inside glass hurricane lamps, pale peach table linens imparted a romantic glow, and a tuxedo-clad sommelier solemnly bore bottles of wine to the various tables as though he were delivering precious elixirs, which he probably was.

As the maitre d' led Carmela to a small, somewhat out-of-the-way table and seated her, she noted that the evening atmosphere at Bon Tiempe was decidedly elegant and romantic. Not exactly conducive to a serious business discussion. Then again, after her somewhat unnerving encounter with the disappearing Billy Cobb, she wasn't sure she could even *conduct* a business discussion with Quigg Brevard tonight. Billy's pop-in, pop-out act had been very strange indeed.

Is he covering up for someone? she wondered. *Does Billy have a suspicion about who murdered Bartholomew Hayward and he's afraid to say? Or is something else going on entirely?*

Carmela brushed her hair back from her shoulders in a symbolic act of clearing her head. *Got to tend to business,* she told herself. Although everywhere she looked, couples were gazing into each other's eyes, enjoying a romantic dinner.

And (Carmela had to admit it) she had dressed up for this meeting, this *encounter* with the rather dashing Quigg Brevard. Studying her reflection in the mirror at home, she'd decided that the black shantung silk dress had maybe looked a little too sexy. So she'd toned down her look with a pashmina shawl tossed casually about her shoulders and replaced the pearl bracelet with two chunky carved Chinese cinnabar bracelets that Ava had given her the previous Christmas. Her leather portfolio, filled with samples and tucked under one arm, had imparted the final business-woman touch.

At least she *hoped* it had. Because as she sat here, still waiting for Quigg Brevard to join her, the headwaiter lit the candles on her table and swooshed a linen napkin onto her lap while, with a grand flourish, the sommelier uncorked a bottle of wine and poured a half-inch of viscous red liquid into a gigantic crystal wine goblet for her approval.

All this for me? Quigg's certainly given orders to pull out all the stops.

"The wine is to your liking, *madame?*" asked the sommelier, who was poised expectantly with the wine bottle.

Carmela took a small sip. The wine was rich and robust, slightly oaky and redolent with the scent of berries.

"This is amazing," Carmela told him. And it was—like drinking ambrosia.

"I knew you'd enjoy that particular wine."

Carmela looked up into the deeply tanned face of Quigg Brevard as he slipped into the chair across from her, then gazed at her with a mixture of curiosity and focused intent. "It comes from a small château in Bordeaux," he told her. "Very limited production. Still, Château Veronique has been turning out fine wines since about seventeen ninety-eight. Napoleon Bonaparte was one of its most ardent fans. So was General George Patton." Quigg's smile turned into a somewhat sheepish grin. "Now you know my little secret. I'm an oenophile *and* a military buff. Weird combination, huh?"

Carmela raised an eyebrow. "This wine must have set you back a hundred dollars a bottle."

"A hundred fifty," said Quigg. "But only if I were paying retail." He gestured for the sommelier to fill his glass, too. "Tonight you dine for my pleasure, *madame.*"

"Something tells me I'll be dining very well," said Carmela. *This is awfully cozy and nice. A girl could get used to this kind of treatment.*

Quigg smiled one of his toothy, fleeting smiles. "So we'll eat first, drink a couple glasses of wine, and enjoy ourselves. Get to know each other. Then, if we're still of a mind, we'll talk business."

"Terrific," said Carmela. She gave a sidelong glance around the table, still not finding a menu at her place.

Quigg caught her glance. "I hope you don't mind, I've already ordered for us. Chef Ricardo will be preparing a couple dishes that *aren't* on the menu. Not yet anyway."

"So I'm your guinea pig," laughed Carmela.

"Think of tonight as a taste test," offered Quigg. "And, seriously, I really do want your honest opinion."

The "couple dishes" Chef Ricardo prepared especially for them turned out to be very special indeed. Their appetizer consisted of a grilled duck liver salad. The *segundo,* or second course, brought tears of joy to Carmela's eyes. Asparagus risotto with freshly shaved Parmesan. The arborio rice was creamy and rich, the asparagus bright green and cooked al dente, and the Parmesan cheese imparted a lovely salty, almost nutty taste.

Their surprise entree turned out to be a pair of perfectly pink veal chops stuffed with Gorgonzola cheese and toasted walnuts.

While none of the servings were particularly large or looked like they would be at all filling, the flavors were so sublime, the ingredients so sinfully rich, that Carmela had to launch a vehement protest when Quigg Brevard beckoned for another small veal chop to be brought out from the kitchen.

"Enough," groaned Carmela. "I never eat this much."

"Nothing wrong with a woman who demonstrates a healthy appetite," Quigg told her.

"That's the problem," said Carmela. "Eating this much is *un*healthy."

"Then have another glass of wine," said Quigg as he hopped up from his chair, "to assist in digestion. And I'm going to sound the alert to Chef Ricardo and have him fire up his chafing dish. Dessert will be prepared tableside tonight."

"Dessert," moaned Carmela. "Oh no."

Carmela and Quigg did end up talking business. And as the brown sugar and brandy sizzled in the brass chafing dish, Quigg explained to Carmela what he had in mind.

"As you well know, dining is a transient experience. People come here for a couple hours, hopefully enjoy their elegant and beautifully prepared dinner, then go home. End of story. Bon Tiempe only remains top of mind for a few hours at best. Or, if our customers had a *really* enjoyable time, they might mention their dinner the next day to their friends." Quigg assumed a contemplative gaze. "How on earth do you capture such a short-lived, almost ephemeral experience? And make it promotable to others?"

Carmela understood exactly where Quigg was headed.

"But if Bon Tiempe had a scrapbook," he continued, "we could capture some of the happy faces of the couples and groups who were celebrating, all the fond memories, and use it to our advantage."

Quigg picked up the bottle of Château Veronique and offered the last inch of wine to Carmela. When she declined, he emptied the few drops into his own wineglass.

"Downstairs we have a lovely party room," continued Quigg. "Decorated in a very contemporary fashion." He pointed across the dining room. "Out those double doors you'll find our patio. Circular fountain, mood lighting, small but lush garden. Both areas will accommodate gatherings that range in size from a dozen to seventy-five people. Think of it," he said excitedly, "we're set up for Mardi Gras parties, wedding receptions, anniversaries, birthdays, office parties, you name it!" He paused, waited as Carmela jotted a few notes.

"Now if we had a nicely designed scrapbook," continued Quigg, "we could better *communicate* our atmosphere and our offerings." He paused. "What do you think?"

"You don't have to sell me," laughed Carmela. "But what you might want to consider is having two scrapbooks."

Quigg rocked back in his chair, an amused smile lighting his face. "Why two?" he asked.

"Make the first scrapbook a straight-ahead promotional book using the group and event photos you have right now. I'm assuming you have some of those?"

"A shoebox full," said Quigg emphatically.

"Good," said Carmela. "Then make the second scrap book a sort of romantic-looking guest book. Pass that book around at lunch or in the evening, allow your guests to write in it. Trust me, people love to leave little notes about a special meal they enjoyed or the occasion they're celebrating."

"Okay . . . ," said Quigg.

"But on, say, every other page of that book, we'll put a beauty shot of a dinner entree or a dessert or something," added Carmela. "And we'll also intersperse some of the nicer photos of groups out on the patio or enjoying the party room. And we'll add captions, too."

"So as folks are signing the so-called guest book, we also make the point that Bon Tiempe is available for special events," said Quigg.

"Exactly," said Carmela. "The guest book, or memory book if you will, plants the seeds."

"And when customers come back to actually *plan* their event, we pull out the straight-ahead event scrapbook," said Quigg. "I love it."

"Really?" asked Carmela. She'd been so busy formulating and putting across her ideas, she wasn't sure he'd actually heard her.

"So you'll put them together for us?" Quigg asked. "The scrapbooks, I mean?"

"Of course," said Carmela, thinking, *Honey, you don't have to twist my arm.*

"Outstanding," said Quigg, smiling at her.

And as Carmela gazed at his handsome face, a tiny little point of pain ignited deep within her heart. *Shamus used to look at me like that,* she told herself. *Shamus used to take me out for romantic dinners that lasted for hours. Shamus would debate over the merits of a Bordeaux or a Burgundy, just to make me happy.*

Carmela blinked, tried to yank herself back to the here and now.

Shamus isn't in my life anymore, she told herself firmly. *Not because I don't want him, but because he doesn't seem to want me. Grow up, girl. Wake up and smell the gumbo. March yourself into a lawyer's office and file for that divorce so you can start living your life again. And start dating nice men like this.*

"Penny for your thoughts," said Quigg.

Carmela stiffened and sat up straight. Looking around hastily, her eyes fell on Chef Ricardo, who seemed to be creating something magical with trout, almonds, and white wine.

"I was thinking what a fabulous dinner we just had," she lied.

Quigg looked pleased.

Carmela nodded toward Chef Ricardo. "I'll bet you wish you could clone him."

Quigg nodded fervently. "The man's an absolute genius. A food alchemist."

Carmela watched as Chef Ricardo slid a fillet knife into the body of the large, plump, butter-browned trout, flipped it open casually, and lifted out the spine. Carmela shivered, imagining that knife sliding into a person.

"Tough being a chef, though," she said. "Working every night. Weekends, too."

"He doesn't work every night. Sometimes we let him off for good behavior."

"Was he working last Saturday night?" Carmela asked.

Quigg's brows knit together. "Why do you ask?"

Carmela shrugged. "No reason."

Quigg rolled his eyes. "Chef Ricardo did *not* stab Bartholomew Hayward," he told her emphatically. "You're being overly suspicious and probably watch far too many episodes of *Law and Order*. Reruns and syndication are *not* necessarily a good thing."

"So he was here," said Carmela.

"As a matter of fact, he was off last Saturday night."

"Really," said Carmela.

Quigg chuckled. "But he'll be doing double duty *this* Saturday night since we're also catering the bash over at the Art Institute." He paused. "Does *that* make you happy?"

"The Monsters & Old Masters Ball?" asked Carmela. *Well, this is a coincidence.*

"That's the one," said Quigg. "Say, you gonna be there?" His dark eyes sparkled. He was obviously amused by Carmela's amateur sleuthing.

Carmela ducked her head. "Yes, I am."

"Terrific," enthused Quigg. "Save me a dance, will you? Or a monster hop or whatever the heck's going on there."

"I don't know," said Carmela playfully. "Are you coming in costume? It's Halloween, after all."

"Are you kidding?" said Quigg. "I'll be the poor sap dressed in a tux. Just think of me as Lurch from *The Addams Family*. Say"—he turned suddenly serious—"how *was* that funeral this morning?"

"Funereal," Carmela told him. "Except for Barty Hayward's wife, Jade Ella, who served as the one bizarre bright spot in the whole thing. She wore a red dress and did everything but dance on Barty's grave." Carmela glanced over at Chef Ricardo, who seemed to be focused intently on their conversation even as he garnished his trout with a medley of asparagus and roasted red pepper.

"Jade Ella has always seemed like a very unusual woman," said Quigg thoughtfully. "She's dined here several times and each time she's been accompanied by a different male escort. I get the distinct feeling *she's* the one who prefers calling the shots."

"Jade Ella's a real pistol," allowed Carmela. *And a viable suspect, too. Not unlike Chef Ricardo.*

"So," said Quigg, smiling at Carmela. "You're willing to put together those scrapbooks? You'll take a stab at it?"

"Interesting choice of words," said Carmela.

Quigg Brevard stood up and shook his head. "I'll get those photos for you, Carmela."

Chapter 13

CLICK CLICK CLICK. Boo's toenails clicked daintily across the floor as Carmela led her into the store on her leash. Outside, rain poured down in sheets. Carmela didn't ordinarily bring Boo to her shop, but today Ava wasn't going to be around to let her out and it was far too blustery to leave Boo outside in the courtyard.

"Hey there, pups," called Gabby as she grabbed a towel and knelt down to wipe Boo's wet paws. In typical shar-pei fashion, Boo immediately gave a good shake, then plopped herself down and scrunched her feet underneath her plump little body, trying to hide her paws.

"How come Boo came along today?" asked Gabby, still struggling to find a paw beneath all those ample wrinkles.

"Ava went to the retail buyers market today. And it didn't seem right to impose on Tyrell."

Tyrell Burton was Ava's sometime assistant. A grad student at Tulane who was studiously earning his MA in history, Tyrell was an African American whose great-grandmother had emigrated from Haiti almost a hundred years ago. Because great-grandma had been known to dabble in voodoo, Tyrell felt himself uniquely qualified to work at Ava's store. His Haitian heritage, combined with a knack for being exceedingly glib, made Tyrell a favorite with tourists. And he never tired of spinning a few good yarns just for their benefit.

Carmela shrugged out of her raincoat and, in a motion not unlike Boo's, gave it a good shake. Droplets of water flew everywhere.

"Hey," scolded Gabby, grabbing a roll of paper towels and kneeling down to wipe the floor. "I don't know which one of you is messier. You or Boo."

"Oops, sorry," said Carmela, bending down to help sop up water. It wouldn't do for unsuspecting customers to slip on the wet floor and take a nasty header.

"No problem," said Gabby, who sometimes seemed happiest when she was cleaning up after someone.

Maybe Stuart is a secret slob, thought Carmela. *Gabby always seems so pleased when there's a mess to clean up. Maybe Stuart, the Toyota King, leaves his underwear in a ball at night or slops toothpaste all over the sink.* Carmela chuckled to herself for a moment, until she remembered the awful truth. *Wait a minute, what am I thinking? All men do that stuff. Somewhere along the line, the sloppiness factor has been embedded in their genetic code.*

"What are you chuckling about?" Gabby asked.

"Nothing," Carmela told her, a little ashamed of her flight of fancy over Stuart's messiness. Carmela gazed toward the back of the store where Tandy and Byrle sat huddled at the big craft table. It didn't look like much scrapbooking was going on, but they were certainly deep in conversation.

"What's the story back there?" Carmela asked.

Gabby rolled her eyes. "Tandy's pretty hysterical about Billy skipping town like he did. And she's waiting to talk to you. She says you're always such a calming influence."

"Me?" Carmela snorted. "First time I've ever heard that. Usually I'm the one who gets accused of upsetting the proverbial apple cart."

"Hey," Gabby grinned, "accept the compliment."

"I will," said Carmela as she strode to the back of the store, Boo scurrying after her.

"Carmela," said Tandy, her hypothyroidal eyes fixing on her. "We have to talk."

Carmela slid into a chair across from Tandy and Byrle. Tandy reached across the table and grasped for Carmela's hands. "Things are *so* bad," she whispered harshly, her lower lip beginning to quiver. "Donny and Lenore are just beside themselves with worry. And I didn't sleep a wink all night myself. I kept turning this whole thing over and over in my mind. Does Billy know something? Is Billy somehow involved?" Tandy's thin hands suddenly slipped out of Carmela's and she swiped at the tears streaming down her thin, pale cheeks. "Sorry," she said. "This is *very* embarrassing."

Byrle patted Tandy's shoulder. "There, there," she said, sympathy in her voice. "What's a few tears in front of friends?"

"We're pretty positive Billy has left the state," said Tandy, snuffling harder. "He's got cousins over in Biloxi, so he could be headed that way." Tandy fumbled in her purse, pulled out a large white hanky, and blew her nose loudly.

Carmela stared at Tandy. Her dear friend was obviously in a world of hurt and she so wanted to help. *But will telling Tandy that I spoke to Billy last night make things any better? I don't know. I really don't know.*

"The thing of it is," continued Tandy, "the police are really on Billy's case now. His little disappearing act has them *convinced* of his guilt."

"Oh, honey," said Byrle, "that's not necessarily true."

"It *is* true," said Tandy. "Now there's a warrant out for Billy's arrest!"

Carmela grimaced. *Tell Tandy? Not tell her?* She held her thumb to her lips, nibbled nervously at a fingernail.

"Tandy . . . ," began Carmela, "someone came . . ." She hesitated. "That is . . . I saw Billy last night." This last part came out in a rush. *There,* thought Carmela. *I finally spit it out. For what it's worth.*

Carmela's words had a profound effect on Tandy. Her eyes went wide as saucers, a tiny hand flew to her birdlike chest. "You *what?*" Tandy was truly shocked. Dumbfounded, in fact.

"Billy knocked on my back door last night," explained Carmela.

Now Tandy put a hand to her mouth. "You actually *talked* to him? Really and truly?"

"Honey," said Carmela, "I wouldn't characterize it as a heart-to-heart talk, but, yes, we spoke. Truth be known, it was a fairly one-sided conversation. I asked Billy a few probing questions, Billy shifted from one foot to the other, pretty much unwilling to answer any of them."

"But he's *okay*," said Tandy. Her eyes gleamed; a healthy color had suddenly returned to her face.

"Physically, Billy seemed fine," said Carmela. "But something has definitely got him running scared. And I get the feeling it's *not* necessarily the police."

"Oh my lord!" exclaimed Tandy. "I've got to call Donny and Lenore immediately."

"No!" protested Carmela, knowing this could turn into a major problem for her.

Tandy stared at Carmela. "Why in heaven's name not?" she asked. "Billy's their only son, they're worried sick about him. And they want him to come home!"

"Listen," said Carmela, "I got the distinct feeling Billy's not about to saunter into Donny and Lenore's house, hang up his baseball cap, and sit down to a nice dish of jambalaya. Billy's definitely on the run and I'm pretty sure he's going to *stay* on the run."

"Dear God," said Tandy in a small, tight voice. "You mean . . . Billy's *never* coming home?"

"Probably not until Bartholomew Hayward's murder is solved anyway," said Carmela. "Until this whole thing gets sorted out."

"But the police aren't *doing* anything," wailed Tandy.

"They do seem incredibly myopic," admitted Carmela. She was miffed that Lieutenant Babcock *still* hadn't gotten back to her about the list she'd given him.

"Then it's up to us," declared Byrle in her typical gung-ho style. But as she delivered her words, she stared pointedly at Carmela.

"Darned right, it's up to us," said Tandy, struggling to get a rein on her emotions. She, too, was staring directly at Carmela.

Why do I get the feeling that "us" suddenly means me? wondered Carmela. *When did I get appointed Sherlock Holmes?* But even as the words free-floated through her brain, she knew the answer. *Because Barty Hayward was killed in back of my store. Because he was probably staggering toward my back door for help.*

"Listen," said Carmela finally, "I'm not making any promises, but there are a couple things I *could* look into. Okay?"

Both women exhaled in unison as they leaned forward expectantly.

"Okay," whispered Tandy.

"But you've got to keep quiet," warned Carmela.

Byrle made a zipping motion across her mouth.

"Mum's the word," promised Tandy.

"And you have to promise you won't breathe a word of this to Donny and Lenore," said Carmela, directing a firm gaze at Tandy.

"I won't," said Tandy.

"Because the last thing I want is a bunch of police swarming around here asking questions," said Carmela. *Would they, really? Oh yeah, they would. And then I'd really be in a pickle. Aiding and abetting a felon and/or fugitive. Withholding evidence. Yipes.*

Tandy's eyes shone brightly. "I knew we could count on you, Carmela."

"What did I tell you?" said Byrle. "Carmela's got more sleuthing ability in her little finger than all of us put together."

"Shhhh," warned Carmela. Three customers had just entered her store and were clustered around a display of foil papers up front. Even though Gabby had rushed to help them, you never knew what might be overheard and passed on.

"We'll make like church mice," said Tandy, suddenly happy.

"We'll work on our scrapbooks," said Byrle as she plunked her craft bag on top of the table and began pulling out a jumble of photos, albums, and scissors.

"Okay," said Carmela. "I'm going to see if Gabby needs any help." She hesitated, waggled a finger at Boo. "And you, my dear girl, had better remain back here for the time being." Boo, who was lying at Tandy's feet, gazed up at Carmela solemnly as if to say, *Pardon me, but I am too well mannered a canine to be receiving such a stern lecture on protocol.*

THE WEEKS before and after a holiday, any holiday, were always frantically busy at Memory Mine. And this pre-Halloween week was no exception. In fact, these three customers, just like all the others, had come in search of stickers, rubber stamps, decorative papers, and ribbon. As Carmela well knew, they'd use some of the craft items for Halloween scrapbooking, others for decorating trick-or-treat bags, rubber-stamping invitations, and making window decorations.

Carmela had laid in a good supply of special Halloween papers and rubber stamps. She knew most of her regulars would be making Halloween scrapbook pages to celebrate the exploits of their own little monsters or, like Tandy and Baby, their grandchildren's Halloween capers. Carmela's stock of rubber stamps now included ghosts, skeletons, and classic movie monsters, while her supply of Halloween paper boasted bats, pumpkins, haunted houses, creeping vines, and star and moon motifs.

Carmela was just sliding sheets of beige kraft paper with large orange pumpkins emblazoned across them into an oversized envelope, when Tyrell Burton came trooping into the shop. And, lo and behold, Sweetmomma Pam was with him.

"Hey, Tyrell," called Gabby from behind the front counter, where she was ringing up a customer. "Haven't seen you in a while." She smiled at Ava's wizened little grandmother. "Hi there, Sweetmomma Pam."

"I've got another customer for you," said Tyrell. He put his hands on Sweetmomma Pam's narrow shoulders and gently pushed her forward, presenting her to Carmela. A tiny woman with curly white hair dressed in an innocuous navy blue pantsuit, Sweetmomma Pam was definitely dwarfed by Tyrell's imposing form.

"Hey there, *dawlin'*," she said, waving to Carmela as a smile lit her lined face.

"Tyrell?" said Carmela. "Is there something going on I should know about?"

"I realize you're extremely busy, Carmela," began Tyrell, "but there are two of you"—his glance quickly flashed to Gabby—"and only one of me. Things are in a tizzy at the voodoo shop, on account of Halloween. And Sweetmomma Pam requires a tad more *chaperoning* than I am able to provide." This explanation was delivered with such tact and delicacy that Carmela had to smile in spite of herself.

"And," continued Tyrell, "Miss Ava assured me that you and your friends would extend every courtesy to Sweetmomma Pam."

Carmela reached out, gently put a hand on the old woman's shoulder. "Of course we will. In fact, we're delighted to have Sweetmomma Pam join us." Ava had been such a good sport about taking Boo out for walks when Carmela couldn't make it home at noon, that Carmela was glad she could finally reciprocate.

Tyrell was visibly relieved. "Ava promised she'd be back by four o'clock at the latest." Spinning on his heels, Tyrell was about to make a hasty exit, when he suddenly paused and turned around. "Thank you, ladies," he said. "And God bless."

Leading Sweetmomma Pam back to the craft table, Carmela made hasty introductions. And, as she got Sweetmomma Pam settled in, she began to formulate a plan. Sweetmomma Pam was the perfect candidate to help her finish up the menu cards. It was an easy project that would keep her guest busy and hopefully amused. If all went well, she'd then be able to zip over to the Art Institute after lunch and deliver said cards to Natalie.

"You got a boyfriend, honey?" Sweetmomma Pam asked Carmela as they sat side by side, Carmela stamping images on her menu cards and Sweetmomma Pam adhering them to the larger card using Carmela's faux finished photo corners.

"No," Carmela told her. "I'm still married."

Sweetmomma Pam squinted in disbelief. "You're *married*? So how come y'all are livin' alone? In that little apartment in back of Ava's?"

"Um . . . actually I'm separated," Carmela explained.

"Separated," snorted Sweetmomma Pam. "That's nothin' but a fancy term for a bad marriage. In my book a woman's either married or she's not. There shouldn't be any middle ground."

Darn it, thought Carmela, *Sweetmomma Pam is probably right. There shouldn't be any middle ground. Either Shamus and I should stick together through thick or thin, or we should get that divorce. So why is it I'm still hovering in marital purgatory? Stuck right smack dab in the middle, not knowing what's going on. Not knowing if we're gonna divorce or reconcile.*

Sweetmomma Pam suddenly turned her attention to Tandy, sitting across the table from her. Tandy was using one of her objets trouvés—found objects. In fact, Tandy was big on found objects. She'd once done an entire scrapbook using fabric scraps, old buttons, and angel charms as accent pieces.

Today Tandy was designing a scrapbook page using the front of a Wheaties box. She had cut away the picture of the sports hero du jour and replaced it with a photo of one of her grandsons whacking out a homer in a Little League game. The headline now read SLUGFEST OF CHAMPIONS.

"Who's that fella?" asked Sweetmomma Pam, poking a finger at the grinning sports hero Tandy had discarded. "The one that got eighty-sixed."

Not a serious sports fan, Tandy shrugged. "I don't really know. Probably some hotshot named Barry or Bobby or Bubba."

Sweetmomma Pam wrinkled her nose and smiled. "This is fun." One of her sharp elbows jabbed at Carmela's ribs.

"Eleven o'clock," a mechanical voice announced brightly.

Tandy jumped in her seat. "What on earth was *that?*"

Sweetmomma Pam stuck her skinny wrist out. "My talking watch. Ain't it a pip? I ordered it off the TV."

"That voice sounds like it's been sucking helium," exclaimed Tandy.

"It's amazing what they can put on a chip these days," added Byrle.

But Sweetmomma Pam's watch had also told Carmela that they were definitely making progress on the menu cards. They'd been at it a half hour and were more than halfway done.

"You're an absolute whiz," Carmela told her. And she was, too. Sweetmomma Pam's gnarled fingers had been working double time, deftly sticking on the little photo corners. In fact, Carmela had finished her stamping and was moving on to her next last-minute project. Glassware for Baby's party.

Baby was in the throes of decorating her palatial Garden District home for Halloween and was planning to throw a huge party for her family on Saturday night, just a few short hours before she and husband Del scampered off to the Monsters & Old Masters Ball. Baby had wanted to create something really special for her dinner table and Carmela (scrapbook and craft masochist that she was) had promised Baby she'd decorate some glassware for her.

So, early this morning, Gabby had accepted delivery of two dozen martini glasses. Not the garden variety kind, but whopping, oversized, long-stemmed martini glasses that you could really serve a serious drink in.

"Watcha gonna do with those, *cher?*" asked Byrle. She eyed the giant martini glasses expectantly as Carmela pulled them from the confines of their carton.

Carmela held up a finger. "Give me a minute and I'll show you."

She opened a stamp pad of black ink, rocked a rubber stamp against it gently, then applied the stamp to the side of one of the martini glasses. When Carmela removed the stamp, there remained the perfect image of a spider.

"A spider . . . cool," said Sweetmomma Pam.

Carmela spun the glass around and carefully added another dozen or so spiders until the little arachnids appeared to be crawling all over the martini glass.

"That's quite a Halloween effect," said Tandy. One eyebrow was raised. She didn't *dislike* the spider effect, it was just taking her a while to warm up to the *idea* of spiders.

"What the heck is Baby gonna serve in that?" asked Byrle.

"Something she calls a Monster Slosh," said Carmela.

"Dear lord, a drink that size, one surely would get sloshed," said Sweetmomma Pam with a gleam in her eye.

"What's *in* a Monster Slosh?" asked Tandy.

"Ginger beer, lime juice, and a shot of dark rum," said Carmela. "Baby's gonna serve it on the rocks with a gummy worm dangling over the side for garnish. And maybe a lump of dry ice for a nice spooky fog effect."

"Baby really loves to go all out," remarked Tandy.

Carmela smiled as she held up her handiwork. "Don't we all," she said.

TWENTY MINUTES later, Carmela's good mood evaporated when a disheveled-looking man entered her shop and introduced himself as Reed Bigelow. Dark haired, dark complected, and seemingly dark tempered, Reed Bigelow had a nose that looked as sharp as the bill of a hawk.

He thrust his embossed business card into Carmela's hand. "I represent the Harget Brown Insurance Company," he told her. "Offices in New Orleans, Baton Rouge, Shreveport, and Alexandria." He rocked back on his heels, the picture of pride and puffery, as he hooked his thumbs in the pockets of his trench coat and waited for Carmela to react.

Carmela studied the man's card, wondering exactly what reaction it was supposed to elicit from her. Stunned silence? Respect? "Life insurance or business insurance?" she finally asked him, since it wasn't readily apparent from his card.

He shrugged. "Does it matter? I just want to ask a few questions."

Carmela gave an answering shrug, then handed the card back to a surprised Reed Bigelow. "Excuse me," she said, "I have customers to attend to."

"Look, lady . . ." The insurance man was suddenly right behind her, dogging her steps.

Carmela stopped and turned. "Oh," she said, a look of surprise registering on her face. "I guess it *does* matter." *Don't try to bully me, friend. I haven't lived in the South all my life and dealt with blustering men without picking up a trick or two. Fact is, it's a little bit like handling bull elephants. Kindness combined with brute force.*

Carmela smiled to herself. Now why couldn't she use that line of reasoning with Shamus? Good question.

He had already backed way off, partly because of Carmela's no-nonsense attitude and partly because of the audience he had suddenly acquired. "Look," he explained, mindful that several pairs of eyes were now focused on him, "I didn't mean to get off on the wrong foot here. It's just that I've got this crazy lady constantly calling my office and haranguing me. *When you gonna mail out the check, Reed? When do you think I'm finally gonna get a settlement?*" By raising his voice and putting a little wheedle into his tone, Reed Bigelow had managed to do a fairly good imitation of Jade Ella Hayward.

"Jade Ella," said Carmela, trying her best to suppress a knowing smile.

"Bingo," he said unhappily, trying to figure out some way to get his business card back into Carmela's hands. Much to his dismay, she had stuck her hands deep into the pockets of the craft apron she always wore when she did rubber stamping.

"When *is* Jade Ella going to get her payoff?" asked Carmela, who was suddenly more than curious. "And I assume this *is* life insurance."

Bigelow nodded as he scrunched his face into a grimace. "That's the thing of it," he said. "These situations are extremely hard to predict. There are no hard-and-fast rules. In most cases, once the deceased is buried, our company cuts a check. However, in situations where a homicide has occurred"—he suddenly lowered his voice—"then we have to make sure that the beneficiary is what you'd call a *noninvolved* party."

"And is Jade Ella a noninvolved party?" asked Carmela, who was starting to enjoy herself in this little cat-and-mouse game with Reed Bigelow.

The man continued to look unhappy. "Not exactly," he said.

"So Jade Ella's a suspect?"

"Not exactly," he told her.

"Let me get this straight," said Carmela. "From what you've determined so far, Jade Ella is a non-noninvolved party, yet she hasn't been elevated to murder suspect."

Bigelow narrowed his eyes. "You got a funny way of putting things, lady."

"So I've been told," said Carmela. The phone next to her shrilled and she casually reached over to pick it up. After listening for a few seconds, Carmela covered the mouthpiece and turned toward the back of the shop.

"It's the Merci Beaucoup Bakery," she called to Tandy, Byrle, Gabby, and Sweetmomma Pam. "They're checking to see if we want lunch delivered today. Do we?"

"Ooh," exclaimed Byrle. "How about muffulettas?"

"Yum," said Tandy.

Besides the po'boy, the muffuletta was the other signature sandwich of Louisiana. Back in the early 1900s, a Sicilian grocer, gastronomically inclined, combined various meats, cheeses, and olive relish onto a round, seeded muffuletta loaf, thus launching a deliciously enduring trend. Although there were endless variations on the muffuletta sandwich, they all shared one thing in common—muffulettas were wonderfully messy to eat.

"Salami and cheese for me," called Tandy.

"Tell 'em to skip the capers on mine," said Byrle.

"I'm *dying* for an oyster po'boy," screeched Sweetmomma Pam.

Carmela smiled sweetly at the unhappy little man who hovered nearby. "This lunch thing will probably take a while to sort out," she told him. "I'm gonna have to get back to you."

Chapter 14

"THESE ARE TERRIFIC," murmured Natalie Chastain as she turned over one of the menu cards and studied it. "Really terrific."

"Thanks," said Carmela. "It's been a fun project." *And praise be for the nimble fingers of Sweetmomma Pam.*

"Where would we be without volunteers like you?" Natalie asked, then quickly grinned and held up a hand. "Don't answer that. I *know* where we'd be. Up a creek without a paddle."

Carmela and Sweetmomma Pam had finished the menu cards and Baby's martini glasses by two that afternoon. Carmela had immediately tossed everything into her car (she'd taken to parking in back of Menagerie Antiques now, since nobody was ever there) and headed across town to the Art Institute. Now, as she stood in Natalie's cramped office, surveying floor-to-ceiling shelves filled with Chinese bronzes, kachina dolls, Greek vases, and various and sundry pieces of antique silver, the large black and white institutional clock that hung on the wall was just creeping toward two thirty.

"I'll have the description tags for you tomorrow afternoon," Carmela told her as she studied the final copy Natalie had just handed her. She also silently thought to herself, *I'm really gonna have to book it.*

Natalie nodded, sublimely pleased. "And I understand you'll also be carving our jack-o'-lanterns." She flashed Carmela a quizzical glance. "Carmela, how do you *manage* it all?"

Carmela shrugged. She had no idea. "Just doing a favor for a friend is all. Jekyl got busy."

"Jekyl got smart and left town," sighed Natalie. "I should follow his good example. The preparations for Saturday night's Monsters & Old Masters are *killing* me. Are killing *everyone* here," she amended.

"Is that Mrs. Meechum I hear?" a friendly voice called from out in the hallway.

Carmela swiveled her head just in time to see Monroe Payne step through the doorway. Dressed in a dark suit, carrying a small painting in his hand, he looked sedate and suave.

"Hello there," Carmela said, pleased to see him again.

Monroe dropped his voice an octave and gave her a warm smile, the kind he usually reserved only for big-buck donors. "Natalie's been telling me what an absolute *angel* you've been, Carmela. Helping us with the menu cards and the description tags . . . Speaking of which, here's our final piece." He handed the small oil painting over to Natalie.

"Wonderful," she said.

"And of course you'll be in attendance Saturday night?" Monroe said, smiling at Carmela. He glanced quickly at Natalie, suddenly flustered. "*Please* tell me we sent complimentary tickets to Mrs. Meechum."

"Carmela. Just call me Carmela." Actually, she had never changed her name to Meechum in the first place. "And don't worry about complimentary tickets. I'm already sitting at Baby and Del Fontaine's table. They invited me way back when. Months ago, really."

Natalie Chastain gently set the oil painting down on her desk, frowned slightly, then pawed through a jumble of papers. She suddenly looked puzzled as something caught her eye. "Don't quote me on this, Carmela, but I think you're going to end up with place cards at *two* different tables. I distinctly remember your husband telling me you'd be sitting with him, since his sister is slated to receive our Founder's Award Saturday night."

"That sounds exactly like something Shamus would do," said Carmela, fuming inside. She was pretty sure she'd made it crystal clear to Shamus that she was sitting with Baby and Del and the rest of the gang.

"Problem?" asked Natalie.

"You'll just have to make like a social butterfly," said Monroe, sensing Carmela's discomfort and trying his best to give the apparent mix-up a light-hearted spin. "And flit freely from one table to another. Maybe even bring a second costume so no one will be the wiser."

"I'll take it under advisement," Carmela told him, although she was really thinking about wringing Shamus's scrawny neck. "Natalie," she said, holding up a finger. "Tags for the art and floral displays tomorrow."

Natalie bobbed her head gratefully. "Thank you *so* much."

RAIN WAS still spattering down when Carmela swung her car back down Napoleon Avenue and headed for the Garden District. Here were sixty-six blocks of palatial splendor, elegant antebellum mansions constructed in the

1840s and '50s to house the socially and financially prominent. Today, most homes were painted in delicate soft pastels and trimmed in white. Many had been made even grander over the years by the addition of Greek columns, expansive verandahs, second-story porticos, and intricate wrought-iron fences and balustrades.

Stately and majestic, the oak tree reigned supreme in the Garden District; its great languid bows formed imposing archways over many of the streets. Lavish gardens surrounding the homes, originally cultivated to shield residents from the stench of nearby slaughterhouses, boasted towering stands of crape myrtle, bougainvillea, oleander, and camellias. In spring, the yards of most Garden District homes were a riot of flowering azaleas.

As Carmela pulled her car in front of Baby's house and got out, she could hear the faint clang of the old streetcar as it rattled its way down St. Charles Avenue, just a few blocks over. Dating back to 1835, it was the oldest streetcar line still operating in the United States and its thirteen-mile route still served as a commuter train for New Orleans residents.

Baby Fontaine lived on Third Street in a palatial Italianate home with double doors of glass and wrought iron. Pale pink silk covered the walls of the front entry hall, where an enormous crystal chandelier dangled and a huge circular stairway curled dramatically upward.

"Carmela!" called Baby as she ran to greet her, all rustling silk and smelling of Joy, the perfume she considered her signature scent. "Come in, come in," she enthused.

Charles Joseph, the Fontaines' longtime maintenance man, had admitted Carmela and was now dispatched to Carmela's car with orders to carefully ferry in the newly decorated glassware. Charles Joseph, who kept the furnace purring, the air conditioner humming, and the ancient copper pipes flowing as well as could be expected in the grand old house, was a tall, solemn, gray-haired man with a heroic handlebar mustache. Carmela thought he looked exactly like one of the old French pirates who had fought alongside Andrew Jackson and Jean Lafitte to help save the city of New Orleans during the War of 1812.

Grabbing Carmela by the hand, Baby dragged her down the center hallway to what she called her office. Carmela found herself being pulled past a grand living room that was impeccably furnished with Louis XVI furniture and hung with original oil paintings, as well as a spectacular cypress-paneled library with floor-to-ceiling bookshelves filled with gleaming leather-bound books.

Baby's office at the end of the hallway was really just a small salon with a cozy brick fireplace. But Baby had set it up with a white silk love seat and matching club chairs, an antique library table for scrapbooking and craft projects, and pink lighting that was highly complementary to a lady's complexion. This was Baby's special retreat where she planned parties, gabbed on the phone, and had a few friends in for tea and gossip. It was also where she kept Sampson, her pet snapping turtle.

"Hello, Sampson," said Carmela, peering into a giant cut-glass bowl at the dark green, humpbacked reptile. Sampson, not known for having particularly good manners or even a decent temper, gave a warning hiss as he regarded Carmela with hooded eyes.

"Careful, honey," said Baby, "don't get too close. Sampson's a little out of sorts today. We didn't have any beefsteak handy, so I had to make do with a slice of chicken. Put the poor dear off his feed, I guess."

Carmela knew Sampson wasn't all that picky. He'd been known to chomp down on a human or two when guests got a little too curious and poked a finger at him.

"Did I tell you?" Baby said excitedly. "Everyone's coming Saturday afternoon." By "everyone" she meant her family. Kids, grandkids, brothers, sisters, cousins, second cousins. She was going to stage a late afternoon Halloween buffet at her house and then scamper off to the Art Institute for the Monsters & Old Masters Ball.

"This year Anne Rice won't have the only big hoo-ha in the Garden District," said Carmela, referring to the big Halloween party that the famous mystery writer traditionally threw.

"Well, it's not like ours is going to go all night," said Baby. "Del and I for sure want to be there for Monsters & Old Masters. Besides, the kids will want to go out trick-or-treating and most of the kinfolk will be going on to other parties."

"I see some nice trick-or-treat bags over there," said Carmela, pointing to a stack of orange and black bags that Baby had gussied up with black cat and bat charms. "What else are you planning for Saturday?"

"The dining room will be draped with *yards* of sheer orange gossamer fabric," said Baby with great enthusiasm. "With matching ribbon tied around the silverware."

"And outside?" prompted Carmela. Baby was always big on outside decor, too.

"I'll do a spectacular arrangement of orange and white pumpkins on the front porch," said Baby. "With garlands of grape vine and bittersweet hung everywhere. And of course we'll be doing pumpkin alley again this year."

Pumpkin alley was something all Baby's neighbors participated in. They got together and brought in a huge truckload of pumpkins, carved faces into them, and then, on Halloween night, lined the street with glowing jack-o'-lanterns. Set every three feet along the curb, the flickering, smiling faces of pumpkin alley were quite a sight to behold.

"How's the carving coming?" asked Carmela, knowing that was the hardest part. Knowing she had to get busy herself pretty soon and carve a couple jack-o'-lanterns of her own.

"I've only got two more left to do," groaned Baby. "But I'm plumb out of ideas. Carmela, I was wondering if you might . . ."

"Your glassware, Miss Baby." Charles Joseph stood at the doorway, boxes piled in his arms. Carmela found it amusing that Charles Joseph never called her Mrs. Fontaine or even Ms. Fontaine, but always Miss Baby. Then again, it was one of those Southern mannerisms that was both peculiar and endearing.

"Here, let me help," said Baby, leaping up from the love seat and grabbing the top box of glassware. Together, she and Charles Joseph set the boxes on the table, then gently opened them.

Carmela said a hasty prayer to Saint Francis Xavier Cabrini, the patron saint of hopeless causes, knowing it would be a miracle if all two dozen martini glasses had survived their period in transit. Not because of her car, which was as smooth-riding as they come, but because the streets of New Orleans were so perilously riddled with potholes. Killer potholes. Had been, in fact, since anyone could remember. Probably since the very colorful Huey P. Long, also known as the Kingfish, had reigned as governor and then senator.

"These are fabulous!" exclaimed Baby as she grasped one of the spider-decorated glasses and held it up for inspection. "Aren't they fabulous, Charles Joseph?"

Charles Joseph bobbed his grizzled head. "Very fanciful, indeed." He gave a faint smile. "Lovely work, Miss Carmela."

"Thank you, Charles Joseph," said Carmela, suddenly feeling as though she were in a stage play where everyone was terribly well mannered and polite.

"Nothing broken?" asked Carmela.

"They're absolutely perfect," smiled Baby, her blue eyes gleaming. "In more ways than one." She put an arm around Carmela. "Thanks for being such a dear friend."

Charles Joseph helped repack the boxes and gathered them up once again. "I shall place these in the pantry, ma'am, if that is agreeable to you."

"Wonderful," cooed Baby, who turned to face Carmela. "Now, about those two pumpkins I have left . . ."

"I've got just the design for you," said Carmela as she grabbed a crayon and a sheet of paper, then sat herself down at the library table and began to sketch.

"Look at that," marveled Baby as Carmela's fingers flew across the page. "A pumpkin face that has a moon for one eye and a star for the other. Where *ever* do you find your inspiration?"

CARMELA ZOOMED down the back alley, pointed her car into the parking space behind Menagerie Antiques, and cut the engine.

Quarter to five. Had she really been gone almost all afternoon? Yes, she had. *But,* she told herself, *I got a whole lot done, too.*

And there's lots more to do, a little voice echoed inside her head as Carmela stuck her key in the lock and pushed her way inside the shop.

"I'm back," she called, throwing her leather bag down atop the clutter of her desk.

Out front, two customers were sifting through a basket filled with colorful stickers while Gabby stood at the front counter, ringing up a purchase for a third customer. Carmela thought Gabby looked absolutely frazzled.

"You've been busy," Carmela remarked after the last customer had finally departed.

Gabby stared at her. "Busy? *Au contraire,* my dear, we've been absolutely frantic. I do believe we did more business today than in all of last week." Gabby blew out a puff of air that lifted her bangs off her forehead, then plunked herself down on one of the stools that had been brought around from the back of the counter. "Halloween," she said. "Amazing. It's been almost as crazy as Mardi Gras."

"Gabby," said Carmela, immediately feeling guilty, "I'm awfully sorry. I had no idea the shop would be so busy today."

Gabby waved a hand. "Not to worry. In a weird way it was kind of fun. Challenging, you know?"

Carmela nodded as she glanced about the shop. Something was missing. Or rather, someone was missing. Boo was still there, curled up in the corner, but . . . "Where's Sweetmomma Pam?" Carmela asked suddenly.

"Gone home," said Gabby, gathering up a handful of hair and pulling it into a ponytail. "Ava stopped by about twenty minutes ago to pick her up. Ava also inquired about your—and I quote—hot date last night." Gabby paused, curious now. "*Did* you have a hot date last night?"

"Not really," said Carmela. "It was more of a business thing. I'm going to do a scrapbook for Bon Tiempe Restaurant."

"Oh," said Gabby, suddenly switching to her disinterested mode. Gabby's forte was helping customers put together family scrapbooks and she was quite content to let Carmela deal with the commercial projects.

Carmela glanced at her watch, a sporty little Tag Heuer that Shamus had given her when they were first married. "Listen, could you stick around for five more minutes? I have to bring some stuff in from my car."

"No problem," said Gabby, beginning to sort through a basket of stickers that had gotten all messed up.

"I stopped by Patterson's Paper Supply and got three more packages of that floral-patterned paper," Carmela called to her as she headed toward the back door.

"Good," said Gabby. "Mrs. Gardette was in a few days ago asking about it."

Carmela had the packs of paper balanced on one knee, and that knee jammed up against the rear bumper of her car, when a truck lumbered down the alley. It was a large, nondescript-looking vehicle with a white cab and a wooden box with a tarp thrown over its contents. Easing up to the back door of Menagerie Antiques, the truck rumbled to a stop, its tailpipes belching diesel fumes.

What's this? Carmela wondered as she wrinkled her nose. *A delivery for*

Bartholomew Hayward? Doesn't this guy know that Barty is dead? Has been
for some five days now?

Resting her packages on the hood of her car, Carmela walked toward the
truck. If memory served her correctly, Barty had been expecting a shipment
the night he was murdered. She wondered if this was the shipment, arriving
late. Or if this same fellow had delivered a *different* shipment on Saturday
night. If so, he might know something.

"Got a delivery," said the trucker, jumping from his cab. He was ample-
bellied and jowly, wearing a gray shirt that barely tucked into baggy khaki
pants. The name DWAYNE was stitched in red over his shirt pocket. No doubt,
Carmela decided, his family and friends pronounced it *Doo*-wayne.

"The owner is away," said Carmela, unsure as to how to proceed. *Yeah,*
he's away. For good.

"No problem," said Dwayne. "As long as somebody can let me in."

Carmela thought of the keys Billy Cobb had passed on to her a few days before. Should she go get those keys and let Dwayne in? Why not? No harm done.

Carmela was back with the ring of keys in two minutes, unlocking the
back door and then ducking inside the back room of Menagerie Antiques. She
pressed a dusty red button and the large garage door creaked and groaned its
way upward.

"You were just here last Saturday?" she asked.

"Nope," said Dwayne. "Haven't been here for a couple weeks."

That might have been so, but Dwayne certainly knew his way around. He
flipped on a few more lights, then shoved a couple wooden crates off to one
side to make room for the new shipment. Then he muscled the half-dozen
pieces of furniture off his truck, slid them onto a dolly, and wheeled the furniture inside. Once he'd dispatched with the furniture, he disappeared into the
bathroom for a few minutes to do his business.

Carmela stood off to the side the whole time, a somewhat reluctant par-
ticipant, still wondering if she'd done the right thing.

And, pray tell, what is the right thing? Tell Dwayne to get lost? Call the
oh-so-strange Jade Ella and tell her to get down here to her dead husband's
shop? Ring up Reed Bigelow, Bartholomew Hayward's insurance agent?

None of the choices seemed terribly appealing. Or all that appropriate. So,
in the end, Carmela just wandered about Bartholomew Hayward's workroom,
gazing at spare chair parts, a peeling fireplace mantel, a small painting on an
easel, and waited patiently for Dwayne to emerge from the rest room.

Dwayne came out, zipping his pants. "You got anything for the return
trip?" he asked nonchalantly.

"What?" asked Carmela, slightly discombobulated by Dwayne's casual
zip-up.

The trucker inhaled deeply. Then he picked up his clipboard and tapped a
metal pen against it, as though he really didn't have time for this. "Mr. Hayward's usually got a pickup for me," he told her.

"Where do you take it?" Carmela asked, wishing Dwayne would stop his annoying tapping.

Dwayne gave an exasperated shrug. "Storage. Where else?"

Carmela rolled her eyes. "I *know* that."

With that the trucker seemed to drop his hard-ass attitude. "The usual place," he told her. "Place over in Westwego, just off River Road."

"Yeah," said Carmela. "Okay." She gave an appraising look around, then flashed Dwayne what she hoped was one of her sweetest smiles. "No, we don't seem to have anything to haul out there today."

"Okay then," he said, passing her the pen and clipboard. "Just put your John Hancock right there."

"Not a problem," said Carmela. She thought about signing a false name, then figured, the heck with it. On the bottom line of the form she carefully penned *Carmela Bertrand accepting shipment for Billy Cobb.*

"Thanks," said Dwayne as he disappeared out the door. "You-all have a good one."

Carmela stood in the back of Bartholomew Hayward's shop and looked around. The shipment Dwayne had left was relatively small. A highboy chest of drawers, a banister-back rocking chair, plus a round dining table with four so-so chairs. Nothing to write home about. Probably the same caliber of stuff Dove Duval had been summarily stuck with.

But that storage place over in Westwego. Now that sounded interesting. Carmela wondered if that could be the place where Billy Cobb was hiding out.

She turned the idea over and over in her head, wondering if Billy was, in fact, hunkered down in Barty Hayward's storage space. Finally, she decided there was only one way to find out. Take a drive out there.

Yeah, but that means I have to go into Barty's office and snoop through his records to locate the exact address.

Was that a smart thing to do?

Good question.

And, of course, the next issue was what to do if she actually found Billy Cobb hiding out there. Then what? Did she try to reason with him? Get him to turn himself in so the whole mess could be sorted out? Lieutenant Babcock seemed like a decent man. Could she convince Billy to turn himself in to him? And then convince the lieutenant that Billy was innocent?

But there was something else bothering Carmela. In the back of her mind hung the unanswered question: *What if Billy Cobb really is a murderer? What if I'm walking into what could end up being a trap?*

Carmela decided she wouldn't dwell on that right now.

The address. First I gotta find the address.

Carmela eased through the swinging doors that led into the shop, decided it probably wasn't a good idea to switch on the lights. If she did, customers walking by would for sure see her rummaging around and knock on the door, seeking admittance.

Moving carefully through narrow aisles of etageres and tea tables crammed with antique silver teapots, pewter pitchers, colorful glass vases, and fanciful lamps with fringed shades, Carmela made her way to Bartholomew Hayward's desk in the center of the room. Hesitantly, she turned on a single Tiffany-style lamp. As it cast its golden light across the top of the desk, Carmela hoped she could locate a Rolodex or address book. If she could, she was fairly certain she'd also find the address.

Unlike Barty Hayward's neatly organized shop, his desktop and business records were a mess. Business cards were heaped in three different Chinese blue and white bowls, messages were written on tiny scraps of paper and scattered seemingly everywhere, files were nonexistent. After twenty minutes of random pawing through office drawers and stacks of papers, Carmela found a small stack of unpaid bills sitting beneath an antique bronze frog that sported large, bugged-out eyes. And, lucky, lucky, lucky, one of the bills just happened to be an invoice for monthly rent of $810 on warehouse space located at 1015 River Road.

"Find anything interesting?" a voice suddenly rasped.

Carmela's heart thudded in her chest and she physically jumped at least a foot. She reared up ramrod straight and whipped her head around to see who'd just spoken to her. Standing just outside her little pool of light was Jade Ella Hayward, staring at her with a curious glint in her eyes.

"Jade Ella," gasped Carmela. She fought to keep her voice easy and conversational even though her heart was still thumping out of control. "You scared me half to death!"

Jade Ella stared pointedly at Carmela. In her crimson embroidered Chinese jacket, tight blue jeans, and beaded high-heeled boots, Jade Ella looked like she was ready to attend the MTV Music Awards. Maybe even vault onstage and belt out a number or two.

"What are you doing here?" Jade Ella finally asked. Not *Hello,* not *How are you,* just *What are you doing here.*

"I . . ." Carmela stuttered, then suddenly remembered she was still clutching a copy of the furniture delivery order she'd just signed.

"I signed for a delivery," she stammered. "A truck pulled up something like ten minutes ago. Did you see the new furniture out back?"

Jade Ella nodded, but Carmela wasn't sure whether Jade Ella was admitting to having seen the furniture, or if she was just encouraging Carmela to continue her explanation. "I was just going to stick this in a safe place where Billy or whoever could find it." Carmela held the piece of paper up as evidence and gave a casual shrug. *There, that sounds awfully reasonable, doesn't it?*

"How'd you get in?" asked Jade Ella.

"Billy gave me a set of keys. Just in case."

Jade Ella took a few steps forward and peered into Carmela's face. Looking for . . . what? For her to flinch? To crack and come clean?

When Jade Ella didn't seem to find what she was looking for, she let loose a long sigh then held up her own set of keys. She jangled them noisily in Carmela's face. "See, I've still got my keys, too."

Carmela stared back at Jade Ella, wondering if Jade Ella had finally received the life insurance check she'd been so anxiously awaiting. Was the case finally settled? Was Jade Ella no longer a suspect? Did she now own Menagerie Antiques lock, stock, and barrel?

Carmela's momma had once told her that the best way to get an answer from someone was to ask them a direct question. That's what Carmela did now.

"Did you get your insurance settlement?" she asked Jade Ella.

Jade Ella's pupils seemed to contract, her eyebrows pinch together. Then, within a split second, she'd composed herself again.

"Why, no, I didn't, Carmela," said Jade Ella. "But it's awfully kind of you to ask." Jade Ella's voice was guarded.

"Reed Bigelow, your insurance agent, stopped by my shop this morning," said Carmela, by way of explanation. "That's why I asked."

Jade Ella's face seemed to relax. "Ah, and what did the tedious Mr. Bigelow want from you?"

"He wanted to ask a few questions concerning Barty's death," said Carmela. "Since I was almost a witness."

"Yes, you were," said Jade Ella. "Almost." Her green eyes bore into Carmela with burning curiosity. "Carmela, you didn't tell Mr. Bigelow that I played any sort of role in Barty's business affairs, did you?" Jade Ella took a step forward and adjusted a small oil painting that sat on an easel.

"We never got around to any kind of Q-and-A session," Carmela told her. "Things just got too busy. And besides, everything's already in the police reports, which I believe he would have access to. Why do you ask?"

Jade Ella folded her arms protectively across her chest. "There's seems to be an itty-bitty problem concerning taxes," said Jade Ella. "Something owed, or unpaid, or carried over," she said. "Anyway . . . Barty's tax issues have absolutely *nothing* to do with the insurance company paying out death benefits."

"Death benefits," repeated Carmela. "Sounds so final."

But Jade Ella had already spun on her glitzy boot heels and was threading her way back through the shop and toward the back door. "Good day, Carmela," she called.

Chapter 15

RAIN BEAT DOWN and a howling wind whipsawed stands of scrawny palmettos as Carmela made her way tentatively down River Road. Bumping along this deserted stretch of road that wound perilously close to the banks of the Mississippi, she'd once again come to the inevitable conclusion that New Orleans and much of its surrounding environs was a very spooky place. Aboveground cemeteries seemed to lurk everywhere. Old buildings emerged from dank mists like silent sentinels. And here in the Crescent City, where humidity often topped out at one hundred percent, trees and vegetation had a nasty habit of running wild. Of stealthily overgrowing brick walls, fountains, and crumbling outbuildings to the point where landmarks were reduced to architectural topiaries.

As Carmela slowed her car and rolled down the window, searching for 1015 River Road, she had the feeling she was time traveling. She'd been on the lookout for a storage space. Hopefully a modern, concrete building that was well lit and offered orderly numbered addresses.

Instead, what she was finding were decrepit old buildings, docks, and warehouses. Very industrial and not the least bit inviting. No sir.

Faded numerals loomed ahead of her. A one, a zero, a blank spot, then a five. Was this 1015? Had to be. Cranking her car into a muddy parking lot, Carmela gazed at the ramshackle wood building and wrinkled her nose.

She was staring at a long, low building with some sort of decaying wooden truck dock stretching along one side of it. A tumble of old machinery was scattered about, most of it hidden by overgrown weeds. This had obviously been some kind of manufacturing plant. But certainly not in recent years.

Carmela cut the engine, listened to the *tick tick tick* of the motor cooling down. Boo, hunched in the front seat next to her, gave a tentative *woof*.

She reached over and ruffled Boo's fur. "Sorry, girl," she told the dog. "Your job is to stay here as lookout and lend a little moral support." Gazing at the ramshackle building once more, she noted that it was sublimely unappealing. "Make that a *lot* of moral support."

Okay, she told herself. *This was your big idea, your grand adventure. You had an inkling that Billy Cobb might be hiding out here. Does this look like the kind of place someone would hide out?*

Ignoring what she deemed to be her own stupid, frivolous questions,

Carmela opened the car door and stepped gingerly onto squishy, muddy ground.

If this is Bartholomew Hayward's storage space, what on earth does he store here?

Slowly, quietly, Carmela made her way to the front door of the building. There were no windows, no lights, no indication of what might be inside.

Putting a hand on the old metal door, Carmela jiggled the handle. No dice. The door was dismally chipped and pockmarked, but it was also sturdy, serviceable, and securely locked. No way was she going to just waltz in the front door for a quick look-see.

That meant searching around back. Looking for a window to slip in or another door that could possibly be jimmied.

Which also meant breaking and entering. Gulp.

Keenly aware she was stepping on broken glass as well as moldering vegetation, Carmela made her way to the back of the building. Here the earth was even more soggy, and with each step, she had to pull her shoes from sucking mud.

Stopping in front of a wooden door, Carmela grasped the handle and gave it a tug. The handle rattled, but this door seemed to be locked securely as well.

But back here was also a row of windows.

Carmela stalked along the back of the building, searching for a possible point of entry. At the last window, she spied a loose molding. Digging her fingers under the wood, she tugged hard and was rewarded with a loud *creak*. The wood, damp and rotting, crumbled easily. Then the entire strip of molding pulled away and the bottom window, dirt-streaked glass set in decayed wood, came crashing down, barely missing her foot.

Ouch! Damn!

Torn between wanting to go back to her car and check her foot for possible splinters, and exploring this strange, deserted building, Carmela hesitated for a moment. Then she braced her hands against the side of the window frame, ducked down, and swung a leg up. Now she was halfway in. From there it was an easy task to balance on the window ledge in a crouching position and propel herself inside.

Crunch. Carmela landed atop broken glass. And decided she probably wasn't the first person or persons to enter uninvited through this window.

Anybody here right now? I sure hope not.

Because suddenly, even the thought of running into Billy Cobb in this spooky, deserted place seemed terribly unnerving.

Wondering what exactly this old place had been, she ventured a few hesitant steps in the dark. The interior of the building was pitch black and she wondered how she'd ever find a light. She'd taken three more nervous steps when something tapped her gently on the shoulder.

What the . . . ?

Carmela's mind conjured up an array of horrors . . . bat, giant spider, mysterious disembodied hand . . . as she brushed wildly at the thing that hung there.

And discovered it was a thick black cord.

An electrical cord? Yeah, could be, she thought shakily.

Carmela took a deep breath, grasped at the loop of dusty cord, and followed it upward? To a power switch. Her fingers fumbled for a second, finally made contact. A quick *click* and a dim yellow light flooded the premises.

Carmela gazed around. Dark, hulking machinery loomed everywhere. Tiny particles of dust and debris danced in the air.

Carmela promptly sneezed. But now she also had a fairly good idea of what this old place had been.

It's an old shrimp-processing plant!

The Gulf waters off Louisiana were rich and fertile with shrimp. White shrimp were netted off the coastal inland waters, usually from September through May. And brown shrimp, a migratory shrimp, were plentiful May through December. As a result, small shrimp-processing plants dotted the landscape.

Carmela's eyes focused on a disintegrating rubber conveyor belt where shrimp had once been sized and sorted. Ten feet down from that conveyor belt was an enormous metal pot, incredibly filthy now, that had probably served as one of the cookers. To her left was the dust-covered guillotine—a nasty-looking machine armed with hydraulic knives that had quickly and efficiently lopped off shrimp heads. Some of the knives lay scattered nearby, looking corroded and dangerous and sharp. That machine, usually operated by a foot pedal, still carried a faded yellow cardboard sign stuck to its side. Printed in black ink was the word WARNING accompanied by an outline of a man's severed hand, obviously lost due to careless operation. An object lesson of sorts.

Carmela continued to peer around. Dust and metal carnage were everywhere. Lots more strange-looking machines, foul-smelling conveyer belts, and toppled-over racks. Against the far wall, two dirt-encrusted metal doors led to what had probably been old blast freezers.

And snugged up against the old freezer doors was a huge jumble of furniture.

So this really is Barty Hayward's storage space.

Walking tentatively toward the furniture, Carmela studied the jumble of highboys, desks, tea tables, and wooden fireplace mantels. And, as she gazed at the wooden furniture, lying there in a rather sorry state, she saw exactly what Bartholomew Hayward had been up to.

New drawer pulls and fittings had been replaced with old ones. Tables inlaid with bits of ivory and mother-of-pearl had been stained with tea for instant aging. Paintings barely older than she was had been restretched on old frames.

And as Carmela gazed at the musty, dusty surroundings, a rueful smile crept onto her face. Because she saw that this place was, indeed, the perfect place to store furniture.

You could take most anything that was newly knocked together out of pine, oak, cedar, or cypress, and store it here for a few months. Given the climate, each and every piece would be warped and slightly malodorous by the end of its incarceration.

Even a rank amateur could bring in a load of brand-new stuff, toss dirt and sawdust all over it, drip a little pigeon poop on it for good measure, then let it all percolate. And the whole lot would end up looking aged, instantly— within six months flat. Guaranteed.

You had a pretty sweet racket going, Barty.

Carmela stood for a moment, taking it all in as the muffled toot of a tugboat drifted in from the river.

What else was stored here? she wondered. Carmela peered into the dimness, mustiness prickling her nose.

There were smaller wooden crates stacked along the back wall. Probably containing prints and paintings. Carmela moved over to these, reached into a rectangular crate that was open on top, and pulled out a painting.

It was a lovely piece, lots of golds and russets and dark greens. A landscape painting that depicted a Tuscan hillside and a villa in the background with a high, squared-off tower. Pretty. She flipped it over, noting a series of numbers marked on the back of the painting: *NMA92107.*

Carmela stared at the numbers, wondering what they meant.

Auction house? Yeah, probably.

She shrugged and slipped the painting back into its wooden case and idly gazed about the old plant.

Who would have known about this? she wondered. Besides Barty. And the delivery guy, Dwayne.

She figured Jade Ella might also have known. As tumultuous as their marriage had been, the woman must have known *some* things about her husband's business.

And on the heels of that thought came another, a real corker. *Did Jade Ella suspect I might be coming out here tonight?*

Carmela racked her brain.

How long was Jade Ella standing there before she spoke to me? Did she watch me shuffle through the invoices, then carefully peruse the storage invoice?

Carmela knew that if Jade Ella was suspicious about her coming out here tonight, she could be watching right now. Which was a very spooky notion.

Time to boogaloo out of here.

It took Carmela considerably less time to exit the back window, prop the lower half back in place, and scamper to her waiting car. Then, the heater roaring like a blast furnace and Boo dozing on the seat next to her, Carmela bumped her way across the muddy lot to the paved road. But all the while she kept one eye on the rearview mirror. Just in case.

* * *

THE PHONE was ringing off the hook when Carmela came rocketing through her front door, Boo right behind her. She scampered, muddy shoes and all, across the sisal carpet to grab the phone.

"Hello?" she said, fully expecting to hear dead air. She didn't for a minute think she'd made it in time. Figured her caller would have gotten frustrated and hung up.

"Carmela," came a rich, male voice. "You're home."

It was Shamus.

"Shamus," she said, feeling somehow reassured at hearing his familiar voice. "Hey there."

"Hey, cupcake, you're still coming Saturday night, right?"

"What are you talking about?" She knew exactly what Shamus was talking about.

"You're going to sit at our table, aren't you?" Shamus twittered excitedly.

Carmela let out a long sigh. She'd already covered this territory with Shamus and the answer had been a big fat no. Putting a hand over the receiver, she dropped it to her chest, wondered why life always had to be so darn complicated. Quigg Brevard had also hinted at the two of them getting together. And she was already committed to sitting with Baby and Del.

Ain't it grand to be wanted?

Carmela put the phone back to her ear. "Shamus, you know I'm not going to be able to do that."

"Aw, honey," came his answer, and Carmela thought how funny it was that his voice had gone from reassuring to wheedling in a matter of thirty seconds.

"No can do, Shamus." Carmela hobbled over to a dining room chair and sat down. Hooking her left toe into the back of her right tennis shoe, she pried the shoe off. Flecks of mud spattered everywhere. Reaching down, she pulled off the other muddy shoe and gave it a toss. Boo, who'd been sitting near the kitchen ever since they'd come in, flashed her a reproachful look. A look that said, *I'd be punished for making this sort of mess.*

"Carmela, I can't tell you how much Glory is looking forward to this very special night. And to have you right there to share it with us would be icing on the cake for her."

Bad metaphor, decided Carmela. It was way too reminiscent of wedding cake. And the fact that she and Shamus had barely made it past their first anniversary.

Carmela glanced down, saw a tiny rip in her gray wool slacks, and frowned. Damn, these were good ones, too. Plucked from the clearance rack at Saks.

"Tell Glory not to get her underwear in a twist," Carmela told Shamus. "I'll be there Saturday night. I'll applaud politely. I'll tell all my friends to applaud politely."

"But we have a place reserved for you at *our* table," Shamus continued in his maddening way. "It's been prearranged."

"Then I'll *post*-arrange it," Carmela laughed, even though she was still gritting her teeth. "Don't you know? I've got a special *in* at the Art Institute."

"Dawlin', I know you do," continued Shamus. "Which is why I'm askin' you to do this one little old favor." Shamus had casually dropped into good old boy mode. "It would mean so much to the family."

The family. Of course it's about the family. It's always about the family. Except when it's really about the family, decided Carmela. Which always made the whole familial landscape slightly Kafkaesque.

The call waiting button on Carmela's phone suddenly burped.

Hallelujah! Saved by the burp.

"Shamus?" said Carmela. "I gotta go. I got another call."

Without waiting for a response, Carmela drove her thumb down on the button, disconnecting Shamus and connecting her other caller. She decided she didn't give a rat's ass if it was a telemarketer calling to hawk a load of aluminum siding. She was still gonna be nice as pie to him.

But it was someone with far more chutzpah than any mere mortal telemarketer. It was Ava.

"Where the hell have you been?" demanded Ava. "I've been calling your place all night. I thought maybe a bunch of rogue Irish folk dancers swept in and kidnapped you."

"No such luck," said Carmela. She tugged at her slightly damp socks, peeled one off. "I was snooping around inside a deserted shrimp-processing plant. Out on River Road. My hair stinks and there's gobs of slithery mud and probably dead shrimp parts stuck to the soles of my shoes. No less than a dozen cats followed me in from my car." She peeled the second sock off and tossed it toward Boo, who dodged it, then quickly scampered out of the way.

"Damn it, girl," said Ava. "Your life reads like an old Doris Day movie. Trippin' all over the countryside, having one merry adventure after another." She paused. "Honey, what were you *doin'* in a nasty old place like that, anyway? Was this some kind of Halloween prank? Wait a minute . . . don't tell me you're playing that crazy Internet game where you get all sorts of clues, then use one of those global positioning doohickeys."

"No, just following up on a Bartholomew Hayward thing," Carmela told her.

"A new lead?" asked Ava.

"Nah, more like a dead end," said Carmela.

"Oh," said Ava, disappointed. "Here I was hoping for big news. Nothing seems to want to break on that Billy Cobb thing, does it?"

"Actually," said Carmela, "Billy paid a surprise visit to my store yesterday."

"Get out!" exclaimed Ava. "So he didn't leave town after all."

"No, but he's threatening to," said Carmela. She sighed. She wanted to help exonerate Billy, but nothing seemed to be gelling. Nothing that told her he was beyond-a-shadow-of-a-doubt innocent. "I checked on the Internet and called around to a few ladies' shoe stores earlier today, trying to follow up on that heelprint thing?"

"And?"

"Seems nobody's ever heard of a brand with the initials GC."

"Hmm," said Ava. "Maybe it's Gina Chanel."

"Who on earth is Gina Chanel?"

"I dunno," laughed Ava. "Coco's little-known stepsister?"

"Hah," said Carmela. "Nice try."

"Say, honey," said Ava, "I'm sorry you got stuck with Sweetmomma Pam today."

"Not a problem," said Carmela. "She was perfectly lovely and turned out to be a big help."

"Really? You don't have to say that just on my account. I can take it, even if Sweetmomma is kinfolk."

"Really, she's welcome any time," said Carmela.

"You think she'd be welcome Saturday night?" asked Ava.

"You mean . . . ?" said Carmela, not quite tumbling at first to what Ava was asking.

"Saturday night," continued Ava. "At Monsters & Old Masters." She sighed heavily. "Here's the big *problema*. First Sweetmomma Pam told me she had a date for Saturday night, now she says she's broken the whole relation-ship off because the guy turned out to be too much of a chauvinist pig."

"You're talking about the fruit guy?" asked Carmela. "The one she was so *hot* for?"

"That's the one," said Ava. "She says it's over. Kaput. Just one more notch in Sweetmomma Pam's belt, such as it is."

"Actually," said Carmela, "I see that as a positive."

"Meaning?"

"Meaning that Sweetmomma Pam probably had her consciousness raised." *Consciousness raising* was a term Carmela's momma had used a lot when she was growing up. And that Carmela had read about when she'd thumbed through the pages of her momma's old *Ms.* magazines. Put into practical usage, Carmela had found that the basic tenets boiled down to two things: Don't let any fella treat you like a doormat. And don't let any fella make you feel like he's smarter or better than you. 'Cause he ain't. Pretty fine advice actually.

"Of course Sweetmomma Pam is welcome Saturday night," said Carmela. "Shouldn't be a problem at all."

"Do you think we could squeeze her in with us?" asked Ava, who had also been invited to sit at Baby and Del's table. "She's just a little bit of a thing. Barely a hundred pounds."

"I'm sure we can work something out," said Carmela.

"Whew," said Ava. "Now all I have to worry about is coming up with a costume for Sweetmomma Pam."

"I doubt that'll be much of a problem for you," said Carmela. Ava's closets looked like the costume department for the combined road companies of *Hello, Dolly!* and *The Lion King.* Over-the-top theatrical with tons of sequins, feathers, and glitter.

"I hope we're still on for our visit to Spa Diva Saturday morning," said Ava. "I'm really looking forward to it."

After her little run-in with Jade Ella earlier in the evening, Carmela had mixed feelings about using the gift certificates they'd been given. Still, Ava seemed to be counting on it.

"Did you get a load of all the spa treatments they offer?" enthused Ava. "It sounds like a hedonistic paradise. Right up my alley."

"They list some treatments I've never heard of," said Carmela. "Paraffin peel, hot lava stones, a Brazilian wax. I know what a bikini wax is, but a Brazilian wax?"

Ava chuckled. "Honey, haven't you seen pictures of those women strutting their stuff on those beaches in Rio? With their teeny-weeny swimsuits kinda scrunched up the crack of their butts?"

Now it was Carmela's turn to giggle. "Yeah."

"You're a smart girl," said Ava. "Figure it out."

Carmela decided it might be more prudent, if not slightly more modest, to opt for the salt glow body wrap instead.

Chapter 16

FRIDAY MORNING DAWNED dark and dreary. Carmela pulled on a pair of gray wool slacks, a peachy-pink sweater, then a lightweight camel-colored suede jacket.

She'd dreamed about that darned shrimp-processing plant all night. Strange, nightmare images that involved knives, dank conveyor belts, and the layer of feltlike dust that seemed mounded over everything.

And she'd thought fleetingly about that number on the back of the oil painting, too. *NMA92107.*

What did it mean exactly?

When she arrived at Memory Mine, Carmela decided the easiest way to do some fast research would be to phone Natalie Chastain. She was a museum registrar, after all. It was her bailiwick to know about such things.

But when she dialed Natalie's number, the phone rang and rang. Carmela was about to give up, when she heard a loud *click* and then someone came on the line.

"Natalie's office," said a male voice.

"Hi there," said Carmela. "Natalie around?"

"Sorry," came the voice. "I'm not sure where she's off to at the moment."

"Mr. Payne?" asked Carmela.

"Yes, this is Monroe Payne. To whom am I speaking, please?"

"It's Carmela, Carmela Bertrand. I'm doing the—"

"The menu cards!" said Monroe with a smile in his voice. "Of course. I'll tell Natalie you called."

"Actually," said Carmela, hesitating slightly, "I had a quick question. Quite unrelated to menu cards."

"Perhaps I can help?" said Monroe.

Should I? wondered Carmela. *Why not? He's a smart guy, too.*

"If you found a series of numbers on the back of a painting, what would that mean to you?" she asked.

"You're talking about acquisition numbers?" asked Monroe.

"I guess that's it," said Carmela. "Hmm."

"Or deacquisiton numbers," continued Monroe.

"*Deacquistion?*" said Carmela. "That's what—getting rid of a piece of art? Do museums ever do that?"

"Actually," said Monroe, "they do it all the time. Have private sales, sell to dealers, sell at auction."

"*All* museums do this?" asked Carmela.

"Unless they've got a storage area with climate-controlled vaults the size of Texas," Monroe laughed. "Good Lord, you'd be surprised at the things people donate to museums. Old photographs, archaeological relics . . . someone once tried to give us an *elephant's* foot."

Carmela chatted with Monroe Payne for a few more minutes, then hung up. His information had been valuable, but it hadn't led anywhere.

Oh well.

"You off now?" asked Gabby as she popped her head into Carmela's office.

Carmela jumped up, grabbing her handbag and digital camera. "Yup. If anybody calls, just tell 'em I'll be hanging out in Lafayette Cemetery No. 1."

CARS RATTLED by on Prytania as Carmela, accompanied by Boo, picked her way through the fog-shrouded graves of Lafayette Cemetery. Two days earlier, when she'd come here for the funeral of Bartholomew Hayward, the place had been fairly well populated by the living: mourners for Barty's funeral, attendees for two other graveside services that had been going on that morning, plus the inevitable flocks of sightseers, tour groups, and amateur vampire hunters. Today, though, just a few stragglers wandered about.

Of all the cemeteries scattered throughout New Orleans, Lafayette Cemetery No. 1 was one of Carmela's favorites. It was incredibly old, highly atmospheric, and chock-full of history.

Established in 1833, Lafayette Cemetery No. 1, like most New Orleans cemeteries, had been borne out of terrible necessity, when pestilence, yellow fever, and cholera ravaged the city. Those epidemics often claimed thousands of lives, all in one hideous swoop.

Because New Orleans had been built below sea level, early residents soon learned a bitter lesson. Bodies of their loved ones that were buried underground had a nasty habit of finding their way back to the surface. So it didn't take long for the aboveground cemetery to be devised. Crypts, mausoleums, and oven vaults were constructed aboveground to receive the bodies of the deceased.

Many of the larger structures bore a keen resemblance to Roman ruins; others spookily sported several stories, like condos for the dead. But what Carmela was most fascinated by were the ancient single tombs. These were three to four feet high and six feet long and resembled whitewashed grave vaults. Many were crumbling and decrepit now, due to the ravages of time, vandalism, and the merciless heat and humidity. Many of these tombs had once been embellished with images of angels, saints, and other heavenly accouterments, which had long since eroded and melted into ghostly forms.

These were the exact images Carmela planned to photograph, then plug into her computer. Once these images were enlarged, she'd print them out on paper as a sort of pattern. Taping these paper patterns to hollowed-out pumpkins, she would use a wood gouge to carve away the background, ending up with a nifty stencil effect. When lights were inserted, her tombstone images would appear in dark outlines against a glowing orange background.

Because there were so many eerie old graves to choose from, Carmela snapped away with her camera, wandering freely among the tombs as Boo trailed on the leash behind her. As she rounded a large multicolumned mausoleum, Carmela ran headlong into Dove Duval.

"Dove!" she exclaimed, putting a hand to her thudding heart.

Dove Duval pulled up short, as well. "Why, hello, Carmela," she said sweetly. "Lovely day for a stroll, isn't it?"

For the third day in a row, rain drizzled down and clouds hung low. The wind delivered a nasty, damp chill and the weather forecasters were still talking hurricane. Lovely day? Carmela figured Dove *had* to be kidding.

Dove held her umbrella aloft and pressed in uncomfortably close to Carmela. "You must be working on one of your little *projects*," Dove purred.

Carmela didn't much like the way Dove said the word *projects*. Tugging on the leash, Carmela instantly telegraphed an alert to Boo. And Boo, never a terribly friendly dog to begin with, slid her gums back over her sharp white teeth and uttered a low growl. *Grrrrrrr.*

Unsettled, Dove took a step backward. "Such a charming creature," she observed dryly. "Is your dog always this friendly?"

"She's a Chinese shar-pei," Carmela explained. "Not exactly your warm fuzzy breed. More on the order of chilly-wrinkley. Shar-peis tend to regard most outsiders as sworn enemies." Carmela kept a grin pasted on her face even though she didn't feel particularly smiley toward Dove. "I think it hearkens back to the invasion of Genghis Khan," she added. *Whatever the heck that means,* thought Carmela.

But Dove Duval, obviously no genius when it came to history, seemed to accept Carmela's remark at face value. "I see," she said.

"And you're just out for a stroll?" Carmela asked, noting that Boo was holding her tail down instead of in its usual tight curl. The dog was definitely not getting good vibes from Dove.

What are you really doing here, Dove Duval? wondered Carmela. *How come you're lurking around Bartholomew Hayward's grave? Have you really come for an innocent ramble through the cemetery or are you here to gloat over your handiwork?*

"Isn't this what folks here like to do?" asked Dove, gazing about in what seemed to be a state of blissful rhapsody. "Wander these marvelous old cemeteries and commune with the dead? Isn't that what *you're* doing?"

"Actually," said Carmela, "I was just snapping a few photos." She didn't much feel like explaining her jack-o'-lantern–carving project to Dove. In fact, she didn't feel like explaining *anything* to her.

"Probably for one of your many scrapbooks," said Dove, poking bits of choppy blond hair behind her ears. "You're *so* creative." She was obviously dying to know more.

But Carmela was not forthcoming.

"You're very tight with Baby Fontaine, aren't you?" Dove said finally.

"She's one of my dearest friends."

Dove cocked her head to one side. "Baby comes from an old family?"

"Pretty old," said Carmela. "Her grandfather was mayor of New Orleans back in the twenties."

"Very impressive," said Dove. "And she's chaired a lot of committees for the Art Institute?"

Carmela nodded. "She's had her share."

"Let me ask you something," said Dove. "I've spoken with Monroe Payne a few times about a possible winter fund-raiser."

"Okay," said Carmela. So that was it. Dove was bound and determined to chair her own fund-raiser. She probably assumed that, once you were chairman of an event, it was a hop, skip, and a jump to a seat on the board of directors. Carmela knew it was actually a very long and arduous leap.

"And although my concept is still a little loosey-goosey," continued Dove, "I've been tossing around the idea of an upscale food event. A tasting, to be precise."

"You mean like a wine tasting?" asked Carmela. "Because the docents at the Zoological Society are already doing that. Have been for five or six years now."

"I was actually considering something a tad more upscale," said Dove, her eyes gleaming. "Perhaps a caviar and vodka tasting. Maybe give it a catchy name. Call it Night of the Czars or something like that. What do you think?"

"Sure," said Carmela. "Might work."

Dove looked at her sharply. "Monroe Payne was *extremely* enthusiastic, Carmela."

"He'd be the one to know. From what I hear, Monroe Payne has definitely got his finger on the pulse of the donors." Carmela tugged at Boo's leash and the two of them started to edge away.

"Yes, he does, doesn't he," said Dove.

"Nice seeing you," said Carmela, deciding she was pretty close to making a clean break.

"Have fun now," said Dove, waggling her fingers and pulling her dark green velvet cape about her shoulders. "See you tomorrow night." She paused. "And Carmela . . ."

Carmela hesitated, a slight frown crossing her face. "Yes?"

"I can't *wait* for you to see my arrangement!"

IT WASN'T until she got back to her shop that Carmela had a chance to take a look at the photographs Quigg Brevard had given her. But first, of course, she had to drop off her car at home, put Boo in the apartment, then pop across the courtyard to say hello to Ava and Tyrell, who were practically going berserk from all the customers who were crowded inside their little incense-filled store. Then Carmela hotfooted it back to Memory Mine on Governor Nicholls Street.

"Hey there," said Gabby, who was demonstrating some new templates for a couple customers. "Help yourself to some pumpkin soup. It's in the back room."

"You cooked?"

Gabby put a hand to her forehead, simulating utter shock. "Surely you jest. No, Baby dropped off a pot of soup earlier. Said she had *tons* of pumpkin meat left over."

"I'll just bet she does," said Carmela.

With a mug of Baby's pumpkin soup heating in the microwave, Carmela sat down at her desk and spread out the photos Quigg Brevard had given her. Most were your fairly typical party shots. Not the lampshade-on-your-head variety, but still all the subjects looked fairly garrulous and affable. Men and women flirting, toasting, hugging, kissing.

There were several shots of a wedding reception, with a bride in a big poufy dress that looked a little like a wedding cake itself. And, surprise, surprise, there were also a few photos of Bartholomew Hayward hosting a summer soiree on the back patio of Bon Tiempe.

The timer on the microwave dinged and Carmela jumped up to fetch her soup. It was steaming like mad, but she took a sip anyway. Wonderful. Baby was a superb cook, even though she was forever claiming she wasn't and usually opted to have her dinner parties catered.

Carmela carried her mug of soup back to her desk and focused, once again, on the photos of Bartholomew Hayward's party. She could faintly recall that the summer before, Barty had staged a big promotion that he'd called his American Painters Expo. It had been by invitation only and she hadn't been one of the chosen. But, judging from the attendees in the photograph, quite a few socially prominent art lovers had RSVP'd and shown up to peruse his selection of rather enchanting paintings.

In two shots Carmela could clearly see that paintings in large, decorative frames had been set up on easels ringing the courtyard. And that the guests were drinking, chowing down, and actually gazing at the paintings with what could only be called rapt attention. Carmela wondered how successful the event had been and then decided that, with the huge resurgence in art collecting and art investing today, Barty had probably made himself a small fortune. She also wondered how authentic they were, although from the looks of things, the paintings looked surprisingly good. Far better than Barty's other merchandise.

"Carmela?"

Carmela turned her head and raised her eyebrows at Gabby. "Need some help?" she asked. She set her mug down. "I can sure . . ."

"It's not that," said Gabby, fidgeting. She dropped her voice. "That *police detective* is back."

"Lieutenant Babcock?"

Gabby gave a tight nod. "He wants to talk to you."

"No problem," said Carmela. "Send the gentleman back."

By the time she'd scooped up all the photos and deposited them in the top drawer of her desk, Edgar Babcock was standing in her doorway.

"Please," she said, indicating a slightly rickety director's chair, "have a seat."

It was tight quarters in her office and the chair was none too comfy, but Lieutenant Babcock didn't seem to mind.

"What brings you back to Memory Mine?" asked Carmela. "Still looking for a birthday gift for that scrapbooking sister of yours?"

He smiled mildly.

Lieutenant Babcock was a pretty cool customer, Carmela decided. Really knew how to play it close to the vest. He was also one of those people who left lots of gaps in the conversation. The kind of gaps an extremely nervous person, someone who had something to hide, would probably struggle to fill in.

"Actually," said Babcock, crossing his legs, "I'm doing a little research on paint." His pleasant smile never wavered. "Gilt paint."

"Would that be the type of gilt paint that was found on a certain scissors?" asked Carmela.

"It would."

"Mm-hm," she said noncommittally.

"It might also be the type of paint used on certain scrapbook pages."

Carmela leaned back in her chair and her heart did a tiny flip-flop.

"I don't believe it's the same type of paint at all," she said. She knew most of her paint was acrylic-based and assumed the paint found on the latex gloves was oil-based. Most paints and stains used in furniture refinishing were oil-based.

"Still," said Lieutenant Babcock, "it might be worthwhile for our lab to run a few tests."

"Is one of my customers under suspicion?" she asked. "Am I a suspect?"

Lieutenant Babcock gave her a mild smile. "Not at all. We're simply attempting to rule people out."

"Like you tried to rule out Billy Cobb?"

"Billy Cobb is no angel," said Babcock.

"Billy Cobb is also not a murderer," replied Carmela.

"You seem awfully sure of yourself."

"Yes, I do. I am." Carmela fought to keep her voice even.

Babcock suddenly leaned forward, an expression of grave concern on his face. "Can I be perfectly frank with you?"

"Please," said Carmela. It had pretty much been her experience that anyone who said they wanted to be perfectly frank with you was probably setting you up for a nice juicy lie.

"We're not making a lot of forward progress in this investigation," said Lieutenant Babcock, as though he were letting her in on a big secret. "We need all the help we can get."

"And you want my help?" said Carmela.

"Do you have any to give?"

Carmela hesitated. Actually, this man *did* seemed rather committed. And, because her bullshit detector didn't seem to be going off too badly, she decided he might even be one of the honest ones. She wondered if there was any way she could bring Billy Cobb together with Lieutenant Babcock. Convince Billy to turn himself in. And, at the same time, convince Babcock to focus on what she deemed was the *real* investigation. If Billy's name could be cleared, the police could get back to searching for the real murderer.

But Billy was hiding out God knew where. And Carmela had no way to reach him. Billy had her phone number, but would he call? That was the $64,000 question.

Lieutenant Babcock cleared his throat. "It would help enormously," he said, "if you could give us sample bottles of all the gilt paint you carry here in your shop."

"To rule us out," said Carmela.

Lieutenant Babcock offered her a sad smile and Carmela wondered for about the twentieth time if she should say something to him about Jade Ella Hayward and Dove Duval. In her book, both women seemed incredibly suspicious. If there was any ruling out—or in—to be done, they were a good place to start.

But she didn't. At this point, it seemed that any accusations on her part would just come across as smoke screen or sour grapes.

BY FIVE thirty, Gabby had already left for the day, and Carmela was ready to call it quits. She'd fiddled unhappily at her computer, torn between wondering about Billy Cobb's innocence and placing a couple Internet orders for restocks on paper and craft boxes. Now, just as she was about to switch the phone over to the answering service, it started to ring.

Rats, she thought as she picked up the phone, *don't let it be another customer. God bless 'em all, but I'm wrecked. Totally wrecked.*

"Carmela?" came a glib-sounding voice. "Carmela Bertrand?"

"Yes?"

"Glad I caught you. This is Clark Berthume from Click! Gallery." There was a pause. "You know our shop?"

"Yes," she said again, wondering what on earth this was all about. And suddenly leaping to the conclusion that perhaps Shamus had finally gotten the photography show he'd wanted. So Clark Berthume was calling to ask . . . what? To design some sort of invitation or poster or something?

"A friend of mine, Jade Ella Hayward, passed along a few photos you took," said Clark effusively. "I daresay, I was absolutely *bowled over* by them."

"You're calling about *my* photos?" said Carmela, suddenly at a loss for words. "What photos?"

"Why, the fashion sequence you did for Spa Diva, of course."

"No, no," protested Carmela. "There was no fashion sequence." She glanced about as if hoping someone would rush to her rescue. No one did. No one was there. "There must be some terrible mistake," Carmela laughed. "I was horsing around in the park a few weeks ago at the same time Jade Ella had a fashion shoot going on. Just for fun, I took a few shots of the models, too. Alongside the hired photographer. The *real* photographer." Carmela took a deep breath. "So you see, they're not fashion shots at all."

"But you printed them and passed them on to Jade Ella."

Carmela racked her brain. She guessed she did. "I guess I did."

"And she used one of them on the cover of her brochure," said Clark Berthume.

Carmela chewed at her lip. "Could be."

"Well, the shots look extremely professional to me," said Clark Berthume. "In fact, you seem to have captured a certain blasé high fashion attitude and quirky sense of style. Which brings me to the reason I'm calling. I was wondering if you'd be interested in having a small show?"

"A show?" Carmela's voice rose in a surprised squawk. "Me?"

There was a polite chuckle. "Well, that would be the general idea, yes."

"Perhaps I didn't completely make my point," protested Carmela, still stunned by the invitation. "I'm not a professional photographer." Photography, to her, still seemed like more of a by-product of scrapbooking. Shamus was the one with professional aspirations, wasn't he?

"Miss Bertrand," said Clark Berthume, "the black-and-white prints I have spread out on my desk at the moment are really quite stunning. They tell me you're a very fine photographer."

Damn Jade Ella, thought Carmela. *Why did she do this? Why did she have to show those stupid photos to Clark Berthume?*

"Can I call you back?" stuttered Carmela.

"Not a problem," said Clark Berthume. "When can I expect to hear from you?"

Next year. Never. "Next week?" asked Carmela.

"Monday afternoon at the latest," cautioned Clark Berthume. "I'm trying to fix the schedule."

Chapter 17

RAIN POUNDED DOWN as Carmela scampered across her courtyard and jammed her key in the door. Mounds of jaunty bright red bougainvilleas that cascaded from twin urns flanking her front door had been knocked flat. The fountain that normally babbled so gently swirled like a storm drain. Overhead, the night sky pulsed with lightning and crackled with thunder. If this was indeed a hurricane, it seemed aptly poised to unleash its full fury.

Carmela almost missed seeing the envelope someone had slid under her door. Tromped right across it and dripped water all over it, in fact, until she flipped on the light and noticed its white glare staring up at her from the floor.

"What's this?" Carmela asked Boo as she bent over to pick it up. "Special delivery?"

Ripping open the envelope, Carmela pulled out a small photo that had been stuck inside. And as she stared at it, received the shock of her life.

The photo was of her and Boo walking in the cemetery. That morning!

That someone had spied on her was creepy enough, but the mysterious photographer had taken it one step further and actually *vandalized* the photo. Carmela's face had been scratched out with a pin until only paper showed through. Then the pin had been stuck clear through the paper into Boo's chest, right about where her heart would be. Crude arrows aimed at both of their heads had been drawn with red grease pencil.

Ohmygod. Someone was watching me today! Was it Dove Duval? Or somebody else? Oh, lordy, this isn't good. This isn't good at all.

Carmela's first thought was to call somebody. Ask them to come over as a sort of reinforcement. Because she sure as hell didn't want to be alone. Feeling threatened and afraid and vulnerable.

Carmela flew to the phone and dialed Ava's number. Nobody home. She was probably out on a date. Or with Sweetmomma Pam.

What about Baby? No, I can't call her. She's busy preparing for her family get-together tomorrow night.

Carmela dialed Gabby's number. She answered on the first ring.

"Gabby," said Carmela, "sorry to bother you, but did anybody call while I was out today?"

"Sure," chirped Gabby. "A couple folks did." She held her hand over the receiver for a couple seconds while she called: "Just a *minute*, Stuart. We'll eat in a *second*."

"A couple?" asked Carmela.

"Well . . . probably more like three or four."

"And you told them . . . ," said Carmela, knowing *exactly* what Gabby had told them.

"Just what you said," responded Gabby. "That they could find you at Lafayette Cemetery No. 1."

CARMELA HUNG up the phone, wondering who else she could call. She glanced over at Boo, who lifted her head expectantly.

Shamus? Ooh, I don't want to do that, do I?

A second look at the scratched and mangled photo changed her mind.

But even after getting Shamus on the phone and explaining her big scare to him, he was not the knight in shining armor she'd hoped he'd be.

"Jeez, Carmela." Shamus's voice was flat. "I was just about to head up to Harrisonburg. There's a Civil War reenactment going on at Fort Beauregard this weekend."

"But it's raining. Pouring buckets, in fact."

"Yeah, but . . ."

"And you for sure were planning to be back tomorrow afternoon anyway," Carmela said. "For Monsters & Old Masters." She hesitated. *Should she? Why not.* "And Glory's big award," she added.

"Well . . . yeah," came his answer. "Of course."

"You could still drive up early tomorrow," she suggested.

"I might miss the cannon salute."

Carmela hung on the phone, not saying a word. Feeling guilty about imposing on him. Feeling even more guilty about the surprise invitation she'd just received from the Click! Gallery. Mustn't let Shamus know about *that*.

"Well, if you're *really* scared . . . ," Shamus finally offered.

"I'm really scared," Carmela told him.

Ten minutes later, Shamus Allan Meechum, Carmela's estranged husband, was wandering barefoot around her kitchen, scratching his stomach and peering into cupboards.

"Got anything to eat?" Shamus asked. He flipped open one cupboard after another, poking his head in. When he'd rifled through everything and still hadn't found anything that appealed to him, he turned to the cluster of canisters and cookie jars that sat on Carmela's kitchen counter just to the left of her stove.

Popping open a ceramic cookie jar, Shamus dug his fist in and helped himself to a dark brown cracker. He munched thoughtfully, then reached in to grab a few more. "Say, these are pretty good," he mumbled. "Got any cheese to put on 'em?" Shamus whipped open the refrigerator door and insinuated his entire head in the refrigerator's cool interior.

"You probably don't want to eat those," Carmela called to him from where she was flaked out, watching TV. "Those are mackerel morsels."

Still surveying the interior of Carmela's refrigerator, Shamus found a half-eaten wedge of cheddar cheese. Greedily, he grabbed a knife and sliced at the cheese, piling it on top of the crackers. Popping them into his mouth, he chewed appreciatively. "Mm-hm, they sure *are* mackerel flavored. And they're *good*. Especially with cheese."

"Shamus, listen to me," said Carmela, starting to laugh. "You're slathering cheese on dog treats."

"What?" came Shamus's strangled cry. He stopped chewing, then suddenly leaned over the sink and turned on both faucets full force. For the next couple minutes, a cacophony of sputtering, splashing, and gargling ensued.

"Why the hell didn't you *tell* me those were dog cookies?" he asked, emerging from the kitchen red-faced and angry. His normally wavy hair stuck up in unruly tufts as Shamus stared accusingly from Carmela to Boo. Boo, as usual, feigned complete innocence. "Who keeps *dog* cookies in a cookie jar?" he groused.

"You know darn well that ceramic doggie is Boo's treat jar," said Carmela. Boo's curlicue tail gave a quick wave as she looked on in mute support.

"Besides," said Carmela, "I had no idea you were going to ransack my kitchen and start chowing down on dog cookies. I'm not exactly psychic."

"No, you're a sadistic prankster," accused Shamus.

"Holy mackerel, Shamus," said Carmela, starting to giggle again. Since the cookies were homemade and wholesome, she knew they were perfectly fine to eat.

Shamus held up a finger. "That's not funny. And damn it, I'm *still* hungry. You surely can't expect a man to go to bed on an empty stomach. He gazed at her meaningfully.

Carmela fixed him with a level gaze. "There's chowder in the freezer, Shamus. Pop a carton in the microwave and it'll be defrosted in six, maybe seven minutes."

The chowder sounded appealing, but Shamus still wasn't convinced.

"What about biscuits?" he asked. "You got any biscuits? Or how about a loaf of nice chewy bread?"

"Nope." Shamus was a carbo freak of the first magnitude. Carmela was, too, but she tried to do without.

"Then I'll bake some bread," said Shamus. "Chowder's no good if you don't have something to dunk in it."

Shamus proceeded to busy himself in the kitchen, pulling out a mixing bowl and then dumping in flour, sugar, and . . . *a bottle of beer?*

"What are you doing?" asked Carmela, deciding this had to be the weirdest recipe ever concocted. Unless Shamus was just making it up as he went along. To jerk her chain.

"I'm making my famous game day beer bread," he replied.

"You're not serious," said Carmela. "You never made *anything* before. And I have certainly never heard you utter a single word about game day beer bread. Please tell me this is some sort of fantasy you read about in a men's magazine. *Soldier of Fortune* or *Penthouse.*"

"They don't put *recipes* in those magazines," Shamus snorted. "Besides, your nose is just out of joint because you think I can't cook." Shamus's voice was heavy with reproach. "And you are so wrong."

"I know I'm not an ardent Julia Child disciple," said Carmela, "or even a Martha fan. But popping open a bottle of beer? Please. That does not constitute *cooking.*"

Yet, a little while later, when Shamus's bread came out of the oven, all hot and steamy and yeasty smelling, Carmela got the surprise of her life.

"This is good," she said, slathering on butter and munching a piece. *Yeah, I guess I'm a bit of a carbo freak, too. Hard to keep a lid on it.*

"You sound surprised." Shamus sounded hurt.

"Actually, I'm astonished," said Carmela. "I had no idea you could cook, let alone bake."

"Well, I *did* reside in a frat house for three years."

"Sure, but you had a housemother. Mrs. . . . what was her name . . . Warlock."

"Murdock," amended Shamus. "Mother Murdock."

"Right," said Carmela, deciding that poor Mother Murdock probably should have been canonized for putting up with all those stinky socks and stinky jocks.

"Honey, I'll have you know that at Tri Delt we had a housemother, two maids, and a handyman."

Carmela shook her head, thinking back to her own college days. It had been your basic four girls crammed into a one-bedroom apartment experience. Endlessly jockeying for the phone and the bathroom, someone always using the last tampon or bit of toilet paper but never owning up to it.

CARMELA'S GOOD humor was once again put to the test when it was time to turn in.

"Jammies?" asked Carmela, eyeing Shamus's hastily packed overnight bag.

"Pardon?" said Shamus, not understanding. Or pretending not to.

"Pajamas," said Carmela. "Did you bring them?"

"Well . . . yeah. I think so."

"Good," said Carmela, ducking into the bathroom. "You change while I take off my makeup and brush my teeth."

Somewhere between the toning and the cleansing routine Carmela heard the phone ring. She tossed her tissue into the trash can and listened, heard Shamus talking in low tones. *Had he given out her number?* she wondered. She straightened up and stared at her bare face in the harsh fluorescent light, thinking, *If this doesn't scare him off, nothing will.* And knowing in her heart that installers of bathroom lighting surely must harbor intense feelings of hostility toward women.

"Some guy named Quigg called," Shamus snorted when she emerged from the bathroom clad in a modest floor-length nightie. "Said you could call him back tomorrow. Quigg." He gave a second disdainful snort. "Sounds like somebody's coonhound. Hey there, Quigg, old buddy, sniff around by that cypress tree and see what you come up with."

Carmela climbed into bed, knowing *this* conversation wasn't going to be productive.

"Say, do you have a date or something with that guy Quigg?" asked Shamus. "Is that why you don't want to, or can't, sit at our table?"

"Not exactly," said Carmela.

"Not exactly," repeated Shamus, suddenly looking very wounded.

Carmela stared at Shamus in wide-eyed amazement, wondering about the green-eyed monster that was suddenly crouched on Shamus's back. She surely hadn't expected this kind of reaction from him. Maybe curiosity, maybe amusement. But certainly not out-and-out jealousy. Hmm.

"Where are your pajamas?" Carmela asked him, but Shamus was still reveling in his full-fledged snit. He peeled down to his T-shirt and jockey briefs, then clambered into bed next to Carmela.

Was this, Carmela wondered, what was meant by the phrase *brief encounter?*

She patted the bed and Boo immediately jumped up and snuggled in between them, a modern-day shar-pei bundling board.

Shamus frowned, lifted himself up on one elbow, and peered across Boo's furry form. "You really owe me for this, you know."

Carmela gazed back at Shamus and shifted about uncomfortably, amazed that a forty-five-pound dog could occupy such a sizable amount of real estate. "What do you mean?" she asked.

"Don't play cute with me," said Shamus. "You know exactly what I'm talking about. Saturday night. Glory's table. Quid pro quo, baby."

Carmela considered this. Shamus had come to her rescue tonight, so it was probably only right that she return the favor. On the other hand, didn't Dr. Phil continually lecture on the danger of married people "keeping score"? *You did this, so I get to do that.* Except she and Shamus weren't exactly your typical married couple. They were your typical on-the-verge-of-divorce couple.

"Okay, Shamus. You got it," said Carmela, trying to stifle a yawn.

Shamus thumped his pillow, flopped over, and let loose a long sigh. "Thank goodness *that's* settled," he mumbled.

As Carmela began to drift off to sleep, the last thing she was aware of were Boo's wet snorts mingled with Shamus's mumbled snores.

Is this the real meaning of family? she wondered. *Maybe. Hard to tell.*

Chapter 18

THE INTERIOR OF Spa Diva looked like it might have taken some of its divine inspiration from the gentlemen's clubs of yesteryear. A leopard print love seat and chairs were clustered around a black ebony cocktail table. Chinese lamps with silk shades of saffron yellow and mandarin red cast a glow against gold-leaf wallpaper. A white flokati rug seemed to undulate on the floor and two life-sized ceramic Chinese warriors from an indeterminate dynasty stood guard on either side of the reception desk.

"Obviously not a glitter-free zone," remarked Carmela as they strolled up to the front desk.

But Ava was never adverse to a little glitz. "I like this," she said. "Very glam-o-rama."

"Very Jade Ella," whispered Carmela.

The receptionist, a skinny, leather-clad blond, accepted their gift certificates and led them each to a treatment room.

Ava had finally decided upon the Banana Frango facial, while Carmela had opted for the full-body mud mask. The brochure, the one with *her* photo adorning the cover, touted the full-body mud mask as a "hedonistic indulgence guaranteed to sleek and slough the skin." She didn't know how much sleekness one could attain in forty-five minutes, but she figured her body could probably do with a little sloughing.

Carmela was shown to a treatment room with gleaming marble floors and walls, recessed glass panels adorned with etched nudes, and a large adjoining shower. Shucking out of her clothing, Carmela climbed onto the vinyl padded table and pulled a sheet about her modestly.

Within moments, a determined-looking woman with gray hair pulled back in a stiff bun entered the room. She carried a pail filled to the brink with green mud.

Uh-oh.

"I am Greta," the woman said by way of introduction. "Roll over, please."

Carmela obediently rolled onto her tummy. The word *please* had been filled with lots of sibilance, but not much warmth.

"The mud draws out *impurities*," explained Greta tersely, slapping a handful of cold, wet goo on Carmela's backside. It smelled earthy and slightly minty. Carmela shivered as she wondered about Greta's accent. Was the inscrutable Greta Swiss? German?

"This is special mud?" asked Carmela, trying to make the best of what suddenly seemed like a slightly embarrassing situation. Maybe that Brazilian wax *would* have been preferable.

"Mineral mud," Greta told her as she patted the goo all across Carmela's back, then turned her attention to Carmela's legs. "Imported from France."

"Ah," said Carmela. "France." It felt like a stupid retort, but she couldn't think of anything better to say as Greta grunted and groaned and tossed handfuls of mud onto her.

"Turn," Greta finally ordered.

Carmela struggled onto her right side, then managed an ungainly flop. Already the mud had begun to harden and form a crusty shell. The treatment table she was reclining on seemed to be heated and she felt like she was slowly becoming a human puff pastry.

More mud was slathered and slapped atop her chest and breasts and when the procedure was complete down to the tips of her toes, Carmela found herself on her back, fully entombed in mineral mud. Greta positioned Carmela's arms close to her sides, then covered her with what looked like a vinyl-coated electric blanket.

Heat, Greta told her, would *activate* the mud's skin-softening properties. She was also instructed to think pure thoughts and not to move a muscle for the next thirty minutes.

The vinyl electric blanket was set at a sleep-inducing eighty degrees and plugged into a master panel that, she was told, electronically controlled the entire procedure. As Greta slipped out the door, the room lights dimmed automatically and Carmela found herself alone in the treatment room.

It wasn't long before Carmela *was* beginning to drift off. The padded treatment table was surprisingly comfortable, the mud had induced a kind of lethargy, and, from somewhere, probably the master control panel, gentle music played over hidden speakers. Quiet, restful, New Age–sounding music. Lots of strings, a gentle pan flute. The kind of music that could transport your brain waves from their normal alpha state into the more relaxed beta state.

As she listened to the gentle notes, Carmela felt each one keenly, could almost *see* the notes floating in the warm air above her. Carmela giggled to herself, aware she was free-associating, not worrying where it was going to take her.

As she sank deeper and deeper into a state of relaxation, Carmela heard a low *click*. She turned her head and sighed, assuming the tape had ended and a new one was going to begin. And let herself tumble, tumble, tumble, like Alice in Wonderland falling down that most intriguing rabbit hole, into a dreamlike state.

But something was crouched on Carmela's chest. Pressing down. Something heavy and hot.

Carmela's eyelids fluttered. She knew she should try to open them, but it seemed like too much trouble.

Trouble.

She was intensely hot. Sweltering.

This time her eyelids really did open.

Nothing was on top of her, but sweat oozed from every pore, coursed down her face in rivulets. She wondered if this was part of the treatment.

No, it couldn't be. She was too hot. Feverish.

Way too hot.

She tried to move an arm, but it stuck fast.

Okay, then try to move your legs, she told herself. *Stand up and the vinyl electric blanket thing that's making you so hot will slide right off.*

She couldn't budge an inch. Now she felt like she was encased in molten lava. Every nerve twanged, every inch of skin seemed to burn.

This isn't happening!

Now what? she wondered. *Now you scream your head off,* her brain replied.

"Help! Anybody!" Carmela shrieked at the top of her lungs. She paused a moment, listened for footsteps. "Get me outa here!"

She gazed longingly at the door, praying for it to open.

"Everything good?" Greta, suddenly chirpy, snicked open the door and peeked her gray head in.

"Get me outa here!" Carmela yelled. "It's too hot, I'm burning up!"

Greta ripped the vinyl electric blanket away, then pulled at Carmela's mud-encrusted arms. There was a slight *crack* as the mud gave way, then, finally, Carmela was free.

"You set the heat way too high!" Carmela screamed, struggling to sit up. She was angry and didn't care who heard her. "I was heading for a meltdown. The darn mud and electric blanket were as hot as Chernobyl!"

"No, ma'am, *you* must have changed the setting." Greta pointed triumphantly to the master control panel. "Almost a hundred degrees." She glowered suspiciously at Carmela. "Too high," she pronounced, as though Carmela were clearly at fault.

Carmela hoisted herself off the treatment table, flung one arm out as much as one could fling a mud-encrusted arm, and pointed toward the door. "Get out!" she thundered.

Knowing a convenient exit when she saw one, Greta scuttled for the door and disappeared.

Angry, hot, feeling like an Egyptian mummy who'd just been released from her sarcophagus after a long slumber, Carmela dragged herself stiff-legged across the room to the shower. She turned the water on full throttle and positioned her mud-encased body under the spray. Then, the cooling water pelting her about the head, shoulders, and back, Carmela waited as the dried mud finally reconstituted itself and changed back to slithery goo. Then the goo finally slid off.

As she stared at the faintly musty green mineral mud swirling about her bare feet toward the drain, Carmela wondered just what the hell had happened. Had there really been a malfunction just now? Or had it been mischief?

Chapter 19

"WHEN WERE YOU going to tell me?" Shamus's voice, filled with hurt, dripping with anger, blasted at Carmela from the telephone.

Carmela grimaced as she stared at the four fat orange pumpkins that squatted on her kitchen counter. And her heart sank.

Does he know about the show? Is that what this call is about?

"Tell you what?" she asked.

"About the show." Shamus's voice cut like a knife.

He knows.

"Oh, that," said Carmela, fighting to keep her voice even. "There's been a mistake."

"Really," said Shamus.

Carmela knew she had to carefully explain what had happened, make Shamus understand that she hadn't gone out and lobbied for this show herself. Hadn't tried to cut out his knees from under him.

"I was fooling around, taking photos a couple weeks ago," she explained as patiently as she could, "at the same time Jade Ella Hayward had this photo shoot going on. So I took a few black-and-white shots of her models. She saw them at my shop and, for some *bizarre* reason, decided to use one on the front cover of her brochure."

"You're a bad liar, Carmela. You always have been."

"And you're a bad listener, Shamus, because I'm telling you the truth!"

"You just *happened* to score a commercial project and you just *happened* to worm your way into having your own show. At Click! Gallery yet." Shamus sighed. "You knew all about this last night and didn't have the decency to tell me."

"There's nothing to tell, Shamus. I don't even *want* the show. I'm not going to *have* a show."

Shamus's voice was like ice. "You know what was nothing, Carmela? Last night was nothing."

His cold callousness sliced at her heart. "Don't say that, Shamus. Don't do this, please," Carmela begged him.

"And another thing," Shamus spat. "You presence is no longer required at our table tonight."

"What about Glory's big award?" cried Carmela. First she'd been strong-armed into participating, now she was being cut out. Very confusing.

"Forget about it," snapped Shamus. "There's no room for traitors and turncoats. Not in the Meechum family anyway."

Carmela flinched as Shamus slammed the phone down.

And thought about their miserable timing. Always that rotten timing.

Why the hell was that, anyway? Crossed wires? Bad luck? Planetary unrest?

She picked up her carving knife and stared at one of the pumpkins she'd just finished carving. It bore the image of a sorrowful angel clutching a cross.

Was this a metaphor for her life with Shamus? Sadness, sorrow, star-crossed lovers?

Carmela sighed. She supposed the night before *hadn't* meant anything to him. She, on the other hand, had woken up this morning feeling light-hearted, ebullient, and a trifle dreamy. She and Shamus had shared a bed, kind words, and a few laughs. Even though they'd hadn't physically made love, she had sensed that their emotional bond was still there, still intact. Yes, she had felt it wash over her in a warm, comforting wave. A hell of a lot of love still existed between the two of them. And she was sure Shamus had felt it, too.

Now . . . Now Shamus's fragile ego had sustained a life-threatening blow. And when Shamus's ego was knocked off-kilter, his psyche seemed to follow. Which meant they were probably back to square one. Completely estranged, on the brink of divorce.

Furious and frustrated, Carmela drove her carving knife into the front of one of the pumpkins, piercing its soft flesh.

It could just as easily have been her heart.

* * *

TWENTY MINUTES later, emerging from the shower, still trying to get rid of the *feel* of that morning's mineral mud treatment, Carmela's phone jingled again.

Slipping into a terry cloth bathrobe, Carmela padded across the slick floor and wondered tiredly if it was Shamus again. Calling to crab at her some more.

But this time it was her cell phone ringing from the depths of her handbag. And the caller turned out to be . . . surprise, surprise . . . Billy Cobb!

"Carmela," he said.

"Yes, Billy," she said breathlessly. She sat down on the edge of her bed, stared down at her well-scrubbed pink toes.

"You've always been friendly and nice to me, Carmela." He paused. "Would you give my family a message?"

"Of course," she told him, even as she warned herself to proceed with extreme caution. "Listen, Billy . . ." She hesitated, wondering how best to phrase this. "Did you by any chance slip something under my door last night?"

"Huh?" said Billy. "No. Why?" When Carmela didn't answer, he said, "I only called 'cause I'm for sure leaving town tonight. If you could tell Aunt Tandy . . ."

"Billy . . . no." Carmela tried to harness her jumbled thoughts. "Listen, Billy, I need to talk to you. In person. Can you meet me at the Art Institute tonight?"

"Why?" asked Billy, suspicion creeping into his voice.

"Because . . . uh . . ." Carmela struggled to come up with a plausible excuse, hated herself for concocting an outright lie. "Because your aunt has something for you."

"Money?"

"I'm not sure . . . I think so." *Oh,* she thought to herself, *this is awful.*

"I guess I could stop by then."

"You know where the Art Institute is?"

"I know where it is," said Billy. "I've been there."

"Okay then," said Carmela. "Nine o'clock. Come to the side door. The one on Perrier Street that leads to the administration offices."

"I'll find it."

With a sigh of relief, Carmela hung up the phone. Now she wondered if it was going to be possible to negotiate something with Lieutenant Babcock. It would be a long shot, but she felt she had to give it a try.

Carmela dug in her purse, found the business card Lieutenant Babcock had given her a few days earlier. Then she phoned the number, was put on hold by a disinterested-sounding officer, and had to wait a good five minutes before the officer told her she was being patched through. Probably to his home number, Carmela decided. It was, after all, Saturday afternoon.

There was a click and a whir and then Lieutenant Babcock was on the line. "Babcock here." He sounded busy and distracted.

Uh-oh, bad timing? Again?

"Lieutenant Babcock? Hello. This is Carmela Bertrand."

"The scrapbook lady," Lieutenant Babcock responded. Now there was a little more warmth to his voice. "Hello, yourself."

"Yeah, hi," Carmela said, flustered. "I was wondering if you came up with anything on your paint tests." She didn't really give a hoot about the paint tests, but it seemed like a good gambit to get the conversation rolling.

"I don't know," said Lieutenant Babcock. "I'm pretty sure the labs are still working on it. Probably gonna take a few days."

Carmela hesitated. "What I'm about to ask you is going to sound a trifle presumptuous, but would you . . ." She fumbled with her question. "I mean *could* you possibly meet me at the Art Institute tonight?"

"I suppose so," he said slowly.

And then, because Edgar Babcock was the smart cookie Carmela knew he was, with a cop's innate savvy and a nose for ferreting out trouble, he asked her directly, "Does this have something to do with Billy Cobb?"

"It does," admitted Carmela. "At least I *hope* it does." She waited, but he didn't ask for any more of an explanation. "Listen, if you have other plans tonight . . ."

"Not anymore," he said.

"Okay then," she said, thinking, *I gotta introduce this guy to Ava. There's something about him that's very appealing. He's got that quiet self-assurance.*

"What time?" Babcock asked.

Carmela asked him to meet her around nine fifteen, figuring that would give her just enough time to convince Billy Cobb to abandon his plan to flee the state. Then she hung up, thinking, *Am I nuts or what? I'm trying to get a guy to turn himself in and I'm also thinking about playing matchmaker at the same time.*

She knew this was precisely the problem with having that Cawegian heritage. Cool rationalization mixed with red-hot emotion. Which meant the wires were definitely crossed.

Chapter 20

THE SKY WAS stormy and restless as Carmela, Ava, and Sweetmomma Pam climbed the steps of the Art Institute. Waiting at the top were flickering jack-o'-lanterns with mirthful grins and a bevy of junior volunteers costumed as ghosts and passing out green glow sticks.

"How'd you get those jack-o'-lanterns here?" asked Ava. She was wearing a skin-tight silver sequined gown that clung to her body seductively. Most of her face was painted silver to match, and her eyeliner consisted of a tiny strip of miniature silver sequins. Her hair was pulled into an updo and threaded with gemstones, giving her the appearance of a fanciful cockatiel.

"Natalie Chastain stopped by and picked them up," said Carmela, who was equally tricked out in a black-and-white harlequin-patterned gown. She'd forgone the face paint, however, and instead wore a black mask with a sparkling pavé surface and black ostrich plumes that curved away from either side of her face. "She's got this big old honkin' Chrysler she calls her jungle cruiser," added Carmela.

"Neato," sang Sweetmomma Pam as she scampered up the stairs, greatly excited by the prospect of attending such a gala ball.

Ava studied the harlequin gown Carmela was wearing. "Your butt looks real good in that dress, honey."

"Thank you," said Carmela. At the last minute she'd changed from a gold peasant-style gown to the more flamboyant harlequin gown. Dressing to catch someone's eye tonight? Could be.

"You still feelin' hot flashes from that mud wrap this morning?" asked Ava.

"Hot flashes!" exclaimed Sweetmomma Pam, who was dressed adorably in a 1920s-era gold flapper dress complete with beaded headband and gold leather bird mask with a wicked-looking curved beak that had to be a good six inches long. "Never had 'em, never will!"

"I think I finally cooled down," said Carmela, fanning herself even though the evening had turned chilly.

Like Cerberus guarding the entrance to Hades, Jade Ella Hayward met them at the entrance to the ballroom. She was glammed out in a jaguar print silk blouse that wrapped around her slim waist, then tied in front with a co-quettish pussycat bow. The blouse topped a pencil thin black leather skirt and what had to be Manolo Blahnik heels, also jaguar-spotted. A very spendy outfit, Carmela decided. Jade Ella must have dipped into the insurance money already.

"Car*mela*," Jade Ella intoned, rolling her eyes and scrunching up her face, getting ready to launch an all-out abject apology. "Greta told me what happened. I'm *soooo* sorry." She nervously fingered the matching jaguar-spotted mask she had clutched in her hands.

"Poor Carmela was almost pan-fried like a catfish," said Ava, jumping in, always at the ready to defend her friend. "She could have been seriously injured!"

"I *know*. I *heard*. We're still having problems with the master control module," Jade Ella explained. "You see, everything at Spa Diva is computerized. From the music to the lighting to the treatment apparatus. Very high tech, but terribly sensitive, too. If something's just the teensiest bit off, well . . ."

"You'd better get your apparatus fixed posthaste," warned Carmela. "Because I went from Defcon Four to Defcon One in about two minutes!" Defcon was slang for the Department of Defense's readiness alert status. Defcon One meant the warheads were about to fly.

"Seven fifteen," announced a loud mechanical voice.

Ava frowned at Sweetmomma Pam. "Will you turn that wristwatch thing *off*?" she hissed.

"Carmela," purred Jade Ella, "please *believe* me when I say it was a terribly unfortunate accident." She laughed nervously. "You *certainly* can't believe anyone wished you harm?"

Carmela shook her head, still highly suspicious of her little "accident" at Spa Diva. She wondered if Jade Ella figured she might be privy to some inside information about Barty's murder. Or did Jade Ella have motives more sinister than that? Carmela knew that if Jade Ella *did* mastermind the malfunctioning control module, that put her squarely in line as the prime murder suspect.

And what on earth was Jade Ella up to with the Click! Gallery—pushing her photographs on Clark Berthume, the owner?

"Jade Ella," said Carmela, "I got a phone call from Clark Berthume yesterday."

A knowing grin spread across Jade Ella's face. "Aren't you thrilled?" she cooed. "I just knew Clark would go ga-ga over your work."

"First of all," said Carmela, "photography's not my life's aspiration. In fact, I do it only for fun. Second, I'm not interested in having any sort of show."

"Oh, Carmela," said Jade Ella, "how can you be so callous? Clark has photographers waiting in line for just this kind of break! Please don't blow it!"

"Carmela." Natalie Chastain tapped her gently on the shoulder and Jade Ella, sensing an opportune moment, slipped into the crowd.

"Natalie, hello," said Carmela. And then, because Natalie looked a little frazzled, even dressed up in her rather elegant Roman robe with a wreath of grape leaves circling her head, said, "It looks like it's going to be a wonderful evening."

"It does?" Natalie brightened considerably. "Good, that's exactly what I needed to hear. Especially after all our last-minute hassles."

Carmela hastily introduced Ava and Sweetmomma Pam to Natalie, and then had to do introductions all over again when Monroe Payne suddenly appeared and joined their little cluster.

Wearing a Peking Opera costume of embroidered crimson silk, Monroe authentically looked the part with his dark hair slicked back and drawn into a Chinese topknot set high upon his head.

"Have you seen the art and floral pairings yet?" Monroe asked them, obviously delighted at how everything had turned out.

"No, but we're going to take a look right now," Carmela told him, as an older couple wearing matching Medieval lord and lady costumes suddenly descended on Monroe in that assured way moneyed people always have.

The selected artworks were hung on the walls of the ballroom and the corresponding floral arrangements placed directly in front of them on square marble pedestals. The description cards Carmela had created were in little Lucite holders directly in front of the floral arrangements.

As fanciful a concept as Monsters & Old Masters was, Carmela had to admit that many of the artwork and floral pairings were really quite clever.

A bouquet of bright red chili peppers mixed with canary grass and accented with boughs of curly willow was set in a flat ikebana-type vase and paired with a dynamic, brightly colored Japanese print that depicted a Samurai warrior in full battle dress.

A bouquet of silvery-green lamb's ear and blue salvia was accented with bright green apples and cinnamon sticks and paired most appropriately with a painting that depicted capering wood nymphs.

And dried yarrow and strawflowers, tied with raffia and displayed in a painted ceramic bowl, were paired with a ceramic Day of the Dead sculpture from Guadalajara, Mexico.

As Carmela moved down the row of floral and art pairings, she suddenly found herself staring into the hard face of Glory Meechum.

"Hello, Carmela," said Glory.

Glory was one of the few guests who hadn't come in costume. She was wearing a boxy navy blazer with an equally boxy matching skirt. On the other hand, if Glory was trying to pass for the dowdy head matron of a women's prison or private girls' school, then she was right on the money costume-wise. Glory also had a nice tall drink clutched firmly in one hand. Probably bourbon and water. From its dark amber appearance, it was obvious the drink had been mixed fairly strong.

"Nice to see you, Glory," said Carmela. She glanced longingly after Ava and Sweetmomma Pam, who had wandered away. "Congratulations again on your Founder's Award."

Glory gave a self-satisfied smile and leaned in slightly. Her eyes were like hard little orbs and she exhaled loudly through her nose. Carmela could smell the bourbon on her breath and sensed that a confrontation might be imminent.

"Too bad you weren't able to *join* us," said Glory. She pulled her mouth into a sneer. "But I guess *family* doesn't mean a whole lot to you anymore."

"Glory . . . ," said Carmela, tiredly, spreading her hands apart in a peace gesture, "I'd be happy to sit at your table tonight." This kind of crap just wasn't worth it, she decided. She'd sit at the damn table and be pleasant if it killed her.

Glory tucked her chin down and peered at Carmela. "That might prove slightly *embarrassing* for you, Carmela. Especially since Shamus elected to bring a *date* tonight. A lovely young woman by the name of Zoe Carvelle, who is most enchanting." The ice in Glory's glass clinked like gnashing teeth. Then Glory flashed a triumphant smile, spun unsteadily on her squatty little navy heels, and tottered away.

Carmela stared after her, stunned by Glory's revelation. Shamus had brought a date. Her estranged *husband* had brought a date. Wasn't that just a trip and a half? She was about to be completely humiliated at one of New Orleans's major social events. Could things get any worse?

A crowd of masked revelers suddenly swirled around her. Of course they could, she decided. This was New Orleans, after all.

A stark white face with waving strands of long black hair floated in close, startling her.

"Hey there, Carmela." Dove Duval's familiar voice suddenly issued forth from this strange apparition. "Having fun?"

Carmela managed to squeak out a one-syllable answer as she took in Dove Duval's costume. Dove wore a Morticia Addams wig of long, black, straight hair. Her face was powdered stark white, like a performer in a Japanese Kabuki theater. Dove's lips were outlined in black then filled in with bloodred lipstick. Her eyes, rimmed in black, lent an eerie stark contrast, making her look enormously predatory and slightly crazed. And she wore a floor-length black witch's gown. *She looks,* Carmela thought, *like that bizarre pop star Marilyn Manson.*

Dove Duval's bloodred lips pulled themselves into a wide smile. "Aren't *you* the liberated woman."

Carmela figured Dove *had* to be referring to Shamus and his date. And decided she seriously didn't want to go there. Instead, Carmela decided to negotiate a countermaneuver. "How did your little photo session go yesterday?" she asked.

Dove blinked rapidly at her. "Pardon?"

"Weren't you also taking photos when we met in the cemetery yesterday?" Carmela stared at Dove. *Someone* had taken the photo of her and Boo, scratched it up, then shoved it under her door.

"Why, no," said Dove. "I don't know the first thing about taking pictures."

Carmela gave a long sigh. Dove wasn't about to give her anything. "Did you finally get your floral arrangement done?" she asked.

That little question produced a flurry of animation and activity. Encouraged by Carmela's apparent interest, infinitely proud to show off her handiwork, aspiring for recognition, Dove Duval grasped Carmela's arm and pulled her down along the wall of artworks.

"Like it, Carmela?"

They stopped in front of the owl painting, *Owl in the Moonlight.* True to her word, Dove had composed an arrangement using poppy heads, dried feverfew, and bright orange Dutchman's trousers.

"Wonderful," replied Carmela, gazing at the moss-filled wire basket that was tied with velvet ribbon from her store.

"I just love being artistic," said Dove. With her exaggerated accent, it sounded like she said *I just love being autistic.*

* * *

IT TOOK a good ten minutes for Carmela to finally pull herself away from Dove Duval, make her way through the crowd, then finally locate the large circular table that Baby and Del had reserved. When she finally got there, feeling more than a little discombobulated, everyone was already seated. Baby and Del. Tandy and Darwin. Gabby and her husband, Stuart. And Ava and Sweet-momma Pam. An extra place setting had been added for Ava's grandmother, and she now sat perched expectantly on a folding chair.

After a flurry of greetings, hugs, and air kisses, Carmela slipped into the chair next to Ava.

"Shamus brought a date," she told her friend in a low whisper.

Ava lifted an eyebrow and held it for a second, letting it quiver in disbelief. "Shamus brought a *date?*" she whispered back. "Date with a capital D?"

"Zoe," said Carmela. The sick, sinking feeling that had begun in her stomach now seemed to have spread through her entire body. "Zoe with a capital Z."

"Oh, honey!" Ava grasped Carmela's hand and gave her a look of pure commiseration.

And, as everyone around her clinked glasses, noshed hors d'oeuvres, and made small talk, Carmela sat and tried to puzzle out what she could do to avoid being introduced to Zoe. Something. *Anything.* Even faking an epileptic seizure would be preferable and slightly less embarrassing than having to smile and shake hands with your husband's date. Especially in a room full of scrutinizing society folk who loved nothing better than watching other people squirm like a bug on a pin.

Ava, her curiosity roused, craned her neck and peered across a sea of tables, trying to catch a look at Shamus's date. "Hmm. I think I see her."

"Dog?" asked Carmela.

"Actually," said Ava, "she's rather striking."

On the pretext of reaching for a decanter of wine, Carmela half-stood and craned her neck as well. Finally she spotted Shamus, then Zoe sitting next to him. There was something familiar about her.

Damn. It's the woman in the keyhole dress. Has to be.

"She certainly is striking," agreed Carmela. "And youthful."

Ava nodded. "Particularly if your taste runs toward emaciated girls with a head full of hair extensions."

"My thoughts exactly," agreed Carmela.

Ava plucked the wine decanter from Carmela's hand and refilled her own glass. "And, if you ask me, I'm thinking her ta-ta's aren't the genuine article, either."

Once the main entree of roast duck had been served, Quigg Brevard and Chef Ricardo stopped by their table. Carmela made hasty introductions and there were handshakes and compliments all around.

"I'd love to take credit for everything," Quigg told them ebulliently, slapping Chef Ricardo on the back, "but my head chef, Chef Ricardo Gaspar, is the real genius."

Baby and Del applauded with great enthusiasm, then everyone at the table joined in, with a spatter of applause coming from surrounding tables as well.

Ava immediately caught the eye of Chef Ricardo. He sped to her side with the swiftness of a man questing after the holy grail. Or, more like, lusting after it.

"You like more sweet potato casserole, miss?" he asked her.

Ava tilted her chin up and eyed him carefully. "I'm fine."

But Chef Ricardo was not to be deterred. "Another glass of wine? I get you *better* wine. *French* wine, not cheap domestic." Obviously, Chef Ricardo considered drinking California wine tantamount to drinking pig swill.

"Now you're talking my language, sweetie." Ava, always delighted to be fawned over, fixed Chef Ricardo with a dazzling smile.

He leaned in close to her and inhaled deeply. "*Lovely* perfume, miss. Very sensual." Chef Ricardo narrowed his eyes and uttered a low Lothario growl. Then he was off on his quest for better wine. French wine.

"What was that all about, *miss*?" asked Carmela.

Ava fanned herself nervously. "I think it's that Banana Frango facial I had earlier. It's still giving off kind of a heady aroma." She gave Carmela a sideways glance. "Honey, do you *still* see Chef Ricardo as a viable suspect? 'Cause, truth be known, I think the man is kinda cute. And, you know, I never was all *that* fond of Bartholomew Hayward."

"Go for it," said Carmela.

As tuxedo-clad waiters cleared away remnants of Chef Ricardo's calorie-loaded desserts—cranberry bread pudding and elegant lemon bars—the orchestra tuned up and the dancing began.

Baby and Del immediately headed for the dance floor to kick off the evening with a tango. Other couples, captivated by the sensuous music, their emotions fueled by the free flow of drinks, rushed to join them. And Carmela finally got her first clear, unobstructed view of Shamus's table.

But Shamus was no longer sitting down. Instead, he was heading determinedly for *her* table. With Zoe in tow!

"Oops," exclaimed Carmela, "gotta run."

"Where you going?" called Tandy.

"Ladies' room," said Carmela. She jumped to her feet, grabbed for her beaded evening bag. But in her state of panic, the bag slipped through her fingers and fell to the floor and she had to dive under the table for what she hoped would be a fast retrieval.

"Carmela," said Shamus. "I'd like you to meet Zoe."

Great, thought Carmela, *Shamus just introduced his date to my butt.*

Embarrassed, Carmela backed out from under the table and scrambled hastily to her feet.

"Hi there, howdja do?" she mumbled hastily. Pumping Zoe's hand, not bothering to really look at her, Carmela tried to make a break for it, but Shamus moved left to block her.

Damn. Guess you can't outflank an old quarterback. Especially one who can still scramble.

"I understand you're very creative," said Zoe politely.

"Carmela did all the menu cards," volunteered Ava. She'd jumped up suddenly to help Carmela in whatever way she could. "And the cards with the floral and art descriptions, too." Now she moved in on Zoe like a lioness circling her prey.

"Zoe manages a clothing store," Shamus told them. "The Hive." He paused. "Perhaps you ladies have heard of it?"

"Nice place," said Carmela, feeling just a tiny ripple of intimidation. The Hive was a very upscale boutique located on Magazine Street. It carried many of the top designers like Versace, Ungaro, and Armani. She'd heard that they'd recently added a men's line, too.

"Listen," said Ava, moving in on Zoe, "I've been looking for a hot pink slip dress. Do you have anything remotely similar to that? Better yet, do you have any hot pink *shoes*? Something strappy and fun." Ava gave a long sigh. "It's so *difficult* to find the perfect designer piece . . ."

Shamus looked on with amusement as Ava rattled away and Zoe rattled back.

Carmela faced Shamus. "You don't have a costume," she told him. He wore a black turtleneck under a black jacket, and Carmela wondered where *that* little fashion *faux pas* had originated. Shamus had always told her he despised turtlenecks.

"What do you think?" he asked, holding his arms out, obviously wanting Carmela's reaction to his new look. Expecting a compliment.

"If you swabbed white greasepaint on your face you could pass for a mime," Carmela snapped.

Shamus looked stung. "You know I *despise* mimes."

Carmela shrugged. *"C'est la vie."*

Shamus glowered at her. "This hostile attitude you've adopted," he said. "It's not one bit flattering. I hope you don't intend to keep it up all night." Shamus was so mad, he stomped off and left Zoe standing there with Ava.

"Only as long as I have to," Carmela called to Shamus's retreating backside.

Ava stopped chattering and the three of them stood staring at each other. Finally Zoe spoke up. "You're very pretty," she told Carmela. "Shamus said you were pretty." She appraised Carmela with a careful eye, like a budding plastic surgery aficionado. "You have very full lips. I've been thinking of having my lips enhanced. There's a plastic surgeon up in Baton Rouge who's supposed to be a genius . . ."

"Implants," replied Ava, gesturing at Carmela's lips.

"Really," said Zoe, narrowing her eyes. "They look very natural."

"You want natural," said Ava, "take a gander at Carmela's cheekbones."

Zoe's eyes widened even more. "Implants, too?"

Ava nodded. "The surgeon made two teensy little incisions inside her mouth, then slipped these little plastic pieces right in. I tell you, the girl's put together with spit and clay."

Zoe was clearly fascinated. "I've heard about cheek implants. Did they hurt?" she asked Carmela.

"Never felt a thing," replied Carmela.

"But if you want realistic," said Ava, "take a gander at Carmela's eyes."

Now Zoe was completely confused. "Her eyes?" She threw Carmela a questioning glance.

Carmela, who'd never had an implant or a collagen injection in her life, just nodded. "Had 'em done two years ago," she said. "Love 'em."

Ava lowered her voice to a conspiratorial whisper. "Carmela was born with brown eyes. Didn't the surgeons do a fabulous job?"

Zoe's pouty mouth formed a perfect O. "Oh yes, they *did*," she marveled. "And I had no idea they could even do a transplant procedure like that. Wow."

"Biosynthetics," purred Ava. "Isn't medical science amazing?"

"Yes, it is," said Zoe, feeling that she'd developed a real kinship with the two women.

"You're evil," Carmela told Ava as Zoe headed back to her table. "Pure, unadulterated evil."

"And you're not?" asked Ava. She gave a slow wink. "Having fun?" she asked.

"I am now," said Carmela. But ten minutes later, Shamus was back in her face, begging for help.

Carmela stared at him, wondering where he found the nerve. "You want *my* help?" she asked. The man was certainly born with an extra helping of chutzpah.

"There's a problem with Glory," Shamus hissed, plucking at Carmela's sleeve. "Hurry up! We've got a dire emergency on our hands!"

As Shamus pulled her across the ballroom, Carmela noted that suddenly, somehow, Shamus considered the two of them complicit again. Now *we* have an emergency. On *our* hands.

Glory Meechum was slumped in her chair, one chubby hand still stubbornly clasped around a glass of bourbon. Her older brother, Jeffrey, a pear-shaped banker in a drab gray suit, stared at her helplessly. Two useless banker cousins sat nervously twiddling their thumbs.

"She just drank too much bourbon!" exclaimed Carmela as she surveyed the situation. Over the past couple years Carmela had seen Glory sock it away pretty good, but she'd never seen her this drunk. Glory's face was doughy and slack, her lipstick smudged and smeared. Not a positive sign.

Shamus put a hand protectively on one of Glory's broad shoulders. "That's not the real problem. She only had a couple drinks this evening, but she's been taking this new medicine for her OCD. My guess is the combination of booze and pills must've packed a real wallop."

"That lady's stoned, all right," said Ava, who had followed Carmela to

Shamus's table. "She's stoned out of her gourd." Ava peered into Glory's glazed eyes. "Oh yeah, look at her pupils. She's gone."

"She's gone," repeated Sweetmomma Pam, who had tagged along as well.

"Carmela, do something!" wailed Shamus.

Startled, wondering why this little family emergency had suddenly been thrust on *her* shoulders, Carmela whipped her head toward him. "Face it, Shamus, Glory's zonked."

"Carmela . . . please! You've got to *do* something," Shamus begged as Baby and Del, curious as to what was going on, sidled up to the table as well.

"The woman's clearly stoned, Shamus, what do you want me to do?" Carmela snapped. "Fire up the light show and throw some Jefferson Airplane on the turntable?"

"You don't have to be so nasty about it," grumped Shamus.

Carmela hesitated. Shamus was probably right. She *was* being a tad bitchy. But wasn't she enjoying this little spectacle as well?

Oh yeah. What goes around comes around, Miss Glory Meechum. Spread enough bad karma around and it'll come back and chomp you in the butt.

"This is Glory's big night," pleaded Shamus. "She's supposed to receive her Founder's Award!"

"Might I offer a suggestion?" said Baby. She stood on the sidelines, looking cool and somewhat detached in her Marie Antoinette costume, but also helping to block this rather embarrassing scene from other prying eyes.

"Whaaaa?" mumbled Glory, rolling her head. Neither eye seemed to be able to focus on the same thing. With her head sunk on her chest and her eyes looking wonky and rolling out to the sides, Carmela thought Glory resembled a Mississippi channel catfish.

"Now mind you," said Baby, "not that I know this *firsthand*. But I *did* attend college in the late sixties."

Ava gave an encouraging nod. "Lots of psychedelics back then. Powerful stuff."

"And I did hear *rumors* . . . realize, these were *only* rumors," said Baby, "that several spoonfuls of sugar dissolved in a glass of orange juice could bring a person down from a nasty high. Something about increasing glucose and balancing blood sugar levels."

"Kind of like a diabetic," breathed Ava. "That's *good*."

"Shamus, go tell Monroe Payne to hold off on that Founder's Award presentation," announced Carmela. She narrowed her eyes, appraising Glory like she was a science project. "Let's go ahead and try Baby's sugar and orange juice suggestion. Glory's in no condition to walk out on a stage. Let alone stumble through an acceptance speech."

"I don't know," said Baby, "I've seen lots of men do it."

"But that's men, honey," interjected Ava. "In the South men are *expected* to get a little tipsy at social occasions. It's their birthright."

"Hear, hear," said Baby's husband, Del, grinning.

Chapter 21

"CARMELA," SAID GABBY, her face scrunched into a worried grimace, "I think Stuart's havin' one of his low blood sugar attacks."

"Um . . . didn't Stuart just eat, Gabby?" Carmela had just poured glass after glass of sugar-enhanced orange juice down Glory Meechum's gullet to revive her, and now Gabby was pressing her about yet *another* health crisis. *What am I? An ER doc?*

Gabby gestured helplessly at her husband, who was sprawled in his chair, staring up at Ava with a foolish grin. "He didn't eat that much," explained Gabby. "He was pretty busy jumping up and down, gallivanting around to neighboring tables, and saying how-do to folks."

"Uh-huh," said Carmela. "Trying to sell cars?"

"Lester Dorian *did* mention that he might be trading in his Cadillac, and Stuart was trying to get him to go for the big Toyota."

"With the luxury package," said Carmela.

"Of course," said Gabby. "And the GPS. Anyway," she continued, "the food's all cleared away and since you're *personally* acquainted with the caterer and his head chef, I thought maybe you could . . . you know . . ."

"Get some food for Stuart," said Carmela.

"Could you do that?" asked Gabby. "I really hate to leave Stuart sitting here all by himself. He's so shaky and rambling. You never know *what* could happen."

Right, thought Carmela. Stuart might get spirited off by forest elves. Or, worse yet, rival car dealers. "Okay, Gabby, but just hold on a minute, okay?"

"How come everybody's droppin' like flies?" asked Ava as she dug in her evening bag for a packet of Clorets. "It's like we're on one of those big cruise ships or something."

"That's right," said Carmela, "the *Voyage of the Damned*. Now, for the pièce de résistance all we need is a rousing case of Legionnaires' disease."

"Chew this," Ava instructed Stuart as she shook a Cloret out of the package and handed it to him. "No, honey, don't just *swallow* it in one gulp, it's not a *pill*." Ava sighed mightily as she passed him another Cloret. "Here. Try it again. And this time *chew*!"

Carmela checked her watch as she sped across the ballroom. Five minutes to nine. Where had the evening gone? Had she even had a few moments to relax and have a bit of fun? Hell no.

In fact, she was beginning to feel like some poor shlub in a Marx Brothers comedy where everything was spiraling out of control. Not only did she have to find a couple bites of food for Stuart, preferably something sweet and chewy, she had to surreptitiously meet Billy Cobb at the side door, try to locate Lt. Edgar Babcock, and *then* see if she could engineer some sort of truce between Billy and the New Orleans Police Department. Could she really pull all that off? Only if she was suddenly brandishing a bright blue Superwoman cape and a pair of silver bracelets.

As Carmela breezed down the corridor that led toward the employee lunchroom and administrative offices, she thought about how she'd been forced to abandon her original plan.

So much for my notion of finding the real killer. I gave it a shot and failed miserably. Ran across a few suspicious people, but never found any concrete evidence that linked them to Barty Hayward's murder. And, Lord knows, you have to have evidence.

Carmela turned into the small kitchen. Two women were beginning the daunting task of washing dishes and stacking plates.

"Is there any bread pudding left?" Carmela asked.

One of the women shrugged. "Check next door."

Carmela popped next door to the employee lunchroom. The long tables were piled with a jumble of boxes, food platters covered with plastic wrap, and half-empty silver serving platters. Waiters rushed in and out, depositing empty wine decanters, serving utensils, and bread baskets. Nobody seemed to notice her.

Poking through the debris on one table, Carmela found a large cake pan that still contained a few lemon bars sprinkled generously with powdered sugar. She searched around, found a small china dessert plate, and scooped two of the lemon bars onto the plate. They were a little squishy by now, but Carmela decided Stuart would just have to rough it.

Glancing at her watch, Carmela saw it was almost time to meet Billy at the Perrier Street door.

Uh-oh, better take care of that first.

Clutching her plate of lemon bars, Carmela slipped out of the lunchroom and made her way farther down the corridor, away from the bright lights and clatter into semidarkness and quiet. Natalie Chastain's office was down this way. So was Monroe Payne's office and those of the various curators.

Carmela's plan was simple if not simplistic: Put Billy at ease, try to get him to come inside with her, then quietly reason with him. And then, at the magic moment, Lt. Edgar Babcock would appear. Helpful and rational. An honest, forthright representative of the New Orleans Police Department who would help straighten things out.

Good heavens, she thought to herself, *isn't this a grand fantasy? I'm really making this guy Babcock into a regular Dudley Do-Right.*

When Carmela was halfway down the corridor, hurrying to meet Billy, one of the lemon bars slipped off the plate. Tumbled end over end and landed with a *splotch*, the white powdered sugar spilling out around it.

Nice going, klutz.

Carmela wrinkled her nose and stared down at the mess.

Okay, one lemon bar down, one to go. We'll deal with this happy little accident on the return trip.

AT FIRST Carmela thought Billy had stood her up. She pushed open the heavy metal door, leaned out, peered into swirling darkness as rain pelted down and lightning strobed in the sky overhead.

Then she saw him. Walking swiftly toward her, splashing haphazardly through puddles of standing water. Billy's head was tucked down and the collar of his dark blue pea coat was turned up against the battering wind and rain.

"Billy, over here," Carmela called, waving to him.

Billy ducked through the doorway in a cold wash of rain, then the door snicked shut behind him.

Carmela put a hand on Billy's shoulder and exhaled slowly. The boy looked cold and drenched, his youthful face tired and drawn. "I was worried you wouldn't show up," she told him. Now that he was actually here, she wasn't sure exactly how to proceed.

Billy faced her as he slowly dripped water on the marble floor. "Do you have the money?" he asked tiredly. His eyes sought out the plate she was clutching. "What's that?"

"Lemon bar," said Carmela, thrusting the plate into his hands. "Listen, Billy, did you know about Barty's storage space across the river?"

Billy accepted the plate and frowned. "I knew about it, yeah."

"You used to go over there with him?" she asked.

The boy shook his head. "Nope."

"But you talked to Barty about it?"

Billy gave a shrug. "Not really. I just heard him mention it a couple times."

"To people in the store?" Carmela asked.

Billy thought for a minute. "More like on the phone, I think."

"On the phone," repeated Carmela.

"Yeah," said Billy. "He was probably talkin' to the delivery guys. I think that's where Barty had 'em take the really crappy stuff."

"You're sure?" asked Carmela as, around the corner, she heard a sudden shuffle of footsteps.

Carmela touched a warning finger to her lips . . . *Shhhh* . . . as she and Billy flattened against the wall.

The footsteps stopped, then there was the distinct jingle of keys. Someone must be letting themselves into one of the offices, Carmela decided. Maybe Natalie?

She peeked around the corner, caught a flash of rich red silk. No, that had to be Monroe Payne in his Peking Opera costume. Probably come to fetch Glory's Founder's Award. The presentation was probably going to kick off fairly soon and Glory would receive her fancy engraved trophy now that she was back on her feet.

Okay now, how am I going to find Edgar Babcock ... and drag Billy to meet him?

There was a sudden cry of dismay, then Monroe uttered a single low word: *"Damn."*

Oops, thought Carmela, *I think Monroe Payne just stepped in that lemon bar.*

She poked her head out slightly to take a look. In the dim light she could see Monroe hopping along, trying to scrape something off the bottom of his shoe. Yellow goop, no doubt.

Sorry, Monroe.

As Carmela and Billy stood there in silence, someone else came clattering down the hallway. There was a low exchange of voices, something about a disgruntled donor, and Carmela also heard Monroe mutter, "Idiot food-service people." Then Monroe and whoever it was that had spoken to him hurried back down the hallway, away from them.

Now it was Billy's turn to stick his head around the corner for a quick peek.

"Are they gone?" hissed Carmela.

Billy nodded.

"Come on, then," said Carmela, plucking at his jacket. "Let's go."

But Billy was suspicious. "Go where?"

"Uh . . . just down the hall a little. We've got to talk."

Reluctantly, Billy allowed Carmela to pull him down the corridor in the direction Monroe Payne had just retreated.

When they got to the now-decimated lemon bar, Carmela glanced down at the mess, then paused. *What the . . . ?*

"What's wrong?" asked Billy.

"Got to get more light," she muttered. "Take a closer look at something."

Monroe Payne's office door was open a couple inches. Voilà. Perfect. In his haste, Monroe had left his office unlocked.

Pushing the door open, Carmela's eyes searched the darkness. A small lamp burned on Monroe's expansive mahogany desk. But not enough candlepower for her purposes. Carmela searched around the door frame for a light switch, finally found it, hit it with her hand.

Yellow light spilled into the hallway and Carmela was finally able to get a good look at the splotched lemon bar.

"What?" asked Billy, shifting nervously from one foot to the other, obviously aching to get the hell out of there.

But Carmela's eyes had traveled to the wide arc of powdered sugar that was spread out around the mess in the corridor.

"Oh no," she breathed.

Carmela bent down on one knee, staring, not quite believing. And like a cartographer reading the latitude and longitude of a map, her index finger traced above a faint gridlike pattern that was imprinted in the spill of powdered sugar.

"What?" asked Billy, picking up on her radical shift in attitude. "You look like you just saw a ghost."

"Close," said Carmela hoarsely. She grabbed Billy by the lapels, pulled him into Monroe's office. "We've got to check something out," she told him.

"What?" he asked.

"*Shhh*," she said as her eyes flicked around his office, taking everything in.

Monroe Payne's office was twice the size of Natalie Chastain's. He had a large executive desk, two leather club chairs facing it, and, over by the window, a nice-looking round wooden conference table with four chairs pulled in around it. Two of his walls had floor-to-ceiling bookcases stacked with oversized art books, Chinese ceramics, pre-Columbian vases, Greek urns, and some rolled-up Japanese hand scrolls. Exactly the mishmash of objects you'd expect to find in a museum director's office.

Carmela's eyes fell on a closet door.

Let's just take a quick look-see.

She pulled at the closet door, grimaced as it swung open with a loud *creak*. And found . . . clothes. Thud.

There was a khaki raincoat, a couple light blue shirts, a gray tweed sport coat, a couple striped rep ties tossed carelessly over a wooden hanger.

Carmela stared at these items, bit her lower lip, exhaled slowly. And wondered if her snap assumption about Monroe Payne had been *that* off base.

Hmm. Maybe.

She dropped to her knees, pawed haphazardly around on the closet floor. And came up with . . . what else? . . . a pair of shoes. Nice brown leather wing tips that looked to be maybe a size ten or eleven. She picked one up and held it for a moment, the leather feeling cool and slick in her hand. Then, pulling in a deep breath, Carmela turned one of the wing tips over.

And saw the letters GC imbedded in the rubber.

GC! Ohmygod!

Carmela righted the shoe, peered inside. Giorgio Cortina. GC was Giorgio Cortina, the shoe's Italian manufacturer. A *men's* shoe manufacturer!

Carmela closed her eyes and a shiver of excitement coursed through her.

Bartholomew Hayward and Monroe Payne must have had business dealings together. Business dealings that went terribly wrong!

Is this enough evidence to tie Monroe Payne to Bartholomew Hayward's murder and clear Billy? It has to be. Carmela paused, thinking hard. *But what about motive?*

No. She decided she had to forgo worrying about motive for now. The first order of business was for her and Billy to get the hell out of this office and find Lt. Edgar Babcock.

"What the hell's going on?" Billy demanded suddenly. He'd been watching her closely, shifting about nervously.

"We've got a big problem," Carmela told him.

"What are you talking about?" he asked, wary.

Carmela stared at him. "I think Monroe Payne killed Bartholomew Hayward."

"What!" It took Billy a few seconds to digest this. "You're talking about that museum guy?" he asked.

"Right," said Carmela. "Did he hang around Menagerie Antiques? Was he a friend of Barty's?"

"Tall guy? Slicked-back hair?" asked Billy.

"Yes, yes!" said Carmela. "Monroe Payne." She glanced about nervously. They really did have to get out of there.

"He was at the shop sometimes," said Billy. "But I wouldn't call them friends." His face contorted. "Jeez, if you think . . . well, shouldn't we call the cops or something?"

"Exactly my thinking," said Carmela, noting how quickly Billy's attitude about cops had flip-flopped. But her heart suddenly sank as she heard footsteps coming back. "Quick," she whispered to Billy as she pawed for the switch and doused the light. "Get in the closet." She gave Billy a rough shove, was about to dive in herself when . . .

Click.

Carmela's heart beat a timpani solo as the office door swung slowly open.

Uh-oh. Bad timing. Very bad timing.

A shadowy figure leaned in.

Could Lieutenant Babcock have somehow found his way to this office? Could she be that lucky? Carmela gazed apprehensively into the darkness, but the tiny spill of light from the desk lamp wasn't enough to illuminate the figure in the doorway.

"Hello, Carmela." The voice rang cold as tempered steel, but held a note of arrogance as well.

Oh no!

Monroe Payne stepped slowly into the light. And any hope Carmela had of Lt. Edgar Babcock magically showing up suddenly died.

Slowly, like a bad dream playing out in slow motion, Monroe Payne raised his arm. He held a gun. An ugly little snub-nosed Beretta. Not a terrible amount of stopping power, but certainly enough to do the job at close range.

Carmela stared at Monroe, feeling stupid, useless, and sick to her stomach. She wanted to cry, to rage, to plead. This wasn't how the scenario was supposed to play out! This was all wrong!

Monroe took a measured step closer to Carmela and his mouth twisted into an angry sneer. "You couldn't leave it alone, could you." He stared at the upended shoe in her hand. "You and your stupid investigating. Had to go *snooping* around! Get suspicious about footprints and acquisition numbers." He waggled a finger at her. "Well, we certainly can't have *that.*"

Still clutching the shoe, Carmela tried to discreetly heft her handbag. Could she smack Monroe in the face with it? Rake him with the sharp beads? Could she rush at him full tilt, then duck and spin past him?

But that would leave poor Billy still hunkered down in the closet.

"You and I are going for a little ride," said Monroe. His voice was cold, menacing. Carmela could imagine the final destination of that little ride. Bayou with quicksand? Mississippi River backwater? Gator-infested swamp?

But now there was the faint sound of more footsteps approaching.

"Carmela?" A tentative voice echoed from down the corridor. It was Ava. "Are you down here, honey?"

"Don't make a sound," snarled Monroe.

Carmela stared at him, took a calculated risk. "Call the police, Ava!" she screamed at the top of her lungs.

There was a moment of stunned silence, then the distinct sound of Ava retreating posthaste. Of her clattering down the corridor and letting out a mighty yell.

"You bitch!" screamed Monroe. Gun raised, he turned toward the door and as he did, Carmela swung her beaded bag at him. If she could rake his cheek, knock him off balance . . .

But *pffft,* like a swift-moving phantom, Monroe Payne was gone. He'd spun on his pricey Italian loafers and slipped out the door as quickly and silently as he'd entered.

Carmela hesitated for a few shocked seconds, then moved toward the door. A second high-pitched scream ricocheted down the marble hallway.

What on earth? thought Carmela. She flung herself around the corner, pounded down the hallway in the direction of the piercing scream.

Thirty feet down, outside the lunchroom, a small knot of people milled about. From the startled looks on their faces, they seemed collectively stunned.

"What happened?" cried Carmela. "Who screamed?"

Chef Ricardo pushed his way through the knot to Carmela, his arms cartwheeled frantically. "He took her! The man with the gun took her!"

Monroe Payne took Ava? No, he couldn't have. Ava's lean and strong from twice-weekly Tae-Bo classes. Plus she had a head start on Monroe.

As if on cue, Ava suddenly appeared. "Sweetmomma Pam!" she cried. "She followed me down here and Monroe Payne grabbed her! He was waving a gun around and he just picked her up like a rag doll and held her in front of him!"

"Like a human shield!" added Chef Ricardo.

Carmela's heart filled with dread. "Quick! Where did they go?" she asked.

"Outside the building!" Chef Ricardo told Carmela, gesturing wildly.

"Where did who go?" asked Shamus, suddenly appearing in the fray.

Ava's face blanched white. "Monroe Payne kidnapped my poor granny!" she shrieked.

"Good Lord," said Shamus, stunned. He looked at Carmela. "Really?"

She gave a sick nod.

Alarmed by the shouting, another glut of people suddenly poured into the hallway. As if in a dream, Carmela saw Baby, Del, Tandy, and Quigg Brevard stream toward them. Billy Cobb hurried down the hallway from the opposite direction, still carrying the plate with the lemon bar.

"Sweetmomma Pam was kidnapped?" cried Baby, putting a hand to her mouth. "Oh my god! That dear sweet lady!"

"We gotta get her back!" shrilled Ava.

"Find Lieutenant Edgar Babcock," Carmela told her. "Now!"

"Where?" pleaded Ava, verging on hysteria.

"He's here somewhere," said Carmela. "Just yell your head off and find him," ordered Carmela. "Shamus'll help you."

"Billy?" called Tandy in a quavering voice as she suddenly caught sight of her nephew. "What are *you* doing here?"

But Billy was roundly ignored for the time being as Ava, now the center of attention, clawed frantically at Carmela's sleeve. "We gotta get her back!" she insisted. "I'll just die if anything happens to her!"

"We'll find her!" said Shamus, who looked clearly confused.

"Nothing's going to happen to Sweetmomma," said Carmela determinedly.

Tears streamed down Ava's face. "Promise me!"

"I swear," said Carmela. "On my daddy's grave. Now *go!*"

Chapter 22

AS CARMELA RACED for her car, she was aware of someone sprinting after her, splashing headlong through puddles. A quick glance over her shoulder told her it was Shamus.

Shamus? What's he up to?

With his longer, more powerful strides, Shamus reached the car at the same time Carmela did. Together, they ripped open the doors and hurled themselves inside Carmela's Mercedes.

"Monroe Payne killed Barty!" Carmela told him between gasps as she fumbled in her beaded bag for her car key. "And now he's kidnapped Ava's granny!"

"Holy shit!" cried Shamus. "Did you see which way he went?" Shamus's voice was tense and he wore his serious game face.

Carmela jammed the key into the ignition and cranked it hard. The Mercedes SL revved immediately with a throaty rumble. "No, but—"

"Hang on, I think we've got company!" yelled Shamus as he tucked his knees up under his chin and yanked at the seat belt.

Momentarily distracted, Carmela whipped her head to the right just as she stomped on the accelerator, building up rpm's and almost red-lining the engine. With her car roaring like a jumbo jet, she was set to double clutch and pop directly into second gear. "What?" she asked him.

There was a moment of yelling and pounding on the outside of her car, then the passenger-side door was ripped open. Quigg Brevard and Chef Ricardo, both breathing heavily, clambered in and squeezed themselves onto what could best be described as a token backseat.

Annoyed, Shamus glanced back over his shoulder. "Who do you guys think you are? The Lone Ranger and Tonto?"

"*Drive*, Carmela!" yelled Quigg, pounding the back of her seat.

"Drive!" echoed Chef Ricardo. His eyes were wild and rolling as he glanced nervously out the rain-streaked back window. Trying to see what had become of Ava, Carmela assumed.

"Where's she supposed to drive *to*?" snarled Shamus. He wasn't particularly happy about the two passengers who had opted to pack themselves in like sardines.

But Carmela's car was moving now, roaring like an Indy car and spinning its wheels wildly as she jammed the accelerator to the floor. They fishtailed fifty yards down Perrier Street, then the Mercedes's extra-wide tires finally found purchase and they really took off.

"Somebody's behind us!" yelled Quigg.

"Is it a squad car?" asked Carmela. "Lieutenant Babcock?" She risked a quick glance in the rearview mirror even as her car rocketed down the street.

"Can't tell," said Quigg. He put a hand on her shoulder as she swerved wide around a corner. "Hey, take it easy. Do you even know where you're going?"

Carmela responded with a tight nod. Yes, she did. In fact, she had a damn good idea of where Monroe Payne had probably spirited Sweetmomma Pam off to.

The shrimp-packing plant! Out on River Road. Has to be.

"HOLY BUCKETS," whispered Shamus as they rolled silently into the little dirt parking lot. Carmela had doused her headlights some five hundred yards out and now they crept in slowly.

"Is that other car still behind us?" asked Carmela.

"I think we lost 'em at the last turnoff," said Quigg. Everyone was talking in hushed whispers now, wondering what the next move should be.

Carmela made the decision for them. Springing lightly from her car, she gathered her skirt up around her knees and tiptoed toward the dilapidated building that Barty Hayward had used as his storage facility.

We can't just sit around and hope Lieutenant Babcock is coming, decided Carmela. *Got to act now!*

"Wait!" called Shamus in a loud whisper. "You can't go in there alone!"

"Watch me," Carmela whispered back. She hadn't bothered to tell him Monroe Payne had a gun. If she had, Shamus probably would've hog-tied her. And then where would Sweetmomma Pam be?

"Damn," said Shamus, scrambling out after her. He hesitated, turned to stare at Quigg Brevard and Chef Ricardo, who were still wedged in, yet making motions like they were going to extricate themselves. "Are you coming?" he groused at them.

"We're *trying,*" said Chef Ricardo as he flailed about, trying to get a little leverage.

Carmela, meanwhile, had disappeared around the building. Tiptoeing through sucking mud in high heels wasn't easy, and she was thankful for the rain as it slapped down upon the metal roof of the building and shook the trees around her. Covered any noise.

Way in back, close to where she'd gone in through the broken window two nights earlier, she found a dark-colored BMW hunkered down. Its nose was pointed into a grove of scrub brush, almost as though the owner had been trying to hide it.

Does this car belong to Monroe Payne?

Carmela ventured over and put a hand on the hood of the car. The metal was still warm to the touch.

Damn straight it's his car. Has to be.

Carmela crept over to the broken window and peered in. Somewhere, toward the front, she thought, a dim light had been turned on.

Is Monroe Payne in there with Sweetmomma Pam? Only one way to find out.

Grasping the broken window, Carmela pulled at it. The sheer weight and bulk stunned her for a moment, then she was able to ease it down onto the ground. Hiking her skirt up above her knees, Carmela eased herself in through the window.

The interior of the shrimp-processing plant was just as dark and dank and dusty as Carmela remembered it. But this time, with her memory to guide her, Carmela was better able to navigate her way through the jumble of machinery and conveyer belts. And, as she edged closer to the giant cooker pot, she knew her hunch had been right. Someone was moving about inside one of the old blast freezers. One of the heavy metal doors was standing partially open, and she could see the gleam of a flashlight as light bounced off the freezer's interior walls.

Darn. I saw those blast freezers before, but didn't bother to look inside. Whatever's in there must be pretty darn valuable if Monroe Payne saw fit to chase all the way over here.

Carmela crouched down behind the old cooker as murmurs from inside one of the blast freezers grew louder. She tried to still her breathing and, at the same time, cock her head at an optimal angle to catch what was being said.

At first she heard just fragments of words, but then she was able to make out a high-pitched, pleading voice.

Sweetmomma Pam!

Sweetmomma's Pam's voice was followed by a deep, angry voice.

Monroe Payne.

But what's he up to? wondered Carmela.

She didn't have to wait long. Monroe backed out of the blast freezer, a clutch of oil paintings in his arms, precariously balancing his flashlight. With his right shoulder, he began to muscle the heavy metal door closed on Sweetmomma Pam, obviously intending to trap her inside.

All the while, Sweetmomma Pam clawed frantically at the door. "Please!" she moaned. "Don't leave me in here!"

That was enough for Carmela. She stood up from behind the cooker and shouted loudly at Monroe, "Back off, buster! Leave her alone!"

Startled, Monroe whirled toward her, dropping his armload of paintings. "What the . . . ?" he called out, then his hand snaked inside his clothing.

Carmela sank down behind the cooker just as he fired and a bullet *plinked* off the rim of the giant metal cauldron.

At that exact moment, the front door crashed open and Lt. Edgar Babcock hurled himself in, landing in a very credible combat stance. He leveled his pistol directly at Monroe. "Drop it!" he shouted.

"Shoot him!" yelled Shamus, who stumbled in directly behind Lieutenant Babcock, wielding an enormous flashlight. There was a scuffle of feet on the wooden landing outside and then Quigg Brevard and Chef Ricardo also appeared.

"Watch out, everybody!" screamed Carmela. "He's got a gun!"

"Back off!" yelled Monroe. In one swift move he reached through the door and grabbed Sweetmomma Pam by the arm, pulling her toward him. Now his gun was pointed directly at her heart, even as his eyes flashed nervously toward Lieutenant Babcock.

Carmela grimaced. When Monroe had hauled Sweetmomma Pam out roughly, the poor dear's mask had slipped down over her face. *She's probably scared clean out of her mind,* worried Carmela. *And please, dear Lord, don't let Lieutenant Babcock surrender his weapon. Under any circumstances.*

"Just everybody back off or the old lady gets it!" With Sweetmomma Pam in his grasp, Monroe Payne was suddenly a lot more confident.

Trying to gauge the situation, Lieutenant Babcock lowered his gun slightly. "Okay now," he said in a cool, reasonable voice, "let's nobody panic. We can work things out."

"You can *get* out!" snarled Monroe, angered by the glut of people who had suddenly appeared at the deserted storage building. He stared coldly at Lieutenant Babcock. "Put the gun down." Spitting out each word hard, Monroe meant his order to be obeyed.

Lieutenant Babcock lowered his gun to his side.

Damn, thought Carmela.

"Ten o'clock!" boomed a tinny, mechanical voice.

Startled, not knowing where yet *another* strange voice was coming from, Monroe jerked his head wildly just as Sweetmomma Pam turned toward him. The sharp beak of her mask caught him squarely in his right eye.

"My eye!" he screamed.

Howling with pain, Monroe clutched at his face and fumbled his gun. Seconds later, it clattered noisily on the wood-planked floor.

"Rush him!" yelled Shamus.

"No!" screamed Lieutenant Babcock. "Stay back!"

Chef Ricardo, never at a loss for action, grabbed one of the rusty knives from the old guillotine table and tossed it. It *whooshed* through the air, then hit with a loud *thwack,* remarkably pinning the fold of red fabric that contained Monroe Payne's upraised arm to the wall.

Everyone gasped. It was a stunt worthy of an Indiana Jones movie.

"Jeez," marveled Quigg, "you hit him."

"I *meant* to," said Chef Ricardo, pleased with what had to be a lucky, once-in-a-lifetime throw.

Lieutenant Babcock scrambled for the dropped gun as Monroe let loose with a second fearsome shriek that would've done a wounded animal proud.

"Yeoow!" he screamed. "I've been stabbed!"

Men, thought Carmela as she rushed forward and swept Sweetmomma Pam into her arms. *Always with the theatrics.*

"Get a doctor!" Monroe's outraged screams had turned to shouts and angry whimpers now. He stared fiercely at Carmela as she led Sweetmomma Pam a safe distance away, even as he held a trembling hand to his injured eye. "She attacked me with her beak!" he snarled. "Pecked me like a nasty bird from an Alfred Hitchcock movie!"

"Shut up," barked Lieutenant Babcock as he wrested the knife from the fabric that pinned Monroe Payne to the wall, then tossed it to the floor out of reach. Then, with little wasted effort, the lieutenant snapped a pair of handcuffs on Monroe.

Monroe stared sullenly at Chef Ricardo. "That idiot threw a knife at me!"

Chef Ricardo stepped forward and peered at the ripped fabric and creased flesh with a proprietary glance. *"Ees nothing,"* he said scornfully. "Barely a *flesh* wound."

"Sweetmomma Pam?" Ava Grieux, hair unpinned and swirling about her shoulders, teetered in the front doorway, a look of pure terror on her lovely face.

"Ava!" said Carmela, startled by her friend's sudden appearance. "Sweet-momma Pam's just fine. But how did *you* get here?"

"She came with me," said Lieutenant Babcock. He pulled a radio from his belt and spoke rapidly into it, requesting a backup squad as well as an ambulance.

Shamus smiled broadly. Sweetmomma Pam was safe, the cops were taking over, the drama seemed to be wrapping up.

But Carmela wasn't finished. Not by a long shot. Bartholomew Hayward had been stabbed. She'd been threatened and shot at. Sweetmomma Pam had been kidnapped. And Billy Cobb had been falsely accused and almost arrested!

Like an overworked image from a grade B horror film, Carmela felt a sheet of red descend before her eyes. And, in the tick of a single synapse, felt herself slip from fear into full-blown rage. Neurons popped like errant fire-crackers inside her brain as a wave of anger engulfed her.

Baring her teeth in a snarl, Carmela hurled herself at Monroe Payne, grabbing tufts of red silk with both fists. "You arrogant asshole," she yelled, "who do you think you are! Murdering . . . thieving . . ."

Shamus's eyebrows shot up. He stepped forward and put a tentative hand on Carmela's shoulder. "Hey, Carmela, take it easy. It's over, you don't have to make a big scene."

But Carmela was not to be deterred. She delivered a sharp kick to Monroe's knees and yanked savagely again at his costume. "Blustering bully!" she screamed. "Kidnapping Ava's grandmother! Stabbing Bartholomew Hayward! You're *pitiful . . . pathetic*!"

Lieutenant Babcock watched her with a slack jaw. This was a side to the seemingly mild-mannered Carmela Bertrand he'd never have guessed at.

"Get her *off* me!" yelped Monroe. "The woman's gone insane!"

Shamus continued to pull at Carmela. "Ease off, Carmela, it's over."

She refused to look at him. "No, it isn't! It's not over 'til *I* say it's over!"

"Come on, honey," Shamus entreated. "Back off, okay? You're scaring the crap out of me . . . and, besides, you're tearing the poor man's dress."

Abruptly, Carmela released her hold on Monroe Payne. He fell back against the wall, angry, shaken, and nervous that a one-hundred-and-twenty-pound woman had been poised to clean his clock.

Carmela turned and stared into Shamus's brown eyes, allowing his words to slowly penetrate her consciousness. "What did you say?" she asked.

He shrugged gently. "You were tearing his dress?"

A hint of a grin dimpled Carmela's face. Shamus stared at her for a second, then his mouth began to twitch as well. "I thought you were gonna kill him," said Shamus. He gave an elaborate mock wipe at his brow. "Cripes."

Then the tension fell away and Carmela and Shamus threw their arms around each other, hugging and patting each other on the back, reassuring one another that everything was okay.

"Did I just miss something?" asked Quigg Brevard, scratching his head.

Ava shook her head. "Jeez, Carmela. Just when it looked like you were over that louse . . ."

Sweetmomma Pam crinkled her old eyes and beamed. "Soul mates," she whispered. "I can see it in their eyes."

Chapter 23

MONROE PAYNE CONFESSED to everything. First in drips and drops, then in a long, rambling, self-effacing story in which he also named two other art dealers from Miami whom he swore were also "embroiled" in the scam.

"So this was all about art forgeries," said Carmela.

Everyone had trooped back to Quigg's restaurant afterward for some rapid decompression. Of course, in New Orleans, rapid decompression could easily allow for generous drinks and seriously fine food.

Baby and Del, Tandy and Darwin, and Gabby and Stuart had also been summoned. And now they were gathered around the tables at Bon Tiempe, as well.

"They found oil paintings with museum labels still on them stashed in those old blast freezers," said Quigg. "Apparently Monroe Payne and Bartholomew Hayward were in cahoots. Monroe would steal an original and paint a forgery. Then Bartholomew Hayward would handle the sale of the original painting via the crooked art dealers in Miami."

"With the forged piece going back on the walls of the New Orleans Art Institute," said Carmela.

Now Lt. Edgar Babcock spoke up. "It looks that way. I think when all this gets out, the board of directors at the New Orleans Art Institute is going to have a lot of explaining to do. They're going to have some very unhappy donors." He looked around at the still-stunned faces. "The Norton Museum, too. In Palm Beach. They had someone working on the inside there, too. With the dealers trading stolen paintings back and forth."

"So no one would recognize them," said Baby. She shook her head sadly and Del clasped her hand. Baby was still stunned that her beloved Art Institute was part of such a terrible scandal.

Carmela took a sip of wine and thought about the photos Quigg had given her. The ones that depicted Barty Hayward hosting his American Painters Expo. Had those been stolen paintings? Probably. Probably stolen from the Norton Museum or whatever other Florida museum had been part of the scam. And she remembered something else, too. Natalie Chastain sitting in her office, accepting a painting from Monroe Payne and frowning when she touched the frame. And . . . what else? Maybe wiping a bit of gilt paint from her hand?

Carmela nodded to herself. Of course. Gilt paint that wasn't completely dry. It was probably the same gilt paint that had been on the murder weapon.

Carmela stood up and wandered over to the marble sideboard to pour herself another glass of wine. No wonder Bartholomew Hayward had such an endless supply of paintings. He was part of a major conspiracy to rob public museums and reap obscene profits. Of course, with such high stakes, it wasn't surprising Barty Hayward and Monroe Payne had gotten into some kind of argument. One that had ended disastrously for Barty Hayward.

Shamus noticed Carmela standing alone and casually walked over to join her. Touching her shoulder gently, he asked, "Are you okay?"

She managed a smile. "I'm fine."

"God, you're feisty." There was nothing but admiration in his voice.

Her smile wavered. "I am? Really?"

Shamus snorted. "'Course you are." He paused, gazed down at his shoes. Normally talkative and glib, Shamus seemed at a loss for words.

Carmela put a hand on Shamus's jacket, then walked her fingers up his lapel. "You don't really look like a mime, you know."

A smile twitched on his face. "Thanks. You had me worried." Shamus looked suddenly sheepish. "Carmela . . . I didn't mean those things I said before. You're still very much a part of the family."

Carmela's voice was soft, barely above a whisper. "I know."

They stood for a few moments, shoulders touching. Carmela noticed that Ava was snuggled in the protective arms of Chef Ricardo. She grinned to herself. Some matchmaker she was. She'd had her eye on Lieutenant Babcock for Ava, but Ava had ended up with the hot-tempered chef. That was the thing about chemistry between men and women. Kapow—you never knew what would happen.

"I've been thinking," said Carmela.

"About what?" asked Shamus.

"A joint photography show."

A look of surprise spread across Shamus's handsome face. "Aren't you the creative thinker."

"Of course, I'll have to go meet with Clark Berthume. Show him your stuff, try to get him to agree to it . . . ," said Carmela.

"He will," said Shamus determinedly. "You're a world-champion finagler, Carmela. Always have been. You can talk anybody into anything."

"You really think so?" said Carmela.

Shamus nodded vehemently. "Oh yeah."

They stood together in silence, shoulders and hips touching now.

Hmm, wondered Carmela. *Could I talk Shamus into giving it another shot? Into giving us another shot?* She gave him a sideways glance. *It's sure worth a try,* she decided. *Well worth a try.*

Scrapbook and Stamping Tips from Laura Childs

Stamping on Glass

You can use your favorite rubber stamps to decorate beverage glasses, glass votive candles, or even mirrors and windows. When it's time to clean up, colorful stamp-pad ink can be removed in a flash using ordinary glass cleaner.

The Fabric of Your Life

Using a piece of fabric as background for your photographs adds texture, dimension, and color. Also consider snippets of embroidery, antique lace, scraps of baby clothing, or a piece from a wedding veil.

Treasure Trove Envelopes

Glassine envelopes, incorporated into your scrapbook pages, are perfect for holding photos, old letters, valentines, beads, trinkets, sand dollars, a bird feather, dried rose petals, a single earring, etc. Envelopes also give your scrapbooks a fun, interactive quality.

Tell a Story

Scrapbook pages are more interesting when you tell the complete story surrounding an event. Get pictures of the before, the during, and the after. For example, a page detailing a child's birthday could be told with the before (getting dressed or decorating), the during (the party), and the after (the family dog lapping a plate of cake crumbs).

Pretty As a Picture

The same scrapbooking techniques you've perfected for your albums can also be used to create beautiful collages that can be framed. Family photos, old letters, and precious documents can be mounted together in a picture frame, then displayed on a wall or desk.

Double-Duty Punches

Use your paper punches to create other interesting shapes. For example, if you have a heart punch and a circle punch, you can create a flower. Punch out a single circle to use as the center, then a dozen or so heart shapes to use as petals.

Food for Thought

Since so many family events center around food, be sure to include recipes in your scrapbook. Use colorful recipe cards or print your recipe on a die-cut (a nice big apple, for example!).

Carmela's Favorite Recipes

Killer Pecan Popovers

POPOVERS
4 eggs
2 cups milk
3 tbsp. butter, melted
2 cups all-purpose flour
½ tsp. salt
½ cup pecans, finely chopped

HONEY BUTTER
2 tbsp. honey
½ cup butter, softened

POPOVERS: Whisk eggs, milk, and melted butter together in a large bowl. Add flour and salt, stirring until smooth. Stir in pecans. Spoon batter into 12 (6 oz.) greased custard cups, filling each cup halfway and placing them on a baking sheet. Bake at 400° for 40 minutes or until firm. Serve immediately with honey butter.

HONEY BUTTER: Stir honey into the ½ cup softened butter, then cover and chill.

Baby's Sublime Applesauce

*12 large Granny Smith apples, peeled and
    chopped*
1½ cups sugar
¼ cup fresh lemon juice

Combine ingredients in a heavy pan and cook over low heat, stirring often, for about 10 minutes. When apples begin to break down, increase heat to medium and cook, still stirring, for another 25 minutes or until thickened. Spoon apple mixture into hot sterilized jars and seal. Yields about 6 cups.

Carmela's Caramel Sauce

1 cup butter
2 cups sugar
2 tsp. fresh lemon juice
1½ cups whipping cream

Melt butter in a heavy saucepan over medium heat, then add sugar and lemon juice. Stir constantly for 6 or 7 minutes or until mixture turns a rich caramel color. Add whipping cream, a little at a time, and continue stirring. Cook for another 1 to 2 minutes. Remove from heat, pour into sterilized jars, and seal. Yields about 3 cups.

Big Easy Shrimp

4 tbsp. butter
1 onion, chopped
2 cloves garlic, minced
½ green pepper, chopped
1 tsp. salt
Dash of pepper
Pinch of Cajun seasonings
1 can tomatoes (14 oz.)
1 lb. shrimp
2 cups cooked rice

Melt butter in large pan. Add onion, garlic, green pepper, salt, pepper, Cajun seasonings, and tomatoes (including juice). Simmer for 12 minutes. Add shrimp and continue simmering until shrimp are cooked through. Pour over rice. Serves 4.

Chef Ricardo's Grilled Duck Liver Salad

1 tbsp. butter
7 oz. duck liver, cut into bite-size bits
2 tsp. whole-grain mustard
1 tsp. fresh chopped parsley
2 tbsp. Marsala wine
2 tsp. white wine vinegar
Salad greens

Heat butter in frying pan, add liver, and sizzle until sealed. Blend together all the other ingredients except salad greens and add to pan, stirring constantly for 3 minutes. Spoon the duck liver over a bowl of salad greens and serve immediately.

Bon Tiempe Asparagus Risotto

1 tbsp. butter
1 large onion, chopped
2 cups arborio rice
½ cup dry white wine
4 cups chicken broth
1 lb. asparagus, chopped in 1-inch pieces
¾ cup water
2 tsp. chopped fresh parsley
1 cup fresh grated Parmesan cheese
Salt and pepper to taste

Melt butter in large saucepan over medium heat. Add onion and sauté until tender. Add rice and stir for 1 minute. Add wine and cook until absorbed (4 to 5 minutes), stirring often. Add ½ cup of the chicken broth and simmer until liquid is absorbed, stirring constantly. Continue to cook, adding more broth by ½ cupfuls and allowing liquid to be absorbed before adding more. This process can take a good 20 minutes and you must remember to stir often. Add asparagus and stir, adding the water as mixture becomes creamy. Keep stirring and give the rice time to cook. When rice is fully cooked and very creamy, add parsley and ½ cup of the Parmesan cheese. Stir, season to taste with salt and pepper, and transfer to serving bowl and sprinkle with remaining Parmesan cheese.

Veal Chops Stuffed with Gorgonzola and Walnuts

4 oz. Gorgonzola cheese (or blue cheese)
2 tbsp. butter, softened
2 tbsp. walnuts, chopped
1 tbsp. fresh chives, chopped
6 veal rib or loin chops, about 1-inch thick

Combine cheese and butter in a small bowl. Add walnuts and chives, mix well. Divide stuffing mixture into 6 equal portions and set aside. Cut a 2½-inch horizontal pocket in each veal chop and insert 1 stuffing portion into each pocket. Close pockets with small skewers or wooden picks. Place chops on rack in broiler pan so meat is approximately 4 inches from heat. Broil 12 to 14 minutes for medium doneness, turning once. (Note: Chops may also be cooked uncovered on an outdoor grill.)

Baby's Monster Slosh

3 oz. ginger beer
Juice of ¼ lime
1½ oz. dark rum
Gummy worm

Into a tall glass filled with ice, pour ginger beer, lime juice, and rum. Stir well and garnish by hanging a gummy worm over the side. (Note: If you want to de-monster your drink, garnish with a thin wedge of lime instead.)

Hearty Pumpkin Soup

14 oz. vegetable broth
1 large onion, chopped
2 carrots, diced
16 oz. pumpkin meat (fresh pureed or canned)
2 cups milk
1 tsp. cinnamon
Salt
Pepper
Nutmeg

Put broth, onion, and carrots in a large pot, and simmer uncovered for 10 to 15 minutes, until carrots are soft. Mix in the pumpkin, milk, and cinnamon, then simmer for another 10 minutes. Season with salt and pepper, sprinkle with ground nutmeg.

Boo's Holy Mackerel Morsels
(These are strictly for dogs!)

1 can (15 oz.) mackerel
½ cup whole-grain bread crumbs
1 tbsp. minced green pepper
2 tbsp. canola oil
1 egg, beaten

Mash mackerel in a bowl with a fork, then add the remaining ingredients and mix well. Roll into walnut-size balls, then press with fork to flatten. Place on well-greased cookie sheet and bake at 350° for 20 minutes. Once they are firm and lightly browned, flip fish cakes and put back into oven for 5 additional minutes to dry them out slightly. Cool completely before storing in refrigerator.

Shamus's Game Day Beer Bread

¼ cup sugar
3 cups self-rising flour
1 bottle (12 oz.) beer

Stir all ingredients together, then spoon dough into a lightly greased 8½" × 4½" bread pan. Bake at 375° for 55 to 60 minutes or until golden brown. Cool in pan on wire rack for 5 minutes, then remove from pan and continue cooling on rack.

Bound for Murder

This book is dedicated to my dear friend,
Diane,
whom I finally reconnected with after almost 30 years.

Acknowledgments

Heartfelt thank-yous to my agent, Sam Pinkus; to Gary, for giving me an office at Mill City Marketing/Survey Value; to my husband, Bob, for his continued support; to the many scrapbook shops that carry my books and invite me in for book signings; to the tea shops that also carry my books and generously promote them via "scrapbook teas" (what fun!); to all the marvelous booksellers who not only stock my books, but recommend them to customers; and to all the wonderful writers, reviewers, web masters, crafts columnists, and editors who have been so kind and generous with their words.

Chapter 1

"HAUNTED?" CRIED CARMELA Bertrand as she and her friend Ava Grieux trundled their packages down a narrow hallway where sagging floorboards creaked and lamps with beaded shades cast a faint pinkish glow. "I don't recall Quigg ever mentioning that Bon Tiempe was haunted." With tall, narrow doors at every twist and turn and canted baroque mirrors that tossed back gilded reflections, the hallway felt more like a funhouse maze.

Putting her shoulder to the door at the far end of the hallway, Carmela nudged it open and the two of them stepped into a small, tastefully furnished business office that had been shoehorned in where a butler's pantry had once existed. Back when Bon Tiempe Restaurant had been a private New Orleans home.

Ava Grieux's expressive brown eyes gave a languid sweep of the small office, taking in the slightly Gothic decor, the Tiffany lamp strewn with dancing dragonflies, and the moss green velvet settee pushed up against one wall. The opposite wall was dominated by an antique roll-top desk with a laptop computer sitting atop it.

"*Feels* haunted," said Ava, hunching her shawl-draped shoulders in a hopeful gesture.

Carmela uttered a soft laugh as she set her box of place cards down on a small marble-topped table, then grabbed the box containing the floral arrangement that Ava, her best friend and female confidante, had been carrying. "Haunted by ghosts of customers past, maybe," Carmela told her, placing the oversized box on the desk. "Before Quigg turned this old Bywater mansion into a hoity-toity restaurant it was a costume shop." Quigg Brevard was the rather dashing proprietor of the fabulously successful Bon Tiempe. A bit of a bon vivant, Quigg was also a man who found Carmela most enchanting, much to her consternation. Because fortunately or unfortunately for Carmela, she was already married. To Shamus Allan Meechum, professional cad, sweet talker, and the youngest of the Crescent City Bank Meechums.

Although Carmela and Shamus were most definitely separated—physically, spiritually, and in all manner of opinion concerning the commonly held definition of matrimonial harmony—they'd simply never gotten around to making their separation formal and legal. Even for a banker, Shamus wasn't all that keen on formal and legal.

"Mmm," said Ava, surveying her wavering image in yet another antique mirror and obviously liking what she saw. "Lots of so-called costumers in

New Orleans." Ava poufed her mass of auburn hair and pulled the front of her cocktail dress down to reveal a tad more of her luscious décolletage. Then, like a lazy, languid cat, Ava eased herself down onto the velvet settee, allowing Carmela an unobstructed view of the amber-tinted glass.

Carmela stared straight ahead as though confronting the lens of a camera. Not unlike what she'd done for her fourth grade class picture when, geeky-looking and skinny, she'd probably taken the worst picture of her life.

Now the image that stared back at her was quite different. Mid-twenties, pretty veering toward stunning, Carmela possessed a unique blend of kinetic energy and quiet confidence. Her looks were further enhanced by her glowing, almost luminous complexion. Her lovely oval face was loosely framed by streaked blond hair. And many thought her grayish blue eyes strikingly similar in color to the flat glint of the Gulf of Mexico.

That's me? Carmela asked herself, always surprised by her now-comely image. Then, suddenly startled, she frowned and peered into the mirror for a closer look. As she studied her image, she realized that the silvering or mercury or whatever you called that shiny stuff on the back of the mirror had either flaked off or been improperly redone. So a faint double image was reflected. A *ghost* image. Carmela gave a slight shiver. *Maybe Ava's premonition wasn't so far-fetched after all.*

Ava dug eagerly into the box Carmela had brought along. "I haven't seen your place card designs yet, *cher*," she said, carefully pulling out a stack of deckled paper cards and studying them.

"Honey, that's because my design isn't *done* yet," Carmela told her, letting loose a mighty sigh. "I ordered ribbon six weeks ago and it only just showed up on my doorstep late this afternoon!" Carmela pulled two spools of peach-colored ribbon from her purse and held them out for Ava's inspection.

"Personalized ribbon," said Ava, narrowing her eyes. "Perfect."

Carmela was the proprietor of Memory Mine, a small scrapbooking shop tucked away on Governor Nicholls Street in the French Quarter. Besides helping her customers create pluperfect scrapbook pages that showcased their precious photos, her talents also shone forth when it came to designing keepsake boxes, party invitations, and personalized albums.

Reaching into her bag again, Carmela produced a small gold snipping scissors. She spun out one of the spools of ribbon until she had a twelve-inch piece on which sparkled the gold-embossed words *Wren & Jamie*. Giving a quick snip, Carmela passed the twist of ribbon over to Ava.

"This is gonna be great," said Ava, studying the ribbon. "I love the script or type font or whatever you call it."

"I could order some for your shop," said Carmela, raising one skeptical eyebrow. Ava owned the Juju Voodoo and Souvenir Shop over on Esplenade Avenue. Voodoo being a thriving cottage industry in New Orleans, Ava's tiny shop was redolent with the heady scents of sandalwood incense, musk oil, and flickering vanilla candles. With its enchanting stock of love charms and tiny silk bags filled with "secret" herb mixtures (mixtures that Ava confided were better suited to seasoning a turkey) the little shop catered shamelessly to tourists who flocked to the French Quarter searching for an authentic voodoo experience.

Ava giggled at the thought of personalized ribbon for her shop. "I think my shop's a little trippy for something this classy." She eyed the twelve-inch hanks of peach ribbon Carmela kept snipping and handing over to her. "So what do you want me to do?" she drawled. "Just twine this stuff through the holes ya'll punched?"

Carmela nodded. "Thread it through and I'll finish up with some neat little bows and judicious trimming." The place cards Carmela had designed for tonight were truly miniature works of art. Four-by-six-inch pieces of floral card stock served as the canvas. Upon this, Carmela had created a mini collage, incorporating tiny Renaissance-style images of angels, pressed flowers, gold heart charms, and the guest's names printed on peach-colored vellum. She'd used a crinkle cutter to create a deckled edge at the bottom of each card. The personalized ribbon threaded through the top would be the final loving touch.

As Carmela worked, she glanced at her watch nervously. She knew the guests were probably arriving right now. And even though they were being hustled into the party room to mix, mingle, and enjoy cocktails and finger food, she still needed to get the place cards on the tables ASAP. After all, Gabby was counting on her. Big time.

As if reading Carmela's mind, Ava glanced up and smiled. "Is Gabby pretty excited about Wren's wedding?" she asked, her nimble fingers continuing to weave ribbon through the punched holes in the place cards.

"Gabby's ecstatic," confirmed Carmela. "She doesn't have any brothers or sisters, and Wren is her absolute favorite cousin."

"It was sweet of you to help with all the arrangements," murmured Ava, trying to keep up with Carmela, who was tying bows and trimming ribbon like a true scrapbook and craft pro.

"It's the least I can do," murmured Carmela. Ever since she'd opened Memory Mine, Gabby Mercer-Morris had served as her highly capable assistant and enthusiastic instructor of scrapbook classes. In fact, the place cards that Carmela and Ava were laboring over right now were a kind of by-product of Gabby's creativity.

Gabby was a paper freak of the first magnitude. She adored the myriad of paper designs they carried for scrapbooking, and positively swooned over the special vellums, mulberry papers, Japanese washi papers, flax and jute fiber papers, and parchment papers they also carried. And, although it had been Carmela's idea to offer their Paper Moon class, an introduction to the amazingly diverse world of paper, it was Gabby who'd hatched the idea for card-making classes. Classes that filled up immediately and taught eager scrapbookers how to apply the same stamping, embossing, and dry brush techniques they'd learned in scrapbooking to create highly personalized greeting cards, thank-you cards, and even place cards.

Now Gabby's cousin, Wren West, was marrying Jamie Redmond this coming Saturday. And Carmela, with a little help from Ava, was doing her utmost to make tonight's prewedding gala an elegant and memorable occasion.

The place cards finished, Carmela let out a low whistle as she lifted the centerpiece Ava had designed from its tissue paper nest inside a cardboard box.

Ava glanced at Carmela. "What?" she asked, anxiously. "It's okay, isn't it?"

"Okay?" exclaimed Carmela. "This is spectacular." Time had run out for Carmela today, so she'd sent out a plea to Ava. And Ava, overachiever and dear friend that she was, had gladly responded. Besides owning a voodoo shop and freelancing as a custom mask maker, Ava was also a rather fine floral designer. For the big prewedding bash tonight, she'd created a floral arrangement using pink ruffle azaleas, foxglove, Louisiana peppermint camellias, and ferns, accented with sprigs of bleeding hearts and set in a cream-colored French crock.

"Twarn't nothin," replied Ava, plucking at the sprigs of bleeding hearts to straighten them. But she was pleased just the same to receive Carmela's compliment.

Twenty minutes later the party was in full swing.

"Interesting crowd," commented Ava, as she sipped a dirty martini, her favorite drink du jour. "I've already been hit on four times."

"Good night for you?" asked Carmela.

Ava shook back her frowzled mane and considered the question. "A little slow," she admitted. Tall and sinewy, with the carriage of a New York runway model, Ava was zipped into a slithery gold dress that most definitely showed off her generous assets. Once crowned Miss Teen Sparkle of Mobile, Alabama, Ava had never abandoned the regal bearing as befitted a Southern beauty queen.

"Give it a few minutes," said Carmela, as the party swirled noisily around them. "Things should pick up." It was a good-sized crowd—exactly sixty people according to the guest list—that had turned out to celebrate the much anticipated wedding of Wren and Jamie. Most were friends of the groom, Jamie Redmond, who'd grown up just south of New Orleans in the little town of Boothville and then moved the seventy or so miles north to attend Tulane University. Wren, Jamie's fiancée and Gabby's first cousin, had moved to New Orleans from Chicago just over a year ago.

"Evenin' pretty ladies," drawled a male voice behind them.

"Hello," said Ava, arching a single eyebrow and turning to appraise their admirer.

"I bet you're Carmela," said the man, a tall, good-looking fellow with dark wavy hair and a pencil mustache. He was clutching a glass of bourbon and weaving slightly.

"I'm Ava, *this* is Carmela," said Ava, setting him straight.

"Blaine Taylor," said the man playfully, leaning in close. "But ya'll can call me B.T."

"You're Jamie's software partner," exclaimed Carmela. She'd heard all about Blaine Taylor from Gabby. Blaine was supposedly a big-time real estate investor as well as former Tulane classmate of Jamie's. Although he didn't look it at the moment, Blaine was also a fairly savvy businessman and had teamed up with Jamie to help investigate potential markets for a software program Jamie had designed.

"Neutron," said Blaine, blowing soft, boozy breath into Carmela's ear.

"Pardon?" she said.

"Neutered?" asked Ava. "*That* doesn't sound good."

Blaine Taylor looked hurt. "Not neutered, *Neutron*," he said, lurching toward Ava and, in the process, sloshing half his drink on the Aubusson carpet. "Oops," he said, a silly smile flitting across his handsome face.

"I see you've made the acquaintance of my erstwhile partner," said Jamie Redmond, suddenly materializing at Carmela's elbow. Tall and elegantly slim, with a fair complexion, pale blue eyes, and ginger-colored hair, Jamie appeared slightly embarrassed by his friend's behavior. "Has B.T. been boring you with tales of our software project?" he asked the two women.

"Mostly he's just been weaving and sloshing," commented Ava, still eyeing Blaine. "So we're kind of reserving judgment."

"What exactly *is* Neutron?" asked Carmela, turning her attention to Jamie.

"It's pretty neat," Jamie responded eagerly. "Neutron is a software program that helps detect bugs and bombs in newly written code."

"Oh," said Ava, suddenly disinterested. "Computer stuff."

"Wait a minute," said Blaine, holding up one finger. "This is cutting-edge stuff!"

"As you can see," said Jamie, making a self-deprecating gesture at the well-worn tweed jacket he wore, "I'm the tweedy, nerdish member of the team. And Blaine's the showy 'suit' side. Very buttoned up." He smiled enthusiastically at the two women. "Would you believe it? Blaine's already got us pow-wowing with a couple heavy-hitter high-tech companies! Both have expressed interest in either licensing or possibly even buying Neutron outright."

"For *big* money," Blaine blurted out, a silly, satisfied grin pasted across his face. "That is, if I can get this self-styled *dilettante* to seriously agree to sell." Blaine spat out the word *dilettante* like he was referring to cattle manure.

Jamie put a hand on Blaine's shoulder to steady him. "I have to admit, as a self-made real estate mogul, Blaine has opened a lot of doors for us."

"You're in real estate?" said Ava, perking up. Here was something a girl could understand and appreciate. Serious, tangible assets.

Blaine bobbed his head eagerly, delighted at Ava's sudden interest. "I'm a private investor," he told her. His words came out *private inveshtur*.

"Honey, you and I should get better acquainted," said Ava, gently pulling Blaine away. "Tell me," she said as they strolled toward the hors d'oeuvre table, "do you hold *lots* of real estate yourself? Or do you mostly just buy and sell it for a tidy profit? Like playing Monopoly?"

Jamie chuckled as they watched Ava and Blaine wander off together.

"Like a lamb to the slaughter," said Carmela. "She'll have a P & L statement from him by evening's end."

"Blaine's a big boy," laughed Jamie. "He'll be fine. His only problem is he *does* like to party. At Tulane, Blaine was an absolute hellion. President of some ultrasecret group called the Phlegethon Society, although I think it was more about drinking than anything else."

"Ava means well, too," said Carmela. "But the prospect of your wedding this Saturday evening has her *altar ego* all in knots. Ava was positive she'd be married and divorced by now."

Jamie smiled at Carmela's little joke.

"With all this talk of selling your software program," continued Carmela, "what's going to happen to your cozy little bookstore?" Jamie owned a bookstore over on Toulouse Street, not far from Carmela's scrapbook shop. He specialized in secondhand books, maps, old engravings, and the occasional rare or antique book.

"*Possibly* selling my software program," said Jamie. "It still needs a bit of fine-tuning. As for the bookstore, I think it might finally be turning a profit."

Carmela nodded knowingly. Although everyone thought owning a shop in the French Quarter guaranteed huge rewards, a lot of proprietors were lucky to eke out a modest living.

"Hey, you two!" cried Gabby, as she rushed over with her cousin Wren in tow.

Jamie wrapped his arms around his bride-to-be and planted a kiss on Wren's forehead. Wren, a petite blond with big blue eyes and short wispy hair, smiled up at him in complete adoration. In her cream-colored wrap dress and citrine chandelier earrings, she looked like anything but a wren.

"Who knew this bookish fellow was also a software genius," said Carmela, smiling as the two of them embraced. *Why,* she wondered, *can't Shamus and I communicate like that? Bear hugs, longing gazes, lots of sexual tension.*

"Genius? No way!" protested Jamie. "I was merely born with a love for the printed word as well as the digital. The luck of the draw."

"And a talent for choosing the right girl, too," said Gabby, obviously pleased at the fine catch her cousin had made. She put a hand on Carmela's arm and lowered her voice. "Your place cards are gorgeous," she said. "Thank you."

"My pleasure," said Carmela. She'd put them out earlier according to Wren and Gabby's seating chart.

Gabby laid a hand across her heart and ducked her head. "You've done so much, Carmela," she said, her dark eyes filled with gratitude. "Designing the wedding invitations, the place cards tonight, helping Wren and Jamie with tons of arrangements . . ."

"How can we possibly thank you?" bubbled Wren.

"Just have a lovely wedding Saturday night and live happily ever after," said Carmela. *After all,* she decided, *isn't that what wedded bliss is really all about? Is* hopefully *all about?*

Carmela smiled at Jamie as he listened attentively to Wren and Gabby chit-chat back and forth. She decided that Jamie seemed like a nice-enough guy, acted like a nice-enough guy. Of course, the true test lay ahead. Could Jamie Redmond, this good-looking, dripping-with-charm bookseller, put away his bachelor habits? Could he slip his old ways into his sock drawer without a single twinge of regret and settle down to a nice, long monogamous relationship?

Carmela shook her head to clear it. Of course he could. What was she thinking? It was Shamus, *her* husband, who'd been unable to succumb to a full-time commitment. Shamus, her adorable husband who swore he loved her, but still craved freedom. Who claimed they were soul mates, yet continued to sling barbed arrows into her heart. Ava had lectured her sternly about proceeding full steam ahead on a divorce, and she was probably right. Still . . .

Gazing across the crowded room, Carmela caught sight of Quigg Brevard, the owner of Bon Tiempe. Darkly handsome and oh-so-suave, Quigg made no bones about the fact that he was interested in Carmela.

But am I interested in him? she wondered. *Yes. And No. Yes, because Quigg is charming and courtly and talks a good game about honesty and relationships. And no, because somewhere, in the dark recess of my aching heart, I still believe Shamus and I might find our way back to each other.*

"Honey," said Ava, coming up behind her, "that man is about as subtle as a Zubaz track suit."

"You're talking about Blaine Taylor?" asked Carmela, slightly amused by Ava's apparent discomfiture. "Old B.T.?"

"We shall henceforth refer to him as Mr. Calamari," snapped Ava. "The man is a veritable *octopus*. Had his grabby little hands all over my sweet little bod. Didn't wait for an invitation or nothin'." Ava smoothed her dress, managing to look both pleased and outraged. "Can't say I care for a man who doesn't wait for my say-so."

"You don't think your come-hither dress and spring-loaded bra aren't the next best thing to an engraved invitation?" asked Carmela. Dressed in her skin-tight gold dress, Ava had caught the roving eye of nearly every man in the joint.

Ava grinned widely. "Sure, I dress to advertise my assets. But what's a girl supposed to do? Skulk around like a *nun*? Wear skirts below her knees?"

Carmela had to choke back a chuckle. For Ava Grieux, whose bursting clothes closet looked like something a drag queen would kill for, there was no middle ground. Dress like a meek Carmelite or boldly strut your stuff. That was it.

Ava nudged Carmela as her eyes roamed the room. "Monsieur restaurateur is gazing your way," she said in a coy voice.

Carmela glanced over toward Quigg Brevard again. Even though he was deep in conversation with one of his high-hatted chefs, he was indeed looking in her direction. Smiling at her, in fact. Carmela waggled her fingers at Quigg in greeting and he waggled fingers back.

"Now *that's* the man you should be involved with," whispered Ava. "A drop-dead gorgeous guy who could sweep you off your feet, maybe even start a rip-roaring scandal or two. Stop you from pining away over silly old Shamus Meechum."

"I'm not pining," said Carmela. "I'm getting on beautifully with my life. It's exceedingly busy. Hectic, in fact."

"You seem to be confusing your thriving business at Memory Mine with your rather dreary personal life," said Ava. "Tell me, what did you do last Friday evening?"

"Nothing," said Carmela, wincing. She had cleaned her refrigerator, a sputtering, vintage Norge that only an unscrupulous landlord would dare stick in a rental unit.

"Aha," said Ava, sounding victorious. "And Saturday evening?"

"Stayed home," muttered Carmela, not liking the gist of this conversation one bit. Truth be known, Saturday night had been a total black hole. Sinking into the abyss of boredom, she'd alphabetized her spice rack.

Ava planted hands on slim hips and stared pointedly at Carmela. "You stayed *home*," she said in an accusing tone. "With Boo." Boo was Carmela's little dog. A Chinese shar-pei.

"Boo is extremely good company," argued Carmela, trying to score a few points. Boo had proved useful at disposing of some stinky, slightly moldy cheese, but had been completely indifferent when presented with the spice rack project.

"Boo doggy is sweet and utterly adorable," agreed Ava. "Unfortunately, she is somewhat lacking in the conversation department. Carmela, you need a man who'll take you out and show you a good time. Jump-start your heart again."

"Jump-start my heart," repeated Carmela. This she wasn't so sure of. Although Ava's enthusiastic pitch did carry a certain appeal.

"That's right, girl," continued Ava in an upbeat, manic manner that seemed to veer between spirited cheerleader and hectoring, lecturing evangelist. "Your poor emotions have been lying dormant for months. Ever since—"

"I know, I know," countered Carmela. "You don't have to say it." *Ever since Shamus slipped into his boogie shoes and disappeared out the back door,* thought Carmela. *Ever since he tromped all over my poor heart, the rat.*

"Take a look around," urged Ava. "What do you see?"

"Ava . . ." pleaded Carmela. This was getting entirely too personal. Even for best friends.

"No, I mean it," insisted Ava.

Carmela surveyed the crowd of friends and well-wishers. Many were people she recognized from around town. Some were folks from the Garden District, the upscale part of town where she'd lived with Shamus before the demise of their so-called marriage. Before Shamus's big sister, Glory Meechum, had so rudely tossed her out of the family home. Other guests she recognized from the French Quarter. Shop owners, long-time denizens of charming courtyard apartments, a couple restaurant owners. And what they all seemed to have in common, what Ava had most certainly been driving at, was that certain sparkle in their eye, a light-hearted *joie de vive* in their attitude.

"They're people having fun," Carmela grudgingly admitted.

"Not just fun, Carmela. They're having a damn *laugh riot*!" exclaimed Ava. "Honey, this is New Orleans . . . the Big Easy. We're the city that care forgot. The poster child for bad behavior! Our war cry is *Laissez les bon temps rouler*. Let the good times roll!"

"Point well taken," said Carmela. "I hereby resolve to have way more fun."

Ava let loose an unlady-like snort. "I don't believe you."

"No, really," persisted Carmela. "I'm going to march over to the bar right now and order a drink."

"Well, hallelujah," said Ava, brightening considerably. "That's a start. Whatcha gonna have, *cher*?"

"Maybe a hurricane," said Carmela. The hurricane was a marvelous concoction of fruit juice and rum that had been invented in New Orleans back in the thirties. Necessity being the mother of invention, the hurricane had come about because an overzealous bar owner had ordered one too many cases of rum and hurricane lamp–shaped glasses.

"You go, girl," urged Ava as Carmela sped off toward the bar. "And please! Smile pretty at all the nice men!"

"YOU LOOK way too serious," a low voice whispered in her ear.

Carmela spun on her barstool to find Quigg Brevard gazing at her. "Why does everyone insist on telling me I'm having a rotten time?" she hissed.

Quigg stared at her as though she were a fragile porcelain angel that had suddenly morphed into a demonic Chuckie doll. "My, we sound cranky tonight," he said, deadpan.

Carmela managed a sheepish smile. "Yeah . . . well . . . sorry. I didn't mean to jump down your throat."

Quigg waved a hand. "Don't apologize. Your feelings are your feelings. And you, my dear Carmela, unlike many people in my circle of acquaintances, have the unique ability to vent your emotions honestly. And with great verbal flair, I might add." He peered at her closely. "I find that unusual in a woman."

"Are you kidding?" responded Carmela, studying his impossibly white Chiclet teeth and noticing the tiny gleam of gel in his hair. "If you listen closely enough, most women let you know *exactly* what's on their mind."

"Okaaay," said Quigg, obviously enjoying this discussion. "Are you implying that men are the ones who are emotionally dishonest?"

"No," said Carmela, "absolutely not. I think men are a remarkable species. Very up-front about what they want."

Quigg smiled ruefully. "I'm probably gonna regret this, but what *is* it you think men are up-front about?"

"Power and sex," said Carmela. "But not necessarily in that order."

"Whew," said Quigg, "you don't pull any punches, do you?"

The bartender slid Carmela's drink toward her. "I try not to," she said. *Now* she felt more like her old self. She took a sip of her drink. "Mmm, good. Strong."

Quigg Brevard fixed her with a rakish grin. "Bon Tiempe aims to please."

"Listen," said Carmela, "I didn't mean to get so . . ." she searched for the right word . . . "*visceral* about things. I'm going through kind of a weird phase right now." She didn't bother mentioning that she'd been going through the same weird phase since she was fourteen. Maybe thirteen.

"No problem," said Quigg. "Like I said, I find your openness extremely refreshing."

Carmela took another sip of her drink, thinking: *Quigg wouldn't be a bad catch. He's handsome, has a good sense of humor, and the man's a gourmet chef. Maybe Ava's right. There could be some merit to exploring relationship options while enjoying a properly prepared soufflé.*

"Bon Tiempe looks enchanting tonight," Carmela told him, suddenly struck by the mellow feel of the old-world bar. Or maybe it was the smoothness of the ninety-proof rum.

"Lots of drawbacks to running a restaurant housed in a crumbing old mansion," said Quigg, "to say nothing of the madness that goes on in our kitchen. But our atmosphere seems to draw customers in like a magnet. Besides your group tonight we've got another forty or so dinner guests and bar patrons."

Indeed, Bon Tiempe dripped with old-world elegance. Antique chandeliers sparkled overhead, oil paintings crackled with age hung on brocade-covered walls, crushed-velvet draperies with golden tassels sectioned off different parts of the restaurant to create cozy, private dining nooks. Throw in the cypress wood paneling and sagging floors, and the overall effect was refined and genteel, tinged with a hint of decadence. A perfect reflection of New Orleans in general.

Quigg glanced at his watch. "I'm gonna check with the kitchen in a couple minutes. Tell 'em to start plating the prime rib."

Three weeks ago, when Carmela, Gabby, and Wren met with Quigg to plan tonight's menu, they had settled on prime rib with ginger peach chutney, bell peppers stuffed with rice and shrimp, and citrus salad. For dessert, Quigg's dessert chef was whipping up a sinfully rich Mississippi mud cake with brandy sauce.

"I'd better get busy and grab the centerpiece for the head table," declared

Carmela. "It's a surprise for Wren, so we've been keeping it under wraps in your office."

"Go grab it," Quigg said enthusiastically, while behind them loud *clinks* sounded with a gaggle of guests raising their champagne flutes in a boisterous toast.

"Here's to our beautiful bride and groom," boomed an exuberant voice.

Carmela and Quigg glanced over their shoulders at a red-faced reveler, a beefy man decked out in an expensive-looking pearl gray suit and showy tartan tie.

"Dunbar DesLauriers," muttered Quigg. "I better tell the kitchen to hold the brandy sauce for that one."

Carmela slipped off her barstool. "I really am going to fetch those flowers."

Moving quickly from the bar into the dining room, she stopped to admire the tables draped in white linen and sparkling with stemmed glassware and silver chargers. White tapers flickered enticingly, tiny silver place-card holders held her cards.

Gorgeous, Carmela thought to herself. *A beautiful prenuptial dinner, lovingly planned right down to the last detail.*

"To Wren and Jamie," came another excited voice.

Carmela heard a faint spatter of applause as she stepped briskly down the hallway. She scooted past the coat check, twisted to the right past the dark little nook with the telephone booth, then jogged left and down to the end of the hallway.

Nudging open the door to Quigg's office, Carmela stopped abruptly in her tracks. Someone had doused the lights so only the eerie green glow from the laptop computer shone in the room.

Then, slowly, as she stood there getting her bearings, Carmela became aware of the presence of someone else. Someone sprawled on the green velvet settee where, just an hour earlier, Ava had reclined in languid splendor.

Some poor soul had too much to drink, was Carmela's first thought. Tiptoeing across the room, she made her way to the roll-top desk where the centerpiece of azaleas, foxglove, and bleeding hearts sat.

But the position of the body on the settee, a funny *something* about the room, made Carmela hesitate.

Is that Blaine? she wondered. *Did the hail and hearty party animal finally veer from merely tipsy into full-fledged blotto?*

Hesitantly, Carmela's fingers tugged the metal chain of the Tiffany lamp. But its forty-watt bulb barely illuminated the amber and purple dragonflies that danced about the lampshade.

Even though the room was mostly still in shadows, Carmela's eyes landed on a tweed jacket laying in a puddle on the floor. And she recognized it instantly.

That's Jamie's jacket. Jamie's asleep on the settee!

Carmela frowned and took a step closer. It *was* Jamie who was just laying there, scrunched forward on his side, arms thrown carelessly over his head.

She wondered if Jamie had fallen ill. Worried that maybe he wasn't used to drinking at all. Because Jamie, poor fellow, hadn't even stirred when she'd turned on the light.

Puzzling over what to do, Carmela decided the best thing was to give him a gentle nudge. Wake Jamie up. It would be infinitely better to share an embarrassed laugh with him now than let the poor guy sleep through dinner. A dinner that was in his and Wren's honor!

Carmela placed a hand on Jamie's shoulder.

Should I really rouse him? she wondered. And a little voice inside answered back, *Of course you should wake him up. Don't be a dimwit.*

Carmela shook Jamie.

Nothing. Poor guy was dead to the world.

Carmela shook him again, harder this time, and was rewarded when Jamie began to slowly roll over. But her expectation of a drowsy awakening suddenly turned to horror as Jamie rolled off the settee and dropped to the floor with a heavy *thud!*

Holy shit! What did I do to him?

Hastily retreating to the doorway, Carmela searched frantically for a light switch. Her fingers skittered across the switch plate, then finally found purchase. Overhead light suddenly flooded the room.

Ohmygod!

Jamie Redmond, mild-mannered bookseller and fiance of Wren West, lay sprawled face down on the floor, a butcher knife jammed in his shoulder. His blue and white pinstripe shirt, that had probably been neat and crisp when he put it on, was now soaked a terrible dark red.

Unable to catch her breath for a moment, Carmela gaped at the hideous tableau. The protruding knife with the dark wood handle. The glut of blood seeping across the floor. The dark, wet stain on the green velvet settee.

Footsteps sounded behind Carmela as she leaned forward to feel for a pulse. *Nothing. Not a tick. Oh Lord!*

"Carmela?" came Quigg's worried voice. "Everyone's about seated. They're waiting for Jamie. They're waiting for *you*," he added.

Carmela whirled about to face him. A lump in her throat the size of a Buick made her words tumble out in a hoarse croak. "Someone's attacked Jamie!" she cried.

"Good Lord!" exclaimed Quigg, catching sight of the fallen man. Quigg threw himself to his knees, did the same quick search for a pulse. Then, shaken at not finding any sign of life, leapt to his feet, whipped his cell phone from his pocket, and punched in 911.

Feeling sick to her stomach, Carmela stepped out of the room as Quigg screamed frantically into the phone. Demanding the police, an ambulance, an EMS team.

"Carmela?" called Ava's soft voice from down the hallway. "What the hell's going on?" Ava was catching snatches of Quigg's frantic conversation.

Carmela caught Ava by the shoulders and halted her before she got too close. "It's Jamie," she said, her voice shaking.

"What?" Ava asked nervously, trying to peek past Carmela. "That boy didn't get cold feet, did he?"

With a stricken look, Carmela stepped aside, allowing Ava to see for herself. Quigg was still on his cell phone, his voice rising in intensity as he spoke with the 911 operator.

"Oh my god!" bellowed Ava when she saw Jamie's body. "He's *dead*?"

Still in shock, Carmela simply nodded. "I think so. No pulse."

Ava pushed a mass of hair off her forehead. "Jeez," she said, looking stunned. "What the hell are we gonna tell Wren?"

Carmela stared in horror at the unreal scenario. One minute Jamie had been alive and laughing and filled with hope. Now he was laying on the floor, a kitchen knife protruding from his shoulder, his fingernails already starting to turn blue. Carmela shook her head in disbelief. *What could have happened? Who could have done this?*

She tried to push her fear aside and concentrate on the here and now. Outside, sirens shrilled as police cars raced toward Bon Tiempe, and Carmela knew that in two more minutes they'd all be standing behind yellow police tape.

Focus, Carmela admonished herself. *Stay cool. For Wren's sake. And Gabby's.*

Carmela crept back into the office, Ava closely shadowing her. *Try to find a clue as to what happened,* she prodded herself. *Look around. Think!*

"Why would anyone . . . ?" began Ava, but Carmela interrupted her.

"What's that on the table?" Carmela asked in a whisper. "Those marks?"

Ava squinted at the small marble table nestled next to the blood-soaked settee. "More blood," she said, sounding horrified.

Carmela took another tentative step in. "Looks like Jamie tried to . . ."

"Mother Mary," breathed Ava, suddenly catching on.

Footsteps thundered in the hallway and Carmela knew a wall of people was poised to descend upon them. "Look," she said, in whispered excitement. "I think Jamie tried to write a message with his own blood!"

Chapter 2

THE WOMEN WHO were crowded around the craft table in the back of Memory Mine the next morning all exuded the expectant air of baby birds. Mouths open, eyes bright, every muscle straining to catch the retelling of the strange and sordid details of the night before.

Carmela and Gabby had both arrived at the shop promptly at 9:00 AM this Thursday morning, even though they'd been up until well past midnight, talking with police and being interviewed by two detectives. Shortly after they'd hung the hand-lettered OPEN sign in the shop window, their "regulars" had come tumbling in. Worried, nervous, and rabid for details.

Baby Fontaine, the fifty-ish, pixielike Garden District socialite, whose manners were superseded only by her good humor, had been the first to arrive. Byrle Coopersmith came in on her heels. And Tandy Bliss had tumbled in shortly thereafter, toting her oversized scrapbooking bag. Skinny with a cap of tight red curls, Tandy was a fanatical scrapbooker and a woman not known for mincing words. As Byrle had once remarked of Tandy, "She never met a subject she couldn't comment on."

Bony elbows propped on the table, chin cupped in her hands, Tandy was demanding more answers than either Carmela or Gabby could provide.

"But you saw the weapon," Tandy was saying. "So you must know *something*." Wren being Gabby's cousin, she had popped into the scrapbook shop frequently over the past few months, so Baby, Byrle, and Tandy had all come to know her fairly well. Plus, Gabby had continually regaled them with details of Wren's upcoming nuptials.

Gabby shivered. "Carmela was the one who saw everything. She and Quigg stumbled upon poor Jamie's body." She held a hanky to her nose and sniffled.

"How grisly," murmured Baby. "Was it really a butcher knife?"

"Afraid so," said Carmela, wondering if she'd ever be able to exorcise that terrible image from her mind. Worse yet, would she ever be able to return to Bon Tiempe without thinking about their gleaming racks of sharpened knives?

"And this happened in Bon Tiempe's business office?" said Tandy, still trying to get the picture clear in her mind.

"In Quigg's office, yes," Carmela said slowly.

"You're sure nobody else was around?" queried Baby. "There were no witnesses who came forth?" It seemed inconceivable to her that a killer had slipped into an upscale restaurant, murdered this well-liked, mild-mannered groom, then disappeared without a trace. Baby was married to Del Fontaine, one of New Orleans's top attorneys, and, in her mind, there *had* to be a witness. There was *always* a witness. Even if you had to pay them.

"Quigg's office is tucked way back," said Carmela, feeling like she was almost offering an apology. "Behind the kitchen." She held a new stencil in her hand, a somewhat intricate design of what could pass for a Garden District home, but she hadn't shown it to anyone yet, so distressed was she. "The office, the hallway, the telephone nook, the coat-check area . . . it's all kind of a rat's maze back there."

"Lots of doors in that hallway," piped up Tandy. "Darwin took me to dinner there one night and I got lost just trying to find the ladies' room. Thought I'd have to take a whiz in the potted palm."

"So what's going to happen now?" asked Byrle. "I mean, I know the police are investigating, but what about the . . ." Her voice trailed off.

"The wedding," said Gabby, in a somber tone. "I'm going to start phoning all the guests."

"Oh no!" the women exclaimed with collective dismay.

"Well, someone has to," said Gabby, a trifle defensively. "You certainly can't expect poor Wren to make those calls. It would break her heart."

"Of course we don't, sweetie," said Baby. "It just sounds like such an awful, sad task. You're very brave to take it on."

"I'm tougher than I look," said Gabby. And she was. At barely twenty-three, with dark hair, dark eyes, pale skin, and a penchant for sweater twin-sets, Gabby came across as the sorority girl–type. Demure, sweet, extremely well mannered. But there was flint beneath that polished exterior. Real fortitude when it was needed.

Tandy shook her head, still turning the whole situation over in her mind. She had read the *Times-Picayune,* scanned the TV stations for coverage, and called everyone she knew, trying to ferret out details. "Jamie Redmond's murder made front-page news in the *Times-Picayune,*" she said, as if everyone hadn't already seen the terrible headlines.

"The media adores bad news," commented Byrle. "Somethin' good happens, they turn a cold shoulder. But a nasty murder or a family tragedy, they eat it up."

"It's about selling papers and garnering ratings," said Carmela who, besides being a realist, had once worked as a graphic artist at the *Times-Picayune.* "They're a business. You can't completely blame them."

"Spoken like a true Republican," muttered Tandy.

CARMELA ASSURED Gabby that it was fine to use her office and to take all the time she needed for her calls. And a grateful Gabby did exactly that, barricading herself inside Carmela's cluttered little cubby hole, tearfully whispering into the phone amidst a jumble of rubber stamps, paper samples, and scrapbook supply catalogs.

Hovering at the front of the store, Carmela waited on customers while she put together a new display featuring Asian-inspired stickers and charms. She was proud of Memory Mine, the little scrapbook shop she'd built on her own. And she loved how it had turned out. The brick walls held floor-to-ceiling brass wire racks filled with thousands of sheets of colorful scrapbook paper. She had one of the best selections of albums in all of New Orleans, and her flat files were filled with elegant, textural, handmade papers laced with linen, hemp, ivy leaves, and banana fibers. Her store had become a meeting ground, a place where friends could come and spend a few hours, roll up their sleeves, and be wildly creative while they enjoyed wonderful commaraderie, too.

Glancing toward the back of the store, Carmela saw that Baby, Tandy, and

Byrle were slowly unearthing their photos, albums, paper, rubber stamps, and stencils and were starting to begin work on their scrapbook pages.

Good, she thought. *Hopefully we can enjoy business as usual. Sort of.*

Even though they'd all gone round and round on the details of Jamie Redmond's murder, there was one thing Carmela hadn't discussed with anyone besides Ava. The strange, squiggly symbols that seemed to be scrawled in Jamie's own blood. The message that had looked like "INA." Or maybe "INE." Or "INAE." She wasn't sure which it was, since, if they were letters at all, they were shaky and not very well defined.

The detective she'd talked with last night, a Detective Jimmy Rawlings, hadn't been terribly impressed with her hot theory that Jamie had scrawled out a final message. He'd yawned into his cup of coffee and copied the symbols down in his little spiral notebook. *Told* her he'd try to check them out. But she still had the impression that Detective Rawlings saw the marks as a kind of random by-product of the victim thrashing around. In other words, he hadn't seen any meaning in them at all.

Maybe so, thought Carmela. *But what if Jamie Redmond had known his attacker? What if, after being stabbed, Jamie had realized he was mortally wounded? So, painfully, carefully, he scuffed out those marks using his own blood.*

Because there were no witnesses, Jamie Redmond had to be his own witness. He had to leave a clue for the living.

It was an unsettling thought for Carmela. Yet one that was highly intriguing. So when Gabby took a break to run out and grab cups of chicory coffee for everyone, Carmela slipped into her back office and grabbed a pen and paper. She scrawled the letters down as best she remembered them and came up with a couple dozen ways to complete them.

INATE? I NEED? INACTIVE? INERTIA? Good heavens. Just what was it Jamie had been trying to convey?

But Carmela was either extremely tired or her neurons just weren't firing all that well today. Because nothing seemed to gel.

As Carmela sat puzzling over her scrawled symbols, the phone rang. Instinctively, she reached for it and answered with a not-so-chipper: *Memory Mine. Can I help you?*

"Carmela."

It was Quigg, who, for some reason, jump-started every phone conversation with a throaty, meaningful growl. In this case, it was actually kind of nice. Interesting, anyway.

"How you doin'?" Quigg asked. "You okay?"

Carmela gazed toward the back of her store where everyone was buzzing away at the big table they'd dubbed Craft Central.

Am I okay? Not really.

"Yeah, I guess so," she lied.

"What a *disaster,*" exclaimed Quigg, obviously referring to last night.

"To have a customer murdered right in my own restaurant! Unsettling, truly unsettling. The police figure it was probably a robbery gone bad. Kids or maybe a junky who slipped in through the kitchen and was searching for the office safe."

"Is there a safe in the office?" asked Carmela.

"No," said Quigg. "But that's something only *I'd* know."

"People could slip past your staff?" she questioned. "In the kitchen?" This seemed totally implausible to Carmela.

"Oh, yeah," said Quigg. "Easy. Pick your area. Kitchen, prep area, pantry, or cooler. Cripes, it's always bedlam back there, and most restaurants have huge turnovers so there's always some new guy lurking about."

Damn, thought Carmela.

"That poor woman," said Quigg, obviously referring to Wren. "I felt so helpless. She seemed inconsolable. If only there was something I could have done!"

"Refunding the money was a nice gesture," said Carmela. Quigg had been so upset last night, he'd written a check on the spot, refunding all the money for the bar tab and dinner. Carmela had the check in her handbag.

"It was nothing," said Quigg, who sounded anguished. "I just wish we could have gotten to Jamie Redmond sooner. Maybe the outcome would have been different."

"Maybe," said Carmela. "You did a lot, though. You were very take-charge."

"The police kept my entire staff until three o'clock this morning. Three bus boys and my damn *sous*-chef put in for overtime, can you believe it?"

She did, and told him so.

"On the plus side," continued Quigg, not sounding one bit happy, "business is suddenly booming."

"You've got to be kidding," said Carmela.

"I never kid about business, dawlin'. It seems everyone and his brother-in-law is burning with curiosity. I guess they want to enjoy a cup of *court bouillon* and bask in the midst of a real-life crime scene." Quigg pronounced it *coo-bee-yon,* which was, of course, the New Orleans pronunciation for that type of spicy fish stew. "Forensics a la carte," continued Quigg. "Sick, no?"

"Sick yes," murmured Carmela, knowing full well that the average citizen seemed utterly fascinated with crime scenes and forensic evidence these days. Case in point, just take a gander at what was being spewed out on TV.

"You've got to keep in mind," said Quigg, "that this is fairly typical for New Orleans. I mean, we're the Roswell, New Mexico, of the macabre. We've got more voodoo shops, ghost tours, haunted buildings, above ground cemeteries, and amateur vampires per capita than any other place in the world!"

"Good point," agreed Carmela. Visitors to the French Quarter were forever wandering into her shop and asking if there were any haunted houses or hotels in the area. Lately she'd been sending them down the street to Amour's Restaurant, a so-so brasserie that had been particularly snippy and pretentious to Gabby and her when they'd tried to order take-away.

"Listen," said Quigg, "I don't know if this is the right time to tell you this, but I'm opening a new restaurant in a couple months. Already leased space over on Bienville Street in a building that used to be an art gallery. Gonna call the place Mumbo Gumbo. Any chance I could talk you into designing the menus? I want the typography and overall look to have a kind of jumbled scrapbook feel."

"Sounds like something I could handle," replied Carmela. She'd turned him down on designing the new menus for Bon Tiempe and he'd ended up with heavy leather menus and old English type so ponderous looking it rivaled the Magna Carta. *So maybe, yeah.*

Carmela set the receiver back in its cradle just as Gabby came scuttling through the front door, carrying a cardboard tray filled with steaming cups of café au lait. She trundled the coffee back to the big square table and began passing out cups while everyone murmured thank-yous.

"Got one for you, too, Carmela," Gabby called.

"Be right there," said Carmela. She grabbed her paper filled with symbols and shoved it into the bottom drawer. She didn't want Gabby to know what she'd been up to. After all, the symbols or words or whatever they were could be nothing at all.

Jumping up, Carmela was eager to accept the little cardboard cup from Gabby. But as she held out her hand, she also stared in amazement at the person pushing her way through the front door.

"Carmela?" said Gabby. At first she thought Carmela didn't want the coffee. Then, suddenly catching on, Gabby quickly turned and followed Carmela's surprised gaze.

"Wren?" cried Gabby, utterly stunned by her cousin's unexpected appearance at the little scrapbook shop. "What . . . what are you doing here?"

As if on cue, Baby, Tandy, and Byrle all swiveled their heads to stare at Wren West, who was hesitantly making her way toward them.

Gabby hurried to meet Wren halfway. "Why honey?" she asked. "What possessed you to come here today?"

Wren looked subdued yet nervous. "I was just over at Jamie's store, a couple blocks away," she explained. "And it was like I could feel his presence."

That was enough for Tandy. She leaped from her chair, bounded over to Wren, and swept her up in her skinny arms. "Oh honey," she urged, "come over here and sit with us. Take a load off."

"You should be at home," murmured Baby, as Tandy hurriedly made room for Wren at their table. "You poor thing."

Like mother hens, they began clucking and cooing over Wren, offering their sympathy, their best wishes, and their assistance, should she need it.

"I really think you should just go home," worried Gabby.

Wren shook her head, looking miserable. "That's Jamie's place, too," she said.

"Oh my," said Tandy, looking perplexed.

"Blaine said he'd help me figure out what to do about the property," said Wren, sipping at the café au lait Carmela had given her.

Tandy's brows shot up in a question mark.

"Blaine Taylor," explained Carmela. "He was Jamie's business partner. Jamie invented a software program and Blaine was helping him market it."

"I didn't know Jamie had another business besides the bookstore," said Baby. "How nice."

"Ya'll are treating me like one of those poor sick kids they send to Disneyworld," said Wren. "Please don't."

"My sincere condolences," said Byrle, reaching over and gently touching Wren's sleeve. "Have you thought about funeral arrangements yet? I know we'd all like to attend."

Wren bit her bottom lip and shook her head. This was obviously a painful subject for her to talk about. "Not really," she said. "Jamie didn't attend one particular church or anything, so I guess I'm just going to have him cremated."

"Cremation is very dignified," said Baby, looking a trifle askance that there didn't seem to be a formal service looming on the horizon.

"Then what?" asked Tandy, handing Wren a Kleenex. "Maybe just have a private burial?"

Wren accepted the Kleenex and gave a defeated shrug. "I don't know. Maybe . . . lay him to rest with his parents?"

"They've both passed on?" asked Byrle.

Wren nodded and daubed at her eyes. "Oh yeah, long time now. Almost fifteen years. Jamie was adopted, and his parents were older." Wren was grasping the Kleenex with both hands now, twisting and turning it like a lifeline. "I mean, Jamie was just six or seven when he came to live with them, and they were both in their mid-forties by then."

"They lived here?" asked Baby, who was always interested in all aspects of parentage and lineage.

"No," said Wren. "Jamie grew up down in Boothville, where his dad ran a small printing shop. His parents were both killed in a car crash, and he doesn't have any other relatives." Wren blinked furiously. "You know, my parents are both dead, too. We called ourselves the two orphans," she told them, tears welling in her eyes.

"Where are Jamie's parents buried, honey?" asked Baby in her gentlest voice.

Wren's lower lip quivered and giant tears slid down her cheeks. "I have no idea!"

Chapter 3

GOLD CHARMS TUMBLED onto the table as Carmela ripped open a little cellophane package. Wren, who'd been sitting at Tandy's elbow for the past hour or so, watching her create a page to showcase her granddaughter's birthday party, looked over with interest. Baby and Byrle had gone off to run errands, but Tandy, determined to add an overlay of sparkling confetti, soldiered on.

"What are those for?" asked Wren.

The wire cords that felt like they'd been stretched tight around Carmela's heart loosened a notch. Wren seemed to have gotten hold of her initial grief, the hard grief that psychologists say can be horribly debilitating. After this morning's tearful revelation that Wren had no idea where Jamie's parents were buried, Carmela had stepped in and offered to help. Born and bred in the New Orleans area, Carmela knew her way around fairly well. She also understood that a few well-placed phone calls could sometimes short-circuit the ponderous beauracratic system that seemed to run rampant in Louisiana's cities and parishes.

"I put my foot in the glue again and volunteered to make two scrapbooks for Gilt Trip," Carmela told Wren.

Gilt Trip was the brainchild of a group of wealthy, good-hearted Garden District ladies who wanted to help raise funds for a new crisis nursery at a women's shelter. They'd decided that every year three or four of them would select an interior designer to completely renovate one room in their home. Once completed, these newly refurbished and hopefully splendiferous rooms would be thrown open to the public for their amazement, enjoyment, and possible envy. Hence the name Gilt Trip.

Tickets would be sold, of course, at ten dollars a pop and all money raised would be donated to the crisis nursery.

As a former Garden District resident, Carmela had been asked to create a scrapbook that highlighted the redone music room at the Lonsdale home. The scrapbook was supposed to showcase the step-by-step transformation of the room and include a few touchy-feely items like wallpaper samples, drapery fabric, and paint chips. It was also supposed to feature selling points about the interior designer and crafts people who completed all the glitzy renovations.

Carmela thought the cause highly worthwhile and the project not too difficult, so she'd gladly said yes. But somewhere along the line, a scrapbook-making volunteer had dropped away and Carmela's one scrapbook project had suddenly morphed into two scrapbooks. Now Carmela knew she really had to hustle to complete both books in time for the start of Gilt Trip next week.

"What I did," said Carmela by way of explanation to Wren, "was create my own album cover."

"Pretty," said Wren, admiring the deep plum-colored velvet that Carmela had stretched over and glued to what had been an ordinary brown vinyl album.

"Then, to sort of set the stage, I'm going to add this free-form piece of gold paper," said Carmela. "You see? I just tore away the edges until I had a sort of circle."

"Then you added that smaller piece of wine-colored organza on top of it," said Wren, watching Carmela work.

"Right," said Carmela. "Those are the redone music room's primary colors. Plum and wine, very deep and rich-looking."

"I've made little boxes that were decorated and dimensional," said Wren, "but I've never tried my hand at something like this."

"It's really not that different," said Carmela. "You just build up a few layers until you have a rich, tactile piece."

"So now what?" asked Wren.

Carmela picked up a two-by-three-inch piece of sheet music that had been torn into another free-form design. "Now I glue this on top, but slightly off center."

"Neat," said Wren.

"And for the piece de resistance, I'll daub a little blue and green paint onto these gold charms to give them some instant age. Then I'll string them on gold wire and anchor them on top of everything." The charms Carmela had selected were a violin, a baby grand piano, and a treble clef, motifs very much in keeping with the theme of the redone music room.

And now, thought Carmela, *if Margot Butler would just stop by with the before and after photos, I'd really be in business.*

"Carmela," called Gabby from where she was perched on a high stool behind the front counter. "Could you come up here a minute?"

"Sure," said Carmela, sliding the album and charms over toward Wren. "You'd be doing me a big favor if you fastened those charms on," she told Wren.

"You trust me?" asked Wren, blinking.

"Absolutely," said Carmela, thinking *This girl needs some TLC and a lot of confidence-building to boot.*

"CARMELA," SAID Gabby in a low voice, "I've been thinking."

"About . . ." said Carmela, although she had an inkling of what might be on Gabby's mind.

"About poor Jamie, of course," said Gabby, her face reflecting her anguish. "Do you really believe that story the police seem to be proposing of a burglary gone awry? That it was completely random?"

"Not sure," said Carmela. The police, the two detectives, and the crime scene team had seemed awfully hasty in their assessment. Then again, they had loads of experience in this arena. She remembered a news story from not too long ago about how a gang of kids sent an old rusty bicycle crashing through the windshield of a car at a stoplight, then murdered the two passengers for a take of less than twenty dollars. So . . . yeah, it was possible. Anything was possible.

"On the other hand," said Carmela, "Baby wangled that little write-up in the *Times-Picayune*. So anyone who had it in for Jamie would have known where to find him last night."

"True," said Gabby, furrowing her brow. "I hadn't thought about that." She was silent for a moment. "But do you *really* think a man like Jamie Redmond had an emeny? He sold books, for goodness' sake. And old maps."

"Maybe there's a lot of money in that," said Carmela. "Or there's more to Jamie than meets the eye."

"Maybe," said Gabby, sounding unconvinced. "But if the assault on Jamie *wasn't* random . . ." She gazed at Carmela with a growing look of horror.

"Then it could have been someone who was a guest last night," finished Carmela. "Yes, I have considered that."

"You have? Really?" asked Gabby. She seemed relieved. "I thought maybe I just had a suspicious nature."

"You don't," Carmela told her. "I'm usually the one who starts babbling conspiracy theory."

Gabby continued to look worried. "What do you think we should do?"

Carmela thought for a minute. "A couple of things," she said finally. "One, let's take a good, hard look at the guest list."

"That's right," breathed Gabby, "we've still got a copy. Because you did the place cards." She put a hand to her heart. "Wouldn't it be *awful* if one of Wren and Jamie's guests wished them harm?"

If one of them had, thought Carmela, *they'd certainly been successful.* But she didn't share that unhappy thought with Gabby.

"And I'm thinking about making a phone call to a certain friend," continued Carmela.

"Would this be a certain Lieutenant Edgar Babcock?" Gabby asked. Lieutenant Babcock had helped them with a sticky situation a few months earlier.

"It would," said Carmela. "But, like I said, I'm still thinking about it. We should probably see how the police investigation proceeds before we interfere too much. See what the police come up with." She stared at Gabby. "But please, give me your word you won't breathe a hint to anyone that I'm going to do a little snooping. Especially to Wren."

"Agreed," said Gabby. She moved her hand to Carmela's shoulder. "What a friend you are," she said as tears sparkled in the corners of her eyes.

The bell over the front door suddenly tinkled.

"Car-*mel*-a," called a somewhat strident voice as Margot Butler, one of New Orleans's most edgy and outspoken interior designers, exploded into their shop. Dressed head-to-toe in black, Margot was rail-thin with large brown eyes and an upturned nose that gave her a slightly snippy air.

Gabby quickly swiped at her eyes. "Margot. Hello." Margot had taken one of Gabby's classes last spring on the pretense of learning all about card making and rubber stamping. Unfortunately, she'd been surreptitiously trolling for new design customers and had proved to be somewhat disruptive.

"Hello Gabby," said Margot, immediately dismissing her and focusing instead on Carmela. She dug into the red messenger bag she had slung across her skinny form and pulled out a bright yellow packet, obviously a pack of photos. "Lookie what I brought you," she sang out.

"For the scrapbooks?" asked Carmela. "Thank goodness."

"For *one* of them anyway," replied Margot, handing the packet over to Carmela. Digging in her bag again, Margot came up with a Chanel lipstick. Clicking open the shiny black case, she swiveled the lipstick up and applied it to lips that looked like they might be collagen-enhanced. Carmela noticed that Margot's lipstick was the exact same shade as her spiffy messenger bag, which looked like very designer-ish and expensive and seemed to be made from some type of reptile skin.

"Just the photos for the Lonsdale house?" asked Carmela. "The music room?"

Margot nodded. "The dining room at the DesLauriers home isn't finished yet." She said it casually, as though they both had all the time in the world.

"You know, Margot," said Carmela, somewhat sternly, "Gilt Trip begins a week from today. And these are *custom* scrapbooks."

"Yeah," answered Margot. "And they're gonna add beaucoup credibility to all the decorated rooms. Plus, we were able to negotiate better prices with the vendors and crafts people, since they're going to be showcased in the book, too. That's what I call smart marketing."

"There isn't going to be *any* marketing if I don't get photos and materials," said Carmela in a firm voice. She tapped her foot to show her impatience. "What's the holdup?" she asked.

Margot frowned. "We're creating an entirely new room, Carmela. Genius can't be rushed."

But I can? thought Carmela. *What a crock.*

"We're awfully busy in the store," said Gabby, leaping to Carmela's defense. "If we don't have all the materials by Monday, I'm not sure we can promise anything." She smiled sweetly at Margot.

Carmela could have kissed Gabby. Usually mild-mannered and demure, this was an entirely new side to Gabby. She wondered where this newfound moxie had come from. *Does adversity really make us stronger? Oh, yes it does. I'm sure it does.*

Margot pursed her lips. "I'll see what I can do, Gabby," she said in a terse voice.

"So you'll stay in touch, let us know?" Gabby pressed her.

Margot dug in her bag, then tossed one of her business cards at Gabby. "Or you can try to reach me," she said, spinning on her boot heels and charging out the door.

"Woof," said Carmela. "*She's* hot and bothered."

"No kidding," said Gabby. "I just hated the way she was treating you. Like hired help."

"Are you kidding?" said Carmela. "I bet that woman doesn't treat her hired help like hired help."

"WHAT DO you think?" asked Wren once Carmela had made her way back to the craft table.

"Terrific." Wren had attached the charms and, as an added touch, curled the top and bottom of the music scrap, then gilded the edges. Now it looked like an old-fashioned piece of sheet music.

Wren gazed up at Carmela. "Can I come back tomorrow?" she asked in a small voice.

Carmela leaned down and put her arms around her. "Of course you can, honey."

"Why don't we make some of those bibelot boxes," suggested Tandy. She seemed to be wiping tears from her eyes as well. "Wren was telling me about a bibelot box she made that's very dimensional and decorated. We did keepsake boxes here once, but they were mostly decoupaged."

"I made my bibelot box for Jamie," said Wren. "I could bring it in and show everyone," she said hopefully.

"Sounds like a wonderful idea," said Carmela, wondering how on earth she was going to investigate a murder, get her scrapbooks done, prepare for the upcoming Scrap Fest, and suddenly run a class on bibelot boxes.

"Then it's settled," declared Tandy. "I'll call Baby and Byrle and maybe CeCe Goodwin, too. Tell 'em the agenda. I just know they'll all want to come!"

Chapter 4

THE FRENCH QUARTER at night is a rare experience. Sultry, sexy, and seductive, it is a place where the residential and the commercial co-exist in a fairly easy truce. Street musicians, sketch artists, and horse-drawn carriages ply narrow cobblestone streets lit by soft, glowing gaslights. Blocks of raucous bars, strip joints, and music clubs, especially along Bourbon Street, come alive with neon bling-bling as carousing visitors stagger from one bar to the other, clutching their ubiquitous *geaux* cups.

The French Quarter yields pockets of unbelievable charm and beauty, as well. Hidden courtyard gardens, elegant Old World hotels, and esteemed restaurants such as Antoine's, the oldest restaurant in America, rub shoulders with posh antique shops brimming with oil paintings, family silver, and the crème de la crème of estate jewelry.

Heartsick after she and Shamus had broken up, finally deciding to settle down in a place of her own, Carmela had turned to her friend Ava Grieux for help. And as luck would have it, there was a little apartment available behind Ava's shop in the tiny, picturesque courtyard with the burbling fountain.

Carmela pounced. The apartment had everything she wanted. Cozy atmosphere, affordable price, and, as they say in real estate, location, location, location.

Inside, of course, the place had been a total disaster. Carmela had to dig deep in her bank of creativity karma to come up with a solution. But dig she did, and now her little apartment exuded a lovely Belle Époque sort of charm. Carmela knocked down crumbling plaster to reveal three original brick interior walls. She painted the one remaining wall a deep, satisfying red to match the jumble of bougainvilleas in her courtyard. And, thanks to a fairly profitable first and second quarter, her early thrift shop finds had recently been replaced with honest-to-goodness real furniture. A gigantic leather chair and matching ottoman that was the exact color of worn buckskin. A marble-topped coffee table. And a fainting couch.

Carmela's walls displayed an ornate, gilded mirror, old etchings of the New Orleans waterfront during the antebellum period, and a piece of wrought iron, probably from some long ago French Quarter balcony, that now served as a bookshelf for her collection of antique children's books.

Imbued with all these loving touches, Carmela's apartment now looked like home, felt like home, was home.

Ducking through the tunnel-like confines of the *porte cochere* to enter her secluded courtyard, Carmela was suddenly aware of just how bone-tired she really was. She'd stayed at Memory Mine till almost six-thirty tonight, trying to get a few pages done on the first Gilt Trip scrapbook. Then she'd stopped at Mason's Market to pick up a few groceries. Potatoes, green onion, cheddar cheese—ingredients for a potato-cheddar soup. Now the clock was edging toward seven-thirty, and the thin January sunlight had long since departed.

Shifting her bag of groceries to the other arm, Carmela dug for her key and hastily jammed it into the lock.

The front door was half open when Carmela froze. There were low voices. Coming from inside her apartment.

Somebody's in there? Boo let somebody in? Must have. Either that or Boo has suddenly become a big fan of Wheel of Fortune.

"Awright," Carmela called out with far greater bravado than she felt. "I've got a gun and it's pointed right at your stupid head."

"No, it's not dawlin'," came a deep male voice. "You're not even close."

Shit, thought Carmela, instantly recognizing the voice. *It's Shamus. Shamus is in my apartment. Why didn't I sprinkle holy water on the doorsill and hang a garland of garlic over the doorway when I had the chance? Ward off the evil jinx of my estranged husband.*

Carmela flipped the light on. Shamus was lounging in her newly acquired leather chair peering at the TV. Boo, curled up on the ottoman at his feet, threw her a sleepy, guilty glance.

"Nice going, Boo," said Carmela. Ambling in, she plunked the groceries down on her small dining table, vowing *not* to invite Shamus to stay for dinner. "Once again you've managed to flunk Watchdog 101."

Like a furry croissant, Boo curled up tighter and feigned sleep.

The leather chair creaked as Shamus shifted his full attention to Carmela.

He was still drop-dead handsome, she decided. Tall, six-feet-two, with a lanky, sinewy body and curly brown hair. But his most insidious traits were dark, flashing eyes and a devilishly charming smile. *Satan, get thee behind me,* Carmela silently commanded.

Yet, like a stupid, silly zombie, she kept moving toward him. *What is wrong with me?* she wondered. *Sure can't be love, because love's supposed to feel good.*

A plush postal worker dog toy with a goofy face and detachable mail sack lay next to Boo. Shamus had brought her a toy.

Nice. Now he's even trying to buy Boo's affections.

Boo had chewed a corner on one of Carmela's Big Little Books last week and she still had mixed feelings about encouraging her dog to freely enjoy a chaw.

"You've still got a key," Carmela said in a flat tone. Their relationship always seemed to be in flux, so keys were constantly being offered, rejected, or hurled back and forth.

Shamus offered his best boyish look of concern, but made no motion to dig said key out of his pants pocket. "You want it back? I've still got one to your shop, too."

Carmela combed her fingers through her hair, thinking. She came up with nothing on the keys, but decided her "do" might be getting a trifle shaggy and that she probably needed to pay a fast visit to Mr. Montrose Chineal at the Looking Glass Salon. Except the last time she'd waltzed in and asked Mr. Montrose to cut it shorter, he'd left her looking strangely like an artichoke.

"No. Yes," said Carmela finally responding. She sat down on the edge of the ottoman next to Boo and let loose a deep sigh. "I don't know."

The fact of the matter was, Shamus had become an enigma to Carmela. He was the man who'd captured her heart, charmed her silly, and begged her to marry him. He was Garden District society, she was Chalmette working class. But they'd clicked. In that magical, comfortable way that instantly tells you it's right.

She'd been intrigued by his manners, mildly impressed that he could navigate his way through a French wine list, and awe-struck that she—little old Carmela Bertrand—had seemingly grabbed this tiger by the tail.

Shamus, in turn, had been wildly smitten and declared her to be amazingly creative as well as the most divine creature he'd ever laid eyes on.

Their courtship had been whirlwind, the wedding ceremony a tableau of shocked relatives (on both sides). And their honeymoon, spent in one of the suites at the Oak Alley Plantation, had been filled with great sex and unbelievable tenderness.

Then all hell broke loose.

Oh, Shamus hadn't stayed out late drinking, hadn't been unfaithful, hadn't been unkind or physically brutish in any way. He'd just . . . changed. Grew quieter, more somber, more unhappy.

Until one day he just left.

She'd likened it to a big cat who'd been caged. A chimera who'd been tamed.

And if I really believe all that hooey, I'm a bigger fool than I thought! mused Carmela.

Reality check? He's an immature cad. A grass-is-greener kind of guy. If Shamus really wanted this marriage to work, he'd make it work. Because Shamus generally gets what he wants.

"I take it you heard about last night?" Carmela asked Shamus, her tone weary.

He nodded. "I'm just back from a trip out to New Iberia to look at some property, but the break-in and murder are still big stuff on tonight's news. Channel Eight, Channel Four, some sketchy stuff on Six. That's why I came over." Shamus put a hand on Carmela's shoulder. "Lean back," he urged.

Warnings exploded in Carmela's head, but she was too tired to heed them. Instead, she leaned back against Shamus. Absorbed his warmth, savored his strength, and snuggled her tired head against the curve of his shoulder. He felt reassuring, infinitely strong, and achingly familiar.

"Tell me," he said. "Some of it was on the news, but I want to hear it in your words."

And so Carmela told him, her voice breaking more than once. About Wren and Jamie. All the planning they'd put in. About how the much-anticipated party at Bon Tiempe had ended up as a crime scene with harsh black and yellow tape stretched everywhere.

"How's Gabby doing?" Shamus asked when she'd finished.

"Upset about her cousin, but hanging in there. She came to work today."

"That's a positive," said Shamus.

Carmela raised an eyebrow. This from a man who'd deserted his post at the Crescent City Bank and stayed away almost six months, pleading the Gauguin precedent?

"And Wren?" Shamus asked. "I don't really know her, but I'm pretty sure I met her once when I stopped at Jamie's bookstore to look for a Faulkner first edition. She worked there, didn't she?"

Carmela nodded. "She's shell-shocked, but I think she'll eventually work her way out of it."

"That's good," said Shamus. "Time heals."

"So they say," said Carmela, looking at him sideways.

Shamus sat for a long moment, then cleared his throat self-consciously. "So what's the deal? Are you seeing that restaurant guy?"

Well, that came out of left field, Carmela decided.

"Quigg Brevard?" she replied. "No. Not really." She'd sat next to Quigg at a dinner party and had gone to dinner at his restaurant a few times, but that wasn't technically *seeing* him, was it?

"Good," declared Shamus. "I don't like him. I don't like him one bit. The man favors European suits and slicks on too much hair gel."

Okay, thought Carmela, *let's add those items to the column labeled Things Shamus Dislikes. A column that seems to expand exponentially with each passing day.*

Carmela picked up the plush postal worker toy Shamus had given Boo. The mailman had a glib smile and a newly shredded belly.

"She already ripped the squeaker out," said Shamus, a silly grin on his face. "Took her thirty seconds flat. It was like watching a crazed surgeon perform open-heart surgery."

"The postman always squeaks twice," muttered Carmela.

Shamus's grin expanded across his handsome face and, inside, Carmela felt a twinge of deep longing.

That was one thing Carmela still adored about Shamus. His sense of humor and whimsy. His quick laughter.

He was also an easy mark, she smirked to herself. Shamus could be taking a slug of Coca-Cola and if she laid a zany one-liner on him quick enough . . . presto . . . he'd hiccup and laugh and Coke would suddenly froth from his nose. It was one of those weird, gross, secret things they did to each other. Try to make Coke spew from each other's noses.

"Listen, babe," said Shamus, suddenly looking intense. "We gotta get together real soon and talk."

Carmela lifted her head and studied him. *We do?* she thought, her heart suddenly stalling a beat. *Really? Does this mean Shamus finally wants to sit down and talk about us? About our marriage?*

"We do?" she finally said. Her mouth felt like it was stuffed with cotton, her palms seemed suddenly damp.

Shamus assumed his serious mortgage banker look. The look that said *We're not convinced your financial underpinnings are quite up to snuff.* "Absolutely," he responded. "The sooner the better."

"And we're going to discuss . . ." she said, trying to lead him.

"The photo show," he said, a bright smile on his face. "We've got a good shot here to have a joint show. I've got my portfolio all pulled together, now it's your turn to get it in gear. You've dragged your feet long enough, honey. We can't keep stringing the Click! Gallery along forever!"

As fast as it had flipped over, Carmela's heart thudded inside her chest. *The photo show. The stupid photo show is his big, fat burning issue.*

Carmela had done some fashion photography for a ritzy day spa by the name of Spa Diva. Clark Berthume, the owner of Click!, had seen her moody black-and-white shots and offered her a show. In a gesture borne out of guilt and graciousness, Carmela had asked Shamus to be part of it. He'd been dabbling in photography for a couple years now and was actually quite talented.

And here I thought that maybe, just maybe, Shamus wanted to talk about us, fumed Carmela. *About our marriage. Or total lack thereof.*

Carmela launched herself out of the chair and headed for the kitchen.

"Carmela," called Shamus. "Something wrong?"

"Nothing," she called. *Nothing that a really nasty divorce lawyer can't fix.*

Chapter 5

"WREN," EXCLAIMED TANDY. "I can't believe you really came in again." Scrapbook bags slung across her slight shoulders like a pack animal, Tandy chugged her way to the battered table at the back of the store.

Wren, who was sitting next to Gabby, helping her sort out packages of stencils, ducked her head shyly. "This is the only place I feel safe," she said in a quiet voice.

"Where do you live?"

"In Jamie's house," said Wren.

Tandy slid a pair of red half-glasses onto her bony nose and peered quizzically at Wren. "And where might that be?"

"Big old house over on Julia Street," said Wren. "I think it used to be a girl's school or convent or something."

"Good grief," responded Tandy. "Please tell me you're not referring to the old Benedictine convent. I didn't think that place was even habitable. Certainly not for *people*, anyway."

Gabby immediately dove to her cousin's defense. "Jamie bought that place eight months ago and was working very hard to renovate it. You'd be surprised, Tandy, it's really quite updated and livable now."

"Just livable or comfy livable?" asked Tandy, looking skeptical.

"Jamie got a special grant from the Preservation Foundation," explained Wren.

"So it *had* been scheduled for the wrecking ball," said Tandy. "I thought so."

"He got a special grant?" asked Carmela, her ears suddenly perking up. She'd been camped nearby in her office, paging through a slew of vendor catalogs, getting ready to place an order for rubber stamps. There were some wonderful new ones available—antique engravings of botanical prints, carriage lanterns, ornate pillars, even French bistro tables. They had a slight Courier & Ives look, without being too New Englandy.

"You ask about the grant like it might be a problem," Wren said to Carmela. "Is it?"

"I honestly don't know," she said, emerging from her office.

"But you've got that worried look on your face," said Gabby, suddenly nervous.

"Sorry," said Carmela.

"And you know about grants and things," persisted Gabby. "You've served on committees."

"Arts committees and a Concert in the Parks committee a couple years ago," said Carmela. "Never anything to do with architectural preservation or renovation." She remembered that particular home on Julia Street as one that had been used as a Benedictine convent for just a few years. Mostly it was a big stone building that had been in a state of disrepair since time immemorial.

"You think the Preservation Foundation is going to want their money back if the work wasn't completed?" asked Gabby.

"No idea," said Carmela, sincerely regretting she'd raised the question.

But Wren was suddenly galvanized by what she perceived as a new threat. "You think I'll get kicked out?" she cried. "It's my home. The only place I've got!"

"Honey," said Carmela, "do you know if the mortgage is in your name, too, or just Jamie's?"

Tears oozed from Wren's eyes. "Not sure. I know I signed *something*."

"Well," said Carmela, "I just happen to have an acquaintance in banking who'd probably be willing to do a little pro bono investigating."

Put that good-for-nothing Shamus to work, she thought to herself. *Although, if the grant had been awarded to Jamie, it might put Wren in a difficult, disputed position. To say nothing of the ownership of the home.*

Gabby gathered together the stencils Wren had sorted. "You look tired," she told her cousin.

"I didn't sleep very well last night," said Wren. "I kept hearing weird noises."

"Those big old homes are awfully creaky," said Tandy. "Or maybe it's just plain haunted."

"Please don't say that," cried Wren. "I'm terrified as it is to stay there all by myself."

"What if I came over and stayed with you tonight?" asked Gabby.

"Would you really?" said Wren, brightening. "That'd be great."

"We could . . ." began Gabby, then stopped abruptly. "Darn. I can't. Stuart's taking his sales managers and their wives out for dinner tonight. He for sure wants me to go along." Stuart Mercer-Morris, Gabby's husband, was the self-proclaimed Toyota King of New Orleans. In fact, Stuart proudly bragged that he owned dealerships in all four parishes that made up the New Orleans metro area: Orleans, Jefferson, St. Bernard, and St. Tammany.

As Carmela watched Wren's face fall, she thought: *It's Friday, and once again, loser that I am, I don't have a date. Or even a semblance of a plan for tonight.*

"Wren," she said. "How about if I came over and stayed with you?"

"Would you really?" squealed Wren. "That'd be great!" The girl did sound delighted.

Maybe I'll even invite Ava, decided Carmela. *Try to get an impromptu slumber party going. Maybe do a quick check of Jamie's home office and see if we can find any papers. See if he put his property in Wren's name, too.*

"Holy smokes," said Gabby, scrambling to her feet. "I've got to get our 'make and takes' ready for Scrap Fest tomorrow." Scrap Fest was a one-day scrapbook event sponsored by a local scrapbook club. Memory Mine was going to have a booth there along with quite a few other vendors. Scrap Fest would also be sponsoring scrapbook classes as well as an all-night crop.

"Aren't you happy you don't have to man the booth by yourself?" Carmela asked Tandy. Since Wren and Jamie's wedding had been scheduled for tomorrow evening, Tandy had volunteered to set up and work at Memory Mine's booth. Now, with no wedding to attend, plans had changed big-time, and both Carmela and Gabby would be going to Scrap Fest.

"Actually," said Tandy, "I was kind of looking forward to working the booth. Hearkens back to my old retail days when I worked at the jewelry counter in Woolworth's."

"Then don't change your plans on our account," said Carmela. "You're always welcome to hang with us."

"Thanks," said Tandy. "Maybe I will."

THE LITTLE bibelot box Wren had brought in proved to be the hit of the morning. It was a stunning little oblong box, painted a midnight blue and embellished with swirls of gold peacock feather designs and decorated with keys that had been painted antique gold. In the center of the lid was a large, sparkling crystal.

"The feather designs look like they were done in gold leaf," marveled Baby. She and Byrle had shown up some fifteen minutes ago. Her daughter, Dawn, and another friend, Sissy Wilkerson, had come along as well.

"It's really just gold paint," said Wren, pleased that everyone was oohing and ahing over her handiwork. "And the keys were just keys that Jamie had laying around."

"Still, you're *very* creative," said Baby.

Wren, not used to being the center of all this attention, gazed around the table at all the eager faces. "Ya'll are so sweet," she said, her voice catching.

Tandy waved a hand. "You're in the sisterhood now, honey. Which means we take care of our own."

"Okay, Carmela," demanded Byrle in a joking tone. "Show us how we can make some of these so-called bibelot boxes. And what exactly does *bibelot* mean, anyway?"

"A *bibelot* is like a bauble or trinket," said Carmela, setting a half dozen empty Altoid tins and three empty Camembert cheese boxes on the table.

Surprised, the women just stared at them.

Finally Byrle spoke up. "You've got to be kidding," she said, puzzled by the strange items Carmela had just dropped before them. Carmela had played tricks on them in the past, and Byrle wasn't exactly sure what was going on.

"Do we collectively have bad breath?" joked Tandy. She reached for one of the Altoid tins and flipped it open.

"It's empty," said Carmela, "all the mints long gone. But . . . once you choose a special theme, then do some painting and decorating, these rather ordinary little boxes are going to be transformed into precious little gems. In other words, bibelot boxes. Smaller than keepsake boxes, but just perfect for stashing a special locket or favorite pair of earrings."

"Now I get it," said Byrle, suddenly enchanted with the notion of turning the utilitarian red and white tin she held in her hands into a thing of beauty. "By the way, the one Wren did is stunning."

"Show us what to do," urged Tandy, settling her glasses on her nose and leaning forward eagerly. That was the thing about Tandy. She might have a sharp tongue, but she was always game for something new.

"First things first," said Carmela. "Select a box."

Hands darted into the middle of the table as each woman grabbed a box.

"I'm going to take this Altoid tin and guide you through a few steps rather quickly," said Carmela. "Then you can take your time, think about what you want to do, and create your own unique design."

"Sounds good," said Baby.

"Paint," said Carmela, unsnapping the lids on a couple jars of acrylic paint. "First I'm going to sponge on some blue, purple, gold, and copper pearlescent paint."

The ladies watched as Carmela deftly sponged on the paint, making the sides of the tin a trifle more bluish and adding a more dramatic hint of purple and copper on the lid.

"While that dries, I'm going to take three small squares of frayed brown burlap and daub them with purple and copper paint."

"Wow," said Baby's daughter, Dawn. "You made them look like antiqued screens or something. Now what? You glue them on?"

Carmela nodded. "And once those three painted squares are attached, I'll glue on a gold aspen leaf, a small gold bee charm, and a small sprig of faux fruit. In this case, frosted purple pears."

"It sure won't resemble an Altoid tin once you're finished," said Tandy. "It really will be a jewel of a box."

"Complete with four crystal beads at each corner for legs," said Carmela. "But don't just copy what I've done, really let your imagination soar. Think about using mosaic tiles or embossing powder. Or even creating a tortoiseshell look."

"Love it," declared Tandy. She had completed more than a dozen scrapbooks and was adept at all the various tricks and tools available to scrappers and crafters.

Carmela hung around the back table for another fifteen minutes or so, offering words of encouragement and giving a few small creative hints. Then she made her way to the front of the store where Gabby was packing up, getting everything ready for tomorrow's Scrap Fest.

"How's it going?" asked Carmela. Actually, she could pretty much see how it was going. Gabby had assembled several large cardboard boxes and was sifting through store merchandise, determining what should be brought along so it could be displayed in their booth tomorrow.

"Do we want to take these stencils?" asked Gabby, holding some up.

"The new ones, yes," said Carmela, gazing about her shop, wishing they could take along the metal racks that were filled with all their wonderful new papers.

"How about this rack of charms and tags?" she asked.

"Ditto," said Carmela.

"And the scissors," murmured Gabby.

"Gotta have those," agreed Carmela.

Gabby turned toward Carmela with a wry grin on her face. "Why don't we just transport the entire store!"

"Great idea," said Carmela. "Beam me up, Scotty!"

AN HOUR later the women at the back table had made remarkable progress with their bibelot boxes. Tandy had covered her box with paisley paper, added a layer of gold mesh, then decorated the whole thing with squiggles of copper wire that had stations of pearlized gold and copper beads. Baby had painted her old Camembert cheese box to resemble Chinese red lacquer, then added a Chinese coin charm, gold tassel, and a tiny matching red tag stamped in gold with Chinese characters. Byrle and the other two girls were all going with romantic themes, incorporating bits of hand-colored photos trimmed to resemble stamps and emblems, mesh ribbon, embossed paper, silk flowers, and dragonfly charms.

"Wow, is that ever cute," said Gabby, looking at Byrle's bibelot box. "Very mauve."

"I'm making mauve my signature color this season," joked Byrle.

"You look like you're all done in," said Wren, glancing up at Gabby, who was still buzzing about the shop. Wren had been content to huddle at the craft table, watching and enjoying as the women created their personal bibelot boxes.

"I'm kind of brain dead," admitted Gabby. "It's tough trying to figure out the merchandise mix. What to take, what to leave behind."

"But you figured it out," interjected Carmela. "That's what counts."

"All I have to do now is tape the boxes closed," replied Gabby. "And therein lies my problem. We have roll after roll of masking tape, invisible tape, and double-stick tape, but, alas, no strapping tape."

"I'll run out and grab some," volunteered Carmela. "When the messenger service arrives to pick this stuff up, we want our boxes to be secure."

"Okay," said Gabby, content to stay and mind the store.

But as Carmela slipped out the front door, ready to head off toward Bultman's Drug Store, where she was pretty sure she'd find a good supply of packing materials, she encountered what seemed like an immovable object on her front sidewalk. A large man.

She tried to duck around him, but he side-stepped to block her.

"Hey there," said the man, definitely capturing her attention. He tucked his chin down and fixed her with a smile. A good show of teeth, she noted. But not much warmth.

"Do I know you?" Carmela asked. Somehow she had the feeling this little meeting wasn't exactly a chance encounter. That this man might have been *lingering* outside her shop.

"I'm looking for Wren West," said the man, staring at Carmela with pale, watery blue eyes. "I was just over at Biblios Booksellers and the darn place is locked up tighter 'n a drum. Figured she might be here."

"How would you figure that?" asked Carmela, curious about this man who seemed to act so casual yet projected an aura of tension.

"I'm Dunbar DesLauriers," he said, pulling himself up to his full height and puffing out this chest.

Dunbar DesLauriers. The name rang a bell. Carmela stared at him for a second, then her brain suddenly made the connection. This was the same man who'd been wearing the tartan tie at Wren and Jamie's ill-fated prenuptial dinner two nights ago. The one who had been swaggering about, making the drunken toast.

"As a collector of rare books, I was Jamie Redmond's best customer," Dunbar drawled.

Carmela stared at him, slightly amused by his pomposity. *He wasn't just one of Jamie's customers, he'd been his* best *customer.*

Dunbar DesLauriers swiveled his oversized head and peered in the front window of Memory Mine. Past the display of spiral-bound journals and calligraphy pens, past the poster that advertised their tag-making class. "She's in there, isn't she?" he said in a low voice.

"Yes, she is," said Carmela, picking up a vibe she didn't much like and suddenly not wanting Wren to be disturbed by this strange, somewhat boorish man. "But she's still very upset. I think we need to respect her privacy." *What I really mean is* you *need to respect her privacy.*

"I'm sorry to hear that," said Dunbar, a touch of hardness coming into his eyes. "About her being so upset, that is. I really wanted to speak with Miss West. Make her a business proposition."

"A business proposition?" asked Carmela. *What is all this about?*

"Yes," said Dunbar, rocking back on his heels. "I was going to offer to buy the inventory. Take the whole mess off her hands."

Carmela stared at him. By *whole mess* he obviously meant Jamie's bookstore.

"I wouldn't exactly call Jamie's bookstore a mess," said Carmela, beginning to get her hackles up at this strangely self-important man. Last time she'd ventured into Jamie's store, it had been a charming mishmash of old wooden bookshelves stuffed with leatherbound books, Oriental carpets on uneven wood-planked floors, antique oak flat files spilling over with old maps, and cozy stuffed chairs tucked into corners. The feeling was similar to being in your grandma's attic. Familiar and warm, a place where you could curl up and read undisturbed for a while. And with classical music perpetually wafting through the air, Biblios Booksellers had seemed a most intriguing shop. Very old-world and charming.

"This probably isn't the time or the place for discussing business deals," said Carmela. Her words came out a little firmer than she'd intended and Dunbar cocked his head at her, registering disapproval.

Could this boorish fellow really have been a friend of Jamie's? Carmela wondered. *Then again, he had been an invited guest at their dinner.*

Dunbar DesLauriers seemed to consider Carmela's words for a while, then he bent forward and gave her a sly wink. "You really should tell that poor girl to sell to me, you know." Dunbar's voice was like butter. "She'd listen to you. She trusts you and that cousin of hers." He paused. "Rest assured, you'd be giving her solid business advice," he said, punctuating his words with another aggravating wink.

Carmela gazed at Dunbar DesLauriers, not liking his condescending attitude one bit, wondering exactly what his game was. "Think so?" she asked.

Dunbar DesLauriers curled his upper lip and sucked air in through his front teeth. "Oh sure," he said, looking extremely pleased with himself.

Carmela could feel her anger rising, could almost picture a cartoon thermometer where the mercury rose up, up, steadily up, then suddenly exploded off the top. She *really* didn't like the subtle pressure Dunbar DesLauriers seemed to be exerting. So why, she wondered, was he exerting this pressure? Why did he suddenly want to buy Jamie's bookstore, lock, stock, and barrel? What was going on? Was he just a businessman used to getting his way? Was there some rare book in Jamie's inventory that Dunbar wanted for his personal collection? Or did he just get off on bullying women? Hmm.

In Carmela's experience there was only one way to deal with a bully. Put 'em on the defensive.

"You know," she said, starting to regret her words even as they tumbled out. "You were probably the last person to be seen with Jamie Redmond on Wednesday night."

The smarmy smile disappeared from Dunbar's lined face in about two seconds flat.

His brows shot up in displeasure, his face suddenly took on the ominous hue of an Heirloom Tomato. "If I didn't know you better, Ms. Bertrand," he sputtered, "I'd say you were veering dangerously close to slander."

"You *don't* know me at all, Mr. DesLauriers," replied Carmela. "But if you did, you'd know I don't veer. I pretty much set a direct course. Now kindly leave us in peace. And if you have any more business proposals to make, perhaps you'd best send them via an intermediary. In other words, have your lawyer talk to Wren's lawyer."

And with that, Carmela took off down the street, leaving Dunbar DesLauriers fuming in her wake.

Chapter 6

BLUESY NOTES DRIFTED out from the Copper Club and hung in the night air on Girod Street. Around the corner on Camp Street, coffee house musicians cranked out their own version of swamp pop, a riotous feel-good blend of rock, Cajun, and country.

In the area once known as the Warehouse District, a proliferation of blues clubs, art galleries, recording studios, and coffee houses had popped up like errant mushrooms, replacing old sugar refineries, tobacco factories, and cotton presses. Red brick row houses that were in disrepair were suddenly deemed highly desirable, and this once-industrial, working-class neighborhood that rubs shoulders with the Central Business District was reborn as the Arts District.

Jamie Redmond had been in the process of restoring a large, rather austere-looking limestone building on Julia Street. Looking more churchlike than residential, it had originally been built as a home then used as a convent for a short period of time.

The interior was dominated by high ceilings, original slate floors, cypress paneling, and a small first-floor rotunda that served as a sort of central hub with the various rooms radiating off from it.

Carmela, Ava, Wren, and Boo lounged in what had been Jamie's at-home library. The battered leather couches were comfortably slouchy, a fire crackled cheerily, but the faces the three women wore were a little grim.

As would be expected, Wren was still stunned and deeply disturbed by her fiance's murder just two days ago. Carmela was troubled by her somewhat bizarre encounter with Dunbar DesLauriers earlier this afternoon. And Ava was pretending to be upset that tonight's date with a legislator from St. Tammany Parish had been canceled. She'd told Carmela and Wren that she'd been counting on a spectacular dinner at NOLA, Emeril Lagasse's famed five-star restaurant in the French Quarter.

"Ava," said Carmela, knowing her friend was trying her darndest to make Wren smile, "the man was *married*, for heaven's sake. You can't count that as a *date*. I think that's technically an affair."

Ava waved a hand distractedly. "Honey, how else am I gonna enjoy the company of a husband unless I borrow somebody else's?"

"You weren't really going to go out with a married man, were you?" asked Wren.

"Sure I was," grinned Ava. "It was going to be kind of a test drive."

"You're trying to cheer me up," said Wren, managing a half smile.

"Is it workin'?" asked Ava, peering at her speculatively.

"Some," admitted Wren.

"Well, good," replied Ava, reaching for a handful of popcorn. "Because I'd stand on my head and whistle Dixie if I thought it'd make you feel any better."

"You're so sweet," said Wren. "Both of you." She was sitting cross-legged on the floor in her pajamas, sipping a cup of hot cocoa. Ava had kindly offered to make dirty martinis for everyone, but Wren hadn't been feeling up to it. And Carmela didn't think the two of them should be merrily imbibing when Wren felt so miserable. It just wasn't appropriate.

"Do the police have any ideas at all?" asked Ava. She'd brought her pajamas along, as well. A black satin negligee with a touch of marabou at the plunging neckline. Not exactly slumber-party attire. Then again, she'd pointed out to Carmela that the gown *was* a sedate black.

"The police are still going over the guest list," Carmela responded. "Apparently trying to run down leads."

"I didn't think there were any leads," said Ava. "The story in this morning's *Times-Picayune* said the police were . . . and I quote . . . 'baffled.'"

"Maybe we shouldn't talk about this," said Carmela, seeing Wren fidget uncomfortably. She seemed to have gone downhill since this afternoon when she was at Memory Mine. Wren had appeared tired and sad then, but was still functioning. Now she looked extremely depressed, almost despondent.

"No," said Wren, in a tired voice. "I *want* to talk about it. The man I was supposed to marry tomorrow evening, the man I planned to spend the rest of my life with, was killed. Murdered. And nobody seems to have any answers."

"Honey," said Ava, "I'm sure the homicide detectives are busting their buns trying to solve this case. They've probably interviewed every guest and kitchen staffer. Even the folks who just dropped by Bon Tiempe for a quick drink at the bar."

"But they're not getting anywhere," said Wren. "I talked to Detective Rawlings earlier this evening and he said they had a short list of suspects but still nothing conclusive." She gazed at Carmela, her face etched with sorrow. "I wish we could do something," she murmured. "I know Gabby talked to you about looking into a few things. You are, aren't you? I mean I *hope* you are."

Carmela gave a tentative nod. "Did she tell you?"

"No," said Wren, "I figured it out by myself. You're . . . just that sort of person. Smart and naturally resourceful."

Carmela smiled at Wren's assessment of her. She'd promised Wren earlier today that she'd try to find out where Jamie's parents were buried. And even though Gabby had talked about going over the guest list, Carmela hadn't intended to do anything much beyond the scope of a little cemetery snooping. Now Wren seemed to be asking if she'd help *investigate* Jamie's murder!

"Wren, I don't pretend to possess any real investigative skills . . ." Carmela began.

"That's not what I hear," said Wren quickly. Her face sagged, but her eyes burned bright. She glanced over at Ava, who threw her an encouraging look. A look that said *Go ahead and ask her*.

"Ava, you didn't," said Carmela. *Of course she had.*

"Face it, sugar, you're a natural," said Ava with enthusiasm. "You pulled old Shamus's butt out of the glue last year. And then your clever thinking helped Tandy out, too." Ava flashed a wide smile, her Miss Teen Sparkle Pageant smile. "We were all *real* proud of you for that."

Carmela shook her head slowly. "Nice try, Ava, but it's not going to work. Those cases were different. Everything just sort off fell into my lap."

"So we'll try to hand you this one on a silver platter," said Ava.

Carmela threw Wren an imploring look. "What has she been telling you?" Clearly Ava had been huckstering her investigative skills.

"That you're smart and feisty and don't take crap from anyone," said Wren.

"I also mentioned you've got a natural built-in bullshit detector, too," added Ava. "Which sure comes in handy."

"There's no way . . ." began Carmela. "I mean, I wouldn't have a clue where to start." She stopped abruptly, seeing the effect her words had on Wren.

A tear slid silently down Wren's cheek, a shudder passed through her body. "I certainly understand if you don't want to get involved," said Wren softly. "I truly do." She reached for a hanky and daubed at her eyes. Boo raised her head, gazed mournfully at Wren, and let loose a deep sigh, as if in sympathy.

Carmela stared at Wren and her heart went out to her. She knew what it was like to lose someone. She'd lost her father in a barge accident on the Mississippi when she was still a little girl. She'd lost Shamus. He hadn't died, of course, but his love for her had seemingly evaporated into thin air. And that had been awful. Losing a fiance as Wren just had . . . Carmela couldn't imagine what kind of gut-wrenching pain the girl must be in.

"Wren," said Carmela cautiously, "what if we just batted a few ideas around? You let me ask a few questions, do a little cautious snooping. I'm not promising anything, but maybe something could turn up." She glanced at Ava and shrugged. "You never know." *Oh dear, why can't I leave well enough alone?*

Wren threw Carmela a hopeful look. "I'd be ever so grateful."

Ava reached over and patted Carmela on the knee. "I knew you'd want to dig in and help, *cher*."

"Okay then," said Carmela, turning her full attention to Wren. "You've been interviewed by the police, correct?"

"Twice," said Wren. "Two nights ago, the night of Jamie's murder, and then most of yesterday afternoon."

"What kinds of questions did they ask you?" asked Carmela.

Wren bit her lip and thought for a moment. "They asked if I knew anyone who might be angry or upset with Jamie. You know . . . family, friends, business acquaintances, old enemies, old girlfriends."

"Ghosts from the past," murmured Ava.

Carmela gave Wren an encouraging look. "And were you able to give them any names?"

Wren shook her head slowly. "Not a one. The thing of it is, everyone *loved* Jamie. He was a terrific person. An all-around good guy."

"I don't want to sound harsh," said Carmela, "or like a traitor to Jamie's memory; but are you positive he never mentioned anything about his past? Something that might have seemed strange or a little bit off?"

"Not that I recall," said Wren. "Then again, he didn't talk much about it."

"What about his family?" Carmela knew that in a murder investigation the first thing police did was take a good hard look at family members.

"He didn't have any blood relatives that he knew about," said Wren. "Remember? Jamie was adopted."

"Hmm," said Carmela. "Do you know if Jamie was ever able to reconnect with his birth parents?"

"I'm almost positive he didn't," said Wren.

"Okay," said Carmela, "how about business partners or investors?"

"The only business partner he had was Blaine Taylor. And that was just for the software thing. Neutron." She took a sip of cocoa. "Blaine's been wonderful. Very solicitous and helpful."

"Think hard, Wren," Carmela pressed. "What about old rivals, a problem in the past, maybe an old enemy? Did he ever mention anything like that? Even in passing? Or maybe in jest?"

"Not really," said Wren. "Like I said, people loved Jamie. He sold *books* for crying out loud!" She looked upset that she was unable to dredge something up. "Sorry," she said contritely.

"He must have been involved in *some* kind of dispute," said Ava. "I mean, half the people I know, people who are really dear friends, drive me nuts *once in a while*." She glanced over at Carmela. "Not you, honey."

"Thanks a lot," said Carmela. Drawing her knees up to her chin, she stared into the crackling fire, wondering if there was some way they could get more of a handle on this. *People didn't just sneak into fancy restaurants and murder a groom at his prenuptial dinner just for sport, did they? No. Someone had to have a motive. Someone had to be angry, jealous, looking for money, or out for revenge. Those always seemed to be the main motives for murder. At least on TV anyway.*

"Wren," said Carmela suddenly. "Does Jamie have a home office?"

Wren nodded. "Sure, next room over. What used to be the chapel back when this place was a convent. There are still a couple statues in there, in fact."

While Boo remained sprawled on the couch, the three of them trooped into the rotunda and across to Jamie's office.

"Spooky," said Ava, as Wren flipped on the light. "Looks like Ozzy Osbourne decorated the place."

Jamie's office had indeed been a former chapel. A circular stained glass window served as backdrop for a large wooden desk that sat where a small altar had probably stood. A computer on a stand was canted to the left of it. On either side of the stained-glass window were small recessed niches with old plaster statues tucked into them. Bookcases lined the side walls. Light fixtures in the shape of electrified candles threw their illumination upward to highlight cove ceilings with peeling paint.

"Jamie thought this place exuded a very Gothic feel," explained Wren. "So he never made any changes."

"Maybe he couldn't make any," said Carmela.

"What do you mean?" asked Ava. She pulled a leatherbound book from a shelf, blew dust from the top of it, then slid it back onto the shelf.

"Jamie received some sort of historic preservation grant from the city," Carmela explained. "Perhaps it stipulated that he had to leave some things as is. Not update them."

"Could be," said Wren. She reached out and tentatively touched one of the almost-ruined statues, an undetermined saint with socketless eyes who valiantly clutched a crucifix. "I've always found this room a little weird, myself. But Jamie said it appealed to him, reminded him of his parents." Wren paused. "Whatever *that* was supposed to mean."

"Maybe they were religious," said Ava.

"Maybe," shrugged Wren.

"I had an aunt who had loads of statues and stuff like this," Ava continued. "She even belonged to the St. Christopher Auto Club, although she hadn't driven her Chevy Bel Air in years. Just left it parked in the garage."

Carmela gazed around the office that was indeed rather Gothic in spirit. She wondered if the words Jamie had tried to scrawl in his own blood had any connection to all this. Had he been Catholic? Did he know Latin? She frowned. Maybe. Maybe not. Nothing seemed to come together.

"Have you looked through Jamie's desk?" asked Carmela, eyeing the scarred wooden desk with its array of drawers. She knew that, sooner or later, Wren would have to bite the bullet and search Jamie's papers. After all, who knew if Jamie had owned this house outright or still carried a mortgage on it? Same for his bookstore. Carmela knew that if they could find mortgage papers, a will, or even the name and address of Jamie's lawyer, they'd be miles ahead.

But Wren hung back. "You look," she urged Carmela. "I know I should, but I feel funny. It's still too soon."

"You're sure?" asked Carmela. "You don't mind me pawing through Jamie's desk?"

Ava knelt down next to Carmela. "Come on, let's have a look. I can't believe we're gonna find anything particularly shocking."

"Agreed," said Carmela. "So you take the left set of drawers, I'll take the right."

"And I'll get to Scotland before you," joked Ava.

Ten minutes later, one of their burning questions had been answered. It turned out that Jamie did have a little bit of equity in the house on Julia Street. He'd put ten thousand dollars down on it, made about four years' worth of mortgage payments, and then refinanced it. It looked like he now owed a balance of approximately one hundred thousand dollars to the bank. Crescent City Bank to be exact. And he *had* added Wren's name to the title. So, whatever else happened, boom, bust, or bear market, Wren would always have a place to live as long as she kept making payments on that mortgage. Or, if she decided she didn't want to live there, couldn't face the memories, it was at least hers to sell and still realize a small profit.

They could find nothing to do with Jamie's business, however. No lease, tax records, or inventory sheets. Carmela figured that information must either be on Jamie's computer or stashed at the bookstore. That issue, however, wasn't quite as pressing. Obviously Jamie owned his inventory of books and maps. And, like every other shopkeeper in the French Quarter, he probably had a landlord that collected rent every month.

"Should we check the computer?" asked Carmela.

"Go ahead," said Wren.

Carmela sat down and clicked open the hard drive. A quick perusal showed that pretty much everything there pertained to Jamie's software program, Neutron. Carmela wondered if the program existed only there, on that computer, or if it was backed up somewhere on CD or zip drive or existed on the Internet in the form of a beta site. She also wondered who owned Neutron. Was it Jamie's program and Blaine Taylor was helping sell it for a piece of the action? Or did both men own an equal share? Frowning, she found a blank CD, stuck it into the computer, and made a backup copy of Jamie's Neutron files. *This is another issue we'll have to sort out sooner or later,* she decided.

As far as clues pertaining to Jamie's background, or any long-forgotten relatives, or even something that alluded to a murky past, there didn't seem to be anything. They found household bills, invoices from trades people who'd done work in rehabbing the house, electric bills, records of sewer and water assessments, and credit card receipts. But that was it.

Carmela also didn't find anything that had to do with Jamie's family. She knew Wren was counting on her to find out exactly where Jamie's parent's were buried, so Jamie could be laid to rest along side them. And she'd been keeping a keen eye out for death certificates, burial information, or even a deed to a cemetery plot, but nothing had materialized so far.

"Except for the mortgage information, we've got zip," said Wren. She was obviously relieved she wasn't going to be kicked out onto the street, but disappointed that nothing else had surfaced.

"What about photos?" asked Ava. "We haven't peeked through any of these yet." She held a stack of photo envelopes, most of them bright yellow and looking fairly recent. A couple cream-colored envelopes at the bottom of her stack looked like they might be a little older.

"Let's scoot back across the hall and take a look," suggested Carmela.

"THESE ARE from the Literary Festival last year," said Wren. "Jamie was on one of the panels." She smiled wistfully. "The one about Mark Twain. He *loved* Mark Twain."

"What about that other packet?" asked Ava. She had given Wren a couple photo packets to look through. She was nosing through the rest of them.

"And these were taken the last time Jamie had an open house at the bookstore," said Wren, shuffling through the photos.

"Y'all are so *academic,*" drawled Ava. "My photos are usually of crazy relatives and such. You know, my brothers and cousins with their souped-up Chevys and aunts with big hair who wear rhinestone cat-eye glasses."

"Sounds like the *Dukes of Hazzard,*" said Carmela.

"You're not far off, sugar," replied Ava.

"Here's something," said Wren, digging into another envelope.

"What?" asked Carmela.

"A bunch of black-and-white photos," said Wren. She frowned. "I've never seen these before. I wonder . . ."

Carmela leaned over and took a look. They were black-and-white photos of what appeared to be an old homestead. A white wood frame house, part of a small barn in the background, what looked like swampland off in the distance. *Could this be the place where Jamie grew up?* Carmela wondered. *Is this his parents' home?*

"Where did you say Jamie was from?" Carmela asked.

"Boothville," said Wren.

"Did he ever take you down there?" asked Carmela.

"Nope," said Wren. "And Jamie didn't talk much about it either. I wonder . . . are the photos dated?"

Carmela flipped one over. "Ten slash eighty-four. October, nineteen eighty-four."

"Mmm," said Wren, studying the photo. "This could be his parents' place. Wonder why he never bothered showing me this stuff."

"Hard to tell with people," murmured Carmela. "Some folks are just more private than others. They need to keep things to themselves."

Sitting across from them, Ava had been quiet for some time.

"Did you find something, Ava?" asked Wren.

"Uh . . . ah . . . no," said Ava. She had a smile pasted on her face, but her eyes darted from side to side.

A warning bell sounded in Carmela's head. Ava was rarely at a loss for words. She had obviously found something fairly sensitive.

"What is it?" asked Wren, curious that Ava wasn't being more forthcoming.

"Just more old photos," said Ava, trying to feign an offhand manner. "From before you guys were engaged." She slid the stack of color photos back in the envelope.

"Can I see?" asked Wren, holding out a hand.

Ava glanced up and met Carmela's eyes. And Carmela had a pretty good idea at that moment what Ava had stumbled upon.

"You don't really need to . . ." began Ava, sounding apologetic.

"But I do," insisted Wren.

Wordlessly, Ava handed Wren the envelope of photos.

Wren pulled the photos out, one by one, studying each shiny image carefully. When she got to about the sixth one, she stared at it for at least a full minute. Then the photo toppled from her hand and landed face down on the carpet. And Wren stood up and abruptly left the room.

You could have heard a pin drop as Carmela and Ava gazed at each other in shocked silence. Then Carmela reached down and plucked the photo from where it lay on the carpet.

Ava edged in closer as Carmela flipped it over. Together they stared at the shocker photo.

His arm draped possesively around a young woman, Jamie was gazing at her with what could only be called unabashed love. The woman wore a dazzling smile on her face and a large, sparkling diamond on her third finger, left hand.

"Can you believe this?" breathed Ava. "Jamie must have been engaged once before! Poor Wren. This ain't exactly what she needs right now. A ghost from Jamie's past."

Carmela stared at the photo, stunned. It wasn't the photo of the deliriously happy couple that took her breath away and made her heart pound a timpani drum solo. It was the smiling woman. Because this was no ghost from the distant past. This woman was very real and very much among the living.

Margot Butler.

Wearing a major bling-bling ring.

Jamie Redmond had once been engaged to Margot Butler.

Carmela grimaced at the thought. Margot Butler, the chatty, pushy, in-your-face interior designer who'd popped by Memory Mine just yesterday afternoon. Who *had* to know that her former fiance had been stabbed to death the night before, but hadn't uttered a peep, hadn't seemed the least bit concerned.

Margot Butler, who'd have to be brain dead not to notice Wren sitting at the back table.

So just what the hell is going on? Carmela wondered. *Because whatever Margot's game is, it's very strange indeed.*

Chapter 7

"YOU REALLY KNOW her?" cried Wren. Her sad eyes searched the faces of Carmela and Ava.

"*I* never met the little hussy," said Ava in her most righteous tone. "But Carmela knows her."

Carmela gave a silent nod. They'd finally coaxed Wren back into the library, and this time Ava *had* mixed up a batch of dirty martinis. Now they each sipped one.

"Jamie was engaged to someone else," said Wren, an incredulous look on her face. "Before me." She seemed to be in a mild state of shock.

"It certainly looks that way," said Carmela. She took a tiny sip of her martini. *Strong. Good. Wren probably needs a strong drink right about now. We all do.*

"I don't think this should change the way you feel about Jamie one bit," said Ava. "After all, this was *before*. It's ancient history. Everyone has previous relationships. God knows, *I've* had my share of previous relationships."

Carmela had to smile. Ava'd had more than her fair share of previous relationships.

"I understand all that," said Wren, "and the rational part of my brain tells me I should be okay with it. But my heart tells me Jamie deliberately hid something from me. That's the part that hurts like hell. It means . . . it means he lied." Wren practically whispered the last part of her sentence.

"Not technically a lie," said Carmela, "more a sin of omission."

"But a sin just the same," insisted Wren.

"Maybe that's why Jamie put his office in the old chapel," offered Ava. "Maybe he was praying for forgiveness." Ava, having been raised a Catholic, prayed often for forgiveness.

"You think so?" asked Wren, brightening some.

"Sure," cooed Ava. "Or maybe he was trying to summon up the courage to tell you," Ava continued. "To come clean."

"Now I'll never know," murmured Wren.

Carmela put a hand on Wren's slim shoulder. "But you *do* know. You know that Jamie loved you. Loved you so much he put the house in your name. And please remember, Jamie didn't go through with his marriage to Margot Butler. He was planning to marry *you*. You've got to hold that truth sacred."

Ava drained her glass and stood up. "Anybody want another one?" she asked.

"I do," said Wren.

"Then I'm gonna put the sausage and cheese and stuff I brought along out on a plate, too," said Ava. "We can have ourselves a little oinkfest."

"I'm stunned," said Wren, turning to Carmela. "There's a lot about Jamie I didn't know."

Carmela peered at Wren. Her eyes looked clear, she was holding her head up again, and she'd stopped daubing at her eyes with a tissue. She looked like she might have possibly rejoined the living. On the other hand, maybe the dirty martinis Ava had whipped up had finally taken the edge off.

"Agreed," said Carmela. "But you look better. More composed."

"This is going to sound weird, but I *feel* better," said Wren. "I mean, I'm still utterly heartbroken, this was the man I loved, after all. But it feels like I'm getting a handle on things."

"Good," said Carmela.

"For one thing, I'm mad," said Wren.

Carmela threw her a quizzical look. "You're mad?"

"Hopping mad," declared Wren. "And I want revenge for Jamie's death."

"Revenge isn't always a positive thing," Carmela said cautiously. *Was this really Wren talking or was it the martini?*

"Okay then, how about justice?" said Wren. "I want justice."

Wren's desire for justice seemed like a very logical and rational emotion, Carmela decided.

"And you will help me, won't you?" asked Wren. "Gabby bragged that you can do anything once you put your mind to it. So did Ava."

Carmela reached over and clasped one of Wren's hands as she heard a whisper of movement out in the rotunda. "I'll try," she said. "I'll give it my best shot." She looked up, expecting to see Ava, but saw only shadows.

"Thank you, Carmela," said Wren. "I know you're not that much older than I am, but I feel like you've become my mentor. Or maybe my fairy god-mother. Not the old-fashioned kind who grants silly wishes, but the smart *to-day* one. The one who watches over you and gives good advice."

Ava appeared in the doorway, laden with a large silver tray. Wedges of bright yellow cheese, rounds of sliced sausage, and stacks of crackers were piled on it.

"Who's ready for some . . ." Ava's words suddenly died in her throat. Eyes round as saucers, blood draining rapidly from her face, she gaped at the floor. "Holy shit!" she suddenly shrieked. "Watch out! Get back!"

"What?" cried Wren, looking around wildly. "What?"

Just as the silver tray crashed to the floor, just as crackers, cheese bits, and sausage rounds exploded everywhere, Carmela caught a flash of gray-brown scales as something raced across the Oriental carpet then slithered un-der the sofa.

"Snake!" came Ava's blood-curdling cry. "Snake!"

Like Lot's wife turned to salt, Wren froze on the sofa. In full-blown panic mode herself, Carmela noted that Boo had jerked awake and let loose a series of panicked barks.

No, Boo! thought Carmela. *Please don't get brave on me!*

Carmela wrapped a hand around Wren's arm just below her elbow and squeezed tightly. With her other hand she got a firm grip on Boo's collar, ready to haul the dog along with her. "On my count, we make a dash," she told Wren harshly, her jaw clenched, her voice hoarse. "One, two, three, NOW!" She jerked Wren's arm and Boo's collar, pulling them both up.

A twinge of pain flickered across Wren's face, then they were bounding gazelle-like across the room and out into the rotunda to join a terrified Ava. From there it was a mad dash to the front door, feet and paws clattering on slate, voices raised in alarm, as they scrambled down the limestone steps.

And rushed headlong into . . . the arms of Blaine Taylor!

"You!" screamed Carmela, freaked out for a second time in the space of about five seconds.

"What's wrong?" yelled Blaine. He seemed as stunned as they were to have run smack dab into them on the sidewalk like this. "Did someone break in? Is everyone okay?"

"Snake!" screamed Wren. She wasn't having any trouble vocalizing now. People coming out of the bar a half a block away looked over in alarm.

"Ava!" screamed Carmela, suddenly realizing her friend wasn't with them.

Carmela spun on her heel and dashed back up the steps.

"No!" screamed Wren, trying to keep Boo from following. "Don't go back in there!"

But Ava was pushing her way out the heavy door. "I'm here. I'm okay," she was gibbering. "I just had to grab my purse in the hallway . . . get my cell phone!"

"Sweet mother of pearl," exclaimed Blaine. "Are you ladies okay?"

"Hell no," snarled Ava. "There's a friggin' snake in there!"

"What!" said Blaine. He took a step back, peered at the house as though the unwelcome reptile was about to come hurtling out at him. "Are you serious?"

"You heard me," said Ava. "Some idiot tossed a cottonmouth into the house."

"A cottonmouth?" said Blaine, still sounding incredulous and trying not to stare at Ava in her negligee.

"We don't know somebody tossed it in," said Carmela. "It could have just been there. It's an old house. Who knows what the hell lives down in the cellar." She knelt down and gently massaged Boo's head, trying to calm the little dog down.

"She's right," said Blaine. "These old places can house any number of varmints. Rodents, snakes . . ."

"Please!" shrilled Ava. "Do us all a favor and kindly skip the rundown!"

"Okay, okay," said Blaine Taylor, slipping an arm around Wren's waist. "Everybody just calm down, okay?"

"By the way," said Carmela, who had pulled herself together and was gazing at Blaine Taylor, noticing that the man seemed to relish his role as the great calmer-downer. "What were you doing out here on the sidewalk?"

"Just dropping by to see how Wren was doing," he said in a sincere tone. "I was worried about her."

"Kind of late, isn't it?" asked Carmela.

"Is it?" asked Blaine, glancing at this watch. "Jeez. After nine. Wow. The thing of it is, I was working at my office and was headed home." He smiled again at Carmela. "I live over on Harmony Street, so I usually take Tchoupitoulas. Just a hop away."

"Uh huh," said Carmela. The coincidence bothered her, but this probably wasn't the time to make an issue of it.

"What are we going to do about the snake?" demanded Ava. "Bribe it to leave? Get it into the witness protection program?" There was a tinge of hysteria in her voice.

Blaine pulled off his jacket, removed the cell phone from the pocket, then draped his jacket around Ava's almost-bare shoulders. "I'm gonna call somebody," he told them. "There's a company called Critter Gitters. Their guys come right to your house and take care of unwanted varmints. They had to come to my place once to retrieve an opossum that got stuck in the chimney."

"Are you serious?" said Ava, seeming to finally calm down. "There's really a company called Critter Gitters?"

"Looks like," said Carmela, as Blaine called information, waited a couple seconds, then was connected to the critter-gitting people. They milled about on the sidewalk for a minute or two, listening as Blaine described the problem, then he clicked off his phone.

"They can be here in thirty minutes," he told them. "You know where the thing is?"

"Hell, yes," said Ava. "Under the sofa. Probably eating our cheese and sausage."

"I don't want you staying here tonight," Blaine said to Wren.

"I don't think I could," responded Wren.

"She can come back to my place," offered Ava, who lived above the voodoo shop and across the courtyard from Carmela. "I've got one of those inflatable beds. You just pull the ripcord and the thing balloons up in about six seconds flat. Sweetmomma Pam ordered it off the TV last time she was in town." Sweetmomma Pam was Ava's granny, a feisty old gal who was addicted to infomercials and the shopping channels. Last they'd heard, Sweetmomma Pam had discovered eBay.

"And you're going to wait here?" Carmela asked Blaine.

Blaine nodded. "I don't mind. I'll have 'em check out the whole house." He stared pointedly at Wren. "Of course, it ain't cheap."

"Just do it," said Carmela.

Blaine nodded. "Right. You never can tell what burrowed in during the hot summer months, then decided to snuggle in and take up residence now that it's cooler. But if there are any more unwelcome guests, I know these guys will find 'em."

"Good," breathed Wren. "Great."

"So you'll call us with an *all-clear* in the morning?" asked Ava.

"You got it," said Blaine. "No problem."

BUT THERE were problems. Lots of strange coincidences and unanswered questions. And it was a long time before Carmela was able to drift off to sleep that night. Swirling images kept sparking her brain. The image of Jamie Redmond felled by a butcher knife seemed indelibly burned in her brain.

And she was haunted by other questions, too. Could Margot Butler have been angry at Jamie because he'd broken off their engagement? Why did the bull-in-a-china shop Dunbar DesLauriers suddenly have a burning desire to buy Jamie's complete inventory of books? And just what the hell was Blaine Taylor doing outside Wren's house on Julia street at nine o'clock at night?

Answers? She didn't have any yet. But she would. God help her, she would.

Chapter 8

THE MEETING ROOMS at the Le Meridien New Orleans pulsed with activity. Dozens of Scrap Fest workshops were underway, demonstrating such scrapping techniques as writing with wire, paper layering, stitching on scrapbook pages, and glitter dusting. Various scrapbook pages were being scrutinized and judged for originality and technique, and more than one competitive finalist bit her nails in anticipation of receiving a coveted purple ribbon.

In the main ballroom, exhibitor booths, most of them manned by manufacturers and suppliers, displayed the very latest in rubber stamps, cutting tools, albums, archival and scrapbook paper, templates, toppers, borders, and punch art.

It was, quite frankly, a scrapbookers heaven. And Carmela and Gabby were reveling in the excitement of it all. Scrapbook clubs from all over Louisiana, as well as Mississippi and Alabama, had descended upon this first-ever Scrap Fest. Manufacturers and suppliers had arrived with their newest and neatest products, which meant that Carmela and Gabby were not only busy manning their own booth, they also were buzzing around, snapping up the latest products to stock in Memory Mine.

"Did you see the new rubber stamps from Kinetic Creations?" asked Gabby breathlessly. She had just returned from a whirlwind tour around the convention floor and looked exhilarated but slightly discombobulated.

Carmela nodded as she rang up customers two at a time. "I already ordered the entire Romance and Renaissance series," she said. "The stamps are absolutely gorgeous."

"Have Baby, Byrle, and Tandy shown up yet?" asked Gabby, looking around.

"Baby and Byrle stuck their heads in the booth for a moment and then disappeared," said Carmela. "They're out making the rounds. And Tandy was just . . ." She glanced around, slightly perplexed. "Well she's here *somewhere*."

"Here I am," screeched Tandy, pushing her way through the crowd and flashing a wide, slightly toothy grin. "I didn't forget. My nimble fingers are poised and ready to dig in."

Carmela checked her watch. In about two minutes, Gabby and Tandy were scheduled to preside over a "make and take." This was a special hands-on demo at their booth where customers could sit down at the craft table and actually work on a project. In this case it was to be a scrapbooky-looking bookmark. Because seats were offered on a first-come basis, customers had already settled onto most of the folding chairs and now stared up at them expectantly.

Noting this, Gabby hurried to the head of the table to deliver a friendly welcome and quick introduction. Tandy hastily gathered up precut paper, strands of fiber, and glue sticks for the actual "make" part.

Carmela knew she could breathe easy for a while; once Gabby started her demo, most of the booth traffic would gather round the table to watch.

"Okay," said Gabby, as Tandy passed out card stock cut into bookmark-sized strips, "we're going to start by stamping a series of designs."

Carmela slid onto a tall stool and relaxed. From where she was perched she could keep an eye on their paper assortment, their rack of watercolor brush markers, and their huge display of faux finishes, embossing powders, ribbons, and tags.

"I thought I'd find you here," said a voice at her elbow.

A smile was instantly on Carmela's face, even though she didn't immediately recognize the stocky, somewhat forceful-looking woman who'd suddenly materialized beside her.

"You're Carmela, aren't you?" asked the woman.

Carmela nodded. "Yes, I . . ."

"Pamela DesLauriers," cut in the woman, extending her hand in a no-nonsense manner. "Dunbar's better half."

Good lord, thought Carmela. *The woman's a virtual clone of her overbearing husband. Right down to the florid complexion and tartan scarf wrapped around her neck.*

"How can I help you?" Carmela asked pleasantly, slipping off the stool to face Pamela DesLauriers.

Pamela responded by dangling a large manila envelope in Carmela's face. "Knock knock," Pamela said, wobbling her head in a slightly ditzy manner. "*You're* doing the scrapbooks for Gilt Trip?" With her expectant, crowing manner, yet slightly condescending gaze, Pamela looked like a cross between a cockateil and a Chinese lap dog.

"And *you're* the owner of Happy Halls," responded a surprised Carmela. "How wonderful." *Crap,* Carmela thought to herself. *This is my other scrapbook project. Why do I suddenly have the feeling things are getting a little too complicated? I've been tapped to do a scrapbook for the wife of the man who's making moves on Jamie's bookstore. And,* she reminded herself, *who was present the night Jamie was murdered.*

"Margot Butler assured me you'd do a wonderful job," gushed Pamela. "Of course, *she's* the designer extraordinaire. Who else could come up with the concept of mixing damask and tulle? The woman's got a brilliant eye. So iconic, so forward thinking.

"I've heard wonderful things about Margot's work," Carmela responded brightly, even as her mind flashed on the photo of Margot and Jamie that they'd stumbled upon last night.

"But back to the scrapbook," said Pamela. "I wanted to bring the photos and fabric materials by personally so I could point out a few key concepts to you." One chubby hand dug into the envelope as Pamela stared at Carmela with hard dark eyes and pencil-thin eyebrows raised in a question mark. "Do you mind?"

"Heavens, no," said Carmela, wondering if the smile on her face looked as forced as it felt.

Pamela DesLauriers wasted no time in spreading out her photos, wallpaper pieces, and fabric swatches on top of Carmela's vellum samples.

"You see," said Pamela, fingering one of the photos. "This was the dining room *before*. Elegant, certainly, but perhaps lacking a certain transcendency."

"Mmm," said Carmela, not about to tell Pamela DesLauriers that her dining room looked pretty much like a dining room and that she had no idea what it was supposed to transcend.

"But *voila*," exclaimed Pamela grandly, pointing to the photograph that was, obviously, the *after* photo. "Look what I have now! Calls to mind the grand salon of an Italian villa, don't you think?"

Carmela studied the photograph. It showed the same dining room, now with earth-toned faux finishing on the walls, a Mediterranean-style chandelier, and a sweep of gold damask drapery at the window. Pretty, but certainly nothing that would get the Medici family in a twist. "Great," said Carmela. "I've got some nifty twelve-by-twelve paper that will pick up that same faux finished feel. Should make a perfect background."

"I just knew you'd benefit from my input," said Pamela, obviously pleased. "Of course, I'll want to see your concepts before the scrapbook is finalized. Before you glue it or fuse it or whatever it is you people do."

"We're on a pretty tight schedule," said Carmela slowly. "I'm not sure that's possible." *And I am doing this as a Gilt Trip volunteer, not your personal employee.*

"Of course it's possible, dear," insisted Pamela in a saccharine tone. "Just give me a jingle and I'll run down to your shop for a quick look-see." Pamela swiveled her head, glancing around. "Is Gabby's little cousin here today?" she asked.

"Wren is back at Memory Mine," said Carmela. "She offered to watch the shop while Gabby and I worked here at Scrap Fest."

"Such a dear, sweet girl," said Pamela. "I know Dunbar always found her so helpful when he stopped by Biblios."

"That sounds precisely like Wren," said Carmela, wondering just what this was leading up to.

"You know," said Pamela, "Dunbar has his heart set on buying Jamie's collection of antique books." She cocked her head and dangly earrings swung from her lobes, grazing her plump cheeks.

Bingo, thought Carmela. *This is what Pamela is leading up to.*

"I'm not sure the books are for sale," said Carmela. "I'm not sure anything's for sale." She knew that if Jamie had also put the bookshop in Wren's name, Wren might decide to keep it and run it. Biblios Booksellers was a viable business, after all. Wren might not feel like putting her heart into it right now, but things could certainly change. Wren had worked there for the past six months, so she already knew the ropes and was well-versed in the realm of antique books.

Pamela laughed out loud at Carmela's words, however. "Honey," she gushed, "the one thing I've learned is that *everything* has a price."

"I'm not so sure about that," cautioned Carmela. *Why is it rich folks always think everything has a price?* she wondered. *When the things that really matter—family, friends, tradition, loyalty—are clearly priceless.*

"But *I* am," responded Pamela. "Besides, I can't imagine that a bunch of dusty old books would fetch all that much money."

"Depends on what they've been appraised at," responded Carmela, thinking this might be the perfect project for Jekyl Hardy, her float-builder friend who was also a licensed art and antiques appraiser.

Pamela waved a chubby hand dismissively. "Honey, when Dunbar puts an offer on the table, people generally accept."

Pamela DesLauriers's visit left a bad taste in Carmela's mouth. So after checking Gabby and Tandy's progress with the demo, Carmela pulled out her cell phone and called Memory Mine. She'd been quite willing to close the store, but Wren had volunteered to work there and keep it open. Carmela said okay, partly because she didn't think it would be terribly busy—all the truly manic scrapbookers would be here at Scrap Fest—and partly because it gave Wren something to do. Helped keep her mind off the fact that today was supposed to have been her wedding day.

Wren answered on the first ring. "Memory Mine. How can we help?"

"You're not busy," said Carmela.

"Oh, but we were," said Wren, instantly recognizing Carmela's voice. "Business has been good. We had a real rush maybe thirty minutes ago. Well . . . *you* had a rush."

"The possessive *we* is just fine," said Carmela, "because you are part of the family."

"So you keep telling me," said Wren. "Thank you. That means a lot to me."

Carmela hesitated. "You've been fielding calls okay? No problems?" She wondered if Dunbar DesLauriers had possibly tracked Wren down and dared to pester her.

"No problems," said Wren. "A fellow by the name of Clark Berthume called for you. From the Click! Gallery."

Oh oh. "Did he leave a message?" asked Carmela.

"He said he was trying to fix a schedule for the gallery's upcoming shows and he wanted to know when you were going to drop by with your portfolio." Wren paused. "Carmela, I didn't know you did photography, too. That's wonderful! You're a regular Renaissance woman!"

"No, I'm just a twenty-first-century gal who's completely overbooked like everyone else," said Carmela. "But I'll try to give him a call." *Try to call him off,* thought Carmela.

"And Blaine Taylor dropped by earlier," added Wren. "He said the house received the all-clear. They caught the snake and, luckily, didn't find anything else wiggling around."

"Good," said Carmela, still a little shaken, as they probably all were, by last night's snake incident.

"Blaine said the Critter Gitter people told him this wasn't at all uncommon. Apparently, snakes and lizards and stuff are often found crawling through pipes and up from basements."

"Really," said Carmela. She'd lived in and around New Orleans all her life and never experienced anything quite like that. "I guess that helps put some perspective on it."

"I'm a little nervous about going home," said Wren, "but I have to face the ordeal sometime."

Poor Wren, thought Carmela, *has to face a lot of tough ordeals.*

"Oh, and I asked Blaine about the software thing," said Wren.

"What about the software thing?" asked Carmela.

"You know. Who owns Neutron Software."

"What did he tell you?" asked Carmela, hating herself for having such a suspicious nature.

"That he and Jamie had drawn up a tentative buy-sell agreement," said Wren, "based on book value of the business."

"Uh huh," said Carmela.

"But they also had a provision," continued Wren, "that should one partner die, proprietary rights automatically revert to the surviving partner."

"Is that a fact," said Carmela. *Interesting little codicil. And oh-so-convenient for Blaine.* "We should get a copy of that agreement and take a look at it," said Carmela. "Better yet, we should have a smart lawyer look at it."

"I don't know if Jamie had a lawyer," said Wren.

"Well," said Carmela, as a spatter of applause erupted from the table nearby and a dozen happy customers popped up with their completed bookmarks. "We're just gonna have to do some snooping. And then we'll find ourselves a good lawyer." *One who isn't tied to Blaine Taylor,* she added silently.

"HOT DIGGITY," said Tandy to Carmela. "You sold a ton of rubber stamps and packages of that crinkley fiber."

"Thanks to the terrific demo you and Gabby did," said Carmela.

"Shoot, it was all Gabby's doing," said Tandy, waving a hand. "She's sweet but so persuasive. Even *I'm* gonna buy some of those new stamps. I mean, I *love* that heritage series."

"Tandy," said Carmela, "can you help Gabby with the booth for about ten minutes?"

"Sure 'nuf," said Tandy. "Whatcha gonna do? Take a spin around the hall again?"

"That's exactly what I'm going to do," declared Carmela. There was a new vendor who was selling templates for pop-ups and she wanted to place an order or at least grab one of their catalogs.

But twenty steps away from her booth Carmela ran smack dab into Margot Butler.

"How do, Carmela," drawled Margot. Looking very much the avant-garde interior designer, Margot was dressed in a slinky black blouse, black leather slacks, and dark green leather boots.

"Margot!" said Carmela, surprised. Fresh in her mind was the photograph of Jamie Redmond with his arm around Margot's waist, looking extremely amorous. And extremely engaged.

"Has Pamela dropped by yet?" asked Margot. "With the photos and such?"

"Maybe ten minutes ago," said Carmela.

"Drat," said Margot. "Looks like I missed her. Oh well . . ."

"Margot," said Carmela, wondering how to phrase her question. *Delicately or plunge right in?*

Carmela decided she was definitely a plunge-right-in type. "Margot," said Carmela again, "I didn't realize you and Jamie Redmond had been engaged."

Margot didn't miss a beat. "Oh, yeah." She gave a dismissive shrug. "Jamie and I were quite the item for a while. But . . . well, things just didn't work out." She paused. "And now look what's happened. Pity."

"Are we talking ancient history, Margot?" asked Carmela, trying to keep her voice light.

But Margot was instantly suspicious. "Why are you asking, Carmela? What business is it of yours? And why this sudden inquisition?" she demanded. "You think *I* had something to do with Jamie's death?"

"We came across an old photo last night," explained Carmela. "At Wren's house. We were just surprised."

"Mmm," said Margot. "Did she see it? Wren?"

"Yes, she did," said Carmela.

Margot chewed at her lower lip. "I imagine it upset her."

"I think it might have," replied Carmela. *Is Margot enjoying this little exchange? Yes, I believe she is.*

"Too bad," said Margot. "But like I said, it's old news."

"You mentioned that," said Carmela. "But I'm still curious about timing. In other words, how long ago were you two an item?"

"Oh, let's see," said Margot, pretending to rack her brain. "Last year."

Last year! thought Carmela. Shamus had skipped out on her more than a year ago, and her wounds still hadn't healed. Hadn't even begun to heal. So, this was the question on the table—had Margot been carrying a torch for

Jamie? Or worse yet, had she been nursing a nasty grudge? One that had stung and festered until she finally took matters into her own hands?

"You know," said Margot, "we're going to need those scrapbooks by next Wednesday at the latest. This is a very important fund-raiser. A lot of people are counting on you."

"They'll be finished," said Carmela. "One way or the other, they'll be finished."

"You're such a pro, Carmela," murmured Margot as she edged away. "Well, toodles, dearie. See you later."

"Margot," said Carmela, just as the designer was about to dash off. "What kind of boots are you wearing? I mean the leather?"

Margot paused a few feet from Carmela and tipped a heel up to show her boots off. "Snakeskin," she purred. "Don't you just love 'em?"

Chapter 9

AVA BRUSHED BACK her frizzled mass of auburn hair and leaned over her Eggs Benedict. "Weird," she murmured. "This Margot person really wore snakeskin boots?"

"Cross my heart and hope to die," said Carmela. "Let's hope she's either a confirmed fashionista or she's planning a guest appearance on the *Crocodile Hunter*."

The two women were sitting on the broad front porch of the Columns Hotel. It was a magnificent structure originally designed by the architect Thomas Sully. In more recent years, giant Doric columns had been stuck onto the front to supposedly add charm and make the whole thing look even more like a Southern mansion.

As they nibbled at their Sunday brunch, Carmela had filled Ava in on some of the newer, stranger revelations. She'd related her encounter with the pushy Pamela DesLauriers who claimed husband Dunbar always got what he wanted. And she told Ava about Blaine Taylor's purported buy-sell agreement with Jamie Redmond. An agreement that didn't just give Blaine first dibs, but seemed to give him carte blanche to the entire Neutron computer program.

And then, of course, they'd rehashed their thoughts on Margot Butler with her broken-off engagement and snakeskin boots.

Ava had pretty much reserved comment until all of the strange news had been spilled out onto the table. Finally, she shook her head in amazement.

"Honey, I hate to say it, but it sounds like any *one* of those folks might have had it in for Jamie Redmond."

Carmela nodded slowly. She, too, was gradually coming to that same conclusion.

"Dunbar and Blaine were *there* that evening at Bon Tiempe," said Ava, "so they'd be tops on my list."

"But don't forget," said Carmela. "Margot of the snakeskin boots knows her way around Bon Tiempe, too. I called Quigg last night and found out that Margot's design firm sold him some of the chandeliers. The small crystal ones hanging in the bar, I think."

"Don't you think it's strange that Blaine Taylor showed up just in the nick of time Friday night?" asked Ava. "That really bothers me."

Carmela sighed. "Me, too."

"Is Wren suspicious about any of this?" asked Ava. "I mean, she knows about Margot being engaged to Jamie, but what about the rest?"

"I don't think she's put anything together yet," said Carmela. "And I wasn't planning to fan any flames, either. She's got enough to worry about."

"You're a girl after my own heart," said Ava. "One who knows how to keep her lips properly zipped."

"Don't you think?" asked Carmela. She was torn between protecting Wren and sharing—or rather spilling—her suspicions.

"A little discretion is always the best policy," said Ava. "The question is, what are you going to do now?"

"Correction; what are *we* going to do," said Carmela.

Ava watched the waiter refill her champagne flute, then picked it up, swirling the elegant golden liquor to release the bubbles. Taking a delicate sip, she contemplated the wine. "Terrific," she finally proclaimed. "Nothing like a dry finish to roll your tongue up like a window shade."

Every Sunday, the Columns Hotel hosted a lovely champagne brunch. However, the champagne they opted to serve was a domestic variety. Ava, claiming she was making a decided effort to expand her cosmic consciousness, had ordered a bottle of Perrier-Jouet, a rather fine French champagne. That's what the two women were drinking now. And Carmela, who was also intrigued by the burst of tiny dry bubbles inside her mouth, had to admit the extra thirty dollars was probably well worth it.

"What if," said Ava finally, "we called that nice detective and had a talk with him? The one that helped you out before. Edgar . . ."

"Babcock," said Carmela, finishing Ava's sentence. "Gabby and I talked about calling Lieutenant Babcock, but we really don't have any concrete evidence to present to him. And we're still pretty much going on hunches and theories."

Ava wrinkled her nose. "We need concrete evidence, huh? What about that photo of Margot and Jamie?"

"Doesn't prove she murdered the guy," said Carmela. "Just means she was in love with him. Or used to be in love with him."

"I wonder," said Ava. "I wonder which one of them broke it off. Margot or Jamie."

"Don't know," said Carmela. "And I don't think it's likely we're ever going to find out. Margot got very prickly when I asked a couple questions about her relationship with Jamie."

"Sounds like a lady with something to hide," said Ava.

Carmela shrugged. "Maybe. Or else she's embarrassed because she got dumped."

"The big D," said Ava. "It can be an ego-crusher."

And it can push some people over the edge, thought Carmela. She knew there was a reason an awful lot of killings were dubbed "crimes of passion."

"I wonder if Margot gave the ring back," mused Ava. "I mean, is there a set protocol on that? I can see where if a woman dumps a guy, she's morally obligated to return the ring." Ava took another sip of champagne, enlivened by her train of thought. "But if a guy dumped me? I don't think I'd be hopping up and down, eager to return my engagement ring like I was taking back a pair of bowling shoes or something. Especially if the ring was in the category of a two karat flawless, colorless stone. Say a marquis or princess cut."

"What would you do with it?" asked Carmela, as her cell phone burped inside her purse and she leaned down to retrieve it.

"Have it reset as a fancy pendant," said Ava promptly. She'd obviously given this careful thought.

"Hello," Carmela murmured into her phone.

"Carmela? It's Wren."

Carmela mouthed *Wren* to Ava, who nodded as if she'd almost expected Wren to call.

"What's wrong, honey?" asked Carmela. She thought Wren sounded slightly panicky.

"Dunbar DesLauriers just called and made an offer on the inventory at Biblios. What do I do now?"

"Do you want to sell?" asked Carmela. "Providing we find out you really do own the inventory?"

"I don't know," said Wren. "I haven't really thought about it, so I need some advice. You and Ava are the only business people I know."

Carmela put her hand over the receiver. "She says we're the only business people she knows," said Carmela.

"God help her," said Ava, rolling her eyes skyward.

"There's Stuart," suggested Carmela. Gabby's husband, Stuart, who owned a chain of car dealerships, was forever being lauded by one or another business club or chamber of commerce. He was knowledgeable, but all his honorary titles, plaques, and pins also tended to make him a bit pompous and overbearing.

A long silence spun out.

"Right," replied Wren finally, "there's Stuart."

"Okaaay," said Carmela. "Let's forget about old Stuart. What kind of advice do you need from me?"

"For one thing, I'm flat broke."

"Explain please," said Carmela.

"After I moved in with Jamie six months ago, I quit my job at the travel agency and was really just helping out at the bookstore."

"You worked there full-time, but didn't take a salary?" asked Carmela.

"Oh, she *does* need our help," said Ava in a low voice.

Wren's voice contained a hint of a quaver. "Yes," she answered. "Do you think I should have taken a salary?"

"There's no hard and fast rule, but . . . yeah, probably," said Carmela. She thought for a moment. "What we need to do is poke around and see if there's money left in the business checking account. If there is, that's your back salary."

"Wow," breathed Wren. "We can do that?"

"Sure we can," said Carmela. She didn't know the legalities involved, but figured she'd find a way. She usually did.

"That'd be just great," said Wren, sounding better already.

"Do you know where Jamie kept his checkbooks and ledgers and all that?" Carmela asked.

"Sure," said Wren, "but I never had anything to do with them. The most I ever did was make change for cash purchases or take credit cards. And even then, all I did was take an impression, fill in the numbers, and file the flimsy."

"Tell you what," said Carmela, "Ava and I are just about finished with brunch, so I'll meet you at Jamie's store in . . ." she glanced at her watch, "let's say an hour. We'll see what we can figure out."

"Is she okay?" asked Ava, after Carmela hung up.

"She sounded a little strung out," admitted Carmela. The two of them sat and watched a cluster of tourists amble up the front sidewalk, cameras poised. The Columns Hotel, with its beveled-glass front door, spectacular main staircase, and stained-glass windows, had been used as a location by filmmaker Louis Malle when he'd shot scenes for the movie, *Pretty Baby*. Just like the *Cat People* house over at Chartres and Esplanade, tourists were forever flocking to this real-life location.

"Pardon me," said a young man in a flat Midwestern accent as he stepped onto the porch. "Can we take your picture?" He ducked his head, suddenly turning shy. "I mean, you girls are real Southern belles, aren't you?"

Inhaling deeply, Ava turned her megawatt smile on the handsome young man. "We sure are, sugar," she told him. "Best the South has to offer."

Chapter 10

BOO STRUTTED ALONG Dauphine Street, her shar-pei head held high, tail curled into a tight, furry doughnut, wrinkles jiggling gently. Carmela had dropped by her apartment earlier and changed into blue jeans and an *I Brake for Whales* T-shirt in anticipation of what would probably prove to be a dusty, dirty prowl. Boo had watched solemnly, her shiny bright eyes following Carmela's every move, hoping for an invitation. And Carmela had figured, *Why not?* Why not bring Boo along to Biblios Booksellers? Because, let's face it, the little dog had already been in half the shops in the French Quarter, and conducted herself quite properly, thank you very much. Except for that tiny little incident with Teddy Morton's Siamese. And who's counting *that*!

Lights were on and Wren was already moving around inside the bookstore when Carmela and Boo arrived.

"Knock knock," said Carmela, rattling the doorknob and peering through the frosted-glass window on which *Biblios Booksellers, Rare and Antiquarian Books & Maps* had been painted in flowing gold script.

Wren came scampering to the door to let them in. She was also dressed in blue jeans and wore a chambray shirt knotted at her waist. "Hey there, Boo Boo," she called, reaching down to scratch Boo's tiny triangle ears. "Make yourself at home. There's a nice cozy sofa up in that half loft if you want." And Boo, ever grateful for an invitation to catch a snooze, scurried up the stairs to investigate.

"Have you started going through Jamie's records yet?" asked Carmela.

"No," said Wren. "I was waiting for you. I didn't know exactly what to look for, and you're . . . well, you've got business experience. So I thought I'd just sit tight."

Carmela gazed about the bookstore. Leatherbound volumes gleamed from tall wooden shelves and faded Aubusson carpets covered the floors. Cozy leather club chairs and worn velvet wing chairs were stuck wherever an impromptu seating area presented itself. To Carmela's right was a huge, ornate wooden flat file that boasted dozens of extra-wide drawers. That, she figured, was probably the repository for the antique maps. To her left, six narrow steps led to the loft where Boo was snuffling about; ten feet ahead and two steps down led to a small business area with a desk, file cabinets, and counters piled high with books.

"I love this place," said Carmela. Her dad, though he'd long since passed away, had instilled in her a deep and abiding love for books, and she had never lost that feeling. Books were her ticket to untold journeys, her storehouse of knowledge, her refuge. To this day, Carmela loved nothing better than to curl up with a good book and a steaming cup of tea.

Carmela's early love for books and short story collections had probably served as the impetus for her collection of antique children's books. After a dozen years of combing flea markets, bookstores, and antique shops, her collection now included three dozen early Nancy Drew books, the thick ones from the thirties where Nancy still drove a spiffy, red roadster; at least two dozen Big Little books; Albert Payson Terhune's entire *Lad, a Dog* series; and an early copy of L. Frank Baum's *The Wizard of Oz*.

"This is an amazing collection, isn't it?" said Wren. Now that she was back in the store and had a purpose, she seemed much more relaxed. Happy almost, to be among these tall, sagging bookshelves.

"Did you know that Jamie also did book binding and book conservation?" asked Wren. "Collectors from all over Louisiana would bring Jamie their precious but ailing books and he would repair the leather bindings. Or sometimes he'd completely rebind them or just get pages unstuck. Then there were the people who'd discover old books that had been stored in attics or stuck in musty old trunks for decades. Jamie would treat the pages with archival preserving spray and try to undo the damage done by mildew, heat, mold, and insects."

Carmela nodded approvingly. She was no stranger herself to working with acid-free paper and archival spray. Old photographs were just as delicate as the pages of old books.

"I keep forgetting what an amazing inventory Jamie had," said Wren. "No wonder collectors from all over sent him letters and e-mails with their want lists."

"*Inventory* is the operative word," said Carmela. "If Dunbar DesLauriers really does want to buy the whole shebang, you've got to get a handle on what you really have here."

"I have an inventory list with Jamie's suggested prices," said Wren. "But that doesn't include the couple hundred books shelved in the rare book cases."

"That's a problem," said Carmela. "And, on a business note, we should regard this as a collection rather than just a store full of books. Collections always command higher prices." She thought about what she'd just said. "I suppose that's because someone has already invested considerable time and effort to bring like-minded pieces together and then categorize everything."

"What if I went on the Internet and tried to get prices on the books that aren't on the price list?" suggested Wren. "Some comparables."

"That's a terrific idea," enthused Carmela. "Then we'd have a ballpark idea of the value of the total inventory." She knew the more information they could give Jekyl Hardy, the easier his task would be to appraise the inventory. Or, if he couldn't do it, Jekyl would find someone who could.

They both looked around at books strewn and shelved everywhere. It suddenly seemed like a daunting task, even for a bookstore pro.

"Of course, I'm going to have to do some organizing first," amended Wren. She, too, seemed suddenly overwhelmed by putting a price tag on all this.

"First things first," said Carmela, realizing they were getting side-tracked. "Job one is we go through Jamie's business papers."

"Which ones?" asked Wren.

Carmela shrugged. "Bank statements, the building lease, payables and receivables, his partnership agreement with Blaine Taylor if we can find it. Hopefully a last will and testament," she said as Wren flinched. "Sorry."

"That's okay," said Wren.

Taking a deep breath, Carmela sat down at Jamie's desk and began to paw through his drawers and files. Jamie hadn't exactly subscribed to the organized desk theory, so Carmela had to sort through a lot of junk, too. Letters from book collectors, price lists, catalogs from other book dealers, invoices that had been marked "paid" but never filed. But in the second drawer, she began to unearth the beginnings of the mother load, finding Jamie's business checkbook.

"Checkbook," said Carmela, laying the green plastic book atop the desk.

"You peek," said Wren. "I'm too nervous."

Carmela flipped through the pages. Jamie's commercial account for Biblios Booksellers wasn't all that different than a personal account. He used the same type of check register to keep track of deposits and the checks he'd written. Carmela figured he probably gave the checkbook to his bookkeeper or accountant and let them get quarterly information that way.

"Is there a balance?" asked Wren.

Carmela's eyes sought out the last number in the column. "Yes, there is," she said. "Sixteen thousand and change."

"Sixteen thousand *dollars*?" said Wren.

Carmela nodded.

"Is that good?" asked Wren.

"It is if the rent, heat, and light bills are paid," answered Carmela, scanning the check register. "And they seem to be. Through January in fact."

"So I've got some breathing room," said Wren.

"You've also got a salary," said Carmela. Her hands went to the adding machine that sat atop Jamie's desk. "Let's see. Forty hours a week times approximately twenty-five weeks is one thousand hours. Times . . . let's say twelve dollars an hour . . . that's twelve thousand dollars due to you, my dear." Carmela turned and looked at Wren. "Or do you want me to figure it at fifteen dollars an hour?"

Wren shook her head. "Twelve is fine."

"Okay then," said Carmela, "back to the search." She looked up at Wren. "If there's something else you want to do, go right ahead."

Wren thought for a few seconds. "Jamie kept an old four-drawer filing cabinet in the basement. What if I go down and look through that? See if there's anything worthwhile?"

"Go for it," said Carmela, as Wren walked to the back of the store and pulled open a door she hadn't noticed before. Wren flipped a switch, then disappeared down a steep set of wooden stairs.

Carmela could hear Wren clattering down the last few steps even as her fingers flicked over a bundle of statements from Kahlman-Douglas Certified Public Accountants. She pulled one out, took a quick look. *Good. Now we know who Jamie's CPA firm was. Gonna make things a whole lot easier.*

The middle drawer was stuffed with inventory lists. But they were all computer printouts, so obviously a master list existed on the Dell computer that sat on Jamie's desk.

It wasn't until Carmela pulled open the bottom drawer of Jamie's desk that she found what she was really looking for. The heart of the matter. Tucked in a light blue legal-sized envelope was Jamie Redmond's Last Will and Testament.

Should I read it? wondered Carmela. *Or give it to Wren? This is, after all, a very personal document.*

Then she figured, *The heck with it. I'm gonna go ahead and read it. That's why Wren asked me to come here in the first place.*

The first few pages were fairly standard, probably boiler-plated by Jamie's attorney. The fifth page was the crux of the matter. The information they really needed to know.

Carmela closed all the desk drawers and did a fairly plausible job of straightening the desktop. Then she climbed the half-dozen narrow steps up to the loft to see what Boo was up to.

When Wren came upstairs some ten minutes later, clutching an armload of dusty file folders, she found Carmela stretched out next to Boo, looking serene, reading from Pablo Neruda's *Twenty Love Poems and a Song of Despair.*

Carmela closed the book and smiled up at Wren. "You own it," she told her.

"What!"

"The bookstore. All of this. It's yours. Jamie put it in your name, same as the house. Except this seems to be free and clear, whereas the house has a mortgage."

File folders slipped from Wren's arms and her knees seemed to grow weak. She crossed one leg over the other and slid to a sitting position on the carpet.

"You okay?" Carmela asked.

"I feel like I just woke up from a bad dream," said Wren. "All this time I've been thinking I had to hurry up and sell all this stuff in order to pay the bills. And that it would be a horrible, gut-wrenching experience. And now I find out that I own it." She gazed around with a startled look on her young face. "And you know what?"

Carmela raised one eyebrow.

"I'm glad," said Wren.

"Good for you," said Carmela. "Now you're showing real spunk."

Wren swiveled her head around, as though she were seeing the bookstore for the very first time. "There's just one problem," she said finally. "I'm terrible at this. Business stuff, I mean."

"Hey, don't sell yourself short," said Carmela. "Business can be fun."

Wren wrinkled her nose and snorted. "Fun? How can you even say that?"

"Don't get me wrong, running a business is a tremendous challenge," Carmela told her. "But it's a real character builder, too. Helps you discover what you're really made of. And, in a funny way, running a business helps you prioritize what's really important in your life."

"That wouldn't be a bad thing," admitted Wren. "But I really don't know any of the . . . what would you call them? Business fundamentals?"

"It's not that tricky," said Carmela. "In your case, you have a retail shop. So your business mission is to deliver a good product, a unique product, and make sure your customer enjoys a positive buying experience. That all relates to inventory and customer service."

"I think I can handle that," said Wren, glancing around.

"You also have to concentrate on sales and marketing," said Carmela. "You have to figure out who your audience is. Who your *market* is. Your target market."

"You mean I shouldn't advertise to everyone and his brother?" said Wren.

"Exactly," said Carmela. "In the case of this bookstore, I'd probably generate a few pieces of direct mail and target area book collectors."

"I think Jamie *did* have some kind of mailing list," said Wren, suddenly sounding hopeful.

"And I'd for sure go after the tourist market," said Carmela. "After all, you've got a fabulous location here in the French Quarter. Tons of people who are knowledgeable about antique collecting flock here every year. Chances are, a good portion of them collect antique books and maps, too."

"You make it sound like fun," said Wren.

"Business can be fun, once you get the hang of things," said Carmela. "The most important thing to remember is there are no hard and fast rules. Some of the best, most serendipitous business opportunities occur when you think outside the box."

Wren gazed around the dusty shop with a hopeful look on her face. "So you really think I could run this place? All by myself?"

"I think with a couple terrific employees you could definitely get Biblios Booksellers humming along," said Carmela.

"What kind of employees?"

"If this were my shop," said Carmela, "I might look for a retired college professor or somebody with a library background. Librarians are very smart cookies, you know. They'd bring organization to the business and lend credibility, too."

"What a good idea," enthused Wren.

"Sounds like you're seriously considering this," said Carmela.

"I am. Wow! I can believe I said that."

"What did you find in the basement?" asked Carmela, making a motion toward the file folders that lay on the carpet next to Wren.

"Not much. Old business records from, like, five years ago, a few old photos, and a bunch of other junk. Looks like letters and old news clippings."

"Let me see," said Carmela.

Wren handed Carmela one of the brown file folders. "These are very old photos," said Carmela, pawing gently through the contents. "Some of them look like they might even date back to the forties and fifties. And there are old negatives, too." She was suddenly formulating an idea. What if she took some of these old negatives and printed them in different ways? Maybe a photo montage effect combined with some of her own photos? Then she could colorize them on the computer or even hand-color them using some of the oil pens she had at Memory Mine.

Would something like that make a nice addition to her somewhat skimpy portfolio? Yeah. Maybe.

Better yet, would producing a few pieces like that get Shamus off her back? And satisfy Clark Berthume from the Click! Gallery? Worth a shot. Definitely worth a shot.

"Mind if I take some of these home?" Carmela asked Wren.

"Be my guest," said Wren. "In fact, you can *have* them. I certainly don't know what I'd do with them."

"Except for this one," said Carmela, peering into another brown folder. "These look like they might be pictures of Jamie." She handed the folder to Wren, who immediately clutched it to her chest.

"I'm not going to sort through this right now," Wren told her. "But I am considering doing some sort of scrapbook in Jamie's memory."

"I think that's a lovely idea," said Carmela, smiling at Wren. The girl seemed to have definitely perked up. Maybe it was the knowledge that she now owned tangible assets. Maybe she was starting to work through her grief.

Boo suddenly let out a loud, wet snort. Startled, the dog sprang from the couch and spun around, ears perked, as if to ask, *Who on earth made such an undignified noise?*

"She woke herself up," said Wren suddenly convulsed with laughter.

"She does that a lot," said Carmela. Shar-peis are soft-palette dogs, renowned for their prodigious sound effects.

Wren reached out and stroked Boo's velvety fur. "This is going to be a very tough decision. Now that I'm back here, I do love the atmosphere. So cozy and welcoming. But I know I'll have some demons to work through, too, if I stay and keep the store going. I'm sure I'll be constantly jumping at shadows. Hoping against hope that Jamie's going to walk through that front door again."

"You'll need some time," admitted Carmela.

"But I don't have much time," said Wren. "Aren't business people always saying 'Time is money'? Well, there isn't a lot of money here. Especially since rent needs to eventually be paid. As well as heat, light, and all those other things you mentioned."

"Come work at Memory Mine for a while," said Carmela.

Wren stared at her, amazed. "What? Are you serious?"

"There's sixteen grand in the business checking account," said Carmela. "That should cover operating expenses for two, maybe three months. Buy you some time. Plus I could really use the help, since Mardi Gras is just around the corner. Besides our usual scrapbook customers and scrapbookers looking for unique gifts, we'll probably be inundated by people who want to create their own cards and party invitations."

"And you'd actually pay me?" said Wren.

"That's the general idea," said Carmela.

"Wow." Wren's face lit up.

"Is that a yes?" asked Carmela.

"Yes!" enthused Wren. She clambered to her knees, leaned forward, and threw her arms around Carmela, giving her a huge bear hug.

Woof!

"Hugs all around!" cried Wren as Boo pounced happily at Wren and, in the process, knocked over a half-filled cup of a cup of coffee that must have been tucked beneath the sofa. "Just wait until I get back to Gabby's," declared Wren. "She'll be thrilled to hear we'll all be working together!"

Carmela dug in her purse for a tissue to mop the spilled coffee. "She sure will," she replied, her smile suddenly frozen on her face. *Please tell me why this coffee smells so fresh?* she asked herself. *Has someone been in this store very recently? Like late last night or earlier today?*

Oh dear. And please don't tell me it could be the same someone who snuck down the hallway at Bon Tiempe and wielded that nasty butcher knife! That would be very bad, indeed!

Chapter 11

CLOUDS OF PINK and blue swirled overhead in a colorful wind-swept sky. The late afternoon sun, glinting orange, threw an extra scrim of light on the Caribbean colors of the French Quarter buildings as Carmela and Boo walked slowly home. The familiar *clip clop* from one of the horse-drawn carriages echoed down the block, a low mournful *toot* sounded from some tugboat anchored over on the Mississippi.

Carmela had been tossing around the notion that someone might have been poking around Biblios Booksellers not long before she and Wren had shown up today. But now, as she sped along, she'd almost succeeded in talking herself *out* of her paranoia.

Probably it was an old cup of coffee, right? That someone had carried in last week. Probably no one has been stretched out on that old sofa in the bookstore's loft.

"Hey there, Boo," said Carmela. "You didn't catch any kind of scent, did you? Someone who might have been sitting on that sofa just before you?"

Boo shook her head and kept chugging along.

A young couple standing in a doorway, locked in a heated embrace, paused for a few seconds to stare as Carmela walked by.

Yeah, I talk to dogs. Because sometimes dogs are the only creatures who truly listen.

Turning into her courtyard, Carmela glanced up at the gracefully arched second story bow window that overlooked the fountain. Ava's apartment was up there. And usually a light burned bright. But right now her place was still dark.

"She probably went out on a date," Carmela told Boo. "She didn't *mention* anything about it, but I bet that's what she's doing. Having a fun date." Carmela unlocked the door to her apartment, nudged it open with her foot so Boo could scramble in. "In fact, that's where I would be, if I wasn't so socially impaired."

Boo immediately sped toward the kitchen, where she parked herself and proceeded to stare intently at the doggy cookie jar that held her dry kibbles.

"Isn't is a little early?" Carmela asked her. "Wouldn't you rather dine fashionably late?" It wasn't quite five. If Boo had her way she'd be eating supper at two in the afternoon.

Boo continued to stare at the jar as if she could levitate the lid, Uri Geller–style.

"Okay, you win," Carmela told her.

She fed a delighted Boo, plopping a spoonful of yogurt on top of the dry kibbles, then changed into a comfy velour track suit that Ava had given her for her birthday. The track suit didn't exactly carry a fancy designer label, but Ava had assured her it was probably made in one of the same overseas sweatshop that did the Juicy Couture or J.Lo line.

Then Carmela settled in at her dining-room table. She finally had a chance to breathe. No major distractions seemed to loom on the horizon, so she was determined to take the plunge and see what could be done about putting her photos in order. The ones Shamus had been so hot and bothered about. The ones that were supposed to go to Click! Gallery to help determine if she and Shamus were really going to have a joint photo show.

Carmela still wasn't completely positive she even wanted her photographs in a show. It wasn't that she was shy about people seeing her work. After all, people looked at her scrapbook pages every day. In her shop, her front display window, and even on her website. It was just that photography was one of her favorite hobbies. Something she could do with her heart instead of her head. And once you turned that hobby into a vocation, treated it more like a business, you really had to start thinking consciously about it. And then it wasn't quite so pure and joyful anymore.

Carmela had just hoisted her black oversized portfolio onto the table when the phone rang. Casting her eyes toward the heavens, she prayed it wasn't anything major.

It was Shamus. So, of course it was major.

"Meet me for dinner," he said, his invitation sounding peppy, just this side of manic.

Carmela stared at the photos spread out before her. She was determined to get through this. "Can't," she told him. "I'm in the middle of something." *Besides, what's the point?* she wanted to say, but didn't.

"I bet you're planning to go out for dinner tonight, aren't you?" said Shamus, taking her refusal as a challenge. "Let me guess. It's that sleazy restaurateur. That Quigg person. Did I guess right? Are you going to slither off to his restaurant and let him ply you with wine and truffles?"

"No," Carmela said, although she had to admit Shamus's little restaurant fantasy sounded pretty damn good. Preferable, certainly, to poking through a bunch of black-and-white photos that she was struggling to get excited about.

"What are you in the middle of?" he asked. Shamus had never been big on subtlety. Or privacy for that matter.

"If you must know," said Carmela, "I'm working on my photos."

"For the show?" exclaimed Shamus. "The one at Click!?"

"You got it," said Carmela, casting a discerning eye at a black-and-white shot of a Mississippi river boat. Not bad, but not stunning either. Maybe a six on a scale of one to ten.

"Good girl," commended Shamus. He'd suddenly revised his tone to bubbly and enthusiastic. "This could be a very big step for us, Carmela. Very major."

"Mmm," said Carmela, noncommittally. Shamus was definitely way more into this show than she would ever be.

But Shamus babbled on. "I don't think I told you this, but Glory liked two of my photos so well that she hung them in the bank lobby. The ones of that Creole-style townhouse on Royal Street. Anyway, I understand they're garnering rave reviews."

"Rave reviews," said Carmela. Shamus was beginning to seriously get on her nerves. "Rave reviews from people who come in to grab twenty bucks from the ATM. Those are pretty high accolades, Shamus. Sounds like you're one step away from having a big show in a fancy New York gallery."

"You're just jealous," said Shamus, sounding hurt.

"Actually, I'm not," said Carmela. "In fact, I'd be delighted if you did this show all by yourself."

"We had a deal, Carmela," said Shamus. Now there was an edge to his voice. He was definitely giving her the Shamus Meechum Seal of Disapproval. "You said we'd do this *together*. You can't just pull out now."

"Why not?" said Carmela. "You pulled out of our marriage." *Oh oh, now I've veered into that old territory again. Oh, shame on me.*

"Totally different situation, Carmela. You know that."

Carmela sighed. "Okay, Shamus, cards on the table. I can't quit, but you can? Where's the fairness in that?" She knew she was being petty, knew she was beating a dead horse, but she couldn't stop. Anger and frustration still burned inside her like a molten ball.

"This is hopeless," fumed Shamus. "Utterly hopeless."

I'm afraid you're right, thought Carmela.

Silence hung between them for a few beats, then Shamus finally said. "So you're going to drop by Click! when?"

"I don't know," said Carmela, who by now had completely lost interest in perusing her photos. "Maybe next Tuesday," she lied. "Wednesday at the latest."

"Good," said Shamus. "Glad to hear it." He seemed to have blanked out their snarling, sniping go-round of ten seconds ago.

Wonderful, thought Carmela. *Shamus is having a senior moment.*

"Be sure to let me know how it goes," urged Shamus. "In fact, call me the minute you're finished."

"Right," said Carmela, knowing she wouldn't. She hung up the phone, stared down at the table. *Crapola.* Any iota of enthusiasm she'd had for this project had just flown right out the window.

So now what?

Carmela exhaled slowly, stared across the room at the chair where her purse and the brown file folders from Jamie's store sat. Maybe take a look through those, she decided. They were one thing she could follow up on.

But after thumbing through the files for a few minutes, Carmela didn't find anything that was particularly interesting. Or enlightening.

Most of the photos were similar to the ones she'd looked at the other night. Black-and-white shots of what had to be Jamie's old homestead down near Boothville. There were a few variations on the same theme, but nothing that knocked her out.

No, these aren't going to work even if I hand-color them. Not thematic enough. Oh well.

There were a few old news clippings tucked in among the photos, too. Most were from the *Boothville Courier* and dealt with high school sports team wins. A baseball conference championship, a football win, a wrestling match.

It looked like Jamie might have been a frustrated scrapbooker, Carmela decided. But then again, lots of people were. They amassed huge amounts of photos, clippings, programs, and letters, but never quite made it to the next logical step, that being scrapbooking, journaling, or creating genealogy albums. Because they never found a logical way to chronicle their jumbled collection of photos and moments, they were never able to fully enjoy them.

Carmela was about to stuff everything back in the folder and fix something to eat, when one of the clippings caught her eye.

A faded news clipping with the headline *Bogus Creek Boys Await Sentencing.*

Bogus Creek Boys? The name had a funny, colorful ring to it. Old-fashioned. Like the bank robbers who populated the American landscape during the twenties and thirties. Bonnie and Clyde. The Al Karpis Gang. Ma Barker and Al Capone.

So who were these Bogus Creek Boys? she wondered. *And why had Jamie Redmond elected to save this particular clipping?*

Carmela scanned down the narrow column, quickly absorbing the gist of the story. A ring of counterfeiters had set up shop near Boothville. In fact, they'd operated out of an abandoned camp house on the banks of Bogus Creek. Hence the moniker, Bogus Creek Boys. They'd been apprehended by a savvy local sheriff, but no printing plates had been recovered.

However, it was the final paragraph that riveted Carmela's attention and caused a sharp intake of breath.

It said, *T.L. Walker and J. Redmond, two members of the counterfeiting gang, are slated for sentencing this Thursday.*

Carmela stared at the clipping in her hands.

J. Redmond. Jamie Redmond? Jamie had been one of the Bogus Creek Boys? Good lord!

Carefully setting the snippet of paper on the table, Carmela tapped it gently with her index finger, as though trying to ascertain if the article were truly genuine.

Jamie Redmond a convicted criminal? A criminal who'd actually served time? Carmela pursed her lips, thinking.

Or was this article about his father? Hadn't his father owned a little printing shop? Sure he had.

She turned the article over, looking for a date. There was nothing that lent a clue as to whether the article was ten years old or twenty-five years old.

So Jamie, or Jamie's father, had a shady past. She wondered if that's why Jamie had been so closed-mouthed about his life in Boothville. And Carmela also wondered if this strange link to a sordid past might hold an important clue as to why Jamie Redmond had been murdered.

Did one of the Bogus Creek Boys get out of prison and come back to target him? Had Jamie or his father plea-bargained? Enough so there might still be anger and bad blood at work?

Worse yet, could someone have been blackmailing Jamie? Extracting money from him in exchange for remaining quiet about his past?

Could it have been Blaine? Or Dunbar DesLauriers? Had Jamie finally cried *enough*? And been murdered because of it?

Had Margot Butler broken off her engagement because she learned of Jamie's past?

Unanswered questions were piling up faster than broken beads and empty *geaux* cups after a Mardi Gras parade.

Carmela stood up, wandered into her kitchen, and plucked the lid off her cookie jar. She stood there nibbling one of her homemade Big Easy chocolate-chip peanut-butter cookies. She usually loved them, but tonight she didn't seem to be getting her usual kick. Tonight she was just too upset.

Chapter 12

"THESE PUMPKIN MUFFINS are heavenly," raved Tandy as she helped herself to a second plump muffin drizzled with cream cheese frosting. "Is this your recipe, Carmela?"

"My momma's," said Carmela, as she sorted through one of her drawers of oversized sheets of paper. Last night, after her unsettling conversation with Shamus and her discovery of the news clipping about Jamie Redmond, she had whipped up a batch of pumpkin muffins to bring to Memory Mine. Baking was one of Carmela's sure-fire ways to let off steam. Short of actually throtting someone to death.

"Well, I want your momma's recipe," declared Tandy. "I swear, I could probably get Darwin to balance on a rubber ball and bark like a seal if I dangled one of these muffins in front of him." Darwin, Tandy's husband of many years, was known for his incurable sweet tooth.

"If I let Stuart barely breathe the aroma from these muffins," said Gabby, "he'd probably go into insulin shock. How much sugar does your recipe call for, anyway?" she asked, taking a nibble.

"Quite a bit," admitted Carmela, glancing about her shop. For a Monday morning, Memory Mine was already pleasantly crowded. Gabby and Wren had shown up for work promptly at 9:00 AM, and Baby and Tandy had arrived some twenty minutes later. Baby was bound and determined to turn out her first batch of Mardi Gras party invitations, and Tandy had decided she wanted to make a second bibelot box for one of her daughters-in-law.

Six more customers had since wandered into Memory Mine and, wicker baskets in hand, were happily browsing the racks of paper and displays of albums, glitter glue, scissors, and oil pens as they tossed various scrapbooking must-haves into their baskets.

Carmela was delighted that Wren has seemingly jumped, feet first, into her new role at Memory Mine. In fact, when one of the customers inquired about scrapbook borders, Wren had quickly produced a book of border designs as well as several of their new adhesive-backed borders. And when another lady asked about embossed paper, Wren was immediately able to pull out a half-dozen samples.

Watching Wren work so diligently, Carmela felt anguished, knowing she'd ultimately have to share her discovery of Jamie's sordid past with her. She had to tell Wren what she'd found because it was the honest thing to do. But she certainly wasn't relishing the task.

"She's good, isn't she?" whispered Gabby. She had noticed Carmela watching Wren.

Carmela nodded. "Wren's a natural. Like you."

Gabby thought for a moment. "But I'm here because I'm a scrapbook fanatic. Whereas Wren seems to genuinely love working with people."

Carmela playfully raised an eyebrow. "And you don't?"

"It's not that," Gabby hastened to explain. "It's simply that Wren seems to connect with them on a completely different level."

"I know what you mean," said Carmela. "We understand scrapbooking and rubber stamping backward and forward, but Wren seems to sense what customers need and knows when they could use a little help or encouragement." She paused. "Or maybe not so much help as a gentle *nudge*. I don't know how to explain it any better."

"You just did," said Gabby.

"Has Wren told you anything about Dunbar DesLauriers's offer?" asked Carmela.

Gabby nodded. "Just that he offered to take the inventory off her hands. Nothing about price or anything like that."

"I think Dunbar figures he can toss out any number he feels like and she'll leap at it," said Carmela. "That's the problem with really wealthy people. They're so focused on money that they think everyone else is, too."

"Well," said Gabby, "Wren was sure tickled that you took so much time with her yesterday, prowling through that old bookstore and giving her real-life business advice. For that I thank you, too. There aren't a lot of female entrepreneurs around, in case you hadn't noticed. Not many role models."

"But more than there used to be," said Carmela. "Which I take as a very positive sign."

Gabby slid her velvet headband forward, shook her hair, then replaced the headband. "Do you really think Wren could run Biblios Booksellers?" she asked. "I thought for sure she'd be hot to unload it, but now she's talking about maybe giving it a shot. Possibly reopening the place sometime in March."

"She could probably handle it," said Carmela. "She'll need help, of course, but there are lots of good people out there."

Gabby smiled, aware that Carmela had just paid her another compliment. "So you don't think she should just sell everything—lock, stock, and barrel? That's what Stuart advised, you know."

"That's Stuart," said Carmela. "No offense, but he's a little hide-bound when it comes to women and business."

"A little!" exclaimed Gabby. "He wasn't all that keen about me working here. I think if Stuart were actually able to execute his master-of-the-universe plan, he'd have me staying home all day wearing a perfect little pink suit and a string of pearls, cultivating roses, and learning how to bake the perfect soufflé."

"Hey," said Carmela. "At least the guy has good taste and he cares."

"Good point," said Gabby, watching Wren ring up a customer at the front counter.

"When it comes to either selling or keeping the bookstore, she'll make the right decision," said Carmela, reaching for the telephone as it let off an insistent ring. "She'll figure it out." Carmela put the phone to her ear. "Good morning," she said. "Memory Mine Scrapbooking."

"Is Wren there?" asked a male caller.

Carmela watched as Wren handed a brown paper bag stuffed with scrapbook goodies over to her customer, then bid her good-bye. "She's with a customer right now," Carmela lied. She had just recognized the voice on the other end of the line "Perhaps I could take a message?"

"Is this Carmela?"

"Yes, it is," she answered sweetly.

"Well, this is Blaine Taylor. And it's imperative I speak with her."

"Old B.T.," said Carmela. "How are you, anyway?"

"Fine, fine, but I—"

"I imagine you're pretty busy these days, anticipating all the money you're going to make selling Jamie's software program," said Carmela.

There was a stunned silence, then a burst of angry static. "What are you talking about?" Blaine demanded.

"I'd love to see that so-called buy-sell agreement you and Jamie drew up," continued Carmela. "You don't have a copy handy, by any chance, do you?"

"That's absolutely none of your business!" cried Blaine. "You have nothing to do with this."

"Actually I'm making it my business," said Carmela. "Wren's asked for my help with a few loose ends. And guess what, pal? You're one of them."

Whether it was Carmela's casual reference to him as a loose end or her bemused yet aggressive stance, Blaine Taylor was suddenly furious.

"You're out of your league," he warned. "Don't even bother getting involved. This has nothing to do with you."

"Here's a grand idea," continued Carmela, not allowing his blustering to faze her. "Why don't you shoot a copy of that buy-sell agreement of yours over to the law firm of Leonard, Barstow, and Streeter," she said, naming one of the top law firms in New Orleans. "In fact, send it to the attention of Seth Barstow, Senior Partner."

"What?" said Blaine, his voice rising in a high squawk. "LBS is your counsel?" He sounded stunned.

Hooray. Score one for the good guys.

"Yup," said Carmela. "They sure are." Of course that particular law firm wasn't *exactly* her lawyer. But they *were* one of the law firms that did work for the chain of Crescent City Banks that Shamus's family owned. And in her mind that was close enough for jazz. Plus, Leonard, Barstow, and Streeter had posh downtown offices and a reputation for pit-bull tenacity, so why not dangle them as a threat? Why not, indeed?

Blaine Taylor was still stuttering and stammering. "Perhaps we could work something out after all, Carmela. You know I don't want to see Wren completely—"

"Do you actually have the software program?" asked Carmela, interrupting him. "Do you have a copy of Neutron?"

"Well, no," stammered Blaine. "Not physically. Although Neutron exists as a *virtual* product." Blaine was still babbling.

Good, thought Carmela. *And it's also a smart thing I made a virtual copy of everything on Jamie's home computer. Just in case.*

"Talk to you later, Blaine," said Carmela. "Be sure to send a copy of that buy-sell to my attorney." She paused. "Or you can drop it by my shop."

"What was *that* about?" asked Gabby, eyeing Carmela suspiciously as she hung up the phone.

"Just that weirdo, Blaine Taylor," grumbled Carmela. "I swear that old boy is trying to pull a fast one on Wren."

Gabby's smile suddenly crumpled. "What?" she said, shock morphing into anger. "What is this, anyway? Let's see how badly we can bash Wren when she's down? First Dunbar DesLauriers wants to ram through a quick sale, now Blaine Taylor, who was *supposed* to be Jamie's good friend, is trying to screw her. Why is this happening?"

Carmela grabbed Gabby by the arm and pulled her into her office. "Take it easy," she said. "Unfortunately for Wren, it's business as usual."

Carmela knew you couldn't compete in business these days without running up against a few nasty, nefarious people. And having your teeth kicked in a time or two. Getting blind-sided was a hard-learned lesson for many business owners. But it was almost a right of passage. Something you couldn't escape. And if you *did* stay under the radar, remain complacent, and play it safe—that seemed to be the kiss of death, too. As her daddy used to tell her, if you want to run with the big dogs, you gotta climb down off the porch.

But as Carmela was giving a whispered explanation to Gabby, Wren suddenly appeared in the doorway.

"You've got a visitor," Wren told Carmela.

Carmela glanced past Wren and her heart sank.

Glory.

Glory Meechum was Shamus's big sister and the senior vice president of the Crescent City Bank chain. She was also hell on wheels. As matriarch and self-appointed leader of the snarling Meechum clan, it was she who'd pinned the blame for Carmela and Shamus's break-up squarely on Carmela's head. Even though Shamus had been the instigator, the one who'd tossed his tightie-whities into his Samsonite jet pack, grabbed his Nikon cameras, and skedad-dled to the family camp house in the Baritaria Bayou. Go figure.

This can't be good, thought Carmela as she strode out to meet Glory Meechum. *Glory never just pops in for a fun, impromptu visit. She's got to have something evil percolating in her strange brain.*

"Carmela," said Glory in a loud bray. "We need to talk." Standing a husky five-feet-ten in her splotchy print dress, with a helmet of gray hair and a countenance reminiscent of an Easter Island statue, Glory presented a formi-dable figure.

She wants to talk about me and Shamus again? Now what's the problem?

"Glory," said Carmela, deciding to grab the bull by the horns. "Why don't you direct whatever inquest you've decided to launch directly at Shamus. He's the one who's been acting like a bad boy in all of this." Carmela kept her voice even, being mindful not to appear challenging or threatening. Bad things happened when you challenged Glory.

"This isn't about Shamus," snapped Glory. "This is about *you.*"

"We've been through this before, Glory," sighed Carmela. "I'll be happy to grant Shamus a divorce. *He's* the one who keeps dragging his size elevens when it comes to putting the paperwork in motion."

Glory's face, already set in a frown, switched to a glower.

Ah, thought Carmela, *there's that famous Meechum Seal of Disapproval again. The family could almost copyright it.*

"Before you go off on a tangent," said Glory, "perhaps you'd give me a chance to speak my peace?"

"Fine, Glory," said Carmela. "What?"

Glory's eyes shifted toward the back of the store where Wren was doling out paper samples to Tandy. "I want you to instruct that girl to sell her collec-tion of moldy old books to Dunbar DesLauriers."

"What!" said Carmela, stunned. Those were not the words she'd expected to come spewing out of Glory Meechum's mouth.

"I know Dunbar will give her a fair price," continued Glory in a nadder-ing tone. "The girl could do a whole lot worse."

"Will you stop calling her *the girl*?" said Carmela. "And why on earth are you remotely concerned with what happens to Wren or Biblios Booksellers? *Good grief, who's going to crawl out of the woodwork next to take a bash at poor Wren?*

"Not that it's any business of yours," said Glory. "But Dunbar DesLauri-ers is an extremely valuable customer at our bank. Which is why I'm willing to do almost anything in my power to keep the dear man happy."

"Uh huh," said Carmela, still stunned by this twist in the conversation.

Glory's unplucked eyebrows formed stormy arcs over hard, beady eyes. "I understand you've been giving the girl some *business* advice," she said.

"Wren," said Carmela. "Please say her name. Wren."

"Wren," snarled Glory.

"Thank you."

Glory slammed her sensible black handbag onto the counter and glared at Carmela. "You think you're a pretty tough cookie, don't you? Well let me give you a word of warning: Don't take me on. Because you'll lose, Carmela." She pronounced her name *Car-mel-la,* spitting out each syllable venomously hard.

"I wasn't aware this was a contest," said Carmela. *Just a contest of wills.*

"You've visited the bookstore, correct?" said Glory.

"Sure," said Carmela.

"And the girl . . . Wren . . . has expressed some interest in selling?"

"She's still deciding," said Carmela.

"Dunbar DesLauriers is prepared to pay seventy-five thousand dollars for the entire inventory," said Glory. "He'll write a check today, in fact."

"You realize," countered Carmela, "Wren hasn't had a chance to bring an appraiser in yet."

Glory shrugged. "A mere technicality in the face of such a generous offer." She rearranged her frown into a friendly grimace. "I can't impress upon you what a valuable customer Dunbar is. I see no reason to upset him with petty dickering."

"That's funny," said Carmela. "Because the only person I've seen upset so far is Wren. Everyone, and I do mean everyone, seems to think they can come cowboying in and strong-arm her."

"I certainly wouldn't do that," snapped Glory. She pulled a handkerchief from her bag and blew her nose into it, letting loose a good, loud honk.

"Of course you would," Carmela fired back. "You are."

Glory stuffed her hanky back into her purse, then rubbed her large hand, palm down, across the top of the counter. When she turned it over, she stared at it for almost a full minute, then wiped it hard against the side of her splotchy print nylon dress. *Wshst wsht.*

She's off her meds again, thought Carmela. Glory had been diagnosed with a mild obsessive-compulsive disorder and was supposed to be taking medicine to help control it.

Carmela let loose a deep sigh. "Tell Dunbar we'll get back to him, Glory."

"When?" demanded Glory, obviously intent on keeping the pressure on.

"I don't know," said Carmela. "Two or three weeks, maybe a month. Like I said, we'll get back to him."

Glory stared hard at Carmela and took a step closer to her. Closer than she'd ever come before, her anger overshadowing the OCD that always kept her a protective arm's length away from everyone. "There are *debts,*" Glory murmured, her eyes glinting like hard marbles. "Outstanding *loans* that Jamie Redmond incurred. All this must be taken into account."

"The debt you refer to is a mortgage," said Carmela.

"A mortgage with *my* bank," said Glory, her thin lips twitching upward slightly. "A variable-rate balloon mortgage that *I* control."

"Don't," said Carmela, holding a finger up. "Don't you dare threaten."

But nothing could wipe the smile of satisfaction from Glory's doughy face.

"WELL *THAT* was good for business," remarked Gabby after Glory had finally stalked out, slamming the door behind her.

Carmela cringed. "Do you think everyone heard us?" They were standing at the front of the shop while most everyone else was grouped at the back.

Gabby shrugged. "Probably not. It was mostly your body language that gave away the tone of the argument. One petite bulldog . . . you. Up against one very large, immovable object . . . Glory."

"She's a fruitcake," admitted Carmela as she and Gabby walked slowly back toward the craft table where Baby, Tandy, and Wren were gathered, heads bent over their various projects.

"And you're a defender of the underdog," said Gabby, her eyes shining brightly. Then, without warning, she gave Carmela a quick hug. "Thank you," she told her.

Carmela nodded. It was flattering to be thought of as *Carmela, fearless defender of underdogs*. Even though her heart was beating like a fluttering dove.

And, of course, she *still* wasn't sure how to break the rather shocking news to Wren about the Bogus Creek Boys news clipping she'd stumbled across. Or tell her about Dunbar DesLauriers's seventy-five-thousand-dollar offer on the bookstore. Or tell her about Glory's nasty threat.

Gulp.

Carmela wiggled her shoulders to dispel the tension, sucked in a deep breath. She'd find a way. She always did.

Chapter 13

"WHY DID I think you were making party invitations?" Carmela asked Baby.

Baby swiveled in her chair and adjusted the Chanel scarf draped around her patrician neck. Here blue eyes looked mischievous, her short blond hair artfully tousled. "Because that's what I told you when I came in this morning. But, surprise surprise, things have changed."

"I guess," said Carmela, gazing over Baby's shoulder at a marvelous array of colorful tags.

The women had sent out for salads from the French Quarter Deli an hour or so ago. Now, the salads munched and the debris cleared away, Tandy and Baby were back at their projects, while Gabby and Wren buzzed about, kibitzing and unpacking boxes of newly arrived scrapbooking supplies.

And while Tandy had made great progress on her bibelot box, Baby was indeed working on an entirely different project.

"Your little tags are gorgeous," Wren told Baby. "But Carmela's right, we all thought you started out with invitations."

"You don't like my photo tags?" asked Baby.

Now Tandy jumped in. "Are you kidding, sweetie? They're *wonderful.*" Tandy was always big on unabashed enthusiasm.

And Baby's photo tags were adorable. She had cut out individual faces from a number of color photos, then matted them with small bits of pebbled card stock so they looked like miniature portraits. Baby then sponge-dyed ink on large colorful tags to achieve a textured, marbleized surface, then mounted each "portrait" on one of the faux-finished tags.

"So now what?" asked Wren. "You're going to put the tags on a scrapbook page?"

"I could do that," said Baby. "But instead I'm going to make a front and back cover from this leather-looking paper, then bind all the tags together with a piece of silk ribbon twined with different fibers. So they become like pages in a book."

"You're creating a little memory book," said Wren, obviously charmed by the craft project. "Very clever."

"Wren," said Tandy. "Show me your bibelot box again, will you? I want to see how you affixed the legs."

Wren popped into Carmela's office to grab her bibelot box while everyone gathered to admire Tandy's handiwork.

Tandy had decoupaged a square tea tin with dark-red mulberry paper that had gold Japanese *kanji* writing on it. Then she had added several colorful postage stamps depicting Mount Fuji and cut-outs of Japanese family crests. Gold fish charms were glued on the sides of the box, and the top featured a lovely red tassel strung with pearls and Japanese blue and white beads.

"It's gorgeous," said Gabby. "Now I'm in the mood to make one."

"Can you believe it started out as an ordinary tea tin?" asked Baby. "Now it looks like something you'd see in one of those expensive gift shops down on Magazine Street."

"I think you should just add four more of those blue and white beads for feet," suggested Gabby. "Right on the corners. Like Wren did on hers."

"Here it is," said Wren, as she set her little bibelot box covered with keys in the middle of the table. "My mystery key box, as I like to call it."

Tandy slid her glasses onto her nose and peered at Wren's bibelot box carefully. "I wouldn't mind making one just like that. Lord knows, I've got a dusty jar filled with antique keys sitting on a shelf in my basement. There's probably still a key in there for my dad's old place over in Westwebo."

"WREN," SAID Carmela in a quiet voice, once things had settled down and everyone was busily working away. "A few things have come up that you need to know about. And some decisions need to be made."

Wren turned toward Carmela. "Tell me."

Carmela cleared her throat. "Ah . . . maybe it would be best if we went and sat in my office?"

"Do we have to?" asked Wren. "I feel like I'm definitely among friends here. In fact, I feel like I'm able to draw strength from everyone's concern and support."

"It's just that one of the items we need to discuss is somewhat personal," pressed Carmela.

Wren shook her head. "I don't care. I can't tell you how much I love and trust this group of women."

"Aren't you sweet," said Tandy, reaching over to pat one of Wren's hands.

"*She's* the love," said Baby, threading a piece of silk ribbon through her photo tags.

"Okay, then," said Carmela, sitting down at the table and putting her hands flat. "There's good and bad news."

"Good news first," said Wren, taking a deep breath.

"Dunbar DesLauriers has put a cash offer on the table for Biblios Booksellers," said Carmela. She hoped this would be perceived as good news.

"Did he really?" exclaimed Gabby, suddenly excited. "How much?"

"Seventy-five thousand dollars," replied Carmela.

"Not bad," Tandy said. "That'd keep a girl in stickers and rubber stamps for a good long while."

Carmela bit her lower lip. "I have to admit seventy-five thousand dollars doesn't sound bad, but we don't really have a handle on the value of the rare book inventory." She looked over at Wren for confirmation.

"They're not all rare," offered Wren. "A lot of them are more like first editions."

"So a first edition would sell for . . . what?" asked Gabby, obviously intrigued by Dunbar's offer. "What would be a ballpark figure?"

Wren shrugged. "Depends. A first edition of, say, *Mosquitoes* by William Faulkner might be three . . . maybe four hundred dollars."

"So Dunbar's offer sounds fair?" asked Carmela. "Maybe even a bit on the high side?"

"It could be," said Wren. "Again, I'd have to check the inventory price sheets that do exist. And maybe run an Internet search for comparables on the rarer books."

"Do we know if Dunbar DesLauriers knows what he's bidding on?" asked Baby. She'd been listening quietly, now she spoke up.

"What do you mean?" asked Wren.

"Dunbar DesLauriers is a rare book collector," said Baby. "He may be just as familiar with the inventory as Jamie was. Or even *more* familiar."

"You think he's trying to put one over on me?" asked Wren.

Baby shrugged. "Don't know." Baby was no stranger to the competitive world of collecting. Her husband, Del, had amassed a spectacular collection of antique Japanese swords. And Baby herself collected miniature oil paintings and antique jewelry.

"I assume there's some play in Dunbar's number," said Carmela. "I see his offer of seventy-five thousand dollars as more of a *suggested* retail price."

"I like the way you think," said Tandy. "Although seventy-five thousand does sound good."

"Unfortunately," said Carmela. "Nothing's ever easy. There's more to this deal than just a straight ahead offer of cash."

Gabby looked at her sharply. "What do you mean?"

Carmela sighed. "There's also an implied threat," she told them.

"Concerning what?" asked Wren.

"Your mortgage. The mortgage on the house on Julia Street," said Carmela.

"The *mortgage*?" said Wren, clearly puzzled. "But Jamie put the house in my name, too, right? So all I have to do is make the monthly payments and I'm okay?" She stared at Carmela. "Right?"

"Well, not exactly," said Carmela. "It seems that the mortgage Jamie has with Crescent City Bank . . . the mortgage *you* now have . . . is an adjustable-rate balloon mortgage."

"Is that why Glory Meechum came storming in here earlier?" asked Baby. "With her underwear all in a twist?"

Carmela nodded. "She claims Dunbar DesLauriers is one of her best customers. That she'd do anything to keep him happy."

"I'll bet," muttered Baby. Glory lived two blocks from Baby in the Garden District, and there was no love lost between the two women. When Glory had been the chairman of their Garden Club's Spring Rose Show, she'd accused Baby of bringing in ringers. Roses that hadn't actually been grown in Baby's garden. Which had been an outright lie, of course. And an accusation that *still* aggravated Baby.

"A balloon mortgage," repeated Wren. She wrinkled her nose. "What a funny name. What is it? What does it mean?"

Carmela took a deep breath. "Basically, it means your monthly payment has nowhere to go but up and that the entire balance is probably due in a matter of months."

"Are you serious?" cried Wren. "You mean I could lose the house!"

"That possibility does seem to exist," said Carmela, hating the fact that she had to break this news to Wren. "Unless, of course, you get busy and pay the mortgage off."

"With the profit I make from selling Biblios Booksellers," said Wren. She crossed her arms and hugged herself tightly. "This feels suspiciously like a trap."

"It sure does," agreed Gabby.

"A catch-22," added Tandy.

"But legal, just the same," said Carmela. She hated to be the one hard-ass in the bunch, but the mortgage *was* completely aboveboard. It may not have been a smart choice on Jamie's part, but it was legal just the same.

"Well, this has been quite a day," declared Wren, looking forlorn.

"Wait," said Carmela, "it's not over." She slid the news clipping across the table.

"What's this?" said Wren.

"I'm afraid it's even more disturbing news," said Carmela. *Who am I kidding? It's beyond disturbing. It's downright crappy.*

Gabby sped around the table so she could read over Wren's shoulder.

"Good lord!" said Wren, when she'd finished the article. Her face was white, her hands were shaking. She slid the article over to Tandy and Baby, who quickly scanned it.

"Oh, my goodness!" declared Baby. She looked over at Wren with pity on her face. "This is quite a shocker."

"When does it end?" stammered Wren. "I thought finding out that Jamie was once engaged to Margot Butler was a terrible shock."

Baby and Tandy quickly exchanged glances. "He was?" asked Tandy. "Wow."

"Now I find out Jamie was a convicted felon!" continued Wren in an agonized voice. "Which is even worse!"

"Don't jump to conclusions yet," warned Carmela. "This could be about Jamie's father."

"No," said Wren. "I'm sure it's about Jamie. That's why he was always so closed-mouthed about his past." She leaned forward, rocking back and forth in her chair as though the pain were almost too much to bear. "I feel awful," she murmured. "Ashamed, almost."

"It's not *your* fault," said Gabby, patting Wren on the shoulder.

"Please don't feel bad," said Tandy. "Try to look on the bright side. Lots of perfectly lovely people have done jail time."

Baby swiveled in her chair, aghast. "Are you *serious*? Name one."

Tandy thought for a moment. "Leona Helmsley."

"Leona Helmsley was dubbed the *Queen of Mean*," snorted Baby. "I don't think her poor ex-employees would characterize her as a lovely person at all."

Tandy pursed her lips. "Well, she certainly *seemed* kind of sweet when Suzanne Plechet played her in the made-for-TV movie."

"Look," said Gabby, "could we please not dwell on this? What's done is done. Even if Jamie served time in jail, he'd put it behind him by the time he met Wren. He paid his debt to society, as they say."

"She's right," murmured Tandy. "Jamie was a lovely person."

"I think for now we have to focus on the positive," continued Gabby. "Keep Jamie's memory sacred and continue in our quest to find his parents' final resting place." She gazed pointedly at Carmela.

I know, I know, thought Carmela. *I was supposed to make a few calls, try to figure out where Jamie's parents are buried, and I still haven't gotten around to it.*

"That's for sure," said Wren, shaking her head, not knowing what to think. "I'm having Jamie cremated, and I still don't know what to do with his ashes."

"When Jamie is finally at rest," murmured Baby, "maybe Wren will rest a little easier, too.

"That's a lovely thought," said Wren. "Thank you."

Gabby gazed at Carmela. "When were you going to look into that grave site thing?"

"Ava and I are gonna take a drive down to Boothville tomorrow," said Carmela. This was going to come as big news to Ava. Of course, it was also big news to Carmela. Until she'd just blurted it out, a trip down to Boothville hadn't been in her forecast. *Oh well.*

"I'm going to light a few candles tonight," said Gabby. "And say a little prayer that everything will work out okay." Gabby took great comfort in lighting the colorful vigil rights that were prevalent in French Quarter shops. Her favorites were Saint Cecilia and Saint Ann.

"Amen," said Tandy, as she inked a rubber stamp and slammed it down hard on a piece of craft paper.

WHEN MARGOT Butler walked in the door at four o'clock, Carmela was thankful Wren had gone home early. She didn't think Wren could deal with seeing Margot in person, knowing the woman had once been engaged to Jamie.

And Wren just might start mulling over the possibility that Margot could be a possible suspect in Jamie's murder. Because I sure am.

Today Margot was bouncy and vivacious, filled with energy and big ideas.

"Pamela DesLauriers is absolutely *thrilled* that you're working on her Gilt Trip scrapbook," Margot enthused.

Carmela, who hadn't had a free moment to even think about the scrapbook, just smiled.

"But some enhancements have been made," said Margot. "In Pamela's dining room. In fact, the photos she dropped off simply don't do it justice."

"What are you suggesting, Margot?" asked Carmela. Margot was kicking up a lot of dust, but they didn't seem to be getting anywhere.

"Could you . . . *would you* . . . stop by in person?" begged Margot. "It would mean so much to us."

"You're retaking photos?" asked Carmela. Margot was still being resolutely obtuse.

Margot suddenly looked unhappy. "Yes, I suppose we're going to have to do that. Although a reshoot is simply not in the budget . . ." She shrugged. "I'm not sure *how* we're going to pull that rabbit out of a hat."

"Maybe I could retake a couple photos," suggested Carmela. It suddenly seemed like a good idea to get inside the DesLauriers home. Maybe take a look to see what kind of book collection Dunbar really had?

"Good heavens, Carmela!" exclaimed Margot. "What a spectacularly brilliant idea! You're a photographer?"

"I've been known to snap a picture or two," said Carmela.

"Tomorrow," said Margot. "You must come tomorrow, then."

"No," said Carmela. "That won't work. I've got to take a quick trip out of town. But I can come on Wednesday. Thursday at the latest."

Margot's bony little hand suddenly gripped Carmela's arm hard. "It's gonna be tight, but I love the idea!"

Carmela had to turn away so Margot couldn't see her amused expression. As long as Margot was getting her way she was sweet as pie. And when she didn't get her way? Well, Carmela had seen *that* side to Margot, too. She wondered if Jamie had also seen that side.

Is that why Jamie broke off the engagement? Carmela wondered. *And Margot, strange little lady that she was, had become totally enraged?*

If Margot couldn't have Jamie, was she crazy enough to make it so that no one could have him?

Carmela shook her head as Margot skittered out the front door, then she headed back to see if Tandy and Baby needed any help finishing up their projects.

"Did you ever notice how much Margot likes snakes?" piped up Baby. "She always seems to be wearing snakeskin shoes or carrying a snakeskin bag."

"Well, heavens to Betsy," shot Tandy. "Look what she named her company."

Carmela, Gabby, and Baby mouthed a collective, "What?"

"Fer de Lance," replied Tandy. When they all continued to stare at her, she set her hot glue gun down and stared at them. "Well for goodness' sake," said Tandy, her tight curls bobbing. "A fer de lance is a snake!"

Chapter 14

THE OIL PENS were put away, the mulberry paper returned to the flat files, the day's receipts tallied and scribbled in the little black ledger Carmela kept to assure herself Memory Mine was indeed a viable business.

And now Carmela was going to follow through on an idea she'd hatched earlier this afternoon.

Just before Wren had left for the day, Carmela had asked for the key to Biblios Booksellers. Wren, of course, had immediately turned it over to her. Which meant Carmela could now pay a second visit to the dusty little bookstore over on Toulouse Street to see if she could unearth anything else that might shed a little light on Jamie Redmond's past. And on his tragic demise.

Clues. Let's call 'em what they really are. They're clues.

But even the most well-intentioned plans are generally fraught with a few problems. Because once Carmela arrived at the store, she realized *her* problem was going to be tiptoeing down the creaky flight of stairs into that musty old cellar.

Standing in the middle of the bookstore, listening to the quiet, she gazed at towering cases of books. Then she slowly let her eyes slide toward the cellar door.

Spiders and mousies and bugs, oh my!

It wasn't that she was *afraid* of these things. Good heavens, no. She was merely . . . well, let's call it apprehensive.

Buck up, girl. You've never backed off from anything in your life!

Carmela walked over to the cellar door, her footsteps echoing in the empty store, half wishing she'd strong-armed Wren to coming back here with her. Putting a hand on the doorknob, she gave a good, firm yank. The door creaked back on its hinges and the smell of mildew and dust immediately assaulted her nose.

Whew. Not exactly eau de magnolia, is it?

Fumbling for the light switch, Carmela flipped it on. She was rewarded with a dim glow at the bottom of the stairs. Slowly, carefully, she headed down the creaky stairs toward the faint puddle of light, one hand gripping the flimsy wooden railing. It wouldn't pay to take a tumble here.

At the bottom of the stairs, Carmela paused. The basement or old root cellar or ancient torture chamber, or whatever it had been, was small. A lot smaller than she'd imagined it would be. The ceiling was low and oppressive, a tangle of furry cobweb-coated beams, and the floor was packed earth. Up against one wall, looking strangely like a log jam, was a ceiling-high jumble of broken bookcases. An old sink, dirty and rusted, hung from another wall. A dusty four-drawer metal file case stood poised in front of her.

This must be where Wren got the file folders with the photos and clippings.

Fighting an urge to sneeze, Carmela slid the top drawer open. Empty. She wasn't surprised. Its former contents were probably the very same files that were stashed at her apartment. Sliding the drawer closed, she heard a faint skittering in the corner.

Mousies? Yeah, probably.

She slid the second and third drawers open. The second drawer was empty, the third drawer was filled with old office supplies. Tape that probably wouldn't stick anymore, an old stapler, a couple jars of hardened Wite-Out, an ancient tube of glue.

Carmela moved on to the bottom drawer, but it was stuck tight.

Which means Wren probably didn't check this drawer. Should I? I can try, anyway.

The grubby-looking sink hanging from the wall was dripping a steady *drip drip drip* that annoyed Carmela, grating on her nerves.

I'm gonna get this done with and get the heck out of here.

Steeling her shoulders, grasping the handle with both hands, Carmela gave a mighty yank. Nothing. Searching around the basement, she finally found a wooden box that had a pile of rusty tools in it.

Good. Maybe there's something here.

She passed on the saw, the hammer, and the broken pliers. But decided the rusty screwdriver just might do the trick.

Carmela went back to the file case, wedged the screwdriver into the edge of the drawer, and put as much muscle behind it as she could.

Creak. The drawer popped out a quarter inch.

Repositioning the screwdriver, Carmela dug it in deeper and tried to lever-age it with all her might.

A high-pitched *creak* dropped to a low *groan* as the drawer slid grudg-ingly open.

Success!

Carmela peered in. A single brown file folder lay in the bottom of the drawer. With one quick motion, she grabbed it, executed a fast spin, and bounded back up the stairs.

Enough of this creepy place!

Back upstairs, Carmela found that the sun had just gone down. And the frosted windows, the ones that always made the place seem so warm and cozy when sunlight filtered through them, now lent a dark, spooky feel.

Hmm, does Wren really want to run this place all by her lonesome?

But Carmela knew where she could find a cozy spot to take a look at the file she'd just retrieved. Climbing the half-dozen stairs to the little loft, she plopped down on the sagging couch. The same couch she'd sprawled on yesterday with Boo.

Feeling old wire springs shift beneath her, Carmela flipped open the file folder and perused its contents.

More photos. Black-and-white photos mingled with a few color Polaroids. But these photos all had a collegiate feel to them. Guys partying, drinking beer, posturing with their arms slung about each other's shoulders.

Boy's bonding, thought Carmela. Maybe from Jamie's earlier days at Tulane?

A phrase Shamus used to toss around bubbled up in Carmela's mind. *Shit-faced.* That's what Shamus had called partying. Only it wasn't really partying at all, but getting drunk. Binge drinking. An epidemic, apparently, on today's college campuses.

Squinting in the dim light, Carmela quickly sifted through the rest of the photos until she came to a thick glob of papers. Here were more photos and papers, but they were all hopelessly stuck together. Pulling at one corner, she immediately tore a piece off. Oops. Not good. This was obviously going to require some careful work on her part. But nothing that she could do now.

Lost in thought, Carmela stared at the jumble of pillows sitting at her feet. Casually, mindlessly, she contemplated the nubby kilim fabric, with its Oriental design and colors of muted blue, green, and purple. And then she suddenly blinked hard.

Why are these pillows piled on the floor?

She stared at them quizzically, knowing something wasn't quite right. Felt a jittery what's-wrong-with-this-picture? vibe suddenly run through her.

Then, sudden comprehension kicked in. And Carmela scrambled to her feet. Some time between late yesterday afternoon and right now, someone had been in the store!

How did she know that for sure? Because whoever this mysterious visitor had been, he or she had removed the cushions and piled them on the floor.

Who? The same person who'd left a half a cup of coffee there yesterday? Yipes!

She knew it hadn't been Wren who moved the pillows, because Wren had been working at Memory Mine all day. Could it have been Blaine Taylor? Searching for something that belonged to Jamie? Something that he desperately needed to find?

Or could it have been Dunbar DesLauriers? As a long-time customer, Dunbar DesLauriers might have known if Jamie had hidden a key somewhere. On a nail out back or under one of the back steps. If it had been Dunbar, maybe he'd come back to check on one of the precious antique books he wanted to buy.

But did that even make sense? wondered Carmela. *If there were two or three books Dunbar specifically wanted, wouldn't he just steal them?*

Carmela gazed around. It was possible Dunbar had already stolen them.

Maybe his big fat offer of seventy-five grand was just his version of a clever smoke screen.

And what about Margot Butler? Carmela wondered if she had a key to the bookstore. Or if Margot had visited the bookstore right before she'd dropped by Memory Mine earlier. Would that have accounted for her manic mood?

Carmela shivered. Margot's snake fetish scared the bejeebers out of her. In Louisiana, snakes were generally given a wide berth.

Scrtch scrtch.

A sudden scratching at the front door startled Carmela.

Now what's going on?

Putting a hand to her chest to calm her beating heart, Carmela realized someone was at the door. Probably a customer, wondering if the bookstore was open.

Carmela descended the few steps and hurried over to the front door where a dark shadow moved on the other side of the frosted window pane.

She pulled the door open, ready to tell whoever it was that the store was closed until further notice, and got the surprise of her life when the unexpected visitor turned out to be Shamus!

"Shamus!" she cried. "You scared me to death!"

Shamus looked totally unapologetic. "Sorry. Didn't mean to."

"How did you know I was here?" she asked. She wasn't sure if she was still angry at him or secretly relieved that he'd turned up like the proverbial bad penny. She'd been talking herself into a pretty good case of the willies.

Shamus shrugged. "When I stopped by the store and you weren't there, I just put two and two together."

"Did Glory send you?" Carmela asked, wary now. "Are you here because of her?" *There's an old adage that warns against shooting the messenger, but I could certainly make an exception in this case.*

Shamus squinted at her. "What are you, loony or something? I'm here because of you."

"Yeah right," said Carmela.

"Are you going to let me in?" he asked, pushing his way through the open door.

Carmela shrugged and retreated deeper into the store. Amazingly, the place didn't seem nearly so gloomy or frightening now. Funny how another warm body can make things feel a whole lot safer.

"Call Glory off, Shamus," said Carmela. "She's been acting very badly. Threatening Wren and making wild assumptions."

"It's just business," said Shamus. "That's how Glory is. She takes everything very seriously." He shook his head, assuming a look of bemused befuddlement. "You have no idea how tough banking is these days, Carmela. People think you've got millions to spread around when actually you're dealing with extremely narrow margins. Banking has become a very demanding business. We're constantly being pushed to our limits."

Carmela folded her arms and threw him a wry glance. "Those pesky usury laws make it *so* hard to earn obscene profits these days, don't they Shamus?" She knew that Louisiana's banking laws were some of the most liberal in the country.

"Carmela," said Shamus. "A word of warning. Glory is dead serious about helping Dunbar DesLauriers get his way. If you have *any* influence with this young lady at all, I think you should advise her to sell. For gosh sakes, wake up and smell the red ink! Small businesses are collapsing all around us. This isn't the go-go nineties anymore. Times are lean. And from what I hear, Dunbar's offer is more than fair."

"Save the *strum und drang* for all the loan customers you give thumbs down to, Shamus," snarled Carmela. "And by the way, when did *you* suddenly evolve into a wise old business sage? You watch maybe thirty minutes of CNN at best and catch a few installments of Lou Dobbs and you think you're a whiz kid. Well you're not, Shamus. Take some advice from someone who's really *in* business. Climb down from your high horse and into the trenches. See what it's *really* like."

Shamus bristled and took a step forward just as a ball of brown and white fur shot through the door and swirled wildly about his knees.

"Holy shit!" shrieked Carmela. "What's that?"

"A dog," said Shamus, suddenly back in nonchalant mode.

Carmela peered at the creature who had, in fact, stopped swirling and was now sitting rather complacently beside Shamus. "I can *see* it's a dog," she huffed. "What's it doing here?"

"It kind of followed me."

"Followed you? Why would it do that?"

"Because I'm lovable?" proposed Shamus.

Carmela ignored his remark. "Followed you for how long?"

"The last few blocks," said Shamus.

"And you just *let* it?" said Carmela, a critical tone creeping into her voice. "Jeez Shamus, the poor thing probably belongs to someone. You probably lured it away from its neighborhood. From its home."

"No, I don't think so," said Shamus. "See, Poobah isn't even wearing a collar."

"Then how do you know the dog's name is Poobah?" asked Carmela, starting to get exasperated.

"Because I named him," said Shamus, looking pleased.

"You named him Poobah," said Carmela. *Obviously, Glory wasn't the only fruitcake in the family.*

Shamus reached down and rubbed the dog under its chin. "You're a good boy, aren't you, Poobah?" he crooned. "You're kind of a scratch-and-dent guy, but you've got a big heart."

Tail thumping like crazy, Poobah snuggled up against Shamus. Carmela rolled her eyes skyward.

"Bet you're hungry, too," said Shamus. He cast a meaningful gaze at Carmela. "This dog needs a decent meal."

"Take him to the Humane Society," advised Carmela. "I'm sure they'll be more than happy to feed him. Probably even help locate his owner. This dog could have an ID chip imbedded under his skin somewhere, you never know."

"I don't think so," said Shamus slowly. "He's clearly a stray." Shamus squinted at Carmela. "What if he stayed with you for a couple days?"

"No," said Carmela, always amazed by Shamus's extraordinary chutzpah. "No way. Take him home with *you*."

Shamus grimaced. "Can't. I'm staying with Glory right now. That sublet over by Audubon Park didn't work out."

In what struck Carmela as a bizarre coincidence, Shamus and the dog both seemed to be gazing at her with the same sad, befuddled looks on their faces. *Same limpid brown eyes, too. Damn.*

"Glory doesn't like dogs," continued Shamus. "But you do. In fact, you're the best person I know with dogs. You're kind . . . tender-hearted. Animals just naturally respond to you. They *love* you."

"What if he's got fleas?" asked Carmela, looking askance at Poobah. The poor guy really did look as though he'd logged some serious time on the mean streets of New Orleans. His fur was matted, one ear looked like it was partially ripped off. Her heart went out to him. "Boo could catch fleas from him," Carmela continued, trying to resist the little stray's charms.

Trying to resist Shamus's.

"I'll bet he's just fine," said Shamus.

"Boo is extremely fastidious," said Carmela. "It would just kill her if she got creepy-crawly fleas."

"Jeez, Carmela," laughed Shamus. "It's not like we're talking about a sexually transmitted disease or something. It's a few lousy fleas!"

"Still . . ." said Carmela.

"Tell you what," said Shamus. "I'll run out and buy a flea collar."

"And if Poobah lays claim to my furniture and *I* get fleas . . . ?"

"I'll buy two collars."

"Shamus . . ." said Carmela, a warning note sounding in her voice. "This is really a terrible idea."

"No, it's not," enthused Shamus. "It's a wonderful idea. This is a terrific little dog. A diamond in the rough. Plus, we'd be giving the poor fella a home."

"*We'd* be giving it a home?" said Carmela. She stared at Shamus. "No. *We're* not doing anything of the sort."

"Pleeease," he cajoled. "Everybody deserves a second chance."

Carmela stared at Poobah. The little dog gazed mournfully back at her, then cocked his head as if to say *Well, what about it? Like the song says, Should I stay or should I go?*

"Good lord," cried Carmela, throwing her hands helplessly in the air. "I'm a sucker . . . a pushover . . . a patsy!"

"You're a love," said Shamus, slipping an arm around her waist and pulling her toward him.

"Promise me you'll run an ad," said Carmela, savoring the way his body felt pressed up against her. "In the lost and found section of the *Times-Picayune*. Promise me you'll try to find this guy's owner."

"Of course I will," said Shamus. "You know I will. Have I ever let you down?"

Oh boy, thought Carmela. *Time to tattoo the word STUPID across my forehead in capital letters.*

Chapter 15

"I WOKE UP and looked in the mirror this morning," began Ava as she climbed into Carmela's Mercedes, "and was utterly shocked to see how awful my lips looked." She pulled down the passenger-side visor and squinted into that mirror. "Look," she cried unhappily. "My lips used to be all plump and full and now they're thin and wrinkled. I'm gettin' *turtle* lips!"

"No way," said Carmela, laughing. "Your lips and every other body part are still utterly gorgeous. In fact, you're the last person in the world who'd ever have to think about getting collagen injections or Botox or whatever the procedure du jour happens to be." Ava, who was not yet thirty, was drop-dead beautiful. No lines or crows feet had dared insinuate themselves on her face, and her lips were decidedly lush.

"You really think so?" queried Ava. "I still have my looks? To say nothing of my lips?"

"You're fine," Carmela assured her. "Now will you please fasten your seat belt so we can get going?"

"That's funny," said Ava. She was still squinting in the mirror and happened to catch the reflection of Boo and Poobah perched on the tiny shelf that served as a rudimentary back seat in Carmela's Mercedes. "Last time I looked you just had the one dog. Now I'm seeing two dogs squished into your back seat."

"Hey," said Carmela, popping the car into gear and squealing away from the curb. "Last time *I* looked I had one dog."

"Uh-oh, sounds like you found yourself some trouble with a capital T," said Ava as they shot down Barracks Street. "What happened?"

"Shamus happened," said Carmela.

Ava rolled her eyes. "Don't tell me . . ."

"Long story short," said Carmela, "he's a stray. Shamus found him. Or claims he did, anyway."

"Let me guess," said Ava, quickly sensing the gist of the story. "Shamus felt sorry for the dog, but in typical Shamus style he foisted the little mutt off on you. Jeez, Carmela, you're not gonna *keep* him, are you?"

"Of course not," said Carmela, wondering if Ava meant Shamus or the dog. And wondering, also, how to extricate herself from yet another Shamus-induced mess. Shamus obviously adored the poor stray, and Boo, the little traitor, had promptly adopted Poobah as her long-lost little brother.

"What's the dog's name?" asked Ava, scrunching around to get a better look at him.

"Poobah," answered Carmela. Upon hearing his name, Poobah was suddenly at full attention, tail wagging, nose quivering, brown eyes shining eagerly.

"Well, he's kinda cute," said Ava. "I like that furry, Muppet look. Except for that one ear that looks like it's about to fall off. Makes his head look all crooked and goofy."

Poobah, delighted to be the center of conversation, eagerly stuck his head over the back seat and licked Ava on the ear.

"Hey, watch it, fresh guy," she warned. "Those are very expensive chandelier earrings you're nuzzling!"

"You got new earrings?" asked Carmela.

Ava tossed her head and her oversized earrings twinkled and danced, catching the light provocatively. "Twelve ninety-nine at Wal-Mart," Ava told Carmela in a conspiratorial tone. "And believe me, honey, with romantic music and soft lighting, you can't tell the difference between these babies and the fancy schmancy Fred Leighton baubles Nicole Kidman wears on the red carpet."

"Works for me," said Carmela, whose jewelry budget these days was just as tight as Ava's.

"SO WHERE are we headed again?" asked Ava. They had entered Plaquemines Parish awhile back and just passed through Port Sulfur, one of the small towns strung along Highway 23.

"Boothville," said Carmela. For the last ten miles or so she'd regaled Ava with her recent discoveries involving Jamie Redmond, as well as all the various and sundry players who'd had walk-on parts in Jamie's life and whom she now deemed as suspects. In other words, Margot, Dunbar, and Blaine.

"You got weird things going on, suspects up the wazoo, and you still want to go lookin' for the graves of Jamie's folks?" asked Ava.

"Of course I do," said Carmela. "Wren had Jamie cremated, and she'd like to put him someplace."

"I suppose," said Ava. "But I know lots of folks who keep their loved ones close by instead of stickin' 'em in some grave or marble mausoleum."

"Kindly explain what you mean by 'close by,'" said Carmela.

"My Aunt Eulalie keeps her dear departed husband, Edgar, in a Chinese ginger jar on her nightstand," explained Ava. "Says it makes her feel like he's still with her. Except now he doesn't snore or hog the remote control. And this fella I used to work with, Carlos? He's got his mother's ashes in a coffee can under the sink. Says he's going to plant her next spring when he puts in new rose bushes."

"A double planting," said Carmela.

"Something like that," replied Ava, peering in the mirror again. "You know, *cher*," she said, frowning, then poking at the tiny wrinkle that formed between her eyes. "That blue car's been on our tail for the last few miles."

Mildly curious, Carmela glanced in her rearview mirror. "This is the only decent highway going south," she said. "He's probably headed down to Pilottown or the Delta Wildlife Refuge."

"Mmm," said Ava, settling back. "Probably."

There was no sign of a blue car when they pulled in to a roadside cafe for a bite of lunch.

"Big Eye Louie's," said Ava, as tires crunched across gravel. "Place looks awful."

"Doesn't it?" agreed Carmela. Big Eye Louie's was a battered, one-story wooden building that could have benefited greatly from a coat of paint. An overhang of rusty corrugated tin stuck out from just below the roof line to shield the front door and the large windows to either side of it.

"Which means we might just get ourselves a decent bowl of gumbo," Ava added gleefully.

"Or jambalaya," said Carmela. She was passionate about the rice-based dish that often featured spicy andouille sausage.

"Dogs okay in the car?" asked Ava.

But Carmela had already left the driver's-side window partially cracked and was making tracks for the front door of Big Eye Louie's.

Once inside, the roadside cafe was everything they expected it to be. Smoky, fairly crowded, hideously decorated. Men with red-and-white checked napkins tucked into their shirt fronts labored over steaming bowls of gumbo. Neon beer signs lent a crazy Times Square feel. Loud zydeco music pulsed from the jukebox. Stuffed possums, alligators, and fish hung overhead. The wooden walls were a veritable rogue's gallery of photos, sports pennants, team jerseys, and trophies. A big-screen TV dominated the back wall of the bar.

"The prototypical sports bar," murmured Ava. "Designed for the sporting gent with a lust for life and an urge to blast away at small animals."

They walked up to the bar where a tall, lean man with curly red hair and a handlebar mustache was briskly wiping glasses. "Help you?" he asked.

"Are you Big Eye Louie?" asked Ava.

"Might be," smiled the man, whose two front teeth were rimmed in gold. "You ladies interested in lunch?" He gave the bar in front of him a neat swipe with his rag, then quickly snapped down two paper place mats and fresh red-and-white checkered napkins. "We got turtle soup today—'the other white meat.' And it's on special."

"Is it really turtle?" asked Carmela. "Or alligator?" She knew that most turtle soups in Louisiana restaurants and cafes contained a good bit of alligator meat. There were over one hundred alligator farms in southern Louisiana, and alligator meat was big business.

The red handlebar mustache twitched faintly. "There's some of that in there, too," he allowed.

"You got gumbo?" Ava asked.

The bartender nodded. "Chef's partial to crawfish and a bit of okra."

"Good enough," said Ava as the two women slid onto barstools. "But I want a bowl, not just a cup."

Carmela opted for the hybrid turtle-alligator soup and they both ordered Dixie longnecks.

"We didn't miss the turn off for Boothville, did we?" Carmela asked, once big steaming bowls had been set in front of them.

"Another mile down," said the bartender. He smiled and slid a plate of hush puppies between them. "Compliments of the house."

Their respective lunches were steamy, hearty, and spicy. And Carmela and Ava soon fell into what Carmela called "the N'awlins feeding frenzy." In other words, the food was so good and hot and spicy that it actually prompted you to eat faster. Whatever the logic behind Carmela's feeding frenzy theory, they both finished their lunches in record time.

"My lips are on fire," remarked Ava. "They feel all puffy."

"That's good, right?" smiled Carmela.

"Yeah," said Ava, poking at one with a manicured finger. "I guess so. I never thought of cayenne and Tabasco as natural lip plumpers, but if they do the trick—great!"

Carmela paid the bill, leaving three single dollar bills on the bar. "You ever hear of a family by the name of Redmond who lived around these parts?" she asked the bartender, after he'd carefully folded the bills, tapped them on the bar in recognition, then slipped them into a glass jar that had a hand-lettered TIPS sign pasted on it.

The man thought for a moment. "Sounds familiar." He nodded toward the wall filled with framed photos. "Seems to me there was one or another Redmond who played football. You might check them pictures over yonder."

Carmela slipped off her barstool and walked over to the wall. She stood there a moment, studying the various photos. There were pictures of guys playing football, guys playing softball, guys hunting, guys fishing, guys cleaning fish.

Louisiana. Sportsman's paradise.

Carmela was halfway through the sportsman's rogues gallery when she found what she was looking for. A photo of one of Boothville High School's football teams.

And there was Jamie Redmond, in a somewhat younger incarnation, staring back at her.

"I think this is him," she called over to Ava.

"Yeah?" Ava slid off the barstool and sauntered across the room. Her mass of auburn hair, lithe sinewy figure, denim mini skirt, and leather jacket were almost too much for the men still sitting at tables.

They stared, gaped, and ogled.

In the silence that spun out, one man snapped the head off a crawfish and sucked the spicy juice. Loudly.

A chorus of *ooohs* rose from the table where he was sitting.

Ava tossed her head nonchalantly. "You *wish*," she sang out.

Which touched off a hearty spattering of applause for Ava.

"Time to go," announced Carmela. She hustled back to the bar, grabbing her denim jacket off the back of the stool.

"You ladies care for a slice of homemade bread pudding with brandy sauce?" offered the bartender, grinning stupidly at Ava. "It'd be compliments of the house."

Ava reached up and fingered a stuffed catfish that dangled overhead. "Thanks," she told him, "but I'm stuffed, too."

The bartender shook his head and grinned at her. "You're a real pistol, aren't you? Why don't y'all come back Saturday night? We got a live zydeko band that cranks up about nine o'clock." He winked at Ava. "We'd show you a real good time."

"Thanks," she said as they headed out the door. "Maybe we will."

"Now wasn't that an amusing little interlude," said Carmela. She pulled the car door open, caught the two dogs by their collars as they struggled to make a break for it, and unceremoniously stuffed them back in. "Vastly entertaining. And such scintillating conversation. With Noel Cowardtype *bon mots*."

"Oh you," laughed Ava. "They're just good old boys havin' fun."

"Maybe a little too much fun, if you ask me."

THEY STOPPED at the local library looking for information. An elderly gent with faded blue eyes and a "Friends of the Library" pin in the lapel of a too-large, slightly frayed blue suit, carefully informed them that the "regular librarians" were still out for lunch.

"What I'm after is a little information," Carmela told him.

He smiled at her politely.

"There was a man named Redmond who used to run a small printing shop in these parts," she began. "I know he and his wife passed on awhile ago, but I'm trying to find out where they're buried. Or perhaps where they once lived." She pulled out a black-and-white photo. "I think this was their house."

The old man pursed his lips and nodded slightly as he glanced at the photo. "I remember the family," he said in a soft voice. "Baptists, I believe." He reached for a pencil and a piece of paper and slowly began sketching a rudimentary map. "You'd want to look for them in this particular cemetery," he told her. With great precision he drew a criss-cross of streets, then placed an X in one area of the map.

"And the homestead?" said Carmela. "I understand the family lived out of town a ways. On Fordoche Road."

The old man bent over his map again. "Turn here," he told her, tapping his pencil. "Lidville Street to Fordoche. Then follow Fordoche, maybe ten miles out."

"You knew them?" Carmela asked. "The Redmonds?"

He gave a faint nod. Carmela couldn't figure out if the old man was trying to cover up for his forgetfulness or was just covering up.

"Anything you can tell me about them?" she asked. "About the family?"

The old man closed his eyes slowly and Carmela was reminded of an old turtle. "Don't like to speak ill of anyone," he told her as he slid his homemade map across the scarred counter to her.

"What was that all about?" asked Ava, once they were back in the car.

"I have no idea," said Carmela.

"Seemed like he wanted to say more, but was too polite," said Ava.

"Seemed to me he was being awfully careful," replied Carmela.

Chapter 16

THE CEMETERY WAS, no pun intended, a dead end. There was no marble gravestone with the name Redmond carved into it, no family marker, no caretaker nearby to query.

They had split into two teams—Carmela with Poobah on a leash, and Ava with Boo—and walked the rows of tombstones for the better part of an hour. But they'd found nothing. The results were disappointing, to say the least.

"At least the dogs got to stretch their legs," said Ava, noticing the glum expression on Carmela's face.

"Us, too," said Carmela.

"We goin' to the house, then?" asked Ava. They had gravitated to a large memorial commemorating all the veterans who'd fought in this country's wars, both foreign and domestic. "That is, if the house is still there."

"We've come all this way," said Carmela. "It'd be a shame to quit now."

Bumping down Fordoche Road, following the map the old man at the library had sketched, Carmela was struck by the raw beauty of the area. On either side of what seemed more like a dike built to keep the bayou at bay than a road were great expanses of brackish water, punctuated by mangrove trees and towering, bald cypress. This was the realm of egrets, herons, ibis, and cormorants. Where the American alligator was most at home, too. The one also dubbed the Mississippi alligator, pike-headed alligator, or just "gator." Whatever the moniker, this contemporary cousin of the dinosaur garnered a good share of respect.

"It's kinda spooky," said Ava. Poobah had wormed his way from the back seat into the front and was now firmly ensconced in Ava's lap. Boo, happy to have the entire back seat to herself, looked on approvingly.

"I truly do love it down here," said Carmela. "Lots of folks get all fidgety and nervous about bayous. They find them haunting and dangerous. But I think they're incredibly beautiful and mysterious."

"Everything's so soggy," said Ava, peering out the window. "I guess I'm more of a dry land gal."

"Are you kidding?" said Carmela. "Of the three hundred sixty-something square miles that make up greater New Orleans, half of that is water."

"Good heavens," exclaimed Ava. "Half? That much, really? Well, I still prefer the dryer things in life. Dry land, dry martinis . . ." She thought for a few seconds. "Dry cleaning."

The sun peeped out from behind high puffy clouds and suddenly illuminated the entire bayou. Greens became brighter and more intense, water riffled by breezes suddenly sparkled like jewels, tendrils of Spanish moss swung gently. Two large heron, both with heroic wingspans, swooped gracefully in front of the car, then settled near a stand of swamp grass.

"Gonna be a nice day after all," said Carmela, feeling upbeat. She had a good feeling about this little trip. She felt sure they'd obtain some sort of resolution. Or new information, at the very least.

Jamie Redmond's home was instantly recognizable from the photographs Carmela had brought along. Though not quite as rustic as a traditional bayou camp house, the two-story building still had that same hunkered down, home-sawed look. Only now, of course, the place was deserted and half falling down.

The front door hung on a single hinge, the little overhang that had sheltered it had tumbled down. Every window pane was broken or gone. Exterior paint had long since been eaten away by heat and unbelievable humidity, beaten away by rain. Pared down to bare wood, the house was a not unattractive silvered gray.

Carmela wondered who owned this property now. Was the title still in Jamie Redmond's name? Or had someone purchased it years ago and maybe just used the land for hunting and fishing? She decided that was something else she might have to look into.

"This is very creepy," said Ava. "Kinda like that old farmhouse in *The Texas Chainsaw Massacre*." She rolled her eyes, ever the devotee of horror flicks. "And you know what happened *there*," she added.

"This isn't Texas and I'll venture to say nobody's fired up a chainsaw around here in years," said Carmela.

"The place does seem a tad overgrown," commented Ava.

Ava's words were a complete understatement. Perched on the edge of a pond, the outbuildings were practically shrouded in kudzu. Mangroves had taken over where the yard had been.

"Look-it," said Ava as they finally climbed out of the car. "Alligators."

Way out in the middle of the pond, a half-dozen little rough humps stuck up out of the water. To the untrained eye they looked like half-sunken logs. Or rocks. But Carmela and Ava knew better. Those were the tell-tale backs of alligators.

Once hunted to the point of endangerment, alligators had made a nice recovery. The hunting season in Louisiana was now just one month long, the month of September. And many commercial alligator farms were required to return up to seventeen percent of their juvenile alligators back to the wild. So the snaggle-toothed *lagato* enjoyed a robust population.

"They won't bother us," said Carmela, "as long as we're active and moving around. But we'll keep the dogs in the car just to be safe."

"So what do you want to do?" asked Ava. "Just snoop? Check the place out and see what we can see?"

"Sounds like a plan to me," said Carmela. "What if I looked inside the house and you took a stroll around the outbuildings?"

"Sure," said Ava. "But be careful. That old place looks like a stiff breeze could bring it crashing down around you."

"Don't worry," said Carmela, heading for the main house. "I'll tread lightly."

DUCKING UNDER fallen boards, Carmela clambered over the front porch and stepped through what was left of the front door.

"Hello," she called out, even though she knew no one was there.

Gazing around, Carmela's first impression was that the place looked like a *Wizard of Oz* house. A house that had been ripped from its foundation, spun around inside an F-6 tornado a few hundred times, then slammed back down to earth. Broken furniture lay everywhere, old pictures hung catty-wampus on walls, plaster had crumbled off to reveal lath board and, in some places, interior wiring.

Ava's right. This place is spooky and looks like it could collapse at any moment.

Glass crunched underfoot as Carmela moved through what must have been the front room, the parlor, and into the kitchen.

There wasn't much left. Wooden cupboards had long since been torn from the walls and pitched outside. Carmela could see what was left of them lying in the overgrown backyard. Twisted black wires, the old connections for an oven that no longer existed, poked from the wall. A sink, rusty and dirty and piled with dust-coated dishes, was the only thing left.

What happened here? wondered Carmela. *When the Redmonds died, was this house rented out to tenants who just let it go? Or was it put on the housing market where it just languished?*

The notion of a house that had once hummed with people and their things, had once been cozy and secure, and then had fallen into utter disrepair, was depressing. Someone had probably hung curtains here once. Had lovingly prepared meals. Had mopped floors and polished wood. Had read books, played music, sang their child to sleep.

Carmela wandered back toward the parlor and carefully made her way up a narrow flight of steps. The upstairs was small and in slightly better condition. Two small bedrooms, a bathroom, and a storage closet occupied this floor. Peeking into one of the bedrooms, Carmela was startled to see what looked like an old sleeping bag.

Or is it just a pile of rags?

She tiptoed in. Well, it was *something*. Maybe a dirty old comforter that had been scrunched up.

Has someone been sleeping up here?

It was certainly possible. And the notion of someone hiding out here gave her a serious case of the creeps.

Time to go. Check around outside, see if I can find a family plot or something.

Descending the stairs, she heard a noise, a faint scuttle, on the front porch. *Ava?*

Bending low as she ducked through the front door, trying to avoid shattered wood and splinters, Carmela was intent on making a fast exit. But as she began to straighten up, her head ran smack dab into a very hard, immovable object. *Whack!*

The blow rocked Carmela's entire being and sent her crumpling to her knees. Still wondering what had happened, not comprehending that she'd just been hit, Carmela uttered a lone groan as she struggled to her feet. She took three, maybe four stumbling steps and then she was falling, falling, falling and the lights winked out.

Minutes later, she was aware of warm sunshine on her face and a buzzing, a terrible reeling in her head. But to move, to actually move, would require an act of sheer heroism.

Ava, where are you? Help me. Something happened. I whacked my head or somebody whacked it for me.

Slowly, like a diver coming up for air, Carmela began to regain consciousness. Struggling mightily, Carmela pushed herself up on one arm. Sunlight glinted off the nearby pond. A gentle breeze riffled her hair. And the alligators, the humpy bumpy alligators that had been way out in the middle of the pond, seemed strangely closer.

Alligators? Are they really there or am I just seeing things? Oh, lord, my head aches.

Carmela closed her eyes and fell back. The pounding in her head was making her almost physically ill, and she had to suck in air quickly to avoid getting dry heaves.

She lay there panting for a few minutes until she was finally able to get a grip on things. But when Carmela finally opened her eyes a second time, they were immediately drawn to the alligators. The humps of their backs were more defined, eyes and snouts protruded just above the surface of the water. They had definitely moved in closer! And this time Carmela understood that they were very, very real!

Got to get out of here! Got to haul ass!

Carmela knew she had to move, but her brain still kept going fuzzy. She could clearly hear Boo and probably Poobah barking off in the background somewhere, but the synapses still weren't firing properly.

Then she was aware of footsteps nearby and a sharp cry of alarm. And warm hands quickly encircling her shoulders.

Ava. Dear, dear Ava.

"Get up!" screamed Ava. "Now! Those damn gators have got you in their sites!" She grabbed one of Carmela's arms and tugged hard. "Holy shit, Carmela, they've moved in at least fifty feet! I think they're still coming!"

Carmela fought for consciousness even as she struggled to her feet. Ava charged a few steps forward, cartwheeling her arms and letting out whoops and hoots that would have been worthy of one of Jean Lafitte's pirates.

"Heeyoo! Get away, gators! Shoo, you ugly buggers!"

The alligators seemed to hesitate a moment, trying to decide what to do. Then they slowly slid backward in the water, their powerful feet and tails acting as silent-running reverse motors. In the alligator universe, anything taller and larger than they were wasn't usually worth the tussle.

Ava came circling back to help Carmela. "Did you fall?" she babbled. "Did you hit your head?"

"Not sure," said Carmela, tentatively. "Somebody could've whacked me one."

"I thought I heard a car," said Ava. "I was walking down this path through the woods 'cause I thought it might lead to a family plot or something. Anyway, I heard it and I thought you might be leaving! I got panicky!"

"I heard someone outside," said Carmela, "and thought it was you!"

"I *knew* that blue car was following us," Ava fumed. "I had a bad *feeling*. Damn, if it turns out to be that weird Margot person, I'm gonna kick her skinny butt from here to next Tuesday."

"What if it was Dunbar? Or Blaine?" asked Carmela. Ava was still pulling her and half carrying her toward the car.

"One thing you should know about me," said Ava fiercely. "I'm an equal opportunity ass-kicker." She looked at Carmela closely and her eyes suddenly teared up. "You're really hurt, aren't you?"

"Don't know," said Carmela, still struggling to walk on her own. Ava let go and Carmela tottered a few steps, stopped, then reached a hand up to gingerly touch the back of her head. She winced. There was an enormous bump that felt like it was growing rapidly larger with each passing second.

"Do you need stitches?" Ava asked as she led Carmela to an old tree stump and eased her down into a sitting position. "Ooh, jeez. It looks like you got bonked pretty hard," she said as she gently parted Carmela's hair.

"It hurts like hell," groaned Carmela, trying to pull away.

"Shush," said Ava. "Keep still and let me take a look."

Carmela finally held still and let Ava inspect her aching head.

"No gash or nothin', *cher*," said Ava. "But you've got a bump the size of a golf ball. You're gonna have a killer headache."

"I already do," said Carmela.

"We better stop and get a can of Coke."

"I don't think I could swallow a drop," protested Carmela. "I still feel woozy and sick to my stomach."

"Not to drink," said Ava, helping Carmela back up and over toward the passenger side of the car. "To hold against your poor little head."

Chapter 17

THREE SQUARES OF melted chocolate formed a rich, dark puddle in the bottom of the sauce pan, as Ava stirred in water, watched the mixture thicken and bubble, then whisked in the rest of her ingredients. When the hot chocolate concoction was perfect, Ava poured a frothy serving into a large ceramic mug and carried it in to Carmela, who was holed up in the bathroom taking an extended hot shower.

"I'm gonna set this on the counter here," Ava told her as she stepped into the warm, steamed-up bathroom.

Carmela's head poked out from behind the shower curtain and billows of steam poured out. "Set what?"

"This cup of bubbling brown sugar hot chocolate," Ava told her.

"What?" squawked Carmela. "You told me you couldn't cook! You told me you never cooked!"

"Making hot chocolate doesn't qualify as cooking," said Ava, squinting at the fogged-up mirror. "It's more like whipping up a little comfort." She paused. "Do I look like I'm gettin' a pimple? Sure I am! I had a teeny little bump this morning and now it's glowing like a tiki torch!"

"Your face looks fine," said Carmela as she reached out, grabbed the mug, and took a sip. The hot chocolate was rich and creamy and redolent with brown sugar. Even with her hair streaming down in wet tendrils and her face sans makeup, Carmela suddenly looked like she was in seventh heaven. "This is delicious!" she exclaimed.

"Of course it is," said Ava. "But I have to tell you, I pretty much follow Sweetmomma Pam's recipe. So it's really her creation, not mine."

"Whatever magic you worked, it's fantastic," said Carmela.

Pulling open the door to Carmela's medicine cabinet, Ava rummaged around and eventually came up with a bottle of Motrin. "No witch hazel or nothin' for my face, huh? Too bad." She snapped the cap off the Motrin and shook out one of the orange tablets into her hand. "Take this," she instructed Carmela as she held the tablet out to the shower curtain.

Carmela's hand came out and grabbed the tablet. She popped it into her mouth and took a follow-up sip of cocoa. "This drink is so *good*," she declared again.

"Good is when we get that nasty bump on your head knocked down a little more," said Ava. "I sure hope your poor brain didn't get all jiggled around inside your skull."

Ducking back under the shower spray, Carmela said: "My brain's been jiggled for years. Why else would I have married Shamus Allan Meechum?"

"Good point," said Ava. "And don't stay in there too long. Looks like your wallpaper's starting to peel. Which could be a serendipitous thing, since you haven't done a lick of decorating for almost two whole months."

Ten minutes later, Carmela emerged from her bathroom wrapped in a white terry cloth bathrobe and smelling of lavender soap. She looked scrubbed, rested, and considerably more relaxed. "Something smells good," she said.

"That something is dinner," Ava told her.

"Now I know I've died and gone to heaven," said Carmela, plopping down at the table where Ava had arranged two place settings and a small array of twinkling votive candles.

"Now don't go gettin' all moony on me," warned Ava. "Because I didn't fix much. Just a little soup."

"You made soup?" Ava never made anything. She either chugged a can of Slim Fast, grabbed takeout, or ate in a restaurant. There was no in between. Certainly no actual *cooking*.

"Pull yourself together and take a closer look at me," said Ava. "Do I look like a fat little Italian granny? Hell no. It's *canned* soup, Carmela. Minestrone. So don't make a big thing of it, okay?"

Carmela smiled. "Okay. But it sure smells good."

"That's because I added a few spices along with some grated cheese and a splash of red wine. Oh, and I ran across the courtyard to my place and grabbed a few extra ingredients. So we're also having bruschetta."

"I love bruschetta," said Carmela as Ava ladled out soup.

"So do those dogs," said Ava.

"Oh, the dogs!" said Carmela, about to jump up. "I didn't feed the dogs!"

"Already taken care of," said Ava. "I gave 'em some of those kibble bits and they went face down like a couple of professional chow hounds."

"That's cause they are," said Carmela. A stock broker friend of Carmela's had once told her that one of the stepping stones to wealth was to never own anything that needed to be fed. And now she had *two* dogs slopping around in her kitchen. Oh well.

Over steaming bowls of minestrone soup and crusty slabs of bruschetta, Carmela and Ava rehashed the afternoon.

"What do you think really happened out there, *cher*?" asked Ava. "Did you just smack your head on one of those tumbled-down timbers or did somebody club you? Somebody who thought you might be gettin' in the way. Doing a little too much investigating."

Carmela nibbled at her bruschetta. It was garlicy and cheesy and smothered with bits of chopped tomato drizzled with olive oil. Fantastic.

"That blue car that you saw earlier," said Carmela. "Who drives a blue car?"

"Aha," said Ava. "Told you so. I thought some yahoo was following us."

"The question is, which yahoo and why?" said Carmela.

"Don't know," said Ava. "But it sure looks like somebody might have been checkin' us out. Trying to figure out what we were doing. Or, if we really want to stretch the bounds of paranoia, trying to *stop* us."

"Maybe," said Carmela. She took another bite of bruschetta, wiped a dribble of olive oil from her chin. "But try this on for size. What if somebody was *looking* for something out there?" Still fresh in Carmela's mind was the nagging feeling that someone had been prowling about Biblios Booksellers yesterday. Looking for something there, too.

"Do you think it was the same somebody who wanted us out of Jamie's house last Friday night?" asked Ava. "When that damn snake just happened to make a guest appearance?"

"Maybe," replied Carmela.

"So . . . this person," said Ava, "and I'd have to say he or she is a very *dangerous* person . . . what are they looking for?"

"Search me," said Carmela. "But it feels like I'm starting to get a slightly clearer picture of what's going on."

"Then kindly tell me what's going on," said Ava. "Because nothing's clear as far as I'm concerned."

"What if Jamie Redmond had something very valuable in his possession?" proposed Carmela.

Ava considered this. "Like what?"

"Don't know," said Carmela. "But it must be something valuable enough to kill for."

Ava frowned. "Whatever it is, they obviously *didn't* get it when they killed Jamie."

"Let me show you something," said Carmela. She got up from the table, found the file with the photos and news clipping about the Bogus Creek Boys, then handed it over to Ava. "Take a look at this."

Ava quickly scanned the clipping. "Right," she said. "You mentioned some of this before. Kind of a shocker for Wren, huh?"

"She was stunned," said Carmela.

"So . . . what are you thinking?" asked Ava. "You think Jamie's got money stashed away somewhere? Counterfeit money?"

"The thought had crossed my mind," said Carmela. "His family was in the printing business."

"And someone knows about this money," said Ava, catching on. "And is looking for it."

"What else could it be?" asked Carmela.

"I have no idea," said Ava. "But now the actions of certain suspects start to make a little more sense."

"Explain," said Carmela, gesturing with her fingers.

"Well, you told me that Dunbar DesLauriers was hot to trot about buying the bookstore from Wren. Why would that be?"

"Because he thinks there's a pile of counterfeit money stashed inside?" answered Carmela.

"Bingo," said Ava. "Cold cash, hot moola, the mother lode."

"But Blaine Taylor doesn't come off looking completely innocent in all this, either," said Carmela. "He was Jamie's business partner in Neutron Software and he's the one who's been oh-so-solicitous to Wren. Offering to help her wherever he can."

"Right," said Ava. "Trying to get close to her. Or close to Jamie's stash, if there is one. Plus, Blaine just happened to pop up right after the snake incident."

"But if this mythical funny money is so important to Blaine, why is he trying to cut Wren out of the Neutron sale, if there ends up being a sale?" asked Carmela. "Doesn't that just draw the wrong kind of attention to him?"

Ava shrugged. "I have no idea. Maybe Dunbar and Blaine are in cahoots."

"Doesn't feel right," said Carmela. She sat there thinking, as rain began to patter down on the roof. "Rats. It's starting to rain."

"It's been threatening to for the last hour," said Ava. She leaned forward, flipped her hair forward, then straightened up and let it settle about her shoulders, suddenly looking like a beauty in a Pre-Raphaelite painting. "What about this Margot Butler? You're the one who thought she was acting so kooky."

"She was . . . is," said Carmela. "Then again, Margot may just be a genuine kook."

"It's not like New Orleans is immune to people with personality disorders," said Ava. "In fact, sometimes I think we're a big fat magnet for them."

"Amen," said Carmela, thinking immediately of Shamus and his nutty family. They were about as dysfunctional as any group could hope to be.

Ava tapped a fingernail against the file folder Carmela had given her. "This is pretty interesting stuff."

"There's more," said Carmela. "I went back to Biblios last night and unearthed another file folder. I just haven't gotten around to looking at everything yet. The contents were in pretty tough shape. All gunked together because of mildew and water damage."

"Well," said Ava. "*You're* supposed to be the expert when it comes to paper restoration and photo conservation, aren't you?" She jumped up to clear the table. "So let's get busy and see what little tricks you can work to remedy the situation."

"Okay," said Carmela, jumping up, too, and heading for the kitchen.

"I'll clear," said Ava as Carmela pulled open the freezer door. "Got a hankering for ice cream, do you?"

"No," said Carmela. "This is where I put the contents of that folder."

"You're kidding," said Ava. "You froze it for safe keeping? Is that kind of like hiding your diamonds in the icebox?"

"Not quite," said Carmela. She pulled out a square tray that held an inch-thick pile of photos and papers. "Freezing wet paper makes it a lot easier to separate."

"Do tell," said Ava, intrigued. "You certainly come up with the darndest things." She followed Carmela to the table, then sat down and watched as Carmela slid a thin steak knife into the top of the pile and pried very gently. Like magic, the top few papers released themselves from the bottom pile.

"Amazing," said Ava. "I would have steamed everything."

"Steaming paper just makes it wet and gloppy," said Carmela. "And it can actually cause paper to disintegrate. But freezing dries papers out. The moisture turns into ice crystals so everything can be easily separated. Well, *sort of* separated. She inserted her knife and pried another few papers loose.

"Now what?" asked Ava.

"Now we separate them again and try to dry them," said Carmela.

The two women worked diligently for several minutes until finally they had a half-dozen photos and five pieces of paper spread out on the dining-room table.

"This one's still folded in half," Ava told her, plucking at it with her fingertips.

"Are you always this impatient?" asked Carmela.

"Always," said Ava. "I'm an instant gratification kind of gal. I like instant coffee, minute rice, and pop-top pudding. When I want something, I want it *now*."

"Then take the bone folder and try and work it in there," Carmela instructed. "If you can get it open, I'll hit it with a shot of archival spray."

"It's working!" exclaimed Ava as she worked the bone folder in and loosened the folded paper. Then, ever so gently, she flipped it open.

"Well done," said Carmela as she went over to the sink to rinse her hands.

Sitting at the table, head bent low over the still-wet piece of paper, Ava studied the sheet intently. "It's a news story," Ava told her.

"From the *Times-Picayune*?"

"Not sure," replied Ava. "There's no newspaper masthead or anything like that."

"What's it about?" asked Carmela.

Ava was hurriedly scanning the story. "Some party that apparently got out of hand."

"Uh huh," said Carmela. Nothing weird there. Lots of parties in New Orleans got out of hand. Especially during Mardi Gras.

"Uh-oh. Guess who's the star of this little article," said Ava, with a note of triumph in her voice.

"Surprise me," said Carmela. Although she didn't think she would be.

"Blaine Taylor," chortled Ava. "Apparently, as a result of rowdy goings-on, old B.T. was arraigned on charges of assault and battery."

Carmela came around to the table and stood next to Ava, drying her hands. "So Blaine Taylor's a regular bad boy, too."

"Looks like," said Ava. "Do you think that's why he and Jamie ended up as business partners in that computer software thing?"

Carmela frowned. Interesting thought. Perhaps theirs *was* a case of two bad boys finding each other. Two rotten eggs who'd connected on a visceral level and then just naturally sought each other out on a business level.

"It's a thought," Carmela told her. "On the other hand, Blaine's bad boy escapades might help explain why he was trying to claim Neutron Software as his own."

"You mean Blaine's a cheat and a jerk and his true character is just shining through?"

"Something like that," said Carmela.

"Do you think Blaine Taylor could have been one of the Bogus Creek Boys?" asked Ava.

"He wasn't mentioned in the article," said Carmela.

"Maybe the authorities just didn't catch him," said Ava. "Or Blaine was what you'd call a silent partner."

"Maybe," allowed Carmela. "Maybe."

TWO HOURS later, a slew of unanswered questions still buzzed like angry bees inside Carmela's head. Ava had cleaned up the kitchen, then slipped out the door and dashed across the courtyard as Carmela drifted off to sleep in her leather chair. Around 9:00 PM Carmela woke up feeling groggy and sore and more than a little discombobulated. Rain was still drumming down on the roof and there was the rumble of thunder off in the distance.

Struggling out of the chair, Carmela padded into the kitchen, figuring a glass of water and another Motrin might be in order. Ava had put the bottle on the kitchen counter so she'd have easy access to it. Plus, she needed to climb into bed, where she could get some proper rest and log some serious REM time.

As Carmela waited for the water to get cold, which always seemed to take an eternity, she noted that Boo and Poobah were snuggled together, muzzle to muzzle, on Boo's comfy L.L. Bean bed. She hoped Boo wasn't getting too attached to the little guy, because there was no way he was going to stay.

Boo attached? What am I thinking? Shamus is the one who's ga-ga over the little stray. But, naturally, I'm the one who's taking care of little Poobah. Or, better yet, I'm the one who was taken in.

Carmela swallowed her pill, downed half a glass of water, and headed for the bedroom. As she passed the dining-room table, a spill of light from the kitchen cast a faint glow, causing her eyes to be naturally drawn there. Drawn toward the articles that had been laid out to dry.

Carmela hesitated. *Had Blaine Taylor been one of the Bogus Creek Boys?* she wondered. No, she didn't think so.

She didn't think Blaine was completely innocent. But was he a murderer? A cold-blooded killer?

Not enough to go on yet. Not enough evidence to make any sort of accusation stick.

The tips of her fingers hovered above the photos and articles that lay there. One photo of Jamie that they'd found—maybe even his graduation picture, since he was neatly dressed in a suit and tie—caught at her heart. He looked so young, so eager, so innocent.

Almost like he had the night of the prenuptial dinner, Carmela decided. The night he was murdered. When he'd looked happy and eager to start a new life with Wren. And very much in love.

A sudden crack of thunder and bright flash of lightning caused Carmela to jump.

Yeeow! That's positively cataclysmic!

Feeling foolish, knowing it was just positive and negative charges cast off from the storm's roiling clouds, Carmela glanced out the window, wondering if Ava had been shaken by nature's heroic display, too.

But what she saw silhouetted in the window rocked her back on her heels!

What the . . . ?

Three more pulses of lightning strobed in rapid succession.

It can't be!

Racing to the window, Carmela pressed her face to the glass and peered into the courtyard. Because just for a flash, just for an instant, she thought she'd seen Jamie Redmond's face at her window!

But I couldn't have, could I?

Nervously, Carmela scanned the dark courtyard, but it was empty. Just rain pounding down on flagstones, pots of drooping bougainvilleas, and a fountain that bubbled furiously even as it filled to capacity.

Pulling herself away from the window, shaking from the tiny shot of adrenaline that had insinuated itself into her nervous system, Carmela told herself she'd seen some kind of optical illusion.

Of course it was. Don't be silly. Don't get all weird.

Had to be her retina picking up the image of Jamie from the photo, then projecting it in her brain. So it caused the *illusion* of seeing him silhouetted in the window.

Just my eyes playing tricks on me.

After all, there was no other logical explanation.

But even after Carmela crawled into bed and settled under her down comforter, it was a good long time before sleep came to carry her away.

Chapter 18

"YOU DIDN'T FIND anything?" asked Gabby. The rainstorm had continued through the night and into the morning, burbling down drain pipes, swirling in gutters and storm sewers, and, in general, snarling up city traffic. Which seemed to set the tone for the day.

Carmela shook her head. "Nothing. Sorry." She debated telling Gabby about the conk on the head she'd received, but decided not to. Things were getting decidedly stranger and there was no reason to panic her.

"And you for sure checked the Boothville Cemetery?" Gabby asked.

"Ava and I walked every row," Carmela assured her, "and found nothing."

Gabby drummed her fingertips on the front counter and gazed toward the back of the store where Wren was showing a customer how to use a template to create a miniature shopping bag. "What are you going to tell Wren?"

"That we tried," replied Carmela. "Which we did. Truly." Carmela sighed. She felt like she'd let Gabby down. She hadn't meant to, of course. It was just that the Redmonds must be buried somewhere else.

"Thank you, Carmela," said Gabby finally. "You took a day off work to do this and here I am being a sourpuss. Sorry."

"No problem," said Carmela, although she appreciated the apology.

"And with this rain pouring down, I can't imagine we're going to be busy today." Gabby shook her head. "There's enough coming down out there to turn Canal Street into a real canal."

"Actually," said Carmela, "I could use a catch-up day."

"Scrapbooks for Gilt Trip?" asked Gabby. She knew that Carmela's life was perpetually over-booked.

Carmela nodded. "Even though you backed Margot off on the deadline, I still have to get them done."

"Today's the deadline," said Gabby.

Carmela shrugged. "I know. But tomorrow's going to have to do."

"Carmela," said Wren as Carmela drifted toward the back of the store. "Can I talk to you?"

Carmela held up a finger. "Hang on a minute, will you?" She wanted to check in with Lieutenant Edgar Babcock. He was her conduit in the New Orleans Police Department, and she wanted to see if they were any closer to naming a suspect or perhaps even making an arrest.

They weren't.

Lieutenant Babcock was sympathetic, courteous, and sincere, all the things Boy Scouts are supposed to be, but he also seemed profoundly down when it came to talking about the case.

"Nothing," he said in a tone that made no bones about the fact that he was disheartened. Not with Carmela. But with the lack of progress.

"We thought for sure you'd be hot on the trail of *someone* by now," said Carmela. She didn't want to come down too hard on Lieutenant Babcock or his colleagues. Criticism and negative pronouncements had a way of discouraging people.

"Jimmy . . . Detective Rawlings . . . and the other officers have gone back and talked to the kitchen employees a half-dozen times," Lieutenant Babcock told her. "And they all tell the same story: Bon Tiempe was a madhouse that night. There were new people being trained in, a *saucier* got fired, several late deliveries were made."

"Your people checked on these deliveries?" asked Carmela.

"Sure did. As I recall, one was from Vincent's Wine Shop, another from Le Fleur; a florist shop, I'd guess. And the third was . . . ah, I'd have to check the case file."

"But nothing," said Carmela. "Nothing out of the ordinary."

"Oh, there's gotta be something," said Lieutenant Babcock. "Or, rather, some*one*. It's just that nobody's pinned him down yet."

"What about the murder weapon?" asked Carmela. It had, after all, been a kitchen knife. Which would seem to indicate a weapon of convenience, grabbed from a drawer or a knife rack in Bon Tiempe's sprawling kitchen.

"We're still looking at that," said Lieutenant Babcock.

Carmela debated telling Lieutenant Babcock about her trip down to Boothville yesterday. About the blue car that had seemed to follow them. And the nasty conk on the head she'd received. But she didn't want Lieutenant Babcock coming down hard on her. Telling her to stay the hell out of the investigation. She was too far in and wanted to see this through to the end. For her own sake as well as Gabby's and Wren's.

"Say," said Lieutenant Babcock, "your friend is still around, right?"

Carmela knew he was referring to Ava. "You mean Ava?"

"That's the one." A silence spun out. "Do you happen to know if she's seeing anyone?"

What to tell him? Ava dated a lot.

"I don't believe she's seeing any *one person* in particular," said Carmela. There. That answer was technically correct.

"Think she'd go out with me?" asked Lieutenant Babcock.

"Why don't you give her a call and find out?" said Carmela. And then, because she thought her answer might sound a trifle flip, she added: "I'm sure she'd love to go out with you."

"Okay, then," said Lieutenant Babcock. "Thanks."

"You'll let us know," said Carmela. "The minute you have something?"

"Count on it," Lieutenant Babcock assured her.

Hanging up the phone, Carmela stared down at the photos and fabric scraps that were sitting on her desk. All stuff to go into the Happy Halls scrapbook for Pamela and Dunbar DesLauriers. She didn't have much of a stomach for completing the scrapbook right now. But a promise was a promise and the Gilt Trip promotion *was* a fund-raiser for the crisis nursery. So . . . she knew it was best to get on with things and focus on the end result, which was a very positive thing. And *not* worry about Margot Butler and her petty posturings. Or Pamela Dunbar and her delusions of grandeur. Still, it was difficult. And maddening, too.

Carmela's phone gave off a single ring and she snatched it up.

"Memory Mine. This is Carmela."

"Good morning," came a carefully modulated voice. "This is Ross Pitot at the Selby Pitot Funeral Home."

"Oh," said Carmela. She *really* wasn't expecting this call.

"Is Miss Wren West available?"

"She's here," said Carmela, "but she's with a customer." This time Wren really was with a customer.

"Perhaps I could call back," said Ross Pitot. "If there's a time . . ."

"This is about Jamie, right?" said Carmela. She paused. "Jamie Redmond. You handled the cremation?"

"That's correct," said Ross Pitot. "And you are . . ."

"I'm Carmela Bertrand. I'm a friend of Wren's. I know the police released Jamie's body a couple days ago, so I'm assuming you have since handled the . . . ah . . . cremation and that Jamie's ashes are ready to be picked up."

"Yes ma'am," said Ross Pitot in a somber voice. "That's exactly why I was calling. The cremains are ready for whatever final disposition Miss West has in mind."

Cremains. What a strange, made-up word, thought Carmela. *Almost clinical sounding. But very final, too.*

"Wren . . . Miss West . . . is still a little upset," said Carmela. "Obviously. But we will be by to pick up the . . . cremains." Carmela grimaced. "I assume there's no immediate rush?"

"Good heavens, no," Ross Pitot assured her. "No hurry at all. Mr. Redmond's cremains are really quite fine here. Tell Miss West to take her time. No problem."

"Thank you," said Carmela. "I'll relay that to her." *I just have to work up my nerve first.*

But Wren seemed to know.

"That was a call about Jamie, wasn't it?" she asked Carmela. Wren was pulling out sheets of sports-themed paper for Tandy and had a stack of photos on the table next to her. "I was going to work on that scrapbook about him," she explained to Carmela, indicating some of the photos of Jamie they'd found at his house. "Over the lunch hour."

"Do it now," said Carmela, suddenly flashing on the image she saw—or thought she saw—in her window last night. *My eyes were just playing tricks on me,* she told herself.

"Are you sure?" said Wren. Carmela didn't seem to be listening, so she said, "Carmela?"

Carmela suddenly snapped out of her strange reverie. "We're not particularly busy," she told Wren. "And you and Gabby did a phenomenal amount of straightening up yesterday, so . . . go ahead." She glanced at the stack of photos with the portrait of Jamie sitting on top. "We just got some new leatherette albums in. One of those might work nicely for what you've got in mind."

Wren gave her a shy smile. "Thank you. And hopefully you'll give me a few pointers, too." She paused. "That call *was* about Jamie, wasn't it? I kind of overheard some of it. I guess his ashes are ready."

Carmela nodded slowly. "You're right, they are. But the fellow at Selby Pitot said there was no hurry."

Wren chewed her lip. "I want to apologize for sending you and Ava on such a wild goose chase yesterday. For some reason, I was sure his parents were buried down in Boothville."

"Not a problem," said Carmela. "I'm just sorry Ava and I didn't find anything." Carmela surreptitiously rubbed the bump on the back of her head. She hadn't found anything, but trouble seemed to have found them.

"Well, if there's no hurry . . ." said Wren. Again Carmela had a strange faraway look in her eyes. But then she was smiling and back to her usual self.

"Don't worry," Carmela told her. "We'll find his parents' grave. It's only a matter of time."

* * *

"GOOD LORD," said Tandy, sliding her red cheaters onto her bony nose. "You've completely covered that page with the most marvelous chintz fabric. I've never seen you do that before."

"That's because I've never done it before," admitted Carmela. "But this is one of the scrapbooks for Gilt Trip, so I really wanted to make a bold design statement."

"You certainly did," said Tandy. "In fact, the end result is pretty fabulous."

"Actually, this isn't quite finished," said Carmela. "I'm about ready to zip down the street to Gossamer & Grosgrain and borrow one of their sewing machines for a few minutes." Gossamer & Grosgrain was the premier fabric and needlecraft shop in the French Quarter. They specialized in elegant silks, damasks, organzas, and satins. And they carried an exemplary array of Venetian point lace and duchesse lace.

"You're going to stitch . . . what?" asked Tandy. Tandy was big on details. In fact, Tandy *demanded* details.

"The whole page," replied Carmela. "I want to create lines of stitchery that will outline each photo."

"Whoa," said Gabby, suddenly interested. "Neat idea. But I thought you weren't going to beat your brains out over this scrapbook. Especially since Margot strong-armed you."

"She didn't beat her brains out," spoke up Wren in a soft voice. "Carmela's pouring her heart into it. Big difference." She flashed a faint, almost triumphant smile at Tandy and Gabby. "Did you really think she wouldn't?"

"I guess not," said Gabby. "Carmela pretty much throws herself wholeheartedly into everything she does."

Don't I wish, thought Carmela. *Don't I wish.*

Chapter 19

THE PROVERBIAL BULL in a china shop was posturing smack dab in the middle of Memory Mine when Carmela returned from her visit to Gossamer & Grosgrain.

Dunbar DesLauriers, arms akimbo and voice in the dangerous decibel range, had seemingly reduced Wren to tears. And Tandy, all skinny one hundred and seven pounds of her, was advancing on Dunbar like an avenging angel.

"What the hell is going on?" Carmela demanded at the top of her voice as she came flying through the front door. Her profane and thunderous approach was designed to startle Dunbar, not upset the others. Unfortunately, it seemed to have the reverse effect.

Dunbar shook his head and rolled his eyes upon seeing her. "Finally!" he cried in a petulant tone. "Someone with a little common *sense.*"

Tandy continued to advance on Dunbar. "Shoo," she told him, flapping her skinny arms at him as though she were trying to oust a flock of disobedient chickens. "Get out. We don't want your kind around here. All you do is bring trouble!"

"Carmela!" demanded Dunbar. "Tell them it's a *business* deal. That it isn't personal, just business. It's the way things are *done.*"

Where have I heard that before? Oh, yeah, in the movie The Godfather. *And always right before they whacked some poor sucker.*

Dropping her newly stitched scrapbook pages onto the counter, Carmela approached the pleading Dunbar. "What are you talking about?" she asked. Then she glanced past Dunbar at Tandy, Gabby, and Wren and extended her hands in what she hoped was a calming gesture. "Let me sort this out," she told them.

"He's an *ass*hole," sniffed Tandy, retreating a few steps and savoring the impact of her words. Reveling in her succinct characterization of Dunbar, Tandy made her pronouncement again: "A total asshole."

"Carmela," pleaded Dunbar, obviously not used to having women ridicule him to such an extent.

"Talk," Carmela ordered, once the three women had retreated all the way to the back craft table.

But Dunbar DesLauriers was still wound up and blustering mightily. "Business," he declared again. He shook his head and his jowls sloshed furiously. "Simply business," he repeated, but his voice resonated with heated anger.

"Why don't you tell me about this little business deal that's got everyone so worked up," said Carmela. A nasty feeling had taken root in the pit of her stomach, but Carmela wasn't about to show any weakness in front of Dunbar DesLauriers.

Never let 'em see you sweat.

Amazingly, she'd learned that valuable lesson from Shamus's sister, Glory.

"I assure you," said Dunbar, whipping out a piece of paper and smacking it down hard on the front counter, "this is all quite legal. All aboveboard."

It had been Carmela's experience that whenever someone went to great lengths to explain how legal and aboveboard something was, it meant they were set to screw you royally.

"What's this, Dunbar?" she asked, snatching up the document and scanning it. "Talk to me. Tell me what's going on."

"Glory sold me the paper," spat out Dunbar DesLauriers. He was fighting to stay in control now. Angry and completely pissed off, he seemed poised to strike, just like the proverbial scorpion.

"The paper on what?" demanded Carmela. The nasty feeling in her stomach was spreading way too fast for comfort.

"Twenty ten Juliet Street," said Dunbar. He sounded angry but suddenly looked slyly pleased. Like an errant little boy who'd just pulled one off.

"On Wren's house," said Carmela. *Oh crap.*

"On the house Crescent City Bank *owned*," said Dunbar. "If you recall, they held the title."

"And now you do," said Carmela. She was seething inside. This was just the kind of dirty, underhanded trick she expected from someone like Dunbar DesLauriers. "I'm sure you're very proud of yourself," she told him.

Dunbar chose to ignore Carmela's biting sarcasm. "I explained to Miss West that we could execute a simple trade," said Dunbar. "A business deal of sorts. The paper on her house for the contents of Biblios Booksellers." Dunbar paused and smiled then, looking all the world like a friendly but ravenous barracuda. "Once she has this paper," he added, "the residence is hers. Free and clear."

"Free and clear," said Carmela, the words almost catching in her throat. "Wrong, pal. Free and clear is when you do the deal *above*board."

"It *is* aboveboard," countered Dunbar.

"You are a despicable weasel," snapped Carmela. "So don't try to take the moral high ground with me. You couldn't just bide your time and maybe do this with a little grace and good faith? For goodness' sakes, Wren might have even *sold* the bookstore to you if you'd let her do it in her own good time and of her own free will. But, no, you've got to come cowboying in here with your conniving ways and dirty tricks. It's probably more *fun* that way, though, isn't it?" Snatching up the piece of paper, Carmela crumpled it into a ball and hurled it at him. "Get out!" she ordered. "Tandy was right. You *are* an asshole."

A spattering of applause erupted from the back of the room as Carmela's ranting came to a rapid conclusion. Chest heaving, face slightly pink, she'd suddenly run out of words.

Dunbar DesLauriers bent swiftly and snatched up the crumpled paper from the floor. He thrust it toward her in a threatening gesture. "This is *legal*," he hissed. "I can call this paper in tomorrow if I want to!"

"Get out!" ordered Carmela.

And with that, Dunbar DesLauriers spun on his heels and caromed out the front door.

"I'M COOKED," said Wren. "Now I don't have any choice." She sat at the table, looking dazed. Gabby and Tandy sat on either side of her, looking supportively morose.

"You're not cooked," said Carmela, still trying to catch her breath after her retaliatory outburst. She was striding around the store, trying to dispel the jittery feeling that had built up inside her from too much adrenaline. Way too much adrenaline. *That's my second hit in the span of twenty-four hours,* she told herself. *Sure hope I don't go into cardiac arrest or something.*

"What if Dunbar wants to call in the loan?" asked Wren, looking dispirited.

"I don't know how much you guys know about real estate foreclosures," said Carmela, "but I used to listen to Shamus endlessly grump and groan about foreclosures. And from the way he carried on about the unfairness of the process, I know it takes a good two or three months. Minimum."

Wren looked up hopefully. "Really? You're sure?"

Carmela nodded. "Yup. And that's after going to court. If you can even get a court date."

"That sounds *good,*" quipped Tandy. "Buys her some time."

"Carmela's right," said Gabby. "Dunbar DesLauriers is a fool and a blowhard. Stuart held a CD on some property and when the tenants didn't make the payments, it took him forever to get it back. Almost six months, I think."

"Six months is even better," said Tandy. She patted Wren's hand. "See, sweetie, you've got plenty of time."

"So what were his histrionics really about?" asked Wren. "Was he just trying to *scare* me?"

"Probably," said Carmela. "Dunbar's a bully, clear and simple. And it's been my experience that bullies always lead with threats and tough talk."

"So what do we do now?" asked Gabby.

Carmela thought for a minute. "Why not call Dunbar's bluff?"

"How on earth can we do that?" asked Wren.

"Well," said Carmela, hastily working through her plan, "why don't you tell him you're going to finalize an inventory list. Make it sound very business-like, but also give him the impression we're knuckling under a bit."

"And our real agenda is . . . what?" asked Gabby.

"We'll ask Jekyl Hardy to do an appraisal on the more-collectible books," said Carmela. "Or, if he can't do it himself, he can recommend one of his friends who's a licensed appraiser."

"Okay," said Wren. "Then what?"

"Not sure," said Carmela. "Maybe you'll end up selling to him after all. Or maybe, in the process of putting a value on the business, you'll be able to walk into another bank and qualify for a mortgage on the house."

"Or a bridge loan for the business," suggested Gabby.

Wren sat quietly for a few moments, then a smile began to spread across her face. "You're right, Carmela," she said quietly. "Business can be fun."

"And it's especially fun," said Carmela, "when you're able to make a tasty profit or hopscotch the other guy!"

Another lesson learned from Glory, thought Carmela. And then she decided that there was no way Glory was going to get away scot-free in all of this.

No way. Glory played a major role in this little fiasco. Her business ethics are cheesy and underhanded at best. She sold the paper on Wren's house to Dunbar DesLauriers, and now she's going to pay the price.

"Carmela," said Gabby, "Quigg Brevard is on the phone."

"Mmm," said Carmela, darting into her office to take his call.

"Hey gorgeous," said Quigg when she picked up the phone. "Whatcha doing tonight?"

All thoughts of staying late to work on the Gilt Trip scrapbook flew out of Carmela's head at the sound of Quigg's voice. Here was a charming, interesting man who sounded like he actually wanted the pleasure of her company. On the other hand, she didn't want to sound *too* anxious.

"I've got some work to finish up," she told him.

"Survey says . . . *wrong*," answered Quigg. "I've got some Chilean sea bass that has your name on it."

"Imagine that," said Carmela. "All the way from Chile. And with my name on it."

"Dinner's at seven," Quigg told her. "And if you're really good, I'll pop the cork on a bottle of Laetitia Pinot Noir."

"How can I say no," said Carmela. *Besides, this gives me one more chance to snoop around Bon Tiempe. I don't expect to find any hot clues, but you never know. It's worth a shot.*

Chapter 20

"WHAT THE . . . ?"

Carmela's first thought when she walked into her apartment was that someone had ransacked the place. Broken in and scattered all the photos and papers she'd laid out so carefully last night.

Then she saw the tiny snippet of paper caught in Poobah's whisker.

Poobah. Oh no. I never pegged you for a chewer.

"Did you do this?" Carmela asked the little dog sharply. Poobah's tail thumped the floor even as his shoulders slumped and he looked evasively away.

"You're a very naughty dog," Carmela told him. Crouching down, she gathered up the mangled remains of the photos and shredded documents. She'd read somewhere that you were never supposed to reprimand a dog after the fact. That they weren't smart enough to put two and two together.

Yeah right. Then why is it dogs universally remember where the treats are kept, how to spell O-U-T, W-A-L-K, and about a hundred other words? And know precisely when you're going to walk through the door? Cripes, most dogs possess the I.Q. of a fourth-grader.

"We're going to take you back to Shamus," Carmela told Poobah. "The nice man who found you. Because the cardinal rule around here is never, ever touch the papers and photos." She put her hands on her hips and continued to lecture Poobah, who really did look penitent. "You see, pal, I'm in the scrap-booking business. And we really can't have you undermining any of my hand-iwork. You understand?"

Poobah rolled his eyes nervously, as if to say *I didn't mean to screw up so badly.* Boo, sensing this was a pivotal moment in canine commiseration, moved in to make her appeal. Eyes bright, paws dancing, Boo pranced in a tight circle around Carmela.

"Sorry, Boo, that's not going to work, either. I'm gonna feed you guys, then take a quick shower and change clothes. While I do that, you two say your doggy farewell's to each other, because Poobah's going back with Shamus tonight. Shamus is in banking, and they don't look as unkindly upon shredded documents as I do."

I'm also gonna kill two birds with one stone, Carmela decided. *When I swing by the Garden District to drop Poobah off, I can say my piece to Glory Meechum. Hoo yeah.*

Carmela nodded to herself, resolute in her mission. Then she dashed off to dig in her closet for the perfect pair of strappy sandals to go with her new black crepe dress.

SIX O'CLOCK in the Garden District was a magical time of night. Gaslights silhouetted stately oaks, and enormous Victorian, Greek-Revival, and French Gothic homes glowed from within. High-ceilinged dining rooms, quiet during the day, suddenly came to life when candles were lit and crystal and silver laid out on damask linen.

Shamus's family had lived in the Garden District for well over fifty years, with various and sundry relatives occupying different homes. Carmela had, of course, lived here with Shamus until they'd split and Glory had driven her out. That former home was now occupied by a Meechum cousin, some poor un-fortunate who'd been conscripted and was probably being groomed for an entry-level slot at one of the banks.

Carmela stood on Glory's wide, graceful verandah and pounded on the front door.

She'd already tried the doorbell three times and got no answer. Probably, Carmela decided, Glory was busy doing a little post-workday touch-up with the vacuum cleaner. Glory's diagnosis of a mild case of OCD meant she was forever cleaning, polishing, nit-picking, and, in general, searching for fly-specks in the pepper.

Suddenly, much to Carmela's surprise, the door flew open and there stood Glory, looking frumpy and frowsled in a splotchy print housedress. "Carmela." She frowned. "What are *you* doing here?"

"Hey there, Glory," said Carmela in hale-hearty greeting. She figured she'd start with a friendly opener, then move in for the kill once she'd gained entrance to Glory's inner sanctum.

But Glory was a tough nut to crack. For one thing, she'd noticed the dog hunkered down at Carmela's side.

"What's that?" she demanded.

"Dog," said Carmela. "Canine."

"You can't bring a dog in here!"

"Sure I can," said Carmela, struggling to maintain her upbeat, semi-friendly ruse. "In fact, it's Shamus's dog."

Glory suddenly looked stunned. "Shamus bought a dog?" The notion seemed inconceivable to her. "He'd never do that! He knows I deplore dog hair and dander. Makes me sneeze and go all itchy."

"Actually," said Carmela, beginning to relish the conversation, "Shamus *found* this dog. It was a stray."

"He *found* a dog?" muttered Glory. She gazed in unabashed horror at the little brown and white mutt at Carmela's side, as though he might be a carrier of the deadly Ebola virus.

"Can we come in?" asked Carmela, brushing past her.

"Absolutely not. Stay right where you are!" ordered Glory. But Carmela breezed on into the living room, definitely inner sanctum territory, then turned to confront Glory. Carmela didn't look quite so friendly now, and Glory, sensing conflict might be imminent, crossed her flabby arms across her broad chest.

"Thanks a lot for selling that mortgage paper to Dunbar," began Carmela. "Your little business deal really helped things along." Her voice dripped with sarcasm.

"It was perfectly legal," snorted Glory. "Standard business practice."

"No, Glory, it was perfectly awful," Carmela fired back. "Wren's fiance was murdered and all you can think about is keeping Dunbar DesLauriers fat and happy. I know customer loyalty and customer relationship management are hot buttons in business today, but I'm not sure your little stunt was the best way to put those principles into practice."

"It's a free country," said Glory. But her words didn't carry their normal dose of venom. Glory was clearly uncomfortable with Poobah in her house. She squirmed, flinched, and one eye seemed to be bouncing around all on its own.

"Right," said Carmela slowly. She knew the "free country" defense was another one of those lame, dumb-ass excuses that really meant *I'm gonna do whatever I want and you can't stop me.*

"Carmela. Glory. What the heck's going on?" Shamus was suddenly in the room with them.

Glory looked relieved. As though reinforcements had arrived just in the nick of time. "Good. You're home," said Glory, edging toward Shamus.

"I brought your dog," Carmela told Shamus.

Looking suddenly uncomfortable, Shamus chose to ignore both of them and focus on Poobah. "Hi, pup," he said, bending down to gently scratch behind the dog's ears.

"Are we quite finished?" asked Glory. She stared belligerently at Carmela. "Because I for one have better things to do than stand around listening to you belly-ache about business that doesn't concern you."

"Don't talk to Carmela like that," said Shamus. "She's still my wife."

"Humph," said Glory, scratching at her neck. "Not for long. If you two don't get divorce proceedings rolling, I'm going to step in and put one of my own lawyers to work. It's high time you . . ."

"Stay out of it," snapped Carmela.

"She's right," said Shamus. "We'll deal with it ourselves."

"In our own sweet time," said Carmela. *Good lord, what am I saying? Our own sweet time? Hasn't this thing dragged on long enough?*

"Mother of pearl!" thundered Glory.

Startled, both Carmela and Shamus jumped at the sound of her strident voice.

"What?" asked Shamus.

Eyes bugged out, looking completely aghast, Glory was leaning forward, pointing to a wet spot on the carpet. "Look! That hideous animal Carmela dragged in here has had an accident! In my *house!*"

"I don't think so, Glory," began Shamus. "Gus was in here earlier watering plants." Gus was Glory's gardener.

"Gus doesn't spill," spat Glory, itching furiously now. "He's not *allowed* to spill."

With a look of panic on his face, Shamus was suddenly back-pedaling like mad. "For cripe sakes, Glory, it's not that big a deal. The dog simply had an accident. A little tinky-poo on the carpet's not going to hurt anything."

Carmela stared at Shamus in utter amazement. First of all, she'd never seen him this panicked, except for the few minutes right before their wedding ceremony. And second, and possibly most startling of all, she'd never ever heard Shamus spout baby talk before. It was extremely odd. And more than a little unnerving. Was this what she had to look forward to if they ever decided to grow old together? Shamus talking about his drinky-winky or his lunchy-munchy? It would be like being forced to endlessly watch the *Teletubbies.*

But Glory wasn't about to be put off by Shamus's suddenly regressive choice of words. "This carpet will have to be replaced," she barked. "It's probably soaked clear through to the foam padding."

"You might have to rip up the floorboards, too," Carmela added helpfully. "Or, at the very least, disinfect them."

Shamus threw her a disparaging glance. "Thanks a *lot!*"

"Don't mention it," Carmela told him sweetly. She was pleased to see that Glory seemed to have developed a full-fledged rash on her neck.

"Take your dog outside now!" Glory commanded Carmela.

"Sorry, but he's not my dog." Carmela tried to hand the leash off to Shamus, but he stood there stubbornly, hands held firmly at his sides.

"Sure he is," whined Shamus. "Poobah's *your* dog. You've been taking care of him."

"Nice try," said Carmela, now finding herself in a face-off with Shamus. "Your mewling and puling might have worked on me once, but not a second time. I'm immune, Shamus. I've found the antitoxin."

"Shamus!" snapped Glory. "If it's your animal, take the damn thing outside!" She pushed out her lower lip and glowered at Shamus like *he* was the one who'd wet the carpet.

Carmela fought to control her glee. Dealing with Glory was a lot more fun when she wasn't on the receiving end of that razor-sharp tongue.

Shamus grabbed the leash from Carmela's hands and headed for the door, Carmela following on his heels. They steamrolled through the doorway together like they were beginning some grand adventure. But Shamus wasn't finished with his petty grumblings.

"You've got to take Poobah home with you," he pleaded, once they hit the front porch.

"No can-do," countered Carmela.

"Pleeease," said Shamus.

"Put a lid on it, will you?" snapped Carmela. She gazed down at Poobah, who was looking a little dazed and confused. *They weren't all going for a walk together? He had to stay in this strange house with the scary lady?*

"Look," said Carmela, "Poobah's a terrific little dog, okay? Maybe, if things were different, I could keep him. But . . . well, it's just not going to work out."

"If things were different," said Shamus, pouncing on her words. "What things?"

"Oh, I don't know," murmured Carmela. "Bigger house, a fenced-in yard . . . just things."

"Us?" Shamus asked sharply. He was grasping Poobah's leash like it were a lifeline.

"Maybe," said Carmela. She was suddenly cautious about the direction this conversation was taking her. *Proceed carefully,* she told herself. *This is dangerous ground.*

"You know I love you," blurted out Shamus. "I always have."

Carmela felt like her head was spinning. Like she was imprisoned on a runaway Tilt-A-Whirl and the ride operator had wandered off somewhere. To have a smoke, or maybe never come back.

"Shamus, telling me you love me is not going to motivate me to keep Poobah." Carmela's words came out harsher than she'd intended and she inwardly cringed. *Great. Lash out and really hit the guy when he's down. Way to go.*

Shamus was peering at her closely now. "Are you going on a date tonight or something?" He'd obviously just noticed her black crepe dress.

"Why do you ask?" *Damn. I thought if I tossed this ratty old sweater on over it he wouldn't notice.*

"You're all dressed up," he said, his tone verging on accusatory. "Your hair looks really cute. And you're wearing makeup. Eyeliner."

The one night Shamus suddenly decides to talk about us, I'm heading off to see another man. Could our timing be any more bizarre? Is this not the story of our entire life together?

Pulling her sweater tightly around her shoulders, Carmela stood on tiptoes and gave Shamus a kiss on his cheek. His skin felt smooth and cool and smelled faintly of spicy aftershave. "Good night, Shamus," she told him. "Good luck with Poobah."

Chapter 21

QUIGG BREVARD CAUGHT both of Carmela's hands in his as he greeted her at the front door. She'd left the ratty sweater in the car and freshened her lipstick, seeing as how it seemed to have worked its way off during her altercation with Glory.

"You look ravishing," Quigg growled. Snazzily turned out in a dark blue suit with a starched white shirt and Chinese red tie, his fashion choice was highly complementary to his dark hair and olive complexion. It also served to make him look a little more handsome, a little more dangerous.

Carmela did what any normal woman would do under the circumstances. She blushed and stammered out a *thank-you*.

"No, I mean it," Quigg told her, slipping an arm about her waist. "Your skin is glowing, your hair looks incredibly blond and fantastic, and I love the dramatic eye makeup."

What's with the comments about makeup? wondered Carmela. *First from Shamus and now Quigg. Do I normally not wear enough makeup? And here I thought I was single-handedly supporting the Chanel and Estee Lauder counters at Saks.*

"Thank you," Carmela murmured again. Quigg's compliments were a far cry from Shamus's almost accusatory remarks about her makeup and hair. But could she really buy into Mr. Oh-so-polished-restaurateur's words? Ah, that was the sixty-four-thousand-dollar question. Quigg Brevard talked a great game and fairly oozed charm, but was he really a one-woman, settling-down kind of guy? Maybe. Or maybe not. Carmela wasn't so sure she wanted to lay her beating heart out there on a silver platter to find out. Been there, done that, as they say. This time, if there was a *this time*, she was determined to proceed with extreme caution.

"This cozy spot right over here," said Quigg, as he hustled Carmela across the dining room, "has been reserved exclusively for *us*."

A table for two, set with white linen, gold chargers, and a virtual hedge of red roses, sat right in front of the marble fireplace and the crackling fire that burned within. The coziest and very best seat in the house. The table that was *the* focal point of the restaurant. Where you could see everyone and they could see you.

Gulp, thought Carmela.

But slipping into her chair, she still couldn't help but be charmed. "You're sure this is just an impromptu little dinner?" Carmela asked him. It sure looked like Quigg had gone out of his way.

"Absolutely," he replied, flashing her a wicked grin. "Worst table in the house. Can't give the darn thing away."

A waiter hustled over to fill Carmela's water glass, gently drape a damask napkin across her lap, deposit of basket of fresh-baked rolls and honey butter at her fingertips, and, in general, fuss over her.

"We'll start with the carpaccio, Gerald," Quigg told him. "And bring the wine right away."

"Very good, sir," replied the waiter.

"No menu tonight," said Carmela. "You must have dinner all figured out."

"We can get you a menu if you prefer," Quigg told her. "But, as I mentioned on the phone, we have some superlative Chilean sea bass fillets that the chef is going to prepare with a barbecue glaze and side of mango salsa."

Carmela shook her head as she suddenly felt faint hunger pangs in her tummy. "Sounds heavenly." She sank back in her sumptuously upholstered chair, watching as Quigg and Gerald went through the wine ritual. Gerald opening and pouring, Quigg sniffing and swirling the contents of his glass.

One of the delights of seeing Quigg was that Carmela *didn't* have to order off the menu. He almost always had a spectacular dinner lined up. Sometimes he surprised her with an exotic appetizer of quail's eggs. Sometimes it was as simple and basic as sliced beefsteak tomatoes with a slice of fresh mozzarella and drizzle of balsamic vinegar.

"The restaurant's packed tonight," she told him. Indeed, every table in Bon Tiempe seemed to be occupied, and Carmela could see a line forming at the front door. Late arrivals waiting for a table or hopefuls praying for a cancellation.

Quigg shrugged. "It's been this way for the past week. Absolutely jam-packed."

"More curiosity seekers?" asked Carmela.

A dark eyebrow shot up. "I prefer to think my menu is the major draw," said Quigg. "But . . . yes, I think so." And then, because Quigg could tell that Carmela really wanted to talk about Jamie's tragic murder, he added: "Curiosity seekers. And amateur investigators, too."

She took a quick sip of wine, put her crystal goblet down. "What you really meant was amateur investigators like me."

Quigg grinned. "You try to look so innocent, but I know you can't resist getting involved."

Carmela's cheeks suddenly flushed with color. "We've all been pretty stunned by this," she told Quigg.

"By *we* you mean your little circle of scrapbookers," said Quigg.

"Well, yes," replied Carmela. "But most especially Wren and Gabby."

"I can't tell you how many times the police have been back here," said Quigg. "The detectives interviewed absolutely everyone who was here that night. Kitchen help, waitstaff . . ."

"And nothing?" said Carmela.

Quigg gave a small shrug. "Apparently not. You've been in contact with the police, too. What do they say?"

"They're baffled."

Carmela hesitated as the waiter set small plates of carpaccio in front of each of them. After he left, she continued.

"You trust all your employees?" she asked Quigg.

Quigg gave a rueful smile. "Hardly," he said. "Then again, I can't say I know them personally. I'm more concerned with their ability to whip up a French remoulade sauce, green tomato relish, or a pan of pecan biscuits than I am with their personal ethics, so I really only know the faces they present here. But lots of people do lead double lives."

"I know they do," she answered. *Case in point: Jamie Redmond seems to have led a bit of a double life himself.*

"How do you like the wine?" asked Quigg. "It's Laetitia Pinot Noir Estate."

"Absolutely superb," Carmela told him.

THEY WERE well through their Chilean sea bass and mango salsa before Quigg circled back to the subject of Jamie's murder.

"Do you still believe Jamie Redmond was trying to scrawl some sort of final message before he died?" Quigg asked her.

Carmela looked pensive. "Don't know," she told him.

"You sure thought so that night," said Quigg. "At least that's what you and Ava were chattering about."

"I know," said Carmela. "But the police pretty much blew that idea out of the water. So I guess I'm not convinced, either."

"It did seem a little far-fetched," allowed Quigg.

"Do you think . . ." Carmela began, then cleared her throat. "Do you think I could have a word with some of the people who were working in the kitchen that night?"

Quigg set his fork down and reached across the table to take her hand. "Carmela, the police really are doing their best. I think your heart is in the absolute right place, but there comes a time when you just have to trust people."

"You're right. I know." She extricated her hand gently, picked up her wine glass, took another sip. *Trusting people isn't something I've had a lot of luck with.*

"And while we're on the subject of hearts and trust," said Quigg, I'd like to say a little something about us."

Carmela almost choked on her wine. *Us? Uh-oh, where is he going with this?*

"I'd like to see you, Carmela," began Quigg. "And I mean more than just an occasional dinner here at the restaurant. And more than just socially."

"Uh huh," she said, knowing she probably sounded like a supreme idiot. But Quigg's words had come out of left field, raining down on her like errant meteorites. *He want to see me more. A lot more. I suppose it was coming, but it still feels like a bit of a shocker!*

Quigg continued to stare at her with great intensity. Until he lobbed the final bombshell. "But you're *married*, Carmela."

"Oh," she said. "That."

"Yes, that," said Quigg. He leaned forward, his voice dropping to a conspiratorial pitch. "Honey, this may be the Big Easy, but the flipside is that New Orleans is very much a God-fearing, church goin' city. In other words, people will eventually start to talk."

And disapprove, she thought. *People love to find something they can disapprove of. It always seems to warm their little hearts.*

Quigg suddenly looked puzzled. "You're getting that weird look on your face," he told her.

"Look? What look?" Carmela asked, innocently. Shamus always told her she got a petulant, mischievous look on her face whenever she was trying to worm her way out of something. He called it her petchevious look.

"It's a look that clearly broadcasts, *I don't give a damn,*" said Quigg. "But I can tell you right now, you should give a damn. Because *I* give a damn, Carmela. So I need to know, are you planning to get a divorce from Shamus Meechum or not?"

There it was. Out on the table. Right alongside the leftover sea bass, spatters of mango salsa, and the empty wine bottle.

Quigg wants to know if I'm getting a divorce, thought Carmela. *And isn't that a good question? I always assumed I was, but I just never seem to get around to the mechanics of it. So what does that really mean? That I'm purposely sabotaging my own divorce? That would make me a complete fruitcake.*

"This silence is lasting way too long for comfort," Quigg said finally.

"Sorry," said Carmela. "Really."

The busboy arrived suddenly to clear away dishes, and they sat quietly, sipping wine, gazing into the fire.

Now we look like we're married, thought Carmela. *Glum looks, zero communication. Isn't this great.*

Once the dishes had been whisked away, Gerald appeared at their table, carrying an enormous dessert tray. He tipped it down for Carmela to inspect, then he carefully and lovingly detailed each small plate filled with lemon truffle, fruit-topped brioche, bread pudding, praline pie, almond cake, and chocolate *gateau.*

The City That Care Forgot never forgets to eat dessert, thought Carmela.

"Have you made a choice yet?" Quigg asked her. His dark eyes stared intently at her across the sugary expanse of the dessert tray.

"No," Carmela told him. "But I will."

Chapter 22

"YOU'RE NOT COMING in this morning?" said Gabby. "That means I'll be here all alone."

"Where's Wren?" asked Carmela. She was trying to watch the road, shift from second gear into third, juggle her cell phone, and navigate Prytania Street all at the same time.

"She went over to the bookstore," Gabby told her. "Apparently you talked to Jekyl Hardy about doing some sort of appraisal on those rare books?"

"I left a message on his answering machine last night," replied Carmela. "I never did talk to him."

"Well, Jekyl called here about twenty minutes ago and told Wren that if she could meet him at Biblios right away he could start on the appraisal. Apparently he had some free time."

"That's terrific," said Carmela. She pulled over to the curb, scanning the homes, reading house numbers.

"Carmela?" said Gabby. "You still there?"

"Sorry," said Carmela. "I'm bumbling around the Garden District trying to do six things at once."

"So you'll be in later?" asked Gabby.

"Yeah, but probably not until late morning. For some bizarre reason known only to myself, I promised Margot Butler I'd take a few more photos of the DesLaurier's newly decorated dining room," said Carmela.

"Ouch," said Gabby. "I guess you volunteered *before* Dunbar bought the paper on Wren's home and tried to call in the loan."

"You got that right," said Carmela.

"I take it you're there now? Traipsing about on eggshells?"

"Not quite," said Carmela. "I'm actually parked at the curb, staring at Casa DesLauriers."

"I thought they called it Happy Halls," chuckled Gabby.

"Please don't remind me," said Carmela.

"What are you going to do if Dunbar's home?" asked Gabby.

"Not sure," said Carmela. "Kick him in the shins? Toss sand in his face? I don't know, I haven't thought it through yet." *So what's new? I don't think a lot of things through.*

"You said Dunbar was just a big bully," said Gabby, "so maybe he got wind you were coming and took off. He's probably long gone."

"Let's hope so," said Carmela. "Facing Pamela Dunbar is bad enough!"

BUT PAMELA Dunbar, dressed rather strangely in a salmon-colored harem pants outfit and dripping with pearls, couldn't have been sweeter as she greeted Carmela at the door of her palatial home.

"Carmela," purred Pamela. "Welcome. I've been so looking forward to your little visit."

You have, really? Then you're the only one. "Sorry I'm a little late. Is Margot here?"

"In the dining room working on a few finishing touches," said Pamela, rolling her eyes expressively. "What an amazing *artiste* that woman is. Always searching for the very best in color and form."

"Uh huh," said Carmela, deciding Pamela *had* to be quoting from Margot's brochure. Nobody really talked like that, did they?

The DesLauriers house was as spectacularly palatial on the inside as it was on the outside. But even though it was expensively furnished, the interior lacked a certain warmth.

It's got that direct-from-the-showroom feel, thought Carmela as she followed Pamela, lugging her scrapbooks, camera gear, and handbag, feeling like an overburdened pack animal. *It's like the furniture movers wheeled in a shitload of stuff, set it down, then took off. Nothing's technically incorrect, but the home just doesn't exude that genteel lived-in feel.*

"Here's our Carmela," announced Pamela in a singsong voice as they arrived at the doorway to her newly refurbished dining room. Coming to an abrupt stop, Pamela cupped both hands together in front of her, then asked in a chirpy voice: "Would you like a cup of coffee? Or small pot of tea?"

"Tea would be nice," murmured Carmela.

"Hey there, Carmela," called Margot, hearing Pamela's announcement, but not bothering to turn around. Margot seemed agitated and lost in thought as she strode to and fro, pondering the placement of a pair of rococo-looking wall sconces that two of her assistants were struggling to hold up. "No, that's way too high," she finally told them. "Slide them down a bit. Everything must feel *accessible*." Margot whirled and threw Carmela a bright smile. "You brought the Lonsdale scrapbook? Showcasing the music room?"

"I did," said Carmela, setting all her gear on the dining room table. "It's all finished." Fact was, Carmela had put a final hour in on the scrapbook last night when she arrived home from Bon Tiempe. Now if she could just get *this* one finished.

Margot immediately grabbed the scrapbook from Carmela and squinted at the cover. "Love it," she declared, then began to page through it. "Good. Good. Good. Perfect," was her verdict. Snapping the scrapbook shut, Margot flashed Carmela another winning smile. "As you can see, we made a few last minute *changes* in the room."

Carmela glanced about. The dining room didn't look all that different from the original photos Pamela had delivered to her. "You sure have," said Carmela, pulling open her camera bag to grab her digital Nikon. "Everything looks great."

"For your first shot," said Margot, "the draperies. You see that lobed medallion design? It was inspired by an Italian Renaissance fabric."

"All righty," said Carmela, snapping away.

"Now step back and get a wide shot," commanded Margot, running a hand across the edge of the dining table. "This table is yew wood. Very rare."

They continued on like that, Margot pointing and explaining the *provenance* of every bit of furnishing, Carmela snapping away.

Once Margot's assistants got the wall sconces screwed firmly in, Carmela took a shot of those, too.

"I talked Carriage House Lighting into donating them," Margot told her in a conspiratorial whisper. "In exchange for being mentioned in the Gilt Trip scrapbook."

"How exactly will the scrapbooks be displayed?" asked Carmela.

"We'll put up the usual velvet ropes and lay down heavy rubber mats to shepherd in visitors," explained Margot. "And then at the end of the tour, we'll have a table set up with the scrapbook and all the brochures and sales sheets from the various vendors. That way, if anyone falls in love with draperies or carpets or wall coverings, they'll know exactly where to get them for their house."

"Gilt Trip isn't a bad way for you to troll for new business, either," remarked Carmela.

Margot gave a slow wink. "That's for sure."

WHEN CARMELA was finished taking pictures, Pamela suddenly appeared, a friendly wraith in harem pants. Somewhere along the line, though, the clanking pearls had disappeared.

"Would you like to see the rest of the house?" Pamela asked Carmela.

"That'd be great," Carmela told her. *I thought you'd never ask.*

Turned out, Dunbar *was* a serious book collector. While the living room was a testament to chintz and prints, the library was very clubby, with Oriental carpets, leather chairs, and wall-to-wall books.

"This is a great library," said Carmela, meaning it.

"Oh, silly old Dunbar and his precious books," said Pamela, waving a hand. "He does so love to collect them."

"Looks like he has a fair amount of first editions," said Carmela scanning the shelves.

"I think he's got his heart set on acquiring quite a few more," said Pamela, giving her a meaningful gaze.

"You know, Pamela," said Carmela, "Dunbar is being awfully pushy about acquiring Biblios Booksellers."

"Honey, that's just Dunbar's way," replied Pamela. "He's just a hard-headed good old boy. He certainly doesn't mean to *offend.*"

"He's not exactly being subtle," said Carmela. "I know what he's doing is considered legal and aboveboard and just business. I've heard all the arguments. But he's just not being very honorable."

Pamela looked almost hurt. "Why on earth would anyone want to run a dusty old bookstore like that anyway? Especially when Dunbar is offering such a great deal."

A great deal, thought Carmela. *That's exactly what John Law, the Scottish financier, told thousands of wealthy Frenchmen as he was bilking them out of their money. His was the very first "swampland deal" in America. And it originated right here in Louisiana. Now Dunbar DesLauriers was doing his best to carry on a proud tradition. Wonderful!*

Chapter 23

"WE WERE JUST about to order out for salads," called Baby as Carmela came flying though the front door of Memory Mine.

"Turkey and baby field greens for me," answered Carmela. "With citrus dressing."

"Got it," said Gabby, who stood poised with pencil and pad.

"Anybody else coming in?" asked Carmela as she dumped her gear on the front counter. "I mean of the regulars?"

"Tandy might drop by later," said Baby. "I think she wants to work on another bibelot box." She laughed. "Tandy's mad for those little things."

"They are pretty neat," admitted Carmela. She grabbed her purse and dug inside for her little Nikon. "I take it Wren's still at the bookstore?"

Gabby nodded. "Yup. She seemed excited, and I think it's good for her mental health to sort through all that stuff."

"It's also good business," said Carmela. "Now she'll know exactly what she has and be able to put a real value on the inventory."

"You're such a smart lady," said Baby. "Always thinking in terms of dollars and cents. Oh," she exclaimed, "what an adorable little camera."

"Isn't it slick?" said Carmela, holding it up.

"Where were you taking pictures?" asked Baby.

Carmela made a face. "Pamela DesLauriers's new dining room."

"Oh you poor thing," laughed Baby. "How'd it go? Is Pamela's house as underwhelming as I've heard?"

"It's not *terrible*," said Carmela slowly. "But it does have that mannered decorator feel. Like every little *tchochke* was placed just so. And her living room definitely looks like a chintz-and-prints factory exploded."

Baby gave a mock shudder.

"Was Dunbar there?" asked Gabby. She'd just phoned in their lunch orders and her ears perked up at Carmela and Baby's conversation.

"No physical sign of Dunbar," said Carmela. "But he was certainly present in spirit."

"I take it Pamela was acting as his little mouthpiece," said Gabby.

"You might say that," said Carmela. "She's under the impression that Dunbar is going out of his way to offer Wren a fantastic deal."

"But you don't think he is," said Baby. "You think he pitched her a low-ball number."

Carmela shrugged. "To be honest, I have no earthly idea what constitutes a fair price. Which is why it's a good thing Wren and Jekyl are huddling at the bookstore today."

"She's been working on a scrapbook about Jamie," spoke up Gabby. Her eyes turned suddenly sad as she stared across the table at the neat little stack of photos Wren had left sitting there.

Baby followed Gabby's gaze. "Such a sweet girl," she murmured. "To tackle such a sad project."

BY TWO o'clock, Carmela finally had a handle on the DesLauriers's Gilt Trip scrapbook. She'd sorted through her digital photos, selected a dozen or so, used Photoshop to do some judicious digital retouching, then printed her photos out on four-by-six and six-by-ten glossy photo paper.

"Too bad we're not getting paid for this," said Gabby, looking over her shoulder.

"Mmm hmm," said Carmela. She received lots of requests these days to design and create what they now referred to as "commercial" scrapbooks.

She'd just designed one for a high-test realtor to showcase all the exceptional properties he'd sold in the past year. And she'd also created a really nifty smaller-sized scrapbook for a woman who guided walking tours through the French Quarter. That scrapbook had been almost collagelike in concept, with photos interspersed between short, fun quotes from satisfied clients.

"Hey, are you still going to design that Mumbo Gumbo menu?" Gabby asked. "For your friend, Quigg?"

Gabby's innocent question seemed to suddenly paralyze Carmela's brain.

My friend Quigg. Is that what he is? A friend? This man who wants to see me more than just socially. Who wants a commitment of sorts. Or, to put it more bluntly, a noncommitment on my part with Shamus.

What am I going to tell Shamus? What does my heart tell me?

No crystal ball, Magic Eight Ball, or tarot cards hold the answer. I'm going to have to figure that out by myself.

Carmela forced herself to tune in to Gabby, who was going on about an idea she had for Mumbo Gumbo's menu. Something about a five-panel booklet that opened up and a cover adorned with embellishments from Ava's voodoo shop.

"Anyway," said Gabby, "what do you think?"

Carmela, embarassed that she had no earthly idea what Gabby had been talking about, said, "I think you're on to something."

"Really?" said Gabby, sounding pleased. "Thanks."

"Hey, you two," called Tandy, who'd shown up about an hour ago. "Get out here and tell me if silver embossing ink is going to work on this gray frosted vellum."

"Yes," said Baby in a mock pout. "It isn't any fun hanging around here if you two are going to huddle in that little office all afternoon."

Grinning, firmly back in the here and now, Carmela carried her photos out to the craft table. "Sorry," she told them, although she knew they weren't really upset.

"Good heavens," exclaimed Tandy when she saw the photos of the DesLauriers's dining room. "Don't you have that last Gilt Trip scrapbook done yet?"

"Tandy!" said Baby, a cautionary note in her voice. "Carmela's been ferociously *busy*."

"She sure has," added Gabby.

Tandy looked contrite. "My apologies, sweetie. I didn't mean to insinuate you were lazy. I just assumed you'd off-loaded that project by now."

"Tonight," sighed Carmela, spreading out a number of twelve-by-twelve sheets of creamy yellow-beige paper that had a Tuscan motif border. "I'm gonna whip through this baby and then Margot Butler's going to stop by here around five o'clock to pick it up. Then my last Gilt Trip scrapbook will be off-loaded, as you so elegantly put it!"

*   *   *

"HEY YA'LL," called Ava as she popped through the back door. Carmela had given Ava a key so she could cut down the back alley.

In unison, Baby, Tandy, and Gabby sang out hearty hellos.

"What are *you* doing here?" asked Carmela. "I thought you had forty cases of saint candles to unpack!" Saint candles were tall jar candles with colorful images of saints either painted on the glass or printed on paper that was wrapped around the glass. They were popular items in French Quarter gift shops.

"Hey," said Ava. "We're workin' our way through the alphabet. Saint Anthony, Saint Bridget, Saint Cecilia . . . well, you get the idea."

"Be sure to save me a Saint Joseph," said Gabby, as she ducked into the office to answer the ringing phone.

"Hey, Ava," said Tandy. "Are you still dating that head chef?"

"You mean Chef Ricardo?" asked Ava.

"That's the one," said Tandy. "He works at Bon Tiempe, right? He should have a little inside information."

Ava shook her head. "He moved to Shreveport last month. Works at a place called Coconut Billie's. It sounds neighborhood, but it's real fancy."

"Too bad," said Tandy.

Ava shrugged. "He was a nice fella, but still kind of a fixer-upper."

"Good lord," said Baby. "He's a man, not a house!"

"I brought you somethin', *cher*," Ava told Carmela. She reached down and gently took Carmela's right hand.

Carmela felt something cool and metallic slither into it. *Jewelry?*

"I ordered this at the last gift show I attended and it just now arrived," said Ava.

"Oh my gosh!" exclaimed Carmela, examining her impromptu gift. "A charm bracelet!"

"Let's see," urged Baby.

Carmela held up a sparkling silver chain bracelet with tiny picture frames dangling from it.

"Little picture frames," said Tandy. "And they're empty! Oh, too cute!"

"Oh, it's a scrapbook charm bracelet," marveled Baby. "You put little photos in there, right?"

"That's the general idea," said Ava. She stood there looking languid and lovely in her tight blue jeans and wraparound brick-red sweater.

"I love it," said Carmela. "I've heard about these, but never got around to sourcing a vendor for them." She reached out and gave Ava a quick hug. "Thank you!"

"You know we're all going to want one," said Baby. She could barely take her eyes off the adorable charm bracelet.

"'Course you do, sweetie," said Ava, reaching into the pockets of her sweater. "Which is why I ordered a half-dozen of them!" She tossed five more plastic packets, each containing a silver charm bracelet, onto the table.

"To die for!" exclaimed Baby, grabbing one immediately. "I can't wait to put my kids' photos in here."

"And grandkids," said Tandy, happily shredding the plastic to get to her bracelet. "You can never forget grandkids."

"WHO WAS on the phone?" Carmela asked Gabby, once Ava had scampered off and Gabby had been presented with *her* very own charm bracelet.

"It was Wren," said Gabby, who suddenly seemed to be glowing with excitement. "And you'll never guess what she and Jekyl found at the bookstore!"

"Tell us," urged Baby, sensing good news.

"A signed first edition of John Steinbeck's *East of Eden* that Wren didn't even know they had!" exclaimed Gabby. "Isn't that great?"

"Terrific," said Carmela.

"I guess some of the first editions got mixed in with the other books," said Gabby. "So now they're hunting for more."

Tandy frowned and slid her glasses on top of her head. "What's something like that worth anyway? Ball park?"

Gabby looked proud. "Jekyl thought the Steinbeck might fetch as much as fifteen hundred dollars."

"That much?" said Tandy. "Very impressive."

"Wonderful," murmured Baby. "It's just like you said, Carmela. Now Wren can put a value on her inventory."

MARGOT CAME sashaying into Memory Mine promptly at five o'clock. Gazing around with mild curiosity, she noted that Carmela was the only one left. "Is it ready?" Margot asked without preamble.

Carmela, who'd been busting her buns to finish the DesLauriers's Gilt Trip scrapbook, wasn't one bit thrilled with Margot's attitude. The woman was rude, demanding, and projected an air of grand entitlement. *Maddening, truly maddening.*

"I hope," said Carmela, "that Gilt Trip succeeds in raising much-needed funds for the crisis nursery." *After all, most of the work, and not just my work, was done on donated time. And it would be a shame if the focus of the fund-raiser shifted away from the very real needs of the crisis nursery and onto Margot's decorating and self-promotion skills.*

"You're such a worrywart, Carmela," chided Margot. "The whole Gilt Trip event is going to be a huge success, you just wait and see."

"Let's hope so," said Carmela, handing over the final scrapbook to Margot.

"Interesting," said Margot, as she accepted the scrapbook. She frowned and knit her brows together as she studied the cover. "I'm surprised you chose a rather plain kraft paper cover for the album." Margot's words were just this side of accusatory.

"To better showcase the accent piece of wrought iron," exclaimed Carmela.

She had run out to a nearby antique shop, done a fast forage through their scratch-and-dent room, and come up with a nice, flat snippet of antique wrought iron. It had been a snap to drill a couple grommets and attach the small curlicue wrought iron piece near the spine. "You see," continued Carmela, "the design is slightly reminiscent of your wall sconces."

"Hmm," said Margot, suddenly warming up to the concept. "You're right." She flipped open the book and began paging through it. "Your photos turned out rather well."

Carmela shrugged. "It's a point-and-click Nikon. Hard to go wrong."

"Still," said Margot, "the mood feels very painterly, and your prints are nice and sharp."

"Good printer," said Carmela. The new color printer *had* been a good investment on her part.

"Very understated," said Margot, continuing to peruse the scrapbook. "But also highly effective. The medium doesn't overshadow the message."

"Right," said Carmela, not exactly sure how to take that comment.

Snapping the book shut, Margot looked pleased. "Thanks, Carmela. Good job."

"You're welcome."

Margot tossed her black portfolio onto the table, unzipped all three sides, then carefully slid Carmela's scrapbook into it for safe transport. "What's this?" Margot asked casually, once she had everything all packed up.

Carmela grimaced. Wren had left her stack of photos sitting on the table alongside one of the Memory Mine coffee mugs. And, of course, Margot's sharp eyes had noticed them. "Just something Wren was working on," Carmela told her.

"A scrapbook on Jamie?" Margot's inquisitive fingers were suddenly riffling through the photos. "How touching."

Carmela decided Margot had to be the only person she knew who could murmur heartfelt works like *how touching* but convey a sense of not really meaning it.

"Well," Margot said, snatching her portfolio up and leaving the little stack of photos in complete disarray. "Life goes on, doesn't it." And then Margot's boot heels were clacking loudly across the wooden floor, and she quickly disappeared out the front door.

Carmela stared at the photos spread out on the table. Deep within her was a sense that Margot had been sublimely disrespectful. That Margot had pawed through this stack of photographs that Wren had lovingly and carefully collected without any regard for feelings or circumstances.

Margot's a cold woman, thought Carmela. *Cold and distant. No wonder her relationship with Jamie ended. No wonder she gives me the creeps.*

Sliding into one of the chairs, Carmela slowly gathered the photos into a pile and began to carefully restack them. As she did so, one of the photos that had ended up on top of the jumbled pile caught her eye. A photo of a middle-aged couple standing in front of the very same house she and Ava had visited! Only in this old photo, the house wasn't nearly as dilapidated as it was now.

These have to be Jamie's adoptive parents. I think Wren said they were already in their late forties or early fifties when he came to live with them.

Her curiosity getting the best of her, Carmela continued to sift through the stack of the photos, studying them. Here was one of Jamie, looking skinny and young in a Tulane softball team jersey.

After his ball-playing days in high school Jamie must have joined the varsity team at Tulane.

Carmela studied the next photo. Here Jamie was posed on a wooden dock in front of what had to be a commercial shrimping boat, since it bore the intricate rigging and hoists that allowed wide, sweeping nets to be lowered from each side.

Hmm.

Flipping the two photos over, Carmela checked the dates that were still faintly visible on the back.

Look at this. Here's Jamie at Tulane, and then, a week later, he's working on a shrimper in the Gulf. Jamie must have been a very industrious, highly motivated fellow to go from finals week right onto a shrimp boat. Then again, with his parents dead, the poor guy probably had to struggle to put himself through school.

The last photo in the stack caused a sharp intake of breath and raised the hair on the back of Carmela's neck.

"What the . . . !"

She stared at an old black-and-white photo that depicted a bizarre grouping of false limbs and crutches!

What on earth does this have to do with Jamie?

Carmela studied the photo, feeling unsettled and a little perplexed. Then, slowly, a distant memory tripped in her brain.

Wait a minute. I know this place, don't I?

She propped it up, resting it against the coffee mug.

It's the chapel at St. Roch!

The St. Roch Chapel was located in the St. Roch Cemetery, one of New Orleans's older cemeteries over on St. Roch and Derbigny Streets. Built to honor St. Roch, intercessor for the sick and victims of the plague, the cemetery had been constructed after the yellow fever epidemic of 1868 ravaged New Orleans. At one time, thousands of people had flocked to the St. Roch Chapel on All Soul's Day to pray for friends and relatives who were sick or in distress. A small side room adjacent to the chapel now contained the *objects curieux* that had been left in St. Roch Chapel. These strange objects included crutches, false limbs, glass eyeballs, plaster anatomical parts, and even medical supplies.

Carmela recalled that, long ago, her dad had taken her to St. Roch for a visit and she'd been terrified by what she'd seen. She had worried that the wooden limbs and glass eyes and strange orthopedic appliances would suddenly come to life, not unlike the dancing broomsticks in that Disney classic, *The Sorcerer's Apprentice.*

Carmela shivered. *Okay, I'm grown up now, and that stuff doesn't freak me out like it used to. But still, the question remains, why is this photo stuck in here with all the other photos of Jamie?*

Carmela let the question percolate in her brain.

Unless . . . this has something to do with Jamie's parent's graves? Could Jamie Redmond's parents be buried in St. Roch Cemetery?

She thought about this for a moment, warming up to the idea.

Yeah, maybe they are. If this photo came from Jamie's old photo collection, then there's an outside chance of it. The question is . . . has Wren seen this photo and possibly asked the same question?

Carmela dialed the number of Biblios Booksellers. It rang once . . . twice . . . three times. *Please be there.*

"Hello?" answered a tentative voice. It was Wren.

"Wren," said Carmela, "you're still there." *Good.*

"We're making terrific progress," chortled Wren. "In fact, Jekyl just ran out to grab us a couple po-boys. We're going to make a major push and try to finish up tonight."

"Wonderful," said Carmela. She paused, unsure how to pose her question. "Wren, that stack of photos you left on the craft table? Have you had a chance to sort through all of them yet?"

"No," said Wren, sounding puzzled. "Is there some sort of problem?"

"Not at all," said Carmela, fighting to make her voice sound breezy and upbeat. "I was just going to tuck them in an envelope for safe keeping."

Wren hasn't seen the photo of St. Roch yet. Good. I don't want to get her hopes up and then disappoint her again. She's had so many disappointments already.

"You're so sweet, Carmela," said Wren. "But I've got a better idea. Why don't you just take the photos home with you and I'll drop by your place later to pick them up. Get all that stuff out of your hair. My photos, the bibelot box I left there. I have a feeling I'm going to be changing careers from scrapbook shop assistant to bookseller real soon."

"That's great, Wren, really great," said Carmela.

"Yeah, well. I guess I really love this place after all." Wren paused. "So you're heading home now?"

Carmela glanced at her watch. Five-fifteen. There was just time enough for a quick run over to St. Roch Cemetery.

"Pretty soon," answered Carmela, crossing her fingers at the little white lie.

"Well, see you later then," said Wren. "And thanks again for all your help."

Carmela hung up the phone and wandered back to the table to stare at the strange photo.

It wasn't much to go on. In fact, this photo taken in St. Roch Chapel might have nothing to do with where Jamie's parents were buried. On the other hand, Carmela knew there was only one way to find out. And if she *did* stumble upon their graves, then Wren and Gabby could finally arrange for Jamie's ashes to be buried along side them.

Lay Jamie to rest, lay Wren's mind to rest. Wouldn't that be nice for a change?

Carmela slipped into her suede jacket and hurried out the door. The sun was sinking fast and she had work to do.

Chapter 24

THIS MIGHT BE a bad idea, Carmela told herself as she pulled her car over to the curb. *A very bad idea.*

New Orleans's cities of the dead had always been considered dangerous territory after dark. Muggers, drug dealers, and all manner of unsavory characters came out at night to claim the spooky aboveground cemeteries as their turf. It was never a great surprise when the occasional tourist, curious but unsuspecting, wandered into one of these cemeteries and had his wallet stolen or ended up requiring a few stitches at a nearby emergency room.

The sun was a red orb sinking behind a screen of bare trees as Carmela pulled her jacket tight around her and stepped smartly through the wrought iron gates of St. Roch Cemetery. The evening was cold and turning colder, the dying shafts of light fading faster than she'd like.

Sundown's in about five minutes, Carmela told herself. *Once that happens, this little foray becomes awfully dicey.*

Gravel crunched beneath Carmela's feet as she hurried down the path to St. Roch Chapel. Mausoleums, vaults, family crypts, and tombstones loomed on either side of her, a spooky setting for an even spookier errand.

At the heavy double doors of St. Roch Chapel, Carmela's fingertips brushed rough wood and she wondered if the building was still unlocked. Then she put a shoulder to the ponderous doors and pushed. Slowly they creaked inward.

Candles flickered on the altar as Carmela hesitantly entered the dim chapel. Her footsteps echoed off the walls and vaulted ceiling, sounding hollow in the cold, still church.

Is there a caretaker around, I wonder?

"Hello," Carmela called out, her voice sounding shaky and shrill. "Anybody here?"

But there was only emptiness. And the moaning of the wind outside.

Slowly, feeling her way carefully in the dim light, Carmela approached the altar, stopping just short of the metal railing. She gazed up at the altar with its statue of St. Roch depicted as a plague victim, skin sores and all. Altar panels on either side illustrated his travels and service to other poor plague victims.

Carmela decided the first order of business was to check out the rather spooky side chapel.

Taking a deep breath, she ducked inside.

The objects adorning the small side chapel were just as strange and disquieting as she remembered. Only now there seemed to be an even more bizarre jumble of items. Leg braces with shoes still attached to them hung on the walls. There were false teeth, replicas of disembodied legs, arms, and hands, and even plaster casts of internal organs. Carmela stared at the strange collection, oddly fascinated. They reminded her of objects that might be found in an old Roman catacomb. Except, of course, there weren't any actual skulls.

Okay, smarty. Now what? No clues are jumping out, nothing says X marks the spot.

Creeping back through the chapel, Carmela slipped back outside, trying to figure out her next move. Coming here had seemed like such a good idea at the time. Now she saw that she might have made a bit of a tactical error. It was dark and dangerous and she probably wasn't going to experience any *aha!* moments stumbling around in the dark.

Still . . . she was here. And that photo had her curiosity working at fever pitch. So maybe a quick peek *was* in order.

Carmela moved down a narrow path that led through a section of larger tombs and mausoleums. A few steps in, the hulking repositories for the dead seemed to lean in on her with a kind of menacing claustrophobia.

She recalled accounts from not so long ago of New Orleans cemeteries that had fallen into terrible disrepair. Tombs that had crumbled, caskets that had disintegrated and broken open to reveal remnants of bones and skulls. She hoped that wasn't the case at St. Roch Cemetery. Prayed there might be a caretaker *somewhere* on the premises.

With thoughts this wild, Carmela's imagination began to work overtime. And a nasty thought bubbled up in her brain.

Did Margot Butler also see the photo of St. Roch Chapel? Would the photo have meant something to her? Could she possibly have followed me?

Carmela cut left past a row of oven tombs, so named for their strange ovenlike shape.

What am I doing here, anyway? This is pure craziness, sheer madness, she fretted. *I better get the hell out of here before they close the gates and lock me in for the night!*

Carmela stopped in her tracks to gather her wits and get her bearings. Glancing left, she saw a faint shaft of light from a street lamp illuminating several whitewashed tombs. She relaxed. A street lamp meant she was probably near the stations of the cross that stretched around the exterior wall of this place. Probably near one of the gates.

Correcting her course, Carmela walked another fifteen feet, glancing about hesitantly. And she suddenly halted dead in her tracks.

There, chiseled into a crumbling crypt that lay directly before her, were the words IN AETERNUM. She stared as something familiar sparked deep in her brain.

Oh my God, can that be the INAE that poor Jamie had tried to scrawl in his own blood? What does it mean? In eternity? Forever?

Hesitantly, nervously, Carmela approached the crypt. It was a good-sized crypt, probably built to hold two coffins, but the structure tilted back like it had settled unevenly over the years. A heavy wrought-iron gate barred the way to an old wooden door.

Door. That means you can go inside. Gulp.

As Carmela reached out to touch the crypt, dry flakes of whitewash crumbled against her fingertips. Then her eyes widened in disbelief and she moved her hand across rough stone. Slowly, her fingers traced the name Redmond.

Oh no! This is where Jamie's parents are buried! Not down in Boothville.

Carmela pulled her hand back, wiped it against her slacks.

But why was this place so important to Jamie? Why did he try to scrawl these words in his own blood?

Her heart thudding like mad, a *swish swish* of blood pounding in her ears, Carmela forced herself to think.

And suddenly, the feeling crept over her that something more important than Jamie's parent's remains was contained within this crypt.

Something's locked inside here! And it's got to be something very important. For the past week, strange forces have been at work. Possibly put into motion by someone who was trying to locate this very place!

Almost on their own, Carmela's hands reached up to grab the rusty lock that hung on the wrought-iron gate.

It was fastened tight. She needed a key.

Carmela thought for a minute. She knew the caretaker probably had a key. But even if she found him and rousted him, there was no way he was just going to hand it over to her. Or even to Wren. In fact, it would probably take a court order to get inside.

As Carmela tugged at the cold metal in her hands, a single thought formed in her head.

What about the keys on Wren's bibelot box? She was very specific about Jamie giving them to her. Does one of those keys fit this padlock? Is there something inside here? Something besides Jamie's dear departed parents that Jamie had wanted to keep safe?

Like a woman possessed, Carmela hurried back to her car. She jumped in, feeling momentarily safe as she sat there thinking. She had the photos and the little bibelot box stashed right there in the back seat. Wren, after all, had asked her to bring those items home with her, so they could be picked up later.

Did she dare? Did she have the courage?

Suddenly, Carmela's cell phone sounded, filling the car's interior with its shrill ring, scaring her half to death.

She pawed for the phone in her bag and pressed the Receive button. "Hello?" she said shakily.

"Carmela?" came an urgent voice. "It's Shamus."

She pressed a hand to her chest, trying to still her fluttering heart. "Shamus? What do you want?"

"I have to talk to you!" Urgency filled his voice.

"Not now," Carmela told him. "I'm busy."

But Shamus was persistent. "It's very important. What are you doing right now?"

"Running an errand." *Am I ever!*

"Are you're still at your shop?" Shamus asked. "Are you at Memory Mine?"

"Uh . . . sure . . . maybe later. Listen Shamus, I'll give you a jingle later tonight, okay?"

"Carmela . . . wait! I have to talk to you! Please, I'm in my car and I could meet you in two shakes!"

But she'd already hung up.

AFTER TWO wrong turns and a moment of sheer mind-blowing panic at what she was about to do, Carmela found her way back to the Redmond crypt.

A sliver of moon had emerged, adding a ghostly glimmer to the cemetery, as Carmela pried the first key off Wren's bibelot box. Taking a deep breath, she stuck the key into the lock. Of course it didn't fit.

Kneeling down, Carmela eyeballed the lock, trying to decide which key might work. Prying off a second key, Carmela stuck that in the lock. Still nothing.

Well this was a bad idea, she told herself. *So far all I've done is manage to ruin a perfectly good craft project.*

But she wasn't about to give up now. She'd come too far, taken too many risks.

Third one's the charm, right?

It was indeed. The key slipped into the padlock and, as Carmela gave it a good hard crank to the right, the rusty hasp fell open.

Holy smokes. I'm in.

She paused for a moment, then swung the wrought-iron door outward. It made a loud creak, and she prayed no one had heard it. Putting a hand on the heavy wooden door, she tripped the outside latch, then pushed inward.

Dust and mustiness assaulted her nose.

Whew. I still can't believe I'm doing this.

Carmela had decided that her actions probably constituted breaking and entering, but maybe not quite to the letter of the law. She figured since she had the key in her possession, it gave her a sort of tacit permission. Sort of.

Carmela took two steps in. One. Two. She switched on the tiny Maglite she'd grabbed from her car's glove box and peered anxiously about.

A pair of coffins, encrusted with a half-inch of furry dust on top, were hunkered side by side.

Oh lord. This is beyond spooky. Now we're entering Twilight Zone *territory.*

Carmela knew she'd found Jamie's parents. But what else was she going to find? Why had Jamie attempted to scrawl a final message? Just what was in here?

Taking a couple more tentative steps, Carmela edged in slowly until she was facing both coffins. She shone the flashlight around. Between the two coffins, she could see a small trapdoor set in the back wall. Carmela shuddered. This was one of the old trapdoors that facilitated removal of bones. As the tradition went, once your dead relatives were finished decomposing and were down to just bare bones, those bones could be disposed of down the chute that led to a pit, or *caveau*, to make room for the tomb's next occupants. It was a strange custom, but one that had been in existence in New Orleans for almost two hundred years.

Interesting cultural and historical trivia, but it doesn't have anything to do with what I'm looking for.

The little Maglite, shone up and down the walls, revealed tangles of cobwebs, more dust. Carmela probed the corners of the crypt, too, but found nothing. And was about to give up, to chalk the night up to a very strange adventure, when her light caught an object on the floor.

Stepping closer to examine this strange lump, Carmela bent down and aimed the full force of her light on the strange object.

What on earth?

A dirty piece of leather seemed to be wrapped around some sort of box.

But what's inside? Please, don't let it be bones or ashes or something funereal.

Tucking the flashlight into the crook of her arm, Carmela reached down and tentatively grabbed a rough edge of the dusty leather. She pulled hard, unwrapping as she tugged. There was a loud clank, and then the hunk of leather was dangling in her hand.

She grabbed for her light and shone it down. Metal engraved images stared back at her.

It took Carmela a few seconds before the realization hit her.

"Counterfeiting plates," she whispered aloud.

Sadness swept over her. This certainly seemed to confirm that Jamie Redmond had been one of the Bogus Creek Boys. And it probably wasn't a great leap of crime-solving logic to assume that one of his fellow gang members had come after him, looking for these very same plates, pressuring him hard for these plates. Probably, Jamie hadn't been so eager to give them up and, in the process, had sealed his fate.

How awful. And senseless.

Maybe now, Carmela decided, the police could pull some records and pick up a trail. But for now, she was going to leave everything just as she'd found it. Maybe wrap the plates back up and . . .

Carmela sensed a presence a split-second before she heard a raspy voice command: "I'll take those."

Stunned, caught completely off guard, Carmela whirled about, aiming the little Maglite toward the dark figure that loomed in the doorway of the musty mausoleum.

You could hear a pin drop when the light hit the man's face.

"You!" Carmela gasped. There, in the narrow doorway, holding a gun and blocking her exit, stood Jamie Redmond!

"Jamie?" Stunned beyond belief, Carmela's words were a terse whisper.

The man reached out and roughly wrenched the Maglite from Carmela's hand.

"Jamie . . . ?" she began again. *It couldn't be, could it? Unless I'm looking at a ghost!*

A low, menacing chuckle filled the dead air of the tomb. "Not quite," he told her.

"Then who . . . ?" began Carmela.

"You mean to say you've never heard of the ne'r-do-well brother?" came a low, sarcastic laugh. "Oh, how that family did love to hide their dirty little secrets!"

"Jamie's brother?" Carmela said, stunned. "I didn't know Jamie *had* a brother."

"And neither will anyone else," said the man, taking a step toward her. "I doubt if even the folks down in Boothville remember Jud Redmond, seeing as how I wasn't around all that much. Unfortunately for them, even though I was the older *frater*, I was also the proverbial bad seed. The one the dear old orphanage foisted off on the Redmonds as part of what you might call a *package* deal. Lucky me, I spent most of my formative years languishing in reform school over in Tallulah." Jud Redmond uttered a harsh laugh.

Carmela was stunned. *Oh my God. J. Redmond of the Bogus Creek Boys hadn't been Jamie Redmond at all. It was Jud Redmond. Poor Jamie was innocent!*

Jud Redmond pressed even closer to her and Carmela could feel the hair on her arms prickle.

"You have no idea what my life has been like," snarled Jud Redmond.

"Tell me," said Carmela, trying to buy time, trying to think. "I really want to know."

"Pollock Federal Prison," Jamie hissed. "Federal. Maximum security."

Carmela nodded. "But they let you out."

Jud just snorted. "Think I'd ever be able to live any semblance of a normal life? Think anyone would hire me? Would ever trust me?" He shook his head with anger. "Think I'd ever win me a pretty little fiancée?"

"I can't answer that," said Carmela, fighting to keep her voice even. "But you're probably going to dig yourself a deeper hole if you go back to counterfeiting." She glanced toward the doorway, wondering if she were quick enough, agile enough to dash by him. She didn't think so. Jud Redmond looked hulking but fast. Like a football player. Like someone who'd had plenty of time on his hands to pump iron.

Seeming to pick up her thoughts, Jud Redmond leaned in toward her. "I never imagined my brother would hide the printing plates here with the folks," he told Carmela in a mocking tone. "Snatching the plates before the Feds discovered them was the only good thing my brother did for me. The only time Jamie gave a rat's ass about me. His fast thinking got me a lighter sentence."

"So Jamie did try to help you," said Carmela, understanding Jamie's motivation, but knowing the law would've looked askance at his actions.

"Yeah, right," said Jud. "When I got out of prison two weeks ago Jamie offered to help me again. This time the boy genius wanted me to learn *computers*." Jud spat out the word. "He wanted me to assume a place among the nine-to-five drones. I told him I wanted one thing." Jud paused. "The plates. All he had to do was hand over the plates and I'd leave him alone. Disappear completely."

"He had to refuse," said Carmela. "Jamie didn't want you breaking the law again. Getting sent back to prison."

"He was a *stupid* man," said Jud angrily.

"He had everything going for him," said Carmela. "And you killed him."

"I didn't mean to," snapped Jud. "He just . . . *refused* to help. He was stubborn."

"Jamie cared for you," cried Carmela. "How could you have murdered him?"

For a split-second Jud Redmond's shoulders seemed to sag and his voice falter. "I was trying to scare him! Who knew the poor jerk was going to grab for the knife. We struggled . . . Jamie twisted the wrong way." Jud paused, more angry than ever now. "It was a stupid, foolish accident!"

"You won't get away with any of this," said Carmela in a voice that sounded far braver than she felt.

Jud Redmond waggled a finger at her. "But I already have. Nobody knows about me, nobody remembers."

"We could go to the police, explain to them what happened. I'll go with you."

"No," said Jud. "That's not gonna happen." He bent forward quickly, gathering up the printing plates. "And unfortunately for you, you've been way too nosy for your own good."

"What are you talking about?" snapped Carmela.

"You made certain *inquiries*," Jud told her, lashing out. "Even when you were warned, you didn't have the common sense to back off."

Carmela thought about the snake, the conk on the head, the face in her window. She recalled the coffee that had been left in the loft at Biblios Booksellers. Jud Redmond had been shadowing their every move, searching for the damned printing plates. In Jamie's house, at the old homestead, at the bookstore. And none of them had had the faintest idea.

"Putting it all together, are we?" taunted Jud. "Pity it's too little, too late."

Carmela rushed him then, launched herself at Jud Redmond with surprising speed and momentum. Fists flailing at his chest, Carmela brought one knee up sharply, connected hard, and was rewarded by Jud's shocked cry of pain and outrage. As he bent forward slightly, dropping the printing plates, she curled her fingers into claws and tore at his eyes.

Suddenly, her jaw exploded in pain and she was flying backward across the interior of the small tomb. She landed hard across one of the coffins.

"You bitch!" screamed Jud. "I'll kill you!"

Her back spasming with pain, Carmela scrambled to her feet and dodged around the coffin, putting it between her and Jud. *If I had a stick, a piece of metal, anything to help defend myself!* But there was nothing.

"Give me the key!" Jud commanded.

Throwing herself to her knees, Carmela dug in her pocket until she felt the cold metal.

"That's it, now hand it over." Jud Redmond was advancing on her.

In one swift motion, Carmela pulled out the key, shoved open the trapdoor in the wall, and tossed the key down. There was a faint metallic *clink*, and then it was gone.

"Not very smart, lady," snarled Jud. "You just sealed your fate." He backed toward the entrance to the crypt, picking up the plates as he went. "Better take some time to get acquainted with the folks," he taunted. "You're going to be their new roommate!"

"Don't you dare!" shrieked Carmela, real terror welling up inside her as she suddenly realized Jud's dark intentions.

"Nighty-night," came Jud's loathsome chuckle as he grabbed the wooden door and tugged it closed. "Enjoy your new home!"

Carmela let out a blood-curdling scream as the heavy wooden door swung shut with a terrible thud.

Chapter 25

CARMELA WAS PRETTY sure her jaw was broken. It not only throbbed like mad, it felt like it was on fire, too. And every time she moved her head, which was every time she screamed, another sharp pain at the back of her neck made her wince.

She'd been screaming for a good twenty minutes now. Standing in the pitch dark, hoping against hope that someone (the caretaker?) would stumble along and hear her through that thick door. But nothing had worked. Not even the muggers, who were *supposed* to populate the cemeteries, had heard her cries.

Now Carmela knew what she had to do.

Try to get that key. Oh lord, but I don't want to.

She wondered if she could do it, then decided she had to give it a shot. After all, she told herself, they're just bones. Ancestral bones.

Ancestral bones. Oh great.

Feeling her way along the floor, Carmela came to the trapdoor. It was a square piece of metal, maybe twelve by twelve inches, hinged at the top.

She laid down, feeling the damp and cold pierce her, hating that she was groveling among dust and mildew. Taking a deep breath, Carmela pushed the trapdoor open and stuck her arm down.

She felt only cold air. *No way. I can't reach.*

Carmela pulled her arm back, shaken. But knew she had to try again.

This time, she shucked her suede jacket off, the better to rid herself of any unnecessary bulk. Then she lay completely flat, head touching the hinged door, and shoved her hand down. This time, her fingertips grazed something hard and brittle. Carmela shuddered.

Bones? Have to be.

But still she couldn't reach.

Easing herself down on her left side, trying to ignore her aching back and jaw, Carmela thrust her right arm back through the trapdoor. Then, driving hard with her legs, she continued to push all the way through until her head and entire right shoulder were wedged inside the top of that terrible vault.

Reaching down, down, down, into the pit, she felt . . . bones. Smooth bones nestled in a pile of dust.

Stifling her revulsion, Carmela searched tentatively with her fingertips.

No . . . no . . . nothing . . . damn. Hey . . . wait a minute.

Carmela took another deep breath and tried to mash herself into the vault another inch or two. Then she forced her hand to dig where she thought her fingertips had felt something.

Trying to blank out the pain in her jaw, the revulsion in her stomach, thoughts of spiders in her hair, Carmela calmly and carefully felt for the key.

Fingers functioning like a hermit crab, scuttling carefully and methodically across the debris, she groped for that all-important treasure.

And, suddenly, there it was. Cool, metallic, infinitely different in texture from the bone fragments she'd been fingering.

Carefully, gently, Carmela curled her thumb and index finger toward each other . . . and snagged the key!

Bringing her arm up carefully, then backing out of the hole with even greater care, Carmela clung tightly to her prize.

Success! Mission accomplished!

Pulling herself into sitting position, Carmela reached for her jacket and wiped her face off as best she could with one of the sleeves.

Then she slipped the jacket back on and edged toward the door.

Okay, she decided, *now that I've got the key, I've got to figure a way out of here.*

Ten minutes of examining the wooden door told her there was no way it could be opened from the inside. It didn't lock, but she recalled that it had a latch that could only worked from the outside. Only if she got the door open could she get to the wrought-iron gate beyond and use her key.

Maybe, she decided, if someone came along tomorrow, they'd hear her screams and get help. Maybe then she could slip her precious key under the door through what seemed to be a tiny gap between the bottom of the wooden door and the stone lintel.

But those were gigantic maybes, and it meant spending the night here. Entombed.

Carmela fought back tears.

Sliding to the floor, she rested her throbbing head against the door. She thought of Boo, who'd be wondering where she was, why she hadn't come home. Carmela thought of Ava, who'd probably call to say hi and figure she was out on a date. She thought about her cell phone that she'd left in her car. And Carmela thought of Shamus, whom she'd pretty much blown off and hung up on earlier. He'd had something important to tell her, but it hadn't been important to her. Then.

Carmela huddled there, thinking how her life had been so topsy-turvey in the past couple years. Marrying Shamus, starting the scrapbook store, separating from Shamus but still feeling a closeness with him.

Closing her eyes, Carmela willed herself to relax. If she was going to keep her wits about her and get through this, she had to somehow calm her still-fluttering heart and quell her anxious mind.

I need a mantra, Carmela decided. *A word I can focus on. Something that makes me happy, something that calms me.*

Scrapbooking.

That was it, she decided. Scrapbooking, made her happy. It released her creativity, drew dear friends together, dispelled tension, touched her soul.

Scrapbooking, she thought to herself. *Let me drift off, thinking about scrapbooking, meditating on the word* scrapbooking.

She tried to clear her mind, to focus on that one word.

Scrtch scrch.

Carmela's brows furrowed. *Not scrtch scrtch. Scrapbooking.*

Scrtch scrtch.

Carmela shook her head, worried that she was imagining sounds. Terrified that Jud had hit her harder than she'd initially thought, had maybe given her a concussion.

Then she heard it for real. A scratching outside the crypt.

Carmela leapt to her feet, screaming at the top of her lungs. "Help! I'm inside! Please get me out!"

"Carmela?" came a very faint voice.

I know that voice!

"Shamus?" she screamed at the top of her lungs. "Shamus!" Her words reverberated inside the crypt.

"Hang on, honey," came his faint reply. "I'll go get help!"

"Wait, Shamus!" shrieked Carmela. "I'm going to try to pass a key out to you!"

"You've got a key?" came his muffled but surprised answer. "Where the hell did you get a key?"

But Carmela was already on her hands and knees, scrambling to shove the hard-won little key through the crack under the door, pushing with the tips of her fingers until they felt numb.

And then the key disappeared. Under the door and . . . she wasn't sure where.

Until there was a sharp crack and a sudden *whoosh* as the wooden door creaked open.

Then she was flying into Shamus's arms, listening to him croon her name over and over again, faintly aware of excited barks and yips.

"Don't ever let go," she told him.

"I'll never let you go," he promised, holding her tight. "But for God sakes, honey, who did this to you?"

"Jamie Redmond had a brother. Jud."

"You're kidding," murmured Shamus, stroking her hair.

"And he murdered Jamie," sobbed Carmela. "His own brother."

"Shh," said Shamus, kissing the top of her head, her eyebrow, her cheek. "Ouch."

Shamus raised an eyebrow. "Ouch?"

"I got smacked hard in the jaw," she told him.

"Oh, my God!" said Shamus, his eyes filled with concern. "We're going straight to the emergency room." Shamus had suddenly assumed the take-charge attitude Carmela had always admired.

"Wait a minute, wait a minute," she cried. The adrenaline was really kicking in now, making her feel schitzy and a little hyper. "How on earth did you find me?" She clung to Shamus like he was her one, single lifeline.

"I went to your shop, looking for you," explained Shamus. "And that weird St. Roch Chapel photo was propped up in the middle of the table. For some reason, I had a hunch . . . you never could keep your nose out of trouble. Anyway, I drove over here and then, of course, spotted your car." Shamus stopped and suddenly held her at arm's length. "But I didn't find you," he said. "Poobah did."

Carmela gazed down at the little brown and white dog with the torn ear. He'd been milling about their knees anxiously.

"Poobah tracked you here," explained Shamus. "He just picked up your scent and dragged me over her." Shamus smiled. "Poobah remembered you. He's the one who really saved the day!"

Carmela knelt down gingerly. "Come here, boy." She held out her hand.

Tentatively, Poobah crept toward Carmela. He stretched out his nose for a sniff, unsure what to do, but anxious for her approval. Then Carmela was gathering him into her arms. Cradling the little dog, hugging him, her tears dampening his furry coat.

"Good boy, Poobah," she told him. "Good boy."

Chapter 26

"THEY GOT HIM," Shamus told her as he hung up the phone.

Carmela was home in bed, cozied up under a down comforter, holding an ice pack to her aching jaw. Boo and Poobah were snuggled at her feet. There had been no mention of fleas.

The doctor in the emergency room at St. Ignatius had taken x-rays and assured Carmela her jaw wasn't broken, but urged her to come back tomorrow to see a specialist. An orthopod. Just because the bone bruise was so severe.

She blinked slowly and turned to stare at Shamus. "They got Jud Redmond?" said Carmela. "Are you serious?"

Shamus nodded, looking pleased. "With major help from you, of course. You gave the police very credible information. A good physical description of Jud Redmond and, of course, the tip on the blue car. And you were dead right about him high-tailing it down to Boothville. They apprehended him on Highway 23, just south of Ironton."

While Carmela was being checked out in the emergency room, Shamus had hastily summoned the state police. Laying on the gurney, feeling tight-jawed and clutching Shamus's hand, Carmela had recounted her abbreviated and somewhat sketchy story, but the police had seemingly jumped on her information.

Carmela shifted the ice pack from her jaw to her cheek, wincing at the cold.

"Call Wren," she told Shamus, her voice a hoarse whisper.

He bent down, frowned slightly. "Now?"

Carmela nodded. "Before she reads something in the newspaper tomorrow or sees it on TV. Before the rumor mill starts cranking out misinformation." She grabbed for his hand. "Please? It's important."

Shamus nodded. "Okay. But you stay here, awright? Tucked in tight."

Carmela gave a faint wave with her hand. She was deliriously content to remain in bed, being ministered to by a very solicitous Shamus. A Shamus who still seemed enormously shaken by her encounter with the dangerous and nasty Jud Redmond.

And, truth be told, Carmela rather liked this subdued Shamus. He reminded her of the Shamus she'd married not so long ago.

Closing her eyes, Carmela wiggled her toes, felt one of the dogs shift slightly. She knew that tomorrow she'd have to fill everybody in. Ava, Gabby, Tandy, Baby—they'd all been part of this, they all had a stake in it.

But for now, she was quite content to lay in her own bed where it was clean and safe and warm. Carmela could hear Shamus on the phone, but couldn't quite make out any words. Oh well . . . he'd be in later to tell her, she decided, as she slid into a light slumber.

"WREN WANTED to hurry right over," said Shamus, breezing into Carmela's bedroom some ten minutes later. "But I told her to hold off until morning. Wait until you're feeling better."

"I'm feeling better now," Carmela croaked. Her voice sounded so bad even she had to laugh. "So how was Wren? How did she take it?"

"She was absolutely stunned," said Shamus. "Had no idea there was a doppelganger brother hanging around. And, of course, she was terribly upset. And I think she felt responsible for what happened to you tonight. But in the end she was mostly grateful. Grateful that Jamie wasn't really a forger or counterfeiter or whatever. Grateful that you stumbled upon his parents' grave, even though the circumstances were certainly not the best."

"Everything turned out okay," murmured Carmela.

"Oh, and she had some good news she wanted to share with you," said Shamus.

"What's that?" asked Carmela. She was starting to yawn now. To feel uncontrollably sleepy again.

"Apparently, in her frenzy of conducting an inventory at the bookstore, Wren stumbled across some sort of Mark Twain book. Not a manuscript per se, but a type of prepublication edition. Jekyl thought it might be worth seventy, eighty grand.

There it is, thought Carmela. *The money Wren needs to pay off Dunbar DesLauriers. The money that will make her home-free and clear. And even help pay back part of that Preservation Foundation grant, if need be.*

"So it's been a night of surprises," said Shamus, exhaling. "One hell of a night."

"I'm still stunned the state police caught up with Jud so fast," Carmela told him. She couldn't believe her misadventure at St. Rochs had wound down so quickly.

"For one thing, it's Federal," Shamus explained to Carmela. "Anything to do with counterfeiting almost always brings in the Secret Service." He shook out a pain pill from the little bottle the hospital pharmacy had given them, then handed her a glass of water. "And it didn't hurt that you were part of the Crescent City Bank Meechums."

"Am I really?" she asked him. "Am I still?"

Shamus sat down on the bed next to her. "Don't you want to be?" he whispered softly.

Carmela nodded her head. Slowly, so her jaw wouldn't hurt any more than it already did. "I do," she said.

"No," said Shamus, tilting her chin up oh-so-gently. "*I* do."

Her eyes locked onto his. "You said those words once before," she reminded him.

Shamus met her gaze with fierce intensity. "This time I sincerely mean them."

Carmela lifted the covers, let him crawl into bed with her. "What were you so fired up about?" she asked as he eased himself down next to her. "When you called me earlier, you said there was something you had to tell me."

They snuggled together, Carmela suddenly feeling happier and content and more hopeful than she had in so many months.

"I want us to move back in together," Shamus whispered in her ear. "Into our old house."

"I thought your cousin was living in that house."

"Not anymore." Shamus reached up and snapped off the bedside lamp. "Real estate being what it is, there's been a sudden vacancy."

Carmela let the icepack plop to the floor as her hands sought him out. *This is it,* she thought. *We've reconciled before, but this is for real. The third time's the charm!*

Scrapbook, Stamping, and Craft Tips from Laura Childs

A Different Kind of Stamping

Colorful postage stamps also look great on scrapbook pages. The U.S. Post Office has issued thousands of colorful and sometimes crazy stamps. Check out Bugs Bunny, Daffy Duck, Elvis, sea turtles, sports stars, even big-eyed cartoon pets.

Scrapbook the Holidays

Why not create a special Holiday Scrapbook every year? Gather cards, photos, bits of gift wrap, menus from holiday dinners, and favorite recipes for party treats. And be sure to have family and guests pen a few lines or recall a favored tradition!

Takin' Care of Business Scrapbooks

If you or someone in your family has a small business that could benefit from a scrapbook, why not create a "commercial scrapbook" just like Carmela does? Florists, caterers, wedding planners, interior designers, landscapers, restaurateurs, and lots more businesses could benefit from displaying their talents and finished products in a beautifully done scrapbook.

Design Your Own Gift Coupons

The same papers, press type, stamps, and stencils you use to create scrapbook pages and cards can be used to create special "gift coupons." Give your husband or special fella a coupon that entitles him to One Free Foot-Rub or a Game Day Snack Extravaganza! Kids love Zoo Day or Pizza Party coupons.

Designer Candles

It's easy to turn ordinary, inexpensive pillar candles into designer candles. To decorate a six-inch pillar candle, cut a two-inch high strip of paper or card stock to wrap completely around it. Gold emboss the edges and stamp designs in the center of the strip. Wrap the strip around the candle and glue the ends together, then tie a gold cord or ribbon around the candle to finish it off. Crinkle paper also looks surprisingly elegant when wrapped around candles and embellished!

Creativity Cubed

You can use your rubber stamps and colored pens to turn ordinary white cubes of note paper into fun desk items. Wrap paper cube with a rubber band to keep paper together, then stamp your favorite motifs on the sides and fill in with colored pens. Four beads hot-glued to the bottom as feet complete your memo cube.

Jump-start Creativity

Ever get "creative block" when it comes to designing new scrapbook pages? You can find fresh ideas in all sorts of places. Art books, graphic design books, and fashion magazines all offer fresh takes on typography and layout.

Favorite
New Orleans Recipes

Bon Tiempe's Bell Peppers Stuffed
With Rice and Shrimp

4 bell peppers
1 lb. shrimp (small to medium-sized)
1 medium onion, chopped
½ clove garlic, chopped
2 tbsp. butter
1 small can tomato sauce
1 cup cooked rice
3 bay leaves
¼ cup parsley, chopped
1 egg
½ cup bread crumbs

Cut tops off bell peppers and clean, then set aside. Sauté shrimp, onion, and garlic in butter until cooked. Add tomato sauce and simmer for 10 minutes. Fold in rice, bay leaves, parsley, egg, and bread crumbs. Gently spoon mixture into peppers and place peppers in baking dish with 1 inch of water in bottom. Bake at 350 degrees for 25 to 30 minutes.

Ava's Dirty Martini

1½ oz. vodka (or gin)
¼ tsp. dry vermouth
2 oz. olive juice
olives for garnish

Pour vodka, vermouth, and olive juice into a martini shaker half-filled with ice. Shake quickly, then strain into martini glass. Garnish with 2 olives.

Mississippi Mud Cake

1 cup butter
1½ cups flour
2 cups sugar
½ cup unsweetened cocoa
⅛ tsp. salt
2 tsp. vanilla
1½ cups chopped peanuts
17 oz. jar of marshmallow cream

Cream butter and sugar until fluffy. Mix in cocoa and salt, then sift flour into creamed mixture. Mix well and add vanilla and peanuts. Pour into greased and floured 9" × 13" pan and bake at 300 degrees for 35 to 40 minutes. Remove from oven and immediately spread marshmallow cream over top of cake. When cake has cooled, cut into squares and place on dessert plates, top with brandy sauce.

Brandy Sauce

1 stick butter
½ cup sugar
2 egg yolks
½ cup heavy cream
¼ cup brandy

Melt butter, then add sugar and egg yolks. Cook over medium heat, whisking constantly for 3 to 4 minutes until sugar dissolves and mixture forms a thick sauce. Remove from heat and add cream and brandy, then continue stirring until mixture is creamy.

Carmela's Big Easy Chocolate Chip Peanut Butter Cookies

2 sticks butter
1 cup sugar
1 cup brown sugar
1 cup peanut butter
2 eggs
1 tsp. baking powder
1½ tsp. baking soda
¼ tsp. salt
½ tsp. vanilla
2½ cups flour
1 cup chocolate chips
1 cup peanut butter chips

Melt butter in microwave, then place in mixing bowl with sugar, brown sugar, and peanut butter. Mix on medium speed until blended. Add eggs and beat mixture for 2 minutes. Reduce speed to low and add baking powder, baking soda, salt, and vanilla. Add the flour, a little at a time, until blended. Add the chocolate chips and peanut butter chips and stir in by hand. Place 1-inch balls of cookie dough on greased cookie sheet. Bake at 350 degrees for 10 minutes or until lightly browned. Yields 4 dozen cookies.

Momma's Pumpkin Muffins

2 cups pumpkin (canned)
1 tsp. vanilla
4 large eggs
1 cup oil
1½ cups sugar
3½ cups flour

1 tsp. baking powder
1 tsp. baking soda
2 tsp. cinnamon
½ tsp. salt
1 cup raisins

Combine pumpkin, vanilla, eggs, oil, and sugar in a bowl, then set aside. Sift flour and combine with baking powder, baking soda, cinnamon, and salt. Combine wet and dry ingredients and beat until batter is smooth. Add raisins. Pour batter into greased muffin tin, filling each cup ⅔ full. Bake for 30 minutes at 350 degrees until lightly browned.

Cream Cheese Frosting

1 3-ounce package cream cheese
1 tsp. vanilla
2 cups sifted powdered sugar
½ cup butter or margarine

Combine all ingredients and mix at medium speed until smooth. Frost pumpkin muffins when cool.

Big Eye Louie's Crawfish Gumbo
(Less adventuresome eaters can substitute crab meat!)

1 lb. crawfish (or crab meat)
2 tbsp. butter
1 large onion, chopped
2 cloves garlic, chopped
½ cup celery, chopped
½ cup carrots, chopped
3 tomatoes, chopped
¼ cup flour
5 cups chicken broth
10 oz. okra (fresh or canned, sliced in rounds)
¼ cup parsley, chopped

Melt butter in sauce pan, then add onion, garlic, celery, carrots, and tomatoes. Simmer gently and stir occasionally until vegetables are tender. Sprinkle flour over mixture and blend well. Gradually add in chicken broth, okra, and parsley. Broil to boil, stirring occasionally, then lower heat and simmer for five minutes. Add crawfish (or crab) and simmer 5 or 6 minutes longer. Season with salt and pepper to taste.

Ava's Bubbling Brown Sugar Hot Chocolate

3 oz. unsweetened chocolate
⅓ cup water
4 cups milk
¾ cup brown sugar (packed)
⅛ tsp. salt

Stir chocolate and water in saucepan over low heat until chocolate melts and mixture thickens. Gradually whisk in milk, then add sugar and salt until blended and bubbly. To serve, pour into mugs, reheating in microwave if necessary. Garnish with peppermint sticks or whipped cream. Yields 4 servings.

Bon Tiempe's Sea Bass with Mango Salsa

MANGO SALSA
2 mangos
4 tbsp minced cilantro
4 tsp. olive oil
2 lemons, juiced
½ red pepper, diced
½ cup green pepper, diced

SEA BASS
4–6 oz. filets of sea bass
1 cup barbecue sauce

MANGO SALSA (Can be prepared one day ahead)

Peel and dice 2 ripe mangos. In mixing bowl, combine mango with cilantro, 2 tsp. olive oil, lemon juice, red pepper, and green pepper.

SEA BASS

Sear sea bass in 2 tsp. olive oil over high heat until lightly browned. Brush each filet with barbecue sauce and transfer to roasting pan. Roast in a 400 degree oven for 5 minutes. Carefully transfer sea bass to serving plates and garnish with mango salsa. Yields 4 servings.